Count Leo Tolstoy was born on September 9, 1828, in Yasnaya Polyana, Russia. Orphaned at nine, he was brought up by an elderly aunt and educated by French tutors until he matriculated at Kazan University in 1844. In 1847, he gave up his studies and, after several aimless years, volunteered for military duty in the army, serving as a junior officer in the Crimean War before retiring in 1857. In 1862, Tolstoy married Sofya Behrs, but their marriage was to become, for him, bitterly unhappy. His diary, started in 1847, was used for self-study and self-criticism; it served as the source from which he drew much of the material that appeared not only in his great novels *War and Peace* (1869) and *Anna Karenina* (1877), but also in his shorter works. Seeking religious justification for his life, Tolstoy evolved a new Christianity based upon his own interpretation of the Gospels. Yasnaya Polyana became a mecca for his many converts. At the age of eighty-two, while away from home, the writer suffered a breakdown in his health in Astapovo, Riazan, and he died there on November 20, 1910.

Priscilla Meyer is Professor of Russian Language and Literature at Wesleyan University, Middletown, Connecticut. She published the first monograph on Vladimir Nabokov's *Pale Fire*, *Find What the Sailor Has Hidden*, and edited the first English translation of Andrei Bitov's work *Life in Windy Weather*. She has co-edited collections on Gogol and Dostoevsky and most recently, with Jane Grayson and Arnold McMillin, *Nabokov's World*. She has written articles on Pushkin, Lermontov, Gogol, D̶o̶s̶t̶o̶...̶b̶okov, and Soviet prose of ...rently writing *How the Ru... ...ins of the Nineteenth-Cent...*

LEO TOLSTOY

Anna Karenina

Translated by David Magarshack
With an Introduction
by Priscilla Meyer

SIGNET CLASSICS
the Chamberlain Bros. edition
a member of Penguin Group (USA) Inc.

CHAMBERLAIN BROS.
Published by the Penguin Group
Penguin Group (USA) Inc., 375 Hudson Street, New York, New York 10014, USA
Penguin Group (Canada), 90 Eglinton Avenue East, Suite 700, Toronto, Ontario M4P 2Y3, Canada (a division of Pearson Penguin Canada Inc.)
Penguin Books Ltd, 80 Strand, London WC2R 0RL, England
Penguin Ireland, 25 St Stephen's Green, Dublin 2, Ireland (a division of Penguin Books Ltd)
Penguin Group (Australia), 250 Camberwell Road, Camberwell, Victoria 3124, Australia (a division of Pearson Australia Group Pty Ltd)
Penguin Group India Pvt Ltd, 11 Community Centre, Panchsheel Park, New Delhi–110 017, India
Penguin Group (NZ), Cnr Airborne and Rosedale Roads, Albany, Auckland 1310, New Zealand (a division of Pearson New Zealand Ltd)
Penguin Group (South Africa) (Pty) Ltd, 24 Sturdee Avenue, Rosebank, Johannesburg 2196, South Africa

Penguin Books Ltd, Registered Offices: 80 Strand, London WC2R 0RL, England

Published by Signet Classics, an imprint of New American Library, and Chamberlain Bros., members of Penguin Group (USA) Inc.

First Signet Classics Printing (Magarshack introduction), 1961
First Signet Classics Printing (Meyer introduction), 2002
First Chamberlain Bros. edition, 2005

An application has been submitted to register this book with the Library of Congress.

ISBN 1-59609-183-5

Printed in the United States of America
10 9 8 7 6 5 4 3 2 1

While the authors have made every effort to provide accurate telephone numbers and Internet addresses at the time of publication, neither the publisher nor the authors assume any responsibility for errors, or for changes that occur after publication. Further, the publisher does not have any control over and does not assume any responsibility for author or third-party websites or their content.

Contents

Introduction   vii

PART ONE   5

PART TWO   139

PART THREE   278

PART FOUR   413

PART FIVE   507

PART SIX   638

PART SEVEN   773

PART EIGHT   885

Selected Bibliography   941

Fact, Fiction, and Film   943

Discussion Points   954

Introduction

In March 1873 Tolstoy began writing *Anna Karenina* as a novel of adultery in the European style, and completed a rough draft in three months. In May 1874, though he felt it would "hardly please others, because it is too simple," he took the first part of the novel to Moscow to be printed. But the novel began to seem "terribly disgusting and nasty" to him; he stopped the printing in June and appeared to have abandoned it until the following November, when the need for ten thousand rubles led him to agree to publish the novel serially in the *Russian Herald*. In the summer of 1875 he finally took up "tedious, banal Karenina" again but had trouble with it because "in order to work, it is necessary that the scaffolding appear," namely "questions of the meaning of life and death." Eventually, the love story that Tolstoy said he had written "in the very lightest, non-severe style" was to become a philosophico-moral novel, as the subject of marriage led him to the problem of the meaning of life; both required the consideration of religious faith.

Thus, the counterpart to Anna's tale became Levin's quest for faith, which reflected Tolstoy's own, and it allowed Tolstoy to complete his novel in 1877. A year earlier he had written to his sister-in-law, "I not only hate and scorn non-belief, but do not see any possibility of living without belief, and even less possibility of dying without it. And little by little I am building my own beliefs, but they are all, though firm, very indefinite and unconsoling. When the intelligence asks, they answer well; but when the heart aches and begs for an answer, there is no support or consolation. With my intellectual demands and answers given by the Christian religion I am in the situation of two hands which would like to join, but the fingers collide."

Tolstoy began his tale of an adulteress who was "only pitiable and not guilty" in the context of intense debates in Western Europe and Russia about the "woman question"—women's rights, the nature of marriage and the proper treatment of the adulteress. Tolstoy followed French literature closely throughout his life, and drew the portrait of his adulteress in response to French texts in particular. Tolstoy's eldest son, Sergei, explains in his memoirs of his father, "My father was a very selective reader, which is not very usual. He remembered everything that he had read, and knew how to get the essence out of a book and what to discard." In *Anna Karenina* Tolstoy recasts what he saw as the social and moral essence of French books on adultery from the late 1850s through the early 1870s. He uses French novels as a baseline against which to consider adultery, taking up not only their arguments but their imagery and motif systems.

Man-Woman (1872), an essay by Alexander Dumas *fils*, was one of the stimuli that led Tolstoy to begin writing a novel on these problems that had bothered him since he had finished writing *War and Peace*. In 1873 Tolstoy wrote to his wife's sister: "Have you read *Man-Woman*? This book startled me. One couldn't expect from a Frenchman such loftiness of understanding of marriage and in general of the relation of man to woman." Anna's adulterous relationship with Vronsky and the counterexample, the successful marriage of Kitty and Levin, are very clearly constructed in dialogue not only with *Man-Woman* but also Dumas' play *Claude's Wife* (1873) in mind. In both, the women are unredeemable, egotistical adulteresses and the men their victims. Thus Tolstoy's first version of the story features a morally and physically repellent adulteress, "fat to the point of disfigurement." But as he worked she grew into the vibrant Anna, and as she became an increasingly sympathetic character, her wronged husband became less of one. During the novel's evolution, Tolstoy seems to have identified with Anna's need for passionate love; her stature grew as his sympathy increased.

Tolstoy's Anna is a complex, sympathetic adulteress with a moral sense. Her dilemma is thrown into relief through the parallel story of Levin, whose quest for how to live draws from Rousseauian ideals and from the Gospels.

In the story of Levin and Kitty, Tolstoy rejects Dumas' overall formulation of the embattled relationship between the sexes, but accepts Dumas' division of woman into three types: women of the temple (virgins), women of the household (wives) and women of the street (courtesans). In the course of *Anna Karenina,* Kitty's friend Varenka remains in the first category; Kitty moves from the first category to the second, in keeping with the church sacraments; and Anna moves from the second to the third, breaking the sacrament of marriage. Both Dumas and Tolstoy condemn their adulteresses to death. Dumas asks what to do with the adulteress and answers his own question: "kill her." The epigraph to *Anna Karenina* ("Vengeance is mine; I will repay," from Romans 12:19) can be read as an answer to this verdict: since for Tolstoy it is precisely the sacrament that is broken, it is for God, not man, to judge. Tolstoy not only rejects a husband's right to avenge himself by murder, but also contradicts the premise of Dumas' essay, that woman wins the grand struggle between the sexes that is marriage. Tolstoy refutes this in the story of Levin's marriage to Kitty, modeling scenes of marital tension and happy resolution on Dumas' negative descriptions.

The scene of Levin and Kitty's wedding is placed at the center of the novel both chronologically and ideologically. The novel's biblical epigraph can have meaning only if marriage is understood as a sacrament, blessed by God, and not merely a civil legality. Levin's doubts about going to confession underscore the importance of the religious dimension of the marriage vows, and hence their irrevocability. In fact, no civil authority could grant divorce in Russia; the Orthodox church could dissolve marriages on the grounds of adultery, either by proof or by confession, as Karenin's lawyer says (child custody was not regulated by Russian divorce law).

Levin's eventual conscious acceptance of God is pre-saged by his intuitive divine rapture on the morning before he makes his formal proposal to Kitty:

> And what he saw then, he never saw again. He was moved particularly by the children going to school, the grayish-blue pigeons flying from the roofs to the pavement, and the little loaves of bread, sprinkled with flour, that some invisible hand had put outside a baker's shop. Those loaves, the pigeons, and the boys were not of this earth.

The pigeons flying from roof to pavement evoke the dove representing the Holy Spirit in paintings of the annunciation; the loaves suggest the sacrament of Communion—Christ's body, offered by an invisible hand. Later Levin's vows are taken in a transcendent state in church following his touching confession to the sweetly reasonable priest (and Tolstoy wrote in a letter that he was "of course, on the priest's side"). The novel defines adultery in relationship to Christianity, as a breach of the sacraments that are the foundation of family life; both men and women (Stiva and Anna) err when they break them.

Tolstoy called *Anna Karenina* a labyrinth of linkages: "If I wanted to say in words all that I had in mind to express in this novel, then I would have to write the very same novel which I have written all over again." One of the ways he makes connections is by the sequence of chapters. In Part One, three characters return from their fateful trips to Moscow: Anna to her husband, Levin to his estate and Vronsky to his friends, and their very different homecomings highlight the contrast among their worlds and values.

The method is most vivid in the parallel between Levin's estate, Pokrovskoye, and Vronsky's, Vozdvizhenskoye. The names characterize the essence of their owners' values: the first comes from the church holiday Pokrova (the word means "cover"), which commemorates the freeing of Constantinople from the Saracens in the tenth century when the Virgin Mary "covered" the city with darkness; the holiday is propitious for weddings, a day for maidens to cover their heads. The name Vozdvizhenskoye comes from the verb "to erect," as a monument, and the hospital Vronsky builds that lacks a maternity ward is more for his own glory than to help its future patients. Levin, in contrast, is concerned about his peasants and works to preserve the land of his ancestors.

In many ways Levin is Leo Tolstoy's self-portrait, a complement to the aspect of himself embodied in Anna, and Pokrovskoye is modeled on Yasnaya Polyana, where Tolstoy was born, lived with his family and wrote *Anna Karenina*. Many details in the novel are taken from life—Tolstoy's wife, Sonya, and her mother had made jam at Yasnaya Polyana in 1871; like Kitty with Dmitri, Sonya had been caught in a thunderstorm with their first baby, Sergei, in the wood on which Kolok is modeled; Tolstoy, like Levin, mowed with his peasants and endured his brother Nikolai's death from consumption in 1860 and subsequent deep depression. Other details too are drawn from life: Tolstoy's enjoyment of ice-skating; all his children getting scarlet fever in 1869; his proposal to Sonya by writing the initial letters of his phrases; her reading of his diaries; his lateness to church caused by the missing shirt. The Goldilocks joke about Kitty being "Tiny Bear" originates in Tolstoy's fondness for the three Behrs sisters, of whom Sonya was the youngest. Even the tooth motif that connects the major characters of the novel—Karenin feels he has had a tooth pulled when Anna confesses her adultery; Vronsky has a toothache when he leaves for Serbia looking to end his life— may originate in the fact that Tolstoy was missing most of his own when at age thirty-four he proposed to eighteen-year-old Sonya.

Similarly, Levin's practical concerns about running his estate reflect the real-life reforms of Alexander II, who liberated the serfs in 1861, initiated judicial reforms and in 1864 established the zemstvos, local administrative councils, so that landowners had to work out new ways to organize agricultural labor and local governance. Tolstoy opposed modernization as destructive of rural life. In Levin's economic analysis, agriculture is the basis of a nation's wealth; his spiritual analysis bases morality in working his land responsibly.

The Levin story is linked to Anna's through her brother, Stiva Oblonsky, whose pleasure-loving nature is contrasted with Levin's devotion to his land. It is emblematic that Oblonsky should arrive at Levin's with an entire separate satchel for cigars, which he calls the "the crown and hallmark of pleasure." It is part of his moral blindness: his smoking is the antithesis of Levin's joy in spring as he sets about manuring the fields. By the time Levin meets Anna, she has acquired a tortoiseshell cigar case; it contains the cigarettes she then smokes, tracing her decline. The drafts for this scene do not contain Oblonsky's satchel for cigars. Instead only "[Oblonsky's] elegant things—straps, suitcase, bag, gun—were carried in." Later Tolstoy gave Oblonsky a cigar case, which finally became a satchel when in 1878 he prepared the first edition of the novel for publication as a separate book. Anna's tortoiseshell cigar case is also absent from earlier drafts of the scene. Tolstoy was careful to complete the tobacco motif that connects the sensuality of brother and sister.

Oblonsky acts as go-between as well as purveyor of accepted views. He summons Anna to Moscow, which incidentally sets her affair with Vronsky in motion; he brings Kitty and Levin together, obtains Karenin's consent for a divorce and introduces Levin to Anna. Tolstoy endows Oblonsky with many lovable characteristics so that the reader tends to accept him as uncritically as Oblonsky's friends do, but nonetheless shows that he has no moral basis for his actions or capacity for independent thought. Most important, Oblonsky, preferring this world to the next, lacks any basis for restraining his sensuality, displayed when he takes Levin to dinner in Moscow at a restaurant whose elegance seems to defile Levin's feelings for Kitty. He orders three dozen oysters: " 'They're not bad,' he said, tearing the slippery oysters from their pearly shells with a silver fork, and swallowing them one after another. 'Not bad, not bad,' he repeated, raising his moist and glittering eyes from Levin to the Tartar and back again."

Anna's vitality is like Oblonsky's. The offspring of a father named Arkady (Arcadia), they share a firm, light tread, a full body and a thirst for sensual love. In this, Anna resembles Flaubert's Emma Bovary. But whereas Emma admires and imitates luxury, Anna already has it. Emma wants a passionate, aristocratic, dashing lover but finds only an imitation of one; Anna gets Emma's wish in Vronsky. Emma wants to be the heroine of a novel;

Anna is seen as one by her peers. Emma fantasizes about eloping to Italy with the pseudoaristocrat Rodolphe (who clenches his teeth in predatory passion); Anna and the truly aristocratic Vronsky (of the "even," "regular" teeth) do in fact go off to Italy. In this way, Tolstoy isolates and distills the moral and psychological aspects of adultery for a young married woman, purifying it of the concern with social status and material luxury that obsesses Emma and positing the most appealing, intelligent heroine he can imagine—one who rejects the accepted practice of deceiving her husband and, unlike Emma, understands that she has cut herself off from God by committing adultery.

Tolstoy's library contained a copy of the Russian translation of *Madame Bovary,* published in 1858. It had been torn out of the journal it appeared in and bound together with Shakespeare's *Othello,* suggesting that Tolstoy read Flaubert's novel in the context of the adultery question that so occupied him in the early 1870s. He follows the same pattern of adaptation in his dialogue with Flaubert's *Madame Bovery* as he does with Dumas. He uses several motifs to characterize Anna that Flaubert had used for Emma. Vronsky's relations with his racehorse, Frou-Frou, are clearly meant to comment on his affair with Anna; Emma's affair with Rodolphe begins when they go riding together on his horses. Both horses and heroines are linked by a bird motif, suggesting the women's captivity: in Tolstoy's novel, after Frou-Frou falls, she begins "fluttering on the ground . . . like a wounded bird" while Anna in the stands is described a few pages later as "fluttering like a caged bird." Emma has a "bird-like step," Rodolphe's house has two "swallow-tailed weathervanes" and Emma's dreams are said to "[drop] in the mud like wounded swallows." Flaubert even names the coach that takes Emma to Rouen for her trysts with Leon the Hirondelle, which means "swallow" in French.

While *Madame Bovary* has the Hirondelle, *Anna Karenina* has the railroad. In a letter to Turgenev in 1857, Tolstoy wrote that "the railroad is to travel as the whore is to love," and starting with the toy train that Oblonsky's children overturn while the household is upset by Stiva's affair with their governess, the railroad is associated with adultery and death. Anna and Vronsky first meet at the station where a peasant is killed by a train; their understanding is sealed during the snowstorm on the platform on the return trip; in Part Eight, back at the Moscow station, we see Vronsky for the last time on his way to war in Serbia.

Anna and Vronsky dream of a dirty peasant with a matted beard, and oddly in both their dreams, he is speaking French. Vronsky "vividly recalled the peasant again and those incomprehensible French words he had been muttering, and a chill of horror ran down his spine." The grotesqueness of the dream has to do with the incongruity of the muzhik (peasant), that essence of Russianness, speaking French, the traditional language of the Russian aristocracy since the time of Catherine the Great. Throughout the novel the corrupt characters speak French, and the innocent ones are distorted by having to use French in elegant society, starting with the Tartar waiter who translates Levin's folksy order of porridge into "porridge *à la Russe*." Like the French language, the railroad is an artificial foreign graft onto Russia causing, as Levin writes, the concentration of wealth in the cities and the distortion of the economy by stimulating industry at the expense of agriculture. He calls Moscow a Babylon, seeing the city as the locus of luxury and debauchery.

Tolstoy's view of the city and urban society was clearly influenced by his devotion to Jean-Jacques Rousseau: "I have read all of Rousseau, all twenty volumes . . . . I made a veritable cult of him: at fifteen, I wore his portrait around my neck like a holy image." Tolstoy listed the group of *Confessions, Emile* and *Julie, or the New Heloise* third on a list of fifteen books that made a big impression on him between the ages of fourteen to twenty. At the end of his life, Tolstoy wrote: "Rousseau has been my master since I was fifteen. Rousseau and the Bible have been the two great and beneficent influences of my life." *Anna Karenina* may reflect *Julie,* whose heroine resists adultery. Her husband, Wolmar, like Levin, works with his peasants, struggles with the question of faith and begins to lose some of his skepticism when faced with the possibility of his wife's death.

In *Anna Karenina* Tolstoy examines the question of the meaning of life in order to consider the problem of adultery, returning to his beloved Rousseau for a basis.

Anna's great tragedy is that she is condemned by the very honesty that constitutes Levin's virtue: both characters adhere to Tolstoy's Rousseauian ideals by refusing to abide by public opinion and meaningless social convention. Levin resists the conventions of society, but comes to accept the wisdom of those related to God. Anna is caught in a web of social, family, moral and religious conventions, which she flouts but is unable to overcome, doomed by the inherent contradictions of her society and of adultery itself. Her candle flares up and goes out, while Levin comes through his near-suicidal condition dazzled by the light of revelation.

In *Anna Karenina* Tolstoy reaffirms Rousseau's views. Levin is a true Emile, learning by his own experience the cost of luxury, the superiority of things made by oneself, the freedom to enjoy black bread and not to be a slave to public opinion. This is Tolstoy's antidote to adultery, an evolving answer to the question of how to live a meaningful life. Responding to the French novel of adultery with Rousseau, Tolstoy is able to reinfuse idealism into the realist novel, which he felt had become distressingly naturalistic. While the romantics insisted on the unattainability of a Platonic ideal in the real world, Tolstoy shows another possibility: the continuous approach toward the ideal in the real. The holy ideal of the beloved can be transformed, painfully and gradually, into the actual wife, and the novel of adultery into a *profession de foi.*

—Priscilla Meyer

Anna Karenina

"Vengeance is mine; I will repay,"
saith the Lord.
—Romans 12:19

Part One

> ∽

CHAPTER 1

All happy families are like one another; each unhappy family is unhappy in its own way.

Everything was in confusion in the Oblonsky household. The wife had found out that the husband had had an affair with their French governess and had told him that she could not go on living in the same house with him. This situation had now gone on for three days and was felt acutely by the husband and wife themselves, by all the members of the family, and by their servants. All the members of the family and the servants felt that there was no sense in their living together under the same roof and that people who happened to meet at any country inn had more in common with one another than they, the members of the Oblonsky family and their servants. The wife did not leave her own rooms, and the husband had not been home for three days. The children ran about all over the house looking lost; the English governess had quarreled with the housekeeper and had written to a friend to ask her to find her a new place; the chef had left the house the day before, at dinnertime; the under-cook and the driver had given notice.

On the third morning after the quarrel Prince Stepan Arkadyevich Oblonsky (Stiva, as he was called by his society friends) woke up at his usual time, that is at eight o'clock, not in his wife's bedroom but on the morocco leather sofa in his study. He turned his plump, well-cared-for body on the well-sprung sofa, as though intending to go to sleep for a long time, hugged the pillow on the other side, and pressed his cheek against it; suddenly he jumped up, sat down on the sofa, and opened his eyes.

"Yes, yes, now how was it?" he thought, trying to remember a dream. "Yes, now how was it? Oh, yes! Alabin was giving a dinner in Darmstadt; no, not in Darmstadt but in some American city. Ah, but in my dream Darmstadt was in America. Yes, Alabin was giving a dinner on glass tables—ah yes, and the tables were singing *Il mio tesoro*. No, not *Il mio tesoro*, something better. And there were some little decanters there, and the decanters were also women," he recalled.

Oblonsky's eyes sparkled gaily and he smiled as he sank into thought. "Yes, it was nice, very nice. There was a lot that was excellent there, but it can't be put into words, or expressed in thoughts, now that I am awake." Then, noticing the shaft of light coming through the side of one of the holland blinds, he briskly thrust his feet down from the sofa to feel for the slippers his wife had given him as a birthday present the year before and which she had worked in gold morocco and, as had been his custom during the last nine years, stretched out his hand without getting up for the place where his dressing gown hung in the bedroom. It was then that he suddenly remembered how and why it was that he was sleeping not in his wife's bedroom but in his own study. The smile vanished from his face and he wrinkled his forehead.

"Dear, oh dear!" he groaned, remembering what had happened. And in his mind's eye he saw again all the details of the quarrel with his wife; he realized the utter hopelessness of his position and, most tormenting fact of all, that it was all his own fault.

"No, she won't forgive me! She can't forgive me! And the worst of it is that it was all my own fault. It is my own fault and yet I'm not to blame. That's the tragedy of it," he thought. "Dear, oh dear!" he kept saying in despair, recalling the most painful aspects of the quarrel.

The most unpleasant moment was the first, when, having returned from the theater happy and gay, with an enormous pear in his hand for his wife, he had not found her in the drawing room. Nor, to his amazement, did he find her in the study. At last he had discovered her in the bedroom with the unfortunate note in her hand that disclosed everything. Dolly, whom he always thought of as preoccupied, busy, and not very intelligent, was sitting motionless, holding the note in her hands, and looked at him with an expression of horror, despair, and anger.

"What is this? This?" she asked, pointing to the note.

And as it often happens, it was, as he recalled it, not so much the event itself that distressed him as the answer he had given to his wife's question.

What happened to him at that moment was what happens to people who are caught red-handed doing something disgraceful. He had not been able to assume the expression that was appropriate to the situation in which he had found himself after the discovery of his guilt by his wife. Instead of taking offense, denying the whole thing, justifying himself, begging forgiveness, or even remaining indifferent (any of these would have been better than what he actually did), his face quite involuntarily ("Reflexes of the brain," thought Oblonsky, who had a liking for physiology), quite involuntarily smiled its usual kind and, for that reason, rather foolish smile.

This foolish smile he could not forgive himself. Seeing it, Dolly gave a start, as though he had hit her, and with her habitual passion burst into a flood of bitter words and rushed out of the room. Since then she had refused to see her husband.

"It's all the fault of that stupid smile," thought Oblonsky.

"But what's to be done? What's to be done?" he asked himself in despair and could find no answer.

CHAPTER 2

Oblonsky was a truthful man in his attitude to himself. He could not deceive himself into believing that he was sorry for his conduct. He could not now feel sorry because he, a handsome and susceptible man of thirty-four, was not in love with his wife, the mother of five living and two dead children, who was only a year younger than himself. He was only sorry not to have been able to hide it from his wife better. But he felt the whole gravity of his position and he was sorry for his wife, his children, and himself. Perhaps he would have been able to hide his peccadilloes from his wife much better had he expected the recent discovery to have had such an effect on her. It was clear that he had never thought the matter out, but had only vaguely imagined that his wife had long since guessed that he was unfaithful to her and preferred not to see what was going on. It even seemed to him that, worn out, old before her time, and plain as she was, and a kind though rather simple and in no way remarkable mother, she ought in all fairness to be indulgent. But it proved to be quite the opposite.

"Oh, it's terrible! Dear, oh dear, it's terrible!" Oblonsky kept repeating to himself, but he could think of no solution. "And how well everything was going before this happened, what a good life we had! She was contented and happy with the children; I did not interfere with her at all, I let her run the house and the children as she liked. True, it wasn't nice that *she* should have been a governess in our house. Not at all nice! There's something sordid and vulgar about making love to one's own governess. But what a governess!" (He vividly recalled Mademoiselle Roland's mischievous black eyes and her smile.) "But after all while she lived in our house I did not permit myself anything. And the worst of it is that she's now . . . It just would happen now. Oh dear, oh dear! What am I to do?"

There was no answer except the usual answer life gives to the most complicated and insoluble questions. This answer is: carry on with your everyday affairs, that is to say, put it out of your mind. He couldn't put it out of his mind, at least not till bedtime, nor could he return to the music sung by the little decanter women; he therefore had to put it out of his mind by the dream of life.

"Well, we shall see what happens," Oblonsky said to himself, and getting up, he put on his gray dressing gown with the pale-blue silk lining, knotted the cord, and drawing a deep breath into his powerful lungs, he walked to the window with his usual springy step, which carried his plump body so lightly, raised the blind, and rang loudly. The bell was answered at once by his old friend and valet, Matvey, who brought in his clothes, boots, and a telegram. Matvey was followed into the room by the barber with shaving things.

"Are there any papers from the office?" asked Oblonsky, taking the telegram and sitting down before the looking glass.

"They are on the table, sir," replied Matvey, with a questioning and sympathetic look at his master, and after a short pause he added with a sly smile: "Someone came from the livery stables."

Oblonsky made no reply, merely glancing at Matvey in the looking glass; from the glance which they exchanged it could be seen at once that they understood each other perfectly. Oblonsky's glance seemed to ask: "Why do you say that? Don't you know what's going on?"

Matvey put his hands into his coat pockets and stood with his legs apart, gazing at his master in silence, good-humoredly and with an almost imperceptible smile.

"I told her to come back on Sunday, sir, and not to trouble you or herself for nothing," he said, obviously repeating a prepared phrase. Oblonsky realized that Matvey was merely trying to be jocular and to draw attention to himself. He tore open the telegram and read it, mentally correcting the usually misspelled words, and his face brightened.

"Matvey, my sister Anna will be here tomorrow," he said, stopping for a moment the plump, shiny hand of the barber, who was combing a rosy parting between his long, curly whiskers.

"Thank God," said Matvey, showing by his answer that he understood the importance of this visit as well as his master, that is to say, that Anna, Oblonsky's favorite sister, might help to bring about a reconciliation between husband and wife.

"Is she coming by herself, sir, or with her husband?" asked Matvey.

Oblonsky could not speak, for the barber was busy with his upper lip and he raised a finger. Matvey nodded to him in the glass.

"By herself. Shall I see that the upstairs room is got ready for her, sir?"

"Tell the mistress. Let her decide."

"The mistress, sir?" Matvey repeated, as though in doubt.

"Yes, tell her. And, here, take the telegram to her and let me know what she says."

"You want to see how she'll react," Matvey understood his master to mean, but he only said:

"Very good, sir."

Oblonsky was washed and combed and was about to dress when Matvey, stepping slowly in his squeaky boots, came back into the room with the telegram in his hand. The barber had gone.

"The mistress told me to tell you, sir, that she's going away," he said, laughing only with his eyes, with his hands in his pockets and his head on one side. "Let him do what he likes, she said, sir."

Oblonsky was silent for a moment. Then a kind, rather pathetic smile appeared on his handsome face.

"Well? Eh, Matvey?" he said, shaking his head.

"Don't worry, sir," said Matvey. "It'll all come right."

"Come right?"

"Yes, sir."

"You think so? Who's that?" asked Oblonsky, hearing the rustle of a woman's dress behind the door.

"It's me, sir," said a firm, pleasant, feminine voice, and Matryona Filimonovna's stern, pock-marked face was thrust in at the door.

"Well, what is it?" Oblonsky asked, advancing towards the door.

Though Oblonsky was entirely in the wrong as regards his wife, and was aware of it himself, everyone in the house, even the nurse, Dolly's best friend, was on his side.

"Well, what is it?" he repeated dejectedly.

"You'd better go down, sir, and tell her again how sorry you are. Perhaps the good Lord will make her change her mind. She is terribly upset, sir, and it's pitiful to see her. And besides, sir, everything is turned upside down. You must take pity on the children, sir. Tell her again how sorry you are, sir. What's to be done, sir? There's no rose without—"

"But she won't see me."

"But you'll have done your part, sir. The Lord is merciful. Pray to him, sir, pray to him."

"Oh, all right, you can go now," said Oblonsky, blushing suddenly. "Well, let's get dressed," he said, turning to Matvey and throwing down his dressing gown determinedly. Matvey, blowing off some invisible speck, held up the shirt, which he gathered up like a horse's collar and with evident satisfaction put it on his master's well-tended body.

CHAPTER 3

Having dressed, Oblonsky sprayed himself with Eau de Cologne, pulled down his cuffs, with a customary movement distributed in different pockets cigarettes, wallet, matches, his watch with its double chain and seals, and shaking out his handkerchief and feeling clean, scented, physically fit, and cheerful in spite of his misfortune, he went, with a slight tremor in each leg, into the dining room where his coffee was already waiting for him. Beside the coffee lay his letters and papers from the office.

He read the letters. One was a very unpleasant one from a merchant who was negotiating the purchase of a wood on his wife's estate. This wood had to be sold; but there could be no question of it until a reconciliation could be effected with his wife. The most unpleasant aspect of it was that a financial consideration had crept into his impending reconciliation with his wife. And the idea that he might be influenced by self-interest, that he might seek a reconciliation with his wife in order to sell this wood, was repugnant to him.

Having finished with the letters, Oblonsky drew towards him the papers from his office, rapidly ran through two of them, made a few notes with a large pencil and, pushing them aside, started on his coffee; while drinking his coffee, he unfolded the morning paper, which was still damp, and began to read.

Oblonsky took and read a liberal paper, not an extreme liberal paper, but one that expressed the views of most people, and although he was not really interested either in science, art, or politics, his views on all these matters were strictly in conformance with the views of the majority and those of his paper, and he changed them only when the majority changed theirs; or rather he did not change them, but they changed imperceptibly of their own accord.

Oblonsky did not choose his politics or opinions, but these seemed to come to him of their own accord, just as he did not change the style of his hat or coat, but always wore those that were in fashion. Living in a certain social environment and feeling the need for some form of mental activity, which usually arises in a person of mature years, to hold views was as necessary to him as to wear a hat. If he had a reason for preferring the liberal to the conservative party, to which many of his circle also belonged, it was not because he considered the liberal outlook more rational, but because it corresponded more closely to his way of life. The liberal party maintained that everything in Russia was bad and, indeed, Oblonsky had many debts and most decidedly not enough money. The liberal party maintained that marriage was an obsolete institution and that it was necessary to reform it, and indeed family life gave Oblonsky very little pleasure and forced him to tell lies and dissemble, which was so contrary to his nature. The liberal party maintained, or rather assumed, that religion was only a curb on the more barbarous part of the population, and indeed Oblonsky could not stand through even a short church service without aching feet, and he could not understand what was the point of all those dreadful, high-flown words about the other world when life in this world was so very pleasant. At the same time, Oblonsky, who liked a good joke, found it very amusing sometimes to shock a mild individual with the suggestion that if one was going to pride oneself on one's birth, one needn't stop at Rurik, the Verangian chief invited by the Slavs to rule over them, and repudiate one's earliest ancestor, the ape. Liberalism had become a habit with Oblonsky and he enjoyed his newspaper as he enjoyed his after-dinner cigar for the slight haze that it produced in his head. He read the leading article, which declared that it was quite ridiculous in our time to raise the cry that radicalism threatened to swallow up all the conservative elements and then demand that the government should take measures for the suppression of the hydra of revolution, but that, on the contrary, "in our opinion the danger lies not in an imaginary revolutionary hydra but in a perverse clinging to tradition which hinders progress," and so on. He also read another article on finance, in which Bentham and Mill were mentioned and subtle attacks were made on the Ministry. With his natural quickness of perception, he understood the point of every stinging remark: where it came from, for whom it was intended, and what had provoked it. And this as usual gave him a certain amount of satisfaction. But today his satisfaction was spoiled by the recollection of Matryona's advice and the fact that things at home were far from satisfactory. He went on to read that Count Beist was said to have left for Wiesbaden, that there was no need to have gray hair, that a light carriage was for sale, and that a young person offered her services. But these bits of information did not give him the quiet, ironical pleasure that they used to before.

Having finished the paper, a second cup of coffee, and a roll and butter, he got up, brushed the crumbs from his waistcoat, and expanding his broad chest, smiled happily but not because he felt particularly pleased; his happy smile was simply the result of a good digestion.

But the happy smile at once reminded him of everything and he grew thoughtful.

Two childish voices (Oblonsky recognized the voices of Grisha, his youngest boy, and Tanya, his eldest daughter) were heard on the other side of the door. They were pushing something along and had dropped it.

"I told you you can't put passengers on the roof," the little girl cried in English. "Now pick them up."

"Everything's in a state of confusion," Oblonsky thought. "Here are the children running wild." And going up to the door, he called them in. They dropped the box, which was supposed to be a train, and came into the room.

The girl, her father's favorite, ran in boldly, threw her arms round him, and laughing, hung round his neck, enjoying as she always did the familiar scent of his whiskers. Having kissed his face, flushed from its stooping position and beaming with tenderness, the girl unclasped her hands and was about to run away, but her father detained her.

"How's Mummy?" he asked, stroking his little daughter's smooth, tender neck. "Hullo," he said, smiling at the little boy who had come up to greet him. He was aware that he did not care as much for the boy as for the girl, and he always tried to treat them in the same way; but the boy felt it and he did not respond with a smile to his father's cold smile.

"Mummy? She is up," replied the girl.

Oblonsky sighed. "So she hasn't slept all night again," he thought. "How is she? Cheerful?"

The little girl knew that her father and mother could not be cheerful, and that her father must know that and that he was pretending when he asked about it so light-heartedly. And she blushed for her father. He realized it at once and he also blushed.

"I don't know," she said. "She told us not to have lessons but go for a walk to Grannie's with Miss Hull."

"Well, run along, darling. No, wait," he said, holding her back nevertheless and stroking her soft little hand.

He took a box of sweets from the mantelpiece where he had put it the night before, and gave her two sweets he knew she liked best, a chocolate and a fruit pastille.

"For Grisha?" said the little girl, pointing to the chocolate.

"Yes, yes." And stroking her shoulder again, he kissed her at the roots of her hair and the nape of her neck and let her go.

"The carriage is ready, sir," said Matvey, "but there's a woman petitioner waiting to see you."

"Has she been here long?" asked Oblonsky.

"About half an hour, sir."

"How many times have I told you to let me know at once!"

"But I must give you time, sir, to finish your coffee at least," said Matvey in the rough, friendly tone which made it impossible to get angry with him.

"Well, ask her in at once," said Oblonsky, frowning with vexation.

The woman, a major's widow by the name of Kalinin, asked him to do something that was absolutely impossible and unreasonable but, as usual, Oblonsky made her sit down, heard her out attentively and without interruption, gave her detailed advice how and to whom to apply, and even wrote her a note in his large, sprawling, attractive, and legible hand to the person who might be useful to her. Having got rid of the major's widow, Oblonsky took his hat and stopped for a moment, trying to think whether he had forgotten anything, but it seemed he had forgotten nothing except the one thing he wanted to forget, his wife.

"Oh yes." He lowered his head and his handsome face

assumed a cheerless expression. "To go or not to go," he asked himself. And an inner voice told him that it would be useless to go, that it would only result in hypocrisy, that it was impossible to patch up or put right their relationship because it was impossible to make her attractive and desirable again or turn him into an old man incapable of love. Nothing could come of it now except lies and hypocrisy; and lies and hypocrisy were contrary to his nature.

"However, I shall have to do it sooner or later," he said, trying to summon up courage, "for it can't be left as it is." He drew himself up, took out a cigarette, lit it, inhaled once or twice, threw it into a mother-of-pearl shell-shaped ash tray, crossed the gloomy drawing room with rapid steps, and opened another door, which led into his wife's bedroom.

CHAPTER 4

Dolly, in a light jacket, her once thick and beautiful hair pinned in thin plaits at the nape of her neck and her frightened eyes looking unusually large in her terribly emaciated face, stood in the midst of the scattered things on the floor in front of an open chest of drawers from which she was taking something. Hearing her husband's steps, she stopped, looked at the door, and tried in vain to look stern and contemptuous. She felt that she was afraid of him and afraid of the coming interview. She had just been trying to do what she had tried to do a dozen times in the last three days: to sort out her own and her children's clothes—to take to her mother's—and again she could not make up her mind to do it; but now, as on the former occasions, she kept saying to herself that it could not go on like that, that she had to do something to punish and humiliate him, to pay him back even a little for the pain he had caused her. She still kept saying that she would leave him, but she felt that this was impossible; it was impossible because she could not break herself of the habit of looking upon him as a husband and of loving him. Besides, she felt that if here, in her own home, she could hardly manage to look after her five children, they would be much worse off where she was taking them. As

15

it was, during the last three days her youngest had fallen ill because he had been given some soup that had gone bad, and the others had gone almost without dinner the day before. She felt that it was impossible for her to go away; but, deceiving herself, she went on sorting out their things and pretending that she would go away.

When she saw her husband she dropped her hand into the drawer of the chest as though searching for something, and she turned around to look at him only when he had come up close to her. But instead of looking stern and determined as she had intended, she merely looked lost and suffering.

"Dolly!" he said in a subdued, timid voice. He drew his head into his shoulders and tried to look miserable, but he could not help radiating freshness and good health.

She cast a quick glance over his fresh, healthy figure. "Yes," she thought, "he is happy and contented, but what about me? And that loathsome good nature of his which people love so much and for which they praise him, how I hate it." She closed her mouth firmly and a muscle started twitching on the right side of her pale, nervous face.

"What do you want?" she said in a rapid, husky, unnatural voice.

"Dolly," he repeated with a tremor in his voice, "Anna is arriving today."

"What do I care?" she cried. "I can't receive her."

"But you must, Dolly . . ."

"Go away, go away, go away!" she shrieked without looking at him, as though the screams were caused by physical pain.

Oblonsky could be calm when he thought of his wife; he even hoped that everything would *come right*, as Matvey expressed it; and he could calmly read his newspaper and drink his coffee. But when he saw her worn-out, suffering face and heard the despair and utter resignation in her voice, he caught his breath, a lump rose in his throat, and his eyes glistened with tears.

"My God, what have I done? Dolly, for heaven's sake! . . . You see . . ." He could not go on; the sobs choked him.

She slammed the drawer to and looked at him.

"Dolly, what can I say? . . . Just one thing: I'm sorry, I'm sorry. Think . . . Cannot nine years of our life make up for a moment, a moment . . ."

16

She dropped her eyes and listened to hear what he would say, as though she were imploring him not to say anything that would prevent her from staying.

"A moment of infatuation," he brought himself to say, and he would have gone on, but at these words her lips tightened again, as though with physical pain, and the muscle in her right cheek began to twitch.

"Go away!" she screamed more piercingly than before, "get out of here and don't talk to me of your infatuations and your abominations."

She was about to leave the room, but swayed and clutched the back of a chair to steady herself. His face widened, his lips swelled, his eyes were filled with tears.

"Dolly," he said, no longer able to restrain himself from sobbing, "for God's sake, think of the children! They've done nothing. I'm the one to blame. Punish me, make me atone for my guilt. I'm ready to do anything I can. I'm to blame. There are no words to express my guilt. But, Dolly, forgive me."

She sat down. He could hear her loud, heavy breathing, and he felt inexpressibly sorry for her. She tried a few times to say something but she could not. He waited.

"You think of the children, Stiva, when you want to play with them. But I'm always thinking of them, and I know that now they are ruined," she said, apparently repeating one of the phrases she had been saying to herself over and over again during the last three days.

She had called him by his pet name, and he gave her a grateful look and made a move to take her hand, but she recoiled from him with disgust.

"I do think of the children and I'd do anything in the world to save them, but I don't know how to save them, whether to take them away from their father or leave them with a depraved father, yes, a depraved father. Tell me, do you really think that after—after what has happened, it is still possible for us to live together? Is it possible? Tell me, is it possible?" she kept repeating, raising her voice. "When my husband, the father of my children, has an affair with his children's governess . . ."

"But what's to be done about it? What?" he said in a miserable voice, hardly knowing what he was saying and dropping his head lower and lower.

"I loathe you, I hate you!" she shouted, getting more and more excited. "Your tears are water! You never loved me! You have no heart, no honor. I loathe you. I hate you. You're a stranger to me, yes, a perfect stranger!" She pronounced the word "stranger," which was so dreadful to her, with pain and hatred.

He glanced at her and the hatred he saw in her face frightened and astonished him. He did not understand that his pity exasperated her. She saw in him pity for herself but not love. "Yes, yes, she hates me, she will not forgive," he thought.

"This is terrible! Terrible!" he said.

At this moment a child, who had probably fallen down in the next room, started crying. Dolly listened and her face suddenly softened.

For a few seconds she seemed to be trying to pull herself together, as though she did not know where she was or what she had to do. Then she got up quickly and moved towards the door.

"But she does love my child," he thought, noticing how her face changed when the child cried. "*My* child. How then can she hate me?"

"Dolly, one more word," he said, going up to her.

"If you follow me I shall call the servants, the children! Let them all know that you're a blackguard! I'm going away today and you can live here with your mistress!"

And she went out, slamming the door behind her. Oblonsky sighed, wiped his face, and went quietly out of the room. "Matvey says it will come right, but how? I don't see any possibility. Oh, how dreadful! And the way she screamed, how unladylike!" he said to himself as he recalled her scream and the words "blackguard" and "mistress." "And the maids may have heard! Terribly unladylike, terribly." Oblonsky stood still for a couple of seconds, wiped his eyes, sighed, and, pushing out his chest, went out of the room.

It was Friday, and in the dining room the German watchmaker was winding the clock. Oblonsky remembered a joke he had once made about this conscientious and punctual bald-headed watchmaker. "The German," he had said, "had been wound up for life to wind up clocks." He remembered it and smiled. Oblonsky was fond of a good joke. . . . "Well," he thought to himself, "perhaps things will come right. What an excellent expression 'come right' is," he thought. "I must tell some-one about it."

"Matvey!" he called. "See that you and Maria get the small drawing room ready for Mrs. Karenin," he said when Matvey appeared.

"Very good, sir."

Oblonsky put on his fur coat and went out on the front steps.

"Will you be in for dinner, sir?" asked Matvey, seeing him off at the front door.

"It depends. Here, take this for the housekeeping," he said, giving him a ten-ruble note from his wallet. "Will that be enough?"

"Enough or not, I suppose it will have to do," said Matvey, slamming the carriage door and moving back to the front steps.

In the meantime Dolly, having soothed the child and realizing by the sound of the carriage that her husband had gone, returned to the bedroom. It was her one place of refuge from the household cares which crowded upon her the moment she left it. Even now, during the short time she had spent in the nursery, the English governess and Matryona had managed to ask her several questions that brooked no delay and which only she could answer: "How are the children to be dressed for their walk? Ought they to have any milk? Should not a new cook be engaged?"

"Oh, please leave me alone," she said and, returning to the bedroom, sat down again in the same chair where she had sat when talking to her husband. She clasped her ema-ciated hands with the rings hanging loosely from her bony fingers, and began going over in her mind the conversation they had had. "He has gone! But what has he done about *her*?" she thought. "He isn't still seeing her, is he? Why did I not ask him? No, no, it will never work. Even if we go on living in the same house, we shall remain strangers. Strangers always!" she repeated again with special empha-sis on the word she found so dreadful. "And how I loved! Good Lord, how I loved him! How I loved! And don't I love him even now? Don't I love him even more than ever now? What's so dreadful is that . . ." she began, but did not finish the thought, because Matryona poked her head through the door.

"Would you like me to send for my brother?" asked Matryona. "He could at least get dinner ready. Otherwise it will be like yesterday again, and the children won't have a bite to eat till at least six o'clock."

"Well, all right, I'll come presently and see about it. And the fresh milk? Has it been sent for?"

And Dolly, absorbed in her daily cares, drowned her grief in them for a while.

CHAPTER 5

Oblonsky had done well at school thanks to his natural abilities, but he was lazy and up to all sorts of mischief and that was why he had come out near the bottom of his class; but notwithstanding his life of dissipation, his rather low rank, and his not very advanced age, he occupied a distinguished and well-paid post as head of one of the Moscow government offices. He had obtained this post through his sister Anna's husband, Alexey Alexandrovich Karenin, who occupied one of the most important positions in the ministry of which this government office was a branch; but even if Karenin had not nominated his brother-in-law for that post, Stiva Oblonsky would have obtained it through a hundred other people—brothers, sisters, relations, cousins, uncles or aunts—or another similar post with a salary of six thousand rubles a year, which, in spite of his wife's considerable fortune, he found necessary, for his affairs were in a precarious state.

Half Moscow and Petersburg were Oblonsky's friends and relations. He was born among the people who were or who became the great ones of this earth. A third of the men who occupied high positions in the state were his father's friends and had known him as a baby; another third were on intimate terms with him; and the remainder were his good friends and acquaintances. As a result of this, the distributors of earthly goods in the shape of government posts, grants, concessions, and the like, were all good friends of his and could not pass over one who belonged to their own circle; Oblonsky had, therefore, no need to be particularly worried about obtaining a remunerative position; all he had to do was not to raise objections or be envious, nor to quarrel or take offense, which, being kindly by nature, he never did. It would have seemed ridiculous if anyone had told him that he would not obtain a post with the salary he required, particularly as he did not demand anything extraordinary; all he wanted was what other men of his age were getting, and he could perform the duties of such a post no worse than anyone else.

Oblonsky was not only liked by those who knew him for his good and cheerful nature and his undoubted integrity, but there was something in him, in his handsome bright appearance, his sparkling eyes, black hair and eyebrows, and pink-and-white complexion that had a physical impact on people who met him and made them feel friendly and cheered them up. "Ah, Stiva! Oblonsky! Here he is!" people almost always exclaimed with a pleased smile when they met him, and if it did occasionally happen that after talking to him people did not feel particularly delighted, they were all as pleased as Punch to see him the next day or the day after.

In the three years that Oblonsky had been head of one of the government departments in Moscow, he had won the affection and the respect of his colleagues, subordinates, superiors, and all who had anything to do with him. The chief qualities which had earned him this universal respect in the service were, first, his extreme indulgence with people, which was based on the fact that he was conscious of his own shortcomings; secondly, his genuine liberalism, not the sort of liberalism he read about in the papers, but that which was in his blood and which made him treat all people the same whatever their financial standing or social position; and, thirdly and chiefly, the complete detachment with which he regarded his work, as a result of which he was never carried away and never made mistakes.

Having arrived at his office, Oblonsky, followed by a respectful commissionaire who carried his portfolio, went straight to his little private office, put on his uniform, and went out into the general office. The clerks and the higher officials all rose and bowed cheerfully and respectfully. Oblonsky, as always, walked quickly to his place, shook hands with the members of the council, and sat down. He joked and chatted for just as long as was seemly and opened the proceedings. No one knew better than Oblonsky how to draw a line between freedom, simplicity, and formality, which is so essential for a pleasant atmosphere during work. The secretary approached with some papers in the cheerful and respectful manner which was characteristic of everyone else in the office, and said in the familiarly liberal tone that Oblonsky had introduced:

"We have at last got the information from the Penza provincial office. Here it is. Would you like, sir—"

"Ah, you've got it at last," said Oblonsky, putting a finger on the paper. "Well, gentlemen . . ." And the official business began.

"If they only knew," he thought, as he bowed his head with an air of importance during the hearing of the report, "how like a naughty boy their president was half an hour ago!" And his eyes laughed while the report was being read. Their work was to continue without interruption until two o'clock, when there would be an adjournment for lunch.

It was not quite two o'clock when the large glass doors of the general office suddenly swung open and someone entered. All the members, glad of the diversion, looked round at the entrance from behind the emperor's portrait and the diamond-shaped glass on which Peter the Great's edicts were engraved; but the doorkeeper immediately ejected the intruder and closed the glass doors behind him.

When the business was concluded, Oblonsky got up, stretched himself, and paying tribute to the liberalism of the times, took out a cigarette in the general office and went into his private office. Two colleagues of his, the crusty old civil servant Nikitin and the Court chamberlain Grinyevich, followed him.

"We shall have plenty of time to finish after lunch," said Oblonsky.

"Yes, I should think so," said Nikitin.

"That Fomin must be a thoroughgoing rascal," said Grinyevich, referring to one of the men concerned in the case they were considering.

Oblonsky frowned at Grinyevich's words, indicating that it was improper to form an opinion prematurely, and made no reply.

"Who came in?" he asked the doorkeeper.

"Someone got in without permission, sir, as soon as

22

my back was turned. He was asking for you. I told him that when the members came out, then . . ."

"Where is he?"

"I expect, sir, he must have gone out into the passage. He was here all the time. There he is," said the door-keeper, pointing to a strongly built, broad-shouldered man with a curly beard who, without taking off his sheepskin cap, was running swiftly and lightly up the worn steps of the stone staircase. One of the officials, who was on his way down with a portfolio, a lean civil servant, stopped, looked disapprovingly at the feet of the stranger, and glanced questioningly at Oblonsky.

Oblonsky was standing at the top of the steps. His face, which was beaming good-naturedly over the gold-laced collar of his uniform, beamed still more when he recognized the man who was running up the stairs.

"I thought so! Levin at last!" he said with a friendly and ironic smile as he gazed at the approaching Levin. "How is it you did not disdain to come and see me in this thieves' kitchen?" said Oblonsky, and not content with pressing his friend's hands, kissed him. "How long have you been in Moscow?"

"I've just arrived and I'm very anxious to see you," replied Levin, looking round shyly and at the same time resentfully and uneasily.

"Well, let's go into my office," said Oblonsky, who was well aware of his friend's touchy and irritable bashfulness; and taking him by the arm, he drew Levin after him as though steering him through some dangerous reefs.

Oblonsky was on equal terms with almost all his acquaintances: with old men of sixty and youths of twenty, with actors, ministers, tradesmen, and adjutants-general, so that a great many people who were on familiar terms with him were at the two extremes of the social ladder and would have been very much surprised to learn that through Oblonsky they had something in common. He was on familiar terms with everyone with whom he drank champagne, and he drank champagne with everyone. And, therefore, whenever he happened to meet any of his disreputable pals, as he jestingly called many of his friends in the presence of his subordinates, his natural tact enabled him to minimize any unpleasant impression his subordinates might have received from this meeting. Levin was not a disreputable pal, but Oblonsky, with his inborn tact, felt that Levin imagined that he might not wish to show his intimacy with him in front of his subordinates and that was why he hurried him into his private office.

Levin was about the same age as Oblonsky and was on intimate terms with him not entirely because they had drunk champagne together. Levin had been his close friend ever since their boyhood days. They were fond of each other in spite of the difference in their characters and tastes, as friends who have known each other since their boyhood mostly are. But in spite of that, as it often happens with men who have chosen different callings, though they might justify each other's career in discussing it, in their hearts they despised it. Each believed that the life he himself led was the only real life and the life led by his friend was nothing but an illusion. Oblonsky could not help smiling ironically at the sight of Levin. He must have seen him a hundred times on his arrival in Moscow from the country, where he did something or other; but what exactly, Oblonsky could never understand or take an interest in. Levin always arrived in Moscow, looking agitated and in a hurry, a little embarrassed and irritated by his embarrassment, and mostly with some totally new and unexpected views on things in general. Oblonsky was amused at this and liked it. Levin too in his heart despised his friend's town life and his official duties, which he considered a waste of time, and he too was amused at it all. But the difference between their points of view was that Oblonsky, doing the same things as everyone else, laughed confidently and good-humoredly, whereas Levin laughed not so confidently and sometimes angrily.

"We've been expecting you for some time," said Oblonsky, entering his office and letting go of Levin's arm, as though wishing to indicate that the danger was over. "I'm very, very glad to see you," he went on. "Well, how are you? What are you doing? When did you arrive?"

Levin was silent, looking at the unfamiliar faces of Oblonsky's two colleagues and especially at the hands of the elegant Grinyevich, who had such long white fingers with such long yellowish nails, curving at the tips, and such huge glittering cuff links. These hands apparently absorbed all Levin's attention and deprived him of freedom of thought. Oblonsky noticed it at once and smiled.

"Oh, I'm sorry, let me introduce you. My colleagues, Philip Nikitin and Mikhail Grinyevich." And turning to Levin he went on, "This is my friend Konstantin Levin, brother of Sergey Koznyshev, an active member of the rural county council, a man with new ideas, an athlete who can lift a hundred-and-twenty-pound weight with one hand, a cattle breeder and a sportsman."

"Very pleased to meet you," said the old man.

"I know your brother," said Grinyevich, holding out his slender hand with its long fingernails.

Levin knit his brows, shook hands coldly, and at once turned to Oblonsky. Although he felt a great respect for his half-brother, a writer famous throughout Russia, he could not bear to be treated as the brother of the famous Koznyshev and not as Konstantin Levin.

"No, I'm no longer a member of the rural council," he said, addressing Oblonsky. "I've quarreled with all of them and I don't attend the meetings any more."

"So soon?" said Oblonsky with a smile. "But how? Why?"

"It's a long story; I'll tell you some other time," said Levin, but he started to tell it at once. "To cut it short, I've satisfied myself that there's nothing the rural district council can or does do," he began, speaking just as though someone had said something offensive to him. "On the one hand, it's nothing but a plaything. They play at being a parliament, and I'm neither young enough nor old enough to be amused by playthings. On the other hand," he stammered, "this—er—is merely a means for the local landowning coterie to make money. We used to have trusteeships and courts of justice, and now we have the rural councils, not bribes, but money in the form of salaries, which they do nothing to earn," he said heatedly as though some of those present had tried to contradict him.

"Aha," said Oblonsky, "I can see that you've now entered a new phase, a conservative one this time. However, we'll talk about this later."

"Yes, later. But I have to see you about something," said Levin, staring at Grinyevich's hand with hatred.

Oblonsky smiled almost imperceptibly.

"Didn't you tell me that you'd never wear European clothes again?" he said, examining Levin's new suit, which was obviously the work of a French tailor. "Yes, I see. A new phase."

Levin suddenly blushed, but not as grown-up people blush, lightly and without noticing it themselves, but as boys blush, conscious that they are making themselves ridiculous by their shyness and in consequence feeling ashamed and blushing still more, almost to the point of tears. And it was so strange to see that intelligent, masculine face in such a childish predicament that Oblonsky tried not to look at him any more.

"But where shall we meet?" asked Levin. "You see, I simply must have a talk with you."

Oblonsky seemed to ponder.

"Tell you what. Let's go and have lunch at Gurin's. We can have our talk there. I'm free until three."

"No," replied Levin, after a moment's thought. "I have to go somewhere else first."

"Very well, let's have dinner together."

"Dinner? But, you see, I've nothing special to talk to you about. Just a couple of words—er—to ask you something. And then we can have a talk."

"Well, in that case, say your couple of words and we'll have our talk at dinner."

"Well, you see . . ." said Levin. "However, it's nothing important."

In his efforts to overcome his shyness his face suddenly assumed a spiteful expression.

"What are the Shcherbatskys doing? The same as usual?" he said.

Oblonsky, who had known for some time that Levin was in love with his sister-in-law Kitty, smiled almost imperceptibly and there was a merry twinkle in his eyes.

"You said a couple of words, but I'm afraid I can't answer in a couple of words, because . . . Excuse me a moment. . . ."

Oblonsky's secretary came in and with a look of respectful familiarity and a certain modest consciousness (common to all secretaries) of his own superiority to his chief in the knowledge of office business, approached the prince with a sheaf of papers and, on the pretext of asking a question, began to explain some difficulty.

Without waiting for him to finish, Oblonsky put a friendly hand on his sleeve.

"I think you'd better do as I asked you," he said, softening his remark with a smile, and explaining in a few words what his view of the matter was, he pushed the papers aside and said: "Please, my dear fellow, do it like that."

The secretary looked embarrassed and withdrew. Levin, who had completely recovered from his own confusion during Oblonsky's talk to the secretary, was standing with his elbows on the back of a chair, a look of sarcastic attention on his face.

"I don't understand, I don't understand," he said.

"What don't you understand?" Oblonsky said with the same gay smile as he took out a cigarette. He was expecting Levin to make some quixotic remark.

"I don't understand what you are doing here," said Levin, shrugging his shoulders. "How can you take this sort of thing seriously?"

"Why not?"

"Why, because there's nothing in it!"

"That's what you think. But, as a matter of fact, we are snowed under with work."

"Paper work. But then you have a gift for that," Levin added.

"Do you mean to say that I lack something?"

"Perhaps you do," said Levin, "but all the same I can't help admiring your grandeur, and I'm proud of having such a great man for a friend. But you haven't answered my question," he added, looking Oblonsky straight in the face with a desperate effort.

"Oh well, all right, all right. Wait a little. You too will come to it. It's all very well with your eight thousand acres in the Karazinsky district and you strong as a horse and fresh as a twelve-year-old girl! But even you will come over to us in the end. Oh yes, about your question. There's no change, but it's a pity you haven't been there for so long."

"Why?" Levin asked in alarm.

"Oh, nothing," replied Oblonsky. "We'll talk about it presently. What exactly brings you to town?"

"Oh," replied Levin, blushing to the roots of his hair, "we'll talk about that too afterward."

"All right," said Oblonsky, "I understand. You see,

27

I'd ask you to come to us, but my wife is not very well. I tell you what, though. If you want to see them, they're quite sure to be in the Zoological Gardens from four to five this afternoon. Kitty skates there. You go there and I'll call for you, and we'll dine somewhere together."

"Very well. Good-by, then."

"Now, look here," Oblonsky called after him, laughing, "I know you, you'll probably forget and rush off to the country suddenly."

"I won't forget."

And remembering when he was already in the doorway that he had not taken leave of Oblonsky's colleagues, Levin left the study.

"Must be a highly energetic gentleman," said Grinyevich after Levin had gone.

"Yes, my dear fellow," said Oblonsky, shaking his head. "He is a lucky beggar! Eight thousand acres in the Karazinsky district, everything before him and what incredible vitality! Not like some of us."

"What have you to complain of, Prince?"

"Oh, I'm in an awful mess," said Oblonsky with a heavy sigh.

CHAPTER 6

When Oblonsky had asked Levin what had brought him to Moscow, Levin had blushed and he had been angry with himself for having blushed because he could not very well reply: "I have come to propose to your sister-in-law," though he had come solely for that purpose.

The Levins and the Shcherbatskys belonged to the old Moscow nobility and had always been on close and friendly terms. Their friendship became even closer during Levin's student years. He had prepared for and entered the university together with young Prince Shcherbatsky, the brother of Dolly and Kitty. At that time Levin was a frequent visitor to the Shcherbatskys' house and he grew fond of the Shcherbatsky family. Strange as it may seem, Konstantin Levin was definitely in love with the entire family, and especially the feminine half of it. Levin himself did not remember his mother, and his only sister was older than himself, so that in the home of the Shcherbatskys he found himself for the first time in the environment of a cultured and honorable old aristocratic family, of which he had been deprived by the death of his own father and mother. All the members of this family, and especially the feminine half, seemed to him as though wrapped in some mysterious poetic veil, and not only did he fail to discover any defects in them, but he imagined behind that poetic veil the most elevated sentiments and every conceivable perfection. Why the three young ladies had to speak French one day and English another; why they had each in turn to practice the piano at certain hours, the sound of which could be heard in their brother's room upstairs where the students were studying; why those masters of French literature, music, drawing, and dancing came to the house; why at certain hours the three young ladies accompanied by Mademoiselle Linon were driven in an open carriage to the Tverskoy Boulevard in their satin fur-lined coats, Dolly in a long one, Natalie in a shorter one, and Kitty in one so short that her shapely little legs in the tightly pulled-up red stockings were exposed to the public gaze; why they had to walk up and down the Tverskoy Boulevard escorted by a footman with a gilt cockade in his hat—all this and much more that happened in their mysterious world he did not understand, but he knew that everything that happened there was perfect and it was with this aura of mystery that he was in love.

As a student he nearly fell in love with the eldest daughter Dolly, but she was soon married to Oblonsky. Then he began falling in love with the second. He seemed to feel that he had to fall in love with one of the sisters, only he could not make up his mind with which. But as soon as she came out, Natalie married the diplomat Lvov. Kitty was still a child when Levin left the university. Young Shcherbatsky joined the navy and was drowned in the Baltic, and Levin's relations with the Shcherbatskys became less frequent, in spite of his friendship with Oblonsky. When, however, at the beginning of the winter, Levin had come to Moscow after a year in the country, and had been to see the Shcherbatskys, he realized which of the three sisters he was really destined to fall in love with.

It would seem that nothing could be simpler than that

he, a man of good family and rich rather than poor, and thirty-two years of age, should propose to the young Princess Shcherbatsky; in all probability he would at once have been considered a good match. But Levin was in love and therefore Kitty seemed to him to be perfect in every respect, a being incomparably above all other human beings, while he himself was so earthly and low a creature that there could be no possibility of anyone, including herself, considering him to be worthy of her.

Having spent two months in Moscow in a dazed condition and seeing Kitty almost every day in society, which he began to frequent in order to meet her, Levin suddenly decided that his marriage to her was impossible, and had gone back to the country.

Levin's conviction that it was impossible was based on the assumption that in the view of her relatives he was not a good or worthy match for the fascinating Kitty, and that Kitty herself could not love him. In the eyes of her relatives he had no ordinary, definite career and position in society, while now that he was thirty-two, his contemporaries were already colonels, aides-de-camp, professors, directors of banks and railway companies, or heads of departments like Oblonsky; but (he knew perfectly well how he must appear to others) he was only a landowner who spent his time breeding cattle, shooting snipe, and erecting farm buildings; in other words, a fellow without talent, who had achieved nothing and who, according to the ideas prevalent in high society, was merely doing what is done by people fit for nothing.

The mysterious and fascinating Kitty could not love such an unattractive fellow as he believed himself to be and, above all, a man who was so ordinary and undistinguished. Besides, his former attitude to Kitty, the attitude of a grown-up person to a child whose brother was a friend of his, seemed to him to be an additional obstacle to love. In his view, an unattractive, kindly man like himself might be liked as a friend, but to be loved with the sort of love he himself felt for Kitty, one had to be a very handsome and, above all, quite a remarkable man.

He had heard that women often fell in love with unattractive and quite ordinary men, but he did not believe it because he judged by himself and he could fall in love only with beautiful, mysterious, and exceptional women.

But after spending two months alone in the country, he realized that this was not like one of the passions he had experienced as a very young man; that this feeling did not give him a moment's peace; that he could not live without having settled the question whether or not she would be his wife; and that his despair was the result merely of his own fancy, and that he had no proof that he would be refused. So now he had come to Moscow with the firm intention to propose to her and marry her if he was accepted, or—he could not imagine what would become of him if she were to refuse him.

CHAPTER 7

Having arrived in Moscow by the morning train, Levin had stopped at the house of his older half-brother Koznyshev, and, having changed, went to the study, intending to tell him at once why he had come and to ask his advice; but his half-brother was not alone. With him was a famous professor of philosophy who had arrived from Kharkov for the express purpose of clearing up some misunderstanding which had arisen between them on a very important philosophical question. The professor was engaged in a heated polemic against the materialists, and Sergey Koznyshev, who had followed this polemic with interest, had, after reading the professor's last article, written him a letter in which he formulated his objections; he reproached the professor for making too great concessions to the materialists; and the professor had immediately come to effect an agreement with him. The discussion concerned the fashionable question of whether there was a dividing line between the mental and physiological phenomena in human activity, and, if so, where?

Sergey Koznyshev welcomed his brother with the coldly affectionate smile with which he greeted everyone and, after introducing him to the professor, went on with the discussion.

A small, sallow man in spectacles, with a narrow forehead, interrupted the conversation for a moment to exchange greetings with Levin and then carried on the discussion without paying any more attention to him. Levin sat down to wait for the professor to go, but soon he became interested in the subject under discussion.

Levin had come across the articles they were discussing in periodicals, and he had read them with the interest of a man who has studied the natural sciences at the university and is familiar with the development of the basic principles of the natural sciences; but he had never himself connected these scientific deductions about man's origin as an animal, about reflexes, biology, and sociology, with the questions concerning the meaning of life and death that had recently come more and more frequently into his mind.

Listening to his brother's conversation with the professor, he noticed that they linked these scientific questions with the spiritual and several times came near to discussing this, but every time they got close to what seemed to him to be the most important point, they immediately beat a hasty retreat and again got involved in the sphere of subtle distinctions, reservations, quotations, allusions, and references to authorities, so that he had difficulty in understanding what they were talking about.

"I cannot admit it," said Koznyshev with his usual clarity and precision of expression and elegance of diction. "I cannot possibly agree with Keiss that my whole conception of the external world is the result of impressions. The most fundamental conception of *being* is obtained by me not through the senses, for there is no special organ to convey this conception."

"Yes, but all of them, Wurst, Knaust, and Pripasov, will tell you that your consciousness of existence arises from the totality of all your sensations, that, in fact, this consciousness of existence is the result of your sensations. Wurst even states plainly that as soon as sensations cease to exist there can be no conception of being."

"I would maintain the contrary," began Koznyshev.

But here again it seemed to Levin that just as they were coming to the most important point of the discussion, they again turned back, and he decided to put a question to the professor.

"So that," he asked, "if my senses are destroyed, if my body dies, no further existence is possible?"

32

The professor glanced at the strange questioner, who looked more like a barge hauler than a philosopher, with vexation, as if his interruption had caused him mental pain, and turned his eyes to Koznyshev as though to ask: "What's one to say to this?"

But Koznyshev, who had not by any means been talking with the same forcefulness and single-mindedness as the professor and whose grasp of intellect was quite sufficient both to answer the professor and at the same time to understand the simple and natural point of view which had inspired the question, smiled and said:

"This question we have as yet no right to settle."

"We haven't the data," confirmed the professor and went on with his arguments. "No," he declared, "all I wish to point out is that if, as Pripasov plainly asserts, sensation is based on impressions, then we ought to make a clear-cut distinction between these two conceptions."

Levin listened no longer, but sat waiting for the professor to go.

CHAPTER 8

When the professor had gone, Koznyshev turned to his step-brother:

"I'm very glad you've come. How long are you going to be here? How are you getting on on the farm?"

Levin knew that his brother took very little interest in his farming and that he had asked him about it merely as a gesture of good will. He therefore told him something about the sale of his wheat and about money matters.

Levin had meant to tell his brother of his intention to get married and to ask his advice. Indeed, he had made up his mind to do so. But when he saw his brother and had listened to his conversation with the professor, and heard the unconsciously patronizing tone in which his brother inquired about their estate (the property they had inherited from their mother had not been divided, and Levin was managing both their shares), Levin felt that for some reason he could not start talking to his brother about his decision to marry. He felt that his brother would not look at it in the way he would have wished.

"Well, how is your rural council getting on?" asked Koznyshev, who was very interested in the rural councils and attached great importance to them.

"I'm afraid I don't know."

"You don't know? But you're a member of the council, aren't you?"

"No, I'm no longer a member, I resigned," Konstantin Levin replied. "And I no longer attend the meetings."

"I'm sorry to hear that," said Koznyshev, frowning.

To justify himself, Levin began to describe what took place at the meetings in his district.

"That's how it always is," Koznyshev interrupted him. "We Russians are always like that. Perhaps it's one of our good national characteristics. I mean this faculty of seeing our own shortcomings. But we overdo it. We comfort ourselves with ironic remarks which are always on the tip of the tongue. All I can say is that if any other European nation had been granted the same rights as those enjoyed by our rural councils, the Germans and the English would have known how to obtain their freedom through them, but we only jeer at them."

"But what was I to do?" Levin said guiltily. "It was my last venture. I did all I could. I can't do any more. I'm sorry. I'm no good at it."

"No," said Koznyshev, "it isn't that you're not good at it. You just don't look on it as you should."

"Perhaps not," Levin replied dejectedly.

"Do you know our brother Nikolai has turned up again?"

Nikolai was Konstantin's elder brother and Koznyshev's half-brother, a social outcast who had squandered the greater part of his fortune, who kept the strangest and most disreputable company, and who had quarreled with his brothers.

"Has he?" cried Levin in horror. "How do you know?"

"Prokofy saw him in the street."

"Here in Moscow? Where is he? Do you know?" Levin got up from his chair, as though intending to go and see his brother at once.

"I'm sorry I told you," said Koznyshev, shaking his head at his younger brother's agitation. "I sent to find out where he was living and sent him back his IOU to Trubin which I had paid. And this is what he writes in reply."

Koznyshev handed his brother a note which he took from under a paperweight.

Levin read in the strange familiar hand: "Please leave me alone. That is the only thing I ask of my beloved brothers. Nikolai Levin."

Levin read it and, without raising his head, stood with the note in his hand in front of Koznyshev.

A struggle was going on in his heart between a desire to forget his unfortunate brother for the moment and the consciousness that this would be wrong.

"He obviously wants to insult me," Koznyshev went on, "but he can't do that. I would have very much liked to help him, but I know it can't be done."

"Yes, yes," repeated Levin. "I understand and appreciate your attitude towards him. I'll go and see him, though."

"Go if you want to by all means, but I don't advise it," said Koznyshev. "What I mean is that so far as I'm concerned, I'm not afraid of it. He won't stir up trouble between us. But for your own sake, I'd advise you not to go. You can't do anything to help him. However, do as you please."

"Quite possibly I can't do anything to help him, but I feel, especially at this moment—but that's a different matter—that I can't be easy in my mind about him."

"Well, that I don't understand," said Koznyshev. "All I know is," he added, "that it's been a lesson in humility. I've come to look differently and more indulgently upon what people call infamy since our brother Nikolai became what he is. You know what he did. . . ."

"Oh, it's dreadful, dreadful. . . ." Levin kept repeating.

Having got his brother's address from Koznyshev's footman, Levin was on the point of going to see him at once, but on second thoughts decided to postpone his visit till the evening. What had to be done first of all to set his mind at rest was to get a definite decision about the matter which had brought him to Moscow. So from his brother's Levin went to Oblonsky's office and, having found out about the Shcherbatskys, drove to the place where he had been told he might find Kitty.

CHAPTER 9

At four o'clock that afternoon, Levin got out of the hired sleigh at the Zoological Gardens and, conscious that his heart was beating fast, went down the path leading to the ice hills and the skating rink, certain that he would find Kitty there, for he had seen the Shcherbatskys' carriage at the entrance.

It was a sunny, frosty day. At the gates there were rows of carriages, private sleighs, sleighs on hire, and policemen. Well-dressed people, their hats shining in the bright sunlight, swarmed at the entrance and along the well-swept paths between the little Russian cottages with their carved eaves; the feathery old birch trees in the gardens, their branches weighed down with snow, looked as if they had been dressed up in new festive vestments.

He walked along the path in the direction of the skating rink and kept saying to himself: "You mustn't get excited! You must keep calm! What are you so excited about? What's the matter with you? Keep still, stupid," he told his heart. But the more he tried to compose himself, the more breathless he became with excitement. A man he knew met and hailed him, but Levin did not even notice who it was. He went up to the ice hills, which resounded with the clanking of the chains by which the toboggans were being pulled up or down, their clatter as they slid down, and the sound of merry voices. He walked a few more steps, and there was the skating rink before him and he at once recognized her among the many skaters.

He knew she was there by the joy and terror that gripped his heart. She stood talking to a woman at the opposite end of the rink. There was apparently nothing striking about her dress or her attitude: but Levin found it as easy to recognize her in that crowd of people as a rose among nettles. Everything became bright in her presence. She was the smile that brightened everything around. "Can I really go down onto the ice and go up to her?" he thought. The spot where she stood seemed to him an unapproachable sanctuary, and there was one moment when he nearly went away, so terrified was he. He had to make an effort and reason with himself that all sorts of people were walking near her and that he himself might have come to skate there. He went down, trying not to look long at her, as though she were the sun, but he saw her, as one sees the sun, without looking.

On that day of the week and at that particular time, people belonging to the same set and all acquainted with one another used to meet on the ice. There were expert skaters there who showed off their skill and beginners clinging to chairs and making awkward, timid movements, boys and elderly people skating for their health; they all seemed to Levin to be a select band of lucky people because they were there near her. Yet the skaters apparently kept overtaking her, catching up with her, and even speaking to her with complete unconcern, and were enjoying themselves quite independently of her, making the best of the excellent ice and the fine weather.

Nikolai Shcherbatsky, Kitty's cousin, in a short jacket and tight trousers, was sitting on a bench with his skates on. Seeing Levin, he called out to him:

"Hullo, Russia's champion skater! Have you been here long? The ice is excellent. Get your skates on!"

"I haven't even got my skates with me," replied Levin, marveling at such boldness and familiarity in her presence, and without losing sight of her for one second, although not looking at her. He felt the sun approaching him. She was turning a corner and, her slender little feet in their high boots at an obtuse angle, quite obviously nervous, she was skating toward him. A little boy in Russian dress, violently waving his arms and stooping low, was overtaking her. She was not skating very steadily; taking her hands out of the muff that hung on a cord round her neck, she held them extended in readiness for any emergency, and looking at Levin, whom she had recognized, she smiled at him, and at her own fears. When she had got round the corner, she gave herself a push with a springy little foot and skated straight up to Shcherbatsky. Catching hold of him with her hand, she nodded smilingly to Levin. She was lovelier than he had imagined.

When he thought about her he could see her vividly in his mind's eye and especially her charming little fair-haired head, poised so lightly on her shapely, girlish shoulders, and her expression of childlike serenity and goodness. It was the childlike expression of her face, combined with the slim beauty of her figure, that made up her special charm that he remembered so well; but what he always found so unexpected about her was the expression of her gentle, calm, and truthful eyes—and especially her smile, which always transported Levin into an enchanted world where he felt softened, and over-flowing with tenderness, as he remembered feeling on rare occasions in his early childhood.

"Have you been here long?" she said, shaking hands with him. "Thank you," she added when he picked up the handkerchief she had dropped from her muff.

"Me? No, not long. I came yesterday, I mean today," replied Levin, who in his agitation did not grasp her question immediately. "I was meaning to come and see you," he went on, and remembering at once what he wanted to see her about, he was overcome with confu-sion and blushed. "I did not know you could skate, and so well."

She looked intently at him, as though wishing to grasp the reason for his confusion.

"Your praise is praise indeed," she said, brushing away with a small black-gloved hand some needles of hoarfrost from her muff. "You've become a legend here as one of our best skaters."

"Yes, once upon a time I was passionately fond of skating. I wanted to be perfect at it."

"You seem to do everything with passion," she said with a smile. "I'd like to see you skate so much. Do put on your skates and let us skate together."

"Skate together! Is that possible?" thought Levin, looking at her. "I'll go and put them on at once," he said, and he went off to get some skates.

"It's a long time since you've been here, sir," said the ice-rink attendant, holding up Levin's foot and screwing the skate onto the heel. "Not one of the gentlemen here is as good as you, sir. Is that all right?" he said, tight-ening the strap.

"Yes, yes, it's all right. Hurry up, please," replied Levin, hardly able to restrain the happy smile which spread over his face in spite of himself. "Yes," he thought, "this is life, this is happiness! Shall I tell her

38

now? But then I'm afraid to tell her because I'm happy now, happy if only in my hopes . . . But afterward? . . . But I have to, I have to, I have to. Away with this weakness!"

Levin got to his feet, took off his overcoat, and taking a run over the rough ice around the hut, glided onto the smooth ice and skated along effortlessly, as though quickening, slackening, and directing his speed by the exercise of his will alone. He approached Kitty timidly, but again her smile reassured him.

She gave him her hand and they set off side by side, quickening their pace, and the faster they skated, the more tightly she squeezed his hand.

"I should soon learn with you," she said to him. "I feel confidence in you for some reason."

"And I have confidence in myself when you lean on me," he answered, and he was immediately frightened at what he had said, and blushed. And indeed, as soon as he had uttered those words, her face all at once lost all its friendliness, like the sun going behind a cloud, and Levin recognized the familiar change in her expression which showed that she was thinking hard: a wrinkle appeared on her smooth forehead.

"You're not worried about anything? However, I have no right to ask," he added quickly.

"No, I'm not worried about anything," she replied coldly, and at once added: "You haven't seen Mademoiselle Linon, have you?"

"Not yet."

"Please, go over and talk to her. She's very fond of you."

"What's the matter? I've upset her. O Lord, help me!" thought Levin and rushed over to the old Frenchwoman with the gray ringlets, who was sitting on a bench. Smiling and showing her false teeth, she greeted him as an old friend.

"Yes, we're growing up," she said to him, indicating Kitty with her eyes, "and getting older. 'Tiny Bear' has grown big now!" the Frenchwoman continued, laughing and reminding him of his joke about the three young ladies, whom he called the three bears of the English fairy tale. "Do you remember when you used to call her that?"

He had not the faintest recollection of it, but she had

been laughing at the joke for the past ten years and enjoyed it.

"Now, off with you, go and skate. Our Kitty is beginning to skate nicely now, isn't she?"

When Levin went back to Kitty her face was no longer stern and her eyes had their former frank and friendly look. But Levin could not help feeling that there was a special, deliberately quiet, emphasis in her friendliness. And he felt sad. After they had talked about her old governess and her eccentricities, she asked him about his own life.

"Aren't you bored in the country in the winter?" she said.

"No, I'm not, I'm very busy," he said, feeling that she was forcing him to assume her own quiet tone of voice, which, as it had been at the beginning of the winter, he would not be able to drop.

"Are you going to stay here long?" Kitty asked.

"I don't know," he replied, without thinking of what he was saying. The thought occurred to him that if he gave in to her tone of calm friendliness, he would again go away without having settled anything, and he decided to make a fight for it.

"You don't know?"

"I don't. It all depends on you," he said and was at once terrified at his own words.

Either she did not hear or did not want to hear his words, but she seemed to stumble and, striking the ice with her foot twice, skated hurriedly away from him. She glided up to Mademoiselle Linon, said something to her, and went off in the direction of the little hut where the ladies took off their skates.

"Good Lord, what have I done? O Lord, help me and teach me!" prayed Levin, and feeling at the same time a need of violent exercise, he took a run and started describing rings within rings.

At that moment a young man, the best of the younger skaters, came out of the coffeehouse with a cigarette in his mouth and his skates on, and taking a run, went down the steps clattering as he jumped from step to step. He flew down and skated away over the ice without so much as changing the easy position of his arms.

"Oh, that's a new trick!" cried Levin, and at once ran up the steps to try it out.

"Don't hurt yourself—it needs practice," Nikolai Shcherbatsky called out.

Levin went up the steps, took a run along the top as fast as he could, and then dashed down, balancing himself with his arms in this unaccustomed movement. He caught his foot on the bottom step but hardly touching the ice with his hand, made a violent effort, righted himself, and with a laugh skated away.

"How sweet and nice he is!" thought Kitty at that moment as she came out of the little hut with Mademoiselle Linon, and she looked at him with a smile of quiet affection, just as if he were her favorite brother. "And am I to blame? Have I done anything wrong? People say I'm just flirting with him, but I know that I don't love him. All the same, I enjoy being with him and he's so nice. Only what made him say that?" she thought.

When he saw Kitty about to leave the ice rink with her mother, who had met her on the steps, Levin, flushed from his rapid exercise, stopped and looked thoughtful. He took off his skates and overtook mother and daughter at the gates of the Gardens.

"I'm very glad to see you," said the princess. "We are at home on Thursdays as usual."

"Today?"

"We shall be delighted to see you," the princess said dryly.

Kitty was upset by this dry tone, and she could not resist the desire to make amends for her mother's coldness. She turned her head and said with a smile: *"Au revoir."*

At that moment Oblonsky, his hat tilted to one side, and with beaming face and eyes, entered the Gardens with the air of a gay conqueror. But on approaching his mother-in-law, he replied to her questions about Dolly's health with a sad and guilty expression on his face. Having exchanged a few words with his mother-in-law in a subdued and dejected tone, he threw out his chest and took Levin's arm.

"Well, shall we go?" he asked. "I've been thinking about you and I'm glad, very glad, you've come," he said, looking significantly into Levin's eyes.

"Yes, let's go, let's go," replied the happy Levin, still hearing her voice saying *"Au revoir,"* and seeing the smile with which it had been said.

"The England or the Hermitage?"

"I don't mind which."

"Well, the England then," said Oblonsky, choosing the England because he owed more there than at the Hermitage, and therefore considered it wrong to avoid it. "Have you a sleigh? Ah, that's excellent, because I let my carriage go."

The two friends were silent all the way to the restaurant. Levin was wondering what the change of expression on Kitty's face had meant, at one moment assuring himself that there was hope and at another falling into despair and clearly realizing that it was madness for him to hope. And yet he felt quite a different man since her smile and the words *"Au revoir."*

Oblonsky was composing the menu of their dinner on the way to the restaurant.

"You like turbot, don't you?" he said to Levin, as they drove up to the restaurant.

"What?" asked Levin. "Turbot? Oh yes, I'm *awfully* fond of turbot."

CHAPTER 10

When they entered the restaurant, Levin could not help noticing a certain peculiarity of expression, a sort of suppressed radiance, on Oblonsky's face and in his whole person. Oblonsky took off his overcoat and, with his hat tilted, walked into the dining room, giving his orders to the Tartar waiters who trod on his heels in their swallow-tail coats, with napkins over their arms. Bowing right and left to his acquaintances, who here as everywhere else greeted him with delight, he went up to the buffet, had a glass of vodka with a bit of fish, and said something to the painted Frenchwoman, all curls, lace, and ribbons, who sat behind the cashier's desk, something that made even this Frenchwoman burst into unfeigned laughter. Levin did not drink any vodka simply because he was outraged by the appearance of that Frenchwoman, who seemed to him made up of false hair, *poudre de riz*, and *vinaigre de toilette.* He moved away from her hurriedly as from some unclean place.

His whole soul was full of memories of Kitty, and his eyes shone with a smile of triumph and happiness.

"This way, sir, this way! You won't be disturbed here, sir," said a particularly obsequious, white-headed old Tartar so broad across the hips that the tails of his coat did not meet. "If you please, sir," he said to Levin, by way of showing his respect to Oblonsky, showing particular attention to his guest also. "If you please, sir."

In a second he had laid a fresh cloth on a round table under a bronze chandelier, although it already had a tablecloth on it, pushed up two velvet chairs, and stood before Oblonsky with a napkin and menu awaiting his order.

"If you would prefer a private room, sir, it will be available in a moment. Prince Golitsyn is there with a lady. We've some fresh oysters in, sir."

"Ah, oysters!"

Oblonsky thought it over. "What about changing our menu, Levin?" he said, keeping his finger on the bill of fare. And there was an expression of serious perplexity on his face. "Are the oysters good? Are you quite sure?"

"They are Flensburg, sir. We've no Ostend ones."

"They may be Flensburg, but are they fresh?"

"They only arrived yesterday, sir."

"What about it? Shall we start with oysters and then change the whole menu? What do you say?"

"I don't mind. I like cabbage soup and buckwheat porridge better than anything, but I don't suppose they have it here."

"Porridge *à la Russe*, sir?" said the Tartar, bending over Levin like a nurse over a child.

"No, seriously, whatever you choose will be all right. I've been skating and I'm ravenous. And don't imagine," he added, noticing a look of dissatisfaction on Oblonsky's face, "that I don't appreciate your choice. I shall enjoy a good dinner."

"I should think so! Say what you like, it's one of life's pleasures," said Oblonsky. "Well then, my good fellow, let's have two, no, three dozen oysters and vegetable soup . . ."

"Printanière," put in the Tartar, but Oblonsky evidently did not wish to give him the satisfaction of naming the dishes in French.

"Vegetable, you know. Then turbot with thick sauce, then . . . er . . . roast beef—and mind it's good—followed, I suppose, by capon and, well, fruit salad."

Remembering Oblonsky's habit of not calling the dishes on the menu by their French names, the waiter did not repeat the order after him, but could not deny himself the pleasure of repeating the whole order after him to himself according to the menu: *"Soupe printanière, turbot, sauce Beaumarchais, poulard à l'estragon, macédoine de fruits . . . ,"* and immediately, as though worked by springs, he put down the menu in one cover and seizing another, the wine list, held it out before Oblonsky.

"What shall we drink?"

"Anything you like, only not too much. . . . Champagne?" said Levin.

"Start with champagne? Well, why not? You like the White Seal?"

"Cachet Blanc," the Tartar put in.

"Yes, bring us that with the oysters and then we'll see."

"Very good, sir. And what table wine?"

"You can give us Nuits, or no, better the classic Chablis."

"Very good, sir. And the cheese? Your special cheese, sir?"

"Oh yes, Parmesan. Or would you like some other kind?"

"No, I don't mind which," said Levin, unable to repress a smile.

And the Tartar, his coattails flying, ran off and five minutes later rushed in again with a dish of oysters, their pearly shells open, and a bottle between his fingers.

Oblonsky crumpled his starched napkin, tucked it into his waistcoat, and putting his arms comfortably on the table, attacked the oysters.

"They're not bad," he said, tearing the slippery oysters from their pearly shells with a silver fork, and swallowing them one after another. "Not bad, not bad," he repeated, raising his moist and glittering eyes from Levin to the Tartar and back again.

Levin ate his oysters, although he would have preferred white bread and cheese. But he could not help admiring Oblonsky. Even the Tartar, having uncorked the bottle and poured the sparkling wine into the thin, wide-lipped glasses, kept looking at Oblonsky with a smile of undisguised pleasure, as he straightened his white tie.

"You don't care much for oysters, do you?" said Oblonsky, draining his glass. "Or are you worried about something? Eh?"

He would have liked Levin to be in good spirits, but Levin, though not in bad spirits, felt constrained. In his present frame of mind, he felt uncomfortable and ill at ease in a restaurant with its private rooms where men took women to dine. And this continuous bustle and running about, these bronzes, mirrors, gaslights, Tartars—all this seemed an affront to him. He was afraid of besmirching that which filled his soul.

"Me? Yes, I am. Besides, all this makes me feel uncomfortable," he said. "You can't imagine how strange all this seems to one like myself who lives in the country. Like the fingernails of that gentleman I saw in your office. . . ."

"Yes, I noticed that you were very interested in poor Grinyevich's nails," Oblonsky said, laughing.

"I can't help it," replied Levin. "Try and put yourself in my place. Look at it from the point of view of a countryman. We in the country do our best to make it easy for ourselves to work with our hands, and so we cut our nails and sometimes roll up our sleeves. But here people purposely let their nails grow as long as they can and wear little saucers for cuff links so that it's quite impossible for them to do anything with their hands."

Oblonsky smiled gaily.

"Yes, it shows that he does not have to do any manual labor. He works with his brain. . . ."

"Perhaps. But all the same it seems strange to me. Just as I can't help regarding it as strange that while we in the country try to get our meals over as quickly as possible so as to be able to get on with our work, you and I are doing our best to make our dinner last as long as possible and for that reason have oysters."

"Well, naturally," Oblonsky put in. "But that's the whole aim of civilization: to make everything a source of enjoyment."

"Well, if that is so, I'd rather be a savage."

"You are a savage as it is. All you Levins are savages."

Levin sighed. He remembered his brother Nikolai and,

45

feeling conscience-stricken and grieved, he frowned; but Oblonsky began to speak of a subject which at once diverted his train of thoughts.

"Well, are you going to see the family this evening? The Shcherbatskys, I mean?" he said, pushing aside the rough, empty oyster shells and drawing the cheese towards him, a meaningful gleam in his eyes.

"Yes, I shall most certainly go," replied Levin. "Although I couldn't help feeling that the princess was not particularly keen on inviting me."

"What nonsense! It's just her manner. . . . Come, my good fellow, let's have the soup now. It's her manner, her *grande dame* manner," Oblonsky said. "I shall be there, too, but first I have to go to a choir practice at Countess Bonin's. But aren't you a savage, though? How is one to explain your sudden disappearance from Moscow? The Shcherbatskys kept asking me about you just as if I ought to know. All I know is you never behave like anyone else."

"Yes," said Levin slowly and with emotion, "you're quite right. I am a savage. But the fact that I am a savage is proved not by my having gone away then, but by having come back now. I have come back now—"

"Oh, what a lucky fellow you are," Oblonsky interrupted, looking Levin in the face.

"Why?"

"The mettlesome steed by his breed, the young lover by his eyes, I recognize," Oblonsky declaimed. "You have everything before you."

"And you have everything behind you?"

"Well, perhaps not, but the future is yours and only the present is mine—and that too only in part."

"Why, what's the matter?"

"Oh well, I'm in a bit of a mess. But don't let's talk about myself. And, anyway, it's impossible to explain it all," Oblonsky said. "Now, why have you come to Moscow? Waiter, take this away," he called to the Tartar.

"Can't you guess?" replied Levin without taking his gleaming eyes off Oblonsky.

"I can guess, but I can't very well break the subject, can I?" said Oblonsky, looking at him with a sly smile. "You can tell from that whether my guess is right or not."

"Well, what have you got to say to me about it?" said

Levin in a trembling voice, feeling that every muscle of his face was quivering. "What do you think my chances are?"

Oblonsky slowly emptied his glass of Chablis without taking his eyes off Levin.

"Me?" said Oblonsky. "I should like nothing better. Nothing. It's the best thing that could happen."

'But you're not making a mistake, are you? You know what you're talking about?" said Levin, looking steadily at Oblonsky. "You think it possible?"

"Yes, I do. Why shouldn't it be possible?"

"Do you really think so? Come, tell me. No, really, tell me what you think. I mean, what if I were to be refused? As a matter of fact, I feel sure that . . ."

"Why should you think so?" said Oblonsky, smiling at his agitation.

"Sometimes I can't help thinking so. You see, that would be terrible for me and for her."

"Well, I don't think there's anything terrible in it for a girl. Every girl is proud of a proposal of marriage."

"Yes, every girl, but not she."

Oblonsky smiled. He knew that feeling of Levin's so well. He knew that for Levin all the girls in the world were divided into two classes: one class included all the girls in the world except her and all of them had all the human weaknesses, and all of them were very ordinary; the other class contained only Kitty alone, a girl who had no weaknesses of any kind and who was above the rest of humanity.

"Wait, have some sauce," he said, holding back Levin's hand, which was pushing the sauce away.

Levin obediently helped himself to sauce, but he did not let Oblonsky go on eating.

"No, wait, wait!" he said. "You must understand that for me it's a question of life and death. I've never spoken to anyone about it, and I can speak to no one about it except you. You see, you and I are different in everything: we've different tastes, opinions, everything. But I know that you like me and understand me and that's why I'm awfully fond of you, too. But for God's sake do be frank with me!"

"I'm telling you what I think," said Oblonsky, smiling. "And let me tell you something more: my wife is a most remarkable woman. . . ." Oblonsky smiled, remembering his present relations with his wife, and went on after a moment's pause: "She has the gift of second sight. She can see people through and through! But that's not all. She knows what is going to happen, especially where marriages are concerned. For instance, she predicted that the Shakhovsky girl would marry Brenteln. No one would believe it, but she turned out to be right. And she's on your side."

"You mean?"

"What I mean is that she's not only fond of you, but that she says that Kitty is sure to be your wife."

At these words Levin's face suddenly lit up with a smile that was indistinguishable from tears of deep emotion.

"She says that?" cried Levin. "I always said that she was a wonderful woman, your wife, I mean. But don't let's talk about it any more," he said, getting up.

"All right, but sit down."

But Levin could not sit still. He strode twice across the little cage of a room, blinking to conceal his tears, and only then sat down at the table again.

"Please, understand," he said, "that this is not love. I have been in love, but this is not the same thing. It is not mere feeling, but a sort of force outside me which has taken possession of me. You see, I left Moscow before because I had made up my mind that it would never be, that such happiness does not exist on earth, do you understand? But I have struggled with myself and I can see now that I can't go on living without it. And it has to be settled."

"Then why did you go away?"

"One moment. Oh, there are so many thoughts, so many questions to ask. Listen. You can't imagine what you have done for me by saying what you did. I'm so happy that I'm becoming positively loathsome. I am forgetting everything. I heard today that my brother Nikolai—you know he's here. . . . And I forgot all about him. I can't help feeling that he is happy too. It's a sort of madness. But one thing is awful. . . . You're married and you must know the feeling. . . . I mean, what is so awful is that we—who are no longer young and have pasts . . . er . . . not of love but of sins—that we find ourselves drawn close suddenly to a pure, innocent

48

being! That's disgusting, and that is why one can't help feeling oneself unworthy."

"Well, you can't have had many sins."

"Oh, all the same," said Levin, "all the same, 'scanning my life with disgust, I tremble, I curse, I bitterly complain. . . .' Yes."

"Well, what's to be done?" said Oblonsky. "That's the way the world is made."

"There's one consolation, though. Just as in that prayer I've always liked, 'Pardon me not according to my deserts, but according to thy loving kindness.' She too could only forgive me that way."

CHAPTER 11

Levin emptied his glass and they were silent for a while.

"There's one thing more that I must tell you," said Oblonsky. "Do you know Vronsky?"

"No, I don't. Why do you ask?"

"Another bottle," Oblonsky said to the Tartar who was filling their glasses and fidgeting round them just when he was not wanted.

"Why ought I to know Vronsky?"

"You ought to know Vronsky because he is one of your rivals."

"Who is this Vronsky?" asked Levin, and the childlike, rapturous expression of his face, which Oblonsky had been admiring, suddenly changed into an angry and disagreeable one.

"Vronsky is one of Count Kyril Ivanovich Vronsky's sons, and one of the best samples of the gilded youth of Petersburg. I got to know him in Tver when I was in the service there, and he came for the levy of recruits. Awfully rich, handsome, influential connections, an aide-de-camp to the emperor and a very charming and good-natured fellow into the bargain. He's even more than just a good-natured fellow. I've got to know him better here. He is a well-educated man and a very intelligent one. He'll go far."

Levin frowned and was silent.

"Well, you see, he appeared here shortly after you left and, as I understand it, he's head over ears in love with Kitty, and you realize that her mother . . ."

"I'm sorry but I don't realize anything," said Levin, scowling gloomily. And he immediately remembered his brother Nikolai and how despicable it had been of him to forget him.

"Wait, wait," said Oblonsky, smiling and touching Levin's arm. "I've told you what I know, and, as far as one can judge, I repeat that in so delicate a matter, affecting a man's tenderest emotions, it looks to me as if the chances are in your favor."

Levin leaned back in his chair. His face was pale.

"But I'd advise you to settle the matter as soon as possible," Oblonsky continued, filling up his glass.

"No thank you, I can't drink any more," said Levin, pushing his glass away. "I shall be drunk. But what about you? How are things with you?" he went on, obviously anxious to change the subject.

"Just one word more: in any case, I advise you to settle the question quickly. I don't advise you to speak of it today," said Oblonsky. "Go and see them tomorrow morning, make your proposal in the classic manner and may the Lord bless you. . . ."

"You've so often expressed the wish of coming for some shooting with me, haven't you?" said Levin. "Why not come this spring?"

He regretted with all his heart that he had started this conversation with Oblonsky. His special feeling was profaned by the mention of some Petersburg officer as his rival and by Oblonsky's conjectures and advice.

Oblonsky smiled. He understood what was going on in Levin's mind.

"I will some day," he said. "Yes, my dear fellow, women are the pivot round which the world turns. My affairs too are in a bad way, very bad, and all because of women. Please, tell me quite frankly," he went on, taking out a cigar and keeping one hand on his glass. "Give me your advice."

"What about?"

"About this. Suppose you're married and you love your wife, but you've fallen in love with another woman. . . ."

"I'm sorry, but I really can't understand that. I mean it's . . . just as incomprehensible to me as if, after having

50

eaten a good dinner now, I were to go into a baker's shop and steal a roll."

Oblonsky's eyes sparkled more than usual.

"Why not? Rolls sometimes smell so good that you can't resist them!"

> *"Himmlisch ist's, wenn ich bezwungen*
> *Meine irdische Begier;*
> *Aber doch wenn's nicht gelungen,*
> *Hatt' ich auch recht hübsch Plaisir!"*

Oblonsky recited these lines with a sly smile. Levin too could not help smiling.

"But joking apart," Oblonsky went on, "just imagine a woman, a charming, gentle, loving creature, poor, lonely, who has sacrificed everything and now when the thing is done—you understand—should one abandon her? Suppose it may be necessary to part from her so as not to break up one's family life, but shouldn't one be sorry for her? Shouldn't one see that she doesn't suffer? Shouldn't one try to soften the blow?"

"I'm sorry. I think you know that so far as I am concerned there are only two kinds of women. Or rather, no . . . there are women and there are . . . I have never seen and I don't think I shall ever see any charming fallen creatures, but women like that painted Frenchwoman at the cashier's desk, the one with the ringlets, such women are vile creatures for me, and all fallen women are the same."

"And the woman in the New Testament?"

"Oh, for goodness sake! Christ would never have spoken those words had he known how they would be misused! Those words seem to me to be the only ones people remember in the whole gospels. However, I'm not saying what I think but what I feel. I have a horror of fallen women. You are afraid of spiders and I am afraid of those horrible creatures. I don't suppose you have made a study of spiders and their habits, and the same is true of me."

"It's all very well for you to talk like that. It's like the character in Dickens who used to throw all embarrassing questions over his right shoulder with his left hand. But the denial of a fact is no answer. What is to be done? Tell me, what is to be done? Your wife is getting old and you are full of life. Before you have time to turn around, you feel that you are no longer in love with your wife, however much you may respect her. Then all of a sudden you fall in love with someone else and you're lost, lost!" Oblonsky repeated with gloomy despair.

Levin smiled.

"Yes, you're lost," Oblonsky repeated again. "But what's to be done?"

"Don't steal rolls."

Oblonsky laughed.

"Oh, you moralist! But try to understand that there are two women: one insists only on her rights and those rights are your love which you can no longer give her, while the other sacrifices everything for you and demands nothing. What are you to do? How are you to act? There's a terrible tragedy here."

"If you want to know what I really think about this, then I can tell you that I don't believe that there is any tragedy here. And for this reason: in my view, love—both kinds of love, which you remember Plato defines in his *Symposium*—both kinds of love serve as a touchstone for men. Some men understand only one kind and others only the other. And those who understand only the nonplatonic love should not speak of a tragedy. For in such a love there can be no tragedy. 'Thank you very much for the pleasure, good-by,' that's the whole tragedy. And neither can there be any tragedy in platonic love, because in that kind of love everything is clear and pure because . . ." At that moment Levin, remembering his own sins and the inner struggle he had lived through, added unexpectedly:

"However, perhaps you're right. Yes, perhaps you are. . . . But I don't know. I really don't know."

"Well, you see," said Oblonsky, "you are a thoroughly earnest and sincere man. This is your strength and your limitation. You are thoroughly earnest and sincere and you want all life to be earnest and sincere too, but it never is. You despise public service because you think its practice ought to be as single-minded as its aims, but that never happens. You want the activity of every single man always to have an aim, and love and family life always to be one and the same thing. But that doesn't happen, either. All the diversity, all the charm, and all the beauty of life are made up of light and shade."

Levin sighed and made no answer. He was thinking of his own affairs and not listening to Oblonsky.

And suddenly both felt that though they were friends and had dined and wined together, which should have drawn them closer, each was thinking only of his own affairs and was not really concerned with the other. Oblonsky had more than once experienced this sort of extreme estrangement instead of intimacy after a dinner with a friend, and knew what to do in such circumstances.

"The bill," he called and went into the next room where he at once saw an aide-de-camp he knew and began talking to him about an actress and her protector. And in his conversation with the aide-de-camp, Oblonsky at once felt relieved and refreshed after his conversation with Levin, who always imposed too great an intellectual and mental strain upon him.

When the Tartar appeared with a bill for twenty-six rubles and some kopecks, with the addition of a tip for himself, Levin, who at any other time, like any other countryman, would have been horrified at his share of fourteen rubles, paid no attention to it now, but settled his bill and set off home to dress and go to the Shcherbatskys, where his fate was to be decided.

CHAPTER 12

Princess Kitty Shcherbatsky was eighteen. She had come out that winter, and her success in society was much greater than that of her two elder sisters and greater even than her mother had expected. Not only were nearly all the young men who danced at the Moscow balls in love with Kitty, but two serious suitors had presented themselves that very first winter: Levin and, immediately after his departure, Count Vronsky.

Levin's appearance at the beginning of the winter, his frequent visits and quite manifest love for Kitty, had led to the first serious discussion between Kitty's parents about her future and to differences of opinion between the prince and the princess. The prince was on the side of Levin and kept saying that he could wish nothing better for Kitty. The princess, with the way women have of going around a question, kept saying that Kitty was too young, that Levin had done nothing to show that his intentions were serious, that Kitty was not in love with him, and she brought all sorts of other objections; but she said nothing about her chief objection, namely that she hoped for a better match for her daughter and that she did not like Levin and did not understand him. When Levin suddenly departed, the princess was delighted and said to her husband triumphantly, "Well, you see, I was right!" When Vronsky appeared on the scene she was still more delighted, confirmed in her opinion that Kitty ought to make not only a good but a brilliant match.

For the mother there could be no possible comparison between Vronsky and Levin. The mother did not like Levin's strange and uncompromising opinions, his awkwardness in society, which she was convinced was due to his pride, and, as she saw it, his uncivilized life in the country with his constant preoccupation with cattle and peasants; nor did she like the fact that, while in love with her daughter, he kept visiting the house for six weeks, waiting for something, looking around, as though he could not make up his mind whether he was doing them too great an honor by proposing to her daughter, and he did not seem to realize that by visiting a house where there was a marriageable girl, he ought to have made his intentions clear. And then suddenly he left without doing so. "What a good thing he is so unattractive and that Kitty did not fall in love with him," thought her mother.

Vronsky satisfied all the mother's desires. He was very rich, intelligent, of noble birth, had a brilliant career before him in the army and at court, and was altogether a most charming person. Nothing better could be wished for.

Vronsky was paying marked attention to Kitty at balls, danced with her, and came to the house, so that there could be no doubt whatever about the seriousness of his intentions. But in spite of that, the mother had been terribly worried and anxious all that winter.

The princess herself had been married thirty years before, and her marriage had been arranged by an aunt. Her future husband, about whom everything was known beforehand, came, looked at his future wife, and was

54

looked at in turn himself; her aunt, the matchmaker, ascertained and reported to each party the impression made on each other; the impression was favorable; then on the appointed day the expected proposal was made to her parents and accepted. Everything had happened very easily and simply. At least so it seemed to the princess. But with her two elder girls she had realized that the seemingly ordinary matter of marrying off one's daughters was not so easy or so simple. The apprehensions she had suffered, the thoughts she had been worried by, the money that had been spent, the clashes with her husband she had to go through when her two elder daughters, Dolly and Natalie, were married! Now, since the youngest daughter had come out, she was going through the same apprehensions and doubts, and having even worse disputes with her husband than she had had over the two elder. Like all fathers, the old prince was particularly punctilious where his daughters' unsullied reputation and honor were concerned; he was unreasonably jealous, especially about Kitty, his favorite, and at every step he would make scenes with the princess for compromising her daughter. The princess had grown used to this at a time when her elder daughters were getting married, but now she felt that the punctiliousness of the prince was more justified. She could see that lately a great deal had changed in the customs of her social circle and that a mother's responsibilities had become still more difficult. She saw that girls of Kitty's age formed themselves into sets, were attending university courses, were more free in their relations with men, drove out alone, that many of them no longer curtsied, and worst of all, that all of them were firmly convinced that the choice of a husband was theirs and not their parents' business. "Today marriages are no longer arranged as before," these young girls thought and said, and even some of their elders said the same thing. But how marriages were arranged now, the princess could not find out from anyone. The French custom, according to which the parents decided the daughter's future, was not accepted and was condemned. The English custom of allowing the girl complete freedom of choice was not accepted either, and indeed was quite impossible in Russian society. The Russian custom of employing a matchmaker was considered disgraceful, and people, including

55

the princess herself, laughed at it. But no one knew how to marry or give in marriage. Everyone with whom the princess discussed this question said the same thing: "Really, in our day it's high time to put an end to all those antiquated customs. After all, it's the young people who get married and not their parents, so the young people must be allowed to manage this business as they think best." But it was all very well for people who had no daughters to talk like that; the princess knew perfectly well that if her daughter were allowed to make friends with any man she liked, she might fall in love with someone who had no intention of marrying or who would not make her a good husband. And however much people tried to persuade her that in our time young people must be allowed to arrange their own lives, she refused to believe it any more than she would believe that loaded pistols could be the best toys for five-year-old children. That was why the princess was more worried about Kitty than she had been about her elder daughters.

Now she was afraid that Vronsky might content himself with paying his addresses to her daughter. She saw that her daughter was already in love with him, but she comforted herself with the thought that he was an honest man and would not take advantage of it. But at the same time she knew that the freedom now in vogue among young people made it easy to turn a girl's head and that in general men thought very little of seducing a girl. The week before, Kitty had told her mother about a conversation she had had with Vronsky while dancing the mazurka with him. This conversation had partly reassured the princess; but she could not be completely reassured. Vronsky had told Kitty that they, that is to say, he and his brother, were so used to obeying their mother in everything that they never made up their minds to do anything of importance without first consulting her. "And now too," he said, "I'm expecting my mother's arrival from Petersburg as something that will make me especially happy."

Kitty had repeated this without attaching any particular significance to his words. But her mother interpreted them differently. She knew that the old woman was expected any day and that she would approve of her son's choice, and she thought it strange that he did not propose to Kitty for fear of hurting his mother's feelings; nevertheless, she was so eager for the marriage itself and above all for the relief from her anxieties, that she believed it. However distressed the princess now was to see the unhappiness of Dolly, her eldest daughter, who was thinking of leaving her husband, the anxiety about her youngest daughter's fate, which was now about to be decided, completely absorbed her. With the appearance of Levin that afternoon, a new anxiety was now added to her worries. She was afraid that her daughter, who at one time had seemed to have been attracted to Levin, might refuse Vronsky out of a feeling of exaggerated loyalty and that, in general, Levin's arrival might complicate and delay matters which were now so near conclusion.

"What is he doing? Has he been here long?" the princess asked, referring to Levin, as they returned home.

"He arrived today, Mother."

"There's one thing I'd like to say . . ." began the princess and from the serious and animated look on her face Kitty guessed what she was going to say.

"Mother," she said, blushing and turning quickly to her, "please, please don't talk about it. I know, I know all about it."

She wanted what her mother wanted, but the motives underlying her mother's desire offended her.

"All I want to say is that having raised the hopes of one person . . ."

"Mother, darling, for goodness sake, don't speak. It's so awful to talk about it."

"Very well, I won't," said the mother, seeing the tears in her daughter's eyes, "but one thing I must say, my dear. You've promised to have no secrets from me. You won't have any, will you?"

"Never, Mother, none whatever," replied Kitty, blushing and looking her mother straight in the face. "But I've nothing to tell you at the moment. I—I—if I wanted to, I should not know what to say or how. . . . I don't know. . . ."

"No, with those eyes she could never tell an untruth," thought the mother, smiling at her agitation and happiness. The princess smiled to think how tremendously important what was going on in Kitty's heart must appear to her, poor child.

CHAPTER 13

After dinner and the beginning of the party, Kitty felt like a young man before a battle. Her heart pounded violently and she could not keep her thoughts fixed on anything.

She felt that this evening, when the two men would meet for the first time, must be the most decisive day of her life. And she kept picturing them to herself, either singly or both together. When she thought of the past, she dwelt with pleasure and tenderness on the memories of her relations with Levin. Memories of childhood and Levin's friendship with her dead brother lent a peculiar poetic charm to her relations with him. His love for her, of which she was quite certain, was flattering and made her feel happy. And she could recall Levin with a light heart. In her memories of Vronsky, on the other hand, there was a kind of strained feeling, though he was a thoroughly well-bred man of the world, a man of even temper; but there seemed to be a sort of insincerity, not in him, for he was very simple and charming, but in herself, while with Levin she felt quite natural and untroubled. On the other hand, as soon as she thought of her future with Vronsky, a dazzling perspective of happiness rose before her; with Levin her future seemed rather misty.

Going upstairs to dress for the evening and glancing into the looking glass, she was pleased to see that this was one of her best days. She was in full possession of all her powers, which was so necessary for what was going to happen; she had a feeling of outward serenity; she felt that her movements were free and graceful.

At half past seven, as soon as she had gone down into the drawing room, the footman announced: "Konstantin Dimitreyvich Levin." The princess was still in her room and the prince had not yet come down.

"This is it," thought Kitty, and the blood rushed to her heart. She was horrified at her pallor as she glanced into the looking glass.

Now she felt certain that he had come so early for the

sole purpose of finding her alone and proposing to her. And now for the first time the whole thing appeared to her in quite a different and new light. It was only now that she realized that the question—with whom would she be happy and who was the man she loved—did not concern her alone, but that in a moment she would have to humiliate a man she was fond of. And humiliate him cruelly. . . . Why? Because he, poor darling, loved her, because he was in love with her. But it could not be helped. It had to be done. It must be done.

"Oh God, must I tell him so myself?" she thought. "But what shall I tell him? Must I really tell him that I do not love him? That would not be true. What then shall I tell him? Shall I tell him that I love another? No, that's impossible! I'd better go away. Yes, go away."

She was walking up to the door when she heard his footsteps. "No, it's not fair! What have I to be afraid of! I've done nothing wrong. What will be, will be. I'll tell the truth. Besides, it's impossible to feel embarrassed in his presence. Here he is," she said to herself as she caught sight of his powerful and diffident figure and his shining eyes fixed on her. She looked straight into his face, as though imploring him to spare her and gave him her hand.

"I'm afraid I have come too soon!" he said, glancing round the empty drawing room. When he saw that his expectations were realized and that there was nothing to prevent him from speaking his mind, his face clouded over.

"Oh no," said Kitty, and sat down at the table.

"You see," he began without sitting down or looking at her, so as not to lose courage, "all I wanted was to find you alone."

"Mother will be down in a minute. She was very tired yesterday. Yesterday . . ."

She spoke without knowing herself what her lips were saying, and she did not take her beseeching tender eyes off him.

He looked at her; she blushed and fell silent.

"I told you I did not know whether I should be here long, that—that—it depended on you."

She dropped her head lower and lower, not knowing herself what she would say to what was coming.

"That it depended on you," he repeated. "What I wanted to say was . . . What I wanted to say . . . You

see, what I have come for is to ask you to be my wife!"
he said, hardly knowing what he was saying; but, feeling
that the worst had been said, he stopped short and
looked at her.

She was breathing heavily and not looking at him. She
was overwhelmed with rapture. Her heart was full to the
brim with happiness. She had never expected that his
declaration of love would have made so strong an impression on her. But that lasted only for a moment. She
remembered Vronsky. She raised her clear, truthful eyes
to Levin and, seeing his desperate face, replied quickly:

"I'm afraid it cannot be. I'm sorry . . ."

How near she had been to him a moment ago and
how important she had been in his life! And how distant
and what a complete stranger she had become to him
now.

"It couldn't have been otherwise," he said without
looking at her.

He bowed and was about to leave.

CHAPTER 14

But just at that moment the princess came in. She
looked horrified at finding them alone together and at
seeing their distressed faces. Levin bowed to her and
said nothing. Kitty was silent. She did not raise her eyes.
"Thank God, she has refused him," thought the mother
and her face brightened with the usual smile with which
she greeted her visitors on Thursdays. She sat down and
began asking Levin about his life in the country. He too
sat down, awaiting the arrival of other guests which
should enable him to slip away unnoticed.

Five minutes later Kitty's friend the Countess Nordston, married the previous winter, came in.

She was a thin, sallow-faced, ailing, and nervous
woman with brilliant black eyes. She was fond of Kitty
and her affection for her, like that of every married
woman for young girls, expressed itself in a desire to
see Kitty married in accordance with her own ideal of
happiness, and for that reason she wanted her to marry
Vronsky. She never liked Levin, whom she had often
met at Kitty's house at the beginning of winter. Her

constant and favorite diversion when she met him was to make fun of him.

"I love it when he looks down at me from his great height; he either breaks off his clever conversation with me because I am too stupid or condescends to stoop to my level. It amuses me very much. I mean, the fact that he talks down to me. I'm very glad he can't stand me," she used to say about him.

She was right because Levin really could not stand her and despised her for the things she was so proud of and considered to be one of her greatest merits—her highly strung temperament, her ultra-refined contempt and indifference for everything that was coarse and middle-class.

The relations between Nordston and Levin were such as are often met with in high society when two people, outwardly remaining on friendly terms, despise each other so much that they are incapable of treating each other seriously, or even taking offense at one another.

The Countess Nordston at once pounced on Levin. "Ah, my dear Mr. Levin, so here you are again in our depraved Babylon!" she said, offering him her tiny yellowish hand and reminding him of what he had said at the beginning of winter about Moscow being a second Babylon. "Well, has Babylon been reformed or have you been corrupted?" she added, glancing round at Kitty with an ironic smile.

"I'm greatly flattered that you remember my words so well, Countess," replied Levin, who had had time to recover himself, and immediately assuming his usually banteringly hostile attitude towards her. "They must have made a very strong impression on you."

"Why, of course, I write them all down. Well, Kitty, have you been skating again?"

And she began talking to Kitty. Awkward as it would have been for Levin to leave just then, he would have preferred it to staying for the rest of the evening and watching Kitty, who kept glancing at him from time to time but avoided catching his eye. He was about to get up, but the princess, noticing that he was silent, turned to him.

"Will you be long in Moscow? I believe you're very busy with your rural council and you can't be away long."

"No, princess, I am no longer busy with the rural council," he said. "I've come up for a few days."

"There's something peculiar about him," thought the Countess Nordston, scrutinizing his stern, serious face. "He doesn't seem to be very keen on expounding his views. But I'll draw him out. I do love to make a fool of him when Kitty's about, and I will."

"My dear Mr. Levin, explain to me, please—you know all about these things—why at our Kaluga estate all our peasants and their womenfolk spend all they possess on drink and never pay us anything now. What's the meaning of that? You always praise the peasants so much."

At that moment another lady entered the room and Levin rose.

"I'm sorry, Countess, but I really don't know anything about it and I'm afraid I can't tell you anything," he said and glanced at the army officer who had come in behind the lady.

"That must be Vronsky," he thought and glanced at Kitty to make sure. She had already had time to have a look at Vronsky and she, in turn, glanced at Levin. From the look of her involuntarily beaming eyes, Levin understood that she was in love with that man, and he understood it as clearly as if she had said so in so many words. But what kind of man was he?

Now, right or wrong, Levin could not but stay; he had to find out what kind of man it was that she loved.

There are people who when they meet a successful rival, no matter in what, are ready to shut their eyes to whatever is good in him and see only what is bad; others, on the contrary, are anxious to find those qualities in their successful rival with which he has prevailed over them, and with aching hearts seek only the good in him. Levin belonged to the second category. But he had no difficulty in finding what was good and attractive in Vronsky. He was immediately aware of it. Vronsky was a dark, thick-set man of medium height with a good-natured, handsome, and extremely calm and determined face. Everything about his face and figure, from his black, closely cropped hair and freshly shaven chin to his wide, brand-new uniform, was simple and at the same time elegant. Having let the lady pass ahead of him, Vronsky went up to the princess and then to Kitty.

As he approached her, his fine eyes began to shine with a special tenderness, and bending carefully and respectfully over her with a barely perceptible happy and (so it seemed to Levin) modestly triumphant smile, he held out his small, broad hand to her.

Having greeted and spoken a few words to everyone, he sat down without once glancing at Levin, who had not taken his eyes off him.

"Let me introduce you," said the princess, pointing to Levin. "Konstantin Dimitreyvich Levin, Count Alexey Kyrillovich Vronsky."

Vronsky got up and, looking amiably into Levin's eyes, shook hands with him.

"I believe I was to have dined with you earlier this winter," he said, with his frank, unaffected smile, "but you had unexpectedly left for the country."

"Mr. Levin despises and hates the town and us townspeople," said Countess Nordston.

"I can see my words must have made a strong impression on you that you remember them so well," said Levin and, remembering that he had made the same remark earlier, he blushed.

Vronsky looked at Levin and the countess and smiled.

"Do you always live in the country?" he asked. "Don't you find it dull in winter?"

"No, not if one has something to do and, besides, I'm never bored in my own company," Levin replied sharply.

"I like the country," said Vronsky, noticing but pretending not to notice Levin's tone.

"But I hope, Count, that you will never agree to live in the country always," said the Countess Nordston.

"I don't know, I've never given it a fair trial," he said. "I had a curious feeling once," he went on. "I've never missed the country, our Russian country, with bast shoes and peasants, so much as when I spent a winter with my mother in Nice. Nice, as you know, is dull in itself, and even Naples and Sorrento are all right only for a short time. But it is there that one has a vivid recollection of Russia and particularly of the Russian countryside. They seem to . . ."

He was addressing both Kitty and Levin, turning his calm and friendly gaze from the one to the other. He was evidently saying whatever happened to come into his head.

Noticing that the Countess Nordston wanted to say something, he stopped without finishing what he had begun and listened attentively to her.

The conversation did not cease for a moment, so that the old princess, who always kept two heavy guns in reserve, namely classical and technological education and universal military service, in case the conversation suddenly flagged, had no need to move them into action; neither had the Countess Nordston any opportunity to tease Levin.

Levin wanted to join in the general conversation, but couldn't bring himself to do so because he kept saying to himself, "Now I'll go," but he did not go, as though waiting for something.

The conversation turned on table rapping and spiritualism, and Countess Nordston, who believed in spiritualism, began to describe the miracles she had witnessed.

"Oh, Countess," Vronsky said with a smile, "you must really take me to a séance next time. I've never seen anything supernatural, though I've been constantly looking for it."

"Very well, next Saturday," replied the Countess Nordston. "But what about you, Mr. Levin? Do you believe in it?"

"Why do you ask me? You know very well what I'm going to say."

"But I'd like to hear your opinion."

"My opinion," replied Levin, "is that this table rapping merely proves that our so-called educated class is no better than the peasants. They believe in the evil eye and spells and witchcraft, while we—"

"Well, then, you don't believe?"

"I cannot believe, Countess."

"But what if I have seen it myself?"

"Peasant women, too, say they have seen house goblins."

"So you think that I'm not telling the truth?"

And she laughed mirthlessly.

"Why no, Mary, Mr. Levin only said he could not believe," said Kitty, blushing for Levin; and realizing it and feeling still more exasperated, Levin was about to reply, but Vronsky, with his frank, cheerful smile, hurried to the rescue of the conversation, which was threatening to become disagreeable.

"So you don't admit that there can be something in it?" he asked. "But why not? We admit the existence of electricity, which we do not know anything about. Why then should there not be some new force as yet unknown to us which—"

"When electricity was discovered," Levin interrupted quickly, "only the phenomenon was discovered; its cause and its effects were unknown. Centuries passed before people thought of applying it. The spiritualists, however, started with tables writing for them and spirits appearing to them and only afterward began to say that it was an unknown force."

Vronsky listened attentively to Levin as he always listened to people, evidently interested in what he was saying.

"Yes, but the spiritualists say at present we don't know what this force is, but there is such a force and it functions under certain conditions. Let the scientists find out what the force is. No, I don't see why there should not be a new force, if it—"

"Because," Levin interrupted, "with electricity every time you rub a piece of resin against wool you produce a certain phenomenon, while here it isn't every time, so that it cannot be regarded as a natural phenomenon."

Probably feeling that the conversation was assuming too serious a character for a drawing room, Vronsky made no reply, but trying to change the subject, he smiled and turned to the ladies.

"Let's try now, Countess," he began, but Levin wanted to finish saying what he had in mind.

"I think," he went on, "that this attempt of the spiritualists to explain their miracles by some sort of new force is most unsuccessful. They speak openly about a spiritual force and yet want to subject it to a material test."

They were all waiting for him to finish and he was conscious of it.

"And I think that you'd make a first-class medium," said the Countess Nordston. "There's something so very ecstatic about you."

Levin opened his mouth and was about to say something, but blushed and said nothing.

"Come, Princess," Vronsky said to Kitty, "let's try table rapping at once, please. You don't mind, do you, Princess?" he asked Kitty's mother.

And Vronsky got up to look for a round table.

65

Kitty got up to fetch a table, and as she passed Levin, their eyes met. She was deeply sorry for him, particularly since she was herself responsible for his unhappiness. "If you can forgive me," her look pleaded, "then please forgive me. I'm so happy."

"I hate everybody, and you and myself," his eyes replied, and he picked up his hat. But he was not to go yet. As soon as the others were arranging themselves round the little table and Levin was about to go, the old prince entered and, after greeting the ladies, turned to Levin.

"Ah!" he began delightedly. "Been here long? I didn't even know you were here, my boy. Very glad to see you."

The old prince sometimes addressed Levin in familiar terms and at other times more formally. He embraced Levin and, while talking to him, did not notice Vronsky, who had risen and was quietly waiting for the prince to turn to him.

Kitty felt that after what had happened her father's cordiality was painful to Levin. She also noticed how coldly her father responded at last to Vronsky's bow and that Vronsky looked at her father with good-natured bewilderment, trying to understand how and why anyone could be so unfriendly to him and failing to understand it, and she flushed.

"Prince, let us have Mr. Levin," said Countess Nordston. "We want to try an experiment."

"What sort of experiment? Table rapping? I'm sorry, ladies and gentlemen, but in my opinion playing quoits is much more amusing," said the old prince, looking at Vronsky and guessing that it was his idea. "There is some sense in a game of quoits, anyway."

Vronsky looked steadily and with astonishment at the old prince and with a faint smile at once began talking to the Countess Nordston about the big ball that was to take place the following week.

"You will be there, I hope?" he said to Kitty.

As soon as the old prince had turned away from him, Levin went quietly away, and the last impression he carried with him that evening was Kitty's smiling, happy face as she answered Vronsky's question about the ball.

CHAPTER 15

After the visitors had gone Kitty told her mother of her conversation with Levin, and in spite of the pity she felt for Levin, the thought that she had received a proposal of marriage made her happy. She had no doubt that she had acted rightly, but she lay in bed a long time unable to sleep. She was haunted by one impression. She kept seeing Levin's face with knitted brows, his kind eyes looking gloomily and dejectedly from under them as he stood listening to her father and now and again glancing at her and at Vronsky, and she felt so sorry for him that tears started to her eyes. But she at once began to think of the man for whom she had exchanged him. She recalled vividly his strong, manly face, his great calm, and his goodness that came out in everything he did; she remembered the love which the man she loved bore her, and she felt happy again and laid her head on the pillow with a happy smile. "I'm sorry for him, I'm sorry, but what can I do about it? It's not my fault!" she kept saying to herself; but an inner voice said something different to her. Was she sorry for having made Levin fall in love with her or for having refused him? She did not know. But her happiness was poisoned by her doubts. "Lord have mercy on me, Lord have mercy on me, Lord have mercy on me!" she repeated to herself till she fell asleep.

At that very moment below, in the old prince's little study, her parents were having one of their frequent scenes about their favorite daughter.

"What? I'll tell you what!" shouted the prince, waving his arms about and immediately wrapping his squirrel-lined dressing gown round him again. "You have no pride, no dignity; you're disgracing, ruining your daughter by this stupid, infamous matchmaking!"

"But for goodness sake, Prince, what in heaven's name have I done?" the old princess was saying, almost in tears.

She had come to say good night to her husband as usual, feeling happy and contented after her talk with her daughter, and though she had not intended to tell him about Levin's proposal and Kitty's refusal, she did hint to him that she believed the matter with Vronsky was quite settled and that he would propose to her daughter as soon as his mother arrived. And it was then, in reply to her, that the prince suddenly flared up and started shouting at her.

"What have you done? I'll tell you what. To begin with, you entice an eligible young man into your drawing room, which of course will become the talk of all Moscow and rightly so. If you give a party, invite everybody and not a selected number of eligible fools. Invite all the brainless puppies" (so the prince called the young men of Moscow), "engage a pianist and let them dance. But don't let us have the sort of thing we had tonight—don't throw them at her head. It makes me sick to look at it. I tell you it makes me sick! And you've got what you wanted, you've turned the poor girl's head. Levin is a thousand times the better man. As for that Petersburg coxcomb, they turn them out by machine. They're all the same, they're all trash. Even if he were a prince of the blood, my daughter has no need to run after him!"

"But what have I done?"

"Why . . ." the prince cried angrily.

"I know that if I were to listen to you," the princess interrupted him, "we'd never see our daughter married. If that's what you want, we might as well go and live in the country."

"I wish we did."

"But be fair! Am I currying favor with them? Not a bit of it! A young man, and a very nice young man, has fallen in love with her and she, too, I believe . . ."

"Yes, you believe. And what if she really falls in love with him and he has no more intention of marrying than I have? Oh, I wish I hadn't seen it! 'Oh, spiritualism! Oh, Nice! Oh, the ball!' . . ." And imagining himself imitating his wife, he curtsied at each word. "And when we have really made Kate unhappy, when she really takes it into her head to—"

"And what makes you think so?"

"I don't think, I know. We have eyes for these things and women haven't. I can see a man who has serious intentions—that's Levin. And I can see a popinjay like that conceited coxcomb who only wants to have a good time."

"Oh well, once you get an idea into your head . . ."

"You'll remember my words, but it'll be too late, just as with poor Dolly."

"All right, all right, we won't talk about it," the princess stopped him, remembering the unhappy Dolly.

"By all means, good night!"

And having made the sign of the cross over each other, husband and wife kissed and went to their separate bedrooms, feeling that each of them remained of the same opinion.

The princess had been at first firmly convinced that this evening had settled Kitty's future and that there could be no doubt as to Vronsky's intentions; but her husband's words disturbed her. And returning to her room, she, like Kitty, repeated a few times to herself, terrified of what the future might hold in store for her: "Lord have mercy on us, Lord have mercy on us, Lord have mercy on us!"

CHAPTER 16

Vronsky had never known what family life was like. In her youth his mother had been a great society beauty who, during her married life and particularly afterward, had many love affairs which everyone knew about. He hardly remembered his father, and he had been educated in the College of Pages.

After leaving the College, a very young and brilliant officer, he at once found himself a member of the wealthy Petersburg military set. Although he occasionally visited Petersburg high society, all his love affairs had hitherto been outside it.

After his luxurious and coarse life in Petersburg, he experienced for the first time in Moscow the charm of a close companionship with a sweet, innocent girl of high society who fell in love with him. It never entered his head that there could be anything wrong in his relations with Kitty. At balls he danced almost always with her and he was a constant visitor at her home. He talked to her about what people usually talk about in society, that is to say, all sorts of nonsense, but nonsense to which he could not help adding a special meaning for her. Although he never said anything to her which could not be said in front of anybody, he felt that she was getting more and more dependent on him, and the more he felt this the more he liked it, and his feeling for her grew more tender. He did not realize that his behavior towards Kitty had a name of its own, that it was the seduction of a girl without the intention of marrying her, and that this kind of seduction is the sort of reprehensible thing common among brilliant young men like himself. He imagined he was the first to discover this pleasure, and he enjoyed his discovery to the full.

If he could have heard what her parents had been saying that night, if he could have put himself in her family's place and learned that Kitty would be unhappy if he did not marry her, he would have been greatly surprised and would not have believed it. He could not possibly have believed that what gave such great and such genuine pleasure to him, and above all, to her, could be wrong. Still less could he have believed that he ought to marry the girl.

Marriage had never presented itself to him as a possibility. Not only did he dislike family life, but in accordance with the views generally held among the bachelor world in which he lived, he regarded the family and particularly a husband as something alien, hostile, and above all, ridiculous. But though Vronsky had no suspicion of what Kitty's parents were saying, he felt, on leaving the Shcherbatskys' house that night, that the secret spiritual ties that existed between him and Kitty had grown so strong that he had to do something. But what he had to do and how he was to do it, he could not imagine.

"What is so charming," he thought as he was returning from the Shcherbatskys', carrying away with him as always a pleasant feeling of purity and freshness, partly due to the fact that he had not smoked all evening, and with it a new feeling of tenderness at her love for him, "what is so charming is that not a word has been said by me or by her and yet we understand each other so well in this unspoken language of glances and intonations that tonight more plainly than ever she told

70

me that she loved me. And how sweetly, how simply, and above all how trustfully! I feel better, purer for it! I feel that I have a heart and that there's a great deal of good in me! Those dear, loving eyes! When she said: 'Oh yes, very much . . .'

"Well, so what now? Nothing. I'm happy and she's happy." And he began wondering where he should finish his evening.

He tried to think of the places where he might go. "The club? A game of bezique? A bottle of champagne with Ignatov? No, I won't go. Château des Fleurs? I should find Oblonsky there. Music-hall songs, the can-can. No, I'm sick of it. What I like so much about the Shcherbatskys' is that I become a better man there. I'll go home." He went straight to his rooms at Deusseaux's, had supper, and after undressing, had scarcely laid his head on the pillow before he fell asleep and, as usual, slept soundly.

CHAPTER 17

At eleven o'clock the next morning Vronsky drove to the Petersburg railway station to meet his mother, and the first person he came across on the steps of the main staircase was Oblonsky, who was expecting his sister by the same train.

"Hello, my dear fellow," Oblonsky cried. "Who is it you're meeting?"

"My mother," replied Vronsky, smiling as everyone did who met Oblonsky. He shook hands and walked up the staircase with him. "She should be arriving from Petersburg today."

"And I waited for you till two o'clock. Where did you go from the Shcherbatskys'?"

"Home," replied Vronsky. "To tell you the truth I was in such a good mood yesterday when I left the Shcherbatskys' that I did not want to go anywhere else."

"The mettlesome steed by his breed,
    The young man in love by his eyes I recognize,"

Oblonsky recited just as he had done earlier to Levin.

Vronsky smiled in a way that showed that he had no intention of denying it, but he immediately changed the subject.

"And whom are you meeting?" he asked.

"Me? A beautiful woman," said Oblonsky.

"Oh?"

"*Honi soit qui mal y pense!* My sister Anna."

"Oh, Mrs. Karenin," said Vronsky.

"I expect you know her."

"I believe I do. Or, perhaps not. I don't really remember," Vronsky replied absent-mindedly, the name of Karenin vaguely suggesting to him something stiff and dull.

"But surely you must know Alexey Karenin, my famous brother-in-law? All the world knows him."

"Well, yes, I know him by repute and by sight. I know he is clever, learned, and a bit religious. . . . But you know this is not—*not in my line*," said Vronsky in English.

"Yes, he's a remarkable man," observed Oblonsky. "A bit of a conservative, but an excellent fellow—an excellent fellow."

"Well, so much the better for him," said Vronsky, smiling. "Oh, there you are," he went on, turning to the tall old footman of his mother's, standing at the door. "Come in here."

Besides liking Oblonsky, as everyone did, Vronsky had more recently felt drawn to him because he associated him in his mind with Kitty.

"Well, do you think we ought to give a dinner for the *diva* next Sunday?" he asked Oblonsky with a smile, taking his arm.

"Most certainly, I'll collect subscriptions. Oh, incidentally, did you make the acquaintance of my friend Levin yesterday?" asked Oblonsky.

"Yes, I did. But he left early for some reason."

"He's a nice fellow," Oblonsky continued. "Don't you think so?"

"I don't know why it is," Vronsky replied, "that there is something blunt about all Muscovites—present company, of course, excepted," he interpolated jestingly. "They all seem to be rearing up on their hind legs losing their tempers, as though they wished to make people realize something or other."

"Yes, that's true enough, they are like that," Oblonsky said, laughing gaily.

"Will the train be in soon?" Vronsky asked a railway official.

"It's left the last station," replied the official.

The approach of the train was made more and more evident by the bustle of preparations in the station, the rushing about of the porters, the appearance of gendarmes and guards, and the arrival of people meeting the train. Through the frosty vapor could be seen workmen in short sheepskins and soft felt boots crossing the network of railway lines. The whistle of an engine on the rails and the movement of something heavy could be heard in the distance.

"No," said Oblonsky, who was very anxious to tell Vronsky of Levin's intentions concerning Kitty, "no, you haven't quite appreciated my Levin. He's a very nervous man and it's true he's sometimes disagreeable, but he can also be very charming. His is such an honest, truthful nature and he has a heart of gold. But yesterday there were special reasons," Oblonsky continued with a significant smile, completely forgetting the genuine sympathy he had felt for his friend the day before and now feeling the same sympathy, only this time for Vronsky. "Yes, there was a good reason why he could have been either particularly happy or particularly unhappy."

Vronsky stopped and asked point-blank: "How do you mean? Did he propose to your *belle-soeur* yesterday?"

"Maybe," said Oblonsky, "I imagined something of the kind yesterday. Yes, if he left early and was in a bad temper, then it must be that. . . . He's been in love with her so long, and I feel very sorry for him."

"So that was it! Well, I think she could make a much better match," said Vronsky and, expanding his chest, resumed his walk. "However, I don't know him," he added. "Yes, it's a painful position. That's why most of us prefer our Claras. If you're unsuccessful there it merely means that you haven't enough cash, but here— here it's your dignity that is at stake. However, here's the train."

And indeed the engine was already whistling in the distance. A few moments later the platform began to vibrate, and puffing out steam driven downward by the frosty air, the engine rolled past, the piston of the middle wheel rising and extending slowly and rhythmically, the bent, muffled figure of the engine driver all covered with hoarfrost; behind the tender came the luggage van with a dog yelping inside it, gradually slowing down and making the platform shake more than ever; at last with a jolt, the passenger coaches slid into the platform and came to a standstill with a jolt.

The dashing guard jumped out blowing his whistle and the impatient passengers began to get down one by one: an officer of the Guards, holding himself erect and looking round sternly; a fidgety tradesman with a bag, smiling cheerfully; a peasant with a sack over his shoulder.

Standing beside Oblonsky, Vronsky watched the carriages and the passengers getting out of them, completely oblivious of his mother. What he had just heard about Kitty excited and delighted him. His chest involuntarily expanded and his eyes sparkled. He felt a conqueror.

"The Countess Vronsky is in that compartment," said the dashing guard, going up to Vronsky.

The guard's words aroused him out of his reverie and reminded him of his mother and his impending meeting with her. He did not really respect his mother and, without being consciously aware of it, did not love her, though in accordance with the ideas of the set in which he lived and with his upbringing, he could not imagine any other relationship to his mother than that founded on absolute obedience and respect. And the more outwardly obedient and respectful he was, the less he respected and loved her in his heart.

CHAPTER 18

Vronsky followed the guard to the carriage and at the door of the compartment he had to stop to make way for a lady who was getting out. With the usual insight of a man of the world Vronsky saw at a glance that she belonged to the best society. He apologized and was about to enter the carriage, but he felt that he had to have another look at her—not because she was very beautiful, not because of the elegance and unassuming grace which were evident in her whole figure, but because there was something specially sweet and tender in the expression of her lovely face as she passed him. As he looked round, she too turned her head. Her brilliant gray eyes, darker because of her thick lashes, rested on his face for a moment and gave him a friendly and attentive look, as though recognizing him, and then at once turned to the approaching crowd as if in search of someone. In that brief glance Vronsky had time to notice the restrained animation of her face, which seemed to flutter between her brilliant eyes and the barely perceptible smile that curved her red lips. It was as though her entire being were brimming over with something that against her will expressed itself now in the sparkle of her eyes, now in her smile. She deliberately extinguished the light in her eyes, but it gleamed in spite of her in her barely perceptible smile.

Vronsky went into the carriage. His mother, a wizened old woman with black eyes and ringlets, screwed up her eyes as she peered at her son and smiled faintly with her thin lips. Getting up from her seat and handing her bag to her maid, she held out her little wrinkled hand to her son to kiss, and lifting his head from her hand, kissed him on the cheek.

"You got my telegram? Are you well? That's good."

"Did you have a good journey?" said her son, sitting down beside her and involuntarily listening to a woman's voice outside the door. He knew it was the voice of the lady he had met as he entered the coach.

"I don't agree with you all the same," said the lady's voice.

"That's the Petersburg way of looking at things, ma'am."

"No, it isn't the Petersburg way, it's simply a woman's way," she replied.

"Oh well, may I kiss your hand, ma'am?"

"Good-by, Ivan Petrovich, and please see if my brother is here and send him to me," said the lady at the very door and came back into the compartment.

"Well, have you found your brother?" Countess Vronsky asked, addressing the lady.

Vronsky realized now that this was Mrs. Karenin.

"Your brother is here," he said, getting up. "I'm sorry I didn't recognize you. Our acquaintance was so short," he said with a bow, "that I don't expect you remember me."

"Oh yes," she said, "I should have recognized you

because your mother and I seem to have talked of nothing but you all the way," she said, at last allowing the animation that was so eager to come out to reveal itself in a smile. "But there's still no sign of my brother."

"Call him, Alyosha," said the old countess.

Vronsky stepped out on the platform and shouted: "Oblonsky! Here!"

Anna did not wait for her brother, but, as soon as she caught sight of him, came out of the carriage with a light, determined step. And the moment her brother went up to her, she flung her left arm round his neck with a movement that struck Vronsky by its determination and grace, drew him quickly to her, and kissed him warmly. Vronsky gazed at her without taking his eyes off her and, without knowing why, smiled. But remembering that his mother was waiting for him, he went back into the carriage.

"She's very charming, isn't she?" said the countess, referring to Anna. "Her husband put her into the compartment with me and I was very glad of it. We talked all the way. Well, and you, I hear . . . *vous filez le parfait amour. Tant mieux, mon cher, tant mieux.*"

"I don't know what you're hinting at, Mother," replied her son coldly. "Well, shall we go?"

Anna entered the carriage again to say good-by to the countess.

"Well, Countess, you've met your son and I my brother," she said gaily. "And I've exhausted all my stories and should have had nothing more to tell you."

"Oh, no," said the countess, taking her hand. "I could travel round the world with you and never be bored. You're one of those charming women with whom it is nice to talk, and nice to be silent. And please don't worry about your son. You can't expect never to be parted."

Anna stood still, holding herself very erect, and her eyes smiled.

"Mrs. Karenin," said the countess in explanation to her son, "has a little son of eight, I believe, and she has never before been separated from him and so she keeps worrying about having left him."

"Yes, we've been talking all the time, the countess and I," said Anna, and again, a smile lit up her face, an affectionate smile intended for him. "I about my son and she about hers."

"I expect it must have been very boring for you," he said, at once catching in its flight the ball of coquetry which she had thrown at him. But she evidently did not want to continue the conversation in that tone, and turned to the old countess.

"Thank you very much. The day has passed so quickly I hardly noticed it. Good-by, Countess."

"Good-by, my dear," replied the countess. "Let me kiss your pretty face. I'm an old woman, my dear, so let me speak plainly to you and tell you that I have grown very fond of you."

Trite as this expression was, Anna evidently believed it quite sincerely and was pleased. She blushed, bent down a little, put her cheek to the countess' lips and then drew herself up again, and with the same smile hovering between her lips and eyes, held out her hand to Vronsky. He pressed the little hand, and the energetic way in which she boldly and vigorously shook his pleased him, just as though it were something special. She went out rapidly, carrying her rather full figure with extraordinary lightness.

"She's very charming," said the old woman.

Her son thought so too. He followed her with his eyes till her graceful figure was out of sight, and the smile still lingered on his face. He saw through the window how she went up to her brother, put her arm in his, and began talking animatedly to him about something that quite evidently had nothing to do with him, Vronsky, and he could not help being annoyed at that.

"Well, and how are you, Mother? Quite well?" he asked again, turning to his mother.

"Everything's all right. Alexander was very nice, and Marie has grown very pretty. She is most interesting."

And she began telling him again about the things that interested her most, her grandson's christening, for which she had gone to Petersburg and the special favor the emperor had shown to her eldest son.

"Here is Lavrenty," said Vronsky, looking out of the window. "We can go now if you like."

The old butler who had traveled with the countess came and announced that everything was ready, and the countess got up to go.

"Let's go," said Vronsky. "There isn't much of a crowd now."

The maid took one bag and the lap dog; the butler and a porter took the other bags. Vronsky gave his arm to his mother, but just as they were getting out of the carriage, several men ran past them with frightened faces. The stationmaster too ran past in his oddly colored cap; evidently something unusual had happened. Passengers who had left the train were running back.

"What? What? Where? Thrown himself under the train? Run over!" the people running past the window could be heard saying.

Oblonsky, with his sister on his arm, came back; both of them also looked alarmed. They stopped at the carriage door to avoid the crowd. The ladies went back into the carriage, while Vronsky and Oblonsky followed the crowd to find out the details of the accident.

A guard, either drunk or too much muffled up against the bitter frost, had not heard the train being shunted back and had been run over.

Even before Vronsky and Oblonsky returned, the ladies had heard these facts from the butler. Oblonsky and Vronsky had both seen the mangled body. Oblonsky was visibly distressed. He wrinkled up his face and seemed to be on the point of bursting into tears.

"Oh, how horrible!" he kept on saying. "Oh, Anna, if you had seen it! Oh, how horrible."

Vronsky was silent and his handsome face was serious but perfectly calm.

"Oh, if you had seen it, Countess," Oblonsky was saying, "and his wife was there too. It was dreadful to see her. She flung herself on the body. They say he was the breadwinner of a large family. What a terrible thing to happen."

"Is there nothing one can do for her?" Anna said in an agitated whisper. Vronsky glanced at her and at once left the carriage.

"I'll be back in a moment, Mother," he added, turning around in the doorway.

When he returned a few minutes later, Oblonsky was already talking to the countess about the new prima donna and the countess kept looking impatiently at the door for her son's return.

"Now we can go," said Vronsky, coming in.

They went out together. Vronsky walked ahead with his mother. Anna and her brother followed behind. At the exit the stationmaster overtook them and said to Vronsky:

"You gave my assistant two hundred rubles. Will you please make it clear whom you intended it for?"

"For the widow," said Vronsky, shrugging. "I don't see why you have to ask me about it."

"Did you give that?" cried Oblonsky from behind, and pressing his sister's arm, added: "Very kind indeed. Don't you think he's a good fellow? Good-by, Countess."

And he and his sister stopped to look for her maid. When they came out of the station Vronsky's carriage had already driven off. The people coming out of the station were still talking about the accident.

"What a terrible death!" said one gentleman as he passed them. "They say he was cut in half."

"On the contrary, I think it's the easiest kind of death, instantaneous," observed another.

"They should have taken proper precautions," said the third.

Anna took her seat in the carriage and Oblonsky noticed with surprise that her lips were trembling and that she was keeping back her tears with difficulty.

"What's the matter, Anna?" he asked when they had driven a few hundred yards.

"It's a bad omen," she said.

"What nonsense!" said Oblonsky. "The chief thing is that you are here. You can't imagine how I'm counting on you."

"Have you known Vronsky long?" she asked.

"Yes. You know we're hoping he'll marry Kitty."

"Oh?" said Anna softly. "Well, now let's talk about you," she added, with a shake of her head, as if wishing physically to get rid of something unwanted that troubled her. "Let's talk of your affairs. I got your letter and here I am."

"Yes, you're my only hope," said Oblonsky.

"Well, tell me everything."

And Oblonsky began his story.

When they arrived at his house, Oblonsky helped his sister out of the carriage, sighed, pressed her hand, and drove off to the office.

CHAPTER 19

When Anna entered, Dolly was sitting in the small drawing room with a fair-haired, chubby-faced little boy, who already looked like his father, and listening to him reading his French lesson. As he read, the boy kept twisting and trying to pull off a button that was hanging precariously from his jacket. His mother had several times taken his plump little hand away, but it always went back to the button. The mother at last pulled the button off and put it into her pocket.

"Keep your hands still, Grisha," she said, and again picked up a counterpane she had been working on for a long time and to which she always returned in times of crisis. Now she was crocheting it nervously, looping the wool with her finger and counting the stitches. Although she had sent word to her husband the day before that it did not matter to her whether his sister came or not, she had got everything ready for her arrival and was waiting anxiously for her sister-in-law.

Dolly was crushed by her sorrow and utterly absorbed by it. Still, she remembered that her sister-in-law, Anna, was the wife of one of the most important men in Petersburg and a Petersburg *grande dame.* And because of that she did not carry out her threat to her husband; that is to say, she did not overlook the fact that her sister-in-law was coming. "After all, Anna had nothing to do with it," thought Dolly. "It's not her fault. I know nothing but good about her and she has shown me nothing but kindness and friendship." True, as far as she could remember her impression when she had visited the Karenins in Petersburg, she had not liked their home; there was something false in the whole atmosphere of their family life. "But why should I not receive her?" thought Dolly. "I only hope she won't try to console me. All these consolations, exhortations, and Christian forgivenesses—I've gone over them a thousand times and it's no use."

All these last days Dolly had been alone with the children. She did not wish to talk about her troubles, but with these troubles on her mind she could not talk of anything else. She knew that in one way or another she was sure to tell Anna everything, and indeed, the thought of how she would tell her pleased her, though she was also furious when she thought of having to speak of her own humiliation to his sister, and to hear her repeat the conventional phrases of exhortation and consolation.

As usually happens, looking at the clock and expecting her to come any moment, she missed the moment when Anna arrived and did not even hear the bell.

Hearing the rustle of a skirt and the sound of light footsteps in the doorway, she looked around, her harassed face involuntarily expressing not joy but surprise. She got up and embraced her sister-in-law.

"Heavens, you're here already!" she said, kissing her.

"Dolly, I'm so glad to see you!"

"I'm glad too," said Dolly, smiling weakly and trying to guess from the expression of Anna's face whether she knew or not. "I'm sure she knows," she thought, noticing the look of sympathy on Anna's face. "Well, come along, I'll show you your room," she went on, trying to put off as long as possible the moment of explanation.

"Is this Grisha? Goodness, how he's grown!" said Anna, and she kissed him and, without taking her eyes off Dolly, stopped short and blushed. "No, please don't let's go anywhere yet."

She took off her scarf and her hat, and, getting it entangled in her black hair which was a mass of curls, she shook her head to loosen it.

"Oh, you look so well!" said Dolly almost with envy. "Radiant with happiness!"

"Me? Yes," said Anna. "My goodness, here's Tanya," she added, turning to the little girl who had run into the room. "Why, Tanya, you're the same age as my Seryozha." She took her in her arms and kissed her. "What a sweet little girl! What a charming child. Do let me see them all."

She not only mentioned them by their names, but she remembered the years and even the months of their births, their characters, and their illnesses, and Dolly could not help being impressed.

"Well, let's go and see them," she said. "It's a pity Vassya is asleep."

Having looked at the children, they went back to the drawing room and, alone now, sat down at the table for coffee. Anna drew the tray towards her and then pushed it away.

"Dolly," she said, "he has told me."

Dolly looked coldly at Anna. She was now waiting for the conventional phrases of sympathy, but Anna said nothing of the kind.

"Dolly, my sweet," she said, "I don't want to speak to you on his behalf, nor do I want to console you. That would be impossible. But, darling, I'm simply sorry for you—sorry with all my heart."

Under their thick lashes her brilliant eyes suddenly filled with tears. She sat down on another chair closer to her sister-in-law and took her hand in her own energetic little hand. Dolly did not draw back, but her face preserved its rigid expression.

She said:

"You can't comfort me. After what has happened, everything is at an end. It's all over."

And as soon as she had said it, her face suddenly softened. Anna raised Dolly's dry, thin hand, and kissed it.

"But," she said, "what's to be done, Dolly, what's to be done? What's the best thing to do in this dreadful situation? That's what you must consider."

"Everything's at an end, that's all there is to it," said Dolly. "And the worst of it is, you see, that I can't leave him. There are the children; I'm tied hand and foot. But I can't live with him. To see him is torture to me."

"Dolly, darling, he told me, but I want to hear it from you. Tell me everything."

Dolly looked at her questioningly.

Anna's face expressed unfeigned sympathy and love.

"All right," she said all at once. "But I shall begin at the beginning. You know how I was married. With Mother's upbringing I was not only innocent, I was stupid. I knew nothing. I know they say husbands tell their wives about their past lives, but Stiva—" she corrected herself: "But your brother told me nothing. You will hardly believe me, but till quite recently I thought I was the only woman he had ever known. I lived like that for eight years. You see, not only did I not suspect any infidelity, but I believed such a thing to be absolutely impossible. And then you can imagine what it meant with such ideas suddenly to find out all this horror, all this nastiness. . . . You see, to be fully convinced of one's happiness and suddenly . . ." Dolly went on, suppressing her sobs, "to come across a letter, his letter to his mistress, my children's governess. No, it's too horrible!" She hurriedly took out her handkerchief and hid her face in it. "I can understand an infatuation," she went on after a pause, "but to deceive me deliberately, cunningly and—with whom? To go on living with me as my husband together with her. That is horrible! You can't understand. . . ."

"Oh, yes, I do understand, I do understand, Dolly dear, I do," said Anna, pressing her hand.

"And do you think he realizes the horror of my situation?" went on Dolly. "Not a bit! He is happy and contented."

"Oh, no!" Anna interrupted quickly. "He is miserable. He is crushed by remorse."

"Is he capable of remorse?" interrupted Dolly, looking searchingly into her sister-in-law's face.

"Yes, I know him. I couldn't look at him without feeling sorry for him. We both know him. He is kindhearted, but he is proud too and now he feels so humiliated. What moved me most of all . . ." (Here Anna guessed what would move Dolly most) "was that he is tormented by two things: he is ashamed because of the children and that, loving you . . . Yes, yes, loving you more than anything else in the world," she went on hurriedly to prevent Dolly from objecting, "he has hurt you so terribly and has made you so unhappy. 'No, no,' he keeps on saying, 'she'll never forgive me.' "

Dolly gazed thoughtfully beyond her sister-in-law as she listened to her.

"Yes," she said, "I quite understand that his position is terrible. It is worse for the guilty than for the innocent, particularly if he feels that he is responsible for all the unhappiness. But how can I forgive him, how can I be his wife again after her? To live with him now will be torture to me, just because I love my past love for him."

And sobs cut short her words.

And as though intentionally every time she softened she again began to speak of what exasperated her.

"You see," she went on, "she is young, she is pretty. Do you realize, Anna, who has robbed me of my youth and my beauty? He and his children. I've served him and all I had went into his service, and he quite naturally finds any fresh, vulgar creature more pleasing now. I expect they must have discussed me when they were together or worse still, ignored me—do you understand?" Again her eyes burned with hatred. "And after that he will tell me . . . Well, what do you think? Can I possibly believe him? Never! No, it's all over, all that was once a comfort to me, a reward for my labors, my sufferings . . . Will you believe me, I've just been teaching Grisha. Before it used to be a joy to me, now it is a torture. Why am I doing all this? Why do I take all this trouble? Why have children? What's so terrible is that my heart has suddenly changed and instead of love and tenderness for him I feel nothing but bitterness. Yes, bitterness. I could kill him and—"

"Dolly, darling, I understand, but don't torture yourself. You are so hurt, so upset, that you don't see many things in their proper light."

Dolly grew quieter and they were silent for a couple of minutes.

"But what am I to do? Think, Anna, help me. I've thought a lot about it and I can't see any way out."

Anna could not think of anything, but every word of her sister-in-law, every expression of her face, went straight to her heart.

"One thing I will say," said Anna. "I am his sister, I know his character, that ability of his for forgetting everything, everything" (she made a gesture with her hand in front of her forehead), "that ability for allowing himself to be completely carried away. But he's also capable of being genuinely sorry for what he has done. He can't believe, can't understand now how he could have done what he did."

"No, he understands, he understood!" Dolly said. "But I . . . You're forgetting me, aren't you? Does it make it any easier for me?"

"Wait. When he was speaking to me, I confess I did not quite realize the whole horror of your position. I only saw his position and that the family was on the point of disintegration. I felt sorry for him, but now that I've talked to you, I, as a woman, realize something else. I see your suffering and I can't tell you how sorry I am for you. But, Dolly, darling, I fully understand your suffering, but there is one thing I do not know: I do not know—I do not know how much love there still is in your heart for him. You alone know that I mean, whether there's enough love for you to be able to forgive him. If there is, then forgive him."

"No," began Dolly, but Anna interrupted her and again kissed her hand.

"I know the world better than you do," she said. "I know how men like Stiva look at these things. You say he spoke to *her* about you. I don't think so. People like him are unfaithful, but their own hearth and home, their own wives are sacred to them. They somehow look upon these women with contempt and they do not let them interfere with the family. They seem to draw a sort of line between their families and those women, a line that can't be crossed. I don't understand it, but it is so."

"Yes, but he has kissed her . . ."

"Dolly darling, listen. I saw Stiva when he was in love with you. I remember the time when he used to come to me and cry when talking about you, and what poetry you were for him and on what a high pedestal he put you. And I know that the longer he has lived with you, the higher you have risen in his esteem. You see, we used to laugh at him sometimes because he would invariably finish every sentence with, 'Dolly is a wonderful woman.' You've always been and you still are his divinity and this infatuation of his has nothing to do with his heart."

"But if this infatuation should repeat itself?"

"I don't think it will."

"Yes, but would you forgive?"

"I don't know. I can't tell . . . Yes, I can," said Anna after a moment's thought, and having summed up the situation and weighed it in her mind, she added: "Yes, I can, I can. Yes, I should forgive. I should not have been the same, but I should forgive, and forgive just as if nothing had ever happened at all."

"Well, of course," Dolly broke in quickly, as though saying what she herself had thought more than once, "it would not be forgiveness otherwise. If one forgives, it must be completely, completely! Well, come along now, I'll show you to your room," she said, getting up and on the way putting her arm round Anna. "My dear, I'm so glad you came. I feel better now, much better."

CHAPTER 20

The whole of that day Anna spent at home, that is, at the Oblonskys'. She did not receive anyone, though several of her acquaintances who had managed to hear of her arrival came to see her. Anna spent the whole morning with Dolly and the children. She just sent a short note to her brother to be sure to dine at home. "Come," she wrote, "the Lord is merciful."

Oblonsky dined at home; the conversation was general and his wife spoke to him, addressing him familiarly, something she had not done before. There was the same estrangement in the relations between husband and wife, but there was no longer any talk of separation, and Oblonsky saw a possibility of an explanation and a reconciliation.

Immediately after dinner Kitty arrived. She knew Anna, but only very slightly, and as she drove to her sister's she could not help feeling a little apprehensive as to how she would be received by this Petersburg society woman of whom everybody spoke so highly. But Anna liked her—she saw that at once. Anna was evidently struck by her youth and beauty and before Kitty could collect herself, she felt not only that she was under Anna's influence, but that she was in love with her, as young girls are capable of falling in love with married women older than themselves. Anna was not like a society woman or the mother of an eight-year-old boy. She would have looked like a girl of twenty, for she possessed the same suppleness of movement, the same freshness and characteristic animation of face which could be detected in her smile or in her glance, were it not for the serious and sometimes sad expression of her eyes which struck Kitty and drew her to her. Kitty felt that Anna was completely natural and did not conceal anything, but that she had another and higher world of complex and poetic interests which were inaccessible to her.

After dinner, when Dolly had retired to her room,

Anna got up quickly and went up to her brother, who was lighting a cigar.

"Stiva," she said to him with a gay twinkle, making the sign of the cross over him and motioning to the door, "go to her and may God be good to you."

He understood her, threw down the cigar, and disappeared behind the door.

When Oblonsky had gone, Anna went back to the sofa where she had been sitting surrounded by the children. Whether because they saw that their mother was fond of this aunt or because they themselves felt the presence of a peculiar charm about her, the two elder children and then the younger ones, as is often the way with children, had clung to their new aunt before dinner and would not leave her now. They had a kind of game which consisted in trying to sit as close as possible to her, to touch her, hold her little hand, kiss it, play with her ring, or at least touch the frills of her dress.

"Very well, let's sit down as we were sitting before," said Anna, resuming her seat.

And Grisha again pushed his head under her arm and leaned against her dress, beaming with pride and happiness.

"When is the ball to be?" said Anna, turning to Kitty.

"Next week, and it's going to be a wonderful ball. One of those balls at which one always enjoys oneself."

"Why," Anna said with tender irony, "are there such balls where one always enjoys oneself?"

"Strange as it may seem, there are. One always enjoys oneself at the Bobrishchevs', also at the Nikitins', but at the Mezhkovs' it is always dull. Haven't you noticed it?"

"No, my dear, there are no more balls for me where I can enjoy myself," said Anna, and Kitty saw in her eyes that peculiar world which was not open to her. "For me there are only balls that are less boring and tiresome."

"How can *you* be bored at a ball?"

"Why shouldn't I be bored at a ball?" asked Anna.

Kitty realized that Anna knew the answer that would follow.

"Because you always look nicer than anyone."

Anna had a propensity to blushing. She blushed and said: "In the first place it isn't true, and, secondly, if it were, what difference would it make to me?"

"Will you go to this ball?" asked Kitty.

"I suppose I shall have to. Here, take this," she said to Tanya, who was trying to pull off the ring which fitted loosely on her thin, white finger.

"I'd be so glad if you would. I should so like to see you at a ball."

"Well, if I have to go I shall at least comfort myself with the thought that it will give you pleasure. Grisha, don't pull my hair, it's untidy enough as it is," she said, arranging a stray strand of hair with which Grisha was playing.

"I imagine you at the ball in lilac."

"Why necessarily in lilac?" Anna asked with a smile. "Well, children, run along now. Don't you hear? Miss Hull is calling you to tea," she said, sending the children away to the dining room.

"I know why you're so anxious for me to go to that ball. You're expecting a lot from this ball, aren't you? And you want everyone to be there to share in it."

"How did you know? Yes."

"Oh," Anna went on, "how wonderful it is to be your age! I remember well that blue mist, like the haze on the mountains in Switzerland. I know it so well. The mist which envelops everything, that blissful time when childhood is just coming to an end and its enormous happy, merry circle becomes a path that grows narrower and narrower, and you feel gay and at the same time fearful as you enter this long avenue of life, though it seems bright and beautiful. Who has not passed through it?"

Kitty smiled in silence. "But how did she pass through it? Oh, I wish I knew the whole romance of her life," thought Kitty, remembering the unromantic appearance of her husband Alexey Karenin.

"I know something. Stiva told me, and I congratulate you. I liked him very much," Anna went on. "I met Vronsky at the railway station."

"Oh, was he there?" asked Kitty, blushing. "What did Stiva tell you?"

"Stiva told me everything, and I would be very pleased. You see," she went on, "I traveled yesterday

88

with Vronsky's mother and she talked about him without stopping. He is her favorite son. I know, of course, how partial mothers are, but . . ."

"What did his mother tell you?"

"Oh, such a lot! And I know he's the favorite, but one can see all the same that he is a chivalrous man. For instance, she told me that he wanted to give all his property to his brother, that as a boy he had done something wonderful, saved a woman from drowning. In short, he is a hero," said Anna, smiling and remembering the two hundred rubles which he had given away at the station.

But she did not mention the two hundred rubles. For some reason the memory of it troubled her. She felt that there was something in this incident that had to do with her, something that should not have been.

"She was very anxious that I should call on her," Anna went on, "and I shall be glad to see the old lady again. I'll call on her tomorrow. Well, thank heaven Stiva is stopping a long time in Dolly's room," added Anna, changing the subject and getting up, looking dissatisfied with something, Kitty thought.

"No, I was first! No!" shouted the children, who, having finished tea, were rushing back to their aunt Anna.

"All together!" said Anna, laughing, and ran towards them, putting her arms round them, and throwing the whole heap of children, struggling and shrieking with delight, on the floor.

CHAPTER 21

Dolly came out of her room for the grown-ups' tea. Oblonsky did not appear. He must have left his wife's room by the back door.

"I'm afraid you will be cold upstairs," observed Dolly, turning to Anna, "I'd like to move you downstairs, and then we shall be nearer one another."

"Please don't bother about me," replied Anna, scanning Dolly's face and trying to find out whether there had been a reconciliation or not.

"You'll find it much lighter here," replied her sister-in-law.

"I assure you I can sleep like a dormouse anywhere and at any time."

"What is it all about?" asked Oblonsky, coming in from the study and addressing his wife.

From his tone both Kitty and Anna knew at once that a reconciliation had taken place.

"I want to move Anna downstairs, but the curtains will have to be changed first. No one knows how to do it, so I shall have to do it myself," replied Dolly, turning to him.

"Goodness knows if they have really made it up," thought Anna, hearing Dolly's cool and calm tone.

"Oh, nonsense, Dolly, you're always making difficulties," said her husband. "I'll do it, if you like."

"Yes, they must have made it up," thought Anna.

"I know how you'd do it," replied Dolly. "You'd tell Matvey to do something that's impossible, and then go off and leave him to make a mess of it," and as she said it the corners of Dolly's mouth puckered up into her usual ironic smile.

"Yes, they've made it up," thought Anna. "A complete reconciliation, thank God." And pleased to have been the cause of it, she went up to Dolly and kissed her.

"Not at all. Why are you so contemptuous of Matvey and me?" said Oblonsky, addressing his wife with a faint smile.

As always, Dolly was faintly ironical towards her husband all the evening, and Oblonsky was contented and cheerful, but careful not to let it show that, having been forgiven, he seemed to have forgotten his offense.

At half past nine the particularly cheerful and pleasant conversation over the tea table at the Oblonskys' was disturbed by an apparently ordinary incident which, however, for some reason struck everybody as peculiar. They were discussing their mutual Petersburg acquaintances when Anna suddenly got up.

"I have her photo in my album," she said, "and I may as well show you my Seryozha, too," she added with the smile of a proud mother.

Toward ten o'clock, when she usually said good night to her son and often tucked him into bed herself before going to a ball, she felt a little sad at being so far from him and, whatever they talked about, her thoughts kept returning to her curly-headed Seryozha. She longed to have a look at his photograph and to talk about him. Taking advantage of the first opportunity she got up and with her light, determined step went out to fetch the album. The staircase to her room on the top floor came out on the landing of the large well-heated main staircase.

As she was coming out of the drawing room there was a ring at the front door.

"Who could it be?" asked Dolly.

"It's too early for me to be fetched and too late for a caller," observed Kitty.

"I expect it must be someone with papers for me," said Oblonsky.

As Anna was walking across the landing a footman came running up to announce a visitor. The visitor himself was standing under a lamp in the hall. Glancing down, Anna at once recognized Vronsky, and a strange feeling of pleasure mixed with a feeling of vague apprehension suddenly stirred in her heart. He was standing without taking off his overcoat, searching for something in his pocket. When Anna was halfway across the landing he raised his eyes, saw her, and a look of dismay and shame appeared on his face. With a slight inclination of her head, she passed across the landing, then she heard Oblonsky's loud voice inviting him to come in, and the quiet, soft, and calm voice of Vronsky refusing.

When Anna returned with her album he had already gone, and Oblonsky was saying that he had called to find out about the dinner they were giving next day to a visiting celebrity.

"What a strange fellow!" Oblonsky added. "He wouldn't come in for anything."

Kitty blushed. She thought that she alone understood why he had called and why he would not come in. "He must have been to our house," she thought, "and not finding me in, thought that I should be here. But he did not come in because he thought it was late and, besides, Anna is here."

They all exchanged glances and without uttering a word began looking at Anna's album.

There was nothing extraordinary or strange about a man who was calling on a friend at half past nine to find out about the details of a dinner they were arranging and refusing to come in; but it seemed strange to all of them. And to Anna most of all it seemed strange and wrong.

CHAPTER 22

The ball was just beginning when Kitty and her mother walked up the large brilliantly lit staircase, decorated with flowers and flanked on both sides by powdered footmen in red liveries. From the rooms came a murmur of movement, as monotonous as from a beehive, and while they put their hair in order and smoothed their gowns before a looking glass among the growing plants on the landing, they could hear the clear notes of the orchestra from the ballroom starting the first waltz. A little old man in civilian clothes, who had been arranging the gray hair on his temples at another looking glass and who smelled strongly of scent, brushed against them on the staircase and stepped aside in undisguised admiration of Kitty, whom he did not know. A beardless youth, one of those society young men whom the old Prince Shcherbatsky called "puppies," in an extremely low-cut waistcoat, straightened his white tie as he walked up the staircase, bowed to them, and, having passed on, returned to ask Kitty for a quadrille. She had already promised the first quadrille to Vronsky and had to give the second to this young man. An army officer, buttoning his glove, made way for them at the doorway, and stroking his mustache, looked admiringly at the rosy-cheeked Kitty.

Although her toilette, coiffure, and all the preparations for the ball had given Kitty a great deal of trouble and thought, she now entered the ballroom in her elaborate gown of tulle, mounted over pink, as simply and naturally as though her rosettes, laces, and all the details of her toilette had not cost her or her maids a moment's attention, as though she had been born in the tulle frock and lace and with that high coiffure with the roses and its two leaves on top.

When, before they were entering the ballroom, her mother tried to straighten a twisted ribbon in her sash,

Kitty moved away a little: she felt that everything on her must be right and graceful and that there was no need to alter anything.

It was one of Kitty's happy days. Her gown did not feel tight anywhere, her lace bertha did not slip down, her rosettes were neither crumpled nor hanging off, her pink shoes with their high curved heels did not pinch but delighted her little feet. The thick bandeaus of fair hair kept up as if it had grown naturally on her little head. All three buttons on each of the long sleeves that fitted closely round her arm fastened without tearing and without pulling them out of shape. The black velvet ribbon of her locket encircled her neck with particular tenderness. The velvet ribbon was lovely and when she looked at it around her neck in the glass at home, Kitty felt that it was eloquent. There might have been a doubt about anything else, but that velvet ribbon was lovely. Kitty smiled again, here at the ball, when she caught sight of it in the looking glass. Her bare arms and shoulders felt as cool as marble, a feeling which Kitty particularly liked. Her eyes sparkled and she could not keep her red lips from smiling at the consciousness of her own attractiveness. As soon as she entered the ballroom and joined the many-hued crowd of beribboned and belaced ladies in tulle dresses who were waiting to be invited to dance (Kitty was never long in that group), she was asked for the waltz, and she was asked by the best dancer, the most exalted person in the ballroom hierarchy, the famous *dirigeur* and master of ceremonies, a handsome, stately married man, Yegor Korsunsky. He had only just left the Countess Bonin, with whom he had danced the first round of the waltz and, surveying his domain, that is to say, the few couples who had begun to dance, he caught sight of Kitty as she entered and rushed up to her with that special free-and-easy ambling gait peculiar only to masters of ceremonies, and bowing, held out his arm to clasp her slim waist without even asking her consent. She looked round for someone to hold her fan, and their hostess took it from her with a smile.

"What a good thing you've come at the right time," he said as he put his arm round her waist. "It's such bad manners to be late."

Bending her left arm, she put her hand on his shoulder

93

and her little feet in their pink shoes began to glide swiftly, lightly, and rhythmically in time with the music over the polished parquet floor.

"One can relax, waltzing with you," he said to her, falling into the first slow steps of the waltz. "It's simply delightful! What lightness! *Précision!*" he said to her, repeating what he said to nearly all the dancing partners he knew well.

She smiled at his praise and continued to scan the ballroom over his shoulder. She wasn't one of those girls at their first ball for whom all the faces blend into one magical impression; nor was she one who had been dragged from ball to ball and to whom all the faces are so familiar that she is bored by them; she was between those two extremes—she was excited and at the same time sufficiently self-controlled to be able to observe everything that was going on around her. She saw the cream of society grouped in the left-hand corner of the room. There was the beautiful Lydie, Korsunsky's wife, bared as far as she possibly could be; there was their hostess; there shone the bald head of Krivin, always to be found with the cream of society; youths, who had not the courage to go near, gazed in that direction; and there she caught sight of Stiva and then saw Anna's charming head and beautiful figure in a black velvet dress. And *he* was there. Kitty had not seen him since the evening she had refused Levin. She recognized him at once with her farsighted eyes and even noticed that he was looking at her.

"Shall we have another turn, or are you tired?" said Korsunsky, a little out of breath.

"No more, thank you."

"Where shall I take you?"

"Mrs. Karenin is over there, I think. Take me to her, please."

"Wherever you please."

And Korsunsky started waltzing, slowing down gradually, straight in the direction of the crowd in the left-hand corner of the room, repeating, *"Pardon, mesdames, pardon, pardon, mesdames,"* steering through the sea of lace, tulle, and ribbons, without touching so much as a feather, and then swinging his partner around sharply, revealing her slim ankles in their openwork stockings and making her train spread out fanwise and across

Krivin's knees. Korsunsky bowed, straightened his broad shirt-front, and offered Kitty his arm to take her to Anna. Flushed, Kitty lifted her train from Krivin's knees and, feeling a little giddy, looked around in search of Anna. Anna was not in lilac as Kitty so much wanted her to be, but in a low-necked black velvet dress which exposed her full shoulders and bosom that seemed carved out of old ivory and her rounded arms with the very small, delicate hands. Her dress was trimmed all over with Venetian guipure. On her head, in the black hair which was all her own, she wore a little wreath of pansies, and there were more pansies on the black ribbon of her sash and threaded through the white lace at her waist. Her hair style was unostentatious. The only ostentatious thing about her was the willful ringlets which always escaped at her temples and the nape of her neck, adding to her beauty. She wore a string of pearls round her firmly molded neck.

Kitty had been seeing Anna every day and was in love with her, and had always imagined her in lilac, but now seeing her in black, she felt that she had never realized her full charm. She saw her now in quite a new and unexpected light. Now she realized that Anna could not possibly have worn lilac, and that her charm lay precisely in the fact that she stood out from her toilette and that her dress was never conspicuous on her. Her black dress with its rich lace was not conspicuous on her, either; it merely served as a frame, and what one saw was Anna alone, simple, natural, elegant, and at the same time gay and animated.

She was standing, as usual, very erect, and when Kitty went up to the little group, she was talking to her host, her head slightly turned toward him.

"No, I'm not going to throw a stone," she was saying in reply to some remark he had made, "though I don't understand," she went on with a shrug of her shoulders, and at once she turned to Kitty with a tender, protective smile. She threw a quick feminine glance over her dress and with a barely perceptible movement, which Kitty at once understood, expressed her approval both of Kitty's dress and her beauty. "You even enter the room dancing," she added.

"This is one of my most faithful assistants," said Korsunsky, bowing to Anna, whom he had not yet seen.

"The princess helps to make a ball gay and beautiful. May I have the pleasure?" he asked Anna, bending towards her.

"Do you know each other?" asked the host.

"Whom do we not know?" replied Korsunsky. "My wife and I are like white wolves, everyone knows us. One turn of a waltz, madam?"

"I never dance if I can help it," she said.

"But tonight you can't help it," replied Korsunsky.

At that moment Vronsky approached.

"Well, if I can't help it then let's go," she said, ignoring Vronsky's bow and quickly putting her hand on Korsunsky's shoulder.

"Why is she displeased with him?" wondered Kitty, noticing that Anna had deliberately ignored Vronsky's bow.

Vronsky went up to Kitty and reminded her about the first quadrille, adding that he was sorry not to have been able to see her for so long. Kitty listened to him and at the same time gazed with admiration at the waltzing Anna. She expected him to ask her to waltz, but he did not do so, and she looked at him with surprise. He flushed and hastily invited her to dance, but scarcely had he put his arm around her slim waist and taken the first step, when the music stopped. Kitty looked into his face, which was so close to her, and then for a long time afterward, for years afterward, that look so full of love which she gave him and which met with no response from him cut her to the heart with tormenting shame.

"*Pardon, pardon!* Waltz, waltz!" cried Korsunsky from the other end of the room and, grabbing the first young girl within his reach, he himself started dancing.

CHAPTER 23

Vronsky and Kitty waltzed several times round the room. At the end of the waltz Kitty joined her mother and she had barely time to exchange a few words with Nordston before Vronsky came for her for the first quadrille. Nothing of any significance was said during the quadrille. They exchanged a few abrupt remarks about the Korsunskys, husband and wife, whom Vronsky described very amusingly as charming forty-year-old children, and about a projected people's theater, and only once did the conversation touch her to the quick—when he asked her about Levin and whether he was at the ball, adding that he had liked him very much. But Kitty had not expected more from the quadrille. She was waiting with a beating heart for the mazurka. It seemed to her that the mazurka would decide everything. That he did not ask her for the mazurka during the quadrille did not disturb her. She was certain that she would dance the mazurka with him as at previous balls, and, indeed, she refused five other partners, saying that she was already engaged. The whole ball, up to the last quadrille, was for Kitty an enchanted dream of gay colors, sounds, and movements. She only stopped dancing when she felt too tired and had to ask for a rest. But while dancing the last quadrille with one of the boring youths who could not be refused, she found herself face to face with Vronsky and Anna. She had not been near Anna since the beginning of the ball, and now she suddenly saw her again looking quite different and such as she did not expect her to see. She recognized the sense of elation with success that was so familiar to herself. She saw that Anna was intoxicated with the wine of admiration she had aroused. She knew the feeling and she knew its signs, and now she recognized them in Anna—she saw the trembling light flashing in her eyes and the smile of happiness and excitement that involuntarily curled her lips and the striking gracefulness, sureness, and lightness of her movements.

"Who is it?" she asked herself. "All or only one?" And without trying to help the harassed youth with whom she was dancing to carry on a conversation the thread of which he had lost and could not pick up again, and outwardly obeying Korsunsky's cheerful and peremptory shouts which hurled them now into a *grand ronde* and now a *chaine*, she watched while her heart sank more and more. "No, it's not the admiration of the crowd that has intoxicated her, but the adoration of someone in particular. And that someone? Can it be *he*?" Every time he spoke to Anna her eyes flashed joyfully and a smile of happiness curved her red lips. She seemed to be making an effort to conceal these signs of joy, but they appeared on her face of their own accord.

"But what of him?" Kitty looked at him and was filled with horror. What Kitty saw so plainly in the mirror of Anna's face, she now saw in him. What had become of his usually calm and firm manner and the carefree and tranquil expression of his face? Every time he turned to her, he bowed his head a little, as if wishing to fall at her feet, and his eyes were full of an expression of submission and fear. "I do not want to hurt you," his every look seemed to say, "I only wish to save myself, and I do not know how." Kitty had never before seen such an expression on his face.

They were talking about their mutual friends, carrying on a most trite conversation, but to Kitty it seemed that every word they uttered was deciding their fate and hers. And the strange thing was that though they were really only talking about how funny Ivan Ivanovich was with his French and how the Yeletsky girl could have made a better match, these words had a special meaning for them and they felt the same as Kitty. The whole ball and the whole world were covered in the mist that enveloped Kitty's heart. It was only the strict school of her upbringing that sustained her and enabled her to do what was expected of her—to dance, to answer the questions put to her, to talk, and even to smile. But before the mazurka began, when the chairs were already being placed for it and several couples moved from the small to the big ballroom, Kitty was overwhelmed by a moment of despair and terror. She had refused five men and now had no partner for the mazurka. She had no hope even of being asked just because she had had much success in society and it could not possibly occur to anyone that she was not already invited. She would have to tell her mother that she was feeling ill and go home, but she had not the strength to do so.

She felt completely crushed.

She went to the far end of a little drawing room and sank into an armchair. The gauzy skirt of her gown lifted in a cloud round her slender waist; one thin, bare, tender, girlish arm dropped listlessly and sank into the pink folds of her skirt; the other hand held a fan with which she fanned her flushed face with rapid short movements. But in spite of her look of a butterfly just settled on a blade of grass and ready at any moment to unfold her rainbow wings and flutter away, her heart was gripped by terrible despair.

"But perhaps I'm mistaken, perhaps it was not so?" And she again recalled all she had seen.

"Kitty, what's the matter?" asked the Countess Nordston, coming up to her noiselessly over the carpet. "I don't understand it."

Kitty's lower lip trembled; she got up quickly.

"Kitty, aren't you dancing the mazurka?"

"No, no," said Kitty in a voice trembling with tears.

"He asked her for the mazurka in my presence," said the countess, knowing that Kitty would understand whom she meant by him and her. "She said, 'Aren't you dancing with the Princess Shcherbatsky?'"

"Oh, I don't care," replied Kitty.

No one except herself understood her situation. No one knew that a few days ago she had refused a man whom she perhaps loved, and refused him because she trusted another.

The Countess Nordston, who was to be partnered by Korsunsky for the mazurka, went and told him to ask Kitty instead.

Kitty danced in the first pair and, fortunately, was not obliged to talk, because Korsunsky ran about all the time giving orders to the dancers. Vronsky and Anna were sitting almost opposite her. She saw them with her farsighted eyes across the room and she saw them close to when they met in couples, and the more she saw them the more she was convinced that her unhappiness was an accomplished fact. She saw that they felt as if they were alone in that crowded ballroom. On Vronsky's face, usually so firm and self-possessed, she saw that expression of submission and bewilderment that had struck her before, an expression like that of an intelligent dog when it feels guilty.

Anna smiled and her smile was reflected on his face. She became thoughtful and he grew serious. A kind of supernatural force drew Kitty's eyes to Anna's face. She looked enchanting in her simple black dress; her full arms with the bracelets were enchanting, her firm neck with the string of pearls was enchanting, the curls of her disarrayed hair were enchanting, the graceful light movements of her small feet and hands were enchanting;

her lovely face was enchanting in its animation; but there was something terrible and cruel about her charm.

Kitty kept looking admiringly at her more than ever and suffered more and more. Kitty felt crushed and her face showed it. When Vronsky saw her as he happened to knock against her during the mazurka, he did not recognize her at first, so changed was she.

"A splendid ball!" he said to her in order to say something.

"Yes," she replied.

In the middle of the mazurka, when they were repeating a complicated figure invented by Korsunsky, Anna stepped into the middle of the circle, chose two men and two women, including Kitty, to join her. Kitty gave her a frightened look as she came up. Anna half closed her eyes, looked at her, smiled, and pressed her hand. But noticing that in reply to her smile Kitty's face merely expressed despair and surprise, she turned away and started talking gaily with the other woman.

"Yes," Kitty said to herself, "there is something strange, devilish, and enchanting about her."

Anna did not want to stay to supper, but their host tried to persuade her to change her mind.

"Do stay, my dear lady," said Korsunsky, taking her bare arm in his, "I have a wonderful idea for a cotillion! *Un bijou!*"

And he moved slowly on, trying to draw her with him. Their host smiled approvingly.

"No, I won't stay," replied Anna with a smile; but in spite of her smile, Korsunsky and the master of the house realized from the determined tone of her voice that she would not stay.

"No, thank you," said Anna, looking round at Vronsky who was standing beside her. "As it is, I've danced more in Moscow at your ball than I have the whole winter in Petersburg. I must have a rest before my journey."

"Are you definitely going tomorrow?" asked Vronsky.

"Yes, I think so," replied Anna, as though surprised at the boldness of his question; but the uncontrollable, tremulous radiance of her eyes and her smile scorched him as she said it.

Anna did not stay for supper, but went home.

CHAPTER 24

"Yes, there is something repugnant and repellent about me," thought Levin as he left the Shcherbatskys' and walked in the direction of his brother's lodgings, "and I don't get on with other people. They say it's pride. No, I haven't even got that. If I had any pride I should never have put myself in such a position." And he thought of Vronsky, happy, kind, intelligent, and calm, who certainly never put himself in such a terrible position as he, Levin, had been in that evening. "Yes, she was bound to choose him. That was only fair and I've no right to complain of anyone or anything. It is my own fault. What right had I to think that she would be willing to unite her life with mine? Who am I? What am I? A nobody, wanted by no one and of no use to anyone." And he recalled his brother Nikolai and was glad to dwell on that recollection: "Is he not right in maintaining that everything in the world is evil and nasty? And I'm sure we were not fair in judging Nikolai. Of course, from the point of view of Prokofy, who saw him drunk and in a tattered fur coat, he is a contempt-ible man. But I know him to be different. I know his soul and I know that I'm just like him. But instead of going to see him, I dined out and then came here." Levin walked up to a street lamp, read his brother's address which he had in his wallet, and hailed a sledge. All the way to his brother's lodgings at the other end of the town, Levin kept recalling vividly all the circum-stances he knew of Nikolai's life. He remembered how in spite of the ridicule of his colleagues his brother had lived like a monk at the University and for a year after, strictly observing all religious rites, going to church, fast-ing, avoiding every kind of pleasure and especially women; and then how afterward something suddenly seemed to break loose inside him and he began making friends with most loathsome people and gave himself up to a life of the utmost dissipation. He then recalled the incident about a little boy his brother had brought from the country to educate and in a fit of rage had beaten

101

so mercilessly that proceedings had been taken against him for inflicting grievous bodily injuries on the child. He next recalled the incident with the cardsharper to whom his brother had lost money and whom he had given an IOU and then prosecuted on a charge of fraud. (It was this debt that Koznyshev had paid.) He further recalled the night his brother had spent at the police station for disorderly conduct. Then there was his disgraceful legal action against his brother Koznyshev, whom Nikolai accused of cheating him out of his share of their mother's estate; and his last adventure when Nikolai had obtained a post in the civil service in one of the western provinces and had been summonsed for beating up a village elder. It was all horrible and disgusting. But to Levin it did not seem to be as disgusting as it must have appeared to those who did not know Nikolai, did not know the story of his life and did not know his heart.

Levin remembered that in his period of piety, fasting, visiting monks, and going to church, when he was seeking for help in religion to curb his passionate nature, Nikolai had not only failed to find anyone to encourage him, but everyone, including Levin himself, had laughed at him. They teased him, called him Noah, a monk; and when he broke out, no one came to his help, but everyone turned away from him in horror and disgust.

Levin felt that his brother Nikolai was at heart, deep inside him, in spite of the depravity of his life, no worse than the people who despised him. It was not his fault that he had been born with an uncontrollable nature and a mind that was scarred by something. But he had always wished to be good. "I will tell him everything, and I'll make him tell me everything. I'll show him that I love and therefore understand him," Levin decided, as he drove up to the hotel shown in the address at eleven o'clock at night.

"On the top floor, twelve and thirteen," the hall porter said in reply to Levin's question.

"Is he in?"

"Yes, sir, I expect so."

The door of number twelve was ajar, and from inside, visible in a shaft of light, came a dense cloud of cheap and foul tobacco smoke and the sound of a voice unfamiliar to Levin; but Levin knew at once that his brother was there—he heard his intermittent cough.

As he entered the room he heard the unfamiliar voice saying: "It all depends on how intelligently and conscientiously the business is conducted."

Konstantin Levin looked into the room and saw that the speaker was a young man with a huge mop of hair, wearing a light, pleated overcoat, pleated below the fitted waist, and that a young pock-marked woman in a woolen dress without collar or cuffs was sitting on the sofa. He could not see his brother. Levin's heart sank at the thought that his brother was living among people who were so alien to him. No one heard him, and as he took off his galoshes, he listened to what the man in the pleated overcoat was saying. He was talking about some enterprise or other.

"Oh, to hell with the privileged classes," his brother's voice said with a cough. "Masha, get us some supper and put the bottle on the table if there's any vodka left or else send for some."

The woman got up, came out from behind the partition, and saw Konstantin.

"There's some gentleman here to see you," she said.

"Who does he want?" Nikolai Levin's voice said angrily.

"It's me," answered Konstantin Levin, coming out into the light.

"Who's *me*?" Nikolai's voice repeated still more angrily.

He got up quickly, brushing against something, and Levin saw facing him in the doorway his brother's familiar, huge, wasted, stooping figure, with the large frightened eyes, which struck him by its wild appearance and ill health.

He was much more emaciated than three years ago when Levin had last seen him. He was wearing a short coat. His hands and bony figure seemed bigger than ever. His hair was getting sparse. The same walrus mustache drooped over his lips, the same eyes looked at the newcomer strangely and naïvely.

"Ah, Kostya!" he exclaimed suddenly, recognizing his brother, and his eyes lit up with joy. But at the same moment he looked round at the young man and made the convulsive movement of his head and neck, as if his tie were too tight, that Levin knew so well; and an entirely different expression, wild, martyred, and cruel, settled on his haggard face.

"I wrote to you and to Sergey that I do not know you and do not wish to know you. What do you want? What do the two of you want?"

He was quite different from what Levin had imagined him to be. When he thought of him, Levin forgot the worst and the most painful sides of his character, which made personal contact with him so difficult; and now when he saw his face and especially that convulsive turn of the head, he remembered it all.

"There's nothing I want to see you about," he replied timidly. "I simply came to see you."

His brother's timidity obviously softened Nikolai. His lips twitched.

"Oh," he said, "so you've just come to see me, have you? Well, come in, sit down. Like some supper? Masha, bring three portions. No, wait. Do you know who this is?" he asked, turning to his brother and pointing to the man in the tight-fitting coat. "This is Mr. Kritsky, my friend from Kiev, a very remarkable man. The police, of course, are persecuting him because he isn't a scoundrel."

And he turned round and looked at everyone in the room, as was his habit. Seeing the woman in the doorway, making a movement as though to go, he shouted at her: "Wait, I said!" And in the awkward and incoherent way of talking Levin knew so well, he again looked round at everyone and began telling his brother all about Kritsky: how he had been expelled from the university for having founded a society to assist poor students and to organize schools on Sundays, and how he had afterward got a job as a teacher in an elementary school and had been driven out of that too, and had then been put on trial for something or other.

"You were at Kiev University?" Levin asked Kritsky, to break the awkward silence that followed his brother's introduction.

"Yes, at Kiev University," Kritsky replied crossly with a frown.

"And this woman," Nikolai Levin interrupted, pointing to her, "is my life's companion, Maria Nikolayevna. I took her out of a house of ill fame," and he jerked his neck as he said this. "But I love and respect her and I'd like all those who wish to know me," he added, raising his voice and frowning, "to love and respect her too. She is the same as a wife to me. Yes, exactly the same. So now you know. You know whom you've got to deal with. And if you think you're demeaning yourself—there's the door and good-by!"

And again his eyes looked around at everybody questioningly.

"Why should I be demeaning myself, I don't understand."

"Oh well, in that case, Masha, order supper for three, vodka and wine. . . . No, wait a minute. . . . Oh, never mind. Go along."

CHAPTER 25

"So you see," went on Nikolai Levin, painfully wrinkling his forehead and twitching. He seemed to find it hard to think what to say and to do. "Well, you see . . ." He pointed to some iron bars tied together with a piece of string in a corner of the room. "Do you see that? That is the beginning of a new undertaking we're starting. A producers' association. . . ."

Levin hardly listened. He kept looking at his brother's sickly, consumptive face, and he was feeling more and more sorry for him, and he could not bring himself to pay attention to what his brother was telling him about the producers' association. He could see that this association was merely a sheet anchor to save his brother's self-respect.

"You know," Nikolai Levin went on, "that capitalism is crushing the worker. Our workers and our peasants bear all the burden of labor and are placed in such a position that no matter how hard they work they cannot escape from their brutish condition. The capitalists rob them of all the profits of their labor by which they might improve their condition and obtain the leisure necessary for getting some education. Everything over and above their wages is taken away from them, and our society is so constituted that the harder they work the greater the profits of the merchants and the landowners, while they remain beasts of burden forever. And this state of affairs has to be changed," he concluded and looked inquiringly at his brother.

"Yes, of course," said Levin, watching the hectic flush spreading over his brother's prominent cheekbones.

"And so we are forming an association of locksmiths, in which all the products and the profits and the main tools of production will be common property."

"Where is your producers' association to be?" asked Levin.

"In the village of Vodrema in the Kazan province."

"But why in a village? I thought that in the villages they had plenty of work as it is. Why a locksmiths' association in a village?"

"Because the peasants are as much slaves now as they ever were and that is why you and Sergey don't like an attempt being made to deliver them from their slavery," replied Nikolai Levin, annoyed at his brother's objection.

Levin sighed, looking round at the dismal and dirty room. The sigh apparently irritated Nikolai still more.

"I know the aristocratic views held by Sergey and yourself. I know that Sergey applies all the power of his mind to justifying the existing evils."

"I don't think so," Levin said with a smile, "and, besides, why do you talk about Sergey?"

"Sergey? I'll tell you why," Nikolai Levin cried suddenly at the mention of Sergey's name. "I'll tell you why! But what's the use of talking? There's only one thing . . . Why have you come here? You despise all this. Very well, why don't you go? Go!" he shouted, getting up from his chair. "Go, go!"

"I don't despise it at all," Levin said timidly. "I don't even dispute it."

At that moment Maria Nikolayevna came back. Nikolai looked round angrily at her. She went up to him hurriedly and whispered something.

"I'm not well and I've grown irritable," said Nikolai Levin, calming down and breathing heavily, "and then you come talking to me about Sergey and that article of his. It's such drivel, such nonsense, such self-deception. What can a man write about justice who doesn't know what justice is? Have you read his article?" he asked, turning to Kritsky, resuming his seat at the table and brushing away some half-filled cigarettes that lay scattered over half of the table, to clear a space for the meal.

"I have not read it," said Kritsky morosely, obviously not wishing to join the conversation.

"Why not?" asked Nikolai, now turning irritably to Kritsky.

"Because I don't think it necessary to waste time on it."

"But if you don't mind my asking you, how do you know it would be a waste of your time? Many people would find the article difficult to understand because it is above their heads. But with me it's different: I can see through his ideas and I know why his article is weak."

They were all silent. Kritsky got up slowly and reached for his hat.

"Don't you want to stay for supper? Very well, goodby. Come with a locksmith tomorrow."

As soon as Kritsky had gone out, Nikolai smiled and winked.

"He's not much good either," he said. "I can see that—"

But at that moment Kritsky called him from outside the door.

"What do you want now?" he asked and went out into the passage.

Left alone with Maria Nikolayevna, Levin turned to her.

"Have you been long with my brother?" he asked.

"Yes, over a year. His health has got worse and worse. He drinks too much," she said.

"You mean?"

"He drinks vodka and that's bad for him."

"Does he drink a lot?" Levin whispered.

"Yes," she said, looking timidly towards the door where Nikolai appeared at that moment.

"What were you talking about?" he said, frowning, and looking from one to the other with frightened eyes. "What was it?"

"Oh, nothing," Konstantin replied, looking confused.

"You needn't tell me if you don't want to. Only I shouldn't talk to her if I were you. She's a streetwalker and you're a gentleman," he said, jerking his neck. "You see," he went on, raising his voice, "you've got a pretty good idea of everything here and I expect you can't help being sorry for the error of my ways."

"Please, Nikolai, please," Maria Nikolayevna whispered again, going up to him.

"Oh, all right, all right! What about supper? Ah, here it is," he said, as he caught sight of a waiter coming in with a tray. "Here, put it down here," he said crossly, and immediately poured himself out a glass of vodka and drank it greedily. "Will you have a drink?" he asked, turning to his brother and brightening up at once. "Well, that's enough about Sergey. I'm glad to see you all the same. Say what you like, but we're no strangers, are we? Come, have a drink. Tell me, what are you doing?" he went on, munching a crust of bread greedily and pouring himself out another glass. "What sort of life do you lead?"

"I live alone in the country as I did before, looking after the estate," replied Levin, watching with horror the greediness with which his brother ate and drank, and doing his best to conceal it.

"Why didn't you get married?"

"I'm afraid I just didn't," replied Konstantin, blushing.

"Why not? For me, you see, everything is over, finished with! I've made a mess of my life. I've said it before and I'm going to say it again: if I had been given my share of the property when I was most in need of it, my whole life would have been different."

Levin hastened to change the subject.

"Do you know that your little Vanya is a clerk in my office at Pokrovsk?" he asked.

Nikolai jerked his neck and sank into thought.

"Tell me, what's happening in Pokrovsk? Is the house still standing, and the birch trees and our classroom? And is Philip the gardener still alive? How well I remember the summerhouse and the sofa! Mind, don't change anything in the house, but hurry up and get married and have everything again as it used to be. I'll come and see you then, if your wife is a nice woman."

"Why not come now?" said Levin. "We'd be so happy there."

"I would come if I were quite sure I shouldn't find Sergey there."

"You wouldn't. I live quite independently of him."

"Yes, but say what you like, you have to choose between him and me," he said, looking timidly into his brother's eyes.

His timidity touched Levin.

"If you want to know what I really think about it," said Levin, "I can tell you that I take no sides in your quarrel with Sergey. You're both in the wrong. You more outwardly and he more inwardly."

"Oh, so you've realized that, have you?" Nikolai cried delightedly.

"But personally, if you want to know, I value your friendship more because . . ."

"Why, why?"

Levin could not say that he valued it because Nikolai was unhappy and was in need of friendship, but Nikolai realized that he meant just that and, frowning, poured himself out another glass of vodka.

"That's enough," Maria Nikolayevna said, stretching out her plump, bare arm to the decanter.

"Let go! Leave me alone! I'll thrash you!" he shouted.

Maria Nikolayevna gave a gentle, kindly smile which evoked the same kind of smile from Nikolai, and she took away the vodka.

"You think she doesn't understand anything, do you? She understands everything much better than any of us. Don't you think there's something good and charming about her?"

"You were never in Moscow before?" Levin said, just to say something.

"Don't be so formal with her. It frightens her. No one but the magistrate, before whom she was brought because she wanted to escape from the house of ill fame, ever spoke politely to her. Dear Lord, what a madhouse the world is!" he cried suddenly. "All these new institutions, magistrate courts, rural councils—what idiotic nonsense!"

And he began to tell Levin about his encounters with the new institutions.

Levin listened to him, and the assertion that there was no sense in all the social institutions, which he shared with him and had often expressed himself, was distasteful to him when he heard it from his brother's lips.

"We shall understand it all in the next world."

"The next world? Oh, I don't like that next world, I

don't like it," Nikolai said, staring at his brother with wild, frightened eyes. "And yet, you see, one would think it would be a good thing to leave all this abomination and muddle, both one's own and other people's; yet I'm afraid of death, I'm terribly afraid of death." He shuddered. "Come and have a drink! Would you like some champagne? Or shall we go out somewhere? Let's go to the gypsies. You know, I've grown very fond of the gypsies and the Russian folk songs."

His speech grew thick and he started jumping from one subject to another.

With Masha's help Levin persuaded him not to go out anywhere, and put him to bed quite drunk.

Masha promised to write to Levin in case of need and to try to persuade Nikolai to go and live with him.

CHAPTER 26

In the morning Konstantin Levin left Moscow and towards evening arrived home. On his way back in the train he talked to his fellow passengers about politics and the new railways and, just as in Moscow, he was overcome by the confusion of ideas, dissatisfaction with himself, and a vague sense of shame; but when he got out at his station, recognized his one-eyed coachman Ignat, with the collar of his coat turned up; when in the dim light from the station windows he caught sight of his upholstered sled, his horses with their plaited tails, and the harness with its rings and tassels; when the coachman Ignat, while still putting his things into the sledge, told him the village news—the arrival of the contractor and the calving of Pava—he felt that the confusion was gradually clearing up, and his self-dissatisfaction and shame were passing off. He felt this at the mere sight of Ignat and the horses; but when he had put on the sheepskin coat Ignat had brought for him, and, well wrapped up, had sat down in the sledge and was driven away, thinking about the new orders he would have to give and now and again glancing at the side horse (a Don saddle horse once, but overstrained, though still a spirited animal), he began to see everything that had happened to him in quite a different light. He felt that he was himself again and he did not wish to be anyone else. All he wanted now was to be better than he had been before. To begin with, he decided that from that day on he would stop looking for any extraordinary happiness such as marriage was to have given him, and that consequently he would no longer think little of what he possessed at present. He would furthermore never again allow himself to be carried away by low passion, the memory of which had so tormented him when he was making up his mind to propose. Then, remembering his brother Nikolai, he made up his mind never to allow himself to forget him, never to let him out of his sight, and to be ready to help him when things should go badly with him. And that would be soon, he felt. Besides, his brother's talk about communism, to which he had paid so little attention at the time, now made him think. He considered a complete change of economic conditions nonsense, but he had always felt the injustice of his own abundance in comparison with the poverty of the peasants, and now decided, so as to feel himself absolutely in the right, that though he had always worked hard and lived far from luxuriously, he would now work harder and allow himself still less luxury. And it all seemed to him so easy to carry out that the whole way home he spent in a most pleasant daydream. Feeling greatly uplifted by this hope of a new and better life, he arrived home before nine o'clock in the evening.

A light from the windows of the room of his old nurse Agafya, who now acted as his housekeeper, fell on the snow-covered drive in front of the house. She was not yet asleep. Kuzma, awakened by her, came running out sleepy and barefoot, onto the front steps. Laska, a setter bitch, ran out too, almost throwing Kuzma off his feet, and, whining, rubbed herself against Levin's knees, jumping up and wishing but not daring to put her forepaws on his chest.

"You've come back soon, sir," said Agafya.

"I was homesick, Agafya," he replied. "Visiting friends is all right, but there's no place like home."

He went into his study, which was gradually lit up by the candle. The familiar objects in the room were revealed: the antlers, the bookshelves, the tiled stove with the ventilator which had long been in need of repair, his father's sofa, the big table with an open book, a broken

111

ash tray, and a notebook with his writing. When he saw all this, he was for a moment overcome by a feeling of doubt of the possibility of starting the new life he had been dreaming of during his drive home. All these traces of his old life seemed to seize hold of him, saying: "No, you won't get away from us, and you're not going to be different; you're going to be just the same as you've always been with your doubts, your everlasting dissatisfaction with yourself, your vain attempts at reform, your falling from grace, and the constant expectation of the happiness you have missed and which is not possible for you."

But this was what the things said to him. Another voice inside him was saying that one must not submit to the past and one can make what one likes of oneself. And obeying this voice, he went to the corner where his two eighty-pound dumbbells lay and started exercising with them, raising and lowering them, trying to put heart into himself. There was a sound of creaking footsteps behind the door. He hastily put down the dumbbells.

The bailiff came in and said that everything, thank God, was most satisfactory, but that the buckwheat had got a little burned in the new drying kiln. This piece of news irritated Levin. The new kiln had been constructed and partly invented by him. His bailiff had always been against it and now announced with badly concealed triumph that the buckwheat had been burned. Levin, on the other hand, was quite certain that if it had been burned, it was only because the precautions he had ordered a hundred times had not been taken. He felt vexed and he reprimanded the bailiff. But there was one important and happy event: Pava, his best cow (he had paid a great deal of money for her at a cattle show), had calved.

"Kuzma, give me my sheepskin, and you, sir," he said to the bailiff, "tell them to bring a lantern. I'll go and have a look at her."

The cowshed for the most valuable cattle was just behind the house. Crossing the yard past the snowdrift by the lilac bushes, he went into the cowshed. There was a warm, steaming smell of dung when the frozen door was opened and the cows, startled by the unaccustomed light of a lantern, stirred on the fresh straw. He caught sight of the broad, smooth, black-and-white back of a Frisian

112

cow. Berkut, the bull, a ring through his nose, was lying down and was about to get to his feet, but changed his mind and only snorted once or twice as they walked past him. Pava, a perfect beauty, as huge as a hippopotamus, turned her back to them, screening her calf from them and sniffing at it.

Levin went into the stall, looked Pava over, and lifted the reddish speckled calf onto its long unsteady legs. Pava, becoming excited, was about to low, but calmed down when Levin put the calf back at her side and, with a heavy sigh, started licking it with her rough tongue. The calf, looking for her udder, kept pushing its nose under its mother's belly and whisking its little tail.

"Bring the light here, Feyodor, here," said Levin, examining the calf. "Like its mother, though its coat is like its sire's. She's a beauty. Big-boned and deep-flanked. She's a beauty, isn't she?" he said to the bailiff, now entirely reconciled with him for the buckwheat under the influence of his satisfaction about the calf.

"She couldn't very well have turned out a bad one, could she? Semyon, the contractor, came the day after you left, sir. You will have to settle with him, sir," said the bailiff. "I believe I told you about the machine."

This single item brought Levin back to all the details of the management of his estate, which was on a large scale, and complicated. He went straight from the cowshed to the office and after talking things over with the bailiff and the contractor, he returned to the house and went straight upstairs to the drawing room.

CHAPTER 27

It was a large, old house, and though Levin was living in it alone he used and heated the whole of it. He knew that this was foolish, he knew even that it was wrong and contrary to his present new plans, but the house was a whole world to Levin. It was the world in which his father and mother had lived and died. They had lived the sort of life which seemed to Levin the ideal of perfection, and which he had dreamed of restoring with a wife and family of his own.

Levin scarcely remembered his mother. The thought

113

of her was sacred to him and in his imagination his future wife was to be a repetition of that enchanting and sacred ideal of womanhood which his mother had been.

He could not imagine love for a woman outside marriage. But he first of all pictured to himself a family and only then the woman who would give him the family. His idea of marriage was therefore quite unlike that of the majority of his friends and acquaintances for whom marriage was only one of many facts of social life; for Levin it was the chief thing in life on which its whole happiness depended. And now he had to give it up!

When he had gone into the little drawing room where he always had his tea and had settled himself in his armchair with a book, Agafya brought him his cup of tea with her usual remark: "Let me sit down for a while beside you, my dear." She sat down on a chair by the window and he felt that, however strange it might seem, he had not given up his dreams and he could not live without them. With her or with another, it would come true. He read his book, thought of what he was reading, stopped to listen to Agafya, who chattered away without stopping; and at the same time all sorts of pictures of his future life in the country and his future family life rose up disconnectedly in his imagination. He felt that deep inside him something was settling down, adjusting and asserting itself.

He listened to Agafya, who was telling him how Prokhor had forgotten the Lord and was spending on drink the money Levin had given him to buy a horse with and had thrashed his wife to within an inch of her life; he listened and he read his book and kept in mind the whole trend of ideas stirred up by what he was reading. It was Tyndall's *Treatise on Heat*. He remembered how he had criticized Tyndall for his conceit about the cleverness with which he made his experiments and for his lack of a philosophic outlook. And suddenly he would be overcome by the joyful thought: "In two years' time I shall have two Frisian cows in the herd and Pava herself may still be alive. I shall have a dozen young cows by Berkut and add the three others—splendid!" He took up his book again.

"Very well, let us say electricity and heat are one and the same thing, but is it possible to substitute one quantity for another in solving an equation? No. Well, so

114

what then? The connection between all the forces of nature can be felt instinctively anyway. . . . It is particularly good that Pava's daughter will be a red-speckled cow and that the whole herd with the addition of those three others . . . Splendid! To go out with my wife and with our guests to meet the herd coming in from the fields. . . . My wife will say: 'Kostya and I reared this calf like a baby.' 'How can you find all this so interesting?' a visitor will ask. 'Everything that interests him interests me.' But who will she be?" And he remembered what had happened in Moscow. "Well, what's to be done about it? It's not my fault. But now everything will be different. It's nonsense to think that life will not allow it, that the past will not allow it. One has to fight for a better life, for a much better life. . . ." He raised his head and sank into thought. Old Laska, who had not yet completely got over her joy at his arrival and who had run out to bark in the yard, came back wagging her tail and bringing with her a smell of fresh air. She came up to him, thrust her head under his hand, whining plaintively and demanding to be stroked.

"She all but speaks," said Agafya. "Only a dog, but she understands that her master has come home feeling depressed."

"Why should I feel depressed?"

"Don't you think I can see, my dear? I ought to know what gentlefolks feel by now. I've grown up among them from a child. Never mind, my dear, as long as you have health and a clear conscience . . ."

Levin looked at her intently, wondering how she understood what was passing in his mind.

"Well, shall I fetch you some more tea?" she said and, picking up his cup, she went out.

Laska kept thrusting her head under his hand. He stroked her and she curled up at his feet, putting her head on her outstretched hind paw. And as a sign that everything was now well and satisfactory she opened her mouth a little, smacked her lips, and, putting her sticky lips more comfortably over her old teeth, lay still in blissful repose. Levin watched this last movement of hers carefully.

"It's the same with me!" he said to himself. "I shall do the same. . . . Never mind. All's well."

CHAPTER 28

Early on the morning after the ball, Anna sent her husband a telegram to say that she was leaving Moscow that very day.

"Yes, I must go, I must go." She explained to her sister-in-law her change of plans in a tone suggesting that she had remembered so many things she had to attend to that she could not possibly enumerate them all. "Yes, it had really better be today!"

Oblonsky was not dining at home. But he promised to be back to take his sister to the station at seven o'clock.

Kitty, too, did not come, sending a note to say that she had a headache. Dolly and Anna dined alone with the children and their English governess. Whether it was that the children were fickle or very sensitive and felt that Anna was not at all the same now as she had been the day they had grown so fond of her, and that she was no longer interested in them, they suddenly gave up their games with their aunt, were no longer in love with her, and showed no interest whatever in the fact that she was going away. Anna was all the morning busy with preparations for her departure. She wrote notes to her Moscow acquaintances, did her accounts, and packed. Altogether it seemed to Dolly that she was in a restless frame of mind, that she was troubled about something. Dolly knew this feeling very well. She had experienced it frequently and mostly without cause and, as a rule, concealed her discontent with herself. After dinner Anna went to her room to dress, and Dolly followed her.

"How strange you are today," said Dolly.

"I? Do you think so? No, I'm not strange, but I feel depressed. It happens to me sometimes. I feel like crying all the time. It's very silly, but it doesn't last," Anna said quickly and bent her flushed face over the tiny bag into which she was packing her nightcap and cambric handkerchiefs. Her eyes were peculiarly bright and were constantly filling with tears. "I did not want to leave Petersburg and now I do not want to leave here."

"You came here and you did a good deed," said Dolly, looking at her searchingly.

Anna looked at her with eyes wet with tears.

"Don't say that, Dolly. I've done nothing and could do nothing. I often wonder why people conspire to spoil me. What have I done and what could I do? There was so much love in your heart that you could forgive . . ."

"Goodness only knows what would have happened without you! How lucky you are, Anna!" said Dolly. "Everything in your heart is so serene and good."

"Everyone has a skeleton in the cupboard, as the English say."

"What skeleton can you have? Everything about you is so clear."

"I have, though!" Anna said suddenly and, quite unexpectedly after her tears, her lips puckered into a sly, ironic smile.

"Well, in that case, your skeleton must be an amusing one and not a gloomy one," said Dolly with a smile.

"No, it's a gloomy one all right. Do you know why I'm going today and not tomorrow? It's a confession and something that is weighing on my mind and I want to make it to you," said Anna, resolutely throwing herself back in her armchair and looking straight into Dolly's eyes.

And to her surprise Dolly saw that Anna was blushing to her ears and to the curly black locks on her neck.

"Yes," Anna went on. "Do you know why Kitty did not come to dinner? She is jealous of me. I've spoiled . . . It was because of me that the ball was a torture instead of a joy to her. But it wasn't really my fault. Truly it wasn't. Or perhaps only a little bit," she said in a thin voice, drawing out the words "a little bit."

"Oh, you said that exactly like Stiva!" Dolly said, laughing.

Anna was offended. "Oh no, oh no, I'm not Stiva!" she said, frowning. "I'm telling you this because I could never allow myself, even for a moment, to doubt myself," said Anna.

But as she was uttering these words, she felt that they were not true; not only did she doubt herself, but the thought of Vronsky disturbed her, and she was leaving sooner than she had intended only because she did not want to see him again.

"Yes, Stiva told me that you danced the mazurka with him and that he—"

"You can't imagine how ridiculous it all turned out to be. All I wanted to do was to arrange a match and—suddenly something different happened. Perhaps I did something in spite of myself that . . ."

She blushed and broke off.

"Oh, they feel it at once," said Dolly.

"But I should be in despair if there were anything serious on his part," Anna interrupted her. "And I'm quite sure that the whole thing will be forgotten and that Kitty will stop hating me."

"But to tell you the truth, Anna, I'm not particularly keen on this marriage for Kitty. I think it would be better if it came to nothing, if he, Vronsky, is capable of falling in love with you in a single day."

"Good Lord, that would be silly!" said Anna, and again a deep flush of pleasure covered her face at hearing the thought that occupied her mind expressed in words. "So here I am, going away, having made an enemy of Kitty whom I like so much. Oh, she is so sweet! But you'll put it right, won't you, Dolly? You will, won't you?"

Dolly could hardly repress a smile. She was fond of Anna, but she was pleased to see that Anna too had her weaknesses.

"An enemy? That's impossible."

"I did so want that you should all love me as I love you. But now I love you more than ever," she said with tears in her eyes. "Oh dear, how silly I am today."

She dabbed her face with a handkerchief and began to dress. Just as she was about to leave, Oblonsky came in late and smelling of wine and cigars, his face red and cheerful.

Anna's emotion communicated itself to Dolly and as she embraced her sister-in-law for the last time, she whispered: "Remember, Anna, I shall never forget what you've done for me and that I shall always love you as my dearest friend."

"I don't know why," said Anna, kissing her and doing her best to conceal her tears.

"You do know and you have understood me. Good-by, my sweet!"

118

CHAPTER 29

"Well, thank God, that's all over," was the first thought that occurred to Anna after she had said good-by for the last time to her brother, who stood blocking up the entrance to the carriage till the third and last bell. She sat down beside her maid Annushka on the upholstered seat and looked round the dimly lit sleeping car. "Thank heaven tomorrow I shall see Seryozha and Alexey, and my life, my nice life, to which I am accustomed, will go on as before."

Still in the same worried frame of mind in which she had been all that day, Anna made herself comfortable with pleasure and deliberation for the journey; with her deft little hands she undid and did up the little red bag out of which she produced a small pillow which she laid on her knees, and wrapping a rug carefully round her legs, she settled herself comfortably. An invalid woman had already settled herself for the night. Two other women began talking to Anna and a fat old woman wrapped up her feet and made some remarks about the heating of the train. Anna said a few words in reply, but not expecting the conversation to be of particular interest, asked Annushka to get out her torch, hooked it onto the arm of her seat, and took a paper knife and an English novel from her handbag. At first she found it difficult to concentrate on her reading. To begin with, the bustle and walking about of the passengers disturbed her, and when the train had started she could not help listening to the noises; then the snow, beating against the window on her left and sticking to the windowpane, and the sight of a muffled-up guard covered with snow passing along the corridor, on the one hand, and the conversation about the terrible blizzard outside, on the other, distracted her attention. And so it went on: the same jolting and knocking, the same snow beating against the window, the same rapid transitions from steaming heat to cold and back again, the glimpses of the same faces in the semidarkness and the same voices, and Anna began to read and understand what she was reading.

Annushka was already dozing, her broad hands, with a hole in one of the gloves, clutching the red bag on her lap. Anna read and understood everything, but she found no pleasure in reading, that is to say, in following the reflection of other people's lives. She was too eager to live herself. When she read how the heroine of the novel nursed a sick man, she wanted to move about the sickroom with noiseless steps herself; when she read of a member of Parliament making a speech, she wanted to make that speech herself; when she read how Lady Mary rode to hounds and teased her sister-in-law, astonishing everyone by her daring, she would have liked to do the same. But there was nothing to be done about it, and she forced herself to read, fingering the smooth paper knife with her little hands.

The hero of the novel was about to attain the Englishman's idea of happiness—a baronetcy and an estate—and Anna was wishing she could go to the estate with him, when she suddenly felt that he ought to be ashamed and that she, too, ought to be ashamed for the same reason. "But what had he to be ashamed of? What have I to be ashamed of?" she asked herself with hurt surprise. She put down the book and leaned against the back of her seat, gripping the paper knife in both her hands. There was nothing to be ashamed of. She went over all her Moscow memories in her mind. They were all good and pleasant. She recalled the ball; she recalled Vronsky and his infatuated, resigned, and submissive face; she recalled all that had passed between him and her: there was nothing to be ashamed of. And yet, at this very point of her recollections the feeling of shame was intensified just as though, when she was thinking about Vronsky, some inner voice said to her: "Warm, very warm, hot." "Well," she said to herself resolutely, changing her position on the seat, "what about it? What does it mean? Am I really afraid to look straight at what passed between us? Well, what did pass between us? Is there really, can there be anything more between myself and that boy officer than there is between me and every one of my acquaintances?" She smiled contemptuously and took up her book again, but this time she could not understand a word of what she was reading. She passed the paper knife over the windowpane, then pressed its cold smooth surface against her cheek and almost

120

laughed aloud, suddenly and unaccountably overcome with joy. She felt that her nerves were being stretched more and more tightly, like strings on violin pegs. She felt her eyes were opening wider and wider, her fingers and toes twitching nervously, something inside her stopping her breath, and all the images and sounds in the swaying half-light struck her with extraordinary vividness. She was constantly overwhelmed by moments of doubt, and she could not make up her mind whether the train was moving forward or backward or had come completely to a standstill. Was it Annushka at her side or a stranger? "What's that on the arm of the seat? A fur coat or an animal? And what am I doing here? Is it me or someone else?" She was terrified of falling entirely under the spell of this semiconscious state. But something seemed to draw her into it, and she was able to give herself up to it or to resist at will. To collect herself, she got up, threw off her rug, and took off the cape of her warm dress. For a moment she did come to and realized that the lean peasant in the long nankeen coat with a button missing, who had just entered the carriage, was the stoker and that he came to look at the thermometer and that the wind and snow burst in after him at the door; but then everything became confused again. . . . The peasant with the long waist started gnawing at something on the wall; the old woman began stretching her legs up and down the whole length of the compartment and filled it with a black cloud; then there was an awful scraping and knocking, as though someone was being torn to pieces; then a red light blinded her; and at last everything was blotted out by a wall. Anna felt as if she had fallen through the floor. But all this was not terrifying but amusing. The voice of a man muffled up and covered with snow shouted something close to her ear. She got up and recovered her senses; she realized that they had stopped at a station and that this was the guard. She asked Annushka to hand her the cape and shawl she had taken off, put them on again, and moved toward the door.

"Are you going out, ma'am?" asked Annushka.

"Yes, I want a breath of fresh air. It's very hot here."

And she opened the door. The snow and wind rushed toward her and struggled with her for the door. And this too seemed great fun. She opened the door and went out. The wind seemed to be waiting for her and whistled merrily and tried to snatch her up and carry her away, but she got hold of the cold handrail with one hand and, holding down her skirt, alighted on the platform and went behind the carriage. The wind was very strong on the steps of the coach, but on the platform, sheltered by the carriages, it was quiet. She drew deep breaths of the frosty, snowy air, breathing deeply and with delight, and, standing beside the carriage, looked around at the platform and at the lighted station.

CHAPTER 30

The terrible blizzard tore and whistled between the wheels of the train and round the posts from behind the corner of the station. The railway carriages, the posts, the people, and everything that could be seen were covered on one side with snow, and the snow piled up more and more. For a moment the blizzard abated, but then blew again with such powerful gusts that it seemed impossible to stand up against it. And yet people were running along, chatting merrily, their boots creaking over the boards of the platform and constantly opening and shutting the heavy station doors. The shadow of a stooping man slipped under her feet, and she heard the sound of a hammer upon iron. "Let me have that telegram!" she heard an angry voice saying from the other side out of the stormy darkness. "This way, please, No. 28!" other voices shouted, and muffled people, covered with snow, ran past. Two men with lighted cigarettes between their lips walked past her. She took another breath to fill her lungs with fresh air and had already drawn her hand out of her muff to take hold of the handrail and get back into the carriage when another man in a military overcoat stepped close beside her and shut out the flickering light from a lamppost. She looked round and at once recognized Vronsky. Putting his hand to the peak of his cap, he leaned over her and asked if she needed anything and whether he could be of service to her? For some time she gazed intently at him without answering and, though he stood in the shadow, she saw, or imagined she saw, the expression of his face and his eyes. It was the same expression of respectful admiration which had made such an impression on her the night before. She had been telling herself again and again during the last two days and, indeed, only a moment ago that Vronsky was no more to her than any of the hundreds of everlastingly identical young men she came across everywhere and that she would never allow herself even to think of him; but now at the first moment of their meeting she was seized with a feeling of joyful pride. It was quite unnecessary for her to ask why he was there. She knew as well as if he had told her that he was there in order to be where she was.

"I did not know that you were traveling too. Why?" she said, letting fall the hand with which she was about to take hold of the handrail. And her face shone with irrepressible joy and animation.

"Why?" he repeated, looking straight into her eyes. "You know that I am going in order to be where you are," he said. "I can't help it."

And at that very moment the wind, as though it had overcome all obstacles, sent the snow flying from the roofs of the carriages, rattled some loose sheets of iron, and in front the deep whistle of the engine began to blow plaintively and mournfully. The whole horror of the blizzard appeared to her still more beautiful than ever now. He had said what her heart desired but what her reason feared. She made no answer, and he saw conflict in her face.

"Forgive me," he said submissively, "if what I said displeases you."

He spoke respectfully, courteously, but so firmly and so insistently that for a long time she could not think of anything to answer.

"What you're saying is wrong and I beg of you, if you are a good man, to forget what you've said as I am going to forget it," she said at last.

"Not one word, not one gesture of yours will I ever forget, nor can I ever forget."

"That's enough, enough!" she cried, vainly trying to impart a stern expression to her face, into which he was gazing eagerly. Taking hold of the cold handrail, she climbed up the steps and quickly went into the corridor of the train. But there she stopped, trying to think of what had just passed. Though she could remember neither her own words nor his, she instinctively felt that this brief encounter had drawn them terribly close together, and this filled her with both dread and happiness. After standing still a few seconds, she entered the compartment and sat down. The tension which had tormented her before not only returned, but increased and reached such a point that she was afraid every minute that something would snap within her under the intolerable strain. She did not sleep all night. But there was nothing unpleasant or gloomy about that tension or the visions which filled her imagination; on the contrary, there was something joyful, glowing, and exhilarating in it. Toward morning Anna dozed off, sitting in her seat, and when she woke it was already broad daylight and the train was approaching Petersburg. She was at once immersed in thoughts of home, of her husband and son and the cares of this day and those that were to follow.

As soon as the train stopped at Petersburg and she got out, the first person to attract her attention was her husband. "Goodness, why are his ears like that?" she thought, looking at his cold, distinguished figure and especially at the cartilages of his ears, pressing up against the rim of his round hat. Catching sight of her, he walked toward her, pursing his lips in his usual sarcastic smile, and looking straight at her with his large, tired eyes. As she met his fixed and tired gaze, her heart contracted painfully with a sort of unpleasant sensation, as though she expected to find him looking different. She was particularly struck by the feeling of discontent with herself which she experienced when she met him. It was that old familiar feeling indistinguishable from hypocrisy which she experienced in her relations with her husband; but she had not been conscious of it before, while now she was clearly and painfully aware of it.

"Well, yes, as you see, your devoted husband, as devoted as in the first year of marriage, is burning with impatience to see you," he said in his slow, high-pitched voice and in the tone in which he almost always addressed her, a tone of derision for anyone who could really talk like that.

"Is Seryozha all right?" she asked.

"And is that all the reward I get for my ardor?" he said. "Yes, he's all right, he's all right. . . ."

CHAPTER 31

Vronsky did not even attempt to sleep all that night. He sat in his seat, either staring straight before him or looking round at the people who got in or out of the carriage, and if before he struck people who did not know him by his air of imperturbable composure, which made them feel uncomfortable, he now seemed prouder and more imperturbable than ever. He looked at people as if they were things. A nervous young man, an official of a district court, sitting opposite, began to detest him for that look. The young man asked him for a light, addressed a few remarks to him, and even pushed against him to make him feel that he was not a thing but a man, but Vronsky continued to look at him as if he were a lamppost, and the young man kept pulling faces, feeling that he was losing self-control under the strain of this refusal to regard him as a human being.

Vronsky saw nothing and no one. He felt like a king, not because he believed that he had made an impression on Anna—he did not believe that yet—but because the impression she had made on him filled him with happiness and pride.

What would come of it all he did not know and did not even consider. He felt that all his powers, till then dissipated and scattered, were now concentrated and directed with fearful energy toward one blissful goal. And that made him happy. All he knew was that he had told her the truth, that he was going where she was, that all the happiness of his life, the sole meaning of his life, he now found in seeing and hearing her. When he had got out of the train in Bologovo to drink a glass of seltzer water and had caught sight of Anna, the first words he said to her involuntarily expressed what he thought. He was glad he had told her that, and she now knew it and was thinking about it. He did not sleep that night. When he returned to his carriage, he kept going over all the positions in which he had seen her and everything she had said. And his heart stood still when he tried to imagine what might happen in the future.

When he got out of the train in Petersburg, he felt, in spite of his sleepless night, as vigorous and fresh as after a cold bath. He stopped by his carriage, waiting for her to come out. "I'll see her again," he said to himself, smiling involuntarily. "I shall see her walk, I shall see her face, she will say something, turn her head, look at me, smile perhaps." But before he saw her, he saw her husband, whom the stationmaster was courteously escorting through the crowd. "Oh, yes, the husband!" It was only now that Vronsky clearly realized for the first time that her husband was a person who was connected with her. He knew she had a husband, but he did not believe in his existence and only fully believed in him when he saw him there, his head, shoulders, and legs in their black trousers; and especially when he saw this husband calmly take her arm with an air of ownership.

When he saw Karenin with his fresh Petersburg face and his sternly self-confident figure, in his round hat and with his slightly stooping back, Vronsky believed in his existence, and he experienced the same disagreeable feeling a man tortured by thirst might feel on reaching a spring and finding that a dog, a sheep, or a pig in it had not only drunk but also muddied the water. Karenin's way of walking on his flat feet, swinging his thighs, seemed particularly offensive to Vronsky. He acknowledged only his own unquestionable right to love Anna. But she was still the same, and the sight of her had the same effect on him physically, exhilarating and stimulating him and filling his soul with happiness. He told his German valet, who came running up from the second class, to get his things and take them home, while he himself went up to her. He saw the first meeting of husband and wife and noticed with the insight of a lover the signs of slight constraint with which she spoke to her husband. "No, she does not love him, she cannot love him," he decided.

Even at the moment when he was approaching Anna from behind he noticed with joy that she became aware of his approach and even looked round for a moment, but on recognizing him, turned to her husband again.

"Did you have a good night?" he said, bowing to her and to her husband and leaving it to Karenin to take the bow as meant for himself and to recognize him or not, just as he liked.

126

"Yes, thank you," she replied.

Her face looked tired and there was not that animation in it that found expression now in a smile and now in her eyes; but for an instant, as she glanced at him, her eyes lit up and though the fire was at once extinguished, that one instant made him happy. She glanced at her husband to see whether he knew Vronsky. Karenin looked at Vronsky with displeasure, trying vaguely to remember who this was. Vronsky's composure and self-confidence struck against Karenin's cold self-confidence like a scythe on a stone.

"Count Vronsky," said Anna.

"Oh, yes, I believe we've met," Karenin said with indifference, holding out his hand. "You traveled there with the mother and returned with the son," he said, enunciating every word distinctly, as though they were worth a ruble apiece. "Back from furlough, I expect?" he said, and without waiting for a reply, turned to his wife and said in his facetious tone: "Well, were many tears shed in Moscow at parting?"

By this address to his wife he gave Vronsky to understand that he would like to be left alone with her and turning to him, he touched his hat; but Vronsky turned to Anna:

"I hope I may have the honor of calling on you," he said.

Karenin looked at Vronsky with a weary eye.

"Very glad," he said coldly. "We are at home on Mondays." Then having dismissed Vronsky finally, he said to his wife:

"What a good thing I had half an hour to spare to meet you and was able to show you my devotion," he went on in the same bantering tone of voice.

"You emphasize your devotion a little too much for me to value it greatly," she said in the same bantering tone of voice, involuntarily listening to the sound of Vronsky's footsteps behind them. "But what has it got to do with me?" she thought, and began asking her husband how Seryozha had been spending his time without her.

"Oh, excellently! Mariette says he's been very sweet and—er—I'm afraid I must disappoint you—er—I mean, he has not missed you—er—as much as your husband. But thank you again, my dear, for making me the pres-

ent of a day. Our dear Samovar will be in ecstasies."
(He called the celebrated Countess Lydia Ivanovna
"Samovar" because she was always getting hot and bothered about something.) "She was asking after you. And,
you know, if I may venture a word of advice, I think
you ought to call on her today. She feels so strongly
about everything. At present, in addition to all her other
troubles, she is very interested in the reconciliation of
the Oblonskys."

Countess Lydia Ivanovna was a great friend of her
husband's and the center of that set in Petersburg high
society with which Anna was most closely connected
through her husband.

"But I wrote to her."

"She wants to know all the details. Do call on her if
you're not too tired, my dear. Kondraty is here with the
carriage for you. I have to go to the committee. Now I
shall not have to dine alone again," Karenin went on,
no longer facetiously. "You can't imagine how I'm used
to . . ." And pressing her hand warmly, he helped her
into the carriage with a meaning smile.

CHAPTER 32

The first person to meet Anna when she got home
was her son. He rushed down the stairs to her, disre-
garding his governess' cries, and with wild enthusiasm
shouted, "Mummy! Mummy!" Running up to her, he
clung round her neck.

"I told you it was Mummy," he shouted to the governess. "I knew!" Her son, like her husband, aroused in
Anna a feeling akin to disappointment. She had imagined him to be nicer than he actually was. She had to
descend to reality to enjoy him as he was. But even as
he was, he was charming with his fair curls, blue eyes,
and plump, shapely little legs in tightly fitting stockings.
Anna felt almost a physical pleasure in his proximity and
his caresses, and morally relieved when she met his artless, trusting, and loving gaze and heard his naïve questions. She unpacked the presents Dolly's children had
sent him, and told her son there was a little girl in Mos-

cow whose name was Tanya and that Tanya could read and write and even teach other children.

"Why, I'm not worse than she, am I?" asked Seryozha.

"To me you're better than anyone in the world."

"I know that," said Seryozha, smiling.

Before Anna had had time to finish her coffee, the Countess Lydia Ivanovna was announced. The countess was a tall, stout woman, with a sickly, sallow complexion and beautiful, dreamy, black eyes. Anna was very fond of her, but today she seemed to see her for the first time with all her faults.

"Well, my dear, did you take them the olive branch?" asked the countess as soon as she came in.

"Yes, it's all over, but it really wasn't as serious as we thought," replied Anna. "My sister-in-law is in general a little too peremptory."

But the countess, who was interested in everything that did not concern her, had a habit of never listening to what interested her. She interrupted Anna:

"Yes, there's a great deal of sorrow and evil in the world, and I'm terribly worried today."

"Why, what's the matter?" asked Anna, trying to suppress a smile.

"I'm getting tired of breaking lances uselessly in the cause of truth, and sometimes I feel quite strung up. The business of the Little Sisters" (this was a philanthropic, religious, and patriotic society) "was going along nicely, but it's impossible to do anything with those gentlemen," the countess added with an ironical air of resignation to fate. "They pounced on the idea, mutilated it, and are now discussing it in such a petty and trivial way. Two or three people, your husband among them, understand the full significance of this affair, but the others simply discredit it. Yesterday I had a letter from Pravdin. . . ."

Pravdin was a well-known pan-Slav agitator abroad, and the countess told Anna the contents of his letter. She then went on to tell her of other unpleasantnesses and of the intrigues against the unification of the churches, and she hurried away because that afternoon she had to be at a meeting of another society and to attend a Slav committee meeting.

"It was always the same before, but how is it that I never noticed it before?" Anna said to herself. "Or is it that she is particularly irritating today? The whole thing is really absurd: her whole life is devoted to charitable affairs, she is a Christian, and yet she is always angry and she always has enemies, and all enemies in the name of Christianity and charity."

After the countess had gone, another friend, the wife of a chief secretary, arrived and gave Anna all the news of the town. At three she too left, promising to return to dinner. Karenin was at the Ministry. Left alone, Anna spent the time before dinner in being present at her son's dinner (he had his dinner separately), in putting her things in order, and in reading and answering the notes and letters that had accumulated on her table.

The feeling of shame she had felt during the journey without any conceivable reason, as well as her agitation, had completely disappeared. In her normal surroundings she again felt steadfast and irreproachable.

She recalled with surprise her state on the previous day. "What had happened? Nothing. Vronsky said something silly, which it was easy to put a stop to, and I replied as I ought to have done. It's quite unnecessary to tell my husband about it. I mustn't do so. To speak about it would be to give it an importance which it does not have." She remembered how she had told her husband about a declaration nearly made to her by a young subordinate of his, and how Karenin had replied that every woman in high society was exposed to that sort of thing, but that he had complete confidence in her tact and would never allow himself and her to be degraded by being jealous. "So there is no need to say anything, is there? Besides, there is nothing to tell, thank God," she said to herself.

CHAPTER 33

Karenin returned from the Ministry at four o'clock but, as often happened, he had no time to go up to her room. He went straight into his study to see the various people who were waiting for him and to sign certain papers brought to him by his private secretary. The Karenins always had two or three people dining with them. This time there was an old lady, a cousin of Karenin's, the Chief Secretary with his wife, and a young man who had been recommended to Karenin for a post in the service. Anna went into the drawing room to entertain them. Punctually at five, before the bronze Peter I clock had finished striking, Karenin entered in evening dress with a white tie and two stars on his coat, as he had to go out immediately after dinner. Every moment of Karenin's life was filled up and carefully apportioned. And to be able to carry out all his engagements he observed the strictest punctuality. "Without haste and without respite," was his motto. He entered the room, exchanged greetings with everyone, and quickly sat down, smiling at his wife.

"Yes, my solitude is over. You wouldn't believe how uncomfortable" (he emphasized the word "uncomfortable") "it is to dine alone."

At dinner he talked to his wife about Moscow affairs, asked with an ironical smile after Stepan Oblonsky, but for the most part the conversation was general and concerned Petersburg official and social affairs. After dinner he spent half an hour with his guests, and having again pressed his wife's hand with a smile, went out and drove off to a meeting of the Council. This time Anna did not go to the Princess Betsy Tverskoy, who, learning of her arrival, had invited her to the theater, where she had a box for the evening. She did not go chiefly because the dress on which she had counted was not ready. On the whole, looking over her wardrobe after the departure of her guests, Anna was very greatly vexed. Before going to Moscow she had sent three dresses to be altered. She was very clever at dressing well on comparatively little money, and these dresses should have been altered three days ago. But it seemed that two dresses were not nearly ready, and the third had not been altered as she wished. The dressmaker came to explain what had happened and insisted that it was better the way she had done it, and Anna lost her temper and said things for which she was now sorry. To regain her composure, she went to the nursery and spent the evening with her son, putting him to bed herself, making the sign of the cross over him and tucking him up. She was glad she had not gone out and had spent the evening so agreeably at home. She felt so calm and light-hearted, she saw so clearly that what had appeared so important in the train had been merely one of those ordinary and insignificant incidents of society life and that there was no reason for her to feel ashamed or uneasy before anyone else. She sat down by the fire with her English novel and waited for her husband. Exactly at half past nine she heard his ring at the front door and he came into the room.

"Here you are at last!" she said, holding out her hand to him.

He kissed her hand and sat down beside her.

"I can see that on the whole your journey has been a success," he said to her.

"Yes, indeed," she replied, and she began telling him everything from the beginning: her journey with the Countess Vronsky, her arrival, the accident at the railway station. Then she told him how sorry she had been first for her brother and then for Dolly.

"I don't quite see how a man like that can be excused even though he is your brother," said Karenin severely.

Anna smiled. She realized that he had said that expressly to show that no family consideration of kinship could deter him from expressing his sincere opinion. She knew that trait in her husband's character, and she liked it.

"I'm glad it's all ended satisfactorily and that you are back again," he went on. "Well, what are they saying there of the new measure I've got passed in the Council?"

Anna had heard nothing about this measure and she felt ashamed that she could so lightly forget what was so important to him.

"Here, on the contrary, it has created quite a stir," he said with a self-complacent smile.

She could see that he was anxious to tell her something agreeable to himself about this affair, and she made him tell her all about it by asking him all the appropriate questions. With the same self-complacent smile he told her of the ovations he had received as a result of getting the measure through.

"It made me very, very happy. You see, it shows that at last we are beginning to take an intelligent and firm view of this matter."

Having finished his second cup of tea and cream and a roll, Karenin got up and went to his study.

"And you didn't go out anywhere, did you?" he said. "I expect you must have found it rather dull."

"Oh, no!" she replied, getting up and accompanying him across the dining room to his study. "And what are you reading now?" she asked.

"At the moment I am reading Duc de Lille's *Poésie des enfers*," he replied. "A very remarkable book."

Anna smiled, as one smiles at the weaknesses of the people one loves, and slipping her hand through his arm, walked with him as far as the study door. She knew his habit, which had grown into a necessity, of reading in the evening. She knew that in spite of his official duties, which took up almost all his time, he regarded it as his duty to follow up everything of note that appeared in the intellectual sphere. She knew, too, that he was really only interested in books on politics, philosophy, and theology, and that art was completely alien to his nature, but that in spite of this, or rather because of this, he never missed anything that created a stir in the world of art and considered it his duty to read everything. She knew that in the sphere of politics, philosophy, and theology he had his doubts or tried to find an answer to the questions that troubled him; but in questions of art and poetry and, especially, music, which he did not understand at all, he held the most rigid and definite opinions. He liked to talk of Shakespeare, Raphael, and Beethoven, and about the importance of the new schools of poetry and music, which he divided up into clearly defined logical sequences.

"Well, enjoy your book," she said at the door of the study, where a shaded candle and a decanter of water had been placed ready at his armchair. "I'm going to write to Moscow!"

He pressed her hand and kissed it again.

"All the same, he's a good man; upright, kind, and remarkable in his own sphere," Anna said to herself when she had returned to her room, as though defending him against someone who was accusing him and maintaining that one could not love him. "But why do his ears stick out so oddly? Has he had a haircut?"

Punctually at twelve o'clock, when Anna was still sitting at her writing desk finishing a letter to Dolly, she heard the even steps of her husband in his slippers. Karenin, who had had his bath and brushed his hair, came in with a book under his arm and went up to her.

"It's time, it's time," he said with a significant smile and went straight into the bedroom.

"And what right had he to look at him like that?" thought Anna, recalling the look Vronsky had given Karenin.

Having undressed, she went into the bedroom, but not only was the animation that had been simply gushing out of her eyes and her smile in Moscow no longer there: on the contrary, the fire in her now seemed quenched or hidden somewhere deep inside her.

CHAPTER 34

On his departure from Petersburg, Vronsky had left his large apartment in Movskaya Street to his friend and favorite fellow officer Petritsky.

Petritsky was a young lieutenant, not of a particularly good family, and not only not wealthy but owing money all around, drunk every evening, and often under arrest for all sorts of absurd and sordid escapades, but a great favorite both of his comrades and superior officers. Driving up from the railway station to his apartment about noon, Vronsky saw a familiar hired carriage outside. When he rang the bell he heard men's loud laughter, a woman's indistinct prattle, and Petritsky's shout: "If that's one of the villains, don't let him in!" Vronsky told his batman not to announce him and went quietly into the first room. Baroness Shilton, Petritsky's girl friend, looking ravishing in her lilac satin dress and with her rosy face and flaxen hair, sat at the round table, making coffee and, like a canary, filling the whole room with her Parisian chatter. Petritsky in his greatcoat and Kamerovsky, a cavalry captain in full uniform, probably straight from parade, sat on each side of her.

"Bravo! Vronsky!" cried Petritsky, jumping up with a clatter from his chair. "Our host himself! Baroness, some coffee for him out of the new coffeepot. We didn't expect you, you see. I hope you're pleased with this ornament to your study," he said, indicating the baroness. "You know each other, don't you?"

"Of course!" said Vronsky, smiling gaily and pressing the tiny hand of the baroness. "Of course! We're old friends!"

"You've come straight home from a journey," said the baroness, "so I'd better be off. Oh, I'll go this minute if I'm in the way."

"You're at home where you are, Baroness," said Vronsky. "How are you, Kamerovsky," he added, shaking hands with him coldly.

"There now!" The baroness turned to Petritsky. "You never say such pretty things."

"Don't I? After dinner I'll say something just as good."

"But there's no merit in it after dinner. Well, all right, I will make you some coffee. Go and have a wash and tidy yourself up," said the baroness, sitting down again and carefully turning the screw in the new coffeepot. "Pierre, pass me the coffee," she addressed Petritsky, whom she called Pierre because of his surname, without bothering to conceal their relations. "I'll put some more in."

"You'll spoil it."

"No, I shan't. Well, and how is your wife?" the baroness said suddenly, interrupting Vronsky's conversation with his fellow officer. "We've been marrying you off here. Have you brought your wife?"

"No, Baroness. A Bohemian I was born and a Bohemian I shall die."

"So much the better! So much the better! Your hand!"

And, without letting Vronsky go, the baroness began telling him all her latest plans, interspersing her story with jokes, and asking his advice.

"He still won't give me a divorce! What am I to do?" (*He* was her husband.) "I want to bring an action. What would you advise me? Kamerovsky, look after the coffee—it's boiling over! Don't you see I'm busy? I want a court action because I want to get back my property. The stupidity of it! Because I'm supposed to be unfaithful," she said contemptuously, "he wants to have the use of my estate."

Vronsky listened with pleasure to this pretty woman's gay prattle, agreeing with what she said, giving her half-jocular advice, and in general at once assuming his usual tone of talking with women of her sort. In his Petersburg world all people were divided into two absolutely distinct and diametrically opposite sorts. One—the lower sort—vulgar, stupid, and above all, ridiculous people, who believed that a husband should live only with the woman he has married, that young girls should be chaste, women modest, men brave, self-controlled, and steadfast; that one should bring up one's children, earn one's living, and pay one's debts, and all sorts of other nonsense like that. They were the old-fashioned and ridiculous people. But there was another sort of people, the real people, to which all his set belonged, in which the main thing was to be elegant, handsome, generous, daring, gay, giving oneself up unblushingly to every passion and laughing at everything else.

Vronsky was only for a moment taken aback after the impressions of quite another world he had brought back from Moscow; but at once, as though putting his feet into old slippers, he entered his former gay and pleasant world.

The coffee did not get made after all, but boiled over and splashed everybody, giving rise to what was required, that is, providing an excuse for much noise and laughter, and splashing the expensive carpet and the baroness' dress.

"Well, I'll say good-by now or you'll never get washed and I shall have on my conscience the worst crime a well-bred person can commit—uncleanliness. So you advise me to put a knife to his throat?"

"Yes, certainly, only hold it so that your little hand is near his lips. He'll kiss your hand and all will be well," replied Vronsky.

"So tonight at the French theater!" and with a rustle of her skirts she vanished.

Kamerovsky got up, too, and without waiting for him to go, Vronsky shook hands with him and went to his dressing room. While he was washing, Petritsky gave him a brief description of his own position insofar as there had been any change in it since Vronsky's departure. He had no money. His father had said he would not give him any and would not pay his debts. His tailor was trying to get him locked up, and someone else, too, threatened to have him jailed. The colonel had told him that if these scandalous affairs in which he got himself involved did not stop, he would have to leave the regiment. He was sick to death of the baroness, especially since she'd taken to offering him money; but there was a girl—he would let Vronsky see her—a real marvel, a beauty, in the purest Oriental style, "the *genre* of handmaiden Rebecca, you understand!" He had had a row with Berkosheu, too, the day before. He was going to send his seconds to him, but of course nothing would come of it. On the whole, however, everything was grand and extremely jolly. And without letting his friend go into the details of his position, Petritsky proceeded to tell him all the interesting news. Listening to Petritsky's all too familiar stories in the all too familiar surroundings of the apartment in which he had lived for the last three years, Vronsky experienced the pleasant feeling of a return to his customary carefree Petersburg life.

"Impossible!" he cried, releasing the pedal of the washstand before which he had been washing his healthy, ruddy neck. "Impossible!" he cried, on being told the news that Laura had thrown over Fentinhof and gone to live with Mileyev. "And is he still as stupid and self-satisfied as ever? Well, and what about Buzulukov?"

"Oh, you should have heard what happened to Buzulukov—it's too wonderful for words!" cried Petritsky. "He has a passion for balls, you know. He never misses a single court ball. Well, so off he went to a grand ball wearing one of the new helmets. Have you seen the new helmets? They're excellent, much lighter. So, there he stood . . . No, listen please!"

"I am listening," replied Vronsky, rubbing himself with a rough towel.

"Well, the grand duchess with some ambassador just happened to pass by and, as ill luck would have it, they were just talking about the new helmets. The grand duchess wanted to show him one of them. They see our dear boy standing there." (Petritsky showed how Buzulukov was standing with his helmet.) "The grand duchess asks him for the helmet, but he won't let her have it. What's the matter? His fellow officers wink at him, nod, frown—give it to her! But he doesn't! Stands to attention—stock-still. Can you imagine it? Then that one—what d'you call him?—tries to take it from him. He won't give it him! So he snatches it away and hands it to the grand duchess. 'This is one of the new ones,' says the grand duchess. She turns it over and—just imagine!—out tumble a pear and some sweets, two pounds of sweets! He'd pinched it all, the dear boy!"

Vronsky shook with laughter. And long afterward, talking of other things, he would, at the thought of the helmet, burst into roars of healthy laughter, showing his strong, even teeth.

Having heard all the news, Vronsky, with the help of his valet, put on his uniform, and went to report to his superiors. After that he intended to go and see his brother and then Betsy, and then pay a few visits so as to show himself in the society in which he could meet Anna. As always when in Petersburg, he left the house not to return till late at night.

Part Two

CHAPTER 1

Towards the end of the winter a consultation took place at the Shcherbatskys' to decide what was the state of Kitty's health and what had to be done to restore her failing strength. She was ill and with the approach of spring grew worse. Their family doctor prescribed cod-liver oil, then iron, and then nitrate of silver, but as none of them did any good and as he advised that she should be taken abroad before the spring, a celebrated specialist was called in. The celebrated specialist, a still comparatively young and very handsome man, demanded to be allowed to examine the patient. He seemed to insist with particular satisfaction that a young girl's feeling of shame was a relic of barbarism and that there was nothing more natural in the world than for a man who was still quite young to touch a girl's naked body. He found it natural because he did it every day and did not, so he thought, feel anything nor think anything wrong when he did it, and that was why he considered a girl's feeling of shame not only a relic of barbarism, but also an affront to himself.

They had to give in, for, although all the doctors studied at the same school and used the same textbooks and knew the same sciences, and although some maintained that this celebrated specialist was a bad doctor, it was for some unknown reason accepted in the princess' household and in her set that this celebrated specialist alone knew something other doctors did not know and that he alone could save Kitty. After having carefully examined and sounded his embarrassed patient, who was overcome with shame, the celebrated specialist carefully washed his hands and stood in the drawing room talking to the prince. The prince frowned and coughed as he listened to the doctor. As a man who had seen something of life and who was neither a fool nor an invalid, he did not believe in medicine and in his heart was furious at the whole of this farcical business, particularly as he was almost the only one who thoroughly understood the cause of Kitty's illness. "A windbag!" he thought, as he listened to the celebrated doctor's chatter about the symptoms of his daughter's illness. The specialist meanwhile found it hard not to show his contempt for this old fool of a nobleman and with difficulty came down to the low level of his intelligence. He knew very well that it was a waste of time to talk to the old man and that the head of this house was the mother. It was before her that he intended to scatter the pearls of his wisdom. At that moment the princess came into the drawing room with the family doctor. The prince withdrew, trying not to show how absurd the whole farcical business seemed to him. The princess was distraught and did not know what to do. She felt guilty toward Kitty.

"Well, Doctor, what do you advise?" said the princess. "Tell me everything." "Is there any hope?" she meant to say, but her lips quivered and she could not utter the words. "Well, Doctor?"

"Let me first confer with my colleague, Princess, and then I shall have the honor of giving you my opinion."

"Shall I leave you then?"

"If you please."

The princess sighed and left the room.

When the doctors were alone, the family doctor began timidly to express his view, that it was the beginning of a tubercular condition, but that . . . etc. The celebrated specialist listened to him and halfway through the speech looked at his large gold watch.

"Yes," he said, "but—"

The family doctor paused respectfully in the middle of what he was saying.

"We cannot, as you know, diagnose the beginning of a tubercular condition. Till the appearance of cavities there is nothing definite to go by. But we may suspect it. The symptoms are there: malnutrition, nervous excit-

140

ability, and so on. The question we have to answer is this: What have we to do to maintain nutrition if there is reason to suspect a tubercular condition?"

"But of course, you know in these cases there are always some hidden moral and psychological reasons," the family doctor permitted himself to remark with a faint smile.

"That goes without saying," the celebrated specialist replied, looking at his watch again. "I'm sorry, is the Yanza bridge back in its place or has one still to drive round?" he asked. "Oh, it's back! In that case I shall be able to do it in twenty minutes. We were saying, weren't we, that the question we have to decide is: How is nutrition to be maintained and the nerves to be strengthened? The two are connected and both have to be dealt with."

"How about a trip abroad?" asked the family doctor.

"I'm against trips abroad. You see, if there is the beginning of a tubercular condition, and of this we cannot possibly be certain, then a trip abroad will be of no use. What we want is some treatment that would keep up the nourishment and do no harm."

And the celebrated specialist explained his plan for a treatment of Soden waters, prescribed chiefly, it would appear, because they could do no harm.

The family doctor heard him out attentively and respectfully.

"But in favor of a trip abroad," he said, "I would put forward the argument that it would be a complete change of scene and the removal of the conditions that may bring back unhappy memories. And, besides, it's what her mother would like."

"Oh, well, in that case, let them go abroad by all means, only I'm afraid those German quacks may do her some harm. . . . You see, they must be made to obey orders. . . . All right, let them go."

He looked at his watch again.

"I'm afraid I must be off," he said and made for the door.

The celebrated specialist told the princess (a feeling of decency suggested it to him) that he would like to see his patient again.

"You don't mean you want to examine her again?" the mother cried in horror.

"Oh no, just a few details, Princess."

"Please come in."

And, accompanied by the doctor, the mother went into Kitty's room. Kitty was standing in the middle of the room, looking emaciated and flushed, and her eyes strangely brilliant after the ordeal she had endured. When the doctor entered she blushed crimson and her eyes filled with tears. Her whole illness and the treatment seemed such a stupid and even ridiculous business. Her treatment, in particular, seemed as ridiculous to her as the piecing together of a broken vase. Her heart was broken. What did they want to dose her with pills and powders for? But she did not want to upset her mother, particularly as her mother considered herself to blame.

"Please, sit down, Princess," said the celebrated specialist.

He sat down opposite her with a smile, felt her pulse, and all of a sudden started asking tiresome questions. She answered him, but suddenly grew angry and got up.

"I'm sorry, Doctor, but this really is a bit too much. This is the third time you've asked me the same thing."

The celebrated specialist was not in the least offended. "Morbid irritability," he said to the old princess, when Kitty had left the room. "However, I had finished. . . ."

And the doctor treated the princess, as an exceptionally intelligent woman, to a scientific exposition of her daughter's condition and concluded with instructions as to how to drink the waters which were completely unnecessary. In reply to the question as to whether they should go abroad, the doctor reflected deeply, as though trying to solve a difficult problem. His solution was at last pronounced: they could go abroad, but they must not believe the quacks and always refer to him about everything.

It was just as though something joyful had happened after the doctor's departure. The mother looked more cheerful when she went back to her daughter, and Kitty, too, pretended to be more cheerful. She often now, indeed almost always, had to pretend.

"Really, I'm quite well, Mother. But if you want to go abroad, let us go!" she said and, trying to show that she was interested in the proposed journey, she began to talk about the preparations for their departure.

Chapter 2

Shortly after the doctor had left, Dolly arrived. She knew that there was to be a consultation that day, and though she had only recently got up after a confinement (she had given birth to a girl at the end of the winter), and though she had many anxieties and troubles of her own, she left her baby and another daughter who was ill, and came to find out what the doctors had to say about Kitty and what was their verdict.

"Well?" she said, coming into the drawing room, without taking off her hat. "You all look very cheerful. Everything is all right, I suppose?"

They tried to tell her what the doctor had said, but it seemed that though he had spoken very fluently and at great length, it was quite impossible to report what he had said. The only thing of interest was that they had decided to go abroad.

Dolly sighed involuntarily. Her best friend, her sister, was going away. Her own life was not particularly happy. After their reconciliation her relations with her husband had become humiliating. Anna's welding had not been strong enough and the domestic harmony had broken again in the same place. There was nothing definite, but Oblonsky was hardly ever at home, there was hardly ever any money, and Dolly was constantly tormented by suspicions of infidelities and she was trying to banish them, afraid of the agonies of jealousy she had been through before. The first outburst of jealousy, once experienced, could not be repeated, and even the discovery of her husband's unfaithfulness could not affect her as strongly as it had done the first time. Such a discovery would merely have disrupted her family life, and she let herself be deceived, despising him and most of all herself for that weakness. Besides, she was constantly worried by the cares of a large family: either something went wrong with the feeding of the baby, or the nurse left, or, as now, one of the children fell ill.

"Well, and how are the children?" her mother asked.

"Oh, Mother, you've plenty of your own troubles. Lily

143

is not well and I'm afraid it's scarlet fever. I've just come out to hear your news, but if, which God forbid, it is scarlet fever, I shall have to stay at home all the time."

After the doctor's departure, the old prince, too, came out of his study and, presenting his cheek to Dolly and exchanging a few words with her, he turned to his wife:

"What have you decided? Are you going? Well, and what do you intend to do with me?"

"I think you ought to stay behind, Alexander," said his wife.

"Just as you like."

"But, Mother, why shouldn't Father come with us?" said Kitty. "He will feel happier and we shall feel happier too."

The old prince got up and stroked Kitty's hair. She raised her face and, forcing a smile, looked at him. She always felt that he understood her better than the rest of the family, though he did not say much to her. Being the youngest, she was her father's favorite, and it seemed to her that his love gave him insight. When her gaze now met his kindly blue eyes looking intently at her, she could not help feeling that he saw right through her and understood the desolation inside her. Blushing, she raised her face toward him, expecting a kiss, but he only patted her hair.

"These silly chignons!" he said. "You can't get to your real daughter. Instead you caress the hair of some defunct female. Well, Dolly, my dear," he turned to his eldest daughter, "what's that fine gentleman of yours doing?"

"Nothing in particular, Father," replied Dolly, realizing that he was referring to her husband. "He's always out. I hardly ever see him," she could not help adding with an ironical smile.

"Hasn't he gone to the country yet to see to the wood?"

"No, he's still getting ready to go."

"I see!" said the prince. "So I'm to get ready too, am I? Very well," he turned to his wife, sitting down again. "As for you, Kitty," he added, addressing his youngest daughter, "you'd better wake up one fine morning and say to yourself: Why, I'm quite well and happy, and I'll go out with Father again for an early morning walk in the frost. Eh?"

144

It seemed that what her father had said was very simple, but his words threw Kitty into confusion and she felt like a criminal who has been caught red-handed. "Yes, he knows everything and he understands everything and what he wants to say to me is that, though I feel ashamed, I must get over my shame."

She could not pluck up courage to say something in reply. She began to say something, but suddenly burst into tears and ran out of the room.

"That's what comes of your jokes!" The princess flew at her husband. "You always . . ." she began her long recital of reproaches.

The prince listened to her remonstrances in silence, but his face grew darker and darker.

"She is so wretched, the poor girl, so wretched, and you don't seem to realize that any reminder of the cause of it hurts her. Oh, dear, to be so mistaken in people," said the princess, and from her change of tone Dolly and the prince understood that she was speaking of Vronsky. "I simply can't understand why there aren't any laws against such vile, dishonorable people."

"Oh, it makes me sick to hear it," the prince said gloomily, getting up from his armchair, as if intending to go away, but stopping at the door. "There are such laws, my dear, and since you have mentioned it, I'll tell you who is to blame for it all: you and you alone. There always have been and there still are things that are done and things that are not done. Yes, and if things had not happened that should not have happened, I—old as I am—would have demanded satisfaction from that young fop. Yes, indeed. And now you can go on trying to cure her and call in these quacks!"

The prince had apparently a great deal more to say, but the moment the princess heard his tone, she, as always happened when things became serious, at once gave in and became penitent.

"Oh, Alexander, Alexander," she whispered, moving nearer to him and bursting into tears.

As soon as she began to cry, the prince calmed down. He went up to her.

"There, that'll do, that'll do! You, too, are unhappy, I know. It can't be helped. There is no great harm done. God is merciful—be thankful . . ." he kept saying, hardly realizing himself what he was saying and responding to the wet kiss of the princess which he felt on his hand. And he went out of the room.

As soon as Kitty left the room in tears, Dolly with her motherly intuition realized at once that there was something here that only a woman could do, and she got ready to do it. She took off her hat and, mentally rolling up her sleeves, went into action. While her mother was attacking her father, she tried to restrain her as far as a daughter's respect for her mother would allow. During her father's outburst, she was silent; she felt ashamed of her mother and tenderness for her father for his immediately returning kindliness; but when her father went out, she set about doing what was most necessary at the moment—to go to Kitty and comfort her.

"I wanted to tell you this a long time ago, Mother. Do you know that Levin was going to propose to Kitty last time he was here? He told Stiva about it."

"Well, what about it? I don't understand . . ."

"Did Kitty refuse him? She did not tell you, did she?"

"No, she said nothing about either of them. She is too proud. But I know that it's all because of that . . ."

"Well, just imagine if she has refused Levin—and I know she wouldn't have refused him, if it hadn't been for the other. . . . And then the other deceived her so terribly."

The princess was too frightened to think how much she was to blame for her daughter's unhappiness, and she got angry.

"Oh, I don't understand anything! Today girls want to do as they like, they tell their mothers nothing, and then . . ."

"I'll go to her, Mother."

"Yes, go. I'm not stopping you, am I?" said her mother.

CHAPTER 3

When she went into Kitty's room—a pretty, little pink room full of *vieux saxe* bric-a-brac, a room as fresh, pink, and gay as Kitty herself had been two months earlier— Dolly recalled how gaily and lovingly they had arranged that room the year before. Her heart sank when she saw

Kitty sitting on a low chair near the door and staring fixedly at a corner of the carpet. Kitty glanced at her sister, and the cold, rather severe expression of her face did not change.

"I'm going home now and I shall have to stay in and you won't be able to come and see me," said Dolly, sitting down beside her. "I want to talk to you."

"What about?" asked Kitty quickly, raising her head in alarm.

"About your troubles, of course."

"I have no troubles."

"Really, Kitty! Do you think I don't know? I know everything. And, believe me, it's so unimportant. . . . We've all been through it."

Kitty was silent and her face looked stern.

"Why should you be suffering for him?" Dolly went on, going straight to the point. "He doesn't deserve it."

"No, because he wouldn't have me," Kitty said in a shaking voice. "Don't talk about it! Please, don't talk about it."

"But who told you that? No one has said that. I'm sure he was in love with you and is in love with you, but . . ."

"Oh, I can't stand these condolences—they're unbearable!" cried Kitty, flaring up suddenly.

She turned around on her chair, blushed, and began moving her fingers rapidly, clenching first with one hand then with another the buckle of a belt she was holding. Dolly knew this trick of her sister's of clutching something in her hands when she flew into a temper; she knew that in those moments of great excitement Kitty was capable of forgetting herself and saying many disagreeable things that had better been left unsaid. Dolly tried to pacify her, but it was too late.

"What do you want me to feel—what?" Kitty was saying rapidly. "That I was in love with a man who didn't care a rap about me and that I'm dying of love for him? And this is said by my sister who thinks that . . . that . . . that she sympathizes with me! I don't want these hypocritical expressions of sympathy!"

"Kitty, you're unfair!"

"Why do you torment me?"

"Why, on the contrary, I—I see that you're unhappy. . . ."

But in her excitement Kitty did not listen to her.

"I've nothing to be distressed or to be comforted about. I've enough pride never to let myself love a man who does not love me."

"But I'm not saying that. . . . Only—tell me the truth," said Dolly, taking her by the hand. "Tell me, has Levin proposed to you?"

The mention of Levin's name seemed to deprive Kitty of the last traces of self-control; she leaped up from her chair and, flinging the buckle on the floor and rapidly gesticulating with her hands, began:

"What has Levin to do with it? I can't understand why you want to torment me. I've said and I repeat that I have some pride and that I shall never, *never* do what you're doing—go back to a man who has been unfaithful to you, who fell in love with another woman. I simply can't understand that! You may do it, but I can't!"

And, having said that, she looked at her sister and, seeing that Dolly was silent, her head bowed sadly, Kitty did not leave the room as she had intended to do, but sat down by the door and, burying her face in her handkerchief, hung her head.

There was silence for a minute or two. Dolly was thinking about herself. The humiliation, of which she was always conscious, was particularly painful now that her sister reminded her of it. She had not expected such cruelty from her sister and she was angry with her. But all of a sudden she heard the rustle of a dress and at the same time the sound of suppressed sobbing, and someone's arms encircled her neck from below. Kitty was on her knees before her.

"Darling Dolly, I'm so, so unhappy!" she whispered guiltily.

And the sweet, tear-stained face hid itself in the folds of Dolly's dress.

As if tears were the necessary lubricant without which the machine of mutual intercourse between the two sisters could not work successfully, the sisters, after having had a cry, began talking, but not of the thing that interested them most; still, though about something else, they understood each other. Kitty realized that what she had said in a fit of anger about Oblonsky's unfaithfulness and about Dolly's humiliation had deeply hurt her sister's feelings, but that she forgave her. Dolly, for her part, learned all she wanted to know. She felt certain that she had guessed right and that Kitty's grief, her incurable grief, was really caused by the fact that Levin had proposed to her and she had refused him, while Vronsky had let her down, and that she was prepared to love Levin and hate Vronsky. Kitty did not say a word about it; she spoke only of her state of mind.

"I've nothing to be unhappy about," she said, when she had calmed down, "but don't you see that everything has become odious, disgusting, and coarse to me, myself most of all? You can't imagine what disgusting thoughts I have about everything."

"What sort of disgusting thoughts can you have?" asked Dolly, smiling.

"Oh, the most disgusting and the coarsest. I can't tell you. It's not that I'm depressed or bored, but much worse. It's as if all that was good in me had hidden itself away and only the most horrible things have remained. I mean—how can I explain it to you?" she went on, seeing the puzzled look in her sister's eyes. "Father began saying something to me just now. . . . It seems to me that all he's thinking of is that I ought to get married. Mother takes me to balls, and I can't help thinking that she only takes me there to marry me off as soon as possible and so get rid of me. I know it's not true, but I can't fight back those thoughts. I can't bear to see the so-called eligible young men. I always imagine they are taking my measure. Before I simply loved going anywhere in a ball dress. I used to enjoy looking at myself. But now I feel ashamed and uncomfortable. Well, what else is there to tell you? The doctor . . . Well . . . ."

Kitty faltered. She was going to say that since this change had come over her, Oblonsky had become unbearable and loathsome to her, and that she could not see him without imagining the coarsest and most disgusting things.

"Well, yes," she went on, "everything appears to me in the coarsest and most disgusting light. That is my illness. Perhaps it will pass. . . ."

"But don't think of it."

"I can't help it. It's only with children that I feel happy—only in your house."

149

"What a pity you can't come and stay with us."

"I will come! I've had scarlet fever and I'll ask Mother to let me."

Kitty insisted on having her own way and went to stay with her sister and nursed the children all through the scarlet fever, for scarlet fever it really turned out to be. The two sisters nursed all the six children successfully through the illness, but Kitty's health did not improve, and in Lent the Shcherbatskys went abroad.

CHAPTER 4

Petersburg high society really forms one set: everyone knows everyone else and all are even on visiting terms with each other. But this large set has its own subdivisions. Anna had friends and close connections with three different sets. One was her husband's official government set, consisting of his colleagues and subordinates in the civil service, who were linked and separated in a most diverse and capricious fashion by their social conditions. Anna found it difficult now to remember the feeling of almost religious awe she at first felt for these people. Now she knew them all as well as people know each other in a small provincial town; she knew the habits and weaknesses of each of them and where the shoe pinched this or that foot; she knew their relations to each other and to the government center; she knew who sided with whom, and how and by what means he did so, as well as who agreed or disagreed with whom and about what; but this set of government, masculine interests could never interest her, in spite of the Countess Lydia Ivanovna's expostulations, and she avoided it.

Another set of people Anna was closely connected with was the one through which her husband had made his career. Its leading light was the Countess Lydia Ivanovna. This was a circle of elderly, plain, virtuous, and religious women and clever, learned, and ambitious men. One of the clever men who was a member of this set christened it "the Conscience of Petersburg Society." Karenin had the highest regard for this circle, and Anna, who had the gift of making friends with all sorts of people, had made friends in it too during the first years of her life in Petersburg. But now, on her return from Moscow, that circle became unbearable to her. She had a feeling that she and all of them were acting a part, and she felt so bored and ill-at-ease in their society that she visited Countess Lydia Ivanovna as little as possible.

The third set with which she was connected was high society proper—the world of balls, dinner parties, resplendent toilettes, the society which clung to the Court with one hand so as not to descend to the *demi-monde*, which the members of that circle affected to despise, though their tastes were not only similar but even identical. Her link with that circle was provided by Princess Betsy Tverskoy, her cousin's wife, who had an income of one hundred and twenty thousand rubles and who had grown very fond of Anna from the first day of Anna's appearance in society, made much of her, and tried to draw her into her own set, making fun of Countess Lydia Ivanovna's set.

"When I'm old and ugly, I shall be like her," Betsy used to say, "but for a young and beautiful woman like you it is a little too early for that almshouse."

At first Anna had avoided Betsy's set as much as she could, as it involved expenses which she could not afford and because at heart she really preferred the other set; but after her trip to Moscow it was the other way round. She avoided her highly moral friends and began to visit her friends in high society. There she met Vronsky and experienced a tremulous joy at every one of their encounters. She met him most frequently at Betsy's, who had been born a Vronsky and was his cousin. Vronsky went everywhere he was likely to meet Anna and spoke to her of his love whenever he could. She gave him no encouragement, but every time she met him her heart was ablaze with the same feeling of exhilaration which had come over her in the train the day she first saw him. She felt herself that at the sight of him her eyes lit up with joy and her lips puckered into a happy smile, and she could not extinguish the expression of that joy.

At first Anna sincerely believed that she was displeased with him for daring to pursue her; but soon after her return from Moscow, having gone to a party where she expected to meet him, and at which he did not turn up, she clearly realized, by the feeling of sadness that came over her, that she had been deceiving herself, that his pursuit was not only not disagreeable to her, but that it constituted the whole interest of her life. . . .

The famous prima donna was giving her second performance and all the fashionable world was at the theater. Catching sight of his cousin from the first rows of the stalls, Vronsky went to her box without waiting for the intermission.

"Why did you not come to dinner?" she said to him. "I'm astonished at the clairvoyance of lovers," she added with a smile so that only he could hear. "*She was not there.* But come after the opera."

Vronsky looked questioningly at her. She nodded. He thanked her with a smile and sat down beside her.

"I remember very well how you used to jeer!" went on the Princess Betsy, who took particular pleasure in following the progress of this passion. "What has become of it all? You're caught, my dear!"

"But all I want is to be caught," replied Vronsky with his calm, good-natured smile. "To tell the truth, if I complain it is only because I have not been caught enough. I'm beginning to lose hope."

"What hope can you have?" said Betsy, taking offense on behalf of her friend. "*Entendons nous . . .*" But little lights danced in her eyes, which said that she knew as well as he what hope he could have.

"None whatever," said Vronsky, laughing and showing his compact row of teeth. "Excuse me," he added, taking the opera glasses out of her hands and looking over her bare shoulder at the row of boxes opposite. "I'm afraid I'm becoming ridiculous."

He knew perfectly well that there was no risk of his becoming ridiculous either in Betsy's eyes or in the eyes of all fashionable people. He knew perfectly well that in their eyes the role of a disappointed lover of a girl or of single women, in general, might be ridiculous; but the role of a man pursuing a married woman, who had made it the purpose of his life to draw her into an adulterous association at all costs—that that role has something grand and beautiful about it and could never be ridiculous, and, consequently, he put down the opera glasses and looked at his cousin with a proud and gay smile playing under his mustache.

"But why didn't you come to dinner?" she said, looking admiringly at him.

"I must tell you about that. I was busy—and what was I doing, do you think? I give you a hundred—no, a thousand—guesses. . . . No, you will never guess it. I was bringing about a reconciliation between a husband and the man who had insulted his wife. Yes, indeed!"

"Well, and did you bring about a reconciliation?"

"Practically."

"You must tell me all about it," she said, getting up. "Come back in the next intermission."

"I'm sorry, I'm going to the French theater."

"From Nilsson?" Betsy asked in horror, although she could not for the life of her distinguish Nilsson from any chorus girl.

"I'm afraid I can't do anything about it. I've an appointment there, well, in connection with my peacemaking."

"Blessed are the peacemakers, for they shall be saved," said Betsy, remembering that she had heard it said somewhere. "Well, sit down and tell me what it is all about."

And she sat down again.

CHAPTER 5

"It's a little indiscreet, but so charming that I simply must tell you," said Vronsky, looking at her with laughing eyes. "I shan't mention names."

"So much the better—I shall guess."

"Now listen: two gay young fellows were driving—"

"Officers of your regiment, I suppose."

"I did not say officers, but simply two young men who had been lunching—"

"Translate: 'had been drinking.'"

"Maybe. So they are on their way to dine with a friend and they are in the gayest of spirits. They see a pretty woman overtaking them in a hired sledge, looking around and, at least so they thought, nodding and laughing at them. They naturally go after her. At a gallop. To their amazement the fair one stops at the entrance of the house they are going to. She runs to the top floor. They only manage to catch a glimpse of a pair of red lips under a short veil and a pair of lovely little feet."

"You describe this with such feeling that I shouldn't be surprised if you weren't one of them."

"And what was it you were saying to me just now? Anyway, the young men go into their friend's apartment. He was giving a farewell dinner. Now there they did perhaps drink a little too much, as is the custom at farewell dinners. During dinner they inquire who lives on the top floor. No one knows. Only their host's valet, in answer to their question whether any *mam'selles* lived upstairs, replies that lots of them live all over the place. After dinner the young men go into their host's study and write a letter to the fair stranger. It was a passionate letter, a declaration of love! Then they take the letter upstairs themselves, in order to explain anything that may not be quite clear in it."

"Why do you tell me such disgusting things? Well?"

"They ring. A maid answers the door. They give her the letter and assure her that they are both so much in love that any moment they may die on the doorstep. The bewildered girl is conducting the negotiations. Suddenly a gentleman with sausage-shaped whiskers and as red as a lobster comes out, informs them that there is no one in the apartment except his wife, and tells them to clear off."

"How do you know that he had sausage-shaped whiskers, as you say?"

"Just listen. I went there today to make peace."

"Well, what happened?"

"That's the most interesting part of the story. It turns out that the happy couple are a civil servant of the rank of titular councilor and his wife. The titular councilor lodges a complaint and I am appointed peacemaker, and what a peacemaker! I assure you, Talleyrand is a sheer nonentity compared with me."

"What was the difficulty?"

"Now, listen. . . . We apologized as well as we could. 'We are in despair. We are deeply sorry for the unfortunate misunderstanding.' The titular councilor with his sausages begins to thaw, but he too wishes to express his sentiments and, as soon as he starts expressing them, he starts getting excited and rude, and I have again to

154

put all my diplomatic talents in motion. 'I quite agree that they behaved badly, but, please, take into consideration their youth, the fact that it was all a misunderstanding; besides, the young men had just dined, you understand. They regret deeply and they ask you to forgive them.' The titular councilor again softens. 'I agree with you, Count, and I am ready to forgive them. But you must understand my wife—my wife, a respectable woman, has been subjected to persecution, insults, and interference by these young louts, these black . . .' And you realize that one of the young louts is standing by my side and I am here to make peace. Again I bring diplomacy into action and again the affair nears its conclusion, my titular councilor gets excited, goes red in the face, his sausages rise, and again I have to bring all my subtle diplomatic arguments into play."

"Oh, you must hear this!" Betsy cried, laughing and turning to a woman who was just coming into her box. "He has been making me laugh so much! Well, *bonne chance*," she added, giving Vronsky a finger that was not engaged in holding her fan, and with a twitch of her shoulders lowered the bodice of her dress, which had wormed its way up a little, so that she might be properly naked when she went up to the front of her box and into the glare of the gaslight and the gaze of all eyes.

Vronsky drove to the French theater, where he actually did have to see the colonel of his regiment, who never missed a single performance at the French theater, to discuss with him his work as peacemaker, which had occupied and amused him for the last three days. Petritsky, whom he was fond of, was involved in this affair, as well as the young Prince Kedrov, a nice fellow and an excellent comrade, who had recently joined the regiment. But the main thing was that the interests of the regiment itself were involved.

Both the young officers were in Vronsky's squadron. The colonel had received a visit from a civil servant, the titular councilor Venden, who had lodged a complaint against the officers for insulting his wife. His young wife, so Venden declared—he had been married six months—was in church with her mother, and suddenly feeling unwell, owing to her interesting condition, could not stand up any longer and had driven home in the first

155

sledge she could hail. It was then that the officers had chased after her; she got frightened and, feeling worse, rushed up the stairs to her apartment. Venden himself had just returned from the office and, hearing a ring at the door and some voices, he had gone out and, seeing a couple of drunken officers with a letter, had thrown them out. He demanded that they should be severely punished.

"No, say what you like," said the colonel to Vronsky, whom he had asked to come and see him, "Petritsky is becoming impossible. Not a week passes without some scandalous incident. That civil servant will not let the matter drop; he will take it further."

Vronsky saw the whole impropriety of the affair and that there could be no question of a duel and that everything must be done to mollify the titular councilor and hush up the affair. The colonel had summoned Vronsky just because he knew him for an honorable and intelligent man and, above all, a man who had the honor of his regiment at heart. They had discussed the matter and decided that Petritsky and Kedrov should go with Vronsky to apologize to the titular councilor. The colonel and Vronsky were both aware that Vronsky's name and the insignia of aide-de-camp to the emperor would be certain to contribute a great deal to mollifying the titular councilor. And, indeed, they were to a certain extent effective; but the result of the peacemaking still remained in doubt, as Vronsky had made it clear.

Arriving at the French theater, Vronsky retired with the colonel to the foyer and told him of his success or lack of success. Having thought it over carefully, the colonel decided to let the matter rest, but for his own satisfaction started asking Vronsky about the details of the interview and could not refrain from laughing as he listened to Vronsky's description of how the titular councilor, after calming down for a while, all of a sudden flared up again as he remembered some detail of the affair and how Vronsky, as soon as a reconciliation seemed on the point of being effected, tried to take advantage of it by effacing himself and pushing Petritsky forward.

"A bad business, but damned funny. You can't expect Kedrov to fight that gentleman, can you? So he was

terribly excited, was he?" he asked again, laughing.
"And how do you like Claire this evening? Marvelous,
isn't she?" he continued, referring to the new French
actress. "However often you see her, every time she's
different. Only the French can do that."

CHAPTER 6

Princess Betsy left the theater without waiting for the
end of the last act. She had hardly time to go to her
dressing room, powder her long, pale face, rub the powder off again, tidy herself, and order tea to be served in
the large drawing room before carriages began driving
up one after another to her huge house in Bolshaya
Morskaya Street. The visitors stepped onto the wide
porch and the fat hall porter, who in the mornings read
newspapers behind the glass front door to impress the
passers-by, noiselessly opened this large door to let them
pass by him.

Almost at the same moment the hostess, with a freshly
made-up face and freshly made-up hair, walked in at
one door and her visitors at the other door of the large
drawing room, with its dark walls, thick carpets, and
brightly lit table gleaming in the light of the candles with
its white cloth, its silver samovar, and its transparent
china tea service.

The hostess sat down at the samovar and took off her
gloves. Moving their chairs with the help of unobtrusive
footmen, the visitors took their seats, dividing themselves into two groups: around the samovar near the
hostess, and at the opposite end of the drawing room
around the wife of an ambassador, a beautiful woman
in black velvet with sharply defined black eyebrows. The
conversation in the two sets wavered, as it always does
for the first few minutes, interrupted by new arrivals,
greetings, offers of tea, as though looking for a subject
to concentrate on.

"She's an extraordinarily good actress," a diplomat
was saying in the group around the ambassador's wife.
"One can see she's studied Kaulbach. You noticed how
she fell, didn't you?"

"Oh, please, don't let's talk about Nilsson! You can't

possibly say anything new about her," said a fat, red-faced, fair-haired woman, who wore an old silk dress and had no eyebrows and no chignon. It was the Princess Myakhky, famous for her simplicity and harsh manners and nicknamed *enfant terrible.* Princess Myakhky sat in the middle between the two groups and, listening to both, took part in the conversation of either the one or the other. "Three different people have said the same thing to me about Kaulbach today, just as though they conspired to do so. I don't know why that should have pleased them so much."

The conversation was brought to a standstill by this remark and they had to think of a new subject.

"Tell us something amusing, but not spiteful," said the ambassador's wife, a past master at the art of polite conversation the English call "small talk," turning to the diplomat who was also at a loss what to say.

"They say that's very difficult," he began with a smile, "that only what is spiteful is amusing. But I will do my best. Give me a subject. Everything depends on that. Once the subject is given, it is easy to embroider it. I often think that the great conversationalists of the last century would have found it difficult to talk cleverly nowadays. People are so sick and tired of everything that smacks of cleverness."

"That's been said long ago," the ambassador's wife interrupted him laughingly.

The conversation had started very pleasantly, but just because it was so pleasant, it came to a stop again. It was necessary to fall back upon the one sure and never-failing expedient: scandal.

"Don't you find there's something Louis Quinze about Tushkevich?" he said, indicating with his eyes a handsome, fair-haired young man standing at the table.

"Why, yes. He matches the drawing room: that's why he comes here so often."

This conversation was kept up for some time since it was full of hints at a subject that could not be discussed in this room, namely, the relations between Tushkevich and their hostess.

Round the samovar and the hostess, too, the conversation at first wavered for some time between these inevitable subjects—the latest piece of society news, the theater, and malicious gossip—and then became fixed on the last subject, that is, scandal.

"Do you know, the Maltishchev woman too—the mother, not the daughter—is having a dress made in *diable rose*?"

"No? That is charming!"

"I'm surprised that a person of her intelligence—and she's not a fool—doesn't see how ridiculous she makes herself!"

Everyone had something disparaging and derisive to say about the unfortunate "Maltishchev woman," and the conversation began crackling merrily like a blazing campfire.

Princess Betsy's husband, a stout, good-natured man and a passionate collector of prints, hearing that his wife had visitors, came into the drawing room for a moment before going to his club. Walking noiselessly over the thick carpet, he went up to Princess Myakhky.

"How did you like Nilsson?" he asked.

"Oh dear, how can you steal up on a person like that?" she replied. "You've frightened me to death. Please, don't talk to me about opera. You don't understand anything about music. I'd better descend to your level of intelligence and talk to you about your majolica and your prints. What treasure have you picked up lately in the flea market?"

"Would you like me to show you? But then you know nothing about it."

"Don't show me. I learned all I want to know about it at those—what do you call them?—bankers. They have some excellent engravings. They showed them to us."

"Why, have you been at the Schüzburgs'?" the hostess asked from her seat near the samovar.

"Yes, *ma chère.* They asked my husband and me to dine and I was told the sauce alone at that dinner cost a thousand rubles," Princess Myakhky said in a loud voice, sensing that they were all listening to her. "And a very disgusting sauce it was—some green dishwater. We had to invite them back and I made a sauce for eighty-five kopecks, and everyone was highly satisfied. I can't afford thousand-ruble sauces."

"She's wonderful!" said the hostess.

"Marvelous!" said someone else.

The effect produced by Princess Myakhky was always the same, and the secret of that effect was that though what she said was often, as now, beside the point, it was simple and had some sense. In the society in which she lived, this was considered to be extremely witty. Princess Myakhky could never understand why it was so, but she knew that it was and made use of it.

While Princess Myakhky was speaking everyone listened to her and the conversation around the ambassador's wife stopped, but the hostess was anxious to draw the whole party together and turned to the ambassador's wife.

"Won't you really have any tea? Why don't you join us?"

"No, thank you, we're very happy here," said the ambassador's wife and resumed the interrupted conversation.

The conversation was very pleasant. The Karenins, husband and wife, were being hauled over the coals.

"Anna has greatly changed since her Moscow trip. There's something strange about her," a friend of hers was saying.

"The change consists mostly in the fact that she's brought back with her the shadow of Alexey Vronsky," said the ambassador's wife.

"What's wrong about that? Grimm has a fable: 'The Man Without a Shadow,' about a man who loses his shadow. That is his punishment for something. I never could understand what sort of punishment it was. But I suppose a woman must feel unhappy without a shadow."

"Ah yes," said Anna's friend, "but women with shadows usually come to a bad end."

"What a beastly thing to say!" Princess Myakhky exclaimed suddenly, hearing these words. "Anna is an excellent woman. I don't like her husband, but I like her very much."

"Why don't you like her husband?" said the ambassador's wife. "He's such a remarkable man. *My* husband says there are few statesmen like him in Europe."

"My husband, too, says the same, but I don't believe it," replied Princess Myakhky. "If our husbands did not say it, we'd see things as they are, and in my opinion Karenin is simply stupid. I say this in a whisper. . . .

Don't you think everything becomes clear? Before, when I was told to consider him clever, I kept wondering why I should and came to the conclusion that I was too stupid myself to see how clever he is. But the moment I said: *He is stupid*, only in a whisper, everything became clear. Don't you think so?"

"How spiteful you are today!"

"Not a bit. I have no other solution. One of us two must be stupid. And, of course, one can never say that of oneself."

"No one is satisfied with his fortune, but everyone is satisfied with his intelligence," the diplomat quoted a French saying.

"Yes, that's true." Princess Myakhky turned to him hastily. "But, you see, I won't give up Anna to you. She's such a fine, sweet person. Is it her fault if everyone is in love with her and if they follow her about like shadows?"

"Why," Anna's friend tried to justify herself, "I never thought of criticizing her."

"If no one follows us about like a shadow, it doesn't mean that we have a right to criticize."

And having administered this dressing down to Anna's friend, the princess got up and, together with the ambassador's wife, joined the group at the table where they were discussing the King of Prussia.

"Whom were you gossiping about there?" Betsy asked.

"The Karenins. The princess gave a forthright description of Mr. Karenin," replied the ambassador's wife, with a smile, sitting down at the table.

"A pity we didn't hear it," said the hostess, glancing at the entrance door. "Ah, here you are at last!" She turned with a smile to Vronsky, who was entering the room.

Vronsky not only knew everybody in the room, but saw them all every day, and that was why he came in with the self-composure of a man coming back to a room full of people whom he has only just left.

"Where do I come from?" he said in answer to the ambassador's wife. "Well, I suppose I'd better make a clean breast of it. From the *opéra bouffe*. I seem to have been there a hundred times and every time with fresh enjoyment. It's delightful! I know it's shameful, but at the opera I go to sleep, while at the *opèra bouffe* I stay to the end and enjoy every moment of it. Tonight . . ."

He mentioned a French actress and was about to tell some story about her, but the ambassador's wife interrupted him with an expression of comic horror:

"Please, don't tell us about those horrors!"

"All right, I won't, particularly as you all know about those horrors."

"They'd all go there, if it were considered the thing to do, like the opera," Princess Myakhky put in.

CHAPTER 7

There was the sound of footsteps at the entrance door and Princess Betsy, knowing it was Anna, glanced at Vronsky. He was looking at the door, and his face had a strange, new expression. Joyfully, fixedly, and at the same time timidly, he gazed at the woman entering the room and slowly rose from his chair. Anna walked into the drawing room. Carrying herself very straight as usual, with quick, firm, and light steps, distinguishing her from other society women, and without changing the direction of her gaze, she took the few steps that separated her from her hostess, shook hands with her, smiled, and with the same smile turned to Vronsky. Vronsky gave a low bow and moved a chair forward for her.

She acknowledged his greeting only with an inclination of her head, blushed, and frowned. But at once nodding rapidly to her acquaintances and shaking the hands extended to her, she turned to her hostess.

"I've just been at Countess Lydia's and meant to come earlier, but I stayed there longer than I had intended. Sir John was there. Very interesting man."

"Oh, that's this missionary?"

"Yes, he was telling us about life in India. It was very interesting."

The conversation, interrupted by the new arrival, again flickered like the light of a lamp that is being blown out.

"Sir John! Yes, Sir John. I've met him. He talks well. Miss Vlasyev is head over ears in love with him."

"Is it true that Miss Vlasyev, the younger girl, is going to marry Topor?"

"Yes, they say it's quite settled."

"I'm surprised at her parents. I'm told it's a love match."

"A love match? What antediluvian ideas you have! Who talks of love nowadays?" said the ambassador's wife.

"What's to be done about it?" said Vronsky. "This stupid old fashion is still popular."

"So much the worse for those who follow that fashion. The only happy marriages I know are marriages of convenience."

"Yes," said Vronsky, "but how often does a marriage of convenience founder just because the very passion that was disregarded makes its appearance."

"But by marriage of convenience we mean marriage in which both parties have already sown their wild oats. It's like scarlet fever. One has to go through it."

"Then we must learn how to inoculate people against love as they are against smallpox."

"I fell in love with a deacon when I was a young girl," said Princess Myakhky. "I don't know whether that was of any help to me or not."

"No, joking apart, I think that to find out what love really is like, one must first make a mistake and then put it right," said Princess Betsy.

"Even after marriage?" said the ambassador's wife jestingly.

"It is never too late to mend," the diplomat said, quoting an English proverb.

"Exactly," Betsy put in. "One has to make a mistake and put it right. What do you think about it?" She turned to Anna, who was listening to the conversation in silence and with a barely perceptible, confident smile on her lips.

"What I think is," said Anna, toying with the glove she had pulled off, "that as there are as many minds as there are heads, so there are as many kinds of love as there are hearts."

Vronsky looked at Anna, waiting with a sinking heart to hear what she would say. He sighed as though the danger he had dreaded had passed with those words of hers.

163

Anna suddenly turned to him.

"I've just had a letter from Moscow. Kitty Shcherbatsky is very ill."

"Is she?" Vronsky said with a frown.

Anna looked severely at him.

"Aren't you interested in this news?"

"On the contrary I am, very much. What exactly do they write, if I may know?" he asked.

Anna got up and went over to Betsy.

"May I have a cup of tea?" she said, stopping behind Betsy's chair.

While the princess was pouring out the tea, Vronsky went up to Anna.

"What do they write to you?" he repeated.

"I often think men do not understand what a dishonorable action means, though they talk so much about it," said Anna, without answering him. "I've been wanting to say that to you for a long time," she added, and taking a few steps, she sat down at a corner table on which lay some albums.

"I don't quite understand the meaning of your words," he said, handing her the cup.

She glanced at the sofa beside her and he at once sat down.

"Yes," she said, without looking at him. "I've been wanting to tell you. You behaved badly, badly, very badly."

"Do you think I don't know that I've behaved badly? But who was the cause of it?"

"Why do you say that to me?" she said, looking at him severely.

"You know why," he answered boldly and joyfully, meeting her gaze and not dropping his eyes.

It was not he but she who became confused.

"That only proves that you have no heart," she said.

But her eyes said that she knew he had a heart and that was why she was afraid of him.

"What you have just been talking about was a mistake and not love."

"Please remember that I've forbidden you to utter that word, that odious word," said Anna, with a shudder; but at once she felt that by that very word "forbidden," she had shown she admitted that she had certain rights over him and by this very fact was encouraging him to

164

speak of love. "I've wanted to tell you this for a long time," she went on, looking resolutely into his eyes and all ablaze with a blush burning her face, "and I came here on purpose this evening, knowing that I should meet you. I came to tell you that this must stop. I've never blushed in front of anyone before and you make me feel as if I were guilty of something."

He looked at her and was struck by a new spiritual beauty of her face.

"What do you want of me?" he said, simply and seriously.

"I want you to go to Moscow and ask Kitty to forgive you," she said.

"You don't want that," he said.

He saw that she was saying what she forced herself to say and not what she wanted to say.

"If you love me as you say you do," she whispered, "then don't do anything that will disturb my peace of mind."

His face brightened.

"Don't you know that you're all life to me? But I don't know peace of mind and I can't give it you. All of myself, my love—yes. I cannot think of you and myself separately. You and I are one to me. And I cannot see any possibility of peace of mind ahead, either for me or for you. I can see the possibility of despair, unhappiness—or I can see the possibility of happiness, what happiness! Is it really so impossible?" he added, only his lips moving; but she heard.

She strained all the faculties of her mind to say what ought to be said; but instead of that she looked at him with eyes full of love and made no answer.

"There it is!" he thought with rapture. "Just when I was beginning to despair and when it seemed that there would be no end to it—there it is! She loves me. She confesses it."

"So please do this for me, never say those words again to me, and let us be good friends," she said, but her eyes said something quite different.

"Friends we shall never be, you know that yourself. But whether we shall be the happiest or unhappiest people on earth, that is in your power to decide."

She was about to say something, but he interrupted her.

165

"I only ask one thing, I ask for the right to hope, to suffer as I do now, but if I can't even do that, tell me to disappear and I will disappear. You won't see me again if my presence makes you unhappy."

"I don't want to drive you away anywhere."

"Only don't change anything. Leave everything as it is," he said in a trembling voice. "Here is your husband."

Indeed, at that very moment Karenin entered the drawing room with his composed, lumbering gait.

Casting a glance at his wife and Vronsky, he went up to his hostess and, sitting down with a cup of tea, began talking in his unhurried, always audible voice, in his habitual jesting tone of voice, poking fun at someone.

"Your Rambouillet is in full strength," he said, looking round at the whole company. "The Graces and the Muses."

But Princess Betsy could not stand that tone of his—*sneering*, as she called it in English—and, like a clever hostess, at once steered him into a serious conversation about universal military service. Karenin was immediately carried away by the subject and began defending in all seriousness the new decree against Princess Betsy, who was attacking it.

Vronsky and Anna continued to sit at the little table.

"This is getting indecent," whispered one lady, indicating Anna, Vronsky, and Karenin with her eyes.

"What did I tell you?" replied Anna's friend.

But not only those two ladies, almost everyone in the drawing room, even Princess Myakhky and Betsy herself, glanced a few times at the couple who sat apart from the general circle, as if that disturbed them. Karenin alone never once glanced in that direction and was not diverted from the interesting conversation he had started.

Noticing the disagreeable impression made on everyone, Princess Betsy slipped someone else into her place to listen to Karenin and went up to Anna.

"I'm always surprised at your husband's lucidity and accuracy of expression," she said. "The most transcendental ideas become clear to me when he's speaking."

"Oh yes!" said Anna, radiant with a smile of happiness and not understanding a single word of what Betsy was saying. She crossed over to the big table and joined the general discussion.

After sitting there for half an hour, Karenin went up to his wife and suggested that they should go home together; but without looking at him, she replied that she was staying to supper. Karenin took his leave of the company and left.

The old fat Tartar, Anna's coachman, in his shiny leather coat, was holding back with difficulty the left gray horse, which had grown restive from the cold and kept rearing up at the entrance of the house. A footman waited, having opened the carriage door. The hall porter stood holding the front door. Anna was trying with her quick little hand to disengage the lace of her sleeve which had caught on a hook of her fur coat and, bending her head, was listening with delight to what Vronsky was saying to her as he escorted her to the door.

"You've said nothing," he was saying. "Very well, I'm not demanding anything, but you know that it is not friendship that I want. There's only one happiness in life for me—the word you dislike so much. Yes, love. . . ."

"Love," she repeated slowly, speaking inwardly to herself, and suddenly, as she unhooked the lace, she added: "The reason why I dislike the word is because it means too much to me, much more than you can understand," and she glanced into his face. "Good-by!"

She gave him her hand and with a quick, resilient step walked past the hall porter and disappeared into the carriage.

Her glance and the touch of her hand went through him like a flame. He kissed the palm of his hand where she had touched him, and drove off home, happy in the knowledge that this evening had brought him nearer to the achievement of his goal than the past two months.

CHAPTER 8

Karenin had found nothing peculiar or improper in the fact that his wife had been sitting with Vronsky at a separate table and talking animatedly about something;

but he noticed that to the other people in the drawing room it seemed rather peculiar and improper, and for that reason it seemed to be improper to him, too. He decided that he had to speak to his wife about it.

On returning home, he went straight to his study, as he always did, sat down in his armchair, and opened a book on the papacy at the place marked by a paper knife, and, as usual, went on reading till one o'clock; only occasionally would he rub his high forehead and shake his head, as though to drive something off. At his usual hour he got up and got ready for bed. Anna was still not back. With his book under his arm he went upstairs; but this night instead of his usual thoughts and considerations about affairs of state, his head was full of his wife and something disagreeable that had happened to her. Contrary to his habit, he did not get into bed, but, his hands interlocked behind his back, began pacing up and down the rooms. He could not lie down, for he felt that he had first to think over carefully the new situation that had arisen.

When Karenin had made up his mind to speak to his wife, it seemed to him easy and simple enough; but now that he began to consider this new situation which had arisen, it looked to him very complicated and difficult.

Karenin was not jealous. Jealousy, in his opinion, was an insult to one's wife, and one should have confidence in one's wife. Why he should have confidence, that is to say, be absolutely convinced that his young wife would always love him, he did not ask himself; but he did not experience any lack of conviction, because he had confidence in her and kept telling himself that he ought to have it. But now, though his conviction that jealousy was a shameful feeling and that he ought to have confidence was as strong as ever, he could not help feeling that he was confronted with something illogical and absurd, and he did not know what to do. Karenin was face to face with life; he was confronted with the possibility that she might be in love with some other person besides himself, and that seemed quite absurd and incomprehensible to him because it was life itself. All his life he had lived and worked in official spheres, dealing with the reflection of life. And every time he had come up against life itself, he had kept aloof from it. Now he experienced a sensation such as a man might experience who, having calmly

168

crossed a bridge over a chasm, suddenly discovers that the bridge has been demolished and that there is a yawning abyss in its place. The yawning abyss was life itself and the bridge that artificial life Karenin had been leading. For the first time the possibility of his wife's falling in love with someone else occurred to him and he was horrified at it.

He did not undress, but walked with his even step up and down over the resounding parquet floor of the dining room, lit by a single lamp; over the carpet of the drawing room, in which the light was reflected only in the large, recently painted portrait of himself, hanging over the sofa; and through her room, where two candles burned, illuminating the portraits of her relations and women friends and the pretty knickknacks on her writing table he had known so well and for so long. Through her room he reached the door of their bedroom and turned back again.

As he walked through each room, and especially over the parquet of the lighted dining room, he stopped and said to himself: "Yes, this must be settled and put a stop to. I must tell her what I think of it and my decision." And he turned back. "But tell her what? What decision?" he said to himself in the dining room and found no answer. "But after all," he asked himself before turning into her room, "what has happened? Nothing. She had a long conversation with him. Well, what about it? Does it really matter if a woman in society talks to someone? And, besides, to be jealous means humiliating both myself and her," he said to himself as he went into her room; but this reasoning, which carried so much weight with him before, carried no weight and had no meaning now. And from the door of their bedroom he turned back again toward the dining room; but as soon as he re-entered the dark drawing room, an inner voice would tell him that it was not so and that if others had noticed it, there must be something in it. And again he told himself in the dining room: "Yes, this must be settled and a stop put to it. I must tell her what I think. . . ." And once again, before turning round in the drawing room, he asked himself: "How am I to settle it?" and then he asked himself once more: "What has happened?" and answered "Nothing!" And remembered that jealousy was a feeling which humiliated a wife, but in the drawing room he was again convinced that something had happened. His thoughts, like his body, went round in a full circle, without arriving at anything new. He noticed that, rubbed his forehead, and sat down in her room.

Here, as he looked at her table with the malachite blotting pad and an unfinished letter lying on it, his thoughts suddenly underwent a change. He began to think of her and of what she was thinking and feeling. For the first time he vividly pictured to himself her personal life, her thoughts, her desires, and the idea that she could and should have a separate life of her own seemed so dreadful to him that he hastened to drive it away. That was the abyss into which he was afraid to look. To transfer himself in thought and feeling into another human being was a mental activity alien to Karenin. He considered such mental activities as equivalent to indulging in harmful and dangerous fantasies.

"And what is so dreadful," he thought, "is that now, just as my work is nearing completion" (he was thinking of the scheme he was in the process of carrying out at the time), "when I need all the peace of mind I can get and when I must muster all my strength, that just now this absurd anxiety should fall upon me. But what's to be done? I am not one of those who can put up with worries and anxieties without having the strength to face them."

"I must think it over, come to a decision, and put it out of my mind," he said aloud.

"Any question of her feelings, of what has taken place or may take place in her heart, is no business of mine; it's a matter for her conscience, and falls within the competence of religion," he said to himself, feeling relieved at having found the paragraph of the statutes where the situation which had arisen belonged.

"And so," said Karenin to himself, "the questions of her feelings and so on are questions for her conscience which have nothing to do with me. My duty is clear enough. As head of the family, I am the person whose duty it is to guide her and who is, therefore, partly responsible for her actions; I must point out the danger I see, warn her, and even exert my authority. I must speak plainly to her."

And he could see clearly now what he had to say to

170

his wife. As he thought over what he was going to say to her, he felt sorry that he should have to waste his time and mental faculties on a domestic matter that could not possibly attract public notice; but, in spite of that, the form and the sequence of the speech he was to make took shape in his head as clearly and precisely as if it were an official report. "I must say and make absolutely clear the following points: first, an explanation of the importance of public opinion and propriety; secondly, an explanation of the religious significance of marriage; thirdly, if need be, a reference to the unhappiness that may befall our son; fourthly, a reference to her own unhappiness." And interlocking his fingers, Karenin stretched them till the joints began to crack.

This trick—the bad habit of clasping his hands and cracking his fingers—always calmed him and restored that meticulous state of mind which he needed so much now. There was the sound of a carriage driving up to the front door. Karenin stopped dead in the middle of the dining room.

A woman's footsteps were coming up the stairs. Karenin, ready to deliver his speech, stood, freeing his interlocked fingers, and wondering whether there would be another crack.

From the sound of her light steps on the stairs he could tell that she was close and, though he was satisfied with his speech, he became frightened of the impending talk with his wife.

CHAPTER 9

Anna walked in with bowed head and playing with the tassels of her hood. Her face shone with a bright glow; but it was not a joyful glow—it was like the terrible glow of a fire on a dark night. On seeing her husband, Anna raised her head and, as though waking from a dream, smiled.

"Aren't you in bed? That is amazing!" she said, throwing off her hood and, without stopping, went into the dressing room. "Time you went to bed," she said from behind the door.

"Anna, I must have a talk with you."

171

"With me?" she said with surprise and she came out from behind the door and looked at him. "What is it about? What is it?" she asked, sitting down. "Well, let's have our talk, if we must. Personally I'd rather go to bed."

Anna was saying the first thing that came into her head and she was surprised, hearing herself, at her own aptitude for lying. How simple and natural her words sounded and how it really looked as though she wanted to go to bed! She felt herself clad in an impenetrable armor of falsehood. She felt that some invisible power was assisting and supporting her.

"Anna, I must warn you," he said.

"Warn me?" she said. "What about?"

She looked so ingenuous and so gay that anyone who did not know her as her husband knew her could not have detected anything unnatural either in the sound of her words or in their meaning. But for him, knowing her, knowing that when he was five minutes late going to bed, she was aware of it and asked the reason; for him who knew that she always immediately told him all her joys, pleasures, and sorrows; for him to see now that she did not care to notice his state of mind or say a word about herself, meant a great deal. He saw that the innermost recesses of her heart, always before open to him, were now closed against him. Moreover, he realized by the tone of her voice that she was not in the least embarrassed by it, but seemed to be saying quite openly to him: yes, it is closed and so it should be and will be in future. Now he felt like a man who returns to his house and finds it closed against him. "But perhaps the key can still be found," thought Karenin.

"I want to warn you," he said in a quiet voice, "that by indiscretion or thoughtlessness you may cause yourself to be talked about in society. Your much too animated conversation this evening with Count Vronsky" (he pronounced the name firmly and with quiet deliberation) "attracted attention."

He spoke and looked at her laughing eyes, which terrified him now by their impenetrability, and even while he was speaking he felt the utter uselessness and futility of his words.

"You're always like that," she replied, as though com-

172

pletely failing to understand him and quite deliberately taking notice only of his last remark. "One day you don't like me to be bored, another day you don't like me to be gay. I was not bored. Does that offend you?"

Karenin gave a start and interlocked his fingers to crack them.

"Oh, please, don't crack your joints!" she said. "I hate it."

"Anna, is this you?" said Karenin, making an effort to control himself and stopping the movement of his hands.

"But what is it all about?" she said with genuine surprise. "What do you want of me?"

Karenin made no answer and passed his hand over his forehead and eyes. He realized that instead of doing what he had intended and warning his wife against making a mistake that would discredit her in the eyes of society, he could not help getting excited about a matter that concerned her conscience, and was struggling against some imaginary stone wall.

"This is what I would like to say," he went on coldly and calmly, "and I'd be glad if you would listen to me. As you know, I regard jealousy as a degrading and humiliating feeling and I shall never allow myself to be influenced by it; but there are certain rules of decorum which cannot be broken with impunity. This evening I did not notice anything of the kind, but, judging by the impression created on everyone there, they all noticed that you did not behave and carry yourself in a manner that was altogether desirable."

"I don't know what you're talking about," said Anna, shrugging her shoulders. "He doesn't care," she thought to herself. "But they noticed it in society and that worries him."

"You are not well, Alexey," she added, getting up and making for the door, but he moved forward, as though wishing to stop her.

His face was more gloomy and forbidding than she had ever seen it. She stopped and, bending her head backward a little and to one side, she began rapidly taking out her hairpins.

"Well, sir, I'm listening to what's coming," she said calmly and sarcastically. "And, indeed, I'm listening with interest because I'd like to know what it is all about."

She spoke and could not help being surprised herself at her calm and natural tone of voice and at her choice of words.

"I have no right to enter into all the details of your feelings and, as a matter of fact, I consider that futile and even harmful," began Alexey Karenin. "In rummaging about in our souls, we sometimes dig up something that might have lain there unnoticed. Your feelings are a matter for your conscience. But I'm in duty bound to you, to myself, and to God to point out your obligations to you. Our lives have been joined not by man, but by God. Only a crime can break that union, and a crime of that kind brings its own heavy retribution."

"I don't understand a thing, and, oh dear, I'm so sleepy too!" she said, rapidly running her fingers through her hair in search of any remaining hairpins.

"Anna, for God's sake, don't speak like that," he said gently. "Perhaps I'm mistaken, but believe me, what I say, I say as much for my sake as for yours. I am your husband and I love you."

For a moment her face fell and the derisive light in her eyes was extinguished; but the words "I love you" again aroused her indignation. She thought: "He loves? Can he love? If he hadn't heard that there was such a thing as love, he would never have used the word. He doesn't know what love is."

"I really don't understand, Alexey," she said. "Tell me exactly what is it you find . . ."

"Let me finish what I was going to say. I love you. But I am speaking of myself. The principal people involved here are our son and yourself. Quite likely, I repeat, you will find my words entirely irrelevant and unjust. Perhaps they've been occasioned by an error on my part. In that case I ask you to forgive me. But if you feel yourself that there is the slightest justification for them, then I beg you to think it over carefully and, if your heart prompts you, to tell me . . ."

Without noticing it himself, Karenin was saying something utterly different from what he had intended.

"I've nothing to say. And, besides," she all of a sudden said quickly, with difficulty restraining a smile, "it really is time we went to bed."

Karenin sighed and, without saying another word, went into the bedroom.

174

When she came into the bedroom, he was already in bed. His lips were sternly compressed and his eyes did not look at her. Anna got into her bed, expecting every moment that he would speak to her again. She was afraid of it and yet she wished it. But he was silent. She waited for a long time without stirring and then forgot him. She was thinking of someone else; she saw him and felt how at the thought of him her heart filled with excitement and guilty joy. Suddenly she heard an even and calm snoring. At first Karenin seemed to have been startled by his own snoring and stopped; but after a couple of breaths the snoring started again with tranquil regularity.

"It's late, late, late," she whispered with a smile. She lay for a long time without stirring and with wide-open eyes, the glitter of which she fancied she could herself see in the darkness.

CHAPTER 10

From that evening a new life began for Alexey Karenin and his wife. Nothing particular happened. As always, Anna went about in society, very frequently visiting Princess Betsy and meeting Vronsky everywhere. Karenin was aware of it, but could do nothing. All his attempts to force her to explain herself were frustrated by the impenetrable stone wall of gay bewilderment which she put up against him. There was no outward change in their life, but their intimate relations were completely altered. Alexey Karenin, a strong man where affairs of state were concerned, felt himself powerless here. Like an ox, his head bent meekly, he waited for the blow of the ax which was raised over him. Every time he began to think about it, he felt that he had to make another attempt, that there was still a hope of saving her, of bringing her to her senses by kindness, tenderness, and persuasion, and every day he made up his mind to have a talk with her. But every time he began talking to her, he felt that the spirit of evil and deceit that possessed her took possession of him, too, and he talked to her about things he had not meant to, and he spoke in a tone he had not intended to use. He

175

spoke to her involuntarily in his habitual tone as if he were mocking those who spoke like that. And in that tone of voice it was impossible to say what had to be said to her. . . .

CHAPTER 11

That which for nearly a whole year had been the sole desire of his life, taking the place of all his former desires; that which for Anna had been an impossible, dreadful, and for that reason all the more fascinating dream of happiness—that desire had been satisfied. Pale, with trembling lower jaw, he stood over her and implored her to be calm, without knowing himself how and why.

"Anna! Anna!" he said in a trembling voice. "Anna, for God's sake!"

But the louder he spoke, the lower she dropped her once proud, gay, but now shameful head, and she bent lower and lower and sank from the sofa on which she was sitting to the floor at his feet; she would have fallen on the carpet if he had not held her.

"Oh God, forgive me!" she said, sobbing and pressing his hand to her bosom.

She felt so culpable and guilty that all that was left to her was to humble herself and beg forgiveness; and since she had no one in the world now but him, she even addressed her prayer of forgiveness to him. Looking at him, she felt her degradation physically and she could not utter another word. He felt what a murderer must feel when he looks at the body he has deprived of life. The body he had deprived of life was their love, the first stage of their love. There was something dreadful and loathsome in the recollection of what had been paid for by this terrible price of shame. Shame at her spiritual nakedness crushed her and communicated itself to him. But in spite of the murderer's great horror before the body of his victim, that body has to be cut up and hidden, for the murderer must enjoy the fruits of his crime.

And the murderer throws himself on the body with a feeling of bitter resentment and as though with passion, and drags it off and cuts it to pieces; so he, too, covered

176

her face and shoulders with kisses. She held his hand and did not stir. Yes, these kisses are what have been bought by that shame. Yes, and this hand, which will always be mine, is the hand of my accomplice. She raised that hand and kissed it. He sank on his knees and tried to see her face; but she hid it and uttered not a word. At last, as though making an effort over herself, she sat up and pushed him away. Her face was still as beautiful as ever, but all the more pitiful for that.

"It's all over," she said. "I've nothing left but you. Remember that."

"How do you expect me not to remember what is life itself to me? For one moment of happiness like this . . ."

"Happiness!" she said with disgust and horror, and her horror involuntarily communicated itself to him. "For God's sake, not a word, not another word!"

She got up quickly and moved away from him.

"Not another word," she repeated, and with a look of cold despair he had never seen on her face before, she left him. She felt that at that moment she could not express in words the feeling of shame, joy, and horror at this entry into a new life, and she did not want to talk about it, to profane this feeling by inexact words. But afterward, too, the next day, and the next, she not only did not find the right words with which she could express the complexity of these feelings, but she could not even find the right thoughts with which she could reflect on all that was in her heart.

She said to herself: "No, I can't think about it now; later, when I am calmer." But that calm for her thoughts never came; every time the thought of what she had done, of what would become of her, and of what she ought to do, occurred to her, she became terrified and she drove these thoughts away.

"Later, later," she kept saying. "When I am calmer."

But when she was asleep and had no control over her thoughts, her situation appeared to her in all its hideous nakedness. She had one and the same dream almost every night. She dreamed that both of them were her husbands and both made passionate love to her. Alexey Karenin wept when kissing her hands and kept saying: "How wonderful it is now!" And Alexey Vronsky was there, too; and he, too, was her husband. And, wondering why this seemed so impossible to her before, she kept explaining to them, laughing, that that was much simpler and that now both of them were happy and contented. But this dream weighed on her like a nightmare, and she woke up in terror.

CHAPTER 12

During the first days of his return from Moscow, when Levin used to start and grow red in the face every time he remembered the disgrace of Kitty's refusal, he had said to himself: "I went red in the face and started and thought that everything was at an end when I did not pass my exam in physics and had to stay for another year at the university; and I also thought that all was over with me when I made a mess of my sister's affairs that I was supposed to look after. And what happened? Now that several years have passed, I recall it all and I can't help being surprised at having taken it so much to heart. The same is going to happen with this grief. Time will pass and I shall regard this, too, with indifference."

But three months had passed and he had not grown indifferent to it, and he felt it was as painful to think about as during those first days. He could not be easy in his mind because after dreaming so long of family life and feeling so ready for it, he was still unmarried and, indeed, was further than ever from marriage. He was painfully conscious himself, as were all around him, that it was not good for a man of his age to be alone. He remembered how, before leaving for Moscow, he had one day said to his cowman Nikolai, a simple-minded peasant, with whom he liked to talk: "Well, Nikolai, I mean to get married," and how Nikolai had promptly replied, as though there could be no doubt about the matter, "And about time, too, sir." But he was now farther than ever from marriage. The place was taken and whenever he put any of the girls he knew in that place, he felt that it was quite impossible. Besides, the recollection of his refusal and the part he had played in that affair tormented him with shame. However much he told himself that he was in no way to blame, the recollection of it, like other humiliating memories of that kind, made him wince and blush. There had been in his past, as in everyone else's, bad actions for which his conscience should have pricked him; but the recollection of his bad actions tormented him much less than these trivial and humiliating memories. These wounds never healed. And cheek by jowl with these memories there was now this refusal and that pitiful condition in which he must have appeared to others that evening. But time and work did their part. The painful memories became more and more overlaid by the simple but important events of country life. With every week he thought less often of Kitty. He was waiting impatiently for the news that she was married or just about to be married, hoping that, like the extraction of a tooth, such news would cure him completely.

Meanwhile, spring had come, beautiful and rapid, without the expectations and disappointments of spring, one of those rare springs which rejoice plants, beasts, and man alike. This beautiful spring pleased Levin still more and confirmed him in his determination to give up all his former plans in order to arrange his solitary life firmly and independently. Though many of the plans with which he had returned to the country had not been carried out, he had observed the main thing—purity of life. He no longer experienced the feeling of shame which usually tormented him after a lapse, and he could look people boldly in the face. Already in February he had received a letter from Maria Nikolayevna to say that his brother Nikolai's health was getting worse, but that he refused medical attention, and in consequence of this letter Levin went to Moscow and succeeded in persuading his brother to consult a doctor and go abroad to some watering place. He was so successful in persuading his brother and lending him money for the journey without irritating him that in this respect he was satisfied with himself. In addition to his work on the estate, demanding special attention in springtime, and his reading, Levin had that winter begun to write a book on farming, the main contention of which was that the character of the agricultural laborer should be treated as something absolute, like climate and soil, and that, therefore, all the conclusions of the science of agriculture should be deduced not from the data of soil and climate only, but from the data of soil, climate, and the given character of the laborer. So that in spite of his solitary existence or as a result of it, his life was extraordinarily full and only from time to time did he experience an unsatisfied desire to communicate the ideas that passed in his mind to someone else besides Agafya, though even with her he often happened to discuss physics, the theory of agriculture, and particularly philosophy; philosophy was Agafya's favorite subject.

Spring was long in coming. For the last weeks of Lent the weather had been clear and frosty. By day it thawed in the sun, and at night there were seven degrees of frost; the crust of the snow was so hard that the peasants drove about on their carts without keeping to the roads. It was a white Easter. Then suddenly, on Easter Monday, a warm wind began to blow, the clouds gathered, and for three days and three nights heavy, warm rain came down in torrents. On Thursday the wind subsided, and a thick gray mist covered the countryside, as if to conceal the mysteries of the changes that were taking place in nature. In the mist the flood waters flowed, the ice floes began to crack and moved down the rivers, and the turbid, foaming torrents flowed faster, until on the following Monday, toward evening, the mist dispersed, the sky was covered with fleecy clouds and then cleared, and real spring had come. In the morning the bright sun rose and quickly devoured the thin ice covering the water, and the warm air all around vibrated with the exhalations of the reviving earth. The old grass turned green again and the young grass thrust out its needle-sharp blades, the buds swelled on the guelder-rose, the currant bushes, and the sticky, resinous birch trees; and in the gold-besprinkled willows the honey bee, which had only just emerged from its hive, flew about humming. Invisible larks broke into song over the velvet of the young, sprouting corn and the ice-covered stubble; peewits began to cry over the marshes and the low reaches of the rivers and streams, still overflowing with brownish water, and cranes and wild geese flew high across the sky, uttering their loud, spring cries. The cattle, their winter coats only partly shed and bald in patches, began to low in the pastures; bandy-legged lambs frisked round their bleating mothers, who were losing their fleece; swift-footed children ran about the quickly drying paths marked with imprints of bare feet; the merry voices of peasant women rose over the pond; and the axes of the peasants repairing their ploughs and harrows rang in the yard. Real spring had come.

CHAPTER 13

Levin put on his big boots and, for the first time, a cloth coat instead of a fur coat, and went about his estate, stepping over streams that flashed in the sun and dazzled his eyes, walking one minute over ice and another over sticky mud.

Spring is the time of plans and projects. And, like a tree in spring which does not yet know how and where its young shoots and twigs, still imprisoned in swelling buds, will spread out, Levin, as he walked out into the yard, had no clear idea what work he would begin on his beloved estate; but he felt that he was full of the most wonderful plans and projects. First of all he went to have a look at the cattle. The cows had been let out into the hot sun and, their new smooth coats glistening, were warming themselves in the sunshine and were mooing, asking to go to the fields. After admiring his cows, familiar to him to the smallest detail, Levin ordered them to be driven into the field and the calves to be let out into the sun. The herdsman ran off blithely to make the necessary preparations. The dairy maids, pulling up the coarse homespun skirts over their bare, white legs, still not sunburned, and with switches in their hands, ran splashing through the mud after the moving calves, crazed with the joy of spring, and chased them into the yard.

After admiring the addition to his herd, which was particularly good this year—the early calves were as big as a peasant's cow and Pava's calf of three months was the size of a yearling—Levin gave instructions for a trough to be brought out and for hay to be put into the racks. But it appeared that the racks made in the autumn in the yard, which was not used in winter, were broken. He sent for the carpenter, who according to his orders should have been at work on the threshing machine. But it appeared that the carpenter was mending the harrows, which should have been mended as far back as Shrovetide. Levin felt very annoyed. It was annoying that there should be a repetition of that everlasting slovenliness in the farm work against which he had been struggling with all his might for so many years. He found out that the racks, which were not wanted in the winter, had been taken into the cart-horses' stable and so had got broken, as they were lightly made for the calves. Besides, it now appeared that the harrows and all the agricultural implements, which he had ordered to be inspected and repaired during the winter, and for which purpose three carpenters had been specially hired, had not been repaired, and the harrows were being mended just when they should have been out in the fields. Levin sent for his bailiff, but, instead of waiting for him to turn up, immediately went to look for him himself. The bailiff, shining as did everything else on that day, was coming from the threshing floor in a warm coat, bordered with lambskin, breaking a straw in his hands.

"Why isn't the carpenter on the threshing machine?"

"I'm sorry, sir, I meant to tell you yesterday: the harrows have to be mended. You see, sir, it's time to be ploughing."

"Why wasn't it done in the winter?"

"But what would you be wanting a carpenter for?"

"Where are the racks for the calves' yard?"

"I gave orders for them to be put back, sir. What is one to do with such people?" said the bailiff, with a wave of the hand.

"Not with such people, but with such a bailiff!" Levin said, flaring up. "Why do I employ you, tell me!" he shouted. But realizing that this would not help matters, he stopped short in the middle of his speech and merely sighed. "Well," he asked after a pause, "can we start sowing?"

"Behind Turkino we might start tomorrow or the day after."

"And the clover?"

"I've sent Vassily and Mishka, sir. They're sowing. I doubt if they'll get through, though. It's very muddy."

"How many acres?"

"Sixteen."

"Why not all of it?" cried Levin.

That they were only sowing sixteen acres instead of fifty-four was still more annoying. Clover, as he knew in theory and from his own experience, only did well when it was sown as early as possible, almost before the fields were free from snow. And Levin could never get this done.

"I haven't the men, sir. What can you do with people like that? Three have not turned up. And there's Semyon . . ."

"You should have taken some men from the thatching."

"I have, sir."

"Where are the men then?"

"Five of them are making compote" (he meant compost); "four are turning the oats over—they might start sprouting, sir."

Levin knew very well that "they might start sprouting" meant that the English oats were already spoiled—again his orders had been disobeyed.

"Why, I told you in Lent to put in chimneys!" he cried.

"Don't worry, sir, we'll get it all done in time."

Levin waved his hand angrily, went to the barns to inspect the oats, and then returned to the stable. The oats were not yet spoiled. But the men were turning them over with spades, while they could be simply discharged into the lower barn; and so giving the necessary orders for it to be done and sending off two men to help with the sowing of clover, Levin recovered from his annoyance with the bailiff. Anyway, the day was so lovely that it was impossible to be angry.

"Ignat!" he shouted to the coachman who, with his sleeves rolled up, was washing the carriage at the well. "Saddle me . . ."

"Which one, sir?"

"I suppose Kolpik will do."

"Yes, sir."

While the horse was being saddled, Levin again called the bailiff, who was hanging about within sight, so as to make it up with him, and began telling him about the coming spring work and the plans for his estate. The manure to be carted earlier so as to have it all done before the first haymaking; the far field to be ploughed

183

continually so as to keep it fallow; and the hay to be got in by outside labor and not half of it by their own laborers.

The bailiff listened attentively and quite obviously tried his best to signify approval of his employer's suggestions, but he still wore the hopeless and despondent expression Levin knew so well and which always exasperated him. This expression seemed to say: "It's all very well, but it's all as God wills."

Nothing exasperated Levin so much as this attitude; but that was the general attitude of all bailiffs he had employed. They all took up the same attitude to his plans, and that was why he was no longer angry, but felt exasperated and all the more stimulated to fight against this sort of elemental force which he could find no other name for than "as God wills" and which he was constantly up against.

"It all depends how we get on, sir," said the bailiff.

"Why shouldn't you get on?"

"We must hire at least fifteen more laborers. They won't come. There were some here today asking seventy rubles for the summer."

Levin was silent. Once more he was up against that force. He knew that however much he tried, he could never manage to hire thirty-seven or thirty-eight—at most forty—laborers at the proper wages. But all the same he could not help carrying on with the fight.

"Send to Sury, to Chefirovka, if they won't come. We have to go and look for them."

"Well, there's no harm in sending, I suppose," the bailiff said gloomily. "And the horses, too, you see, sir. They're not strong enough."

"We'll buy some more. But, you see, I know," he added, laughing, "you're always satisfied with less and poorer quality. But this year I'm not going to let you have your own way. I'll see to everything myself."

"Well, I don't think you waste much time asleep, as it is. We always feel happier, sir, when the master's about."

"So they are sowing clover on the other side of the Birch Valley? I'll go and have a look," he said, mounting the little light bay Kolpik, which the coachman had led up.

"You won't get across the stream, sir," the coachman shouted after him.

184

"Very well, I'll go through the wood, then."

And Levin rode out of the muddy yard through the gate and out into the fields at a brisk amble, his good little horse, who had become restive from inactivity, snorting at the puddles and pulling at the bridle.

If Levin had felt happy in the cattle yard and the barns, he felt even happier in the open country. Rhythmically swaying on his good little ambler and drinking in the warm, fresh scent of the snow and air, he rode through the wood here and there over the crumbly, sinking snow with melting tracks, rejoicing in every one of his trees with its swelling buds and the moss coming to life again on their bark. When he had ridden out of the wood, a vast expanse of green winter corn spread out before him like a smooth, velvety carpet without a single bare patch anywhere and only stained here and there in the hollows with remnants of melting snow. He did not lose his temper either at the sight of a peasant's horse and cart trampling his young winter corn (he told a peasant he met to drive them off), nor by the derisive and stupid answer of the peasant Ipat, whom he happened to meet, who in reply to his question, "Well, Ipat, shall we be sowing soon?" said, "We must get the ploughing over first, sir." The further he went, the happier he felt, and all sorts of plans for the estate, each better than the last, presented themselves to him: to plant willow trees along the south sides of the fields, so that the snow should not lie long under them; to divide the fields, keeping six, under manure for tilling and three under grass; to build a cattle yard at the far end of the field and to dig a pond; and for the purposes of manuring to make movable pens for the cattle. Then he would have over eight hundred acres of wheat, two hundred and seventy acres of potatoes, and four hundred of clover, and not a single acre exhausted.

With such dreams as these, carefully guiding the horse along the borders of the fields so as not to trample his young winter corn, he rode up to the laborers who were sowing the clover. The cart with the seed was not standing on the border but in the middle of a field of winter wheat, which was torn up by the wheels and trampled by the horse. Both the laborers were sitting on the boundary between the fields, probably sharing a pipe of tobacco. The earth in the cart, with which the seed was

185

mixed, was not crumbled, but had become caked or was frozen into lumps. When they saw the master, the laborer Vassily walked toward the cart and Mishka began to sow. This was bad enough, but Levin seldom lost his temper with the hired laborers. When Vassily came up, he told him to take the horse and cart to the boundary of the field.

"Don't worry, sir, the wheat will recover."

"Please, don't argue," said Levin, "but do as you're told."

"Yes, sir," answered Vassily, taking hold of the horse's head. "But the sowing, sir," he said, ingratiatingly, "is first-rate. But it's awful hard walking! You drag along half a hundredweight on each bast shoe."

"And why hasn't the earth been sifted?" said Levin.

"But we do crumble it up, sir," replied Vassily, taking a handful of seed and rubbing the earth between his hands.

Vassily was not to blame that they had given him unsifted earth, but it was annoying all the same.

Having more than once successfully put to the test the method he knew of curbing his annoyance and making all that seemed wrong right again, Levin applied it now. He watched Mishka striding along and dragging enormous lumps of earth that stuck to each foot, dismounted, took the seed basket from Vassily, and prepared to sow.

"Where did you stop?"

Vassily pointed to a mark with his foot and Levin walked along, scattering the seeds and earth as best he could. The walking was difficult, like walking through a swamp, and having done a row, Levin, wet with perspiration, gave back the seed basket.

"Well, sir, I hope you won't blame me for that row when summer comes," said Vassily.

"Why?" asked Levin gaily, feeling that his method had fully justified itself.

"You'll see when the summer comes, sir. It'll look different, it will that, sir. You look where I sowed last spring. See how I scattered the seed! You see, sir, I'm working as hard for you as for my own father. I don't like to do things badly myself and I won't let others do it. For if the master's happy, we're happy too. Look over there, sir!" said Vassily, pointing to the field. "It does your heart good."

"It's a fine spring, Vassily."

"Aye, sir, it's a spring the old men don't recall the like of. I've been home and my old man has sown wheat too, about an acre of it. You can't tell it from rye, he says."

"Have you been sowing wheat long?"

"Why, sir, it was you taught us the year before last. You gave me a bushel of wheat yourself. We sold a quarter of it and sowed the rest."

"Well, mind you crumble up the lumps," said Levin, going up to his horse. "And keep an eye on Mishka. And if it comes up well, you'll have fifty kopecks for every acre."

"Thank you, sir. We've a lot to be thankful to you for as it is."

Levin mounted his horse and rode to the field where clover had been sown the year before and to the one which had been ploughed up for sowing the spring wheat.

The clover was coming up splendidly in the stubble field. It had already recovered and looked quite green among the broken stalks of last year's wheat. The horse sank into the mud up to its pasterns and drew each foot out of the half-thawed earth with a smacking sound. It was quite impossible to ride over the ploughed field: the ground was firm only where there was a little ice, and in the thawed furrows the horse's feet sank over its pasterns. The ploughed land was in perfect condition; in a couple of days it would be possible to harrow and sow. Everything was splendid; everything was gay. On his way back Levin forded a stream, hoping that the water would have gone down. And to be sure, he rode across, starting two ducks. "There ought to be snipe too," he thought, and just at the turning to his house he met the keeper, who confirmed his supposition.

Levin rode home at a trot to be in time for dinner and to get his gun ready for the evening.

CHAPTER 14

As he rode up to the house in high spirits, he heard the sound of harness bells from the direction of the main entrance.

"Why, that's from the railway station," he thought. "Just the right time to arrive from the Moscow train. . . . Who can it be? It couldn't be Nikolai, could it? He did say he might go to a spa or come to see me." At first he felt dismayed, for he feared that his brother's presence might upset his happy spring mood. But he was ashamed of that feeling, and immediately he seemed to open out his spiritual arms, waiting with tender joy and hoping with his whole soul that it might be his brother. He spurred on his horse and, as he rounded the acacia trees, saw a hired sledge drawn by a team of three horses from the station and in it a man in a fur coat. It was not his brother. "Oh, if only it's some agreeable fellow with whom one can have a talk!" he thought.

"Hullo!" Levin cried joyfully, raising both his arms. "What a welcome guest! I'm so glad to see you!" he exclaimed, recognizing Stepan Oblonsky.

"Now I shall be able to find out for certain," he thought, "whether she's married or when she's going to be married."

And on this lovely spring day he felt that the memory of her did not hurt him at all.

"You did not expect me, did you?" said Oblonsky, getting out of the sledge, with specks of mud on the bridge of his nose, his cheeks and eyebrows, but beaming with cheerfulness and health. "I've come to see you—for one thing," he said, embracing and kissing Levin. "To do a spot of shooting—for another. And to sell the Yergushovo forest—for a third."

"Excellent. What a spring, eh? How did you manage to get here in a sledge?"

"It would have been much worse in a cart, sir," remarked the driver, whom Levin knew.

"Well, I'm very, very glad to see you," said Levin with a childlike, happy smile.

Levin led his visitor into the spare bedroom, where Oblonsky's things—his bag, a gun in a case, and a cigar box—were also brought. Leaving him to wash and change, Levin went to the office to give orders about the ploughing and the clover. Agafya, always greatly concerned about the honor of the house, met him in the hall with questions about dinner.

"Do just as you like, only be quick," he said, and went out to see the bailiff.

When he returned, Oblonsky, washed and brushed and his face beaming with smiles, was coming out of his room, and they went upstairs together.

"Well, I must say I'm jolly glad to have got to you at last! Now I shall understand what mysteries you perpetrate here. But, seriously, I envy you. What a house! How splendid everything is! So light and gay!" said Oblonsky, forgetting that it was not always spring and that the days were not always sunny as on that day. "And your old nanny is so sweet! I must say I'd prefer a pretty maid with a little apron, but I agree that with your severe style and monastic life this is good enough."

Oblonsky told Levin a great deal of interesting news and one piece of news of especial interest to Levin, namely that his half-brother Sergey Koznyshev was planning to come and stay in the country with him that summer.

Not one word did Oblonsky say about Kitty or the Shcherbatskys; he only delivered greetings from his wife. Levin was grateful to him for his tact and was very glad of his visitor. As always, a mass of ideas and feelings he could not share with those around him had accumulated during his solitude, and now he poured out to Oblonsky the poetic joy of spring, his failures, his plans for the estate, and his thoughts and ideas on the books he had read, and particularly, the idea of his own book, the basis of which, though he was unaware of it himself, was a criticism of all previous works of agriculture. Oblonsky, always nice and quick to understand everything—a hint was sufficient—was particularly nice on this visit; and Levin noticed a new trait in him, a kind of respect and a sort of tenderness towards him, by which he was rather flattered.

The combined efforts of Agafya and the cook to make sure that the dinner was especially good only resulted in the two hungry friends sitting down to the hors d'oeuvres, filling themselves up with bread and butter, smoked goose, and pickled mushrooms, and in Levin's ordering the soup to be served without waiting for the pasties with which the cook had particularly meant to make his visitor's mouth water. But though Oblonsky was used to very different dinners, he found everything excellent: the herb brandy, the bread and butter, and especially the smoked goose, and the mushrooms, and the nettle soup, and the chicken in white sauce, and the white Crimean wine—everything excellent and marvelous.

"Splendid, splendid!" he said, lighting a thick cigarette after the roast. "I feel as though I had landed from a noisy and shaking steamer onto a tranquil shore. So you maintain that the laborer should be studied as an independent factor on which the choice of the agricultural methods depends? Well, you know, I am an ignoramus in these matters, but it seems to me that a theory and its application ought to have an influence on the laborer too."

"Yes, but wait a bit. I'm not talking of political economy, but of the science of agriculture. It must be like the natural sciences and observe existing phenomena and the laborer with his economic and ethnographic—"

At that moment Agafya came in with some jam.

"Why, my dear Agafya," said Oblonsky, kissing the tips of his plump fingers, "that smoked goose of yours was delicious, and what herb brandy! . . . Well, Kostya," he added to Levin, "don't you think it's time?"

Levin glanced through the window at the sun setting behind the bare trees of the wood.

"Yes, it's time, it's time!" he said. "Kuzma, get the trap ready!" and he ran downstairs.

Oblonsky, too, went down, carefully removed the canvas cover from the varnished gun case, and opening it, began putting together his expensive gun, which was of the latest type. Kuzma, anticipating a large tip, never left Oblonsky's side, putting on his stockings and his boots for him, which Oblonsky willingly let him do.

"Please, Kostya, will you tell them that if Ryabinin the dealer turns up—I told him to come here today—they should ask him in and let him wait."

"Are you selling the wood to Ryabinin?"

"Yes. Do you know him?"

"Know him? Of course I know him. I've done business with him 'finally and positively.' "

Oblonsky laughed. "Finally and positively" was the dealer's favorite expression.

"Yes, he uses the most extraordinarily funny expressions. She knows where her master is going," he added, patting Laska, who was whining and jumping round Levin, now licking his hand, now his boots and his gun.

The trap was already at the front steps when they went out.

"I told them to get the trap ready though it's not far. You wouldn't like a walk, would you?"

"No, let's drive," said Oblonsky, walking up to the trap.

He got in, sat down, wrapped a tiger-skin rug round his legs, and lit a cigar.

"Why don't you smoke?" Oblonsky asked. "A cigar is not just a pleasure, but the crown and hallmark of pleasure. Ah, this is life! How wonderful! This is how I should like to live!"

"Who prevents you?" asked Levin with a smile.

"Yes, sir, you're a lucky fellow! You have everything you like. You like horses—you have horses. Dogs—you have dogs. Shooting—you get it. Farming—you've got that too!"

"Perhaps it's because I appreciate all I have so much that I don't worry about what I haven't got," said Levin, thinking of Kitty.

Oblonsky understood, looked at him, but said nothing.

Levin was grateful to Oblonsky because, with his usual tact, noting that Levin was afraid of talking about the Shcherbatskys, he said nothing about them; but now Levin wanted to find out about the matter that tormented him so much, but he dared not mention it.

"Well, and how are things with you?" said Levin, feeling how wrong it was of him to be thinking only of himself.

Oblonsky's eyes began to sparkle merrily.

"You, of course, don't agree that one can eat one's cake and have it, too. You think it's a crime. But I don't admit life without love," he said, interpreting Levin's question in his own way. "I'm afraid I'm made like that. And, as a matter of fact, it does so little harm to anyone and gives so much pleasure to oneself. . . ."

"Why, is there anything new then?"

"Yes, my dear fellow, there is! You see, I suppose you must know the Ossian type of woman . . . the sort of woman one only sees in dreams. . . . Well, such women actually exist and—er—these women are terrible. You see, woman is the sort of thing that however much you study it, it's always quite new."

"In that case, it's much better not to study it."

"No, sir. Some mathematician, I believe, has said that true pleasure lies not in the discovery of truth, but in the search for it."

Levin listened in silence and, however much he tried, he could not penetrate into his friend's mind and understand his feelings, nor the fascination he felt for studying women of that kind.

CHAPTER 15

The place of the shoot of migrating game birds was not far off, in a small aspen wood by a stream. When they had reached the wood, Levin got down and led Oblonsky to the corner of a mossy and marshy clearing, already free from snow. He himself took up a position by a double birch tree at the other end of the clearing and, leaning his gun against the fork of the lower branch, took off his coat, tightened his belt, and tried to see if he could move his arms freely.

The old, gray-haired Laska, who followed close on his heels, sat down warily opposite him and pricked up her ears. The sun was setting behind the large wood and the small birch trees scattered among the aspens stood out clearly against the sunset with their drooping branches and their swollen buds about to burst into leaf.

From the thicket, where the snow was still lying on the ground, the water still flowed almost soundlessly in narrow, winding streamlets. Small birds chirped and from time to time flew from tree to tree.

In the intervals of silence last year's leaves could be

heard rustling, stirred by the thawing earth and the growing grasses.

"How do you like that! One can hear and see the grass growing!" Levin thought to himself, noticing a wet, slate-colored aspen leaf moving near a blade of young grass. He stood listening and looking down now on the wet, mossy ground, now at the alert Laska, now at the sea of bare treetops stretched out before him at the foot of the hill, and now at the darkening sky covered with white streaks of clouds. A hawk, slowly flapping its wings, flew high over the distant woods; another identical one flew in the same direction and vanished. The birds in the thicket chirped louder and louder and more fussily. Somewhere nearby a long-eared owl hooted and, starting, Laska took a few cautious steps and, putting her head on one side, began listening intently. A cuckoo called from the other side of the river. It twice uttered its usual call and then gave a hoarse, hurried call and then grew confused.

"How do you like that! The cuckoo already!" said Oblonsky, coming out from behind a bush.

"Yes, I can hear," replied Levin, reluctantly disturbing the stillness of the wood, his own voice sounding unpleasant to him. "It won't be long now."

Oblonsky's figure disappeared behind the bush again, and all Levin saw was the flare of a match, followed by the red glow of a cigarette and a puff of blue smoke.

Click! Click! came the sound of Oblonsky cocking his gun.

"What's that cry?" Oblonsky asked, drawing Levin's attention to a long-drawn whine like the high-pitched whinnying of a colt in play.

"Don't you know? It's a jack hare. But no more talking! Listen, they're coming!" Levin almost shouted, cocking his gun.

A shrill, whistling sound came from the distance and, two seconds later, at exactly the usual interval so familiar to the sportsman, came the second and the third, and after the third they could already hear the sound of a hoarse cry.

Levin threw a quick glance to the right and to the left, and there before him against a dull, light-blue sky, over the interlaced tops of the aspens, appeared a flying bird.

It was flying straight toward him: the hoarse cry, which sounded like the even tearing of some tautly stretched cloth, sounded close to his ear; he could already make out the long beak and neck of the bird and, just as Levin took aim, there was a red flash from behind the bush where Oblonsky was standing, and the bird dropped like an arrow and then soared upward again. Another flash, followed by the sound of a hit, and, flapping its wings, as if trying to keep up in the air, it remained stationary for a moment and then fell with a heavy thud on the marshy ground.

"Did I miss it?" cried Oblonsky, who could not be seen for the smoke.

"Here it is!" said Levin, pointing to Laska, who, raising one ear and wagging the tip of her fluffy tail, was bringing the dead bird to her master, walking slowly, as though wishing to prolong the pleasure and almost seeming to smile. "Well, I'm glad you got it," said Levin, at the same time feeling envious that he had not shot the woodcock himself.

"A bad miss with the right barrel," replied Oblonsky, loading his gun. "Sh-sh . . . here it comes!"

And indeed, they heard two shrill whistles following in quick succession. Two woodcock, playing and racing each other, whistling and not calling, flew almost over the sportsmen's heads. Four shots rang out and, like swallows, the woodcock turned swiftly and disappeared from sight.

The shooting was excellent. Oblonsky brought down another brace, and Levin got two, of which one could not be recovered. Low down in the west, Venus, bright and silvery, was already shining behind the birch trees with gentle brilliance, and high up in the east somber Arcturus coruscated with its red fires. Overhead Levin caught sight of the stars of the Great Bear and then lost them again. The woodcock had ceased flying; but Levin decided to stay a little longer till Venus, which he could still see below a birch-tree branch, should rise above it and all the stars of the Great Bear should be visible. Venus had risen above the branch, and the chariot of the Great Bear with its shaft was clearly visible against the dark-blue sky, but he still waited.

"Isn't it time to go?" asked Oblonsky.

It was quiet in the wood and not a bird stirred.

"Let's stay a little longer," replied Levin.

"As you like."

They were standing now some fifteen feet apart.

"Stiva," Levin said suddenly and unexpectedly, "why don't you tell me whether your sister-in-law is married or when she will be?"

Levin felt so calm and self-possessed that he thought that no answer, whatever it might be, could agitate him. But he never expected the reply Oblonsky gave him.

"She has not thought and is not thinking of getting married, but she's very ill and the doctors have sent her abroad. They are even afraid she may not live."

"Good Lord!" exclaimed Levin. "Very ill, is she? What's the matter with her? How did she . . ."

While they were talking, Laska, pricking up her ears, kept looking up at the sky and then reproachfully at them.

"What a time to choose to talk," she thought. "And here comes one. . . . Yes, here it is. They'll miss it."

But at that very instant both of them suddenly heard the shrill whistle, which seemed to strike them across the ears, and both immediately seized their guns, and there were two flashes and two reports at one and the same moment. The woodcock that was flying high up instantly folded its wings and fell into the thicket, bending down the young shoots.

"Excellent! Both together!" cried Levin and ran into the thicket with Laska to look for the woodcock. "Oh yes—what was it? Some bad news. . . ." He tried to remember. "Why, of course, Kitty's ill. . . . I'm afraid there's nothing I can do about it—I'm very sorry," he thought.

"Found it? Clever dog," he said, taking the warm bird from Laska's mouth and putting it into the game bag that was almost full. "I've found it, Stiva!" he shouted.

CHAPTER 16

On their way home Levin asked Oblonsky to tell him all the particulars of Kitty's illness and the Shcherbatskys' plans, and though he would have been ashamed to admit it, he was pleased at what he found out. He was pleased because there was still hope and even more because she, who had made him suffer so much, was suffering herself. But when Oblonsky began to speak of the cause of Kitty's illness and mentioned Vronsky's name, Levin interrupted him.

"I have no right whatever to know all these family affairs and, to tell the truth, I'm not interested in them, either."

Oblonsky smiled almost imperceptibly on catching the instantaneous change, so familiar to him, in Levin's face, which became as gloomy as it had been cheerful a moment before.

"Have you quite settled with Ryabinin about the wood?" asked Levin.

"Yes, I have. An excellent price. Thirty-eight thousand. Eight at once and the rest over the next six years. It's been a long business. No one would give more."

"Which means that you're just giving it away," Levin said gloomily.

"Why giving it away?" said Oblonsky with a good-natured smile, knowing that everything now would seem wrong to Levin.

"Because the wood is worth at least one hundred and eighty-five rubles an acre," replied Levin.

"Oh, these farmers!" Oblonsky said jokingly. "Your tone of contempt for us poor city dwellers! But when it comes to business, we do it better than anyone. Believe me, I've taken everything into account," he went on, "and the wood has been sold for a good price. Indeed, I am afraid he may change his mind. You see, it's not standing trees," said Oblonsky, hoping by the term "standing trees" to convince Levin of the unfairness of his doubts, "but mostly only good for fuel. And it won't yield more than about forty cubic yards of wood per acre, and he's paying me at the rate of seventy rubles the acre."

Levin smiled contemptuously. "I know," he thought, "this manner of all townsmen, and not his only, who, after paying two or three visits to the country in ten years, pick up two or three expressions and go on using them whether it's to the point or not, firmly convinced they know everything. 'Standing trees,' 'yield,' 'forty cubic yards.' He uses words, but understands nothing about the business!"

"I wouldn't try to teach you what you write about in your office," he said, "and if I should need your help, I'd come to you for advice. But you are so sure you understand all there is to know about timber. It's a difficult science. Have you counted the trees?"

"Counted the trees?" said Oblonsky, laughing, still anxious to draw his friend out of his bad humor. "To count the grains of sand, the planets' rays, though a lofty mind were able . . ."

"Well, Ryabinin's lofty mind is able, you see. No dealer will ever buy a wood without counting the trees, unless, of course, someone is giving him it for nothing, as you're doing. I know your wood. I go shooting there every year, and it's worth over one hundred and eighty rubles an acre, cash down, and he's paying you seventy in installments. Which means that you've made him a present of about thirty thousand rubles."

"Don't exaggerate, please," Oblonsky said piteously. "Why didn't anyone offer me so much?"

"Because he's in league with the other dealers. He's bought them off. I've had business dealings with all of them. I know them. They're not genuine dealers, they're profiteers. He wouldn't consider a deal if he only got ten or fifteen per cent profit; he waits till he can make eighty per cent pure profit."

"Come, come, you're in a bad mood today."

"Not at all," said Levin gloomily, as they drove up to the house.

At the front steps stood a cart tightly braced with iron and leather and a well-fed horse harnessed with broad, tightly stretched straps. In the cart sat Ryabinin's clerk, who was also Ryabinin's driver, red-faced and tightly belted. Ryabinin himself was already in the house and met the two friends in the hall. Ryabinin was a tall, spare, middle-aged man, with a mustache, a protruding shaven chin, and prominent lackluster eyes. He wore a long-skirted blue coat with buttons very low at the back, high boots crinkled round the ankles and straight over the calves, and a large pair of galoshes over them. He wiped his face all round with a handkerchief and drawing his coat closer round him, though it fitted him very well as it was, greeted the new arrivals with a smile, holding out his hand to Oblonsky, as if he were trying to catch something.

"So you've arrived," said Oblonsky, giving him his hand. "Good!"

"I dare not disobey your orders, sir, though the roads are in a disgraceful state. I positively walked all the way, but I've arrived in time. How do you do, Mr. Levin, sir?" he addressed Levin, trying to catch his hand too.

But Levin, scowling, pretended not to notice his hand and began taking the woodcock out of the game bag.

"I see you've been amusing yourself with shooting," he went on. "What kind of bird would that be, sir?" he added, looking contemptuously at the woodcock. "A tasty bit of fowl, I don't think," and he shook his head disapprovingly, as if doubting very much whether the game was worth the candle.

"Would you like to go into my study?" said Levin to Oblonsky in French, with a grim frown. "Go into my study. You can talk business there."

"Thank you, sir, anywhere you like," said Ryabinin with disdainful dignity, as if wishing to make them understand that others might find it difficult to know how to behave, but that he had never been in any difficulties about anything.

On entering the study, Ryabinin looked round from force of habit as though to find the icon, but when he found it he did not cross himself. He glanced at the bookcases with the same doubtful expression which he bestowed on the woodcock, smiled disdainfully, and shook his head disapprovingly, this time absolutely refusing to admit that the game could be worth the candle.

"Well, sir, have you brought the money?" asked Oblonsky. "Won't you take a seat?"

"Don't you worry about the money, sir. I've come to see you and talk matters over."

"What's there to talk over? Do sit down, please."

"I don't mind if I do," said Ryabinin, sitting down and leaning his elbows on the back of the chair in a most uncomfortable fashion. "You see, Prince, you must come down a little. It's only fair. The money's all ready, positively to the last kopeck. No trouble about the money, sir. None whatever."

Levin, who had been putting away his gun in a cupboard, was on the point of leaving the room, but on hearing the dealer's words he stopped.

"You're getting the timber dirt cheap as it is," he said. "He came to me too late, or I'd have fixed the price."

Ryabinin got up and, without uttering a word, looked Levin up and down.

"Very tight about money, Mr. Levin is, sir," he said with a smile, addressing Oblonsky. "It's positively impossible to buy anything from him. Wanted to buy some of his wheat, I did. Offered him a good price, too."

"Why should I give you my goods for next to nothing? I didn't find it on the ground, neither did I steal it."

"But, my dear sir, nowadays it's positively impossible to steal anything. Nowadays, sir, everything is finally brought before a judge and jury. Yes, indeed, everything's honest and aboveboard now. Stealing indeed! We've talked it over honorably. You're asking too much for the wood. There's no profit in it. I must ask you, sir, to knock off something, even if it's only a little."

"But is the thing settled or not? If it's settled, it's no use bargaining; if not, I'm buying the wood."

The smile suddenly disappeared from Ryabinin's face. It assumed a hawklike, predatory, hard expression. He rapidly unbuttoned his coat with long fingers, revealing a shirt, brass waistcoat buttons, and a watch chain, and quickly took out a fat, old wallet.

"If you please, sir, the wood is mine," he said, crossing himself quickly and holding out his hand. "Take the money; the wood's mine. That's how Ryabinin does business, no bargaining over kopecks," he said, frowning and flourishing his wallet.

"I shouldn't be in a hurry if I were you," said Levin.

"But, my dear fellow," Oblonsky said with surprise, "I've given my word!"

Levin went out of the room, slamming the door. Ryabinin looked at the door and shook his head with a smile.

"Young, that's what he is! Positively childish. You see, sir, believe me, I'm buying it just for the hell of it. I mean so that Ryabinin and no one else should buy Oblonsky's wood. God only knows if I can make a profit. Yes, sir, I put my trust in God. Now, sir, if you would be so good as to sign the agreement. . . ."

An hour later Ryabinin, well wrapped up in his coat

199

and his overcoat buttons carefully buttoned, and with the agreement in his pocket, got into his tightly iron-bound cart and drove home.

"Oh, these gentry!" he said to his clerk. "What a queer lot!"

"That's right, sir," replied the clerk, handing over the reins and hooking up the leather apron of the cart. "And how about the purchase, sir?"

"Not too bad, not too bad. . . ."

CHAPTER 17

Oblonsky went upstairs, his pocket bulging with the treasury notes the dealer had paid him three months in advance. The business of the wood was completed, the money was in his pocket, the shooting had been excellent, and Oblonsky was in the best of spirits, and therefore he was particularly anxious to dispel the ill humor that had descended on Levin. He wanted to finish the day at supper as agreeably as he had begun it.

Levin really was in a bad mood, and in spite of his desire to be friendly and courteous to his dear guest, he could not pull himself together. The intoxication of the news that Kitty was not married was gradually beginning to have an effect on him.

Kitty was not married and was ill, ill for love of a man who had slighted her. This insult somehow rebounded on him. Vronsky had slighted her and she had slighted him, Levin. Therefore Vronsky had a right to despise Levin and was therefore his enemy. But Levin did not think it all out. He vaguely felt that there was something insulting to him in all this, and was angry not with what had upset him but tried to find fault with everything that came to his mind. The stupid sale of the wood, the fraud that Oblonsky had fallen a victim to and which had taken place in his house, exasperated him.

"Well, have you finished?" he said when he met Oblonsky upstairs. "Will you have supper now?"

"Yes, thank you. The appetite I get in the country, marvelous! Why didn't you ask Ryabinin to stay to supper?"

"Oh, to hell with him!"

"I must say the way you treat him is a bit much!" said Oblonsky. "You didn't even shake hands with him. Why not shake hands with him?"

"Because I don't shake hands with a footman, and a footman is a hundred times better than he."

"You are a reactionary, aren't you?" said Oblonsky. "And how about the merging of the classes?"

"Anyone who likes merging, let him merge by all means. It sickens me."

"I see you really are a reactionary."

"I don't think I've ever given much thought to what I am. I am Konstantin Levin—that's all."

"And Konstantin Levin in a very bad temper," said Oblonsky with a smile.

"Yes, I'm afraid I'm in rather a bad temper and do you know why? Because—I'm sorry to say—of your stupid sale. . . ."

Oblonsky wrinkled his face good-naturedly, like a man whose feelings are hurt and who is being upset for no fault of his own.

"Now, really," he said, "have you ever met a man who sold anything without being told immediately afterward that it was worth much more? While he's trying to sell it, nobody offers him more. I'm sorry, but you seem to bear a grudge against that unfortunate Ryabinin."

"Perhaps I do. And do you know why? You'll again call me a reactionary, or some other dreadful name, but I can't help feeling hurt and vexed when I see on all sides the growing impoverishment of the nobility to which I belong and to which, in spite of the merging of the classes, I'm glad to belong. . . . And an impoverishment not as a result of luxurious living—that does not matter so much; gracious living is the sort of thing the nobility is good at and only the nobility knows how to do. At present the peasants around here are buying land; I do not mind that. The landowner does nothing; the peasants work and squeeze out the idler. That is as it should be. And I'm very glad for the peasant. But it hurts me to see this impoverishment as a result of—what shall I call it?—a sort of innocence. Here a Polish tenant buys a wonderful estate for half its value from a lady who lives in Nice. There land worth ten rubles an acre is leased to a merchant for one ruble. And now you, without any reason whatever, have made that rogue a present of thirty thousand rubles."

"Well, what would you have me do? Count every tree?"

"Certainly count them. You have not counted them, but Ryabinin has. Ryabinin's children will have the means to live and to get an education, while yours may not!"

"I'm sorry, but there's something despicable in this counting. We have our business, they have theirs, and they must make their profit. However, the thing's done and there's an end to it. Oh, and here come the poached eggs, my favorite egg dish. And Agafya will give us some of that wonderful herb brandy. . . ."

Oblonsky sat down to the table and began joking with Agafya, assuring her that he had not tasted such a dinner and supper for a long time.

"Well, sir, you appreciate it at least," said Agafya, "but Mr. Levin, whatever you gave him, if it was only a crust of bread, would just eat it and be off."

However much Levin tried to pull himself together he remained morose and silent. There was one question he wanted to ask Oblonsky, but he could not bring himself to do so, and he could not find the right moment or the right words in which to put it. Oblonsky had gone down to his room, undressed, washed again, put on his goffered nightshirt, and got into bed, but Levin still lingered in his room, talking of all sorts of trifles, and unable to bring himself to ask what he wanted to know.

"What wonderful soap they make," he said, unwrapping and examining a cake of scented soap which Agafya had prepared for the visitor, but which Oblonsky had not used. "Just look: why, it's a work of art!"

"Yes," said Oblonsky with a moist and blissful yawn, "everything has been brought to a pitch of perfection nowadays. Theaters, for instance, and those—er—amusement—er—er—er!" he yawned. "Electric lights everywhere—ah-h!"

"Yes, electricity," said Levin. "Yes. Well, and where's Vronsky now?" he asked, suddenly putting down the soap.

"Vronsky?" said Oblonsky, ceasing to yawn. "Vronsky is in Petersburg. He left shortly after you did and he hasn't been in Moscow once since then. And you know, my dear fellow, I'll be quite frank with you," he went on, leaning his elbow on the table and laying his handsome, rosy face on one hand, his moist, good-natured, sleepy eyes shining like stars. "It was your own fault. You took fright at a rival. But as I told you at the time I don't know which of you two has the better chance. Why didn't you go straight for it? I told you at the time that . . .." he yawned with his jaws only, without opening his mouth.

"Does he or doesn't he know that I proposed?" thought Levin, looking at Oblonsky. "Yes, he does. There's something sly and diplomatic in his face"; and feeling himself blush, he looked in silence straight into Oblonsky's eyes.

"If there was anything on her part at the time," Oblonsky went on, "it was merely a passing infatuation. You see, the fact that he is such a perfect aristocrat and his future position in society had made an impression on her mother, but not on her."

Levin frowned. The humiliation of the refusal he had suffered went like a burning flame through his heart, as though it were a fresh wound he had just received. But he was at home and at home the very walls are a great help.

"Wait, wait," he began, interrupting Oblonsky. "You say he's such a perfect aristocrat. But I should like to ask you why Vronsky or anybody else is so great an aristocrat that I should be slighted because of it? You consider Vronsky an aristocrat. I don't. A man whose father was a sycophant and a timeserver, and whose mother had been the mistress of goodness knows how many men. . . . I'm very sorry, but I consider myself and people like me true aristocrats, people who can point back to three or four honorable generations, all with the highest standard of education (talent and intelligence are a different matter), and who never fawned upon anyone, never depended upon anyone, who lived as my father and grandfather did. And I know lots of people like that. You think it despicable of me to count the trees in my woods, while you make Ryabinin a present of thirty thousand rubles; but you get rent from your tenants and I don't know what else, and I am not getting any, and that's why I value what belongs to me either by birth or labor. . . . We are the aristocrats, and not those who can only exist by the sops thrown to them by the mighty ones of this world and who can be bought for sixpence."

"Well, but whom are you attacking? I agree with you," said Oblonsky, sincerely and gaily, though he could not help feeling that by those whom Levin claimed could be bought for sixpence he also meant him. He was genuinely pleased by Levin's animation. "Whom are you attacking? Though much that you say of Vronsky is not true, I won't speak about that now. I tell you candidly that in your place I'd go to Moscow now with me and . . ."

"No, I don't know if you know it or not, and I don't care, but I will tell you—I proposed and was refused and Kitty is now only a painful and humiliating memory to me."

"Why, what nonsense!"

"But don't let's talk about it. I'm sorry if I've been rude to you," said Levin. Now that he had told everything he became once more as he had been in the morning. "You're not angry with me, Stiva, are you? Please don't be angry," he said, taking his hand and smiling.

"Why, no! I'm not at all angry. There's nothing to be angry about. I'm glad we've had this talk. And do you know, the shooting in the early morning is often very good. Shall we go? I wouldn't go to bed afterward, but go straight from there to the station."

"An excellent idea!"

CHAPTER 18

Though Vronsky's entire inner life was taken up by his passion, his external life ran unalterably and irresistibly along the old customary rails of social and regimental connections and interests. The interests of his regiment occupied an important place in Vronsky's life because he was fond of his regiment and still more because his regiment was fond of him. Not only were they fond of him in the regiment, they also respected him and were proud of him—proud that this immensely rich man, a man of excellent education and abilities, before whom the road lay open to every kind of success that would satisfy ambition and vanity, had disregarded all that and of all life's interests had the interests of his regiment and his comrades nearest to his heart. Vronsky was aware that his comrades were of that opinion of him, and besides liking the life, he felt it to be his duty to uphold their view of him.

It goes without saying that he never spoke of his love to any of his fellow officers, that he did not betray his secret even in the wildest drinking bouts (though, indeed, he was never so drunk as to lose control of himself), and silenced those of his thoughtless comrades who tried to hint at the liaison. But although his love was known to all the town—everyone guessed more or less correctly what his relations with Anna were—most of the young people envied him just on account of what was the most painful aspect of his love affair, namely Karenin's high position and, consequently, the prominence that this liaison might acquire in society.

The majority of the young women, who envied Anna and had long been annoyed at hearing her described as *irreproachable*, were pleased at what they supposed to be the truth and were only waiting for public opinion to turn before coming down on her with the whole weight of their scorn. They were already preparing the lumps of mud they would throw at her when the time came. Most of the older people and people in high positions were unhappy about the imminent social scandal.

Vronsky's mother was at first pleased when she heard of her son's liaison, both because in her opinion nothing gave such a finishing touch to a brilliant young man as an affair in high society and because Mrs. Karenin, whom she had liked so much and who had talked so much about her little son, was after all just like all other beautiful and well-bred women, according to the Countess Vronsky's ideas, that is. But latterly she had found out that her son had refused a post of great importance to his career only because he wished to remain with his regiment and be able to see Anna; she found out that exalted personages were dissatisfied with him; and so she changed her opinion. She was also displeased that, as far as she could gather, this affair was not the brilliant, graceful society liaison she would have approved of, but as she was told, a sort of desperate Werther-like passion, which might involve him in all sorts of foolish situations.

She had not seen him since his sudden departure from Moscow, and she sent him word through her eldest son to come and see her.

The elder brother was also dissatisfied with the younger. It did not matter to him what kind of love it was, great or small, passionate or not, guilty or pure (though the father of a family, he kept a ballet girl himself, and therefore took a lenient view of the matter); but he knew that this love affair displeased those whom it was necessary to please, and he therefore did not approve of his brother's conduct.

Besides his regimental and social occupations, Vronsky had still another occupation—horses, of which he was passionately fond.

That year there was to be an officers' steeplechase. Vronsky had entered for it, bought a thoroughbred English mare; and in spite of his love affair, he showed a passionate, though restrained, interest in the coming races.

The two passions did not interfere with one another. On the contrary, he had to have an occupation and an interest apart from his love to help him to refresh himself and have a rest from the emotions that agitated him so violently.

CHAPTER 19

On the day of the Krasnoye Selo races, Vronsky came earlier than usual to the officers' mess to eat his beefsteak. It was not necessary for him to train strictly, as his weight was exactly the regulation 160 pounds; but he had to be careful not to put on weight and he therefore avoided sweets and starchy foods. He sat with his coat unbuttoned over a white waistcoat, his elbows on the table, waiting for the steak he had ordered and looking at a French novel that lay open on his plate. He only looked at the book in order not to have to talk to the officers coming in and out of the room. He was thinking.

He was thinking of Anna's promise to meet him that day after the races. But he had not seen her for three days and as her husband had just returned from abroad he did not know whether she would be able to keep the appointment that day or not, and he did not know how to find out. He had seen her last at his cousin Betsy's country cottage. He went to the Karenins' country cottage as seldom as possible. Now he wanted to go there and he was wondering how to do so.

"Of course I can say that Betsy sent me to find out whether she was coming to the races. Yes, of course, I'll go," he decided, raising his eyes from the book. And his face was radiant as he vividly imagined the happiness of seeing her.

"Send to my house at once and tell them to harness the troika immediately," he said to the waiter who had brought him a steak on a hot silver plate; and drawing the plate toward him, he began to eat.

From the billiard room next door came the click of balls, the sound of talk and laughter. Two officers appeared at the door: one a young fellow with a weak, thin face, who had recently joined the regiment from the Page's Corps; the other, a plump, elderly officer with a bracelet on his wrist and bloated little eyes.

Vronsky glanced at them, frowned, and as though not noticing them, kept his eyes on the book, eating and reading at the same time.

"What? Fortifying yourself for the job?" asked the plump officer, sitting down beside him.

"As you see," replied Vronsky, frowning, wiping his mouth and not looking at him.

"Aren't you afraid of putting on weight?" he went on, turning a chair round for the young officer.

"What?" said Vronsky angrily, making a grimace of disgust and showing his even teeth.

"Not afraid to put on weight?"

"Waiter, sherry!" said Vronsky, without answering, and, moving his book to the other side, he continued to read.

The plump officer took the wine list and turned to the young officer.

"You choose what we're going to drink," he said, handing him the wine list and looking at him.

"Suppose we have some hock," said the young officer, casting a timid glance at Vronsky and trying to catch hold of his budding mustache. Seeing that Vronsky did not turn around, he got up.

"Let's go into the billiard room," he said.

The plump officer got up obediently and they made their way toward the door.

At that moment Captain Yashvin, a tall, handsome cavalry officer, entered the room and, having given a contemptuous backward nod to the two officers, went up to Vronsky.

"Ah, here he is!" he exclaimed, slapping him heavily on the shoulder strap with his large hand.

Vronsky looked up angrily, but his face brightened at once into its characteristic look of calm, steadfast friendliness.

"That's clever of you, Alexey," the captain said in a loud baritone. "Have something to eat now and drink one small glass."

"I don't feel like eating."

"Just have a look at the inseparables," added Yashvin, glancing sarcastically at the two officers who were just leaving the room.

He sat down beside Vronsky, and his legs, encased in tight riding breeches, being too long for the chair, bent at a sharp angle at the hip and knee. "Why did you not come to the Krasnensky Theatre? Numerova was not at all bad. Where were you?"

"I'm afraid I stayed late at the Tverskoys'."

"Ah!" said Yashvin.

Yashvin, a gambler and a rake, not only a man without principles, but one with immoral principles—Yashvin was Vronsky's best friend in the regiment. Vronsky liked him both for his extraordinary physical strength, which he demonstrated mostly by his ability to drink like a fish and go without sleep and be as fresh as ever; and for his great moral strength, which he demonstrated in his relations with his comrades and superior officers, who feared and respected him, and in his card playing when he staked tens of thousands of rubles and always, however much he might have drunk, with such skill and self-possession that he was considered the best player at the English Club. Vronsky respected and liked Yashvin particularly because he felt that Yashvin liked him not for his name and money but for himself. Of all the people he knew, Yashvin was the only one with whom he would have liked to talk about his love. He felt that Yashvin, though apparently despising all kinds of emotion, was the only one who could understand the powerful passion that now filled his whole life. He was, besides, convinced that Yashvin certainly found no pleasure in gossip and scandal, but understood his feelings properly, that is to say, knew and believed that love was not a joke or a pastime, but something more ecstatic and important.

Vronsky did not talk to him of his love, but was aware that he knew all about it and understood it in the right way, and he found it agreeable to see it in his eyes.

"Ah, yes!" Yashvin said on hearing that Vronsky had been at the Tverskoys', and with a twinkle in his black eyes he began twisting his left mustache into his mouth, a bad habit he had.

"Well, and what were you doing last night? Win anything?" asked Vronsky.

"Eight thousand. But three of them are not quite certain. I'm afraid he won't pay up."

"Well, I suppose you can now afford to lose on me," said Vronsky, laughing. (Yashvin had placed heavy bets on Vronsky's horse.)

"I'm quite sure I won't lose. Makhotin's the only danger."

And the conversation turned on the expectations of the day's races, the only thing Vronsky could think about now.

"Let's go, I've finished," said Vronsky, and he got up and walked toward the door.

Yashvin, too, got up, stretching his huge legs and long back.

"It's too early for me to dine, but I must have a drink. I'll follow you directly. Hey, there, wine!" he exclaimed in his rich voice, so famous on the parade ground, which made the windowpanes rattle. "No, I don't want any," he shouted again. "You're going home, so I'll come with you."

And he and Vronsky went out together.

CHAPTER 20

Vronsky was billeted in a roomy, clean, Finnish peasant cottage divided into two by a partition. Petritsky lived with him in camp, too. Petritsky was asleep when Vronsky and Yashvin came into the cottage.

"Get up, you've slept enough," said Yashvin, stepping

behind the partition and shaking by the shoulder the disheveled Petritsky, who was lying with his nose buried in the pillow.

Petritsky jumped suddenly to his knees and looked round.

"Your brother's been here," he said to Vronsky. "Woke me up, damn him, and said he would come back." And he again drew up his blanket and threw himself back on the pillow. "Leave me alone, Yashvin," he said, getting angry with Yashvin, who was pulling the blanket off him. "Leave me alone!" He turned round and opened his eyes. "You'd better tell me what to drink. I've got such a nasty taste in my mouth that . . ."

"Vodka's better than anything," Yashvin said in his deep voice. "Tereshchenko, vodka and pickled cucumbers for your master," he shouted, evidently fond of hearing the sound of his own voice.

"Vodka? Think so?" asked Petritsky, making a wry face and rubbing his eyes. "Will you have a drink, too? Very well. We'll have a drink together. Vronsky, will you have a drink?" said Petritsky, getting up and wrapping a tiger-skin rug round himself under the arms.

He went through the door in the partition, raised his hand, and began singing in French, " 'There was a king in Thu-u-le' . . . Will you have a drink, Vronsky?"

"Go to blazes," said Vronsky, putting on the coat his valet handed him.

"Where are you off to?" asked Yashvin. "There's your troika," he added, as he saw the open carriage drive up to the door.

"To the stables," said Vronsky, "and then I have to go to see Bryansky about the horses."

Vronsky had really promised to go and see Bryansky, who lived some seven miles from Peterhof, and pay him for the horses; and he did intend to go there too. But his fellow officers realized at once that he was not only going there.

Petritsky, still singing, winked an eye and pouted his lips, as if to say, "We know what sort of Bryansky it is."

"Mind you're not late," Yashvin merely said, and to change the subject: "How's my roan? Is he doing well?" he asked, looking out of the window at the middle horse, which he had sold to Vronsky.

"Wait!" shouted Petritsky to Vronsky, who was already going out. "Your brother left a letter for you and a note. Wait, where are they?"

Vronsky stopped.

"Well, where are they?"

"Where are they? That's the question!" Petritsky declared solemnly, raising his forefinger upward from his nose.

"Come on, tell me. This is silly!" said Vronsky, smiling.

"I haven't lighted the fire. They are here somewhere."

"Stop playing the fool! Where's the letter?"

"I'm sorry, I've forgotten. Or was it all a dream? Wait, wait! What's the use of getting angry? If you had emptied four bottles a head as we did last night, you too would have forgotten where you were lying. One moment—I'll remember it directly."

Petritsky went behind the partition and lay down on the bed.

"Wait! I was lying like this and he was standing there. Yes, yes, yes, yes. . . . Here it is!" and Petritsky pulled the letter from under the mattress where he had put it.

Vronsky took the letter and his brother's note. It was what he had expected: a letter from his mother full of complaints for not having gone to see her and a note from his brother to say that they must talk things over. Vronsky knew that it was all about the same thing. "What business is it of theirs?" thought Vronsky, and crumpling up the letters, he pushed them in between the buttons of his coat, intending to read them carefully on the way. In the passage he met two officers, one of his own and one of another regiment.

Vronsky's lodgings were always the haunt of all the officers.

"Where are you off to?"

"To Peterhof. Afraid I have to."

"Has the mare arrived from Tsarskoye?"

"Yes, but I haven't seen her yet."

"They say Makhotin's Gladiator has gone lame."

"Nonsense! But how will you be able to race in this mud?" said the other.

"Here are my rescuers!" shouted Petritsky on seeing the newcomers. An orderly stood before him with vodka and a pickled cucumber on a tray. "Yashvin here has told me to have a drink to freshen myself up."

211

"Well, you certainly had a merry time there last night. You didn't let us sleep all night."

"Just listen how we finished up," said Petritsky. "Volkor climbed out onto the roof and said he felt sad. I said, 'Let's have music—a funeral march!' And he fell asleep up there on the roof under the strains of the funeral march."

"Come and drink, drink your vodka and then soda water and a lot of lemon," said Yashvin, standing over Petritsky like a mother making a child take its medicine. "And after that a little champagne—oh, a small bottle will do."

"Now that's the first sensible thing you've said. Wait, Vronsky, let's have a drink."

"No, thank you. Good-by, gentlemen, I'm not drinking today."

"Why not? Afraid of putting on weight? Very well, we'll drink by ourselves. Let's have the soda water and the lemons."

"Vronsky!" shouted someone as Vronsky was already going out into the passage.

"What?"

"You'd better have a haircut. Your hair's too heavy, especially on the bald patch."

Vronsky was really beginning to get prematurely bald. He laughed gaily, showing his row of regular teeth, and drawing his cap over the bald patch, went out and got into the open carriage.

"To the stables!" he said and was about to take out the letters, but he changed his mind, not wishing to be distracted before examining his horse. "Later! . . ."

CHAPTER 21

The temporary stable, a wooden shed, had been erected close to the racecourse, and it was there the mare was to have been brought the day before. He had not yet been to see her. During the last few days he had not exercised her himself, but let the trainer do it, and now he simply did not know what her condition was when she arrived and how she was now. No sooner had he stepped out of the carriage than his groom, having recognized it from a distance, had called out to the trainer. A lean Englishman in top boots and a short jacket, with only a tuft of beard left under his chin, came to meet him with the clumsy gait of a jockey, his elbows turned outward and swaying from side to side.

"Well, how is Frou-Frou?" asked Vronsky in English.

"All right, sir," the Englishman replied from somewhere inside his throat. "Better not go in," he added, touching his cap. "I've put a muzzle on her and the mare's fidgety. Better not go in, it excites the mare."

"I'm going in. I want to have a look at her."

"Come along," the Englishman said, frowning, and as before, without opening his mouth, he led the way, swinging his elbows and walking with his loose gait.

They entered a little yard in front of the shed. The stable lad on duty, a smart, well-dressed boy in a clean jacket, met them with a broom in his hand and followed them. In the shed five horses stood in their separate stalls, and Vronsky knew that his chief rival, Makhotin's sixteen-hand chestnut, Gladiator, must have been brought that day and should be standing there too. Vronsky was eager to see Gladiator, whom he had never seen, even more than his own mare; but he also knew that horse-racing etiquette not only made it impossible for him to see it, but improper for him even to inquire about it. As he was walking along the passage, the stable lad opened the door of the second horse box to the left, and Vronsky caught sight of a big chestnut horse with white legs. He knew that this was Gladiator, but like a man who turns his eyes away from another man's open letter, he turned away and went up to Frou-Frou's box.

"That's the horse of Mak—Mak—I never can pronounce his name," said the Englishman over his shoulder, pointing a big finger with a dirty nail to Gladiator's box.

"Makhotin?" said Vronsky. "Yes, that's my only serious rival."

"If you were riding him, I'd back you," said the Englishman.

"Frou-Frou is more high-spirited and he's the more powerful horse," said Vronsky, smiling at the compliment to his riding.

"In a steeplechase everything depends on the riding and the pluck," said the Englishman.

213

Pluck, that is, energy and courage. Vronsky felt that he had enough and to spare, but what was much more important, he was firmly convinced that no one in the world could have more *pluck* than he had.

"Are you quite sure more exercise was unnecessary?"

"Quite unnecessary, sir," replied the Englishman. "Please, don't talk so loud. The horse is nervous," he added, motioning toward the closed horse box, before which they were standing and from which they could hear the trampling of feet in the straw.

He opened the door, and Vronsky went into the box, which was dimly lit by one small window. In the box stood a dark bay mare with a muzzle on, stepping from foot to foot in the fresh straw. Having got used to the dim light of the box, Vronsky once more mechanically took in at one comprehensive glance all the points of his favorite mare. Frou-Frou was of medium size and by no means faultless. She was small-boned, and though well arched, her chest was narrow. Her hindquarters tapered a little too much, and her legs, especially her hind legs, were perceptibly turned inward. Neither her forelegs nor her hindlegs were particularly muscular, but on the other hand she was quite extraordinarily broad in the girth, which was particularly noticeable now owing to her strict training and the leanness of her belly. Seen from the front, her cannon bones seemed no thicker than a finger, but seen sideways, they looked unusually wide. Except for the ribs, she seemed to be all squeezed in at the sides and drawn out in depth. But she possessed in the highest degree a quality which made one forget all her faults; that quality was *blood*, the sort of blood that *tells*, as the English saying has it. The muscles, clearly showing under the network of sinews, stretched in the fine, mobile skin, smooth as satin, and they seemed as hard as bone. Her lean head with the prominent, bright, sparkling eyes, broadened at the muzzle into protruding nostrils with their inner membrane filled with blood. Her whole figure, and particularly her head, conveyed a definite feeling of energy and at the same time gentleness. She was one of those animals who appear not to speak only because they have not the organs of speech.

To Vronsky at any rate it seemed that she understood all he was feeling while he was looking at her.

214

As soon as Vronsky entered, she drew a deep breath and, rolling her prominent eye sideways till the white became bloodshot, looked from the other side of the box at the newcomers, shaking her muzzle and shifting resiliently from leg to leg.

"There, you see, sir, how nervous she is," said the Englishman.

"Oh, you darling!" said Vronsky, moving up to the horse and soothing her.

But the nearer he came, the more nervous she grew. It was only when he got up to her head that she suddenly calmed down, and the muscles began to quiver under her fine, delicate coat. Vronsky stroked her firm neck, set to rights a lock of mane that strayed to the wrong side of her sharply defined withers, and brought his face close to her dilated nostrils, fine as a bat's wings. Her tense nostrils loudly inhaled and exhaled the air; then, with a shudder, she set back one of her pointed ears and stretched out a firm black lip towards Vronsky, as though wishing to catch hold of his sleeve. But remembering the muzzle, she shook it and once more began stepping from one of her finely-chiseled legs to the other.

"Be quiet, darling, be quiet!" he said, stroking her flank again, and left the box in the happy knowledge that the horse was in the very best condition.

The mare's excitement had communicated itself also to Vronsky; he felt the blood rushing to his heart and that he, too, like the horse, wished to move about and to bite; it was both terrifying and joyful.

"Well, then, I rely on you," he said to the Englishman. "At half past six on the course?"

"All right," replied the Englishman. "But where are you going, my lord?" he asked, quite unexpectedly addressing him as "my lord," which he hardly ever did.

Vronsky raised his head in astonishment and looked, as he knew how to, not into the Englishman's eyes but at his forehead, astounded at the impudence of the question. But realizing that in asking this question the Englishman had regarded him not as an employer, but as a jockey, he replied:

"I have to see Bryansky. I shall be at home in an hour."

"How many times have I been asked that question

today?" he said to himself, and blushed, a thing he rarely did. The Englishman looked at him attentively and, as though he knew where Vronsky was going, added:

"The important thing is to keep calm before a race. Don't be put out or upset by anything."

"All right," replied Vronsky, smiling, and getting into the carriage, he told the coachman to drive to Peterhof.

He had only gone a few yards when the clouds, which had been threatening since morning, broke and there was a downpour of rain.

"That's bad," thought Vronsky, raising the hood of the carriage. "It was muddy before, but now it will be a swamp." Sitting all alone in the carriage, he took out his mother's letter and his brother's note and read them through.

Yes, it was the same thing all over again. All of them, his mother, his brother, all of them considered it necessary to interfere in his private affairs. This interference made him angry, a feeling he rarely experienced. "What business is it of theirs? Why does everybody think it his duty to worry about me? And why do they pester me? Because they see that this is something they cannot understand. If it had been an ordinary, vulgar society liaison, they would have let me alone. They feel it is something different, that it is not just a pastime, that this woman is dearer to me than life. And it is this they cannot understand and that is why they are so annoyed. Whatever our fate is or may be, we have made it and we do not complain of it," he said, associating Anna and himself in the word "we." "No, they have to teach us how to live. They have no idea of what happiness is, they don't understand that without this love there is no happiness nor unhappiness—there is no life for us," he thought.

He was angry with them all for their interference just because at heart he felt that they were right, every one of them. He felt that the love which bound him to Anna was not a momentary infatuation, which would pass as all society liaisons pass, without leaving any trace in the lives of the one or the other, except some pleasant or unpleasant memories. He felt all the torment of his and her position, all the difficulty, exposed as they were to the eyes of the whole of the particular world in which they lived, of concealing their love, of indulging in lies

216

and deception. How could they lie, deceive, scheme, and constantly think of others, when the passion which united them was so powerful that they both forgot everything but their love?

He remembered distinctly the oft-repeated occasions when lies and deceptions, so contrary to his nature, had been necessary; he remembered most distinctly the feeling of shame he had more than once detected in her at this necessity for deception and lying. And he experienced a strange feeling which had sometimes come upon him since his liaison with Anna. It was a feeling of revulsion against something: against Karenin, against himself, against the whole world—he was not sure which. But he always drove away this strange feeling. And now, too, after giving himself a shake, he continued with the trend of his thoughts.

"Yes, she was unhappy before, but proud and calm. Now she cannot be calm and dignified, though she does not show it. Yes, this must stop," he decided.

And for the first time he realized clearly that it was necessary to put an end to all this falsehood, and the sooner the better. "We must throw up everything, both of us, and hide ourselves away somewhere alone with our love," he said to himself.

CHAPTER 22

The rain did not last long and when Vronsky arrived at his destination—with the shaft horse at full trot, pulling the side horses through the mud and galloping without traces—the sun appeared again and the roofs of the summer cottages and the old lime trees in the gardens on both sides of the main street glittered with wet brilliance, and the water dripped merrily from the branches and ran down from the roofs. He was no longer thinking of the shower spoiling the racecourse, but was glad because, thanks to the rain, he was certain to find her at home and alone, for he knew that Karenin, who had recently returned from a spa abroad, had not moved from Petersburg.

Hoping to find her alone, Vronsky, as he always did, to avoid attracting attention, got off before crossing the little bridge and walked to the house. He did not enter it from the front steps in the street, but went through the yard.

"Has your master returned?" he asked a gardener.

"No, sir," said the gardener. "The mistress is at home. But you'd better go in at the front door, sir. The servants are there and they'll open it."

"Never mind. I'll go through the garden."

And having made sure that she was alone and wishing to take her by surprise, as he had not promised to come that day and she would certainly not expect him to come before the races, he went, holding up his sword and stepping cautiously along the sand-strewn, flower-bordered path to the terrace overlooking the garden. Vronsky had not forgotten everything he had thought on the way about the burden and difficulty of his position. All he thought of was that he would see her immediately not merely in his imagination, but alive, all of her, as she was in reality. He was already going in, stepping on the whole of his foot so as not to make a noise, when he suddenly remembered what he was always forgetting and what was the most agonizing side of his relations with her—her son with his questioning and, as it seemed to him, hostile eyes.

The boy, more than anyone else, stood in the way of their relations. When he was present, neither Vronsky nor Anna allowed themselves to speak about anything that they might not have repeated to everyone, and did not even allow themselves to hint at anything the boy would not have understood. They had not come to an arrangement about this; it had come about by itself. They would have considered it an affront to themselves to deceive the child. In his presence they talked like acquaintances. But, in spite of this precaution, Vronsky often noticed the child's attentive and perplexed gaze fixed upon him and the strange timidity and uncertainty—now affectionate, now cold and bashful—of the boy's attitude toward him. It was as though the child felt that between that man and his mother there was some important relationship, the significance of which he could not grasp.

And, indeed, the boy felt that he could not understand this relationship. He tried his utmost but could not make out what sort of feeling he ought to have toward that

218

man. With a child's sensitiveness to what other people felt, he saw clearly that his father, his governess, and his nurse not only disliked Vronsky, but regarded him with fear and revulsion, though they never said anything about him, but that his mother regarded him as her best friend.

"What does it mean? Who is he? How ought one to feel for him? If I don't understand," thought the child, "then it must be my fault, and I am a silly or a bad boy." And that was the reason for his searching, questioning, and to some extent hostile expression, and the timidity and uncertainty which made Vronsky feel so ill at ease. The presence of the child invariably aroused in Vronsky that strange feeling of blind revulsion which he had experienced of late. The presence of the child aroused both in Vronsky and in Anna a feeling such as a sailor might have on seeing by the compass that the direction in which he was swiftly sailing diverged widely from his proper course, but that it was beyond his powers to alter course, and that every moment was taking him further and further astray, and that to admit to himself that he was off course was tantamount to admitting that all was lost.

This child with his naïve outlook on life was the compass which showed them the degree of their divergence from what they knew was right, but did not want to see.

This time Seryozha was not at home, and she was quite alone, sitting on the terrace waiting for the return of her son, who had gone for a walk and been caught in the rain. She had sent a manservant and a maid to look for him, and sat waiting. She wore a white dress with wide embroidery, and was sitting in the corner of the terrace behind some flowers and did not hear him. Bending her dark curly head, she pressed her forehead against a cold watering can that stood on the balustrade, holding onto the can with both her beautiful hands with the rings he knew so well. The beauty of her whole figure, her head, her neck, and her arms took Vronsky every time by surprise. He stopped, gazing at her with admiration. But just as he was going to take a step toward her, she felt his approach, pushed away the watering can, and turned her flushed face toward him.

"What's the matter? Aren't you well?" he said in French as he came up to her.

He wanted to run up to her, but remembering there might be other people about, he looked around at the balcony door and blushed as he always did when he felt that he had reason to be apprehensive and circumspect.

"No, I'm all right," she said, getting up and pressing his outstretched hand firmly. "I did not expect—you."

"Good heavens, what cold hands!" he said.

"You frightened me," she said. "I'm alone and was waiting for Seryozha. He's gone for a walk. They will return this way."

But though she was trying to be calm, her lips trembled.

"Forgive me for coming, but I could not let the day pass without seeing you," he went on, speaking French to her, as he always did, trying to avoid using "you," which sounded impossibly cold in Russian, or the dangerously intimate second person singular.

"What is there to forgive? I'm awfully glad."

"But you're unwell or worried," he went on, without letting go of her hands and bending over her. "What were you thinking about?"

"Always of the same thing," she said with a smile.

She spoke the truth. Whenever, at whatever moment, she was asked what she was thinking about, she could have answered unhesitatingly that she was thinking of one thing only—her happiness and her unhappiness. Just now, when he took her by surprise, she was wondering why for others, Betsy, for instance (whose secret liaison with Tushkevich she knew about), it was all so easy, while for her it was so agonizing. For certain reasons this thought troubled her particularly today. She asked him about the races. He answered her and, seeing that she was agitated, tried to distract her and began telling her in the most matter-of-fact tone all the particulars of the preparations for the races.

"Shall I tell him or not?" she thought, looking at his calm, caressing eyes. "He's so happy, so preoccupied with his races, that he won't understand it properly, won't understand all the significance of that event for us."

"But you haven't told me what you were thinking about when I came in," he said, interrupting his account. "Please tell me!"

She made no answer and, bending her head a little,

220

looked wonderingly and mistrustfully at him, her eyes shining from under their long lashes. Her hand, toying with a leaf she had torn off, trembled. He saw it and his face assumed that look of submissiveness and slavish devotion that so captivated her.

"I can see something has happened. Do you think I can be calm for a moment knowing you have some trouble I am not sharing? Tell me, for God's sake!" he repeated beseechingly.

"I shall never forgive him if he doesn't understand all the significance of it. Better not tell him. Why put him to the test?" she thought, still looking at him in the same way and feeling that her hand with the leaf was shaking more and more.

"For God's sake!" he repeated.

"Shall I?"

"Yes, yes, yes!"

"I'm pregnant," she whispered softly and slowly.

The leaf in her hand trembled more violently, but she did not take her eyes off him, watching to see how he would take it. He turned pale, was about to say something, but stopped short, let go of her hand, and lowered his head. "Yes, he understands the full significance of this event," she thought and pressed his hand gratefully.

But she was wrong in thinking that he understood the significance of the news as she, a woman, understood it. At this news he felt with tenfold force the onrush of that strange feeling of revulsion for someone; but at the same time he realized that the crisis he had wished for had now come, that it was no longer possible to conceal their relationship from her husband, and that it was necessary to put an end to this unnatural situation somehow or other. But, besides this, her agitation communicated itself to him physically. He gave her a tender, submissive look, kissed her hand, got up and silently paced up and down the terrace.

"Yes," he said, coming up to her resolutely. "Neither you nor I regarded our relations as a pastime and now our fate is sealed. We must put an end," he said, looking round, "to the lie which we are living."

"Put an end to it? But how, Alexey?" she said softly. She was calm now and her face shone with a tender smile.

"Leave your husband and unite our lives."

"They are united as it is."

"Yes, but entirely, entirely."

"But how, Alexey? Tell me how," she said, with mournful derision at the hopelessness of her position. "Is there a way out of such a position? Am I not the wife of my husband?"

"There is a way out of every position," he said. "One has to make up one's mind. Anything would be better than the position in which you find yourself now. Don't you think I can see how you torture yourself over everything—society, your son, and your husband?"

"Oh, not over my husband," she said with an unaffected smile. "I don't know him, I don't think about him. He doesn't exist."

"You're not speaking sincerely. I know you. You are tortured over him too."

"Why, he doesn't even know," she said, and suddenly a vivid flush suffused her face. Her cheeks, her forehead, her neck turned red and tears of shame started to her eyes. "And don't let us talk of him."

CHAPTER 23

Vronsky had tried several times, though not as determinedly as now, to get her to discuss her position and each time encountered the same superficiality and lightness of judgment with which she had replied to his challenge. It was as if there were something about it that she could not, or would not, make clear to herself; as if the moment she began to speak about it, she, the real Anna, retreated somewhere inside herself and another woman appeared, a woman he did not know, a stranger, whom he feared and did not love and who rebuffed him. But now he determined to speak his mind.

"Whether he knows or not," said Vronsky in his usual firm and quiet tone, "whether he knows or not, does not concern us. We cannot—you cannot remain like this, especially now."

"What's to be done then, in your opinion?" she asked with the same light irony.

She, who had been so afraid that he might take her

pregnancy too lightly, was now annoyed that he should infer the need for doing something from it.

"Tell him everything and leave him."

"Very well, suppose I do so," she said. "Do you know what the result will be? I can tell you all in advance," she went on, and a malicious light came into her eyes which a moment ago had been so tender. " 'Oh so you love another and have entered into a guilty relationship with him?' " (She was mimicking her husband and put a particular stress on the word "guilty," as he would have done.) " 'I warned you of the consequences from the religious, civil, and family points of view. You have not listened to me. Now I cannot let my name be disgraced . . .' "—she was going to say "and my son," but she could not jest about her son—" 'my name be disgraced' and something more in the same vein," she added. "He will say with his statesmanlike manner, clearly and precisely, that he cannot let me go, but will take all measures in his power to prevent a scandal. And he'll do, quietly and accurately, what he says. That's what will happen. He is not a human being, but a machine, and a spiteful machine when he is angry," she added, calling to mind Karenin with every detail of his figure, his way of speaking, and his character, and making him responsible for everything bad she could find in him, forgiving him nothing because of the terrible thing she had done to him.

"But, Anna," said Vronsky in a persuasive, gentle voice, doing his best to calm her, "he must be told all the same and afterward be guided by what he does."

"Then you think I ought to run away?"

"Why not run away? I can't see how we can possibly carry on like this. And not on my account—I can see you are suffering."

"So you really think I ought to run away and become your mistress, do you?" she said spitefully.

"Anna!" he said with a reproachful tenderness.

"Yes," she repeated, "become your mistress and ruin everything!"

Again she wanted to say "ruin my son," but could not bring herself to utter the words.

Vronsky could not understand how she, with her strong, honest nature, could tolerate this state of deceit and not want to escape from it; but it never occurred to him that the chief cause of it was the word "son," which she could not bring herself to utter. When she thought of her son and his future attitude to the mother who had given up his father, she was so terrified at what she had done, that she no longer reasoned but, like a woman, only tried to reassure herself with false arguments and words in order that everything should remain as before and she could dismiss from her mind the dreadful question of what would happen to her son.

"I ask you, I implore you," she said suddenly in quite a different tone, sincerely and tenderly, taking him by the hand, "never to speak of this again."

"But, Anna—"

"Never. Leave it to me. I know all the degradation, all the horror of my position, but it is not so easy to decide what to do as you think. Leave it to me and do what I say. Never speak to me about it. Promise? No, no, promise!"

"I promise everything, but I cannot help being uneasy, especially after what you have said. I cannot help being uneasy when you are feeling uneasy."

"Me!" she exclaimed. "Yes, I do worry sometimes, but this will pass provided you never speak to me about it. When you speak to me about it, it only makes me unhappy."

"I don't understand," he said.

"I realize," she interrupted him, "how hard it is for your honest nature to lie, and I'm sorry for you. I often think that you've ruined your life for me."

"I was just thinking the same," he said, "wondering how you could sacrifice everything for my sake. I can't forgive myself that you are unhappy."

"Me unhappy?" she said, drawing near to him and gazing at him with a rapturous smile of love. "I am like a hungry man who has been given food. He may be cold, his clothes may be tattered, he may feel ashamed, but he is not unhappy. Me unhappy? No, this is my happiness. . . ."

She heard the voice of her son, who was coming back from his walk, and glancing quickly round the terrace, she rose impulsively. Her eyes lit up with the light he knew so well; she raised her beautiful, beringed hands with a quick movement, took hold of his head, gave him a long look, and, putting her face near his, with parted, smiling lips quickly kissed his mouth and both eyes, and pushed him away. She wanted to go but he kept her back.

"When?" he said in a whisper, gazing rapturously at her.

"Tonight, at one o'clock," she whispered and, with a heavy sigh, went to meet her son with her light, rapid step.

Seryozha had been caught in the rain in the park, and he and his nurse had taken shelter in the pavilion.

"Well, good-by," she said to Vronsky. "It will soon be time to start for the races. Betsy has promised to call for me."

Vronsky looked at his watch and went off quickly.

CHAPTER 24

When Vronsky looked at his watch on the Karenins' balcony he was so greatly disturbed and preoccupied that he saw the hands and the face of the watch, but was unable to realize what time it was. He went out into the road and, stepping carefully over the mud, made his way to his carriage. He was so full of his feeling for Anna that he never thought what o'clock it was and whether he still had time to go and see Bryansky. He only retained, as often happens, an automatic reaction of memory which indicated what he had decided to do next. He went up to his driver, who had dozed off in the already slanting shadow of a thick lime tree, gazed for a moment at the dancing swarms of midges hovering over the perspiring horses, and, having waked the driver, jumped into the carriage and told him to drive to Bryansky's. It was only after he had gone over five miles that he recollected himself sufficiently to look at his watch and to realize that it was half past five and that he was late.

There were to be several races that day; a Life Guards' race, followed by the officers' mile-and-a-half race, a three-mile race, and then the one for which he had entered. He could be in time for his own race, but if he went to see Bryansky, he could only just manage

225

it and he would arrive when the whole Court was already there. That was not the correct thing to do. But he had promised Bryansky to call and he therefore decided to go on, telling the driver not to spare the horses.

He arrived at Bryansky's, spent five minutes with him, and drove back at a gallop. The quick drive calmed him. All that was distressing in his relations with Anna, all the vagueness that remained after their conversation, everything slipped out of his mind. He now thought with enjoyment and excitement of the race, that he would be in time after all, and from time to time the expectation of the happiness that night's meeting would give him flashed dazzlingly across his mind.

He was seized more and more by the excitement of the approaching race as he drove further and further into the atmosphere of the races, overtaking the carriages of the people who were driving to the racecourse from Petersburg and from the surrounding country resorts.

He found no one at his quarters; they had all gone to the races and his valet was waiting for him at the gate. While he was changing, his valet told him that the second race had already started, that many people had been to inquire for him, and that the stable lad had twice run over from the stables.

Having changed without hurry (he never hurried or lost his self-control), Vronsky told his coachman to drive him to the stables. From there he could see a whole sea of carriages, pedestrians, and soldiers, surrounding the racecourse, and the covered stands swarming with people. The second race was most probably on, for as he entered the stable he heard the bell ring. As he approached the stables, he met Makhotin's white-legged chestnut Gladiator, which was being led to the course in a blue-bordered orange horse cloth and with what looked like enormous ears edged with blue.

"Where's Cord?" he asked the stable boy.

"In the stables, saddling."

In the open stall, Frou-Frou stood ready saddled. They were just going to lead her out.

"I am not late?"

"All right! All right!" answered the Englishman. "Don't excite yourself."

226

Vronsky cast another glance at the lovely lines of his favorite mare, who was trembling all over, and tearing himself with difficulty from this sight, went out of the stable. He walked towards the stand at the most favorable moment to avoid attracting anyone's attention. The mile-and-a-half was practically over and all eyes were fixed on the officer of the horse guards in front and on a hussar officer behind, who were urging on their horses and approaching the winning post. From inside and outside the ring everyone was crowding toward the winning post, and a group of the horse guards—officers and men—were expressing with loud shouts their joy at the expected triumph of their officer and comrade. Vronsky got in unnoticed to the middle of the crowd almost at the very moment the bell rang to announce the end of the race and the tall, mud-bespattered horse-guards officer, who had come in first, was bending down in the saddle and letting go the reins of his gray stallion, which was dark with sweat and panting heavily.

The stallion, putting his feet down with an effort, slowed down the speed of his enormous body, and the horse-guards officer, like a man waking from a heavy sleep, looked round and forced himself to smile. A crowd of friends and strangers surrounded him.

Vronsky deliberately avoided the select, fashionable crowd which moved and chatted freely, though with restraint, in front of the stands. He knew that Anna, Betsy, and his sister-in-law were there, but to avoid distracting himself he purposely did not go near them. But he continually met acquaintances who stopped him, told him about the races, and asked him why he was so late.

When the winners were called up to the grandstand to receive their prizes, Vronsky's elder brother, Alexander, a colonel with shoulder knots, of medium height, as thickset as Alexey, but handsomer and ruddier, with a red nose and a drunken, open face, came up to him.

"Did you get my note?" he asked. "One can never find you."

Alexander Vronsky, in spite of his dissipated and, in particular, drunken life, for which he was notorious, was a perfect courtier.

Now, while talking to his brother about a matter extremely disagreeable to him, knowing that many eyes might be fixed on them, he wore a smiling expression, as if he were joking with his brother about something of little importance.

"I did," said Alexey, "but I really don't understand what *you* are so worried about."

"What I'm worried about is that people have just re- marked to me that you were not here and that you were seen in Peterhof on Monday."

"There are things which only concern those who are directly interested, and the matter you are so worried about—"

"Yes, but in that case one should resign from the army, or—"

"I ask you not to interfere—that's all."

Alexey Vronsky's frowning face turned pale and his protruding lower jaw twitched, which did not often hap- pen to him. Being a kindhearted man, he very rarely got angry, but when he did and when his chin twitched, then he was dangerous, as Alexander Vronsky knew. Alexan- der Vronsky smiled gaily.

"I only wanted to deliver Mother's letter. Answer her and don't upset yourself before the race. *Bonne chance*," he added with a smile and went off.

But after he had gone, another friendly greeting stopped Vronsky.

"So you don't want to know your friends, do you? How are you, *mon cher?*" Oblonsky said, here, amid all the Petersburg magnificence, no less than in Moscow, shining with his rosy face and glistening, well-combed whiskers. "I arrived yesterday and I'm very glad I shall witness your triumph. When shall we meet?"

"Come to the mess tomorrow," said Vronsky, and apologetically pressing the sleeve of Oblonsky's over- coat, moved off to the center of the racecourse, where the horses were already led out for the steeplechase.

The sweat-covered, exhausted horses which had run in the last race were being led away by their grooms, and one after another the fresh ones were appearing for the next race, most of them English horses, which in their hooded cloths and their tightly girthed stomachs looked like some strange, enormous birds. On the right the lean and beautiful Frou-Frou was being led up and down, stepping as on springs on her elastic and rather long pasterns. Not far from her they were taking the horse cloth off the lop-eared Gladiator. The big, exquisite, perfectly regular lines of the stallion with his wonderful hindquarters and quite extraordinarily short pasterns just over the hoofs, involuntarily arrested Vronsky's attention. He was about to go up to his horse, but he was again stopped by an acquaintance.

"Ah, there's Karenin," said the acquaintance with whom he was chatting. "He's looking for his wife, and she's in the center of the pavilion. You haven't seen her, have you?"

"No, I haven't," replied Vronsky, and without even glancing at the pavilion, where his friend was pointing Anna out to him, went up to his horse.

Vronsky had just managed to examine the saddle, which had to be seen to, when the competitors were summoned to the pavilion to draw their numbers and places. With serious, stern, and in many cases pale faces, seventeen officers assembled in the pavilion and drew their numbers. Vronsky got number seven. The order was given: "Mount!"

Feeling that together with the other riders he was the center upon which all eyes were fixed, Vronsky went up to his horse in the highly strung state in which his movement usually became calm and deliberate. In honor of the races, Cord had put on his best clothes: a black, buttoned-up coat; a stiffly starched collar, pressing hard against his cheeks; a black bowler hat; and top boots. He looked calm and grave as usual and, standing in front of the mare, was himself holding both her reins. Frou-Frou continued to tremble as though in a fever. Her fiery eye glanced sideways at the approaching Vronsky. Vronsky slipped a finger under the saddle girth. The mare turned her eyes a little more, bared her teeth, and put back her ears. The Englishman creased his lips, wishing to convey by a smile his surprise that anyone should go to the trouble of testing his saddling.

"You'd better mount, sir. You won't feel so nervous."

Vronsky cast a last glance at his rivals. He knew that he would not see them again during the race. Two were already riding towards the starting point. Galtsin, one of his dangerous rivals and a friend of Vronsky's, was struggling with a bay horse which would not let him mount. A short hussar in tight riding breeches was galloping along, crouching on his horse like a cat in his desire to imitate an English jockey. Prince Kuzovlyov sat pale-faced on his thoroughbred mare from the Grabovsky stud, while an English groom led her by the saddle. Vronsky and all his best friends knew Kuzovlyov and his peculiarity of "weak" nerves and his terrible vanity. They knew he was afraid of everything, that he was afraid of riding an ordinary trooper's horse; but now, just because it was so terrifying, just because people broke their necks, and there was a doctor standing at each obstacle, and an ambulance with a red cross and a hospital nurse, he had made up his mind to take part in the race. Their eyes met and Vronsky gave him a friendly and encouraging wink. The only one he did not see was his chief rival Makhotin on Gladiator.

"Don't be in a hurry, sir," Cord said to Vronsky. "And remember one thing: do not hold her back at the obstacles and don't urge her on. Let her do as she likes."

"Very well, very well," said Vronsky, taking the reins.

"Take the lead if you can, sir. But don't despair till the last minute, sir, even if you are behind."

Before the mare had time to stir, Vronsky with a powerful, lithe movement put his foot into the notched steel stirrup and placed his well-knit, wiry body tightly and firmly on the creaking leather of the saddle. Having got his right foot too into the stirrup, he straightened out the double reins between his fingers with a practiced movement, and Cord let go. As though not knowing which foot to put forward first, Frou-Frou, stretching the reins with her long neck, started, as if on springs, slightly rocking her rider on her supple back. Cord quickened his step and followed them. The restive mare, trying to deceive her rider, pulled at the reins, now to one side, now to the other, and Vronsky tried in vain by voice and hand to soothe her.

They were already approaching the dammed-up stream on their way to the starting point. Several of the riders were in front and several behind, when suddenly Vronsky heard the sound of a horse galloping through the mud behind him and he was overtaken by Makhotin on his white-legged, lop-eared Gladiator. Makhotin smiled, showing his long teeth, but Vronsky looked at him angrily. He had always disliked him and considered him now as his most dangerous rival. He was annoyed with him for galloping past and exciting his mare. Frou-

230

Frou kicked up her left leg and broke into a canter. She gave two leaps and, angered by the tightened reins, changed into a jerky trot, jolting her rider. Cord, too, frowned and followed Vronsky at a run.

CHAPTER 25

There were altogether seventeen officers taking part in the steeplechase. It was to take place over a large three-mile elliptical course in front of the grandstand. There were nine obstacles on that course: the brook; a barrier nearly five feet high in front of the grandstand; a dry ditch; a water jump; a hillside; an Irish bank (one of the most difficult obstacles), consisting of a bank with brushwood on top and a ditch on the other side which the horse could not see, so that it had to clear both obstacles or come to grief; then two more water jumps and one dry ditch. The winning post was opposite the grandstand. But the start was not in the elliptical course proper, but about two hundred and fifty yards to one side of it; and the first obstacle, the dammed-up brook seven feet wide, was there. The riders could either ford or jump it at their own discretion.

Three times the riders lined up, but each time someone's horse got out of line, and they had to line up again. The expert starter, Colonel Sestrin, was beginning to lose his temper, when at last, at the fourth try, he shouted, "Go!" and the race began.

All eyes, all field glasses were turned on the motley group of riders while they were getting into line.

"They're off! They're off!" was heard on all sides after the hush of expectation.

And small groups of people as well as single individuals began running from place to place to get a better view. In the first minute the field spread out and could be seen approaching the brook in twos and threes and one behind another. It had looked to the spectators as though they had all started together, but for the riders there was a difference of seconds which was of great importance to them.

The excited and over-nervous Frou-Frou was left behind in the first moment and several horses started ahead of her, but even before reaching the brook, Vronsky, who was holding back the mare, tugging at the reins with all his might, easily overtook three riders, and in front of him there was only Makhotin's chestnut Gladiator, whose hindquarters moved lightly and regularly just in front of him, and, in front of them all, the exquisite Diana, carrying Kuzovlyov, who was more dead than alive.

In the first moments of the race Vronsky had no control either of himself or of his mare. Up to the first obstacle, the brook, he could not direct her movements.

Gladiator and Diana approached the stream together and almost at one and the same moment; within less than a second they rose above it and flew across to the other side; lightly, as if on wings, Frou-Frou rose up behind them, but at the very moment that Vronsky felt himself in the air, he suddenly saw, almost under his mare's feet, Kuzovlyov, who was floundering with Diana on the other side of the stream (Kuzovlyov had let go of the reins after the jump and the horse fell, sending him flying over her head). These details Vronsky learned later, now he only saw that right under him, where Frou-Frou had to alight, Diana's legs or head might be in the way. But Frou-Frou, like a falling cat, made an effort with her legs and back while still in the air and, clearing the other horse, raced on.

"Oh, the darling!" thought Vronsky.

After the stream Vronsky regained full control over his horse and began holding her in, intending to cross the big barrier behind Makhotin and try to overtake him only on the flat five hundred yards before the next obstacle.

The big barrier was right in front of the imperial pavilion. The emperor, the whole court, and crowds of people were all looking at them, at him and at Makhotin, who was a full length ahead of him, when they approached the Devil (as the dense barrier was called). Vronsky felt these eyes directed on him from all sides, but he saw nothing except the ears and neck of his mare, the ground racing towards him and Gladiator's hindquarters and white legs rapidly beating time before him and keeping always the same distance ahead. Gladiator rose in the air without touching anything, swished his short tail, and disappeared from Vronsky's view.

"Bravo!" shouted someone's single voice.

At the same moment the planks of the barrier flashed before Vronsky himself, before his very eyes. Without the slightest change of movement, the mare rose under him; the planks disappeared and only behind him was there the sound of a knock. Excited by Gladiator racing in front of her, the mare had risen a little too soon at the barrier and had knocked against it with her hind hoof. But her pace did not change and Vronsky, hit in the face by a lump of mud, realized that he was again at the same distance behind Gladiator. He again saw in front of him Gladiator's hindquarters, short tail, and, once more always at the same distance, his rapidly moving white legs.

At the very moment that Vronsky was thinking that it was time to pass Makhotin, Frou-Frou, already understanding what was in his mind, without any urging, considerably increased her speed and began drawing near to Makhotin on the most advantageous side, the side of the rope. Makhotin, however, would not let him pass that way, and no sooner had Vronsky considered the possibility of overtaking him on the outside than Frou-Frou changed course and began doing just that. Frou-Frou's shoulder, which was already beginning to grow dark with sweat, drew level with Gladiator's hindquarters. They ran side by side for a few lengths. But before the obstacle they were approaching, Vronsky, not wishing to have to go round in a wide circle, started working at the reins, and rapidly overtook Makhotin on the hillside. He caught a glimpse of his mud-bespattered face and even thought he saw him smile. Vronsky passed Makhotin, but he felt that he was close behind him, and he kept hearing behind his very back the regular gallop of Gladiator's feet and the abrupt, still quite fresh, breathing of his nostrils.

The next two obstacles, a ditch and a fence, were taken easily, but Vronsky heard Gladiator's gallop and snorting closer. He urged on his mare and felt with joy that she had increased her speed easily, and he heard the sound of Gladiator's hoofs again at the same distance as before.

Vronsky now had the lead, as he had wished and as Cord had advised, and now he was confident of success. His excitement, his joy, and his tenderness for Frou-Frou

233

grew stronger and stronger. He felt like glancing round and he dared not do so, and he tried to keep calm and not urge his mare so as to let her retain the same reserve of strength as he felt Gladiator still had. There remained only one more obstacle, the most difficult one; if he cleared it in front of everybody else, he would come in first. He was galloping up to the Irish bank. He and Frou-Frou saw the bank from a distance and both of them, the man and the mare, were for a moment seized with doubt. He noticed the mare's hesitation by her ears and raised his crop, but he felt at once that his doubt was unfounded: the mare knew what she had to do. She increased her speed and calmly, as he had anticipated, reared and, giving herself a push from the ground, surrendered herself to the impetus of her leap, which carried her far beyond the ditch. Then, at the same speed, without effort and without changing feet, Frou-Frou continued her gallop.

"Bravo, Vronsky!" he heard the voices of a small group of people—he knew they were his fellow officers and friends—who were standing by the obstacle; he could not help recognizing Yashvin's voice, though he did not see him.

"Oh, my beauty!" he thought, addressing Frou-Frou and listening to what was happening behind. "He's over!" he thought, hearing behind him Gladiator's gallop. There remained only the last water jump of a yard and a half across. Vronsky did not even look at it, but wishing to get in first by several lengths, began working at the reins with a circular movement, raising and lowering his mare's head in rhythm with her stride. He felt that his mare was using her last reserve of strength; not only were her neck and shoulders wet, but on her withers, her head, her pointed ears the sweat stood in beads, and her breath came in short, abrupt gasps. But he knew that her reserve of strength was more than enough for the remaining five hundred-odd yards. Only because he felt that he was nearer to the ground and by the special smoothness of her movement did Vronsky know how much his mare had increased her speed. She flew over the ditch as though she did not notice it. She flew over it like a bird; but at that very moment Vronsky to his horror felt that, unable to keep up with his mare's pace, he had for some inexplicable reason made the bad, unpardonable mistake of dropping into the saddle. His position had suddenly shifted and he realized that something terrible had happened. Before he was aware of what exactly had happened, the white legs of the chestnut horse flashed by him and Makhotin passed at a rapid gallop. Vronsky was touching the ground with one foot and his mare was falling heavily on that foot. He had scarcely time to free his leg before Frou-Frou fell on one side; gasping painfully and making vain efforts with her delicate, sweat-covered neck to rise, she began quivering on the ground at his feet like a wounded bird. Vronsky's awkward movement had broken her back. But this he only understood much later. Now he only saw that Makhotin was rapidly disappearing, while he stood staggering alone on the muddy, immobile ground, and before him Frou-Frou lay breathing heavily and, bending her head toward him, gazed at him with her beautiful eyes. Still not understanding what had happened, Vronsky was pulling the mare by the reins. The mare again began to struggle like a fish, creaking with the flaps of the saddle, and got her front legs free, but, unable to lift her hindquarters, at once began to struggle and again fell on her side. His face distorted with passion, pale, and with his lower jaw trembling, he kicked her in the belly and once more began pulling at the reins. But she did not move and, nuzzling the ground, only gazed at her master with eloquent eyes.

"Oh-h-h!" Vronsky groaned, clutching at his head. "Oh, what have I done!" he cried. "The race lost! And it was my own shameful, unforgivable fault! And this dear, unhappy mare ruined! Oh, what have I done!"

People, a doctor, a male nurse, and officers of his regiment, ran toward him. To his misfortune, he felt he was sound and unhurt. The mare had broken her back and it was decided to shoot her. Vronsky was not able to reply to questions; he could not bring himself to talk to anyone. He turned away and, without picking up the cap that had fallen from his head, walked away from the racecourse without knowing where he was going. He felt miserable. For the first time in his life he experienced the worst kind of misfortune, a misfortune that was irretrievable and for which he was himself responsible.

Yashvin overtook him with his cap and escorted him

home, and half an hour later Vronsky came to himself. But the memory of that steeplechase for a long time remained in his heart the most painful and most galling memory of his life.

Chapter 26

Outwardly Alexey Karenin's relations with his wife remained the same. The only difference was that he was even more busy than before. As in former years, he went with the beginning of spring abroad to a spa for his health, which each year suffered from the heavy strain of the previous winter's work. And as usual he returned in July and at once took up his customary work with increased energy. As usual, too, his wife had moved to the summer residence in the country while he remained in Petersburg.

Since their conversation on the night after the Princess Tverskoy's party, he had never spoken to Anna about his suspicions and jealousy, and that habitual tone of his, as if he were acting someone, was perfectly suited to his present relations with his wife. He was rather colder toward her. He merely seemed to be a little displeased with her for that first night's talk which she had evaded. In his attitude toward her there was a shade of vexation, but nothing more. "You did not wish to have a frank talk with me," he seemed to say, mentally addressing her. "So much the worse for you. Now you will be asking me to talk frankly to you, but *I* shall refuse to do so. So much the worse for you," he thought, like a man who having vainly tried to put out a fire might be angry with his own vain exertions and say to it: "Serves you right! You'll burn out for it!"

He who was so intelligent and shrewd in the affairs of state did not realize the insanity of such an attitude to his wife. He did not realize it because he found it too terrible to realize his real position, and he had locked and bolted that compartment of his heart which contained his feelings for his family, that is, his wife and son. He who was such a conscientious father, had since the end of that winter become particularly cold toward his son and had the same bantering attitude to him as to his wife. "Ah, young man!" was how he addressed him.

Karenin thought and said that in no previous year had he had so much official business as this year; but he was not conscious of the fact that this year he invented work for himself, that this was one of the ways of not opening the compartment where lay his feelings for his wife and son as well as his thoughts about them, which became more terrible the longer they lay there. If anyone had taken upon himself to ask Karenin what he thought of his wife's conduct, the mild and meek Karenin would have made no answer, but would have been very angry with the man who asked this question. That was why there was something stern and proud in the expression of Karenin's face whenever anyone inquired after his wife's health. Karenin simply did not wish to think about his wife's conduct and feelings and, in fact, he just did not think about them.

Karenin's permanent summer residence was in Peterhof and generally the Countess Lydia Ivanovna spent the summer there in a nearby cottage and was in constant touch with Anna. This year the Countess Lydia Ivanovna refused to live in Peterhof, did not once call on Anna, and hinted to Karenin at the impropriety of Anna's intimacy with Betsy and Vronsky. Karenin stopped her severely, expressing the opinion that his wife was above suspicion and from that time began to avoid the countess. He did not see and did not want to see that many people in society already looked askance at his wife; he did not understand and did not want to understand why his wife so particularly insisted on moving to Tsarskoye Selo, where Betsy lived and which was not far from Vronsky's camp. He did not permit himself to think about it, and he did not think about it; but at the same time deep inside him, though he never admitted it to himself nor had any proof or suspicions of it, he knew for certain that he was a wronged husband, and that made him terribly unhappy.

How many times during the eight years of happy married life, looking at other men's unfaithful wives or a deceived husband, had Karenin said to himself: "How could they let it come to that? How is it they don't put an end to such a hideous situation?" But now that the misfortune had fallen on his own head, he not only did not think of how to end it, but refused to recognize it at all; he refused to recognize it just because it was too terrible, too unnatural.

Since his return from abroad Karenin had been twice to their country cottage. Once he dined there and the other time he spent the evening with some visitors, but he had never stayed the night, as he used to do in former years.

The day of the races was a very busy one for Karenin; but in the morning when he drew up his timetable for the day he decided that immediately after an early dinner he would join his wife at the country cottage and then go to the races, at which the whole Court would be present and at which he too ought to put in an appearance. He would go to see his wife because he made up his mind to visit her once a week to keep up appearances. Besides, he had to give her money that day for her housekeeping expenses, which, according to established order, he did every fifteenth of the month.

With his usual control over his thoughts, having considered it all about his wife, he did not allow them to stray further about anything that concerned her.

Karenin had a very busy morning. The day before, the Countess Lydia Ivanovna had sent him a pamphlet by a famous traveler in China, who was now in Moscow, with a letter asking him to receive the traveler himself, a man who was for various reasons very interesting and important. Karenin had not had time to read the pamphlet through in the evening, and he did so next morning. Then he received people with petitions, heard reports, saw different persons by appointment, assigned posts, ordered dismissals, allotted rewards, pensions, salaries, attended to correspondence—the routine business, as Karenin called it, which took up so much of his time. After that came business of his own, a visit from his doctor and one from his estate steward. The steward did not take up much of his time. He only handed Karenin the money and gave a brief account of the state of his affairs, which was not particularly good, for as it happened much more had been spent that year because they had been away from home a good deal, and there was a deficit. But the doctor, a celebrated Petersburg doctor, who was on friendly terms with Karenin, took up a great

238

deal of time. Karenin had not even expected him that day and was surprised to see him, and still more so when the doctor questioned him very closely about his state of health, sounded his chest, and tapped and felt his liver. Karenin did not know that his friend Lydia Ivanovna, noticing that he was not in his usual good health that year, had asked the doctor to go and see him. "Do it for my sake," the Countess Lydia Ivanovna had said.

"I will do it for the sake of Russia, Countess," the doctor had replied.

"An invaluable man," said the Countess Lydia Ivanovna.

The doctor was very dissatisfied with Karenin. He found the liver considerably enlarged, signs of undernourishment, and no beneficial effect whatever from the water cure he had undergone. He prescribed as much physical exercise and as little mental strain as possible and, above all, no worries, which for Karenin was as impossible as not to breathe, and he went away, leaving Karenin with the disagreeable feeling that something was wrong with him and that nothing could be done about it.

On his way out the doctor ran across Slyndin, Karenin's private secretary and an old acquaintance of his. They had been at the university together and, though they very seldom met, they respected one another and were good friends, and that was why Slyndin was the only person to whom the doctor would have expressed his honest opinion about the patient.

"I'm so glad you've been to see him," said Slyndin. "He's not so well and I believe—er—well, what do you think?"

"What I think is this," said the doctor, waving over Slyndin's head to his driver to bring the carriage round. "It's this," said the doctor, taking a finger of his kid glove in his white hand and pulling it. "If you don't stretch a violin string taut, you will find it very difficult to break it, but strain it to the utmost and it will break under the pressure of your finger. And he, with his assiduity and conscientiousness, is strained to the utmost, and there is a pressure from outside, and a heavy one," concluded the doctor, raising his eyebrows significantly. "Will you be at the races?" he asked, as he walked down the front steps to his carriage. "Yes, yes, of course, it takes a long time," replied the doctor to some remark of Slyndin's which he had not quite caught.

After the doctor, who had taken up so much time, came the famous traveler, and Karenin, thanks to the pamphlet he had just read and his previous knowledge of the subject, astonished the traveler by the depth of his knowledge and the breadth of his enlightened views.

At the same time as the traveler, a provincial marshal of nobility, with whom Karenin had to discuss certain matters, was announced. When he, too, had left he had to finish some routine business with the secretary and he had further to call on a certain important personage to discuss some grave and important affair. Karenin only managed to get back at five, his dinnertime, and having dined with his private secretary, he invited him to drive with him to his country cottage and go to the races.

Without acknowledging it to himself, Karenin now looked for an opportunity of having a third person present at his meetings with his wife.

CHAPTER 27

Anna was upstairs, standing in front of a looking glass, pinning with Annushka's help the last bow to her dress, when she heard the wheels of a carriage grating on the gravel at the front door.

"It's too early for Betsy," she thought and, looking out of the window, saw the carriage and poking out of it a black hat and Karenin's all too familiar ears. "What a nuisance! He isn't going to stay the night, is he?" she thought, and the consequence of what might result from his stay appeared so awful and terrible to her that, without a moment's hesitation, she went to meet them with a gay and beaming face; and feeling within herself the presence of the familiar spirit of falsehood and deceit, she immediately gave herself up to it and began speaking without knowing herself what she was going to say.

"Oh, this is nice!" she said, giving her hand to her husband and greeting Slyndin, practically a member of the family, with a smile. "You're staying the night, I hope?" were the first words the spirit of deceit prompted her to say. "And now we can go together. It's a pity I promised to go with Betsy, though. She'll be coming for me."

Karenin frowned slightly at the mention of Betsy's name.

"Oh, I'm not going to separate the inseparables," he said in his usual bantering tone of voice. "Slyndin and I will go together. The doctors have ordered me to walk. I'll walk part of the way and imagine that I'm still at the spa."

"There is no hurry," said Anna. "Would you like some tea?"

She rang.

"Tea, please, and tell Seryozha that his father is here. Well, and how are you? I don't think you've been here before," she went on, addressing Slyndin. "Look how lovely it is out on my terrace."

She spoke very simply and naturally, but too much and too fast. She felt it herself, particularly as she noticed by the inquisitive way in which Slyndin looked at her that he seemed to be watching her.

Slyndin at once went out on the terrace.

She sat down beside her husband.

"You don't look very well," she said.

"I'm afraid I don't," he replied. "The doctor came to see me today and wasted an hour of my time. I can't help thinking that one of our friends must have sent him: so precious is my health. . . ."

"But what did he say?"

She asked him about his health and what he had been doing and tried to persuade him to take a rest and come and stay with her in the country.

She said it all gaily, rapidly, and with a peculiar brilliance in her eyes; but Karenin did not now attach any importance to this tone of hers. He only heard her words and gave them only their literal meaning. And he answered her simply, though jokingly. There was nothing special in this conversation, but Anna could never afterward recall that brief scene without a profound feeling of shame.

Seryozha came in, preceded by his governess. If Karenin had taken the trouble to observe what was happening around him, he would have noticed the timid, perplexed look which the child cast first at his father and then at his mother. But he did not want to, and he did not see anything.

"Ah, young man! He's grown. He's really getting quite a man. How do you do, young man?"

And he held out his hand to the frightened boy.

Seryozha, who had always been timid with his father, now, ever since Karenin began calling him "young man" and since he had begun to wonder whether Vronsky was a friend or an enemy, shunned him. He looked round at his mother, as if asking for protection. He only felt happy with his mother. Meanwhile Karenin, while talking to the governess, was holding onto his son's shoulder, and Seryozha felt so painfully uncomfortable that Anna saw that he was on the verge of tears.

Anna, who had blushed when her son came in, noticing that Seryozha was distressed, got up quickly, lifted Karenin's hand from her son's shoulder, and kissing the boy, led him out onto the terrace and returned at once.

"Well, it's time we were going," she said, glancing at her watch. "Why isn't Betsy here, I wonder."

"Oh yes," said Karenin and, getting up, clasped his hands and cracked his fingers, "I also came to bring you some money, since, as the Russian proverb has it, nightingales are not fed on fables," he said. "I expect you must know it."

"No, I don't. . . . Yes, I do," she said, not looking at him and blushing to the roots of her hair. "But I suppose you'll be coming back here after the races."

"Yes, of course," answered Karenin. "And here's the ornament of Peterhof, Princess Tverskoy," he added, looking out of the window at the approaching carriage of English make, drawn by horses with blinkers and with a tiny lady placed very high. "What elegance! Charming. Well, I suppose we'd better be off too."

Princess Tverskoy did not get out of her carriage; only her footman, in his black hat, cape, and gaiters, jumped down at the front door.

"I'm going, good-by," said Anna, and giving her son a kiss, she went up to Karenin and held out her hand to him. "It was very nice of you to come."

Karenin kissed her hand.

"Well, good-by, then. Come and have tea. Splendid!"

she said and went out, gay and radiant. But as soon as she no longer saw him, she became conscious of the place on her hand his lips had touched and she gave a shudder of revulsion.

Chapter 28

When Karenin arrived at the racecourse, Anna was already sitting beside Betsy in the grandstand where all the highest society had assembled. She caught sight of her husband when he was still far off. Two men, her husband and her lover, were the two centers of her life, and without the aid of her external senses she was aware of their presence. She was conscious of the approach of her husband when he was still a long way off, and could not help following him with her eyes in the surging crowds through which he was making his way. She saw him approaching the grandstand, now condescendingly replying to obsequious bows, now exchanging friendly greetings with his equals, now sedulously trying to catch the eye of the great ones of this world and raising his big, round hat that pressed on the tips of his ears. She knew all those ways of his and she thought them all disgusting. "Nothing but ambition, nothing but the desire to get on—that's all he cares about," she thought, "and those high ideals of his, love of enlightenment, religions, these are only means to an end."

She guessed from the glances he cast at the ladies' pavilion (he was staring straight at her, but he did not recognize her in the sea of muslin, ribbons, feathers, parasols, and flowers) that he was trying to find her, but she pretended not to notice him.

"Mr. Karenin," the Princess Betsy called to him, "I'm sure you don't see your wife—here she is!"

He smiled his frigid smile.

"There's so much splendor here that one's eyes are dazzled," he said and approached the stand.

He smiled at his wife as a husband should smile when meeting the wife he had met only a short while ago, and exchanged greetings with the princess and other acquaintances, giving to each what was due, that is, exchanging pleasantries with the ladies and greetings with the gentlemen. Below, at the foot of the stand, stood an adjutant-general, highly respected by Karenin and noted for his intellect and wide education. Karenin entered into conversation with him.

There was an interval between two races and so nothing interfered with their conversation. The adjutant-general disapproved of racing. Karenin replied, defending it. Anna listened to his high-pitched, smooth voice, without missing a single word, and every word seemed false to her and grated painfully on her ear.

When the three-mile steeplechase was about to begin she leaned forward and did not take her eyes off Vronsky while he went up to his horse and mounted it, and at the same time she heard the repulsive, never-ceasing voice of her husband. She was tormented by anxiety for Vronsky, but a still greater torment to her was what seemed to be the incessant flow of her husband's high-pitched voice with its familiar intonations.

"I'm a bad woman, a lost woman," she thought, "but I dislike lies, I can't stand lies, while *he* (her husband) thrives on them. He knows everything, he sees everything; what then does he feel if he can talk so calmly? If he were to kill me, if he were to kill Vronsky, I should respect him. But no. All he cares about is lies and keeping up appearances," Anna said to herself, without considering what exactly she wanted of her husband or what she would have liked him to be. Nor did she realize that Karenin's peculiar loquaciousness that day, which so exasperated her, was merely an expression of his inner anxiety and uneasiness. As a child who has been hurt jumps about to bring his muscles into motion and deaden his pain, so Karenin needed mental activity to suppress the thoughts of his wife, which in her presence and in the presence of Vronsky and at the constant repetition of his name forced themselves upon his attention. And as it was natural for a child to jump about, so it was natural for him to talk well and cleverly. He said:

"The danger in military, that is, cavalry steeplechases is a necessary concomitant of racing. If England can point to the most brilliant cavalry charges in military history, it is only because she has historically developed this capacity in her men and horses. Sport in my opinion

244

has great value, and, as usual, we only see what is its most superficial aspect."

"Not quite superficial," observed Princess Tverskoy. "I'm told one of the officers has broken two ribs."

Karenin smiled his usual smile, which showed his teeth but expressed nothing.

"Let us assume, Princess," he said, "that it is not quite superficial, not so much external but internal. But that is not the point," and he turned again to the general with whom he was talking seriously. "Don't forget that it is military men who are racing and who have chosen that career, and you must admit that every calling has a reverse side to its medal. This is part of their military duty. The disgraceful sport of prize fighting or bull-fighting is a sign of barbarism. But specialized sport is a sign of progress."

"No, I shan't come again," said Princess Betsy. "It excites me too much. Don't you think so, Anna?"

"It is exciting," said another lady, "but one cannot tear oneself away. If I'd been a Roman, I should never have missed a single circus."

Anna said nothing. She looked steadily at the same spot without putting down her binoculars.

At that moment a highly placed general made his way through the grandstand. Interrupting his speech, Karenin hurriedly, but with dignity, got up and bowed low to the general as he passed.

"Aren't you racing?" joked the general.

"My race is a harder one," Karenin replied respectfully.

But though the answer did not mean anything, the general looked as though he had heard a clever reply from a clever man and fully appreciated *la pointe de la sauce.*

"There are two sides to it," continued Karenin, "that of the performers and that of the spectators. The love of such spectacles, I quite agree, is a sure sign of low development in the spectators, but—"

"Princess, a wager!" came the voice of Oblonsky from below, addressing Betsy. "Who are you backing?"

"Anna and I are betting on Prince Kuzovlyov," replied Betsy.

"I'm for Vronsky. A pair of gloves."

"It's a bet."

245

"And what a pretty scene, isn't it?"

Karenin was silent while the others were talking near him, but went on again immediately.

"I agree, but manly sports . . ."

But at that moment the race started and all conversation ceased. Karenin, too, fell silent, and everybody stood up and turned toward the brook. Karenin was not interested in the race and therefore did not watch the riders, but began absently looking at the spectators with his tired eyes. His eyes rested on Anna.

Her face was pale and stern. She quite obviously saw nothing and nobody except one man. Her hand convulsively clasped her face, and she held her breath. He looked at her and hurriedly turned away, scrutinizing other faces.

"Yes, that woman too, and those others, are very excited: it's very natural," Karenin said to himself. He tried not to look at her, but his eyes were involuntarily drawn to her. He again looked intently at her face, trying not to read what was so plainly written on it, but against his own will he read on it with horror what he did not want to know.

The first fall—Kuzovlyov's at the stream—excited everyone, but Karenin saw plainly on Anna's pale, triumphant face that the man she was watching had not fallen. When, after Makhotin and Vronsky had jumped the big barrier, the officer following them fell on his head and lay unconscious on the ground and a murmur of horror ran through the whole crowd, Karenin saw that Anna did not even notice it and with difficulty understood what the people around her were talking about. But he looked at her more and more often and with greater persistence. Anna, wholly absorbed by the sight of the galloping Vronsky, felt her husband's cold eyes fixed upon her from one side.

She looked around for an instant, gave him a questioning look, and frowning slightly, turned away again.

"Oh, I don't care!" she seemed to say to him, and never once looked at him again.

The steeplechase was unlucky: more than half of the field of seventeen were thrown and hurt. By the end of the race everyone was in a state of perturbation, which was increased by the fact that the emperor was displeased.

CHAPTER 29

Everyone was loudly expressing disapproval and everyone was repeating a phrase someone had uttered: "All we want now are gladiators and lions." Everyone was feeling horrified, so that when Vronsky fell and Anna uttered a loud gasp, there was nothing extraordinary about it. But immediately after a change came over Anna's face which was positively indecent. She completely lost her head. She began to flutter like a captured bird: now getting up to rush off somewhere, now turning to Betsy.

"Let's go, let's go!" she kept saying.

But Betsy did not hear her. She was leaning over and talking to a general who had come up to her.

Karenin went up to Anna and courteously offered her his arm.

"Let us go if you wish," he said in French.

But Anna was listening to what the general was saying, and did not notice her husband.

"He, too, has broken a leg, they say," said the general. "This is unheard of!"

Without replying to her husband, Anna raised her binoculars and looked at the place where Vronsky had fallen; but it was so far off and so many people had crowded there that it was impossible to make anything out. She put down her glasses and was about to go; but at that moment an officer galloped up and was reporting something to the emperor. Anna leaned forward to listen.

"Stiva! Stiva!" she called to her brother.

But her brother did not hear her. She was again about to go.

"I again offer you my arm if you wish to go," said Karenin, touching her arm.

She recoiled from him with a look of revulsion and, without looking at him, replied:

"No, no, leave me alone! I'm staying!"

She now saw an officer running to the grandstand from the place where Vronsky had fallen. Betsy waved her handkerchief at him. The officer brought the news that the rider was unhurt but the horse had broken its back.

When Anna heard this, she quickly sat down and covered her face with her fan. Karenin saw that she was weeping and that she was unable to keep back either her tears or the sobs that were shaking her bosom. Karenin shielded her from view to give her time to recover herself.

"For the third time I offer you my arm," he said after a while, turning to her.

Anna looked at him and did not know what to say. The Princess Betsy came to her rescue.

"No, sir," she said, interposing, "I brought Anna here and I've promised to take her back."

"I'm sorry, Princess," he said, smiling courteously but looking her firmly in the eyes, "but I can see that Anna is not very well and I should like her to come with me."

Anna looked round in dismay, got up obediently, and put her hand on her husband's arm.

"I'll send to him and find out, and will let you know," Betsy whispered to her.

On leaving the grandstand Karenin as usual spoke to those he met and, as usual, Anna had to reply and make conversation, but she was not herself and walked as in a dream, holding her husband's arm.

"Is he hurt or not? Is it true? Will he come or not? Shall I see him tonight?" she was thinking.

She took her seat in her husband's carriage in silence and drove out of the crowd of carriages in silence. In spite of what he had seen, Karenin still did not allow himself to think of his wife's real position. He only saw the outward signs. He saw that she had behaved improperly and deemed it his duty to point it out to her. But he found it very difficult to say that and nothing more. He opened his mouth to say that she had behaved improperly, but involuntarily said something different.

"How predisposed we are to these cruel spectacles, though," he said. "I notice—"

"What? I don't understand," said Anna contemptuously.

He was offended and at once began to say what he had intended.

"I must tell you . . ." he began.

248

"Here it comes," she thought and she felt frightened.

"I must tell you that you've behaved improperly today," he said to her in French.

"How did I behave improperly?" she said aloud, quickly turning her head and looking him straight in the eyes, but no longer with her former gaiety that seemed to conceal something, but with a determined air under which she concealed with difficulty the terror she felt.

"Don't forget," he said to her, pointing to the open window behind the driver's box.

He rose and pulled up the window.

"What did you find so improper?" she repeated.

"The despair you were unable to conceal when one of the riders fell."

He waited for her to answer, but she was silent, looking straight before her.

"I've asked you before to conduct yourself in society in such a way that no evil tongues might be able to say anything against you. There was a time when I spoke of inner relationships; I'm not speaking of them now. I speak now only of external relationships. Your conduct was improper, and I do not wish it to occur again."

She did not hear half of what he said. She was afraid of him and wondered whether it was true that Vronsky was not hurt. Was it of him they were speaking when they said that the rider was unhurt, but that the horse had broken its back? She only smiled with feigned irony when he finished, and said nothing in reply because she had not heard what he said. Karenin began to speak boldly, but when she realized clearly what he was talking about, the fear she was feeling communicated itself to him. He saw that smile and a strange delusion possessed him.

"She's smiling at my suspicions. Why, she's going to tell me now what she told me that time: that there is no foundation for my suspicions, that it's ridiculous."

Now that the disclosure of everything was imminent, he wished nothing so much as that, as before, she should answer derisively and tell him that his suspicions were ridiculous and were without foundation. What he knew was so terrible that he was now ready to believe anything. But the expression on her face, which looked frightened and somber, did not now even hold out the hope of deception.

249

"I may be mistaken," he said. "In that case I'm sorry."

"No, you're not mistaken," she said slowly, glancing despairingly at his cold face. "You're not mistaken. I was and I cannot help being in despair. I am listening to you and thinking of him. I love him. I am his mistress. I cannot endure you. I am afraid of you. I hate you. Do what you like with me."

And throwing herself back in the corner of the carriage, she burst out sobbing, covering her face with her hands. Karenin did not stir or change the direction in which he was looking. But his whole face suddenly assumed the solemn immobility of a dead man, and that expression did not change all the way to the country cottage. As they reached the house, he turned his head to her still with the same expression.

"I see. But I demand that the external conditions of propriety be observed till"—his voice trembled—"till I take measures to protect my honor and inform you of them."

He got out first and helped her out. In the presence of the servants he pressed her hand in silence, got back into the carriage, and drove off to Petersburg.

After he had gone Betsy's footman arrived with a note for Anna.

"I sent to Alexey to inquire how he was. He writes that he is safe and sound, but in despair."

"So *he* will be here!" she thought. "What a good thing I told him everything."

She looked at the clock. She had still three hours to wait, and the memories of what had passed at their last meeting fired her blood.

"Dear me, how light it is! This is dreadful, but I love to see his face and I love this eerie light. . . . My husband! Ah, yes. . . . Well, thank God, everything's over with him."

CHAPTER 30

As in every place where people gather together, so in the small German spa, to which the Shcherbatskys had come, the usual crystallization, as it were, of society took

250

place, each member of that society being assigned his definite and unchangeable place. As definitely and unchangeably as a drop of water exposed to the frost assumes the familiar form of a snow crystal, so each newcomer who arrives at a spa is immediately assigned to his proper place.

Fürst Shcherbatsky *sammt Gemahlin und Tochter*, by the lodgings they occupied, by their name, and by the people they mixed with, were immediately crystallized into a definite and preordained place.

There was a real German *Fürstin* at the spa that year, in consequence of which the crystallization was accomplished more vigorously than ever. Princess Shcherbatsky was very anxious to introduce her daughter to the German princess, and performed this rite on the second day of their arrival. Kitty made a low and graceful curtsy in the *very simple*, that is, very smart summer gown ordered from Paris. The German princess said: "I hope the roses will soon return to this pretty little face," and for the Shcherbatskys a definite way of life was at once firmly established from which there was no escape. The Shcherbatskys made the acquaintance of the family of a titled English lady, of a German countess and her son, wounded in the last war, of a Swedish savant, and of M. Canut and his sister. But the people with whom the Shcherbatskys chiefly associated consisted of a Moscow society woman, Maria Yevgenyevna Rtishchov, and her daughter, whom Kitty disliked because she, too, had got ill as a result of a love affair; and a Moscow colonel, whom Kitty had known from her childhood and always seen in uniform and epaulettes and who here, with his little eyes and open neck and flowered cravat, looked extraordinarily funny and was boring because it was impossible to get rid of him. When all this had become firmly established, Kitty felt terribly bored, especially after her father had gone to Carlsbad and she was left alone with her mother. She was not interested in the people she knew, feeling that nothing new would come from them. Her only real interest at the spa consisted of observing the people she did not know and making guesses about them. Kitty's character was such that she always assumed that people possessed the most excellent qualities, especially those she did not know. And now, when trying to guess who was who, what were the relationships between them and what sort of people they were, Kitty imagined them to have the most wonderful and splendid characters and found confirmation in her observations.

Among those people she was interested most in a Russian girl, who had arrived at the spa with an invalid Russian lady—Madame Stahl, as everyone called her. Madame Stahl belonged to the highest society, but she was so ill that she could not walk and only on exceptionally fine days appeared on the promenade in a wheel-chair. But it was not so much from illness as from pride—as the Princess Shcherbatsky explained— that Madame Stahl had not made the acquaintance of any of the Russians. The Russian girl looked after Madame Stahl and besides that, as Kitty observed, made friends with all the people who were seriously ill, of whom there were so many at the spa, and waited on them in the most natural way. This Russian girl, according to Kitty's observations, was not a relation of Madame Stahl, but neither was she a paid companion. Madame Stahl called her by her pet name Varenka, and other people called her Mademoiselle Varenka. But apart from the fact that Kitty was interested in observing the relations of this girl with Madame Stahl and with other unknown persons, Kitty, as often happens, felt an inexplicable attraction to Mademoiselle Varenka, and when their eyes met she realized that the girl liked her too.

Mademoiselle Varenka was not in the first flush of youth; she seemed to be a person who had never been youthful. She might be nineteen or she might be thirty. If one examined her features, she was, in spite of her sickly complexion, good-looking rather than plain. She would have had a good figure, too, had she not been so thin and her head a little too large for her medium height; but then she was not the type of girl who was attractive to men. She was like a beautiful flower which, though its petals had not yet begun to drop, was already faded and without fragrance. Besides, she could not be attractive to men because she lacked that which Kitty had too much of—the suppressed fire of life and the consciousness of her own attractiveness.

She seemed always busy with some important work, and therefore she could not apparently be interested in anything else. Kitty was especially attracted by this contrast to herself. Kitty felt that in her, in her way of life, she could find the pattern she herself was so painfully seeking; interest in life, dignity of life—outside the relations of girls with men in high society, which now seemed so disgusting to Kitty and which she regarded as a shameful exhibition of goods in expectation of buyers. The more Kitty observed her unknown friend, the more convinced she was that this girl really was the most perfect creature she imagined her to be, the more she desired to make her acquaintance.

The two girls used to meet several times a day, and every time they met, Kitty's eyes said: "Who are you? What are you? You are the delightful person I imagine you to be, aren't you? But for goodness' sake," her look added, "don't think that I'm trying to force myself on you. I simply admire you and love you." "I love you too and you are very, very sweet. And I should love you still more, if I had time," answered the unknown girl's eyes. And, indeed, Kitty saw that she was always busy, either taking the children of a Russian family home from the wells, or carrying an invalid's rug and wrapping it round her, or trying to divert an irritable patient, or choosing and buying cakes for somebody's coffee.

Soon after the arrival of the Shcherbatskys two new persons, who attracted general and unfriendly attention, began to appear at the wells in the morning. They were a very tall, stooping man with black, naïve, and rather terrifying eyes and huge hands, who wore an old overcoat too short for him, and a slightly pock-marked, pleasant-looking woman, very badly and tastelessly dressed. Recognizing them as Russians, Kitty was already beginning to make up a beautiful and touching romance about them. But her mother, finding from the visitors' list that they were Nikolai Levin and Maria Nikolayevna, explained to Kitty what a wicked man that Levin was, and all Kitty's dreams about those two people vanished. It was not so much because of what her mother had told her as because the man was Konstantin's brother that these two people suddenly seemed ex-

tremely disagreeable to Kitty. This Levin aroused in her
now an irrepressible feeling of aversion by his habit of
jerking his head.

It seemed to her that his big, terrible eyes, which followed her persistently, were full of hatred and derision,
and she tried to avoid encountering him.

CHAPTER 31

It was a rainy day. It rained all morning and the patients with their umbrellas crowded into the covered
gallery.

Kitty was walking with her mother and the Moscow
colonel, gaily showing off in his short European coat,
bought ready-made in Frankfort. They kept to one side
of the gallery, trying to avoid Levin, who was taking a
walk on the other side. Varenka, in her dark dress and
black hat with turned-down brim, was walking along the
whole length of the gallery with a blind Frenchwoman,
and every time she met Kitty they exchanged friendly
glances.

"Couldn't I speak to her, Mother?" asked Kitty, following her unknown friend with her eyes and noticing
that she was walking toward the well and that they might
meet there.

"Why, yes, if you want to so much," her mother replied. "Let me first find out about her and I will go up
to her myself. What is it you find so special about her?
A lady's companion, I expect. If you like I will make
Madame Stahl's acquaintance. I used to know her sister-
in-law," added the princess, raising her head proudly.

Kitty knew that her mother was offended that Madame Stahl seemed to avoid making her acquaintance.
Kitty did not insist.

"What a wonderfully nice person she is!" she said,
looking at Varenka, who was just then handing a tumbler to the Frenchwoman. "Look, how everything about
her is so simple and charming."

"I can't help laughing at your infatuations," said the
princess. "No, no, we'd better go back," she added, noticing Levin coming toward them with his companion

and a German doctor, to whom he was saying something in a loud and angry voice.

They were just turning to go back, when they suddenly heard not only loud talk, but a shout. Levin had stopped and was shouting at the doctor, and the doctor, too, was getting excited. A crowd was gathering around them. The princess and Kitty hurried away, but the colonel joined the crowd to find out what was happening.

A few minutes later the colonel caught up with them.

"What was the matter?" asked the princess.

"It's simply disgraceful!" replied the colonel. "The one thing you're afraid of is meeting Russians abroad. That tall man has been quarreling with the doctor, had the impudence to tell him that his treatment was all wrong, and started shaking his stick at him. It's a disgrace!"

"How awful!" said the princess. "Well, how did it end?"

"Luckily that girl with—er—with the mushroom hat intervened. She's Russian, I believe," said the colonel.

"Mademoiselle Varenka?" Kitty asked, looking pleased.

"Yes, yes. She found the right thing to do before anybody else. She took the fellow under the arm and led him away."

"You see, Mother," said Kitty, "and you're surprised that I admire her."

The next day, watching her unknown friend, Kitty noticed that Mademoiselle Varenka was already on the same terms with Levin and his woman as she was with her other *protégés*. She went up and talked to them and acted as an interpreter for the woman, who could not speak any foreign language.

Kitty implored her mother more than ever to allow her to make Varenka's acquaintance. And however disagreeable the princess found it to appear to take the first step toward getting acquainted with Madame Stahl, who for some reason gave herself such airs, she made inquiries about Varenka. The facts she found out about her led her to conclude that though there might be little good there would be no harm in the acquaintance and she went up to Varenka and introduced herself to her.

Choosing a time when her daughter had gone up to

the well and Varenka had stopped outside a bakery, the princess went up to her.

"Allow me to introduce myself," she said, with her dignified smile. "My daughter is simply raving about you," she went on. "I don't suppose you know me. I am—"

"It's more than mutual, Princess," Varenka was quick to reply.

"What a good deed you performed yesterday for our poor fellow countryman," said the princess.

Varenka blushed.

"I don't remember," she said. "I don't think I did anything."

"Why, you saved that Levin from a disagreeable scene."

"Well, yes, his companion called me and I tried to calm him: he's very ill and he was dissatisfied with his doctor. You see, I'm used to looking after that kind of patient."

"Yes, I've heard that you live in Mentone with your aunt, I believe, Madame Stahl. I used to know her sister-in-law."

"No, she is not my aunt. I call her *maman*, but I'm not related to her. I was brought up by her," Varenka replied, blushing again.

This was said so simply, so charming was the truthful and frank expression of her face, that the princess understood why her Kitty was so fond of this Varenka.

"Well, and what about that Levin?"

"He's leaving," replied Varenka.

At that moment Kitty came up from the well, beaming with delight that her mother had become acquainted with her unknown friend.

"Well, Kitty, your great wish to know Mademoiselle . . ."

"Varenka," prompted Varenka, smiling. "Everyone calls me that."

Kitty blushed with joy and long and silently pressed her new friend's hand, which did not return her pressure but lay motionless in hers. But though her hand did not return the pressure, Varenka's face shone with a soft, pleased, though rather sad smile, disclosing her large but fine teeth.

"I've long wished it myself," she said.

256

"But you're so busy. . . ."

"Oh, I'm not at all busy," replied Varenka, but at that very moment had to leave her new friends, because two little Russian girls, the children of one of the invalids, ran up to her.

"Varenka, Mummy's calling!" they shouted.

And Varenka went after them.

CHAPTER 32

The facts the princess learned about Varenka's past and her relations with Madame Stahl and about Madame Stahl herself were as follows:

Madame Stahl, about whom some people said that she had worried her husband to death and others that he had worried her to death by his immoral conduct, had always been an ailing and hysterical woman. When, after having been divorced from her husband, she gave birth to her first baby, the baby had died almost immediately, and her relations, knowing how highly strung she was and afraid that the news might kill her, substituted for her dead child one that was born the same night in the same house in Petersburg, the daughter of a palace chef. That child was Varenka. Madame Stahl learned afterward that Varenka was not her daughter, but she continued to bring her up, particularly as Varenka soon lost all her relations.

Madame Stahl had been living continuously abroad in the south for more than ten years, never leaving her bed. Some people said that she had made herself a name by pretending to be a virtuous and highly religious woman; others said that she really was the highly moral being, living only to do good, which she represented herself to be. No one knew what her religion was, Roman Catholic, Protestant, or Greek Orthodox; one thing, though, was certain: she was on the most friendly terms with the highest dignitaries of all the churches and denominations.

Varenka lived with her all the time abroad and all who knew Madame Stahl knew and liked Varenka, as everybody called her.

Having learned all these facts, the princess found nothing to object to in her daughter's friendship with

Varenka, particularly as Varenka's manners and education were excellent: she spoke admirable French and English and, what was most important, apologized for Madame Stahl, who regretted being deprived by her illness of the pleasure of making the princess' acquaintance.

Having become acquainted with Varenka, Kitty became more and more attracted to her friend, finding new things to admire in her every day.

When the princess heard that Varenka was a fine singer, she invited her to sing to them one evening.

"Kitty plays and we have a piano, though not a good one, I'm afraid, but you would give us great pleasure," said the princess with her affected smile, which was especially distasteful to Kitty now, because she noticed that Varenka had no desire to sing.

But Varenka did come in the evening and brought some music with her. The princess had also invited Maria Yevgenyevna with her daughter and the colonel.

Varenka did not seem to mind in the least that there were people there she did not know and went straight to the piano. She could not accompany herself, but she could sight read excellently. Kitty, who played well, accompanied her.

"You have an exceptional talent," said the princess to her after Varenka had sung the first song admirably.

Maria Yevgenyevna and her daughter thanked her.

"Look," said the colonel, glancing out of the window, "what an audience has gathered to hear you."

And, indeed, there was quite a big crowd under the windows.

"I am very glad it gives you pleasure," said Varenka, simply.

Kitty looked at her friend with pride. She was entranced by her art, her voice, her face, but most of all by her manner, by the fact that Varenka evidently did not think much of her singing and was completely indifferent to their praises. All she seemed anxious to know was whether they wanted her to sing again or whether they had had enough of it.

"If it were me," thought Kitty, "how proud I should feel! How delighted I should be to see that crowd under the windows! But she is quite indifferent. All she is anxious about is not to refuse and to give Mother pleasure. What has she got that gives her this power to disregard everything and be so serenely independent? How I should like to know and to learn it from her!" thought Kitty, gazing into that calm face.

The princess asked Varenka to sing another song, and Varenka sang it just as calmly, distinctly, and well, standing straight at the piano and beating time on it with her thin, dark-skinned hand.

The next song in the book was an Italian one. Kitty played the prelude, and looked round at Varenka.

"Let's skip this one," said Varenka, blushing.

Kitty fixed her eyes anxiously and inquiringly on Varenka's face.

"All right, another one, then," she said hurriedly, turning over the pages and realizing at once that there was something connected with that song.

"No," said Varenka, putting her hand on the music and smiling, "no, let's sing that one."

And she sang it as calmly, coolly, and well as the other songs.

When she had finished, they again thanked her and went to have tea. Kitty and Varenka walked out into the little garden beside the house.

"Am I right in thinking that you have some memory connected with that song?" asked Kitty. "Don't tell me about it," she added hurriedly. "Only say if I am right."

"Why ever not? I will tell you," said Varenka simply and, without waiting for a reply, went on: "Yes, I have. A rather painful memory, I'm afraid. I was in love with a man and I used to sing that song to him."

Kitty gazed at Varenka with wide-open eyes, deeply moved and in silence.

"I loved him and he loved me, but his mother objected to our marriage and he married another. He is living not far from us now and I see him sometimes. You didn't think I had had a love affair, too, did you?" she said, and on her beautiful face there was a faint glimmer of that fire which, Kitty felt, had once lighted up her whole being.

"Indeed, I did! If I were a man I could not have loved anyone else after knowing you. I just can't understand how, to please his mother, he could forget you and make you unhappy. He was quite heartless."

"Oh no, he's a very good man and I'm not unhappy. On the contrary, I am very happy. Well," she added, going back toward the house, "I don't suppose we shall be singing any more today."

"Oh, you're so good, so good!" cried Kitty and, stopping Varenka, she kissed her. "I wish I were even a little like you!"

"Why should you be like anyone? You're nice as you are," Varenka said, smiling her gentle, tired smile.

"No, I'm not nice at all. But tell me . . . Please, wait, let's sit down," said Kitty, making her sit down again on the garden seat beside her. "Tell me, don't you really think one ought to feel humiliated at the thought that a man has scorned your love, that he didn't want you?"

"But he did not scorn it. I am sure he loved me, but he was an obedient son. . . ."

"Yes, but what if—if he did it not because his mother did not want it but because he himself wanted it?" said Kitty, feeling that she had given away her secret and that her face, burning with shame, had already betrayed her.

"Then he would have behaved badly and I should not regret him," replied Varenka, evidently realizing that they were not talking of her but of Kitty.

"But the humiliation?" said Kitty. "One can't forget the humiliation," she said, remembering the look she gave Vronsky at the ball when the music stopped.

"Where is the humiliation? You didn't do anything wrong, did you?"

"Worse than wrong—shameful."

Varenka shook her head and put her hand on Kitty's. "What's so shameful about it?" she said. "You couldn't tell a man who was indifferent to you that you loved him, could you?"

"Of course not. I never said a word, but he knew. No, no! There are looks and ways of behaving. If I live to be a hundred I shall never forget it."

"But why not? I don't understand. Surely, the point is whether you love him now or not," said Varenka, calling everything by its name.

"I hate him. I can't forgive myself."

"Why not?"

"The shame, the humiliation."

"Dear me," said Varenka. "If everyone were as sensitive as you are! There is no girl who has not been through the same thing. And it's all so unimportant."

"What then is important?" asked Kitty, looking at her face with surprised curiosity.

"Oh, lots of things," said Varenka, smiling.

"But what?"

"Oh, lots of things are more important," replied Varenka, not knowing what to say.

But at that moment they heard the princess' voice from the window:

"Kitty, it's chilly! Either get a shawl or come back."

"Yes, I really must be going," said Varenka, getting up. "I've still to call on Madame Bertha. She asked me to."

Kitty held her hand and with passionate curiosity and entreaty questioned Varenka with her eyes: "What is it, what is it that is so important? What is it that gives you such calm? You know, tell me!" But Varenka did not even understand what Kitty's eyes were asking. She only knew that she had to call on Madame Bertha and then be back in time for tea with her *maman* at midnight. She went in, collected her music, and having said goodby to everybody, was about to go.

"Allow me to see you home," said the colonel.

"Yes, indeed, you can't go home alone at night like that," agreed the princess. "Let me at least send my maid Parasha with you."

Kitty saw that Varenka could hardly restrain a smile at the suggestion that she needed anyone to escort her home.

"No, thank you," she said, taking up her hat. "I always go about alone and nothing ever happens to me."

She kissed Kitty again and, without telling her what was important, walked briskly away with the music under her arm, and disappeared in the twilight of the summer night, carrying away with her the secret of what was important and what gave her that enviable calm and dignity.

CHAPTER 33

Kitty made the acquaintance of Madame Stahl, too, and this acquaintance together with her friendship with Varenka not only had a great influence on her, but also comforted her in her sorrow. She found this comfort in that, thanks to this acquaintance, an entirely new world had opened up to her, a world that had nothing in common with her past, an exalted beautiful world, from the heights of which it was possible to gaze calmly at that past. It was revealed to her that besides the instinctive life to which she had given herself up till now, there was also a spiritual life. That life was disclosed in religion, but a religion that had nothing in common with the religion Kitty had known since childhood and which found expression in morning and evening Mass at the Widows' Home, where she could meet her friends, and in learning Slavonic texts by heart with the priest; this was an exalted, mysterious religion connected with a whole series of beautiful thoughts and feelings, in which it was not only possible to believe because one was told to, but which one could love.

Kitty discovered it all not from words. Madame Stahl talked to Kitty as to a dear child one likes to have about because it reminds you of your own past, and only once did she remark that love and faith alone bring consolation in all human sorrows and that no sorrows were too trivial for Christ's compassion, and immediately changed the subject. But in Madame Stahl's every movement, in every word, in every, as Kitty called it, heavenly look of hers, and especially, in the whole story of her life, which she learned from Varenka, Kitty discovered what was "important" and what she had not known before.

But, lofty as was Madame Stahl's character, touching as was the story of her life, and exalted and moving as was her speech, Kitty could not help noticing certain things about her that seemed rather perplexing. She noticed that, when questioned about her family, Madame Stahl had smiled scornfully, which did not accord with Christian charity. She further noticed that she once met a Roman Catholic priest at her house, and Madame Stahl had taken great care to keep her face in the shadow of the lampshade and had smiled rather peculiarly. Insignificant as these two observations were, they troubled Kitty and she had her doubts about Madame Stahl. Varenka, on the other hand, lonely, without kith and kin, without friends, with her sad disappointment, desiring nothing and regretting nothing, was regarded by Kitty as the perfec-

262

tion she could only dream of. Varenka made her realize that it was only necessary to forget oneself and love others in order to be at peace, happy and good. And such a person Kitty wanted to be. Having now already understood what was *most important*, Kitty was not content merely to admire it, but immediately devoted herself with all her soul to the new life that was revealed to her. From what Varenka had told her about the work of Madame Stahl and of others whom she named, Kitty had formed a plan of her future life. Like Madame Stahl's niece, Aline, about whom Varenka had told her a great deal, Kitty would seek out those who were unhappy, wherever she might be living, help them as much as she could, distribute Gospels, and read the Gospel to the sick, the criminals, and the dying. The idea of reading the Gospel to criminals, as Aline did, appealed to Kitty particularly. But all these were secret dreams, which Kitty did not speak of either to her mother or to Varenka.

However, while waiting for the time when she could carry out her plans on a large scale, Kitty, here at the spa where there were so many sick and unhappy people, easily found opportunities to apply her new principles in imitation of Varenka.

At first the princess merely noticed that Kitty was under the strong influence of her *engouement*, as she called it, for Madame Stahl and especially for Varenka. She saw that Kitty not only imitated Varenka's activities, but unconsciously copied her manner of walking, speaking, and blinking her eyes. But afterward the princess noticed that, quite apart from this infatuation, a serious spiritual transformation was taking place in her daughter.

The princess noticed that in the evening Kitty read the New Testament in French, given her by Madame Stahl, which she had never done before; that she avoided her high-society acquaintances and was making friends with the invalids who were under Varenka's protection, and especially with the family of Petrov, a poor, sick painter. Kitty evidently was proud to be carrying out the duties of a sister-of-mercy in that family. All this was very well and the princess had nothing against it, particularly as Petrov's wife was a respectable woman and as the German princess, having noticed Kitty's activities, praised her, calling her a ministering angel. All this would have been very well if Kitty had not gone a little too far. For the princess saw that her daughter was running to extremes, which, indeed, she did not fail to point out to her.

"Il ne faut jamais rien outrer," she said to her.

But her daughter said nothing in reply; she only thought that one could not speak of going too far where Christianity was concerned. How could one possibly go too far in following the teaching which bids one turn the other cheek when smitten on one cheek, and give one's coat when one's cloak was taken? But the princess did not like this running to extremes, and she disliked it all the more because she felt that Kitty did not care to open her whole heart to her. And, indeed, Kitty hid her new views and feelings from her mother. She hid them not because she did not respect and love her mother, but just because it was her mother. She would have revealed them to anyone sooner than to her mother.

"It seems a long time since Mrs. Petrov was here," the princess said one day to Kitty. "I invited her, but she appears to be displeased about something."

"I haven't noticed anything, Mother," Kitty said flushing.

"How long is it since you went to see them?"

"We're planning an excursion into the mountains tomorrow," replied Kitty.

"That's nice," said the princess, looking intently into her daughter's embarrassed face and trying to guess the cause of her embarrassment.

That same day Varenka came to dinner and said that Mrs. Petrov had changed her mind about going to the mountains tomorrow. And the princess noticed that Kitty blushed again.

"Kitty, you haven't had any unpleasantness with the Petrovs, have you?" said the princess when they were alone again. "Why has she stopped sending the children here and coming to see us herself?"

Kitty replied that nothing had happened between them and that she had no idea at all why Mrs. Petrov seemed to be displeased with her. Kitty spoke the truth. She did not know the reason of the change in Mrs. Petrov's attitude toward her, but she guessed it. She suspected that it was something she could not very well tell her mother, something she could hardly say to herself. It was one of those things which you know, but which you never speak about even to yourself; so dreadful and shameful it would be to make a mistake.

Again and again she went over in her mind all the relations she had had with that family. She remembered the naïve pleasure expressed in Mrs. Petrov's round, good-natured face whenever they met; she remembered their secret consultations about the patient, their plots to draw him away from the work which the doctors had forbidden and take him for walks; the attachment of the youngest boy, who called her "my Kitty" and who would not go to bed without her. How nice it all was! Then she remembered the terribly emaciated figure of Petrov in his brown coat, with his long neck, his thin, curly hair, his questioning blue eyes, which seemed so terrible to Kitty at first, and his painful efforts to appear cheerful and animated in her presence. She remembered how at first she had to force herself to overcome the revulsion she felt for him, as for all consumptives, and her efforts to think of something to say to him. She remembered the timid look, full of emotion, with which he gazed at her, and her strange feeling of pity and awkwardness, followed by the consciousness of her own virtuousness that she had felt at the time. How nice it all was! But that was only at first. Now, a few days ago, everything was suddenly spoiled. Mrs. Petrov now met Kitty with simulated politeness and kept watching her husband and her.

Could his touching joy at her approach be the cause of Mrs. Petrov's coolness?

"Yes," she remembered, "there was something unnatural about Mrs. Petrov and something quite unlike her usual kindness, when the day before yesterday she said with a note of annoyance in her voice: 'There, he has been waiting for you all the time and would not drink his coffee without you, though he has grown so dreadfully weak!'

"Yes, perhaps she was also upset when I gave him his rug. It was really nothing, but he accepted it so awkwardly, he thanked me so much that I myself felt awkward. And then my portrait which he did so well. And,

most of all, that look of his—so embarrassed and tender!
Yes, yes, it is so!" Kitty said to herself with horror. "No,
it can't be, it mustn't be! He's so pathetic!" she said to
herself a moment later.

This doubt poisoned the delight she took in her new
life.

CHAPTER 34

Before the end of the spa season Prince Shcherbatsky,
who had gone from Carlsbad to Baden and Kissingen to
see some Russian friends, "to get a breath of Russian
air," as he expressed it, returned to his family.

The views of the prince and the princess on life abroad
were diametrically opposed. The princess found everything admirable and, in spite of her well-established position in Russian society, did her utmost when abroad to
be like a European lady, which she was not, because she
was a typical Russian grand lady; she had therefore to
play a part which was rather a strain. The prince, on the
other hand, found everything foreign to be bad and life
abroad burdensome, kept to his Russian habits, and purposely tried to appear less of a European than he
really was.

The prince returned looking thinner, with loose bags
of skin on his cheeks, but in the gayest of spirits. His
spirits were still better when he saw Kitty completely
recovered. The news of Kitty's friendship with Madame
Stahl and Varenka and the account the princess gave
him of some change she had observed in Kitty disturbed
the prince and aroused in him his usual feeling of jealousy of everything in which she took a keen interest
without his knowledge and a fear that his daughter might
escape from his influence into regions that were inaccessible to him. But these unpleasant reports dissolved in
the sea of good-natured cheerfulness which was always
within him and which was increased by the Carlsbad
waters.

The day after his arrival the prince in his long overcoat, with his Russian wrinkles and baggy cheeks, supported by a starched collar, went out with his daughter
to the well in the gayest of spirits.

It was a lovely morning: the neat, bright houses with small gardens, the sight of the red-faced, red-armed, beer-drinking German housemaids, working away cheerfully, and the clear sunshine gladdened the heart; but the nearer they got to the well, the more frequently did they come across sick people, and their appearance seemed ever sorrier amid those ordinary surroundings of well-ordered German life. Kitty was no longer struck by this contrast. The bright sunshine, the gay glitter of the green foliage, and the sounds of music were for her the natural setting of all these familiar figures, and of the changes for better or worse, for which she watched. But to the prince the light and glitter of the June morning, the sound of the band playing a popular gay waltz, and particularly the appearance of robust maidservants seemed somehow indecent and monstrous side by side with these dejectedly moving living corpses gathered from all parts of Europe.

In spite of his feeling of pride and the sense of renewed youth he experienced when walking arm-in-arm with his favorite daughter, he could not help feeling uncomfortable and almost ashamed of his powerful stride and his large, fat limbs. He almost felt like a man appearing naked in a crowd of people.

"Introduce me, do introduce me to your new friends," he said to his daughter, pressing her arm with his elbow. "I have even taken a liking to your nasty Soden because it has done you so much good. Only it's sad here—very sad. Who's that?"

Kitty told him the names of the people she knew and those she did not know whom they met. At the very entrance to the gardens they met the blind Madame Bertha with her guide, and the prince was pleased to see the tender look on the Frenchwoman's face when she heard Kitty's voice. She at once began talking to him with the French excess of politeness, saying that he ought to be glad to have such a wonderful daughter, praising Kitty up to the skies to her face and calling her a treasure, a pearl, and a ministering angel.

"Well then, she must be angel number two," said the prince, smiling. "She calls Mademoiselle Varenka angel number one."

"Oh, Mademoiselle Varenka is a real angel, *allez*," said Madame Bertha.

In the gallery they met Varenka herself. She was walking hurriedly toward them with an elegant red bag in her hand.

"Here's Father," Kitty said to Varenka. "He's just arrived."

Varenka, simply and naturally, as she did everything, made a movement between a bow and a curtsy, and at once began talking to the prince, as she did to everyone else, unconstrainedly and naturally.

"Of course I know you, I know you very well," the prince said to her with a smile, by which Kitty realized with joy that her father liked her friend. "Where are you off to in such a hurry?"

"*Maman* is here," she said, addressing Kitty. "She slept all night and the doctor advised her to go out. I'm taking her some work."

"So this is the angel number one," said the prince, when Varenka had gone.

Kitty saw that he would have liked to make fun of Varenka, but that he could not do so because he liked her.

"Well, let us see all your friends," he added, "including Madame Stahl if she will do me the honor of recognizing me."

"Why, do you know her?" asked Kitty with dismay, noticing an ironic twinkle in the prince's eyes at the mention of Madame Stahl.

"I used to know her husband and her, too, a little, before she'd joined the Pietists."

"What are Pietists?" asked Kitty, already alarmed to find that what she prized so greatly in Madame Stahl had a name.

"I'm afraid I'm not quite sure myself. All I know is that she thanks God for everything, for every misfortune. Thanks God, too, that her husband died. Which is rather funny, for they did not get on well together.

"Who's that? What a pathetic face!" he said, noticing a sick man of medium height, sitting on a bench in a brown coat and white trousers which fell in strange folds over his wasted legs.

The man raised his straw hat above his thin, curly hair, revealing a high forehead with an unhealthy red mark where that hat had pressed it.

"That's Petrov, an artist," replied Kitty, blushing.

"And there's his wife," she added, indicating Anna Petrov, who, as though on purpose, went off after a child who had run away along the path.

"Poor fellow, and what a nice face he has!" said the prince. "Why didn't you go up to him? I think he wanted to say something to you."

"All right, let's go up then," said Kitty, turning back determinedly. "How are you today?" she asked Petrov.

Petrov rose, leaning on his stick, and looked timidly at the prince.

"This is my daughter," said the prince. "Allow me to introduce myself."

The artist bowed and smiled, showing strangely glistening white teeth.

"We were expecting you yesterday, Princess," he said to Kitty.

He staggered as he said it and, repeating the movement, tried to make it appear as though he had done it intentionally.

"I meant to come, but Varenka said that Mrs. Petrov sent word that you were not going."

"Not going?" Petrov said, flushing and immediately beginning to cough and looking round for his wife. "Anetta, Anetta!" he exclaimed in a loud voice, and the veins in his thin white neck stood out like cords.

Mrs. Petrov came up.

"Why on earth did you send word to the princess to say we were not going?" losing his voice, he whispered to her angrily.

"How do you do, Princess?" said Mrs. Petrov with an affected smile, so unlike her former way of talking to her. "Very pleased to meet you." She turned to the prince. "You've long been expected, Prince."

"Why on earth did you send word to the princess to say we were not going?" the painter whispered hoarsely again, still more angrily, evidently feeling exasperated that his voice had failed him and he could not give his words the expression he would have liked to.

"Oh, goodness me, I thought we were not going," his wife replied with vexation.

"But how . . . when . . ." He started coughing again and gave it up with a wave of his hand.

The prince raised his hat and walked away with his daughter.

"Oh dear," he said with a deep sigh, "the poor wretches!"

"Yes, Father," replied Kitty. "And you ought to know that they have three children, no servants, and hardly any means. He gets something from the Academy," she went on with animation, trying to suppress the excitement aroused in her by the strange change in Mrs. Petrov's attitude toward her.

"And there's Madame Stahl," said Kitty, pointing to a wheel chair in which something in gray and light blue was lying under a parasol, propped up by pillows.

That was Madame Stahl. Behind her was a scowling, sturdy German workman who pushed the wheel chair. At her side stood a fair-haired Swedish count, whom Kitty knew by name. Several patients lingered near the wheel chair, gazing at this woman as if she were something extraordinary.

The prince went up to her. And immediately Kitty noticed that ironic gleam in Madame Stahl's eyes that disconcerted her so much. The prince went up to Madame Stahl and addressed her extremely politely and nicely in that excellent French so few speak nowadays.

"I don't know if you remember me, but I feel I must remind you of myself in order to thank you for your kindness to my daughter," he said, raising his hat and not putting it on again.

"Prince Alexander Shcherbatsky," said Madame Stahl, lifting up to him her heavenly eyes, in which Kitty detected an expression of displeasure. "Very pleased to meet you. I've grown very fond of your daughter."

"Your health, madam, is still not very good?"

"No, but I'm accustomed to it," said Madame Stahl, and introduced the Swedish count to the prince.

"You're very little changed, ma'am," said the prince to her. "I'm afraid it must be ten or eleven years since I had the honor of seeing you."

"Yes, sir. God sends the cross and sends the strength to bear it. I must say I often wonder why my life drags on. . . . The other side!" she said crossly to Varenka, who was not wrapping the rug round her feet to her satisfaction.

"To do good, no doubt," said the prince, laughing with his eyes.

"That's not for us to judge, sir," said Madame Stahl,

noticing the faint expression of irony on the prince's face. "So you will send me that book, my dear count? Thank you very much," she addressed the young Swede.

"Hullo!" cried the prince, catching sight of the Moscow colonel standing nearby and, taking leave of Madame Stahl, he walked off with his daughter and the Moscow colonel who had joined them.

"That is our Russian aristocracy," said the Moscow colonel, wishing to be sarcastic, for he had a grudge against Madame Stahl, who did not wish to be acquainted with him.

"The same as ever," replied the prince.

"Did you know her before her illness, Prince? I mean before she became bedridden?"

"Yes, I knew her when she first took to her bed."

"I'm told she hasn't been on her feet for ten years."

"She doesn't get up because her legs are too short. She had a very bad figure. . . ."

"Father, it's not possible!"

"Evil tongues say so, my dear. And your Varenka must be having an awful time of it," he added. "Oh, these invalid grand ladies!"

"Oh no, Father," Kitty objected heatedly. "Varenka adores her. And, besides, she does so much good! You can ask anyone you like. Everybody knows her and Aline Stahl."

"Maybe," said the prince, pressing her arm with his elbow. "But, you see, it's much better to do good in a way that no one knows anything about it."

Kitty made no answer not because she had nothing to say, but because she did not want to reveal her secret thoughts even to her father. Yet, strange to say, although she was quite determined not to give in to her father's views and not to let him into her holy of holies, she felt that the divine image of Madame Stahl, which she had carried for a whole month in her heart, had vanished irrevocably just like a figure formed by some flung-down clothes vanishes when one realizes that it is only the way the clothes are lying. All that was left was a woman whose legs were too short and who was always lying down because she was malformed and who tormented poor, meek Varenka for not tucking the rug the way she liked. And by no efforts of imagination could the former Madame Stahl be revived.

CHAPTER 35

The prince communicated his high spirits to the members of his family, his acquaintances, and even to his German landlord.

On his return with Kitty from the well, the prince, who had invited the colonel, Maria Yevgenyevna, and Varenka to come and have coffee with them, had a table and chairs brought into the garden under a chestnut tree and lunch laid there. The landlord and the servants brightened up under the influence of his cheerfulness. They knew his generosity, and half an hour later the sick Hamburg doctor, who lived on the top floor, was looking with envy from his window at this cheerful company of healthy Russians gathered under the chestnut tree. Under the trembling shadows of the circles of the leaves, at one end of the table covered by a white cloth and set with coffeepot, bread, butter, cheese, and cold game, sat the princess in a cap with lilac ribbons, handing out cups of coffee and sandwiches. At the other end sat the prince, eating heartily and talking loudly and cheerfully. The prince had spread out his purchases in front of him: carved boxes, knickknacks, all sorts of paper knives, of which he had bought large quantities at all the watering places and was giving away to all and sundry, including the maid Lischen and the landlord, with whom he cracked jokes in his comical, broken German, assuring him that it was not the waters that had cured Kitty, but his excellent food, especially his prune soup. The princess laughed at her husband's Russian ways, but was more lively and gay than she had been all the time she had spent at the spa. The colonel smiled, as always, at the prince's jokes; but as regards Western Europe, which he thought he had studied thoroughly, he was on the side of the princess. The good-natured Maria Yevgenyevna shook with laughter at every amusing joke the prince made; and Varenka, whom Kitty had never seen like this before, became quite limp with the infectious laughter at the prince's jokes, which everybody succumbed to and she could not resist.

All this cheered Kitty, but she could not help being troubled. She could not solve the problem involuntarily posed by her father's satirical view of her friends and the life she had grown so fond of. To this problem was added the change in her relations with the Petrovs, which had so clearly and unpleasantly become manifest that morning. Everybody was cheerful, but Kitty could not be cheerful, and that worried her still more. She experienced the feeling she had known in childhood when she had been shut up in her room as a punishment and heard the gay laughter of her sisters.

"Why on earth did you buy all those things?" asked the princess, smiling and handing her husband a cup of coffee.

"Well, my dear, you go out for a walk, come to a shop, and they ask you to buy something. *Erlaucht, Excellenz, Durchlaucht.* Well, by the time they get to *Durchlaucht*, I can hold out no longer: ten thalers are gone."

"That's only because you're bored," said the princess.

"Naturally. I get so bored, my dear, that I don't know what to do with myself."

"How can you be bored, Prince?" asked Maria Yevgenyevna. "There's so much that is interesting in Germany now."

"But I already know everything that is interesting: prune soup and peas pudding. I know everything."

"Say what you like, Prince," remarked the colonel, "but their institutions are interesting."

"What is so interesting about them? They are as pleased as Punch: they've conquered everybody. Well, why should I be pleased about it? I have not conquered anybody, but have to take off my own boots and put them outside the door myself. In the morning I have to get up, dress at once, and go to the dining room to drink horrible tea. It's different at home. You wake up, you're in no hurry, you get a bit cross about something, you grumble, come to your senses properly, turn things over in your mind quietly and without hurrying."

"But time's money," said the colonel. "You forget that."

"Is it? Why, there are times when you'd gladly give a whole month for half a ruble and there are times you wouldn't sell half an hour at any price. Isn't that so, Kitty? Why are you so serious?"

"I'm all right."

"Where are you off to?" he said to Varenka. "Stay a little longer."

"I'm afraid I must get home," said Varenka, getting up and bursting out laughing again.

When she had recovered, she said good-by and went into the house to get her hat. Kitty followed her. Even Varenka seemed different to her now. She was not worse, but different from what Kitty had imagined her to be before.

"Oh dear, I haven't laughed like that for a long time," said Varenka, collecting her parasol and bag. "What a dear your father is!"

Kitty was silent.

"When shall I see you?" asked Varenka.

"Mother was going to call on the Petrovs. Will you be there?" asked Kitty, putting Varenka to the test.

"Yes," replied Varenka. "They are getting ready to leave and I promised to help them pack."

"Well, I'll come too."

"No, please don't. Why should you?"

"Why not? Why not? Why not?" asked Kitty, opening her eyes wide and holding Varenka's parasol to prevent her going. "No, wait! Why not?"

"Oh, well, your father has come and, besides, they don't feel at ease with you."

"No, tell me why you don't want me to be often at the Petrovs. You don't, do you? Why?"

"I didn't say that," said Varenka quietly.

"No, please tell me!"

"Tell you everything?" asked Varenka.

"Everything! Everything!" Kitty exclaimed.

"Well, actually there's nothing much to tell, except that Mr. Petrov had wanted to leave earlier and now he doesn't want to leave at all," said Varenka, smiling.

"Well, go on!" Kitty hurried her, looking darkly at her.

"Well, and for some reason Mrs. Petrov said that he did not want to go because you were here. Of course, that was absurd, but there was a quarrel because of that—because of you. And you know how irritable these sick people are."

Kitty, frowning more than ever, was silent, and Varenka alone spoke, trying to soften the blow and calm her, for

274

she anticipated an outburst, whether of words or tears she did not know.

"So I think it's better for you not to go. . . . You understand, don't you? Don't be offended. . . ."

"Serves me right! Serves me right!" Kitty said quickly, snatching the parasol from Varenka and looking past her friend's eyes.

Varenka felt like smiling at her friend's childish anger, but she was afraid of offending her.

"Why does it serve you right?" she said. "I don't understand."

"It serves me right because it was all a sham, because it was all pretense, and did not come from my heart. What business was it of mine to interfere in the private affairs of a stranger? And now it seems that I am the cause of a quarrel and that I did something nobody asked me to do. And because it's all a sham, a sham, a sham!"

"But why should you have pretended?" Varenka said quietly.

"Oh, how stupid, how horrible!" she kept saying, opening and shutting the parasol. "There was no need at all for me to do that. It's all a sham!"

"But why?"

"To appear better to people, to myself, to God. To deceive everybody. No, I shall not be taken in again! Let me be bad, but at least not a liar, not a humbug!"

"But who is a humbug?" Varenka said, reproachfully. "You're talking as if . . ."

But Kitty was in one of her fits of temper. She would not let Varenka finish.

"I'm not talking of you—not of you at all. You are perfection. Yes, yes. I know you are perfection. But how can I help it if I am bad? This would never have happened if I were not bad. Very well, then. Let me be bad, but I'm not going to pretend any more. What do I care about Mrs. Petrov? Let them live as they like, and let me live as I like. I can't be different. And yet it's not that—it's not that!"

"What is not that?"

"Everything. I can't live except as my heart dictates, but you live according to rules. I have grown fond of you just because I felt like it, but I expect you did so only in order to save me, to teach me."

275

"You're being unfair," said Varenka.

"But I'm not saying anything about anybody else, I'm merely speaking of myself."

"Kitty!" her mother called from outside. "Come here and show your father your coral necklace."

Kitty took her coral necklace in its box from the table and with a proud look, without making it up with her friend, went to her mother.

"What's the matter? Why are you so flushed?" her mother and father cried with one voice.

"It's nothing," she replied. "I'll be back in a jiffy," and ran back into the house.

"She's still here," she thought. "What am I to say to her? Oh dear, what have I done? What have I said? Why have I offended her? What am I to do? What am I to say to her?" thought Kitty, stopping at the door.

Varenka, with her hat on, sat at the table examining the spring of her parasol which Kitty had broken. She raised her head.

"Varenka, I'm sorry. Please forgive me!" whispered Kitty, going up to her. "I don't remember what I said. I . . ."

"I really didn't mean to upset you," said Varenka, smiling.

Peace was made. But with her father's return, all the world in which she had been living was completely changed for Kitty. She did not renounce all that she had learned, but she realized that she was deceiving herself in imagining that she could be what she wanted to be. She seemed to have recovered consciousness; she felt without hypocrisy or boastfulness the whole difficulty of remaining on the heights to which she had wished to rise; in addition, she felt the heavy burden of that world of grief, sickness, and death in which she was living; the efforts she had made to force herself to love it seemed appalling to her now, and she longed to get back quickly to the fresh air, back to Russia, to Yergushovo, where, as she had learned from a letter, her sister Dolly had already gone with the children.

But her love for Varenka did not diminish. When she said good-by to her, Kitty begged her to come and stay with them in Russia.

"I'll come when you get married," said Varenka.

"I'll never get married."

"Well, in that case I won't come."

"Well, in that case I will get married for that reason only. Mind you don't forget your promise," said Kitty.

The doctor's prediction was fulfilled. Kitty returned home to Russia completely cured. She was not as carefree and gay as before, but she was calm and serene. Her Moscow cares and anxieties had become no more than a memory.

Part Three

CHAPTER 1

Sergey Ivanovich Koznyshev wanted a rest from his mental work and, instead of going abroad as usual, went to stay with his brother in the country at the end of May. Country life, he was convinced, was the best sort of life. He had now arrived at his brother's to enjoy that life. Konstantin Levin was very pleased, particularly as he did not expect his brother Nikolai that summer. But in spite of his affection and respect for Koznyshev, Levin felt ill at ease with his half-brother in the country. He felt ill at ease and, indeed, annoyed to see his brother's attitude to the country. To Levin the country was a place where one spent one's life, that is to say, a place where one rejoiced, suffered, and worked; to Koznyshev, however, the country was, on the one hand, a place of rest from work and, on the other, a useful antidote to depravity, which he accepted with pleasure and with a consciousness of its usefulness. To Levin the country was good because it was an occupation which provided you with the opportunity of doing undoubtedly useful work; to Koznyshev the country was particularly good because there one could and should do nothing. Besides, Koznyshev's attitude to the peasants jarred on Levin. Koznyshev always said that he knew and liked the peasantry, and he often chatted to the peasants, and he did it very well, without dissembling and without affectation, and from every such conversation he deduced general conclusions in favor of the peasants and as a proof of his knowledge of the common people. Levin did not like

278

such an attitude to the peasants. Levin looked upon the peasants more as the chief partner in a common enterprise, and in spite of all the respect and deep affection for the peasant, which, as he himself expressed it, he had probably imbibed with the milk of his peasant wet nurse, he, as their partner in a common enterprise, though sometimes full of admiration for the strength, meekness, and fairness of these men, was very often, when the common enterprise called for other qualities, furious with the peasant for his carelessness, untidiness, drunkenness, and lying. If he had been asked whether he liked the peasant, Levin would certainly not have known what to answer. He both liked and did not like the peasant, just as he liked and disliked people in general. Of course, being a kindhearted man, he liked people more than he disliked them, and the same was true of the peasants. But like or dislike the common people as if they were something apart he could not, for he not only lived among them and all his interests were bound up with them, but he also regarded himself as part of the common people, did not see any special qualities or shortcomings that distinguished himself from the common people, and could not see any difference between himself and them. Moreover, though he had long lived in the closest relations with the peasants, as their master, arbitrator, and, what was more, adviser (the peasants trusted him and would come thirty miles to seek advice from him), he had no definite views concerning them, and would have found it as difficult to answer the question whether he knew the common people as the question whether he liked them. To say that he knew the common people would have been for him the same as saying he knew men. He was constantly observing and getting to know people of all sorts, including peasant people, whom he considered good and interesting men, continually discovering new traits in them, changing his former opinions and formulating new ones. It was quite the reverse with Koznyshev. Just as he liked and praised country life as being the opposite of the life he did not like, so he liked the common people as being the opposite of the class of people he did not like, and so, too, he knew the common people as something in contrast to humanity in general. In his methodical mind definite views of peasant life had been clearly formed, and these were partly deduced from that life itself, but chiefly from contrast with other ways of life. He never altered his opinions about the common people or his sympathetic attitude toward them.

In the dispute which took place between the brothers when discussing the peasant, Koznyshev was always victorious just because he had definite views about them, their characters, qualities, and tastes; while Levin had no definite and fixed ideas, so that in their arguments Levin was always convicted of contradicting himself.

To Koznyshev his younger brother was a splendid fellow, with his heart in the right place, as he expressed it in French, but with a mind which, though rather quick, was too much under the influence of the impressions of the moment and, therefore, full of contradictions. With an elder brother's condescension, he sometimes explained to him the meaning of things, but could find no pleasure in arguing with him because he defeated him too easily.

Levin regarded his brother as a man of great intellect and vast knowledge, noble in the highest sense of the word and endowed with the faculty of working for the general good. But in his heart of hearts, the older he grew and the more intimately he knew his brother, the more and more often it occurred to him that this faculty of working for the general good, which he felt he completely lacked, was perhaps not so much a quality as a lack of something, not a lack of kindly, honest, and noble desires and tastes, but a lack of the life force, of what is called heart, the impulse which drives a man to choose one out of all the innumerable paths of life open to him and to desire that one only. The more he got to know his brother, the more he noticed that Koznyshev and many other people who worked for the general good were not led to this love for the general good by their hearts, but because they had reasoned out in their minds that it was a good thing to do that kind of work and did it only because of that. Levin was confirmed in this supposition by noticing that his brother did not take the question of the general good or the immortality of the soul any more to heart than a game of chess or the clever construction of a new machine.

Something else that made Levin feel uncomfortable in his brother's presence in the country was that in the

country, especially in summer, Levin was always busy
with the farm and the long summer day was too short
to do all that there was to do, while Koznyshev was just
resting. But though he was resting now, that is to say,
he was not working at his book, he was so used to mental activity that he liked to put into elegant and concise
form the ideas which occurred to him, and he liked having someone to listen to him. His most usual and natural
listener was his brother. And therefore, in spite of the
friendliness and simplicity of their relations, Levin felt
uncomfortable at leaving him alone. Koznyshev liked to
lie on the grass in the sun, basking and chatting lazily.

"You can't imagine," he used to say to his brother,
"what a real pleasure this Ukrainian laziness is to me.
Not a thought in my head—a complete void."

But Levin was bored sitting and listening to him, particularly because he knew that in his absence manure
was being carted into fields which were not ploughed
into strips ready for it and being heaped up anyhow if
he were not there to see; that they would not screw the
shares into the ploughs but let them come off and then
say that the ploughs were a silly invention and could not
be compared to the good old Russian wooden plough,
and so on.

"Haven't you walked about long enough in the heat?"
Koznyshev would say to him.

"Oh, I have just to run down to the office for a minute," Levin would reply and he would run off to the
fields.

CHAPTER 2

At the beginning of June it so happened that Agafya,
Levin's old nurse and housekeeper, as she was carrying
to the cellar a jar of mushrooms she had just pickled,
slipped and fell and sprained her wrist. The district doctor, a talkative young man who had only just qualified,
arrived, examined the hand, said it was not dislocated,
made a compress, and staying to dinner, was evidently
delighted to have a talk with the celebrated Sergey Koznyshev. To show off his enlightened views, he told him
all the gossip of the district and complained of the unsat-

isfactory condition of the rural district councils. Kozny-shev listened attentively, asked questions, and stimulated by the presence of a new listener, became quite talkative and made some pointed and weighty remarks, which were respectfully appreciated by the young doctor, and got into that state of animation his brother knew so well, into which he generally got after a brilliant and lively conversation. After the doctor's departure Koznyshev expressed the wish to go to the river with his fishing rod. He was fond of angling and was apparently proud of being fond of such a stupid occupation.

Levin, who had to go to the fields and the meadows, offered to give his brother a lift in the trap.

It was the time of year—the turn of the summer—when one already has a good idea of what the harvest will be like that year, when the next year's sowings have to be planned, and when the time for haymaking is drawing near; when the gray-green rye waves its formed but not yet swollen ears in the wind; when the green oats, interspersed with clumps of yellow grass, stand unevenly in the late-sown fields; when the early buckwheat spreads out and hides the ground; when the fallow land, trodden as hard as stone by the cattle, is half ploughed, leaving long strips untouched by the plough; when the fields in the early morning smell of dried heaps of manure mingled with the honeyed fragrance of the grasses, and the lowland meadows, waiting for the scythe, stretch far and wide like a sea by the banks of the river, with here and there blackening heaps of weeded sorrel stalks.

It was the time of that brief lull in the work on the farms before the beginning of harvest, repeated every year and every year claiming the total strength of the entire peasant population. The harvest promised to be excellent, the days clear and hot and the nights short and dewy.

The brothers had to drive through the woods to reach the water meadows. Koznyshev was all the time full of admiration for the beauty of the woods under the thick foliage of the trees, pointing out to his brother an old lime tree, looking dark on the shady side, but gay with yellow stipules and ready to burst into flower or the brilliant emerald-green shoots of this year on the trees. Levin did not like talking or hearing about the beauty of nature. Words for him detracted from the beauty of what he saw. He agreed with what his brother said, but he could not help thinking of other things. When they came out of the woods, his entire attention was concentrated on a fallow field on a hillside, here and there yellow with grass, or broken up and cut into squares, or dotted in some parts with heaps of manure, or even ploughed. A string of carts were moving across the field. Levin counted the carts and was pleased to see that all that was wanted would be brought, and at the sight of the meadows his thoughts turned to the haymaking. He always felt particularly excited at the thought of haymaking. When they reached the meadow, Levin stopped the horse.

The morning dew still lingered on the thick undergrowth of the grass and Koznyshev, afraid of getting his feet wet, asked his brother to drive him across the meadow to the willow clump near which perch could be caught. Loath as Levin was to crush his grass, he drove across the meadow. The tall grass twined softly about the wheels and the horse's legs, leaving its seeds on the wet spokes and hubs.

Koznyshev sat down under a bush, sorted out his tackle, while Levin led the horse away, tied it to a tree, and stepped into the vast gray-green sea of grass, unruffled by the wind. The silky grass with its ripening seeds reached almost to his waist where the meadow had been flooded in spring.

Walking right across the meadow, Levin came out on the road where he met an old man with a swollen eye carrying a swarm of bees in a hive.

"Well, have you found one, Fomich?" he asked.

"Found one, sir? I'd be glad to keep my own. This is the second time a swarm has got away. It's them lads there I have to thank for getting it. Ploughing your field, they were, sir. So they unharnessed a horse and galloped after it."

"Well, what do you say, Fomich? Shall we start mowing or wait a little longer?"

"Well, sir, our custom is to wait till St. Peter's Day. But you, sir, always mow earlier. Well, why not? The grass is good. There'll be more room for the cattle."

"And what do you think of the weather?"

"Well, sir, it's all in God's hands. Maybe it will keep fine."

Levin went back to his brother. Koznyshev had caught nothing, but he was not bored and seemed in the best of spirits. Levin saw that, excited by his conversation with the doctor, he was eager to go on talking. Levin, on the other hand, was impatient to get home in order to make arrangements about getting the mowers for next day and make up his mind about the haymaking, a matter that was of great concern to him.

"Well, let's go," he said.

"What's the hurry? Let's sit here a little. How wet you are, though! I've had no bite, but it's lovely here. Every kind of sport is good because it brings you in touch with nature. Oh, look how lovely this steely water is!" he said. "These grassy banks," he went on, "always remind me of that riddle—do you know it? The grass says to the water: we shall go on waving, we shall go on waving."

"I don't know that one," answered Levin, wearily.

CHAPTER 3

"You know, I've been thinking about you," said Koznyshev. "From what that doctor told me, and he is not a stupid fellow by any means, what's going on in your district is simply disgraceful. I've told you before and I say it again: it is wrong of you not to go to the meetings of your rural council and in general to take no part in its activities. If decent people keep away, goodness only knows what's going to happen. We pay our dues; the money is all spent on salaries, and there are no schools, no male nurses, no midwives, no dispensaries—nothing!"

"I've tried, you know," Levin replied quietly and reluctantly, "but I can't any more. I'm afraid that's all there is to it."

"But what is it you can't do? I confess I don't understand. I realize that there can be no question of indifference or inability. Is it simply laziness?"

"Neither the one nor the other, nor the third," replied Levin. "I have tried and I see I can do nothing."

He was not paying much attention to what his brother was saying. Looking attentively at the ploughland on the other side of the river, he made out something black,

284

but he was not sure whether it was only a horse or the bailiff on horseback.

"Why can you do nothing? You've made an attempt and because you don't think it was a success, you give up. I wonder you haven't got more self-respect."

"Self-respect?" said Levin, touched to the quick by his brother's words. "I don't understand what that has to do with it. If they had told me at the university that others understood the integral calculus and I didn't, that would have been a question of self-respect. But here one has first to be sure that one possesses the necessary ability for this sort of business and, above all, that this business is of the utmost importance."

"Well, and isn't it important?" said Koznyshev, feeling hurt that his brother should not consider important something that interested him and particularly that he was quite obviously only half listening to him.

"It does not seem important to me and, I'm afraid, it doesn't excite me particularly—I'm sorry," replied Levin, having at last made out that what he saw was the bailiff, who had apparently taken the peasants off the ploughing. They were turning the ploughs over. "They couldn't have finished ploughing, could they?" he thought.

"But, look here," said his elder brother with a frown on his handsome, intelligent face, "there's a limit to everything. It's all very well to be an eccentric, to be a sincere man, and to dislike hypocrisy—I know all about that. But, you see, what you are saying either has no sense at all or very bad sense. How can you consider it of no importance that the peasants whom, as you assure me, you love—"

"I never assured you of anything of the kind," thought Levin.

"—are dying without help? Ignorant midwives cause the deaths of babies and the peasants stagnate in ignorance and are at the mercy of every village clerk. You have been given the means of remedying it and you don't do anything to help because you don't consider it important."

And Koznyshev confronted his brother with this dilemma: "Either you are so intellectually backward that you cannot see all that you could do, or you don't want to sacrifice your peace of mind, your vanity, and I don't know what else, to do it."

Levin felt that he had either to submit or to acknowledge his lack of love for the common cause. And that offended and hurt him.

"It's both the one and the other," he said resolutely. "I don't see that it is possible. . . ."

"What do you mean? Impossible to organize a medical service if the money is properly distributed?"

"Yes, impossible. At least so it seems to me. To organize a medical service over the three thousand square miles of our district, with our roads covered in deep slush when the snows begin melting, with our blizzards, and the high pressure of work in the fields is, I maintain, impossible. Besides, I have no great faith in medicine, anyway. . . ."

"But, come now, that's not fair. I can give you thousands of examples. Well, and what about the schools?"

"What do you want schools for?"

"What are you saying? Can there be any doubt about the advantage of education? If it's good for you, it's good for everybody else."

Levin felt himself morally concerned and he therefore grew excited and involuntarily blurted out the chief reason for his indifference to social questions.

"All this may be very good," he said, "but why should I worry about the establishment of medical clinics which I should never make use of and schools to which I should never send my children, to which the peasant would not want to send his either, and to which, as a matter of fact, I'm not at all sure that they ought to be sent?"

Koznyshev was for a moment startled by this unexpected view on the matter, but he at once formed a new plan of attack.

He paused for a minute, drew out one line, cast it again, and turned to his brother with a smile.

"But," he said, "you must admit that, to begin with, there is a need for a medical clinic. You see, we sent for the district doctor for Agafya, didn't we?"

"Well, I think her hand will remain crooked all the same."

"That remains to be seen. . . . Then a peasant who can read and write is more useful to you and is worth more."

"Oh no," Levin replied categorically. "Ask anyone you like. A literate peasant is far worse as a laborer.

And it's impossible to mend the roads, and as soon as a bridge is built, it is stolen."

"However," said Koznyshev, frowning, for he did not like people to contradict him and especially those who kept continually going off at a tangent and introducing new arguments so that it was impossible to decide which to answer first, "however, that is not the point. Let me ask you this: do you admit that education is a good thing for the people?"

"I do," said Levin without thinking, and at once realized that he had not said what he really thought. He felt that if he were to admit it, it would be proved to him that he was talking meaningless nonsense. How it would be proved to him he did not know, but he knew that it would certainly be proved logically to him, and he waited for that proof.

The argument turned out to be far simpler than Levin had anticipated.

"If you admit it to be good," said Koznyshev, "then, as an honest man, you cannot help caring for, and sympathizing with, this work and wishing to work for it."

"But I don't yet admit that this work is a good thing," said Levin, blushing.

"You don't? But you have just said—"

"What I mean to say is that I do not admit that it is either good or possible."

"But you can't tell without having tried it."

"Well, let us assume," said Levin, though he did not assume it at all, "let us assume that it is so. Still, I don't see why I should be bothered with it."

"You mean?"

"Oh no, since we have started discussing it, you'd better explain it to me from the philosophical point of view," said Levin.

"I don't see what philosophy has got to do with it," said Koznyshev in a tone—so at least Levin thought—that made it seem as though he did not recognize his brother's right to talk about philosophy. And that made Levin cross.

"This is what it has to do with it," he said, getting excited. "I believe the chief motive of all our actions to be, when all is said and done, our personal happiness. As a nobleman, I can see nothing in our rural councils today that could contribute to my well-being. The roads are not better and could not be better, and my horses carry me well enough over the bad ones. I don't require doctors and medical clinics. I don't need a magistrate— I never applied to him and never will. I not only do not require schools, but as I have explained to you, they would even do me harm. To me rural councils mean nothing but a tax of six kopecks an acre, my having to spend a night in town eaten by bedbugs and listening to all sorts of rubbish and nastiness, and my personal interests do not induce me to do it."

"But really," Koznyshev interrupted him with a smile, "personal interests did not induce us to work for the liberation of the peasants, but we did work for it."

"Oh no," Levin interrupted, getting more and more excited, "the liberation of the peasants is quite a different matter. There, personal interests did come in. We wanted to throw off a yoke that weighed heavily upon us all, upon all decent people. But to be a member of a rural council, to discuss how many scavengers are needed and how the drains should be laid in a town in which I don't live, to be a juryman and try a peasant who has stolen some bacon and listen for six hours on end to all sorts of nonsense jabbered by the counsel for the defense and the public prosecutors and hear the president of the court ask our old village idiot Alyoshka: 'Prisoner at the bar, do you plead guilty or not guilty to the indictment of having stolen the bacon?' . . . 'Eh-h-?' "

Levin got carried away and began impersonating the judge and the village idiot Alyoshka; it seemed to him that it was all to the point.

But Koznyshev shrugged his shoulders.

"Well, what do you mean to say by that?"

"What I mean to say is simply that the rights that concern me—my interests I shall always defend with all the power at my command; that when the police came and searched us students and the gendarmes read our letters, I was ready to defend with all the power at my command these rights, to defend my right to education and liberty. I can understand compulsory military service which affects the fate of my children, my brothers, and myself; I am ready to discuss the things that concern me; but to discuss how to dispose of forty thousand rubles of district council money or try the village idiot Alyoshka, I neither understand nor can take part in it."

Levin spoke as if the floodgates of his speech had burst open. Koznyshev smiled.

"And tomorrow you may have to appear in a court of law: would you really prefer to be tried in the old criminal court?"

"I am not going to appear in a court of law. I'm not going to cut anybody's throat, so I don't want anything of the kind. Let me tell you," he went on, again going off at a tangent, "our rural self-governing institutions and the rest of it are like the little birch trees we stick in the ground on Trinity Sunday to look like the wood which has grown up by itself in Europe, and quite honestly I can't bring myself to water these birch trees or believe in them."

Koznyshev only shrugged his shoulders to express by this gesture his surprise at the sudden appearance of those birches in their discussion, though, of course, he had at once grasped what his brother meant.

"Look here," he observed, "one really can't conduct an argument like that."

But Levin was anxious to justify himself for the failing of which he was conscious, namely his indifference to the common good, and he went on:

"It is my belief that no activity can endure for any length of time if it is not based on self-interest. That is the common, philosophic truth," he declared, emphasizing the word "philosophic," as if he wanted to show that he had as much right as anyone else to talk about philosophy.

Koznyshev smiled again. "He, too," he thought, "has some sort of philosophy of his own at the service of his inclinations."

"Well, you know," he said, "you'd better leave philosophy alone. The main task of philosophy has been always, in all ages, to find the necessary connection existing between personal and general interests. But that's beside the point. The point is that all I have to do is to correct your comparison. The little birch trees have not been stuck in the ground. Some of them have been planted and we must treat them with great care. Only those peoples have a future, only those peoples can be called historic, who have an intuitive sense of what is important and significant in their national institutions and who value them."

And Koznyshev carried the discussion into the realm of philosophy and history and showed him how utterly erroneous his views were.

"As for your not liking it, that, I hope you don't mind me saying, is nothing but our Russian laziness and aristocratic habits, and I'm quite sure that in your case it is merely a temporary error and will pass."

Levin was silent. He felt that he had not been left a leg to stand on, but at the same time he could not help feeling that his brother had not grasped what he wanted to say. He only did not know why it was so: whether it was because he could not express clearly what he wanted to say, or because his brother would not or could not understand him. But he did not pursue the matter any further and, without replying to his brother, began to think of a quite different and personal matter.

Koznyshev wound in his last line, untied the horse, and they drove back home.

CHAPTER 4

The personal matter that occupied Levin during his conversation with his brother was this: the year before, while visiting a field during haymaking, he lost his temper with his bailiff and to calm himself had made use of a remedy of his own—he took a scythe from one of the peasants and himself began to mow.

He liked this work so much that several times he went to mow himself: he mowed all the meadow in front of his house and this year ever since early spring he had planned to mow with the peasants for whole days together. Since his brother's arrival, however, he had been wondering whether to go mowing or not. He did not like to leave his brother alone for days on end and he was also afraid that his brother might laugh at him. But walking across the meadow and recalling the impressions mowing had made on him, he almost made up his mind to go. After his irritating conversation with his brother he again remembered his intention.

"I must have some physical exercise," he thought, "or my character will most certainly get spoiled," and he decided that he would go and do some mowing, however uncomfortable his brother and the peasants might make him feel.

In the evening Levin went to the office, gave orders about the work and sent to the villages to summon the mowers for the next day to cut the hay in the Kalina meadow, the largest and finest he had.

"And please send my scythe to Titus to be set and have it brought round tomorrow," he said, trying not to look embarrassed. "I may do a bit of mowing myself."

The bailiff smiled and said: "Very good, sir."

That evening at tea Levin told his brother, too.

"It looks as if the weather has settled," he said. "To-morrow I start mowing."

"I like that work very much," said Koznyshev.

"I like it awfully. I've occasionally mown with the peasants myself, and tomorrow I want to mow all day."

Koznyshev raised his head and looked at his brother with interest.

"How do you mean? All day, just like the peasants?"

"Yes, it's very pleasant," said Levin.

"It's an excellent physical exercise, but I don't think you'll be able to stand it," said Koznyshev without the slightest irony.

"I've tried it. At first it's a bit hard, but you get drawn into it afterward. I don't think I shall lag behind."

"I see. But tell me, how do the peasants look on it? I expect they must laugh up their sleeves at their master's absurd whims."

"I don't think so. But it's such cheerful work and at the same time so hard that one hasn't time for thinking."

"But how can you have dinner with them? It would be a bit awkward to send you roast turkey and a bottle of Lafitte out there, wouldn't it?"

"Oh no, I'll just come home when they have their midday rest."

Next morning Levin got up earlier than usual, but giving orders about the farming delayed him, and when he came to the meadow the mowers were already doing their second row.

From the top of the hill he could already see below the shady part of the field that had been cut, with the grayish heaps of mown grass and dark piles of coats thrown down by the mowers where they had started on the first row.

As he rode nearer, the peasants came into sight, mowing slowly one behind the other, in a long line, each swinging his scythe in his own manner, some with their coats on and some in their shirts. He counted forty-two of them.

They moved unhurriedly over the uneven bottom of the meadow, where a weir had once been. Levin recognized some of his own men. There was old Yermil in a very long white shirt, swinging his scythe with his back bent; there was the young lad Vaska, whom Levin employed as a coachman, who mowed the whole width of a swath with one mighty swing of his arm; there was Titus, Levin's instructor in the art of mowing, a thin little peasant, walking in front of the mowers without stooping and cutting his wide swath as if playing with his scythe.

Levin dismounted and, tethering his horse by the roadside, went up to Titus, who, fetching another scythe from behind a bush, gave it to him.

"Here it is, sir. Sharp as a razor, cuts by itself," said Titus, taking off his cap and smiling as he handed the scythe to Levin.

Levin took the scythe and began trying it out. As they finished their rows, the peasants, perspiring and cheerful, came out into the road one after another and smilingly exchanged greetings with their master. They all looked at him, but no one made any remark until a tall old man with a wrinkled, beardless face, in a sheepskin jacket, stepped out onto the road and addressed him.

"Mind, sir," he said, "it's too late to back out now, so you'd better not lag behind," and Levin heard smothered laughter among the mowers.

"I'll do my best not to," Levin said, taking his place behind Titus and waiting for his turn to start.

"Mind you do, sir," repeated the old man.

Titus made room for Levin, and Levin went after him. The grass was short and close to the road and Levin, who had not done any mowing for a long time and was disconcerted by so many eyes turned on him, mowed badly at first, though he swung his scythe with vigor. He heard voices behind him:

"It's not been properly put on, the handle's too high, look how he has to stoop," said one.

"Press more on the heel, sir," said another.

"Never mind," said the old man. "It's all right. He'll get into it. See? There he goes. . . . Taking too wide a swath, sir. You'll tire yourself out. . . . Must do it right, seeing as how he's the master. Working for himself, he is. Mind the edge of the swath, sir! That's what the likes of us used to get hit on the back for!"

The grass became softer and Levin, listening but not answering back, tried to mow as well as possible as he walked behind Titus. They advanced a hundred yards. Titus was going on without stopping and without showing any signs of fatigue; but Levin was already beginning to fear that he would not be able to keep up: he felt so tired.

As he swung his scythe he felt his strength almost giving out and he decided to ask Titus to stop. But at that very moment Titus stopped of his own accord and, bending down, picked up a handful of grass, wiped his scythe, and began whetting it. Levin straightened himself and, heaving a sigh, looked around. The peasant behind was obviously also tired, for he stopped before he got up to Levin and started whetting his scythe. Titus whetted his own scythe and then Levin's, and they went on.

The next time it was the same. Titus went on swinging his scythe, sweep after sweep, without stopping and without tiring. Levin followed, trying not to lag behind, and he found it getting harder and harder till the moment came when he felt that he had no more strength left, but at that very moment Titus stopped and whetted the scythe.

So they passed all along the first row. And this long row seemed particularly difficult to Levin; but when the row was finished and Titus, his scythe slung over his shoulder, turned about and slowly retraced his steps, taking care to place his feet in the tracks left by his heels on the mown grass, Levin walked back in the same way along his own swath. Though the sweat was pouring down his face and dripping from his nose and his back was as wet as if it had been soaked in water, he felt happy. What pleased him particularly was that now he knew that he would be able to hold out.

The only thing that marred his joy was the fact that his row was not good. "I must swing the scythe less with my arms and more with my whole body," he thought, comparing Titus' swath, cut close to the ground and evenly along the whole of its length, with his own scattered and uneven swath.

The first row, as Levin had noticed, Titus mowed especially quickly, probably to put the master to the test, and it happened to be a long one. The next rows were easier, but Levin had still to strain every nerve not to drop behind the peasants.

He thought of nothing and wished for nothing except not to drop behind the peasants and to do his work as well as possible. He heard nothing, except the swishing of the scythes and saw the erect figure of Titus receding in front of him, the curved half-circle of the mown grass, the grasses, and heads of flowers slowly falling in waves about the blade of his scythe, and ahead of him the end of the swath where there would be an interval of rest.

Suddenly, without knowing what it was or whence it came, he became conscious in the middle of his work of a pleasant sensation of coolness on his hot, perspiring shoulders. He looked up at the sky while his scythe was being sharpened. A dark cloud had spread low over the sky and large drops of rain were falling. Some of the peasants went to put on their coats; others, like Levin, merely moved their shoulders up and down joyfully, glad of the refreshing coolness.

They mowed one row after another. They moved along long rows and short rows, rows with good grass and with bad grass. Levin lost all consciousness of time and had no idea whatever whether it was late or early. His work was undergoing a change which gave him intense pleasure. There were moments in the middle of his work when he forgot what he was doing, he felt quite at ease, and it was at those moments that his row was almost as even and good as Titus'. But as soon as he began thinking of what he was doing and trying to do better, he became at once conscious of how hard his task was, and his row turned out badly.

He finished yet another row and was about to go back again to start the next, when Titus stopped and, going up to the old man, whispered something to him. Both of them looked at the sun. "What are they talking about and why doesn't he start another row?" Levin thought, without realizing that the peasants had been mowing for four hours and that it was time for their breakfast.

"Breakfast time, sir," said the old man.

"Already? All right, breakfast, then!"

Levin handed his scythe to Titus and with the peasants, who were going to their coats for the bread, walked across the long stretch of mown grass, slightly sprinkled with rain, to his horse. It was only then that he realized that he had been wrong about the weather and that the rain was wetting his hay.

"The hay will be spoiled," he said.

"Don't worry, sir," said the old man. "Mow in rain, rake when it's fine!"

Levin untied his horse and rode home to his coffee. Koznyshev had only just got up. Before he had time to dress and come to the dining room, Levin had gone back to the haymaking.

CHAPTER 5

After breakfast Levin found himself placed not behind Titus as before, but between the old man, who was fond of cracking jokes and who now invited him to be his neighbor, and a young peasant who had only got married last autumn and who was mowing this summer for the first time.

The old man, holding himself erect, walked in front, moving with wide, even strides, his feet turned out and with precise, regular motion, which apparently cost him no more effort than swinging his arms in walking, as though in play, laid the grass in a high, level ridge. It was as though it were not he but the scythe itself that went swishing through the juicy grass.

Behind Levin came the lad Mishka. His good-looking, young face, a twist of grass bound around his hair, worked all over with the effort; but the moment one looked at him, he smiled. He quite obviously would have died rather than admit that it was hard work for him.

Levin walked between them. In the heat of the day the mowing did not seem such hard work to him. The

295

perspiration in which he was drenched cooled him, and the sun, which burned his back, his head, and his arm bare to the elbow, gave strength and added perseverance to his labor; and more and more often now came those moments of insensibility when it was possible not to think about what one was doing. The scythe cut of itself. Those were happy moments. More joyous still were the moments when they reached the river at the end of the swaths and the old man wiped his scythe with a handful of wet grass, rinsed its blade in the fresh water of the stream, scooped up some water in his whetstone box, and offered it to Levin.

"Come on, sir, have some of my kvass! Good, isn't it?" he would say with a wink.

And, indeed, Levin had never tasted a drink so delicious as this warm water with bits of grass floating in it and a rusty flavor from the tin box. And immediately after that came the blissful, slow walk with his hand on the scythe, during which one could wipe away the excessive perspiration, fill one's lungs with air, and look over the whole long line of mowers and what was going on all around in the woods and the fields.

The longer Levin went on mowing, the oftener he experienced those moments of oblivion when it was not that his arms swung his scythe, but that the scythe itself made his whole body, full of life and conscious of itself, move after it, and as though by magic the work did itself, of its own accord and without a thought being given to it, with the utmost precision and regularity. Those were the most blessed moments.

The work became hard only when one had to put a stop to this unconscious motion and think; when one had to mow round a mound or an unweeded cluster of sorrel. The old man did it easily. When he came to a mound, he would change his action and cleared the mound on both sides with short strokes first with the end and then with the heel of the scythe. And while he did this, he kept examining and observing everything that came to light before him: sometimes he would pick some plant and eat it or offer it to Levin; sometimes he threw a twig out of the way with the end of his scythe, or examined a quail's nest from which the hen bird had flown up from right under the scythe; sometimes he caught a snake that happened to cross his path and, lifting it with the scythe as though with a fork, showed it to Levin and then threw it away.

For Levin and for the young village lad on the other side of him such changes of movement were difficult. Both of them, having adapted themselves to one strained movement, were in the grip of feverish activity and were quite incapable of altering the movement and at the same time observing what was before them.

Levin did not notice how time passed. Had he been asked how long he had been mowing, he would have said half an hour, while actually it was getting on to dinnertime. As they were about to start on another row, the old man drew Levin's attention to the little girls and boys, approaching from different sides along the road and through the tall grass, hardly visible above it, carrying bundles of bread, which dragged their little arms down, and jugs of kvass stoppered with rags.

"Look at the midges crawling along, sir," he said, pointing to the children and glancing at the sun from under his hand.

They mowed two more rows; the old man stopped.

"It's dinnertime, sir," he said firmly.

And on reaching the river, the mowers went across the rows of cut grass to where their coats lay and where the children who had brought them their dinner were waiting for them. The peasants gathered together, those who had come from a distance in the shadow of their carts and those who lived nearer under a willow bush, over which they threw grass.

Levin sat down beside them; he did not feel like going home.

All constraint in the presence of the master had vanished long ago. The peasants began preparing for dinner. Some had a wash, the young lads had a bathe in the river, and others arranged places for their after-dinner rest, untied their bundles of bread, and unstoppered their jugs of kvass. The old man crumbled up some bread in a cup, mashed it with the handle of a spoon, poured some water from his whetstone box over it, broke up some more bread, and having sprinkled it with salt, turned to the east to say his prayer.

"Come, sir, have some of my grub," he said, squatting on his knees in front of his cup.

The rye bread and water were so delicious that Levin

changed his mind about going home to lunch. He shared the old man's meal and got into conversation with him about his family affairs, taking the keenest interest in them, and telling him about his own affairs and all the circumstances which would interest the old peasant. He felt much nearer to him than to his brother and could not help smiling at the affection he felt for this man. When the old man got up again, said his prayer, and lay down under a bush, putting some grass under his head, Levin did the same, and in spite of the clinging flies and midges that were so persistent in the sunshine and that tickled his perspiring face and body, he immediately fell asleep and only woke up when the sun had gone round to the other side of the bush and reached him. The old man had long been awake and sat setting the scythes of the younger lads.

Levin looked round and could not recognize the place: everything had changed so much. An enormous expanse of meadow was already mown and it shone with a peculiar fresh glitter with its sweet-smelling hay in the slanting rays of the evening sun. And the bushes at the river had been cut down, and the river itself, not visible before, shining like steel along its winding course, and the peasants getting up and moving about, and the steep wall of the yet uncut grass of the meadow, and the hawk hovering over the bare meadow—all of it was completely new. Fully awake, Levin began to calculate how much had been mown and how much could still be done that day.

Quite a considerable amount had been done by the forty-two men. The whole of the big meadow which used to take thirty men two days to mow in the days of serfdom had been cut. Only the corners where the rows were short remained to be done. But Levin was anxious to get as much mowing done that day as possible and he felt it was a pity that the sun was setting so quickly. He was not feeling at all tired; all he wanted was to go on working and finish as much as was possible in the short time that still remained.

"Could we do Mashkin Heights today, do you think?" he said to the old man.

"Aye, we might do that. The sun's getting low, though. What about giving the lads a little vodka?"

About teatime, when the mowers were sitting down

again and those who smoked lit their pipes, the old man told the men that if they mowed Mashkin Heights, there would be vodka.

"Mow it? Of course we'll mow it! Come on, Titus! We'll do it in no time. You can eat your fill at night. Come on!" shouted voices, and the mowers went back to the next row, finishing their bread as they went.

"Now then, lads, steady does it!" said Titus, running on ahead almost at a trot.

"Go on, go on," said the old man, hurrying after him and easily catching him up. "Mind, I'll cut you down!"

And the young and the old mowed with a will as if racing one another. But though they were in a hurry, they did not spoil the grass and the swaths fell just as cleanly and precisely as before. The little patch left in the corner was whisked off in five minutes. Before the last mowers had time to finish their swaths, those in front, their coats slung over their shoulders, were crossing the road toward Mashkin Heights.

The sun was already setting behind the trees when, their tin whetstone boxes rattling, they entered the small wooded ravine of Mashkin Heights. The grass in the middle of the ravine was waist-high, tender, soft, and broad-bladed, speckled here and there among the trees with wild pansies.

After a brief consultation, whether to mow the ravine lengthwise or straight across, Prokhor Yermilin, also a famous mower, a huge, darkish peasant, went on ahead. He mowed a swath up to the top of the ravine, then turned back again and started mowing. The rest proceeded to fall into line behind him, going downhill through the glen and uphill right to the edge of the wood. The sun had set behind the wood. The shadows had fallen, and the mowers were in the sun only at the top of the hill; below, at the bottom of the ravine from which the mist was rising, and on the opposite side, they moved along in the fresh, dewy shade. Work was in full swing.

The cut grass fell with a succulent sound in high, sweet-scented rows. On the short swaths the mowers, crossed together on every side, their tin boxes rattling, their scythes ringing every time they happened to touch, urged each other on with merry shouts.

Levin was mowing as before between the young peasant and the old man. The old man, who had put on his sheepskin jacket, was as jolly, jocose, and free in his movements as before. In the wood they continually came upon birch mushrooms, which had swelled in the succulent grass and which were cut down by the scythes. But whenever the old man came upon a mushroom, he bent down, picked it up, and put it inside his jacket. "Another present for my old woman," he kept saying.

Easy as it was to cut the wet, soft grass, it was hard work going up and down the steep slopes of the ravine. But the old man was not in the least troubled by it. Swinging his scythe just as usual, he climbed slowly up the steep slope, taking short, firm steps with his feet shod in large bast shoes, and though his whole body and his loosely hanging trousers below his long shirt shook, he did not miss a single blade of grass or a single mushroom, and went on cracking jokes with the peasants and Levin. Levin, who followed him, often thought that he would certainly fall as he climbed up the steep hillock with his scythe, for it would have normally been hard to reach the top even without a scythe. He felt as if some external force were setting him in motion.

CHAPTER 6

Mashkin Heights were mown, the last swaths finished. The peasants put on their coats and were gaily walking home. Levin mounted and, regretfully taking leave of the peasants, rode back home. He looked back from the top of the hill; they could no longer be seen in the mist rising from the valley, but he could hear their merry, rough voices, their loud laughter, and the sound of clanking scythes.

Koznyshev had his dinner long ago and was drinking iced lemon and water in his room, looking through the newspapers and magazines which had just arrived by post, when Levin burst in, his matted hair clinging to his perspiring forehead and his back and chest black with moisture.

"We've mown the whole meadow!" he cried joyfully. "Oh, I feel so good, so wonderful! And how did you spend your time?" he inquired, completely forgetting their unpleasant conversation of the previous day.

"Good heavens, what a sight you are!" said Koznyshev, turning round and looking rather displeased at his brother at first. "And the door, do shut the door!" he cried. "You must have let in a dozen at least."

Koznyshev could not bear flies and in his own room he only opened the windows at night and kept the door carefully closed.

"Not one, I swear. And if I have, I'll catch it. You can't imagine what a delight it was! How did you spend the day?"

"Oh, all right. You haven't really been mowing the whole day, have you? You must be as hungry as a wolf. Kuzma has got everything ready for you."

"No, I'm not hungry. I had something there. I will go and have a wash, though."

"Yes, go, go, I'll join you presently," said Koznyshev, shaking his head as he looked at his brother. "Run along, then," he added, smiling, and he gathered his book and prepared to go too. He suddenly felt quite gay himself and he did not want to part from his brother. "But where were you when it was raining?"

"Raining? Only a drop or two. Well, I'll be back in a couple of minutes. So you had a nice day? That's excellent." And Levin went off to dress.

Five minutes later the brothers met again in the dining room. Though Levin had imagined that he was not hungry and sat down to dinner simply because he did not want to hurt Kuzma's feelings, when he began to eat the food seemed extraordinarily appetizing to him. Koznyshev could not help smiling as he looked at him.

"Oh, by the way, there's a letter for you," he said. "Kuzma, fetch it please. It's downstairs. And, mind, shut the door."

The letter was from Oblonsky. Levin read it aloud. Oblonsky wrote from Petersburg: "I have had a letter from Dolly. She's at Yergushovo and she does not seem to be able to get things straight. Please, ride over and see her and help her with your advice—you know all about everything. She will be so glad to see you. She's quite alone, poor thing. My mother-in-law and all the others are still abroad."

"That's splendid! I'll certainly go and see her," said Levin. "Or shall we go together? She's such a nice woman. Don't you think so?"

"Are they not far from here?"

"About twenty-five miles. Maybe even thirty. But the road is excellent. We'll have a nice drive."

"I'll come gladly," said Koznyshev, still smiling.

The sight of his younger brother had immediately put him in a good humor.

"You certainly have an appetite!" he said, looking at his dark red, sunburned face bent over the plate.

"Splendid! You can't imagine what a wonderful regimen it is for every kind of folly. I'm thinking of enriching medicine with a new term: *Arbeitskur*."

"Well, I don't think you're in need of it."

"No, but people suffering from nervous diseases do."

"Yes, it ought to be tried. You know, I almost went to have a look at you haymaking, but the heat was so unbearable that I got no further than the forest. I sat there a little and then walked through the woods to the village, where I met your wet nurse and sounded her as to what the peasants think of you. So far as I could make out, they don't approve of it. She said, 'It's not the sort of thing a gentleman ought to do.' It seems to me that the peasants have a very definite idea of what the gentry should and should not do. And they object to the gentry going outside the bounds which, according to them, have been set for them."

"Perhaps, but, you see, it's a pleasure such as I've never experienced in my life before. And there's nothing wrong about it, is there?" replied Levin. "I can't help it if they don't like it. Still, I don't think it matters. Do you?"

"I can see," Koznyshev went on, "that on the whole you are very satisfied with your day."

"Yes, very satisfied indeed. We finished the meadow. And I made friends with such a wonderful old man there. You can't imagine what a delightful fellow he is!"

"Well, so you are satisfied with your day. Me too. First of all, I solved two chess problems. One is a real beauty—opens with a pawn. I'll show you. And then I thought over our conversation yesterday."

"Did you? Our conversation yesterday?" said Levin, who had finished dinner and sat blissfully blinking and puffing and quite unable to remember what yesterday's conversation had been about.

"I think that you're partly right. Our difference of opinion is mainly due to the fact that you make personal interest the chief incentive, while I believe that every man with a certain degree of education ought to be interested in the common good. You may be right in thinking that activity supported by material interest might be preferable. Your nature is altogether too impulsive, too *primesautière*, as the French say. You must have either passionate, energetic activity or nothing."

Levin listened to his brother and understood absolutely nothing and did not wish to understand. He was only afraid his brother might ask him some question which would make it clear that he did not hear anything.

"That's how it is, old fellow," said Koznyshev, touching him on his shoulder.

"Why, of course!" Levin answered, with a childlike, guilty smile. "But what does it matter? I don't insist on my view." And he thought: "What was it I was arguing with him about? Of course, I'm right and he's right, and everything in the garden is lovely. Only I must go round to the office and see what has to be done." He got up, stretching himself and smiling.

Koznyshev, too, smiled.

"If you want to go for a little stroll, let's go together," he said, not wishing to part from his brother, who was simply exuding freshness and good spirits. "We could even look in at the office, if you want to."

"Good heavens!" cried Levin so loudly that Koznyshev was startled.

"What's the matter?"

"How's Agafya's wrist?" said Levin, slapping his head. "I'd forgotten all about her."

"It's much better."

"Well, I'll run down and see her all the same. I'll be back before you have time to put your hat on."

And he ran downstairs, clattering his heels like a rattle.

CHAPTER 7

Oblonsky had arrived in Petersburg to perform a most natural and necessary duty, a duty familiar to all civil servants, though incomprehensible to outsiders, without the performance of which it is quite impossible to get on in the civil service, that of reminding the Ministry of his existence. To carry out this duty Oblonsky had taken almost all the money there was in the house and was now having a most enjoyable time at the races and the country houses of his friends. Meanwhile, Dolly moved to the country with the children to cut down expenses as much as possible. She went to Yergushovo, the estate that had been part of her dowry, the same estate where the wood had been sold in the spring and which was about forty miles from Levin's Pokrovskoye.

The large old country house at Yergushovo had been pulled down long ago, and the old prince had enlarged and done up the cottage standing sideways to the drive. Twenty years before, when Dolly was a child, the cottage had been roomy and convenient, though, like all cottages of that kind, it did not face south. But now it was old and derelict. When Oblonsky had gone down in the spring to sell the wood, Dolly had asked him to look over the house and have all the necessary repairs done. Like all guilty husbands, Oblonsky was very concerned about his wife's comfort and he looked over the house himself and gave what he considered to be the necessary instructions. According to his ideas, all the furniture had to be recovered with new cretonne, curtains had to be put up, the garden tidied up, a little bridge built by the pond, and flowers planted. But he forgot many other things which were essential and the want of which later caused Dolly a great deal of trouble.

Try as he would to be a solicitous father and husband, Oblonsky never could remember that he had a wife and children. He had the tastes of a bachelor and he took only these into account. On his return to Moscow, he told his wife with pride that everything had been arranged, that the house would be something marvelous, and that he strongly advised her to go. His wife's departure to the country was highly agreeable to Oblonsky in every way: it was good for the children, expenses would be cut down, and he would be freer. Dolly, too, considered going to the country for the summer as absolutely necessary for the children, particularly for the little girl, who did not seem to be able to recover after the scarlet fever, and also as an escape from petty humiliations and small debts owing to the wood merchant, the fishmonger, the shoemaker, which made her life a misery. Besides this, she liked the idea of going away to the country because she hoped to get her sister Kitty, who was to return from abroad in midsummer and who had been ordered bathing, to join her there. Kitty wrote from the spa that nothing would please her more than to spend the summer at Yergushovo, which was full of childhood memories for both of them.

Dolly found the first days in the country very difficult. She used to live in the country as a child and the thing that had stuck in her mind was that the country was a place of refuge from all the sources of irritation in town, that though life there was not particularly wonderful (Dolly was easily reconciled to that), it was cheap and comfortable: there was plenty of everything there, everything was cheap and easy to get, and it was good for the children. But now, coming to the country as mistress of the house, she saw that things were not at all as she expected.

The day after their arrival it rained and during the night the water came through in the corridor and the nursery so that the children's beds had to be carried into the drawing room. There was no kitchen maid. Of the nine cows, according to the dairymaids, some were in calf, others had calved for the first time, still others were old, and the rest hard-uddered. There was not enough butter or milk even for the children. There were no eggs, either. It was impossible to get any hens, and they had to roast and boil tough, old, purple-colored roosters. No peasant women could be got to scrub the floors—they were all out in the potato fields. It was impossible to go for a drive because one of the horses was restive and refused to run in harness. There was no place for bathing because the whole riverbank had been trampled by the cattle and was open to the road; it was not even possible to walk in the grounds because the fence was broken and the cattle got into the garden, including a terrible bull who bellowed and might therefore be expected to gore someone. There were no proper wardrobes; such as there were would not shut or else burst open when anyone passed. There were no pots or pans; there was no copper in the wash house, and not even an ironing board in the maids' room.

At first, instead of finding peace and rest, confronted by what, from her point of view, were terrible calamities, Dolly was driven to despair: she did all she possibly could, but feeling the hopelessness of the situation, had to hold back the tears that kept starting to her eyes. The bailiff, a retired cavalry sergeant-major, whom Oblonsky had taken a fancy to and promoted from hall porter to bailiff because of his handsome and respectful appearance, showed no concern for Dolly's misfortunes, but merely kept saying respectfully, "It's no use, ma'am, the peasants here are such a bad lot," and did nothing to help her.

The position seemed hopeless. But in the Oblonsky household, just as in all families, there was one inconspicuous but most important and useful person—Matryona Filimonovna. She comforted her mistress, assured her that everything would "come right" in the end (it was her usual expression and Matvey had got it from her), and, without hurry or fuss, set to work herself.

She at once made friends with the bailiff's wife and on the very first day of their arrival in the country had tea with her and the bailiff under the laburnums and reviewed the whole position. Soon a club was established under the laburnums, consisting of Matryona, the bailiff's wife, the village elder, and the office clerk, and by means of this club the difficulties of existence were by and by smoothed out and in a week's time everything had really "come right." The roof was repaired, a kitchen maid, a good friend of the village elder's, was found, hens were bought, the cows began to give milk, the garden was fenced in with stakes, the carpenter made a mangle, hooks were put in the wardrobes and they no longer burst open of their own accord, and an ironing board covered with army cloth lay across the back of a chair and a chest of drawers, and the maids' room was soon pervaded by the smell of flat-irons.

"There, you see, ma'am!" said Matryona, pointing to the board. "And you were in despair."

Even a bathing hut was made out of straw frames. Lily started bathing, and Dolly's expectations were at least partly fulfilled, if not of a peaceful, then of a comfortable life in the country. Peaceful Dolly's life could not be, not with six children. One would fall ill, another would be in danger of falling ill, a third could not get something he had to have, a fourth would show signs of a bad character, etc., etc. Rare indeed were the brief periods of peace. But these cares and anxieties were the only kind of happiness possible for Dolly. But for them she would have been left alone with her thoughts about her husband who did not love her. And besides, painful though the fear of illnesses, the illnesses themselves, and the sorrow of detecting signs of evil tendencies in her children were for the mother, the children themselves were beginning to repay her even now with small joys for her trials and tribulations. The joys were so small that they were quite imperceptible, like grains of gold in sand; but there were also good moments when she saw nothing but joy, nothing but gold.

Now, in the solitude of the country, she became more and more often aware of these joys. Often, looking at them, she did her utmost to persuade herself that she was mistaken, that, being their mother, she was prejudiced in favor of her children; all the same she could not help saying to herself that she had delightful children, all six of them in their different ways, but such as are seldom met with—and she was happy in them and proud of them.

CHAPTER 8

At the end of May, when everything was more or less in order, she received an answer from her husband to her complaints about the disorderly state of affairs she had found in the country. He wrote apologizing for not having thought of everything and promised to come down at the first opportunity. The opportunity, however, did not arise and till the beginning of June Dolly lived alone in the country.

On the Sunday before St. Peter's Day, Dolly drove to Mass and took all her children to Communion. In her heart-to-heart philosophical talks with her sister, her mother, and her friends, Dolly often astonished them by the freedom of her views on religious matters. She had a strange faith of her own in transmigration of souls, in which she firmly believed, and was little concerned about the dogmas of the church. But in her family she was strict—not only to set an example, but with her whole heart—about carrying out all that was demanded by the church, and she was greatly troubled because the children had not been to Communion for about a year. So, with Matryona's fullest approval and sympathy, she decided to take them now in the summer.

Several days before, Dolly carefully considered the question of how the children should be dressed. Frocks were made or altered, hems and frills let down, buttons sewn on, and ribbons got ready. Tanya's dress alone, which the English governess had undertaken to alter, was the cause of much bad blood. In altering the dress, the English governess had put the tucks in the wrong place, cut the armholes too big, and nearly spoiled the whole dress. But Matryona hit on the happy idea of putting in gussets and adding a little cape on top. The frock was put right, but there nearly was a quarrel with the English governess. Next morning, however, everything was all right again and shortly before nine o'clock—the hour till which the priest had been asked to wait with the Mass—the children, beaming with joy, stood in their smart dresses on the front steps before the carriage, waiting for their mother.

Instead of the restive Raven, the bailiff's horse Brownie had been harnessed at the intercession of Matryona, and Dolly, who had been delayed by the worries about her own dress, came out in a white muslin gown and took her seat in the carriage.

Dolly had done her hair and dressed, feeling anxious and excited. There was a time when she used to dress for her own sake to look beautiful and be admired; later on, the older she grew, the less and less pleasure she took in dressing up: she saw that she was losing her good looks. But now she was beginning to feel pleasure and excitement again in dressing. Now she was not dressing for her own sake, not to look beautiful, but so that, as the mother of all those charming children, she should not spoil the general effect. And looking at herself for the last time in the glass she was satisfied with herself. She looked beautiful. Not as beautiful as she had wished to look when going to a ball, but beautiful enough for the purpose she had now in mind.

In the church there was no one except the peasants, the servants, and their wives. But Dolly saw, or she thought she saw, the admiration aroused by her children and herself. The children were not only lovely to look at in their fine clothes, but they also behaved themselves beautifully. Alyosha, it is true, did not stand very well: he kept turning round and trying to see the back of his jacket; but he was wonderfully sweet all the same. Tanya stood like a grown-up person and looked after the little ones. But the smallest, Lily, was charming in her naïve wonder at everything, and it was hard not to smile when, after taking the sacrament, she said in English, "Please, some more."

On the way home the children felt that something solemn had taken place and were very quiet.

All went well at home, too; but at lunch Grisha began whistling and, what was much worse, refused to obey the English governess and had to go without his pudding. If she alone had been present, Dolly would not have permitted any punishment on such a day; but she had to support the English governess and she confirmed her fiat that Grisha was to have no pudding. This spoiled the general rejoicing a little.

Grisha cried, declaring that it was Nikolinka who had whistled but they did not punish him, and that he was not crying about the pudding—he didn't mind that—but because he had not been treated fairly. That was a little too sad, and Dolly decided to speak to the governess and get her to forgive Grisha, and she went to find her. But as she was passing through the drawing room she beheld a scene which filled her heart with such joy that tears started to her eyes and she pardoned the little culprit herself.

The punished little fellow was sitting on the sill of the corner window; beside him stood Tanya with a plate. Under the pretext of wishing to give her dolls some dinner, she had obtained the governess' permission to take her portion of the pudding to the nursery and had

309

brought it to her brother instead. Still crying over the injustice of the punishment inflicted on him, he was eating the pudding and kept muttering through his sobs: "Have some too . . . let's eat it together . . . together. . . ."

Tanya, affected by her pity for Grisha and then by the consciousness of her own good deed, also had tears in her eyes; but she did not refuse and ate her share.

When they saw their mother, they were frightened; but looking at her face, they saw that what they were doing was right and, with their mouths full of pudding, they burst out laughing and began wiping their smiling lips with their hands, smearing their beaming faces with tears and jam.

"Heavens, your new white frock! Tanya! Grisha!" exclaimed their mother, trying to save the frock, but, with tears in her eyes, smiling a blissful, rapturous smile.

The new dresses were taken off, the little girls were told to go and have their blouses put on and the boys their old tunics, and orders were given for the trap to be made ready—again to the bailiff's chagrin—and Brownie to be harnessed, for the whole family to go mushroom gathering and bathing. The nursery was filled with the rapturous squealing of the children, and the noise did not subside till they set out for the bathing place.

They gathered a basketful of mushrooms and even Lily found a birch mushroom. Before, it was usually Miss Hull who found one and showed it to her; but this time Lily herself found a fine big one and there was a general shout of delight: "Lily has found a mushroom!"

Then they drove to the river, left the horses under the birch trees, and went into the screened-off bathing place. Terenty, the coachman, tied to a tree the horses that were swishing their tails to drive away the flies, lay down on the grass crushed under his weight in the shade of a birch tree and smoked his shag, while from the bathing hut came the never-ceasing shrieks of delight of the children.

Though it was rather a job looking after all the children and making sure they did not get into mischief, though it was difficult to remember whose were all those little stockings, drawers, and shoes and not to mix them up, and to untie, unbutton, and then to do up again the

310

tapes and buttons, Dolly, who had always been fond of bathing and considered it good for the children, enjoyed nothing so much as bathing with the children. To hold in her hands all those plump little legs, to pull on their stockings, to take the naked little bodies in her arms and dip them in the water and to hear their happy and frightened squeals, to see her little cherubs with their wide-open, frightened, and merry eyes gasping and splashing, was a great joy to her.

When half of the children were dressed again, some peasant women in their Sunday best, who had been gathering angelica and spurgewort, came up to the bathing hut and stopped shyly. Matryona called to one of them to ask her to dry a towel and a shirt that had fallen into the water, and Dolly began to talk with the peasant women. These women, who at first had been laughing behind their hands and not understanding her questions, soon plucked up courage and began talking freely and at once won over Dolly by their frank admiration of her children.

"Isn't she a little beauty? White as sugar!" said one, gazing admiringly at Tanya and shaking her head. "But why is she so thin?"

"She's been ill."

"You've been bathing that one too, I see," another one said, looking at the baby.

"No, I haven't," Dolly replied with pride. "He's only three months old."

"Is he now!"

"And have you any children?"

"I had four, but I've only two living, a boy and a girl. I weaned her just before Shrovetide."

"How old is she?"

"She's turned two."

"Why did you nurse her so long?"

"It's our custom, ma'am: for three fasts."

And the conversation became very interesting for Dolly: what was her confinement like? What illnesses had her babies had? Where was her husband? How often did he come home?

Dolly did not want to part from the peasant women, so interested was she in her conversation with them, so absolutely identical were their interests. What pleased Dolly most of all was that she saw clearly that what the

311

women admired most was the number of her children and how lovely they were. The peasant women amused Dolly and offended the English governess because she was the cause of their laughter, which she did not understand. One of the young women was watching the governess, who was dressing after all the others, and when she put on her third petticoat, she could not refrain from remarking: "Just look at her! Putting on and putting on and can't put enough on, it seems!" she said, and they all roared with laughter.

CHAPTER 9

Surrounded by all her children, their heads still wet from their bath, Dolly with a kerchief around her was driving up to the house when the coachman said:

"There's a gentleman coming, ma'am. Looks like the gentleman from Pokrovskoye."

Dolly leaned out and was pleased to see the familiar figure of Levin in a gray hat and gray coat coming to meet them. She was always glad to see him, but now she was specially glad that he should see her in all her glory. No one could appreciate her splendor better than Levin.

On seeing her, he found himself face to face with one of the pictures of the sort of family life he himself imagined.

"You're like a hen with her chicks, my dear lady," he said.

"Oh, I'm so glad to see you!" she said, holding out her hand.

"Glad to see me, but you never sent me word. My brother's staying with me. I had a note from Stiva that you are here."

"From Stiva?" Dolly asked in surprise.

"Yes, he wrote that you moved to the country and he thought that you wouldn't mind if I were to offer my assistance to you," said Levin, and, having said it, suddenly felt embarrassed and, stopping short, walked on in silence by the trap, breaking off lime-tree twigs and biting them.

He felt embarrassed because he thought that Dolly might not like to accept help from a stranger in a matter that should have been attended to by her husband. And, indeed, Dolly did not like Oblonsky's habit of foisting his family responsibilities upon strangers. And she immediately grasped that Levin realized it. It was for his fine perception and delicacy of feeling that Dolly liked Levin so much.

"I realized of course that this simply meant that you would like to see me, and I was very pleased. I can well imagine how odd everything must appear to you here, used as you are to keep house in town, and if you require anything to be done, I'm entirely at your service."

"Thank you," said Dolly, "but it was only at first that things were a little difficult. Now everything is as nice as can be, thanks to my old nurse," she said, indicating Matryona, who, realizing that they were speaking of her, smiled brightly and amiably at Levin.

"Won't you get in, sir?" she said to him. "We can squeeze up a little here."

"No, thank you, I'll walk. Children, who'd like to race the horses with me?"

The children did not know Levin very well and did not remember when they had seen him, but they did not show toward him any of that strange shyness and hostility children so often feel toward grownups who pretend to like them and for which they are so often painfully punished. Any kind of pretense may deceive the cleverest and most perspicacious of men; but the most backward child will recognize it, however skillfully it may be disguised, and be repelled by it. Whatever shortcomings Levin may have had, there was not a trace of pretense in him and that was why the children showed him the same friendliness that they saw in their mother's face. At his invitation two of the eldest at once jumped down and ran along with him as naturally as they would have done with their nurse, with Miss Hull, or with their mother. Lily begged to go too and her mother handed her to him. He put her on his shoulder and ran on.

"Don't be afraid, don't be afraid!" he shouted to Dolly, smiling cheerfully at her. "I won't hurt her or let her fall."

And looking at his deft, strong, carefully considerate, and extremely guarded movements, the mother lost her fears and looked at him with a bright smile of approval.

Here in the country, with children and in Dolly's

agreeable company, Levin relapsed into the mood of childlike gaiety, which came upon him very frequently and which Dolly liked so much in him. As he ran about with the children, he taught them gymnastics, amused Miss Hull with his broken English, and talked to Dolly about rural occupations.

After dinner, sitting with him alone on the balcony, Dolly began to speak about Kitty.

"Do you know? Kitty is coming here to spend the summer with me."

"Is she?" he said, flushing, and to change the subject at once added: "So shall I send you two cows? If you insist on paying me you can let me have five rubles a month, but I warn you: I shall resent it."

"No, thank you. We're quite all right now."

"Well, in that case I'll have a look at your cows and, if you don't mind, I'll tell your people how to feed them. Everything depends on the feeding."

And to make sure the conversation did not go back to Kitty, Levin went on to explain to Dolly his theory of dairy farming according to which the cow was only a machine for converting fodder into milk, etc.

While saying all this, he was at the same time passionately longing to hear all the news about Kitty and yet dreading it. He feared that the peace of mind he had acquired with such difficulty might be destroyed.

"Yes," Dolly replied with reluctance, "I suppose all this has to be looked after, but who's going to do it?"

Now that she had got her household into satisfactory working order with the help of Matryona, she was loath to change anything. Besides, she had no confidence in Levin's knowledge of farming. The argument that a cow was a milk-producing machine was suspect to her. She could not help feeling that such arguments could not be of any real use to farming. It seemed to her that everything was much more simple, that all that was necessary was, as Matryona had explained, to give Spotty and Whiteflank more food and drink and to make sure the cook did not take all the kitchen slops to the laundrywoman's cow. That was clear. But arguments about meal and grass feeding were highly suspect and far from clear. Above all, she wanted to talk about Kitty.

CHAPTER 10

"Kitty writes to me that all she wants is peace and solitude," said Dolly after a pause in the conversation.

"And how is she—better?" asked Levin, agitatedly.

"Thank God, she's quite recovered. I never believed that there was anything wrong with her chest."

"Oh, I'm so glad!" said Levin, and Dolly thought there was something pathetic and helpless in his face when he said it and looked silently at her.

"Look here," Dolly said, with her kind, though slightly ironic smile, "why are you angry with Kitty?"

"Me? I'm not angry with her," said Levin.

"Yes, you are. Why didn't you call either on us or on them when you were in Moscow?"

"My dear Princess," he said, reddening to the roots of his hair, "I'm surprised that a person who is so kind as you should not feel it. How is it that you don't even feel sorry for me when you know . . ."

"Know what?"

"That I proposed and was refused," said Levin, and all the tenderness he had been feeling for Kitty a moment ago was changed into a feeling of anger at the indignity he had suffered.

"Why do you suppose that I know?"

"Because everybody knows it."

"That's where you are mistaken. I did not know, though I had my suspicions."

"Oh well, you know it now."

"All I knew was that something had happened that made her terribly unhappy and that she asked me never to speak to her about it. And if she did not tell me, she certainly did not tell it to anyone. But what did happen between you? Tell me."

"I've told you what happened."

"When?"

"When I was there the last time."

"Do you know," said Dolly, "I'm terribly, terribly sorry for her. You're only suffering because of your hurt pride. . . ."

"Perhaps," said Levin, "but . . ."

She interrupted him.

"But for her, poor darling, I'm terribly, terribly sorry. Now I understand everything."

"Well, you must excuse me," he said, getting up. "Good-by, *au revoir.*"

"No, wait," she said, seizing him by the sleeve. "Wait, sit down, please."

"Please, please don't let us talk about it," he said, sitting down and at the same time feeling that a hope that seemed dead and buried to him was rising and stirring in his heart.

"If I were not fond of you," said Dolly, and tears started to her eyes, "if I did not know you as well as I do . . ."

The feeling that seemed dead was coming more and more to life again, rising and taking possession of Levin's heart.

"Yes, now I understand it all," continued Dolly. "You can't understand it. To you men, who are free to choose whom you like, it's always clear whom you love. But a girl in a state of suspense, with her feminine, maidenly modesty, a girl who sees you men from afar, takes everything on trust—a girl may and sometimes does feel that she does not know what to say."

"Yes, if her heart does not tell her. . . ."

"No, the heart does tell her, but just consider for a moment: you men are interested in a girl, you come to the house, you become more closely acquainted, you watch her, you wait to see whether you've found what you love, and then, when you are quite sure you love her, you propose. . . ."

"Well, it isn't quite like that."

"Never mind! You propose when your love is ripe and when the odds are in favor of one of your two choices. But a girl is not asked. She is expected to choose for herself, but she cannot do so and can only answer yes or no."

"Yes, the choice between me and Vronsky," thought Levin, and the dead thing that was reviving in his heart died again and only weighed painfully on his heart.

"That's how one chooses a dress," he said, "or some other purchase, not love. The choice has been made and so much the better. . . . And there can be no repetition."

316

"Oh, pride, pride!" said Dolly, as though despising him for the meanness of that feeling compared to the feeling which only women know. "At the time you proposed to Kitty she was just in that state when she could not give an answer. She was hesitating: you or Vronsky. She saw him every day; you she had not seen for a long time. Now, of course, if she had been older—I, for instance, would not have hesitated in her place. I never liked him and I was right, considering how it all ended."

Levin remembered Kitty's answer. She had said: "No, it cannot be. . . ."

"My dear Princess," he said dryly, "I appreciate your confidence in me, but I think that you are mistaken. But whether I am right or wrong, this pride of mine, which you so despise, makes any thought of your sister impossible for me. You understand, absolutely impossible."

"I will only say one more thing: you realize, of course, that I am speaking of my sister whom I love as I love my own children. I'm not saying that she loved you. All I want to say is that her answer at that time does not prove anything."

"I don't know!" said Levin, jumping up. "If you only knew how you were hurting me! It's just as if a child of yours had died, and people kept saying to you: 'He would have been such a lovely boy, and he might have lived, and he would have made you so happy. . . .' But he's dead, dead, dead! . . ."

"How absurd you are," said Dolly with a mournful smile, in spite of Levin's agitation. "Yes," she went on pensively, "now I see it all more and more clearly. So you won't come to see us when Kitty is here?"

"No, I won't. I shan't, of course, avoid meeting her, but I shall do my best to spare her the pain of my presence as far as I can."

"You are very, very absurd," repeated Dolly, gazing tenderly at his face. "All right, then, let it be as though we had never spoken about it. What is it, Tanya?" Dolly said in French to the little girl who had come in.

"Where's my spade, Mummy?"

"I'm speaking French and you must answer in French."

The girl wanted to, but she had forgotten the French for "spade"; her mother told her and then told her in French where she would find her spade. And all this struck Levin as rather disagreeable.

317

Everything in Dolly's house and children struck him now as not at all as charming as before.

"And why does she talk French with the children?" he thought. "How unnatural and preposterous it is! And the children feel it. Teach French and unteach sincerity," he thought to himself, not knowing that Dolly had thought it all over again and again and had still decided, even at the cost of the loss of some sincerity, that her children should be taught in that way.

"But why be in such a hurry to go? Stay a little longer."

Levin stayed to tea, but his good humor had all gone and he felt ill at ease.

After tea he went out into the hall to order his horses to be harnessed, and when he came back he found Dolly upset, with a worried look on her face and tears in her eyes. While Levin had been outside, something had happened that had suddenly destroyed all the happiness she had been feeling that day and her pride in the children. Grisha and Tanya had a fight about a ball. Dolly, hearing a scream in the nursery, had run in and had found them in a terrible state. Tanya was pulling Grisha's hair, and Grisha, his face distorted with rage, was hitting out at her blindly with his fists. Something snapped in Dolly's heart when she saw this. A great shadow seemed to have fallen over her life: she realized that these children of hers of whom she was so proud were not only quite ordinary, but even bad, ill-bred children, with coarse, brutal propensities, wicked children, in fact.

She could not think or talk of anything else, and she could not help telling Levin of her trouble.

Levin saw that she was unhappy and tried to comfort her, saying that it did not prove that there was anything wrong with them and that all children fought; but while saying this, he was thinking to himself: "No, I won't try to show off and talk French with my children, but then my children won't be like that; one must never spoil or deform children, and they'll be delightful. No, my children won't be like that."

He said good-by and drove away, and she did not try to keep him.

CHAPTER 11

In the middle of July the village elder on Levin's sister's estate, about fifteen miles from Pokrovskoye, came to see Levin to report on the state of affairs there and on the hay harvest. The chief income from his sister's estate came from the water meadows. In former years the peasants used to buy the grass for seven rubles the acre. When Levin took over the management of the estate, he had looked over the grasslands and decided that they were worth more and fixed the price at eight rubles. The peasants refused to pay that price and, as Levin suspected, discouraged other buyers from paying it. Then Levin had gone there himself and arranged to have the meadows mown partly by hired labor and partly by paying the peasants in kind. The peasants on the estate did all they could to oppose this innovation, but his plan was put into operation and in the first year the income from the meadows almost doubled. The next year and the year after—that is, last year—the peasants still kept up their active opposition and the harvest was got in by the same means. But this year they had agreed to do all the haymaking for a third of the harvest, and now the village elder came to inform Levin that the hay had been cut and that, for fear of rain, he had asked the clerk at the estate office to be present while he had divided the hay and had already put up eleven stacks of the owner's hay. From the elder's vague replies to Levin's question of how much hay the big meadow had yielded, from the elder's haste to divide up the hay without waiting for permission, and from the whole way the peasant had behaved, Levin realized that there was something wrong about the division of the hay and decided to go over and investigate the matter himself.

Having arrived at the village at dinnertime, Levin left his horse at the cottage of an old peasant, the husband of his brother's wet nurse and an old friend of his. He went to see the old man at his apiary, wishing to find out from him all the particulars about the hay harvest. Parmenovich, a talkative, handsome old peasant, was genuinely pleased to see him, showed him all over his hives, and told him everything about his bees and the swarms of that year; but to Levin's questions about the haymaking he gave vague and reluctant answers. This still more confirmed Levin in his suspicions. He went to the hayfields and examined the stacks. There could not be fifty cartloads in each stack. To show up the peasants, Levin ordered the carts on which the hay had been moved to be fetched at once, to lift one stack and carry it to the barn. There were only thirty-two loads in the stack. In spite of the elder's protestations that the hay had been saturated with water and that it had settled down in the stacks and his swearing that everything had been fair and aboveboard, Levin insisted that the hay should not have been shared out without his orders and that, therefore, he would not accept this hay as fifty cartloads to a stack. After long arguments it was agreed that the peasants should take those eleven stacks, counting them as containing fifty loads each, and that the owner's share should be measured afresh. These negotiations and the apportioning of the hayricks went on till the late afternoon. When the last of the hay had been apportioned, Levin entrusted the rest of the supervision to the office clerk, sat down on a haycock marked by a willow twig, and, fascinated, watched the meadow teeming with peasants.

Before him, in the bend of the river behind the marsh, moved a gaily-colored line of peasant women, chattering loudly and merrily, while the scattered hay was rapidly rising into gray, zigzag ridges on the pale-green stubble. Men with hayforks followed the women, and the ridges grew into tall, wide, and round haycocks. To the left carts were already rumbling over the bare meadow and the haycocks disappeared one after another, picked up in enormous forkfuls, and their places were taken by heavy carts with loads of scented hay hanging over the horses' hindquarters.

"Make hay while the sun shines and the hay you'll get will be lovely," said the old beekeeper, squatting down beside Levin. "What lovely hay, sir! Tea, not hay. Look, sir, at the way they pick 'em up! Like scattering grain to the ducks," he added, pointing to the growing haycocks. "They've carted a good half of it since dinnertime. Is that the last?" he shouted to a young fellow who was driving by, standing on the front part of a cart, flicking the ends of his hempen reins.

"The last one, Dad!" shouted the young fellow, reining in the horse and, smiling, looked round at a cheerful, rosy-cheeked peasant woman, who was sitting inside the cart and also smiling, and drove on.

"Who's that? A son of yours?" asked Levin.

"My youngest," said the old man with an affectionate smile.

"A fine fellow!"

"The lad's all right."

"Married already?"

"Yes, sir. Two years last St. Philip's Day."

"Well, have they any children?"

"Children! Why, sir, for over a year he didn't understand anything and he was too bashful into the bargain," replied the old man. "What lovely hay! Tea, not hay!" he repeated, wishing to change the subject.

Levin looked more attentively at Ivan Parmenov and his wife. They were loading their cart not far away. Ivan stood on the cart, receiving, leveling and stamping down huge trusses of hay, which his pretty, young wife deftly handed up to him, first in armfuls and then on the pitchfork. The young woman worked easily, cheerfully, and with skill. The heavy, compressed hay could not be lifted at once on the pitchfork. She first loosened it with the prongs, then stuck the fork in, then with a quick and resilient movement, leaning all the weight of her body on the fork, forthwith straightened her back with its red belt around the waist and stood erect, her full bosom thrown forward under the white overall, and, turning the fork with an adroit movement, pitched the hay high onto the cart. Ivan, evidently anxious to spare her every minute of unnecessary exertion, hurriedly caught the hay in his outspread arms, and smoothed it evenly in the cart. When she had handed him the remaining hay with a rake, she shook the chaff from her neck and, straightening the red kerchief that had slipped over her white, unsunburned forehead, crawled under the cart to help fasten the load. Ivan was telling her how to do it and roared with laughter at something she said. And in the expression of both their faces could be seen strong, young, and newly awakened love.

CHAPTER 12

The cart was roped. Ivan jumped down and led the good, well-fed horse by the bridle. His wife threw her rake on top of the cart and with a vigorous step, swinging her arms, went to join the other women who had gathered in a ring. Ivan, having come out on the road, took his place in the line of loaded carts. The women, carrying their rakes over their shoulders, bright in their vivid colors, walked behind the carts, their gay voices ringing merrily. One of the women started a song in a harsh, gruff voice and sang it as far as the refrain, when half a hundred powerful voices, some gruff, others shrill, took it up from the beginning again.

The singing women were approaching Levin, and he felt as if a thundercloud of merriment were bearing down upon him. The cloud bore down, enveloped him and the haycock on which he sat; and the other haycocks, the carts, and the whole of the meadow with the faraway fields all seemed to sway and vibrate to the rhythm of that wild, exhilarating, merry song with its loud shrieks, whistling, and whoops of joy. Levin was envious of this healthy merrymaking and he felt like taking part in that expression of gladness in life. But he could do nothing but lie and look and listen. When the peasants with their songs vanished out of sight and hearing, a heavy feeling of despondency at his loneliness, his physical idleness, and his hostility to this world came over Levin.

Some of those very peasants who had most disputed with him over the hay, those whom he had wronged, and those who had wanted to deceive him, those very peasants had bowed cheerfully to him, quite obviously not bearing, and indeed unable to bear, any grudge against him, or any remorse, or any recollection even of having intended to cheat him. All that had been dissolved in the sea of joyous common toil. The Lord had given them the day and the Lord had given them the strength. And the day and the strength had been dedicated to labor, and the labor was its reward. Who was

322

the labor for? What would be its fruits? These were irrelevant and idle questions.

Levin had often admired this kind of life, had often envied the people who lived this kind of life, but today, especially under the impression of what he had seen of the relations between Ivan Parmenov and his young wife, the idea occurred to him clearly for the first time that it depended on himself alone whether or not to change his wearisome, idle, and artificial personal life for that hard-working, pure, and delightful life.

The old man who had been sitting beside him had gone home long ago; the peasants had all dispersed. Those who lived near had gone home, and those who lived a long way off gathered for supper in the meadow where they were to spend the night. Levin, unnoticed by the peasants, remained lying on the haycock, looking on, listening, and thinking. The people who had stayed in the meadow kept awake almost all the short summer night. At first there was the sound of general merry chatter and laughter over supper, then again songs and more laughter.

The whole long day of hard work had left on them no trace of anything but merriment. Before dawn everything became quiet. All one could hear were the incessant nocturnal sounds of the croaking of frogs in the marsh and the snorting of horses in the meadow when the mist began to rise before the morning. Waking up, Levin rose from the haycock, and looking up at the stars, realized that the night was over.

"Well, so what am I going to do? How am I going to do it?" he said to himself, trying to put into words all he had been thinking and feeling in that short night. All that he had been thinking and feeling could be separated into three different trains of thought. The first was the renunciation of his old life, of the useless knowledge he had acquired, and of his utterly futile education. This renunciation was a source of pleasure to him and was easy and simple. Then there were the ideas and thoughts concerning the life he wished to live now. He was fully conscious of the simplicity, purity, and integrity of this life and he was convinced that in it he would find satisfaction, peace, and dignity, the absence of which he felt so painfully. But the third series of thoughts revolved round the question of how to bring about this transition from his old life to the new. And here nothing was clear to him. "Take a wife? Have work and the necessity to work? Leave Pokrovskoye? Buy land? Join a peasant commune? Marry a peasant girl? How am I going to do that?" he asked himself again and again and found no answer. "However, I haven't slept all night and I can't get any clear idea of anything," he said to himself. "I'll get it all sorted out later. One thing is certain, though: this night has decided my fate. All my old dreams of married life were nonsense, not the real thing," he said to himself. "Everything is much simpler and better. . . ."

"How beautiful!" he thought, looking up at the curious mother-of-pearl shell of white, fleecy clouds which seemed to hang motionless right over his head in the middle of the sky. "How lovely everything is on this lovely night! And when did this shell have time to form? A short while ago I looked at the sky and there was nothing there, only two white strips. Yes, exactly in the same way my views of life have imperceptibly changed!"

He left the meadow and walked along the highroad towards the village. A light wind was rising and everything looked gray and dull. It was the moment of half-light that usually precedes daybreak, the complete victory of light over darkness.

Shivering with cold, Levin walked fast with his eyes fixed on the ground. "What's that? Somebody's coming!" he thought, hearing the jingling of harness bells, and he raised his head. Within forty paces of him a four-in-hand with luggage on top was driving toward him along the grassy highroad on which he was walking. The wheel horses were pressing in toward the pole away from the ruts, but the skillful coachman, who was sitting sideways on the box, kept the pole over the ruts so that the wheels ran on the smooth part of the road.

That was all Levin noticed and, without wondering who the travelers might be, he glanced absently at the coach.

In the carriage an elderly woman was dozing in one corner, while at the window sat a young girl, who had evidently only just awakened, holding the ribbons of her white cap in both hands. Bright and thoughtful, full of an exquisite, complex inner life to which Levin was a stranger, she gazed beyond him at the glow of the sunrise.

At the very moment when the vision was about to disappear, a pair of truthful eyes glanced at him. She recognized him and a look of amazement and joy lit up her face.

He could not be mistaken. There were no other eyes in the world like those. There was only one being in the world who was able to concentrate for him the whole world and the meaning of life. It was she. It was Kitty. He realized that she was on her way to Yergushovo from the railway station. And everything that had been agitating Levin that sleepless night, all the decisions he had taken—everything vanished in a trice. He recalled with disgust his ideas of marrying a peasant girl. There alone, in the rapidly disappearing carriage that had crossed to the other side of the road, there alone was the only possible solution to the riddle of his life which had been weighing so agonizingly on him of late.

She did not look out again. The sound of the sprung wheels could no longer be heard; the jingling of the bells grew fainter. The barking of dogs told him the carriage had passed through the village, and around him only the empty fields remained, the village ahead of him, and he himself, lonely and a stranger to everything, walking solitary on the deserted highroad.

He looked up at the sky, hoping to find there the shell he had been admiring and which symbolized to him the whole trend of his thoughts and feelings that night. There was nothing resembling a shell in the sky. There in the unfathomable height a mysterious change had already taken place. There was not a trace of the shell to be seen, but half across the sky there spread a smooth carpet of fleecy clouds which were growing tinier and tinier. The sky had turned blue and much brighter and responded to his questioning gaze with the same tenderness, but also with the same remoteness.

"No," he said to himself, "however good that simple life of toil may be, I cannot return to it. I love *her*."

CHAPTER 13

No one but those who knew Karenin most intimately had any idea that this apparently cold and sober-minded man had one weakness which was quite inconsistent with the general trend of his character. Karenin could not remain indifferent when he saw or heard a child or woman crying. The sight of tears threw him into confusion and he completely lost his power of calm reasoning. The chief of his department and his private secretary knew this and warned women who came with petitions not to give way to tears on any account if they did not want to spoil their case. "He will get angry and will not listen to you," they would say. And, indeed, the emotional disturbance produced in Karenin by the sight of tears found expression in outbursts of anger. "I can't, I can't do anything. Please go!" he would usually shout on these occasions.

When, on their way home from the races, Anna informed him of her relations with Vronsky and immediately afterward had burst out crying, hiding her face in her hands, Karenin, in spite of his feeling of anger against her, became at once aware of an upsurge of the emotional discomfort which tears always produced in him. Knowing this, and knowing, too, that any expression of his feelings at that moment would be incompatible with the situation, he tried to suppress any manifestation of life in him and therefore neither moved nor looked at her. That was the cause of that strange deathlike expression on his face which had so struck Anna.

When they drove up to the house he helped her out of the carriage and, making an effort to control his feelings, took leave of her with his usual civility and uttered the words that did not commit him to anything: he said that he would inform her of his decision the next day.

His wife's words, confirming his worst suspicions, had hurt him cruelly. His pain was made more acute by the strange feeling of physical compassion for her evoked by her tears. But, left alone in the carriage, Karenin, to his relief and joy, felt completely relieved of his pity and of the doubts and torments of jealousy that had plagued him of late.

He felt like a man who had had a tooth out that had been hurting him for a long time. After terrible pain and a sensation of something enormous, larger than his whole head, being pulled out of his jaw, he suddenly, scarcely able to believe his good fortune, feels that the thing that had so long been poisoning his existence and absorbing all his attention is no longer there, and he can again live, think, and be interested in other things besides his tooth. It was this sort of feeling that Karenin experienced. The pain had been strange and terrible, but now it was gone; he felt he could live again and think not only of his wife alone.

"Without honor, without heart, without religion—a depraved woman! I have always known it and I have seen it all along, though out of pity for her I tried to deceive myself," he said to himself. And he really thought that he had always seen it. He recalled all the details of their past life which had not seemed to him to have been wrong before, but now all those facts showed clearly that she had always been a depraved woman. "I made a mistake when I bound up my life with her, but there is nothing reprehensible in my mistake and that is why I ought not to be unhappy. It is not I who am guilty," he said to himself, "but she. But I have nothing to do with her any more. She does not exist for me."

Whatever might happen to her and to his son, toward whom his feelings had changed as much as toward her, no longer interested him. The only thing that did interest him now was how he could best, in a way that was most decent and convenient for himself and hence also most fair, shake off the mud with which she had bespattered him in her fall, and then carry on along his path of active, honest, and useful existence.

"I cannot possibly be unhappy because a despicable woman has committed a crime; I merely must find the best way out of the painful situation in which she has placed me. And I shall find it," he kept saying to himself, frowning more and more. "I'm not the first and I shall not be the last." And to say nothing of the historical instances going back to Menelaus, refreshed in everybody's memory by the recent revival of *La Belle Hélène*, a whole number of instances of the infidelities of modern wives in high society occurred to Karenin: "Daryalov, Poltavsky, Prince Karibanov, Count Paskudin, Dram . . . yes, even Dram, such an honest capable fellow . . . Semyonov, Chagin, Sigonin," Karenin remembered. "It is true a kind of unreasonable *ridicule* falls on these men, but I never saw anything but a misfortune in it and I always felt nothing but sympathy," Karenin said to himself, though it was quite untrue and he had never sympathized with misfortunes of that kind, and the more often he came across cases of wives being unfaithful to their husbands the more highly he had thought of himself. "It is a misfortune that may befall anyone. And this misfortune has befallen me. All that matters is to make the best of the situation." And he began reviewing in his mind the line of action pursued by the men who found themselves in the same position as he.

"Daryalov fought a duel. . . ."

In his youth the idea of a duel had particularly fascinated Karenin just because he was physically a timid man and perfectly aware of it. He could not think without horror of a pistol's being leveled at him and had never used any kind of weapon in his life. This horror had in his youth often set him wondering about duels, and he tried to imagine himself in a situation in which he would have to expose his life to danger. Since he had achieved success and an established position in life, he had long ago forgotten that feeling. But the old habit now reasserted itself and the fear of his own cowardice proved even now so strong that Karenin spent a long time considering and toying with the idea of a duel, though he knew perfectly well that he would never under any circumstances fight one.

"There can be no doubt that our society is still so uncivilized" (not as in England) "that very many" (and among the many there were not a few whose opinions Karenin particularly valued) "would regard a duel with approval, but what object would be gained? Suppose I challenge him," Karenin went on, and conjuring up a vivid picture of the night he would spend after the challenge and of the pistol leveled at him, he shuddered and realized that he would never do it. "Suppose I challenge him. Suppose," he went on musing, "they showed me how to shoot, put me in position, I pull the trigger," he said to himself, shutting his eyes, "and it so happens that I kill him," Karenin said to himself and shook his head to drive away such foolish thoughts. "What sense is there in killing a man in order to define one's relation to a guilty wife and a son? I should still have to decide what I ought to do with her. But what is much more likely, and indeed quite certain, is that it is I who would be killed or wounded. That would be more senseless still. And this is not all. A challenge to a duel on my part would be hardly honest. For don't I know that my friends would never allow me to fight a duel, that they would never allow the life of a statesman whom Russia needs to expose himself to danger? What, then, would happen? Why, that knowing beforehand that the matter would never go as far as endangering my life, I would simply try to cover myself with false glamour by such a challenge. That would be dishonest. It would be false. It would be deceiving myself and others. A duel is unthinkable and no one expects it of me. My aim is to safeguard my reputation, which I need for the uninterrupted pursuit of my work." His work at the Ministry, which had always been of great importance in Karenin's eyes, now seemed of particular importance to him.

Having considered and rejected the idea of a duel, Karenin turned to the consideration of divorce, another expedient chosen by some of the betrayed husbands he remembered. Going over all the cases of divorce he knew (there were very many of them in the highest society with which he was familiar), Karenin failed to find one in which the purpose of the divorce was the one he had in mind. In all those cases the husband had ceded or sold his unfaithful wife, and the very party which had been found guilty of adultery and had therefore no legal right to contract a new marriage, entered into fictitious, pseudo-legal relations with a new partner. In his own case Karenin saw that a legal divorce, that is to say, a divorce in which only the guilty wife would be repudiated, was impossible to obtain. He saw that the complex conditions of the life he led made it impossible to obtain those coarse proofs of a wife's infidelity which the law demanded; he saw that the ultra-civilized veneer of that kind of life would not allow him to bring forward such proofs, even if he had them, and that to bring forward such evidence would injure him more than it would her in the eyes of the public.

An action for divorce would only lead to a great deal of damaging publicity, which would be a godsend to his enemies, an opportunity for the spreading of scandalous stories about him and the lowering of his high position in society. And the main objective, the clarification of his position with the least possible amount of disturbance, could not be secured even by divorce. Moreover, in the event of a divorce or an action for divorce it was evident that the wife severed all relations with her husband and went to live with her lover. And yet, in spite of the complete and contemptuous indifference he thought he felt for his wife, Karenin kept alive one feeling for her—a reluctance to let her live unhindered with Vronsky and in this way let her profit from her crime. The very thought of it so enraged him that he groaned with inner pain, and rose and changed his place in the carriage, and for a long while after sat frowning, wrapping his bony legs, which were very sensitive to cold, in his fluffy rug.

"Besides a formal divorce, one might do the same as Karibanov, Paskudin, and that good fellow Dram, that is to say, just separate," he continued revolving the matter in his mind after he had regained his composure. But this measure too entailed the same inconvenience of a public scandal as a divorce and, above all, it would throw his wife into Vronsky's arms quite as much as a formal divorce. "No, that's impossible, impossible!" he said aloud, wrapping his rug round his legs again. "I may have to be unhappy, but neither she nor he must be happy."

The feeling of jealousy that had tormented him during the period of uncertainty had left him the moment the tooth had been extracted with great pain by his wife's words. But this feeling had been replaced by another: the desire that she should be punished for her crime, let alone that she should not triumph. He did not acknowledge it to himself, but in his heart of hearts he wanted her to suffer for having destroyed his peace of mind and his honor. And having once again reviewed the conditions inseparable from a duel, a divorce, and a separation and once again rejecting them, Karenin came to the conclusion that there was only one solution to his problem: to keep her with him, concealing from the world what had happened and taking all the necessary measures to put a stop to her love affair and, above all, though he did not admit it to himself, to punish her. "I must inform her of my decision and make it clear to her that after considering the painful situation in which she has placed her husband and son, any other solution would be worse for both sides than a *status quo* existing in name only, and that I am prepared to observe it on the strict condition that she agrees to obey my wish, that is, to cease all intercourse with her lover." And as proof that his decision, after it had been finally taken, was the right one, a further important argument occurred to Karenin. "It is only by taking such a decision," he said to himself, "that I act strictly in accordance with my religious beliefs and do not cast off a guilty wife, but give her a chance of repairing the damage she has done and, however painful it may be to me, I shall devote part of my energies to her redemption and salvation."

Though Karenin knew very well that he could have no moral influence on his wife, that nothing would come of all his attempts to redeem her but lies, and though throughout all these painful moments it never once occurred to him to seek guidance in religion, now that his decision, as he thought, corresponded to the demands of religion, this religious sanction afforded him complete satisfaction and some peace of mind. He was pleased to think that in a question of such vital importance no one would be able to say that he had not acted in accordance with the principles of that religion whose banner he had always held aloft amid the general apathy and indifference. Considering further details, he could not see, indeed, why his relations with his wife should not remain almost the same as before. No doubt, he would never be able to treat her with the same respect as before, but there was not and there could not be any reason why he should spoil his own life and suffer because she was a bad and unfaithful wife. "Yes, time will pass, time which puts everything right in the end, and the old relations will be restored," he said to himself. "I mean restored insofar as I shall not feel in any way disconcerted for the rest of my life. She has to be unhappy, but I am not guilty and therefore I cannot be unhappy."

CHAPTER 14

By the time he reached the outskirts of Petersburg, Karenin had not only made up his mind to stick to his decision, but had even composed in his head the letter he would write to his wife. Going into the porter's room, Karenin glanced at the letters and papers sent from the Ministry and ordered them to be brought to his study.

"Tell him to unharness and I will receive no one," he

said in reply to the porter's question, emphasizing with a certain pleasure the words "no one," which was a sign that he was in a good mood.

Karenin walked twice up and down his study and then halted at the enormous writing desk on which his valet, who had preceded him into the room, had placed and lighted six candles. Cracking his knuckles, he sat down and arranged his writing materials. Placing his elbows on the table and bending his head to one side, he thought for a moment and then began to write without pausing for a second. He wrote without addressing her directly, in French, using the plural pronoun "you," which has not the same feeling of coldness as it has in Russian.

At our last conversation I told you of my intention to inform you of my decision in regard to the subject of that conversation. Having thought it over carefully, I now write with the object of carrying out my promise. My decision is as follows: Whatever your conduct may have been, I do not consider myself justified in severing the bonds with which a Higher Power has bound us. The family cannot be broken up at the caprice, the will, and pleasure, or even the adultery of one of the partners of that marriage, and our life must go on as before. This is necessary for me, for you, and for our son. I am quite sure that you have repented and are repenting of what has been the reason for this letter and that you will cooperate with me in eradicating the cause of our dissension and forgetting the past. If not, you can easily imagine what awaits you and your son. I hope to talk all this over with you in more detail in a personal interview. As the summer season is drawing to a close, I would ask you to return to Petersburg as soon as possible, not later than Tuesday. All the necessary preparations shall be made for your return. I beg you to note that I attach particular importance to your compliance with this request.

A. KARENIN

P.S.—I enclose some money, which may be needed for your expenses.

He read the letter over and was satisfied with it, especially that he had remembered to enclose money; there was not a cruel word, not a reproach in it, but there was

332

no undue indulgence, either. Above all, there was an excellent bridge for a return. Having folded the letter and smoothed it with a massive ivory paper knife, and put it in an envelope with the money, he rang the bell with the feeling of pleasure that his well-arranged writing materials always gave him.

"Give this to the courier to be delivered to Mrs. Karenin tomorrow at her country cottage," he said and got up.

"Very good, sir. Shall tea be served in your study, sir?"

Karenin ordered tea to be brought to the study and, toying with the massive paper knife, went to his armchair, beside which a lamp had been placed for him and a French book about the Eugubine tables. Above the armchair hung a portrait of Anna in a gilt oval frame beautifully painted by a famous artist. The impenetrable eyes looked derisively and insolently at him as they had the last evening they had had their talk together. To Karenin the black lace on the head, admirably done by the painter, the black hair, and beautiful white hand with its third finger covered with rings looked quite intolerably insolent and challenging. After looking at the portrait for about a minute Karenin shuddered so violently that his lips began to quiver, making a sound like "brr," and he turned away. He sat down hurriedly and opened the book. He tried to read but could not revive his former keen interest in the Eugubine inscriptions. His eyes were fixed on the book, but he was thinking of something else. He was thinking not of his wife, but of a certain complication that had recently arisen in his official activity which at present constituted the chief interest of his work. He felt that he could now go more deeply than ever into the nature of that complication, and that a capital idea (he could say that without flattering himself) was burgeoning in his head which would clear up the whole business, raise him in his official career, discomfit his enemies, and therefore be of the greatest benefit to the country. As soon as the footman, who had brought in the tea, had left the room, Karenin got up and went to the writing table. Moving to the middle of the table the brief case containing current business, with a scarcely perceptible smile of self-satisfaction, he took a pencil from the stand and settled down to the reading of the intricate papers he had sent for, relating to the impending complication. The complication was this. Karenin's characteristic quality as a statesman, that special characteristic feature peculiar to every rising civil servant, was that with his pertinacious ambition, self-control, honesty, and self-confidence, he also possessed an utter contempt for red tape, a desire to cut down every kind of correspondence, a love of economy, and, as far as possible, an endeavor to achieve a direct relation with real facts. It so happened that the famous Commission of the Second of June had to deal with the question of irrigation of lands in the Zaraisky Province, which pertained to Karenin's department, and presented a striking example of unproductive expenditure and the uselessness of red tape. Karenin knew that this was so. The business of the irrigation of lands of the Zaraisky Province was initiated by the predecessor of Karenin's predecessor. And, indeed, a great deal of money had been spent and was still being spent quite unproductively, and it seemed clear that the whole scheme would lead to nothing. When Karenin had taken up his present post, he had immediately perceived this and had wished to stop it; but at first, while he was still feeling insecure in his position, he knew that too many interests were involved and that it would be unwise to do so; then, being occupied with other matters, he had simply forgotten the business. Like all such matters, it went on by itself, by the mere force of inertia. (Many people made a good living by it, particularly one highly moral and musical family, in which all the daughters played stringed instruments. Karenin knew the family and gave away one of the daughters at her wedding.) For another ministry to raise this question was, in Karenin's opinion, dishonest, because in every ministry there were much worse things which no one ever questioned, out of a sense of loyalty to the service. But now that the gantlet had been thrown down, he would pick it up boldly and demand the appointment of a special commission to investigate and report on the working of the Committee of Irrigation in the Zaraisky Province; at the same time he was determined to give no quarter to those gentlemen, either. He would demand that another special commission should be set up to inquire into the question of regulating the affairs of the native popula-

334

tion. The question of the regulation of the affairs of the native population had been brought up incidentally in the Committee of the Second of June and had been backed up energetically by Karenin as a matter of the highest urgency in view of the lamentable condition of the natives. In the Commission this question had been a matter of bitter contention between several ministries. The ministry that was hostile to Karenin argued that the condition of the natives was very prosperous and that the proposed reorganization might destroy their prosperity, and that if there really was anything wrong, it was due to the failure of Karenin's ministry to put into effect the measures prescribed by law. Now Karenin intended to demand: first, that a new commission be appointed to study the condition of the natives on the spot; secondly, should the conditions of the natives prove to be such as they appeared from the official documents in the hands of the commission, that another scientific commission be appointed to investigate the causes of this deplorable condition of the natives from the (a) political, (b) administrative, (c) economic, (d) ethnographic, (e) material, and (f) religious points of view; thirdly, that information should be demanded from the hostile ministry about the measures taken by that ministry during the last ten years to avert the unfavorable conditions in which the natives now found themselves; and, fourthly and finally, that the ministry should be asked to explain why it had acted in direct contradiction to the letter and the spirit of the fundamental law, Volume . . ., Article 18, and footnote to Article 36, as was evident from the statements submitted to the commission and filed under the numbers 17015 and 18308, of December 5, 1863, and June 7, 1864. A flush of excitement spread over Karenin's face as he rapidly jotted down a summary of these ideas. Having covered a sheet of paper, he rang and sent off a note to his chief secretary, asking for some necessary papers relating to this business to be sent to him. Getting up and taking a turn around the room, he again glanced at the portrait, frowned, and smiled contemptuously. After reading a little more about the Eugubine inscriptions and renewing his interest in them, at eleven o'clock Karenin went to bed and, thinking as he lay there about the situation with his wife, he no longer saw it in such a gloomy light.

CHAPTER 15

Though Anna had angrily and obstinately contradicted Vronsky when he said that her position was an impossible one and tried to persuade her to tell her husband everything, in her heart of hearts she regarded her position as false and dishonest and wished with all her soul to change it. On her way back with her husband from the races, in a moment of excitement, she had told him everything; in spite of the pain it had caused her, she was glad of it. After he left her she told herself that she was glad, that now everything would be resolved and at least there would be no more lying and deception. It seemed to her absolutely certain that her position would now be cleared up for good. It might be bad, this new position of hers, but it would be clear; there would be no vagueness or falsehood about it. The pain she had inflicted on herself and her husband in uttering those words would be compensated for now by the fact that everything would be settled unequivocally. She saw Vronsky the same evening, but did not tell him what had passed between her and her husband, though to clear up the position she should have told him.

When she woke next morning, the first thing that came into her mind was what she had said to her husband, and her words seemed to her so awful that she could not understand now how she could possibly have brought herself to utter such strange, coarse words and she was quite unable to think what would come of it. But the words had been uttered and Karenin had gone away without saying anything. "I saw Vronsky and did not tell him. At the very moment he was leaving I wanted to call him back and tell him, but I changed my mind because it would have looked so strange that I had not told him at the beginning. Why did I not tell him, though I wanted to?" And in reply to this question a hot flush of shame spread all over her face. She understood what had stopped her; she realized that she had been ashamed. Her position, which seemed to have been cleared up the night before, suddenly struck her now not only as not cleared up, but as absolutely hopeless. She was terrified of the disgrace, which she had not even thought of before. The very thought of what her husband might do put the most terrible ideas into her mind. She fancied that presently the bailiff would come and turn her out of the house, that her disgrace would be proclaimed to all the world. She kept asking herself where she would go when she was turned out of the house, and could find no answer.

When she thought of Vronsky, it seemed to her that he no longer loved her, that he was already beginning to find her a burden, that she could not offer herself to him, and she hated him for it. It seemed to her that the words she had spoken to her husband, which she kept repeating to herself in her imagination, she had said to everyone and that everyone had heard them. She was afraid to look into the eyes of the people she lived with. She was afraid to ring for the maid and still less to go downstairs and see her son and his governess.

The maid, who had long been listening at the door, at last came in of her own accord. Anna looked inquiringly into her eyes and blushed with fright. The maid excused herself for coming in and said that she thought she had heard the bell. She brought a dress and a note. The note was from Betsy. Betsy reminded her that she was expecting Lisa Merkalov and Baroness Stolz with their admirers, Kaluzhsky and old Stremov, for a game of croquet that morning. "Do come if only to study the manners and customs. I shall expect you," she concluded.

Anna read the note and sighed deeply.

"Nothing, I want nothing," she said to Annushka, who was rearranging the bottles and brushes on the dressing table. "You can go now. I will get dressed and come down at once. No, thank you, I want nothing, nothing at all."

Annushka went out, but Anna did not start dressing, but remained sitting in the same position, her head and arms drooping, and her whole body shuddering now and then, as if she wished to make some movement or to say something, and again sinking into immobility. She kept repeating: "My God! My God!" but neither "God" nor "my" had any meaning to her. The thought of seeking help in her trouble in religion was as uncongenial to her as looking for help from Karenin himself, though she had never doubted the truth of the religion in which she had been brought up. She knew perfectly well that she could expect no help from religion unless she gave up that which made up the whole meaning of life for her. She felt not only wretched, but was beginning to be afraid of a mental state she had never experienced before. She felt that everything in her mind was beginning to be doubled just as objects sometimes appear double to strained eyes. She did not know at times what she was afraid of and what she desired. Was she afraid of or did she desire what had happened or what was going to happen, and what it was she desired she did not know.

"Oh, what am I doing?" she said to herself, feeling a sudden pain in both sides of her head. When she came to she discovered that she was holding her hair at her temples with both hands and was pulling it hard. She jumped to her feet and began pacing up and down the room.

"Coffee is ready and Ma'm'selle and Seryozha are waiting, ma'am," said Annushka, coming in again and again finding Anna in the same position.

"Seryozha? What about Seryozha?" Anna asked with sudden animation, remembering her son's existence for the first time that morning.

"I think, ma'am, he's been naughty," Annushka replied with a smile.

"Has he? How?"

"Well, ma'am, there were some peaches in the corner room and it seems he has eaten one of them on the quiet."

The thought of her son suddenly helped Anna out of the hopeless position in which she found herself. She remembered that partly sincere, though greatly exaggerated, role of a mother living for her son, which she had assumed during the last few years, and she felt with joy that in the position in which she found herself she had someone to hold on to, someone to care for, quite independent of her relationship with her husband and Vronsky. This was her son. Whatever position she might find herself in, she could not give up her son. Let her husband disgrace her and turn her out, let Vronsky love her no longer and continue to live his own independent life (she thought of him again with bitterness and reproach), she could not leave her son. She had an aim in life. And she must act, act to ensure her position with her son, so that he might not be taken away from her. She had to act quickly, as quickly as possible, while they still had not taken him away from her. She must take her son and go away. That was the one thing she had to do now. She had to be calm and get out of this agonizing situation. The thought of direct action connected with her son, the idea of going away with him somewhere immediately, gave her this calm.

She dressed quickly, went downstairs, and with determined steps walked into the dining room, where Seryozha and his governess were waiting breakfast for her as usual. Seryozha, all in white, was standing at a table under a looking glass and, with bent head and back, was arranging some flowers he had brought with an expression of concentrated attention which she knew so well and in which he resembled his father.

The governess was looking unusually stern. Seryozha exclaimed in a shrill voice, as he often did, "Oh, Mummy!" and stopped short, unable to make up his mind whether to go and greet his mother and leave the flowers or to finish the garland he was making and go up with it to her.

Having said good morning to Anna, the governess began a long and circumstantial account of Seryozha's misconduct, but Anna did not listen to her. She was wondering whether to take her with her or not. "No," she decided, "I won't take her. I'll go alone with my son."

"Yes, that was very bad," said Anna and, taking her son by the shoulder, looked at him, not with a stern but with a timid expression that confused and delighted the boy, and kissed him. "Leave him alone with me," she said to the surprised governess and, without letting go of her son's hand, sat down at the table, where coffee was set ready for her.

"Mummy, I . . . I . . . didn't . . ." he said, trying to find out from her expression what he could expect for eating the peach.

"Seryozha," she said as soon as the governess had gone out of the room, "it was wrong of you to do it, but you won't do it again, will you? You love me, don't you?"

She felt the tears starting to her eyes. "Could I help

339

loving him?" she said to herself, gazing intently into his frightened and at the same time happy eyes. "Is it really possible that he would take sides with his father to punish me? Will he not take pity on me?" The tears were now streaming down her cheeks and, to conceal them, she got up abruptly and ran out onto the terrace.

After the thunderstorms of the last few days the weather had grown clear and cold. In spite of the bright sunshine, pouring through the rain-washed leaves, it was cold outside.

She shivered both with cold and with the terror inside her which seized her with fresh force in the open air.

"Go, go to Mariette," she said to Seryozha, who had come out after her, and began walking up and down the straw matting of the terrace. "Is it possible that they won't forgive me, that they won't understand that it could not possibly have been otherwise?" she said to herself.

Stopping dead and looking at the tops of the aspens swaying in the wind, with their rain-washed leaves glittering brightly in the cold sunshine, she realized that they would not forgive her, that everything and everybody would be as merciless to her as this sky, these green trees. And again she felt that everything inside her was beginning to be split in two. "I mustn't, I mustn't think," she said to herself. "I must start packing. But where am I to go? When? Who am I to take with me? Why, I must go to Moscow by the evening train. Take Annushka and Seryozha and only the most necessary things. But first of all I must write to them both." She went quickly indoors to her room, sat down at the table and wrote to her husband:

"After what has happened, I cannot remain any longer in your house. I am going away and taking my son with me. I don't know the law and therefore I don't know which of the parents should get the custody of the son; but I take him with me because I cannot live without him. Be generous and let me have him."

Up to that point she wrote quickly and naturally, but the appeal to generosity, which she did not think was in him, and the necessity of finishing the letter on a pathetic note, stopped her.

"To speak of my guilt and my repentance I cannot because . . ."

She stopped again, unable to find any cohesion in her thoughts. "No," she said to herself, "this is quite unnecessary," and tearing up the letter, she wrote it again, leaving out the reference to generosity, and sealed it.

Another letter had to be written to Vronsky. "I have told my husband," she began, and sat for a long time unable to write any more. That was so coarse and unwomanly. "Anyway, what can I write to him?" she said to herself. Again she blushed. She remembered his calm composure, and a feeling of annoyance with him made her tear the sheet of paper with the one sentence written on it into little bits. "There is no need to write to him at all," she said and, closing her blotting pad, went upstairs, told the governess and the servants that she was going to Moscow, and at once began packing her things.

CHAPTER 16

In all the rooms of the country cottage, house porters, gardeners, and footmen went about carrying things out. Cupboards and chests of drawers stood open; twice people had to be sent out to the shop for balls of string; the floor was strewn with newspapers. Two trunks, several bags and strapped-up rugs had been taken down to the entrance hall. A carriage and two hired cabs were waiting at the front steps. Anna, who had forgotten her worries while supervising the packing, was standing at a table in her room packing her traveling bag, when Annushka drew her attention to the sound of an approaching carriage. Anna looked out of the window and saw Karenin's courier at the front steps, ringing the bell.

"Go and see what it is," she said and, calmly prepared for anything, sat down in an armchair with her hands folded in her lap. A footman brought in a thick envelope addressed in Karenin's hand.

"The courier has been told to wait for an answer, ma'am," he said.

"Very well," she replied and, as soon as he had gone out of the room, she tore open the envelope with shaking hands. A packet of new banknotes in a paper band fell out of it. She took out the letter and started reading it from the end. "All the necessary preparations shall be made for your return. . . . I attach particular importance to your compliance with this request," she read. She read on, then back, read it all through, and once more read it right through from the beginning again. When she had finished, she became aware that she was shivering with cold and she realized that a calamity more terrible than she had ever expected had befallen her.

In the morning she had been sorry she had told her husband and only wished she had never spoken those words. And here was this letter treating her words as unspoken and giving her what she had wanted. But now this letter appeared more terrible to her than anything she could have imagined.

"He's in the right! In the right!" she said. "Of course, he's always in the right! He's a Christian! He's magnanimous! Yes, the mean, disgusting man! And no one understands it except me. No one will ever understand it. And I can't explain it. They say, 'Oh, he's such a religious, moral, honest, intelligent man!' But they don't see what I've seen. They don't know how for eight years he has crushed my life, crushed everything that was alive in me, that he has never once thought that I was a live woman who was in need of love. They do not know how at every step he has slighted me and remained self-satisfied. Haven't I tried, tried with all my might, to find some kind of justification for my life? Haven't I tried to love him, to love my son when I could no longer love my husband? But the time came when I realized that I couldn't deceive myself any longer, that I was alive, that I couldn't be blamed that God had made me so, that I have to love and live. And now? If he'd killed me, if he'd killed him, I could have borne anything, I could have forgiven anything, but no! He . . .

"How didn't I guess what he would do? He'll do what is consistent with his mean nature. He'll be in the right, while he will do his best to ruin and disgrace me more than ever, ruined and disgraced though I am already. . . .

" 'You can easily imagine what awaits you and your son,' " she recalled the words from the letter. "That is a threat that he will take my son away from me, and I shouldn't wonder if, according to their stupid laws, he could do it. But don't I know why he says it? He doesn't even believe in my love for my child and he despises it (he always sneered at it), despises that feeling of mine, but he knows that I will not give up my son, that I cannot give him up, that there cannot be any life for me without my son even with the man I love. He knows that were I to run away and abandon my son, I should be behaving like a wicked, infamous woman. He knows that and he knows that I could never bring myself to do it.

" 'Our life must go on as before,' " she recalled another sentence of the letter. "This life was sheer agony even before, and more recently it was simply awful. What, then, will it be like now? And he knows all that, he knows that I cannot repent that I breathe, that I love; he knows that nothing but lies and deception can come of it; but he simply has to go on torturing me. I know, I know that, like a fish in water, he swims and delights in deceit. But no! I will not give him that pleasure. I shall tear down the spider web of lies in which he wants to entangle me, come what may. Anything is better than lying and deceit!

"But how? Oh God, oh God! Was ever a woman as unhappy as I am?

"No, I shall tear it down, I shall tear it down!" she cried, jumping up and forcing back her tears. And she went up to the writing table to write him another letter. But deep down she already felt that she would not have the strength to tear down anything, that she would not have the strength to escape from her former position, however false and dishonest it might be.

She sat down at the writing table, but instead of writing she folded her arms on the table, put her head on them, and burst into tears, sobbing and her breast heaving, like a child crying. She wept because her dream of clearing up and defining her position had been shattered forever. She knew perfectly well that everything would remain as it was and, indeed, would be much worse than before. She felt that the position she enjoyed in society and which had appeared so unimportant to her that morning, that this position was precious to her and that she would not have the strength to change it for the disreputable one of a woman who has deserted her husband and child to join her lover; that however much she tried, she could not be stronger than herself. She would never know the meaning of the freedom of love and would always remain the guilty wife, continually threatened with exposure, deceiving her husband for the sake of a shameful liaison with a man who remained independent and a stranger and whose life she could never share. She knew that it would be so, and yet it was so awful that she could not even imagine how it would end. And she cried, unable to restrain her tears, as children weep when they are punished.

The sound of the footman's footsteps made her come to herself, and hiding her face from him, she pretended to be writing.

"The courier is asking for an answer, ma'am," the footman said.

"An answer?" said Anna. "Oh yes, let him wait. I'll ring."

"What can I write?" she thought. "What can I decide by myself? What do I know? What do I want? What do I love?" Again she felt that her mind seemed to be splitting in two. She was again frightened by the sensation and seized upon the first pretext for action that occurred to her to distract her thoughts of herself. "I must see Alexey," as she called Vronsky, when she thought of him. "He alone can tell me what to do. I shall go to Betsy's, perhaps I shall see him there," she said to herself, completely forgetting that when she had told him the day before that she was not going to Princess Tverskoy's, he had said that in that case he would not go, either. She went up to the table, wrote to her husband, "I have received your letter.—A.," rang, and gave the note to the footman.

"We are not going," she said to Annushka, who had come in.

"Not going at all?"

"No, but don't unpack till tomorrow, and let the carriage wait. I'm driving over to the princess'."

"What dress shall I put out?"

CHAPTER 17

The croquet party to which the Princess Tverskoy had invited Anna was to consist of two ladies and their admirers. The two ladies were the chief representatives of a very select new Petersburg circle, nicknamed, in imitation of an imitation of something, *les sept merveilles du monde*. These ladies belonged to a circle whose members, though of the highest society, were hostile to the members of the circle which Anna frequented. Moreover, old Stremov, one of the most influential people in Petersburg and Lisa Merkalov's admirer, was Karenin's enemy in the service. All these considerations had made Anna reluctant to come, and it was to her refusal that the hints in the Princess Tverskoy's note had referred. But hoping to see Vronsky, Anna was now anxious to go.

Anna arrived at the Princess Tverskoy's before the other visitors.

As she was going in, Vronsky's footman, whose side whiskers were combed like a court chamberlain's, was also coming in. He stopped at the door and, taking off his hat, let her pass. Anna recognized him and only then remembered that Vronsky had said the day before that he was not coming. She supposed that he had now sent a note to say so.

As she was taking off her outdoor things in the hall she heard the footman, who even pronounced his *r*'s like a court chamberlain, say, "From the count to the princess," as he delivered the note.

She was anxious to ask him where his master was. She would have liked to have gone home and sent him a note to come and see her or to go and see him herself. But she could do none of these things, for already she heard bells ringing ahead of her to announce her arrival and Princess Tverskoy's footman was already standing half-turned at the open door waiting for her to pass into the inner rooms.

"The princess is in the garden, ma'am," said another footman in the next room. "She will be informed immediately. Would you care to go into the garden, ma'am?"

She was in the same state of indecision and uncertainty as she had been at home; indeed, it was much worse because she could do nothing, she could not see Vronsky, she had to stay here in a company of people who had nothing in common with her and whose mood was so contrary to hers; but she wore a dress that she knew suited her; she was not alone, for all around her was the all too familiar setting of luxury and idleness and she felt more at ease than at home. She did not have to consider what she was to do. Everything did itself. When she met Betsy coming toward her in a white gown that impressed Anna by its elegance, Anna smiled just as usual. Princess Tverskoy was accompanied by Tushkevich and a young girl, a relation, who, to the great delight of her parents in the provinces, was spending the summer with the famous princess.

There must have been something special about Anna, for Betsy noticed it at once.

"I had a bad night," answered Anna, gazing at the footman who came to meet them with, she could only suppose, Vronsky's note.

"I'm so glad you were able to come," said Betsy. "I'm tired and was just going to have a cup of tea before the others arrive. Won't you and Masha go and try the croquet lawn where they have cut it?" she said to Tushkevich. "We shall have time to have a heart-to-heart talk over our tea. We'll have a cozy chat, won't we?" she added in English, turning to Anna with a smile and pressing the hand with which she held a parasol.

"Yes, especially as I cannot stay long. I'm afraid I have got to go and see old Countess Wrede. I promised to see her ages ago," said Anna, to whom lying, so alien to her nature, had become not merely simple and natural in society, but positively a source of satisfaction.

Why she had said something which a moment before she had not even thought of, she could not have explained. She had said it merely because, since Vronsky was not coming, she had to secure her freedom and try to see him in some other way. But why exactly she mentioned the old lady-in-waiting Wrede, to whom, among many other people, she owed a visit, she could not have explained; and yet, as it turned out afterward, even had she tried to think of the most cunning means of seeing Vronsky, she could not have thought of anything better.

"No, I won't let you go on any account," replied Betsy, looking intently at Anna's face. "I should be really hurt if I were not so fond of you. Really, it's as if you were afraid that my company might compromise you. Tea in the little drawing room, please," she said to the footman, screwing up her eyes as she always did when speaking to servants. Taking the note from him, she read it. "Alexey has let us down," she said in French. "He writes that he can't come," she added in such a natural and matter-of-fact tone as though it never entered her head that Vronsky had any other interest for Anna than a partner in a game of croquet.

Anna knew that Betsy knew everything, but when she heard her speak of Vronsky she was always momentarily convinced that Betsy knew nothing about it.

"Oh," said Anna indifferently, as if not greatly interested, and went on, smilingly: "How could your company compromise anyone?" This playing with words, this concealment of a secret had a great fascination for Anna, as it has for all women. And it was not the necessity for concealment, nor its purpose, but the very process of concealment that fascinated her. "I cannot be more Catholic than the Pope," she said. "Stremov and Lisa Merkalov—why, they are the cream of society. They are received everywhere, and *I*"—she laid special stress on the *I*—"have never been severe and intolerant. I simply have not the time."

"I don't believe you. It isn't by any chance that you don't want to meet Stremov, is it? Let him and your husband break lances in the committee room—that's nothing to do with us. In society he is the most amiable man I know and a most ardent croquet player. You will see. And in spite of his ridiculous position as Lisa's elderly lover, you ought to see how he carries it off! He's very charming. You don't know Sappho Stolz, do you? Oh, she's quite the last word in fashion."

While Betsy was saying all this, Anna realized from her bright, intelligent look that she was to a certain extent aware of her situation and that she was devising something. They were in the small drawing room.

"But I suppose I'd better write to Alexey." And Betsy sat down at the table, wrote a few lines, and put her note in an envelope. "I've asked him to come to dinner. I have one lady too many. See if I've made it persuasive enough. I'm sorry, I must leave you for a minute. Please seal it and send it off," she said from the doorway. "I have something to see to."

Without giving it another thought, Anna sat down at the table with Betsy's letter and, without reading it, added at the bottom: "I must see you. Come to Wrede's garden. I shall be there at six o'clock." She sealed the envelope and when Betsy returned, sent it off in her presence.

And, indeed, over their tea, which was brought on a tea trolley in the cool little drawing room, the two women had *a cozy chat*, as promised by Princess Tverskoy before the arrival of her visitors. They were retailing the latest scandal concerning those who were expected, and their conversation dwelt in particular on Lisa Merkalov.

"She's very charming and I always liked her," said Anna.

"Oh, you simply must! She raves about you. Yesterday she came up to me after the races and was in despair that she had missed you. She says you are a real heroine out of a novel and that, if she were a man, she would have committed a thousand follies for your sake. Stremov says she's committing them as it is."

"But tell me, please, I never could understand it," said Anna after a little pause and in a tone of voice which clearly showed that she was not putting an idle question, but that she was asking what was more important to her than it should have been, "tell me, please, what are her relations with Prince Kaluzhsky, whom they all call Mishka? I'm afraid I don't know them too well. What exactly are they?"

Betsy smiled with her eyes and looked intently at Anna.

"It's the new fashion," she said. "They've all adopted it. They've kicked over the traces. But, of course, there is fashion and fashion, and there are ways and ways of kicking over the traces."

"Yes, but what are her relations with Kaluzhsky?"

Betsy quite unexpectedly burst out into a gay, uncontrollable peal of laughter, which very rarely happened to her.

"I'm afraid you're encroaching on Princess Myakhky's territory. It's the sort of question an *enfant terrible* might ask." And however much she tried, Betsy could not help bursting out into the kind of infectious laughter that is peculiar to people who rarely laugh. "You'd better ask them," she said through tears of laughter.

"No, really, you laugh," said Anna, who burst out laughing too, in spite of herself, "but I never could un-

348

derstand it. What I don't understand is the part the husband plays in it."

"The husband? Lisa Merkalov's husband carries her rugs after her and is always at her beck and call. But what there is besides no one really cares to know. As you know, in good society people do not talk or even think about certain details of the toilet. It's just the same in this case."

"Will you be at Rolandaki's fete?" asked Anna, to change the subject.

"I don't think so," answered Betsy and, without looking at her friend, began carefully pouring fragrant tea into little transparent china cups. Moving one of the cups toward Anna, she took out a cigarette and, putting it into a silver holder, lit it. "You see," she said, no longer laughing, as she took up her cup, "I'm in a fortunate position. I understand you and I understand Lisa. Lisa is one of those naïve natures who, like children, do not know the difference between right and wrong. At least she did not understand it when she was very young. And now she knows that this failure to understand becomes her. Now, perhaps, she does not understand on purpose," Betsy said with the ghost of a smile. "But it becomes her all the same. You see, one can look at a thing tragically and turn it into a torment or one can look at it simply and even gaily. Perhaps you are inclined to take things too tragically."

"Oh, how I wish I knew other people as I know myself," said Anna seriously and thoughtfully. "Am I worse than others or better? Worse, I think."

"Enfant terrible, enfant terrible!" Betsy repeated, "but here they are."

CHAPTER 18

They heard sounds of footsteps and a man's voice, then a woman's voice and laughter, and after that the expected visitors came in: Sappho Stolz and a young man, bursting with health, known as Vaska. It was evident that a diet of underdone steak, truffles, and Burgundy did him a world of good. Vaska bowed to the ladies and glanced at them, but only for a second. He had followed Sappho into the drawing room and then walked behind her across the room, as though he were tied to her, and did not take his glittering eyes off her as though he would like to eat her. Sappho Stolz was fair and had black eyes. She walked with brisk little steps in high-heeled shoes and shook hands with the ladies vigorously, like a man.

Anna had never met this new celebrity and was struck by her beauty, by the extravagant nature of her getup, and by the boldness of her manners. On her head there was such a superstructure of soft, golden hair—her own and others'—that her head looked as large as her well-developed and overexposed bosom. The impetuosity of her movements was such that at every step the shape of her knees and thighs was clearly visible under her dress and one could not help asking oneself the question as to where under the heaped and swaying mountain of material at her back the real, graceful little body, so overexposed in front and so hidden behind and below, really came to an end.

Betsy hastened to introduce her to Anna.

"Can you imagine it, we nearly ran over two soldiers," she began telling them at once, winking and smiling and throwing back her train which she had jerked too much to one side. "I was driving with Vaska. . . . Oh, I'm sorry, I don't believe you know each other. . . ." And she introduced the young man by his surname and, blushing, she burst into ringing laughter at her mistake in speaking to him as Vaska to a stranger.

Vaska again bowed to Anna, but said nothing to her. He turned to Sappho.

"You've lost the bet. We got here first. Pay up!" he said, smiling.

Sappho laughed still more merrily.

"Not now, surely," she said.

"Never mind, I'll have it later."

"Very well, very well. Oh, incidentally," she suddenly turned to her hostess, "I'm so sorry, I'm a nice one. . . . I quite forgot. . . . I've brought you a visitor. Here he is."

The unexpected young visitor, whom Sappho had brought and whom she had forgotten, was, however, so important a personage that, in spite of his youth, both ladies got up to greet him.

It was Sappho's new admirer. Like Vaska, he now followed at her heels.

Shortly afterward Prince Kaluzhsky arrived, and Lisa Merkalov with Stremov. Lisa Merkalov was a thin brunette, with a languid, Oriental type of face and lovely and mysterious (as everybody said) eyes. The style of her dark dress, as Anna immediately noticed and appreciated, was in perfect harmony with her beauty. As much as Sappho was hard and stately, so Lisa was soft and limp.

But to Anna's taste, Lisa was far the more attractive. Betsy had told Anna that Lisa had adopted the pose of an ingenuous child, but when Anna saw her she felt that it was not true. She really was an ingenuous and spoiled, but a sweet and gentle, creature. It is true, her behavior was the same as Sappho's: like Sappho, she had two admirers, one young and one old, who followed her about as if tacked onto her and who devoured her with their eyes; but there was something in her that was superior to her surroundings—she had the sparkle of a real diamond among paste. This sparkle shone out of her lovely and really mysterious eyes. The weary and at the same time passionate gaze of those eyes, ringed with dark circles, was striking in its perfect simplicity. Looking into those eyes one could not help feeling that one knew her entirely and, knowing her, could not but love her. At the sight of Anna her whole face lit up with a joyful smile.

"Oh, I'm so glad to see you!" she said, going up to Anna. "Yesterday at the races I was trying to get near to you when you went away. I did want to see you so much, especially yesterday. Wasn't it awful?"

"Yes," said Anna, blushing. "I never thought it would be so exciting."

At that moment the company rose to go into the garden.

"I won't go," said Lisa, smiling and sitting down beside Anna. "You won't go, either, will you? Who wants to play croquet?"

"I like it," said Anna.

"Tell me, how do you manage not to feel bored? To look at you makes one feel cheerful. You live, but I am bored."

"You bored?" said Anna. "Why, yours is the gayest set in Petersburg."

"Perhaps those who are not in our set are still more bored. But we—I at any rate, do not feel gay, but terribly, terribly bored!"

Sappho lit a cigarette and went out into the garden with the two young men. Betsy and Stremov stayed at the tea table.

"Bored!" said Betsy. "Sappho said they had a very jolly time at your house yesterday."

"Oh dear, it was so terribly dull," said Lisa Merkalov. "We all went back to my place after the races. And always the same people! Always the same people! Always doing the same things! We spent the whole evening sprawling about on sofas. What's so gay about that? Please," she returned to Anna again, "do tell me how you manage not to get bored? One has only to look at you to see that there's a woman who may be happy or unhappy, but who is not bored. Tell me how you do it."

"I don't do anything," replied Anna, blushing at these persistent questions.

"That's the best way," Stremov interposed.

Stremov was a man of about fifty, getting gray but still vigorous-looking, with a very plain but intelligent face full of character. Lisa Merkalov was his wife's niece and he spent all his leisure hours with her. On meeting Anna, he, an enemy of Karenin's in the service, did his best, like a clever man and a man of the world, to be particularly nice to her, the wife of his enemy.

" 'Don't do anything,' " he repeated, with a subtle smile. "That's the best way. I always told you," he turned to Lisa Merkalov, "that if you don't want to be bored, you mustn't think that you're going to be bored. It's the same as you mustn't be afraid of not going to sleep if you're afraid of insomnia. That's exactly what Mrs. Karenin has just said."

"I should have been pleased to have said it because it is not only wise but true," said Anna with a smile.

"No, you'd better tell me why one can't go to sleep and why one can't help being bored."

"To sleep one has to do some work first, and to enjoy oneself one has to have done some work too."

"But why should I work when no one wants my work? And I can't and won't just pretend to work."

352

"You're incorrigible," said Stremov without looking at her, and again turned to Anna.

As he rarely met Anna, he could say nothing but platitudes to her, but he said them, about when she was thinking of returning to Petersburg and how fond the Countess Lydia Ivanovna was of her, in a way that expressed his sincere desire to be agreeable to her and to show his respect for her, and even more.

Tushkevich came in to say that everybody was waiting for the croquet players.

"No, please, don't go," begged Lisa Merkalov when she heard that Anna was leaving.

Stremov joined her in begging Anna to stay.

"The contrast will be too great," he said, "if you go from here to old Mrs. Wrede. Besides, you will only give her a chance to talk scandal, while here you arouse quite different feelings of a most praiseworthy kind, feelings which are as contrary to scandal as can be."

Anna hesitated for a moment. The flattering words of this clever man, the naïve, childish sympathy which Lisa Merkalov expressed for her, and all the familiar high-society surroundings—it was all so easy, and what awaited her was so difficult that for a moment she remained undecided whether to stay and put off the painful moment of explanation. But remembering what was in store for her alone at home if she did not come to some decision, remembering that gesture—terrible for her even in memory—when she had clutched her hair with both hands, she took her leave and went away.

CHAPTER 19

Vronsky, in spite of his apparently frivolous life in society, was a man who hated disorder. While still quite young and in the Corps of Pages he had experienced the humiliation of refusal when, having got into debt, he had asked for a loan, and since then he had never again allowed himself to get into such a position.

In order to keep his affairs straight, he was in the habit, some four or five times a year according to circumstances, of shutting himself up and putting his affairs in order. He called it his day of getting even with the world, or the day for doing the washing, or *faire la lessive*.

The morning after the races he woke late and, without having a bath or shaving, he put on a white cotton tunic with stand-up collar, and, spreading out on the table his money, his bills, and letters, set to work. Petritsky, who knew that he was apt to be cross on such occasions, dressed quietly when he saw Vronsky at the writing table and went out without disturbing him.

Every man who is familiar to the last detail with all the complexity of his own circumstances involuntarily assumes that the complexity of these circumstances and the difficulty of clearing them up are of an accidental nature peculiar to himself alone, and it never occurs to him that other people have to deal with personal circumstances which are just as complicated as his. So it seemed to Vronsky. And not without a feeling of inward pride, nor without reason, did he think that any other man would have long ago got head over ears in debt and been forced into some dishonorable action had he found himself in as difficult a position as he. But he felt that it was now especially that he had to take stock of his affairs and clear them up so as to keep out of trouble.

The first thing Vronsky tackled was the easiest one to settle, namely his financial affairs. Noting down in his small handwriting on a piece of notepaper all he owed, he proceeded to add it up and found that it came to 17,000 and a few hundred rubles, which he left out for the sake of simplicity. He then counted his money and looked over his bankbook and found that all he had left was 1,800 rubles, and there was no prospect of getting any more before the new year. Going over his list of debts, Vronsky copied it out, dividing it into three categories. To the first belonged the debts that had to be paid at once, or at any rate, for which he would have to have money kept ready so that they could be paid on demand without a moment's delay. These debts amounted to about 4,000: 1,500 for a horse, and 2,500 as surety for a young fellow officer, Venevsky, who had lost that sum to a cardsharper in Vronsky's presence. Vronsky had wanted to pay the money at once, but Venevsky and Yashvin had insisted that they would pay and not Vronsky, who had not been playing. That was all very fine, but Vronsky knew that in this sordid affair, in which he was involved merely because he had given a verbal guarantee to Venevsky, he had to have the 2,500 rubles ready in order to be able to throw them to the swindler and have nothing more to do with him. So that for this category of urgent debts he must have 4,000 rubles. The 8,000 rubles in the second category were less urgent: these were the debts incurred in connection with the racecourse stables, for oats and hay, to his English trainer, to the saddler and others. Of these too he would have to pay out about 2,000 rubles to be quite free from worry. The last category comprised debts to shops, hotels, and his tailor, and there was no need to worry about them at all. So that he had to have at least 6,000 rubles for current expenses, and he only had 1,800. For a man with an income of 100,000 a year, which was what everybody thought his fortune was worth, it would seem that such debts could hardly be embarrassing; but the trouble was that he was far from having the 100,000 rubles. His father's immense fortune, which alone brought in 200,000 rubles a year, was owned jointly by the two brothers. At the time when his elder brother, who owed a large amount of money, married the Princess Varya Chirkov, the daughter of a penniless Decembrist, Alexey let his brother have the entire income from their father's estates, reserving for himself only 25,000 a year. Alexey had told his brother that this would be enough for him till he married, which he would most probably never do. His brother, commanding one of the most expensive regiments and newly married, could not refuse this gift. His mother, who had her own fortune, made Alexey an allowance of 20,000 a year, in addition to the 25,000, and Alexey spent it all. More recently, his mother, who had quarreled with him about his affair with Anna and his departure from Moscow, had discontinued his allowance. And because of that Vronsky, who was in the habit of spending 45,000 rubles a year, having received only 25,000 this year, found himself in difficulties. He could not ask his mother for money to help him out of them. Her last letter, which he had received the day before, had particularly irritated him, for it contained hints that she was willing to help him to obtain further success in society and in the army, but not to lead a life that scandalized all good society. His mother's attempt to buy him off deeply offended him and made him grow still colder to her. But he could not go back on his generous promise, though he could not help feeling now, dimly foreseeing certain eventualities of his liaison with Anna, that he had been rather thoughtless in giving his promise and that, though unmarried, he might need all the 100,000 of his income. But he could not go back on his word. He had only to think of his brother's wife, he had only to recall how that dear, nice sister-in-law of his reminded him at every favorable opportunity of how she remembered and appreciated his generosity, to realize how utterly impossible it was to withdraw what he had given. It was just as impossible as beating a woman, stealing, or lying. There was only one thing he could and must do, and Vronsky made up his mind to do it without a moment's hesitation: to borrow 10,000 rubles from a moneylender, which he could do without any difficulty, to cut down his expenses, and to sell his race horses. Having decided this, he at once wrote a note to Rolandaki, who had more than once offered to buy his horses. Then he sent for his English trainer and the moneylender, and divided the money he had among the different accounts. Having finished this business, he wrote a cold and sharp reply to his mother. Then he took out of his pocketbook three notes from Anna, read them again, burned them, and recalling his yesterday's conversation with her, sank into thought.

CHAPTER 20

Vronsky's life was particularly fortunate in that he had a code of rules which defined without question what should and what should not be done. The code covered only a very small number of contingencies, but, on the other hand, the rules were never in doubt, and Vronsky, who never thought of infringing them, had never had a moment's hesitation about what he ought to do. The rules laid it down most categorically that a cardsharper had to be paid, but a tailor had not; that one must not tell a lie to a man, but might to a woman; that one must not deceive anyone but one may a husband; that one must not forgive an insult but may insult others, etc. All these rules might be irrational and bad, but they were absolute, and in complying with them Vronsky felt that he need not worry and could hold his head high. Only quite lately, in regard to his relations with Anna, Vronsky had begun to feel that the code of his rules did not cover every contingency and that the future presented doubts and difficulties for which he could find no guiding principle.

His present attitude towards Anna and her husband was clear and simple to him. It was clearly and precisely defined in the code of rules by which he was guided.

She was a respectable woman who had given him her love and he loved her; therefore she was for him a woman deserving of as much, if not more, respect than a lawful wife. He would have let his hand be cut off rather than allow himself to insult her by word or hint, or fail to show her all the respect a woman had a right to expect.

His attitude to society also was clear. Everyone might know or suspect, but no one must dare to speak of it. If they did, he was ready to silence the speaker and make him respect the nonexistent honor of the woman he loved.

Clearest of all was his attitude toward her husband. From the moment that Anna fell in love with Vronsky, he considered his right over her unchallengeable. The husband was only a superfluous person and a nuisance. He was no doubt in a pitiable position, but what was to be done about it? The only right the husband possessed was to demand satisfaction with weapon in hand, and that Vronsky was prepared to give him from the first moment.

But more recently something new had appeared in his inner relations with Anna, which frightened Vronsky by their vagueness. It was only the day before that she had told him that she was pregnant. And he felt that this news and what she expected of him called for something that was not fully defined in his code of rules. And, to be sure, he was taken by surprise and at the first moment when she told him of her condition his heart had prompted him to beg her to leave her husband. He had said so, but now, on thinking it over, he saw clearly that it would be better to manage without it; and yet, at the same time, while he told himself so, he feared that this might be wrong.

357

"If I told her to leave her husband, it meant that she should come and live with me. Am I ready for that? How can I take her away now that I have no money? Supposing I could arrange that . . . but how can I go away with her while I am in the army? If I were to tell her to do that, I must be ready to do these things, that is to say, I must get the money and resign my commission."

And he fell into thought. The question whether or not to resign his commission brought him to the other, almost the chief, interest of his life, known only to him, for he had kept it a dead secret all through his life.

Ambition was the old dream of his childhood and youth, a dream which he was loath to admit even to himself, but which was so strong that even now this passion of his was contending with his love. His first steps in society and the service had been successful, but two years ago he had made a great mistake. Wishing to show his independence and in this way gain promotion, he had refused a post in the hope that his refusal would enhance his value; but it turned out that he had been too bold and he was passed over; and having willy-nilly taken up the position of an independent man, he kept it up very adroitly and cleverly, behaving as though he had no grudge against anyone, did not feel at all injured, and only wished to be left alone because he was enjoying life. But as a matter of fact he had stopped enjoying life as long ago as the year before, when he went away to Moscow. He felt that this independent attitude of a man who could have done anything but wanted nothing was getting a bit frayed at the edges, that many people were beginning to think that he could never be anything more than an honest, good fellow. His love affair with Anna, which had caused such a sensation and attracted general attention, had invested him with fresh glamor and for a while soothed the gnawing worm of ambition in him, but a week ago that worm had reawakened with renewed vigor. A childhood friend of his, who belonged to the same social set and had been at the Corps of Pages with him, Serpukhovskoy, who had graduated with him and had been his rival in the classroom, in the gymnasium, in mischief, and in ambitious dreams, had just returned from Central Asia, where he had been twice promoted and had won a distinction rarely awarded to so young a general.

As soon as he arrived in Petersburg, people began to

talk of him as a rising star of the first magnitude. A schoolfellow of Vronsky's and of the same age as he, Serpukhovskoy was a general and was expecting an appointment that might have an influence on the affairs of state, while Vronsky, though independent and brilliant and loved by a charming woman, was only a cavalry captain who was allowed to be as independent as he pleased. "Of course I am not jealous and could not be jealous of Serpukhovskoy, but his promotion proves that a man like me has only to wait for the right opportunity for his career to be made very quickly. Three years ago he was in the same position as I am now. If I resign my commission, I burn my boats. By remaining in the service I lose nothing. She said herself that she did not want to change her position. And with her love I cannot be envious of Serpukhovskoy." And twisting his mustache with a slow movement of the hand, he got up from the table and took a turn around the room. His eyes shone particularly brightly and he was conscious of that resolute, calm, and happy frame of mind which always came when he had made his position clear to himself. Everything was neat and tidy, as after his former stocktakings. He shaved, had a cold bath, dressed, and went out.

CHAPTER 21

"I've come to fetch you," said Petritsky. "Your toilet has taken a long time today. Well, is it done?"

"Yes, it's done," replied Vronsky, smiling with his eyes and twirling the ends of his mustache carefully, as though any too bold or rapid movement might upset the order into which he had brought his affairs.

"You always look as if you've come out of a bath after it," said Petritsky. "I've come from Gritsky" (that was what they called their colonel). "They're expecting you."

Vronsky looked at his comrade without answering, thinking of something else.

"I see. Is that where the music is from?" he said, listening to the familiar strains of brass instruments playing waltzes and polkas. "What's up?"

"Serpukhovskoy has arrived."

"Oh," said Vronsky, "and I didn't know."

The smile in his eyes gleamed still more brightly.

Once having decided that he was happy in his love, that he sacrificed his ambition to it, or, at least, having assumed that role, Vronsky could no longer feel envious of Serpukhovskoy nor vexed with him for not coming first to him on reaching the regiment. Serpukhovskoy was a good friend and he was glad to welcome him.

"Oh, I'm so glad."

Colonel Demin occupied a large country house. The whole party were on the spacious lower balcony. In the courtyard the first thing to meet Vronsky's eyes was the choir of soldiers in their white cotton tunics, standing beside a cask of vodka, and the hale and hearty figure of the C.O., surrounded by officers: having gone out on the top step of the balcony, he was shouting loudly above the music of the band (which was playing an Offenbach quadrille), giving some orders, and waving his arms at a few soldiers standing on one side. A group of soldiers, a sergeant-major, and some noncommissioned officers came up to the balcony together with Vronsky. After returning to the table, the colonel went out again onto the steps with a glass in his hand and gave a toast: "To the health of our old comrade, the gallant general, Prince Serpukhovskoy. Hurrah!"

The colonel was followed by Serpukhovskoy, who came out with a glass in his hand and smiling.

"You're growing younger every day, Bondarenko," he addressed the ruddy-cheeked, smart-looking sergeant-major, doing his second term of service, who was standing just in front of him.

Vronsky had not seen Serpukhovskoy for three years. He was more mature, had grown side whiskers, but he was as tall and slender as ever, not strikingly handsome, but with a face and figure that were quite remarkable for their gentleness and nobility. One change Vronsky noticed in him was that quiet, continuous radiance which settles on the faces of people who are successful and who are confident that their success is recognized by everyone. Vronsky knew that kind of radiance and immediately noticed it in Serpukhovskoy.

As he was coming down the steps, Serpukhovskoy caught sight of Vronsky. A smile of pleasure lit up his face. He jerked his head backward, raised his glass, greeting Vronsky and indicating by his gesture that he could not help going up first to the sergeant-major, who had drawn himself up and was already puckering up his lips for a kiss.

"Ah, here he is!" exclaimed the colonel. "And Yashvin told me that you are in one of your dismal moods."

Serpukhovskoy kissed the smart-looking sergeant-major on his moist, fresh lips and, wiping his mouth with his handkerchief, went up to Vronsky.

"Well, I am glad!" he said, pressing his hand and drawing him to one side.

"Look after him!" the colonel shouted to Yashvin, pointing to Vronsky, and went down to the soldiers.

"Why weren't you at the races yesterday?" said Vronsky, examining Serpukhovskoy. "I expected to see you there."

"I did come, but I was late. Excuse me," he added and turned to his aide-de-camp. "Please see that this is divided among the men."

And he hurriedly took three hundred-ruble notes from his wallet and blushed.

"Vronsky," said Yashvin, "will you eat something or have a drink? Hey, there, bring the count something to eat. And, here, drink this!"

The party at the colonel's went on for a long time. They drank a lot. They lifted and tossed Serpukhovskoy several times. Then they did the same to the colonel. Then the colonel and Petritsky danced in front of the singers. Then the colonel, feeling a bit tottery, sat down on a bench in the yard and began proving to Yashvin Russia's superiority over Prussia, especially in cavalry attack, and the revelry quieted down for a moment. Serpukhovskoy went indoors to the cloakroom and found Vronsky there. Vronsky was pouring water over his head. He had taken off his coat and put his hairy red neck under the tap and was rubbing his head with his hands. When he had finished, he sat down beside Serpukhovskoy. Both of them sat down on a small sofa and began a conversation of great interest to both of them.

"I used to hear all about you from my wife," said Serpukhovskoy. "I am glad you have been seeing a great deal of her."

"She is a friend of Varya's and they are the only

women in Petersburg I really enjoy meeting," Vronsky replied with a smile. He smiled because he foresaw the turn their conversation was going to take and it pleased him.

"The only ones?" Serpukhovskoy asked, smiling.

"I've heard of you too and not only through your wife," said Vronsky, checking the hint by a serious look. "I was delighted by your success, but not a bit surprised. I expected even more."

Serpukhovskoy smiled. He was quite obviously pleased by such an opinion of him and he did not find it necessary to hide it.

"And I did not expect so much. I frankly admit it. But I'm pleased, very pleased. I'm afraid I'm ambitious. That's my weakness and I don't mind confessing it."

"Perhaps you would if you were not successful," said Vronsky.

"I don't think so," said Serpukhovskoy, smiling again. "Mind you, I do not say that it would not be worth living without it, but it would be dull. I may be mistaken, of course, but I think I have a certain ability for the career I have chosen and that power of any kind in my hands will be better than in the hands of a good many people I know," declared Serpukhovskoy with beaming consciousness of success. "And that is why the nearer I am to getting it, the better pleased I am."

"Perhaps it is so for you, but not for everyone. I thought the same, and yet here am I living and finding that it's not worth living for that alone," said Vronsky.

"Now it's out! It's out!" cried Serpukhovskoy, laughing. "You see, I began by saying that I used to hear about you. Well, I heard about your refusal. Of course, I approved of it. But there's a way of doing a thing and I can't help thinking that while what you did was right, you didn't do it quite in the right way."

"What's done is done and you know I never go back on what I've done. And, besides, I'm all right as I am."

"You're all right for a time. But you won't be satisfied with that. I should not say that to your brother. He's a dear child, just like our host here. Look at him!" he added, listening to the cries of "Hurrah!" "He's having a hell of a good time, but that wouldn't satisfy you."

"I didn't say it would."

"And that's not all. Men like you are wanted."

"By whom?"

"By whom? By society. Russia needs men. She needs a political party. Without it everything goes and will go to the dogs."

"What exactly do you mean? Bertenev's party against the Russian communists?"

"No," said Serpukhovskoy, frowning with vexation at being suspected of such stupidity. *"Tout ça est une blague.* That's always been and always will be. There are no communists. But scheming people have always to invent some harmful and dangerous party. It's an old trick. No, what is wanted is a party of independent people like you and I who know how to wield power."

"But why?" Vronsky named several men who wielded power. "Why aren't they independent men?"

"Simply because they have not, or have not had from birth, independent means, they've not had a name, they weren't born as near the sun as we were. They can be bought either by money or by favor. And to keep their position they have to invent some sort of idea, a policy in which they don't believe themselves and which does harm; and all their policy amounts to is that it provides them with a free government house and so much income. *Cela n'est pas plus fin que ça*, when you get a peep at their cards. I may be worse and more stupid than they, though I do not see why I should be worse. But you and I have one important advantage over them: we cannot be bought so easily. And such people are needed more than ever."

Vronsky listened attentively, but what interested him was not so much the substance of Serpukhovskoy's words as his attitude, for Serpukhovskoy was already planning a struggle with the powers-that-be and already had his likes and dislikes in that world, while his interests in the service were confined to his squadron. Vronsky realized, too, how powerful Serpukhovskoy might become with his undoubted ability for thinking things out and understanding them, as well as his intelligence and gift of words so rarely met with in the circle in which he moved. And, ashamed as he was of it, he could not help feeling envious.

"All the same I lack the most essential thing," he replied. "I lack the will for power. I had it, but I'm afraid it's gone."

363

"I'm sorry," Serpukhovskoy said, smiling, "but it isn't true."

"It is true, it is—now," added Vronsky, wishing to be sincere.

"Yes, it is true *now*, that's a different thing, but that *now* won't go on forever."

"Perhaps," said Vronsky.

"You say *perhaps*," Serpukhovskoy went on, as though guessing his thoughts, "and I tell you *for certain*. And that's why I wanted to see you. You acted rightly. I quite understand that. But you ought not to *persevere* in it. All I ask you is to give me carte blanche. I'm not patronizing you. . . . Though why shouldn't I patronize you? You've often patronized me. I hope our friendship is above that sort of thing. Yes," he said tenderly, like a woman, smiling at him. "Give me carte blanche, leave the regiment, and I shall get you in imperceptibly."

"But please understand I want nothing," said Vronsky, "except that everything should remain as it is."

Serpukhovskoy got up and stood facing him.

"You say you want things to remain as they are. I understand what that means. But listen. We are the same age. Perhaps you've known more women than I have." Serpukhovskoy's smile and gestures indicated that Vronsky ought not to be afraid, and that he would touch the tender spot tenderly and carefully. "But I'm married and, believe me, knowing only your wife, as someone has said, whom you love, you will know women much better than if you knew thousands of them."

"We'll come in a minute!" Vronsky shouted to an officer who looked in at the door to call them to the colonel.

Vronsky was anxious to hear the rest of what Serpukhovskoy was going to say.

"And here's my opinion. Women are the chief stumbling block in a man's career. It is difficult to be in love with a woman and do anything. There is only one way of loving in comfort and without hindrance—marriage. Now, how am I to tell you what I mean?" said Serpukhovskoy, who was fond of similes. "Wait, wait! You can only carry a load and use your hands at the same time if the load is tied to your back—and that is marriage. And that's what I felt when I married. Suddenly my hands were free. But to drag that load about without marriage, your hands will be so full that you won't be able to do anything. Look at Mazankov, look at Krupov. Both have ruined their careers because of women."

"But what women," said Vronsky, recalling the Frenchwoman and the actress with whom the two men mentioned were connected.

"But don't you see that the more secure the woman's position in society, the worse it is. That's much the same as not merely carrying the load in your arms, but having to wrench it away from someone else."

"You've never been in love," murmured Vronsky, looking straight before him and thinking of Anna.

"Perhaps not. But remember what I've told you. And another thing: women are all more materialistic than men. We make something tremendous out of love but they are always *terre-à-terre.*"

"Coming, coming!" he said to a footman who had come into the room.

But the footman had not come to call them again as he thought. He brought Vronsky a note.

"From the Princess Tverskoy, sir."

Vronsky opened the note and flushed crimson.

"I'm afraid I have a headache," he said to Serpukhovskoy. "I'm going home."

"Well, good-by. Do you give me carte blanche?"

"We'll talk it over another time. I'll look you up in Petersburg."

CHAPTER 22

It was already past five and in order not to be late and at the same time not use his own horses which were known to everyone, Vronsky got into Yashvin's hired carriage and told the driver to drive as fast as possible. The old fourseater was very roomy and he sat down in a corner, put his legs on the front seat, and sank into thought.

A vague sense of the orderly fashion in which his affairs had been cleared up, a vague recollection of Serpukhovskoy's friendship and flattery in considering him a man whom his country needed, and above all, the anticipation of his meeting with Anna, all combined into one general impression of a joyous sense of life. This feeling was so strong that he kept smiling involuntarily. He dropped his legs, crossed one leg over the other, and taking it in his hand, felt the springy muscle of the calf, where he had hurt it in the fall the day before, and, throwing himself back, he drew several deep breaths.

"Oh, it's good, very good!" he said to himself. He had often before had this joyous sense of physical well-being, but never before had he been so fond of himself, of his own body, as at that moment. It gave him pleasure to feel the slight pain in his strong leg, it was pleasant to feel the muscular sensation of movement in his chest as he breathed. The same bright and cold August day which made Anna feel so hopeless seemed exhilarating and invigorating to him and refreshed his face and neck, which were still glowing after the drenching he had given them under the tap. The scent of brilliantine on his mustache seemed to him particularly pleasant in the fresh air. Everything he saw through the window of the carriage, everything in that cold and pure air, in that pale light of the sunset was as fresh, bright, and vigorous as he himself: the roofs of the houses glittering in the rays of the setting sun, the sharp outlines of fences and corners of buildings, the figures of passers-by and carriages they occasionally met, the motionless verdure of the trees and grass, the fields with their evenly drawn furrows of potato plants, and the slanting shadows that fell from the houses and trees and bushes and the furrows of potato plants. Everything was beautiful, like a pretty landscape painting which has been only recently finished and varnished.

"Faster! Faster!" he said to the driver, putting his head out of the window, and taking a three-ruble note out of his pocket he thrust it into the driver's hand as the latter turned round. The driver fumbled with something near the lamp, the whip cracked, and the carriage rolled away rapidly over the smooth highroad.

"I want nothing, nothing but this happiness," he thought, staring at the ivory knob of the bell in the space between the windows and seeing Anna in his mind as he had seen her last time. "And the longer it goes on, I love her more and more. Well, here at last is the garden of Wrede's country house. But where is she? Where? Why? How? Why did she fix on this place for a meeting, and why does she write in Betsy's letter?" he thought for the first time, but there was no longer time for thinking. He stopped the driver before reaching the avenue and, opening the door of the carriage, jumped out while the carriage was still moving and walked up the avenue leading to the house. There was no one in the avenue; but looking round to the right, he saw her. Her face was covered by a veil, but he took in with a joyous glance that special manner of walking peculiar to her alone, the droop of her shoulders and poise of her head, and at once he felt a thrill passing like an electric current through his body. He became conscious of himself with renewed force, from the elastic movements of his legs to the motion of his lungs as he breathed, and something set his lips twitching.

When she got up to him, she clasped his hand firmly.

"You're not angry that I sent for you? I simply had to see you," she said, and at the sight of the serious and severe way her lips were set under the veil his mood changed at once.

"Me? Be angry? But how did you get here? Where shall we go?"

"Never mind," she said, putting her hand on his arm. "Come, I've got to talk to you."

He realized that something had happened and that this meeting would not be a happy one. In her presence he had no will of his own: without knowing the cause of her anxiety, he felt that the same anxiety had communicated itself to him.

"What is it? What?" he asked, pressing her arm with his elbow and trying to read her thoughts on her face.

She walked on a few steps in silence, trying to pluck up courage, and then suddenly stopped.

"I didn't tell you last night," she began, breathing rapidly and painfully, "that on my way home with my husband I told him everything. . . . I told him that I could no longer be his wife, that . . . and told him everything."

He listened to her, leaning forward involuntarily with his whole figure, as though wishing in this way to alleviate the gravity of her position. But the moment she had said it, he suddenly straightened himself and his face assumed a proud and stern expression.

"Yes, yes, that's better, a thousand times better!" he said. "I realize how hard it must have been for you," he added.

But she was not listening to his words; she was reading his thoughts from his face. She could not guess that the expression of his face arose from the first idea that occurred to Vronsky—that a duel was inevitable. The idea of a duel never entered her head and she, therefore, explained that fleeting expression of severity in a different way.

When she got her husband's letter, she knew in her heart of hearts that everything would remain as it was; that she would not have the courage to set at naught her social position, to give up her son and go and live with her lover. The afternoon spent at the Princess Tverskoy's had further confirmed it. But this meeting was still of the utmost importance to her. She hoped that it would bring about a change in their position and save her. If, when he heard this news, he would say to her resolutely, passionately, and without a moment's hesitation: "Give up everything and run away with me!" she would give up her son and go away with him. But the news had not had the effect on him she had expected: he only looked as if he had been offended by something.

"It was not at all hard for me," she said irritably. "It all happened of itself, and here . . ." She pulled her husband's letter out of her glove.

"I understand, I understand," he interrupted her, taking the letter, but not reading it and trying to calm her. "The one thing I wanted, the only thing I prayed for was to put an end to this situation, so as to devote my life to your happiness."

"Why do you tell me this?" she said. "You don't think I could doubt it, do you? If I doubted it . . ."

"Who's that coming?" said Vronsky suddenly, pointing to two ladies walking toward them. "They may know us!" And he moved quickly into a side walk, drawing her along with him.

"Oh, I don't care!" she said. Her lips quivered. And he fancied that her eyes looked at him from under her veil with strange malevolence. "As I was saying, that's not the point. I cannot doubt that. But see what he writes to me. Read it." She stopped again.

Again, as at the first moment when he heard the news of her break with her husband, Vronsky, on reading the letter, could not help giving in to the natural impression aroused in him by his attitude to a wronged husband.

Now as he held the letter in his hand, he could not help imagining to himself the challenge which he would in all probability find waiting for him at home that evening or next day and the duel itself, in which, with the same cold and proud look that his face bore at that moment, he would fire into the air and then wait for the shot from the wronged husband. And at that very instant the thought flashed through his head of what Serpukhovskoy had just been saying to him and what had occurred to himself that morning—that it was better not to get involved, and he knew that this thought he could not tell her.

Having read the letter, he raised his eyes, and there was no firmness in his look. She realized at once that he had been thinking of what he should say. She knew that whatever he might say to her, he would not tell her all he thought. And she realized that her last hope had failed her. It was not what she had expected.

"You can see the sort of man he is," she said in a trembling voice. "He—"

"Forgive me, but I am glad of it," Vronsky interrupted. "For God's sake, let me finish," he added, his eyes beseeching her to give him time to explain what he meant. "I am glad because it can't possibly go on as he imagines."

"Why can't it?" said Anna, fighting back her tears and quite obviously attaching no importance whatever to what he was going to say. She felt that her fate was sealed.

What Vronsky wanted to say was that after what he considered to be the inevitable duel things could not go on as before, but what he said was different.

"It can't go on. I hope that now you will leave him. I hope," he looked embarrassed and blushed, "that you will let me arrange and plan our life. Tomorrow—" he began.

But she did not let him finish.

"And my son?" she cried. "You see what he writes! I should have to leave him, and I can't and won't do that!"

"But for heaven's sake, which is better? To leave your son or keep up this degrading position?"

"Degrading for whom?"

"For everyone and most of all for you."

369

"You say degrading . . . don't say that. Such words have no meaning for me," she said in a trembling voice. She did not want him to say something which was not true. His love was the only thing left to her and she wanted to love him. "You must understand that from the day I loved you everything has changed for me. There is only one thing in the world for me: your love. If that's mine, I feel so uplifted and so determined that nothing can be degrading to me. I am proud of my position because, well, I am proud of being—proud . . ." She could not say what she was proud of. Tears of shame and despair choked her. She stopped and burst into sobs.

He also felt that a lump was rising in his throat, that he was beginning to sniff, and for the first time in his life he felt like crying. He could not have said exactly what had moved him so; he was sorry for her and he felt that he could not help her, and at the same time he knew that he was the cause of her trouble, that he had done wrong.

"Isn't a divorce possible at all?" he said weakly. She shook her head without answering. "Couldn't you take your son and still leave him?"

"I could, but it all depends on him. Now I must go to him," she said dryly. Her foreboding that everything would remain as it was had not deceived her.

"I shall be in Petersburg on Tuesday and everything will be decided."

"Yes," she said. "But don't let us talk about it any more."

Anna's carriage, which she had sent away and ordered to return to the gate of the Wrede garden, drove up. Anna said good-by to him and drove home.

CHAPTER 23

On Monday there was the usual meeting of the Commission of the Second of June. Karenin walked into the hall where the meeting was held, exchanged greetings with the members and the president, as usual, and sat down in his place, putting his hand on the papers that had been prepared for him. Among these papers were the references he wanted and a draft of the statement he intended to make. He did not really require the references. He remembered everything and he did not consider it necessary to go over in his mind what he was going to say. He knew that when the right moment came and when he saw his opponent facing him and trying in vain to look indifferent, his speech would come pouring out of itself better than he could prepare it now. He felt that what he was going to say would be so important that every word he uttered would be significant. Meanwhile, as he listened to the usual report he had a most innocent and innocuous look. No one, looking at his white hands with the swelling veins and his long fingers so delicately feeling the edges of the white paper that lay before him, and at his head bent wearily to one side, would have thought that in another moment words would pour from his lips that would raise a terrible storm and make the members shout each other down and the president call them to order. When the report was over, Karenin declared in his quiet, thin voice that he had certain considerations of his own to submit in regard to the question of the settlement of the natives. The attention of the members was turned on him. Karenin cleared his throat and without looking at his opponent, but choosing, as he always did when making a speech, the first person sitting opposite him, a quiet little old man who never had any opinion to express in the commission, began to expound his ideas on the subject. When he got as far as the fundamental and organic law, his opponent jumped up and began to raise objections. Stremov, who was also a member of the commission and who was also stung to the quick, started defending himself, and altogether the meeting became a stormy one. But Karenin got what he wanted and his motion was carried. Three new commissions were appointed and next day in a certain Petersburg circle the meeting of the commission formed the only subject of conversation. Karenin's success was even greater than he expected.

When he woke on Tuesday morning, Karenin recalled with satisfaction his victory of the previous day and could not help smiling, though he wished to appear indifferent when his chief secretary, anxious to flatter him, told him of the reports that had reached him about what had happened in the commission.

Busy with his secretary, Karenin quite forgot that it

371

was Tuesday, the day he had fixed for Anna's return, and he was startled and unpleasantly surprised when a footman came in to inform him of her arrival.

Anna arrived in Petersburg early in the morning; the carriage had been sent to meet her in accordance with her telegram and Karenin should really have known of her arrival. But when she arrived he did not come out to meet her. She was told that he had not yet gone out but was busy with his secretary. She sent word to her husband that she had arrived, and went to her drawing room and began unpacking her things, expecting that he would come in to see her. But an hour passed and he did not come. She went into the dining room on the excuse of giving some orders and purposely spoke in a loud voice, expecting him to come out, but he did not come out, though she heard him go to his study door to see off his secretary. She knew that in his usual way he would soon leave for his office and she wanted to see him first so that their relations might be defined.

She passed through the ballroom and made resolutely for his study. When she entered it, he was sitting in his civil-service uniform, evidently ready to leave, with his elbows on a little table, staring wearily in front of him. She saw him before he saw her and knew that he was thinking about her.

When he saw her, he was about to rise, but changed his mind, then he flushed, something Anna had never seen him do before. He got up quickly and went toward her, looking not at her eyes but a little above them, at her forehead and hair. He went up to her, took her by the hand, and asked her to sit down.

"I am very glad you have come," he said, sitting down beside her, and evidently wishing to say something, he stopped short. He tried to speak several times, but stopped. Although when she was preparing for that interview she had been schooling herself to despise and blame him, she did not know what to say to him and she felt sorry for him. And so the silence went on for some time. "Is Seryozha well?" he asked, and without waiting for a reply, went on: "I shall not be dining at home today and I'm afraid I have to go at once now."

"I had thought of going to Moscow," she said.

"Oh no, you were quite right, quite right to come," he said, and again fell silent.

Seeing that he could not bring himself to begin, she began herself.

"Alexey," she said, looking at him and not dropping her eyes under his gaze fixed on her hair, "I am a guilty woman, I am a bad woman, but I am the same as I was before, as I told you then. I've come to tell you that I cannot make any change."

"I did not ask you about that," he said suddenly, resolutely, and with hatred looking straight at her face. "I had thought so too." Under the influence of anger he apparently regained full possession of his faculties. "But I repeat again what I told you then and wrote to you subsequently," he declared in a harsh, shrill voice, "that I am not obliged to know it. I ignore it. Not all wives are so kind as you to be in such a hurry to communicate such *agreeable* news to their husbands." He put particular emphasis on the word "agreeable." "I am going to ignore it so long as it is not known to the rest of the world and so long as my name has not been besmirched. And therefore I simply warn you that our relations must remain as they have always been and that only if you *compromise* yourself shall I be forced to take steps to safeguard my honor."

"But," Anna said timidly, looking at him with dismay, "our relations cannot be the same as always."

When she saw again his quiet gestures, heard his shrill, petulant, and sarcastic voice, her aversion for him destroyed the pity she had felt for him, and she was merely frightened and was anxious to make her position clear at all costs.

"I cannot be your wife when I . . ." she began.

He gave a cold, spiteful laugh.

"I'm afraid the kind of life you have chosen has affected your ideas. I feel both respect and scorn at the same time—I respect your past and despise your present—so much so that I was very far from the interpretation you give my words."

Anna gave a sigh of relief and dropped her head.

"I must say, though," he went on, getting heated, "that I can't understand how, being so independent as you apparently are and informing your husband outright of your infidelity, you find nothing as reprehensible in it as you seem to find in performing a wife's duties to her husband."

"Alexey, what do you want of me?"

"What I want is not to meet that person here and for you to conduct yourself in such a way that neither *society* nor the *servants* could accuse you of anything—for you not to see him. I think that is not much to ask. In return you will enjoy the privileges of an honest wife without fulfilling her duties. That's all I have to say to you. Now I must be going. I shan't be back for dinner."

He got up and went toward the door. Anna got up too. He bowed in silence and let her pass.

CHAPTER 24

The night Levin had spent on the haycock had not passed without leaving its mark: he was sick of the way he farmed his land and had lost all interest in it. In spite of the excellent harvest he had never, or at least he thought he had never, had so many failures, so much hostility between him and the peasants, as that year, and he was now quite clear about the reasons for those failures and that hostility. The delight he had taken in the work itself as a result of having drawn nearer to the peasants, his envy of them and their life, the desire to adopt that way of living, which that night had been no longer a dream but an intention, the details of which he was considering—all this had so changed his ideas about his own farming methods, that he could no longer feel any interest in them and could not help seeing the disagreeable relationship that existed between him and his laborers and that was at the bottom of all the trouble. Herds of cattle of an improved breed like Pava, the land well manured and ploughed with the best ploughs, the nine level fields surrounded with willows, the 240 heavily manured acres, the seed drills, and all the rest—all that would have been excellent, if it could be done by himself alone or with the assistance of friends who were in sympathy with him. But he clearly saw now (his work on the book of agriculture, in which the chief element in farming was to be the agricultural laborer, helped him a great deal in this), he saw clearly now that his present farming methods were based on a harsh and bitter struggle between him and his hired laborers, a struggle in which on the one side—on his side—there was a continuous and strenuous effort to remodel everything in accordance with what he thought to be a better method, and on the other side the natural order of things. And he saw that in this struggle, while he made the greatest efforts and his laborers made no effort whatever and, indeed, had no intention of making any, the only result was that neither side derived any profit from the farm and that fine implements, splendid cattle, and excellent soil were uselessly spoiled. But the chief thing was that not only was the energy expended on this work wasted, but that he could not help feeling, now that the meaning of his farming activities was laid bare to him, that the aim of his energy was a most unworthy one. For what, after all, was the struggle about? He was fighting for every penny he could get (and he had to do so because the moment he slackened his efforts he would not have had the money to pay his laborers), and they were fighting to be allowed to work quietly and comfortably or, in other words, as they were used to work. It was to his interest that every man should do as much work as possible and that he should not for a moment forget what he was doing and try not to break the winnowing machines, the horse rakes, or threshing machines, that he should keep his mind on what he was doing; the laborer, on the other hand, wanted to work under most agreeable conditions, with intervals for rest and, above all, without worrying or applying himself too much, in fact, without thinking. Levin saw this at every step that summer. He sent the men to mow some clover for hay, picking out the inferior fields overgrown with grass and wormwood and no good for seed; and time and again they mowed the best seed clover fields, justifying themselves by saying that the bailiff had told them to do so and comforted him with the assurance that he would get excellent hay; but he knew that they had done it because those fields were easier to mow. He sent out the tedder to turn the hay and it got broken in the first few rows, because the peasant found it dull to sit on the box under the rotating blades. And he was told: "Don't worry, sir, the women will toss it in no time." The ploughs turned out to be of no use because the peasant never thought of raising the share before turning around at the end of the furrow, and by forcing it around he tired the horses and spoiled the ground; and they told him not to worry! The horses were allowed to stray into the wheat because not a single laborer wanted to be a watchman, and though forbidden to do it, the laborers took turns watching the horses at night, and so Ivan, who had been at work all day, fell asleep, and admitting that he had been at fault, kept saying, "You can do what you like with me, sir!" Three of his best calves died through overfeeding, because they had been let out into the meadow where the clover had been cut, without any water to drink, and they simply refused to believe that they had been blown out by the clover and by way of consolation kept telling him that one of his neighbors had lost a hundred and twenty head of cattle in three days. All this was done not because anyone wished ill to Levin or his farm; on the contrary, he knew that they liked him and considered him a simple gentleman (the highest praise from a peasant); but it was done simply because they all wanted to work gaily and lightheartedly and his interests were not only of no account and incomprehensible to them, but also flatly opposed to their own most justified interests.

Levin had long felt dissatisfaction with his attitude toward the work on his estate. He could see that his boat was leaking, but he had not found or looked for the leak, perhaps purposely deceiving himself. But now he could no longer deceive himself. The farming of the land, as he was managing it, had not only ceased to interest him but had become loathsome to him, and he could not devote himself to it any longer.

Added to this, there was Kitty Shcherbatsky not twenty-five miles away, and he wanted to meet her and yet could not. Dolly, when he called on her, had asked him to come over; to come with the object of once more proposing to her sister, who, as she gave him to understand, would accept him now. Levin himself knew from the glimpse he caught of Kitty that he had never ceased to love her; but he could not bring himself to call on the Oblonskys knowing she was there. The fact that he had proposed to her and that she had refused him had put an insuperable barrier between them. "I cannot ask her to be my wife just because she cannot be the wife of the man she wanted," he kept saying to himself. The thought of this made him feel cold and hostile toward her. "I shall never be able to speak to her without a feeling of reproach, to look at her without resentment, and she will hate me more than ever, and rightly so! And, besides, how can I now, after what Dolly told me, call on them? How could I help showing that I know what she told me? And I shall arrive looking so magnanimous— to forgive her, to pardon her! Me to stand before her in the role of one who forgives her and graciously consents to offer her his love! What made the Princess Oblonsky tell me that? I might have met her accidentally and then everything would have come to pass naturally, but now it is impossible, impossible!"

Dolly sent him a note, asking for the loan of a sidesaddle for Kitty. "I'm told you have a sidesaddle," she wrote. "I hope you will bring it over yourself."

That was more than he could stand. How could an intelligent woman, a woman of any delicacy, so humiliate her sister? He wrote a dozen notes and tore them all up and sent the saddle without any reply. To write that he would come, he could not, because he could not bring himself to go there; to write that he was sorry he could not come because he was busy or had to go away, was still worse. He sent the saddle without an answer and conscious that he was doing something shameful, and next day handed over the hateful business of looking after his estate to the bailiff and set off to a remote district to visit his friend Sviazhsky, who had first-class snipe marshes near his estate and had quite recently written to him to keep a long-standing promise to pay him a visit. The snipe marshes in the Surov district had long tempted Levin, but he kept putting off the visit because of the work on his estate. Now, however, he was glad to get away from the proximity of the Shcherbatskys and, most of all, from his farm work, and especially on a shooting expedition which always served as the best solace in all his troubles.

CHAPTER 25

There was no railway or post-chaise connection with the Surov district, and Levin drove there with his own horses in his own four-wheeled carriage with a leather top.

He stopped halfway at a well-to-do peasant's to feed his horses. A bald-headed, fresh-complexioned old man, with a broad, red beard graying round the cheeks, opened the gates, pressing close to the post to let the three horses pass. After showing the coachman to a place in a lean-to in a large, clean, and tidy yard with some charred wooden ploughs, the old man invited Levin to come into his house. A cleanly dressed young peasant woman with galoshes on her bare feet was scrubbing the floor in the passage. The dog that ran in after Levin frightened her; she uttered a little scream but at once laughed at her own alarm when assured that it would not hurt her. After pointing to the door of the parlor with her bare arm, she bent down again, hiding her pretty face, and went on scrubbing the floor.

"Would you like the samovar, sir?" she asked.

"Yes, please."

The parlor was a large room with a Dutch stove and a partition dividing the room into two. Under the shelf with the icons stood a table decorated with a painted pattern, a bench, and two chairs. By the door stood a dresser with crockery. The shutters were closed, there were no flies, and the room was so clean that Levin was worried that Laska, who had been running after the carriage and rolling in puddles, would make the floor dirty and told her to lie down in the corner by the door. Having looked round the room, Levin went out into the back yard. The good-looking young woman in galoshes, with two empty pails swinging from a yoke, ran down in front of him to fetch water from the well.

"Look lively, there!" the old man shouted after her cheerfully, and went up to Levin. "Well, sir, is it to Nikolai Ivanovich Sviazhsky you're going?" he began, evidently eager to strike up a conversation and leaning on the railing of the steps. "He too stops at our place."

In the middle of the old man's account about his acquaintance with Sviazhsky, the gates creaked again and the laborers drove in from the fields with their ploughs and harrows. The horses harnessed to the ploughs and harrows were big and well fed. The farmhands were clearly members of the household: two of them were young and wore print shirts and peaked caps; the two others, an old man and a young fellow, were hired laborers and wore homespun shirts. Leaving the front steps, the old man went up to the horses and began to unharness them.

"Been ploughing?" asked Levin.

"Earthing up the potatoes, sir. We too rent a little land. Don't let the gelding out, Fedot. Take him to the trough. We can harness the other."

"Have the ploughshares I ordered been brought, Father?" asked a tall, healthy-looking young fellow, evidently the old man's son.

"There—in the sledge," answered the old man, winding up the reins he had taken off and throwing them on the ground. "Put them on while they are having dinner."

The good-looking young woman, her shoulders weighed down by the two full pails of water, returned and went into the house. Some more women, young and handsome, middle-aged, old and plain, some with children, others without, appeared from somewhere.

The samovar was beginning to sing. The hired laborers and the family, having attended to the horses, went to have their dinner. Taking some provisions out of his carriage, Levin invited the old man to take tea with him.

"Thank you, sir, I've had some today already," said the old man, obviously pleased to accept the invitation. "Well, just for the company, then!"

Over their tea Levin learned all about the old man's farm. Ten years before, the old man had rented about three hundred acres from the lady landowner, and the year before he had bought them and rented another nine hundred from a neighboring landowner. A small portion of the land—the worst—he let, and about a hundred and twenty acres of arable land he cultivated himself with his family and two hired laborers. The old man complained that he was doing badly. But Levin knew that he only did so for the sake of propriety and that his farm was in a flourishing condition. Had he really been doing badly, he would not have bought land at thirty-five rubles an acre, would not have married three of his sons and a nephew, would not have rebuilt twice after fires, nor rebuilt it better each time. In spite of his grumbling, it was evident that the old man was justly proud of his prosperity, proud of his sons, his nephew, his daughters-in-law, his horses, cows, and particularly of the fact that he could keep it all going. From his talk with the old man, Levin gathered that he was not opposed to new methods either. He had planted a lot of potatoes, and his potatoes had already flowered and were beginning to set, as Levin had noticed when driving past the fields, while Levin's own potatoes were only just beginning to flower. He earthed up the potatoes with the latest model of plough which he borrowed from the landowner. He sowed wheat. Levin was particularly struck by one small point: the old man used the thinnings of the rye as fodder for the horses. Many a time Levin had seen this invaluable fodder wasted. He had tried to have it gathered up, but had found that for some reason or other it was impossible. The old peasant, however, got it done, and he could not find words to praise this fodder.

"What is there for the young women to do? They carry the heaps out to the roadside and the cart comes along and picks them up."

"I'm afraid we landowners have great trouble with our laborers," said Levin, handing him a tumbler of tea.

"Thank you, sir," said the old man, but refused sugar, pointing to a little nibbled bit of lump he had still left. "How can you get your work done with hired laborers?" he said. "It's ruination. Take Sviazhsky, now. We know the sort of soil he has—black as poppy seed, but he's not particularly happy about his harvests. It's not looked after properly, that's what it is."

"But you are employing hired laborers, aren't you?"

"Well, sir, we be peasants, we be. We look after everything ourselves. If a man's no good, we sack him. You see, sir, we can manage by ourselves all right."

"Finogen wants some tar fetched, Dad," said the young woman in galoshes, coming in.

"That's how it is, sir," said the old man, getting up, and after crossing himself several times he thanked Levin and went out.

When Levin went into the back room to call his coachman, he saw the old man's entire family at dinner. The women served standing. The young, healthy-looking son, his mouth full of buckwheat porridge, was telling some funny story and they were all roaring with laughter, the woman in the galoshes louder than anyone, as she refilled his bowl with cabbage soup.

It is very possible that the pretty face of the young woman in the galoshes had contributed greatly to the

380

impression of well-being this peasant household made on Levin, but the impression was so strong that Levin could not get rid of it. And all the way from the old peasant's to Sviazhsky's he would find himself again and again thinking of this peasant household, as though there were something in this impression that demanded his special attention.

CHAPTER 26

Sviazhsky was the marshal of the nobility in his district. He was five years older than Levin and had been married for some time. His young sister-in-law, whom Levin rather liked, lived in his house. And Levin knew that both Sviazhsky and his wife would have greatly liked to see him married to her. He knew it for certain, as so-called eligible young men always know it, though he would never have as much as hinted it to anyone. He knew, too, that although he wanted to get married and although everything showed that this very attractive girl would make an excellent wife, he could no more marry her than fly, even if he had not been in love with Kitty Shcherbatsky. And this knowledge spoiled the pleasure he hoped to get from his visit to Sviazhsky.

When he got Sviazhsky's letter with the invitation for shooting, Levin immediately thought of this, but he decided nevertheless that whatever Sviazhsky's real intentions were, they were based on an unfounded assumption, and so he would go all the same. Besides, in his heart of hearts he wanted to put himself to the test and once again see what effect that girl had on him. Sviazhsky's home life was extremely pleasant, and Sviazhsky himself, the best type of man who took an active part in rural affairs that Levin knew, was very interesting to him.

Sviazhsky was one of those people who always amazed Levin because their extremely logical, though never original, ideas were kept in a watertight compartment and had no influence whatever on their extremely definite and stable lives, which went on quite independently and almost always diametrically opposed to them. Sviazhsky was an extremely liberal person. He despised the nobility and considered the majority of noblemen to be secretly in favor of serfdom, though too cowardly to express their views openly. He considered Russia to be a doomed country like Turkey and the Russian government so bad that he did not think it worth his while to criticize its actions; yet he was a civil servant, a model marshal of the nobility, and when he traveled he always wore a peaked cap with a red band and a cockade. In his opinion civilized life was only possible abroad, where he went at every opportunity, and yet at the same time he carried on a very complex and improved system of farming in Russia and followed everything with deep interest and knew everything that was being done in Russia. He regarded the Russian peasant as being in the transitional stage of development from ape to man, and at the same time he seemed more pleased than anyone else to shake the hand of a peasant at the elections to the rural councils and to listen to his opinions. He believed neither in God nor the devil, and yet he was very concerned about the question of improving the condition of the clergy and the reduction of the size of their parishes, and was particularly anxious that the church should remain in his village.

On the woman question he sided with the extreme advocates of the fullest freedom for women and, particularly, their right to work; yet he lived with his wife so happily that everyone admired their affectionate, childless family life, and he arranged his wife's life in such a way that she did nothing and could do nothing except share her husband's efforts to spend their time as gaily and as happily as possible.

Had Levin not been in the habit of putting the best possible interpretation on people, Sviazhsky's character would have presented no difficulty or problem to him: he would have dismissed him as a fool or a knave and everything would have been plain. But he could not call him a fool, for there could be no doubt that Sviazhsky was not only an intelligent, but also a highly educated man, who carried his erudition with extreme modesty. There was no subject with which he was not acquainted; but he showed his knowledge only when forced to do so. Still less could Levin say that he was a knave, for Sviazhsky was undoubtedly an honest, kindhearted, and clever man, who was always cheerfully and animatedly engaged on work highly esteemed by all around him and

382

who most certainly never consciously did or could do anything bad.

Levin tried but never could understand him and always regarded him and his life as a living enigma.

He and Levin were friends and that was why Levin allowed himself to sound Sviazhsky and try to get to the very basis of his philosophy of life; but it was always in vain. Every time Levin tried to penetrate further than the doors of the reception rooms of Sviazhsky's mind, which were wide open to all, he observed that Sviazhsky became slightly embarrassed; there was a hardly perceptible look of alarm in his eyes as though he were afraid lest Levin should understand him, and he would meet Levin with a good-humored and cheerful rebuff.

Now, after his disillusionment with the way he farmed his estate, Levin was particularly pleased to be staying with Sviazhsky. Quite apart from the fact that the sight of this happy, loving couple, so pleased with themselves and everyone else, and their comfortable home had a cheering effect on him, he was anxious, now that he was so dissatisfied with his own life, to get at the secret which gave Sviazhsky such a clear-cut, definite, and cheerful outlook on life. Moreover, Levin knew that he would meet neighboring landlords at the Sviazhskys' and he felt that it would be particularly interesting for him to talk and hear about farming, crops, the hiring of labor, etc., the sort of conversation which he knew was regarded for some reason as very low, but which seemed to him now the only subject of importance. "This might not have been so important in the days of serfdom or may not be important in England. In both cases the conditions themselves were or are firmly established, but with us now when everything is in a state of upheaval and is only just beginning to settle, the question of how these conditions will be settled is the only important question in the whole of Russia," thought Levin.

The shooting did not prove as good as Levin had expected. The marsh had dried up and there was no sign of any snipe. He walked about the whole day and only brought back three birds; on the other hand, he brought back, as he always did after a day's sport, an excellent appetite, excellent spirits, and that heightened intellectual condition which with him always accompanied physical exertion. And when out shooting, at a time when he seemed not to think of anything in particular, he found himself again and again thinking of the old peasant and his family, and the impression of them seemed to claim not only his attention, but also the solution of some problem connected with it.

In the evening at tea the very interesting conversation Levin had looked forward to began in the presence of two landowners who had driven over in connection with some business of trusteeship.

Levin was sitting beside his hostess at the tea table and had to keep up a conversation with her and her sister, who was sitting opposite. His hostess was a short, round-faced, fair-haired woman, all dimples and smiles. Levin tried to find out through her the answer to the riddle presented by her husband, which was so important to him, but he did not possess full freedom of thought because he felt terribly embarrassed. He was so terribly embarrassed because Sviazhsky's sister-in-law was sitting opposite him in a dress that seemed to him to have been put on specially for his benefit, with a particularly low, square-cut *décolletage*, showing her white bosom; this square-cut *décolletage*, though her bosom was so white, or perhaps because it was so white, deprived Levin of his freedom of thought. He imagined, probably quite mistakenly, that the bodice had been cut so low especially for him, and he felt that he had no right to look at it, and he did his best not to look at it. But he could not help feeling that it was his fault that it was cut so low. He could not help feeling that he was deceiving somebody, that he ought to explain something, but that it was quite impossible to explain it, and that was why he kept blushing and was restless and uncomfortable. His discomfort communicated itself to the pretty girl. But his hostess did not appear to notice it and insisted on drawing her into the conversation.

"You say," his hostess continued the conversation he had started, "that my husband cannot be interested in anything Russian. Well, you're wrong. It is true he is happy abroad, but he is never so happy as he is here. Here he feels in his own element. You see, he has so much on his plate and he has the gift of interesting himself in everything. But you haven't seen our school, have you?"

"I saw it. It's the little ivy-covered house, isn't it?"

"Yes, that's Nastya's work," she said, pointing to her sister.

"Do you teach there yourself?" asked Levin, trying to look beyond the low neck, but feeling that wherever he looked in that direction he was bound to see it.

"Yes, I have been and still am teaching there, but we have a wonderful schoolmistress. And we have started gym lessons too."

"No, thank you, I won't have any more tea," said Levin, and though feeling that he was being uncivil but incapable of keeping up the conversation any longer, he got up blushing. "I hear a very interesting conversation there," he added, and went to the other end of the table, where Sviazhsky was sitting with the two landowners.

Sviazhsky sat sideways, leaning his elbow on the table and turning his cup round with one hand, while with the other he gathered his beard into his fist, raising it to his nose, as if smelling it, and letting it drop again. He looked with his glittering black eyes straight at the excited landowner with the gray mustache and was evidently hugely amused by his words. The landowner was complaining about the peasants. It was clear to Levin that Sviazhsky knew the answer to the landowner's complaints that would at once demolish his whole argument, but that owing to his position he could not give that answer and listened not without pleasure to the landowner's comic speech.

The landowner with the gray mustache was evidently a rabid defender of serfdom, a passionate farmer who had spent all his life in the country. Levin saw signs of this in his dress, an old-fashioned, threadbare coat that he evidently did not wear very often; in his intelligent, frowning eyes; in his well-turned Russian; in his authoritative tone, evidently acquired by long practice; and in the resolute gestures of his fine, large, sunburned hands, with an old engagement ring on his third finger.

CHAPTER 27

"If only I had not been sorry to give up what has been acquired with so much trouble, I—er—I'd let it all go, sell up and—er—and go off like Nikolai Ivanovich to—er—to hear *La Belle Hélène*," said the landowner, a pleasant smile lighting up his shrewd old face.

"But as you don't give it up," said Nikolai Ivanovich Sviazhsky, "it must not be worth your while."

"The only thing that is worth my while is that I live in my own house, which has neither been bought nor rented. Besides, I still keep hoping that the peasants will come to their senses. As things are now, it's wholesale drunkenness and depravity. Their land has been shared out again and again. They have not a horse nor a cow left. A man may be starving, but try to hire him as a laborer, and he'll do his best to destroy everything he lays his hands on and drag you before the magistrate into the bargain."

"But, surely, you too will summons him," said Sviazhsky.

"Me? Not for the world! It would give rise to such talk that I'd be sorry I ever started it. At the mill, for instance, they took money in advance and cleared off. What did the magistrate do? Why, he acquitted them. The only thing that keeps them in order is the village tribunal and the village elder. He'll thrash them in the good old style. But for that you'd have to give up everything and run to the ends of the earth."

The landowner was obviously trying to provoke Sviazhsky, but, far from getting angry, Sviazhsky seemed to be amused by his talk.

"But we do, you know, manage our estates without such drastic measures," he said, smiling. "Levin and I and our neighbor."

He pointed to the other landowner.

"Yes, he carries on, but just ask him how? Do you call that rational farming?" said the landowner, evidently showing off his advanced views on farming by the use of the word "rational."

"My farming methods are very simple, thank God," said the other landlord. "All I am trying to get out of my farm is enough money to pay the autumn taxes. The peasants come along and say, 'Sir, help us out!' Well, of course, they're our own peasants, my neighbors, and one can't help being sorry for them. So I advance them one-third of their dues; only I say to them: 'Remember, lads, I've helped you, so you must lend me a hand when I need your help—whether at oats-sowing or haymaking or harvest time.' And, well, we agree for so much work

386

from each family. But it's quite true there are some among them who are quite unscrupulous."

Levin, who had long been aware of these patriarchal methods, exchanged glances with Sviazhsky and interrupted the second landowner, turning again to the landowner with the gray mustache.

"So what do you think?" he asked. "How is one to farm one's land at present?"

"Why, either go half and half with the peasants or rent the land to them. You can do that all right, but that's how the wealth of the country is being destroyed. Where my land used to yield ninefold under serfdom and with good management, it will only yield threefold under the half-crop system. The emancipation of the serfs has been the ruin of Russia!"

Sviazhsky looked at Levin with smiling eyes and even made a just perceptible ironical sign to him; but Levin did not find the landowner's words funny—he understood them better than did Sviazhsky. A great deal of what the landowner went on to say to show that Russia was ruined by the emancipation of the serfs even appeared to him to be very true, new, and so far as he could see, undeniable. The landowner was evidently expressing his own thoughts, which people rarely do, and thoughts to which he had been led not by a desire to find some occupation for an idle brain, but which had grown out of the conditions of his life, which he had hatched in his rural solitude and considered from every angle.

"You see, what it comes to is that every kind of progress can be achieved only by the exercise of power," he went on, evidently wishing to show that education was not something foreign to him. "Take the reforms of Peter the Great, Catherine, and Alexander. Take European history. Still more so progress in agriculture. Take the potato—it, too, had to be introduced into our country by force. The wooden plough has not always been used, either. It, too, had to be introduced and, no doubt, by force at the time of the independent principalities in medieval Russia. Now, in our own day, we, the landowners, applied all sorts of improved methods of farming under serfdom: drying kilns, threshing machines, manure carting, and all sorts of implements—we introduced it all because we had the power to do so, and the peasants resisted at first and afterward copied us. But today, gentlemen, with the abolition of serfdom we have been deprived of power, and our rural economy, where it had been raised to a high level, must needs sink back to the most savage and primitive condition. That's how I see it."

"But why?" asked Sviazhsky. "If it's rational, you can carry on with hired labor."

"We haven't the power, sir. How am I to do it? Where am I to get the labor?"

"Now we've got it," thought Levin. "Labor is the chief element in agriculture."

"Hired laborers," replied Sviazhsky.

"Hired laborers don't want to work well, and they don't want to use good tools. Our Russian laborer understands one thing only—to get drunk like a hog, and you can be sure that when drunk he'll ruin everything you put into his hands. He'll ruin your horses by watering them at the wrong time, tear good harness, barter a wheel with an iron tire for one without, drop a bolt into the threshing machine in order to break it. He hates to see anything that is not what he is used to. That's why the whole standard of agriculture has fallen. The land has been neglected, overgrown with wormwood, or given to the peasants, and where a million bushels used to be produced, you get only a hundred thousand. The wealth of the country has decreased. If the same thing had been done, only with proper care . . ."

And he began to develop his own plan of emancipation, by which all these objectionable features might have been avoided.

This did not interest Levin, but when he had finished, Levin returned to his first proposition and, turning to Sviazhsky, tried to get him to express his serious opinion.

"That the standard of agriculture is dropping," he said, "and that our relation to the agricultural laborers being what it is, it is quite impossible to make farming on a rational basis pay, seems to me to be absolutely true."

"I don't think so," Sviazhsky replied quite seriously. "All I can see is that we do not know how to get the best out of the land and that our system of agriculture under serfdom, far from being too high, was too low. We have neither agricultural machinery, nor good

388

horses, nor proper management, nor do we know how to keep accounts. Ask any landowner and he won't be able to tell you what's profitable and what's not."

"Italian bookkeeping!" the landowner said ironically. "Keep your accounts any way you like, if they destroy everything you've got, you won't have a profit."

"Why should they destroy it? They will break one of your rotten threshing machines, your absurd Russian treadmill, but they won't break my steam threshing machine. They'll spoil your typically Russian horse of— what do you call it?—drag-tail breed, the breed of horse who has to be dragged along by the tail, but get some Flemish drays or good Russian cart horses and they won't spoil them. And so it is with everything. We have to raise agriculture to a much higher level."

"Yes, if one could afford it! You're all right, but I have a son at the university to keep, pay for my little sons' education at the secondary school—how do you suppose I can buy Flemish drays?"

"That's what the banks are for."

"The banks? And finish up by being sold up under the hammer? No, thank you."

"I don't agree that it is necessary or possible to raise the level of agriculture," said Levin. "It's my business and I have means, but I never could do anything about it. I don't know to whom banks are useful. So far as I'm concerned, however much money I spend on farming, it's always been a loss: my cattle, a loss; my machinery, a loss."

"That's true enough," said the landowner with the gray mustache with a laugh.

"And I'm not the only one," went on Levin. "I could quote you the opinions of all landowners who carry on rational farming. All of them, with rare exceptions, make a loss on it. But tell us what about your estate—does it pay?" said Levin, and he at once noticed that momentary expression of alarm in Sviazhsky's eyes which he had noticed before whenever he had tried to penetrate beyond the reception rooms of Sviazhsky's mind.

Besides, this question on Levin's part was not quite fair. His hostess had just told him at tea that they had that summer engaged a German bookkeeping expert from Moscow, who had audited their accounts for a fee of five hundred rubles and found that they were losing

389

three thousand–odd rubles a year on their farming. She did not remember the exact figure, but the German seemed to have worked it out to a quarter of a kopeck.

At the mention of profit on Sviazhsky's farming the landowner with the gray mustache smiled, evidently well aware of the sort of profit his neighbor and marshal was able to make.

"Maybe it doesn't pay," replied Sviazhsky. "But that only proves that I'm either a bad farmer or that I spend capital to increase the rental value of my land."

"Good Lord, rental value!" Levin exclaimed with horror. "There may be such a thing as rental value in Europe, where the land has been improved by the labor put into it, but with us the land is getting poorer from the labor put into it, which, of course, means that there's no such thing as rental value."

"No such thing? But it's a natural law."

"In that case we're outside the law: rental value explains nothing to us; it only causes confusion. No, you'd better tell us how the theory of rental value can—"

"Would you like some sour milk? Masha," he said, turning to his wife, "can't we have some sour milk or raspberries? Extraordinary how long the raspberries are lasting this season."

And Sviazhsky got up in the best possible spirits and walked away, apparently assuming that the conversation had come to an end at the very point where Levin supposed that it was only beginning.

His chief opponent in the discussion having gone, Levin continued the conversation with the landowner, trying to prove to him that all their difficulties arose from the fact that they did not wish to know the characteristics and habits of the Russian agricultural laborer. But the landowner, like everyone else who has an independent mind and thinks for himself, was slow in seeing another man's point of view and tenacious of his own. He insisted that the Russian peasant was a pig and liked to behave like a pig, and that the only way to get him out of his swinishness was the exercise of power, and there was no such power. What was needed was a stick, but they were all such liberals now that they had exchanged the thousand-year-old stick for lawyers and prisons, in which the good-for-nothing stinking peasants were fed with excellent soup and provided with so many cubic feet of air.

"Why do you think," Levin said, trying to get back to the subject under discussion, "that it is impossible to find some sort of relationship to labor which would make the work productive?"

"That can never be done with the Russian people," replied the landowner. "We haven't the power."

"What new conditions could be found?" said Sviazhsky, who, having had his sour milk, lit a cigarette, and returned to the disputants. "All the possible relations to labor have been studied and defined," he said. "What is left of barbarism, the primitive commune with its mutual guarantees is disintegrating by itself, serfdom has been abolished, and there is nothing left but free labor. The agricultural laborer, the hired man, the farmer—you can't get away from that."

"But Europe is dissatisfied with this system."

"Dissatisfied and is looking for new methods. And, no doubt will find them."

"That's exactly my point," replied Levin. "Why shouldn't we look for them ourselves?"

"Because it would be just the same as inventing again the way of constructing a railway. It's been invented; it's ready."

"But what if it doesn't suit us?" said Levin. "What if it is stupid?"

And again he noticed the expression of alarm in Sviazhsky's eyes.

"Why, this is just a bit of chauvinism: we've discovered what Europe is looking for! I know all that, but, forgive me, do you know what has been done in Europe with regard to the question of organization of labor?"

"No, I'm afraid not very well."

"This question is now occupying the best minds in Europe. There is the Schulze-Delitsch movement. . . . There is the vast literature on the labor question, with the most liberal Lassalle tendency. . . . The Mulhausen system—that's already a fact, as you probably know."

"I have some idea of it, but very vague."

"Oh, I suppose you're just saying this. I'm sure you know as much about it as I do. I'm not a professor of sociology, of course, but I'm interested in it and if it interests you, you'd better make a study of it."

"But what conclusions have you arrived at?"

"I'm sorry. . . ."

The landowners had got up and Sviazhsky, once more checking Levin in his unpleasant habit of prying beyond the reception rooms of his mind, went to see his visitors off.

CHAPTER 28

Levin felt terribly bored by the ladies that evening; he was worried, as never before, by the idea that the dissatisfaction with the methods of farming he now experienced was not exceptional but the general feeling about the condition in which the farming industry found itself in Russia, and that some arrangement that would make the laborers work as they did for the peasant at whose house he had stopped to have his tea was not a daydream but a problem that had to be solved. And he felt that it could be solved and that an attempt had to be made to solve it.

Having said good night to the ladies and promising to stay the whole of the next day in order to ride over to the crown forest with them to inspect an interesting landslide, Levin went to his host's study before going to bed to borrow the books on the labor question that Sviazhsky had recommended. Sviazhsky's study was a huge room lined with bookcases. There were two tables there—one a massive writing table, standing in the middle of the room, and the other a round table on which newspapers and periodicals in different languages were arranged starlike round the lamp in the center. Beside the writing table was a little filing cabinet with gold-labeled drawers containing all sorts of business papers.

Sviazhsky got out the books and sat down in a rocking chair.

"What is it you are looking at?" he asked Levin, who had stopped at the round table and was looking over the periodicals. "Oh yes, there's a very interesting article there," he added, referring to the periodical Levin was holding in his hand. "It would appear," he went on with gleeful animation, "that the man chiefly responsible for the partition of Poland was not Frederick at all, but . . ."

And with characteristic clearness he gave a brief account of the new and highly important and interesting discoveries. Though Levin was at that moment wholly occupied with the problem of agriculture, he kept asking himself while listening to his host: "What is there inside him? And why, why is he so interested in the partition of Poland?" When Sviazhsky had finished, Levin could not help asking him: "Well, and what of it?" But there was nothing. The only interesting thing was that "it appeared" to be so. But Sviazhsky did not explain, nor did he find it necessary to explain, why he was so interested in it.

"Yes, and I was very interested by that irascible old landowner," said Levin with a sigh. "He's intelligent and a lot of what he said is true."

"Oh, go away with you!" said Sviazhsky. "He's a rabid supporter of serfdom at heart like the rest of them."

"Whose marshal you are. . . ."

"Yes, only I'm marshaling them in the opposite direction," said Sviazhsky, laughing.

"What interests me very much is this," said Levin. "He's right in claiming that our rational farming is a failure and that only usurious methods, like those of that quiet fellow, or the most elementary ones, are successful. Whose fault is it?"

"Ours, of course. And, besides, it is not true that it's a failure. It's successful with Vassilchikov."

"A factory . . ."

"But I still don't know what you are surprised at. The peasants are at so low a level of material and moral development that they're clearly bound to oppose everything that's strange to them. In Europe rational farming is a success because the people are educated. It follows that all we have to do is to educate the common people—that's all."

"But how are we to educate them?"

"To educate the peasant we want three things: schools, schools, and schools."

"But you just said yourself that the peasants are on a low level of material development. How would schools help that?"

"You know, you remind me of the story of the advice given to a sick man. 'You should try an aperient.' 'I have, and it made me worse.' 'Try leeches.' 'I have, and they made me worse.' 'Well, in that case you'd better pray to God.' 'I have, and that made me worse.' It's the

393

same with us. I say political economy, you say it makes things worse. I say socialism—still worse. Education— still worse."

"But how will schools help?"

"They'll give them fresh needs."

"Now that I never could understand," Levin cried heatedly. "How will schools help the peasant to improve his material condition? You say schools, education, will give them fresh needs. So much the worse, because they would not be able to satisfy them. And in what way knowledge of addition and subtraction and the catechism will help him to improve his material condition, I never could understand. The other evening I met a peasant woman with a baby in her arms and I asked her where she was going. 'I been to see the wise woman, sir,' she said. 'The boy had convulsions and I took him to be cured.' I asked her how the wise woman treated her baby for convulsions. 'She puts the baby on the hen roost and mumbles something.' "

"Well, there's your answer! To make sure she doesn't take her baby to put it on the hen roost," Sviazhsky said with a merry smile, "to cure of convulsions, we must—"

"No!" Levin said with annoyance. "That treatment seems to me just like trying to cure the peasant's ills by schools. The peasants are poor and uneducated; this we can see as clearly as the peasant woman sees her baby is ill because it screams. But why schools should cure the ills of poverty and ignorance is as incomprehensible to me as why hens on their perches should cure convulsions. A cure must be found for their poverty."

"Well, in this at least you agree with Spencer, whom you dislike so much. He too argues that education may result from increased prosperity and comfort, from frequent ablutions, as he puts it, but not from being able to read or write."

"Well, I'm very glad, or rather very sorry, to be of the same opinion as Spencer. Only, you see, I've known it for a long time. Schools will not help. What will help would be an economic organization under which the common people would be better off and have more leisure. Then schools will come."

"But all over Europe education is now compulsory."

"And how is it you agree with Spencer in this matter?" asked Levin.

But the look of alarm flashed in Sviazhsky's eyes and he said with a smile:

"Yes, that cure of convulsions is splendid! Did you really hear it yourself?"

Levin saw that he would never find a connection between that man's life and his ideas. It was evident that he did not really care what conclusions his reasoning led to; all he was interested in was the process of reasoning. And he did not like it when the process of reasoning brought him to a blind alley. That was the only thing he did not like and avoided by changing the conversation to something agreeable and amusing.

All the impressions of the day, beginning with the impression of the peasant he had had tea with on the way, which seemed to serve as the basis for all his other impressions and ideas, agitated Levin greatly. There was this charming Sviazhsky, who made use of his ideas only for social purposes and whose life was apparently guided by other principles that remained a mystery to Levin, while together with the crowd whose name is legion he guided public opinion by means of ideas he did not share; that embittered old landowner, whose views, wrested painfully from life, were perfectly sound, but who was wrong to feel bitter against a whole class, and that the best class in Russia; his own dissatisfaction with his own activities and his vague hopes of finding a remedy for all these things—all this merged into a feeling of inward restlessness and expectation of a speedy solution.

Left alone in his room, lying on a spring mattress that bounced unexpectedly whenever he moved an arm or a leg, Levin could not fall asleep for a long time. He was not interested in a single thing Sviazhsky had said, though he had said a great deal that was clever; but the landowner's arguments required careful consideration. Levin could not help remembering all that he had said, and he corrected in his imagination the answers he had given.

"Yes, I ought to have said to him: You say that our farming industry is a failure because the peasant hates every kind of improvement and that improvements must be introduced by force; but if farming did not pay at all without these improvements, you would be right. But it does pay, and it pays only where the laborer is working in conformance with his habits, as in the case of the old

395

man halfway here. Your and our common dissatisfaction with farming shows that it is we and not the laborers who are at fault. We have for a long time been trying to run the industry in our own way—in the European way—without bothering about the nature of the labor force at our disposal. Let us try looking upon labor not as an abstract labor force but as the *Russian peasant* with his instincts, and let us organize our farming industry accordingly. Imagine—I ought to have said to him—that you are running your farm like that old man's, that you have found a way of interesting your laborers in the success of the work and have discovered the golden mean in the improvements which they are willing to accept; then, without impoverishing the soil, you will double and treble the crops you got before. Divide equally and give half the produce to labor, and the share left for you would be larger and the labor force would receive more too. And to do this we must lower our present farming standards and interest the peasant in the success of the work. How this can be done is a question of detail, but there is no doubt whatever that it can be done."

This idea made Levin very excited. He lay awake half the night, thinking over the details necessary to put this idea into practice. He had not meant to leave next day, but now he decided to leave early in the morning. Besides, that sister-in-law with her low-cut dress made him feel ashamed and repentant just as if he had committed some bad action. The chief reason, however, why he was so anxious to get home without delay was that he wanted to present his new plan to the peasants before the winter corn was sown, so that the sowing might be done under the new conditions. He made up his mind thoroughly to reorganize his former methods of farming.

CHAPTER 29

The carrying out of Levin's plan presented many difficulties; but he did his best and if he did not achieve what he wanted, he achieved enough to be able to believe without deceiving himself that the thing was worth doing. One of the main difficulties was that the work on the farm was going on and it was impossible to stop everything and start afresh, and the machine had to be improved while it was working.

When on his return home he told his bailiff the same evening of his new plans, the bailiff with undisguised satisfaction agreed with his argument that everything that had been done till then was stupid and unprofitable. The bailiff declared that he had always said so, but that nobody would listen to him. As for Levin's proposal that he and the laborers should participate as shareholders in the new farming enterprise, the bailiff's reactions were rather gloomy and he did not offer any definite opinion, but immediately started talking of the necessity of carting the last sheaves of rye next day and of starting the second ploughing, so that Levin felt that this was not the right moment for discussing his plans.

When discussing his plans with the peasants and offering them land on the new terms, he at once came up against the same main difficulty: they were so busy with the current labor of the day that they had not time to consider the advantages and disadvantages of the new venture.

One simple-minded peasant, the cowman Ivan, seemed to have fully understood Levin's proposal to let him and his family take a share in the profits from the dairy farm and was entirely in agreement with the plan. But when Levin pointed out to him the benefits that would accrue to him in the future, a look of alarm came into Ivan's face and he said he was sorry he could not stop to listen to it all, and he quickly found himself some task that could not be put off: he either seized a pitchfork to remove the hay from the stalls, fetched water to fill the troughs, or cleared away the manure.

Another stumbling block was the invincible distrust of the peasants, who could not believe that the landowner could have any other aim than to get all he could out of them. They were firmly convinced that, whatever he might say, his real aim would always be hidden in what he did not tell them. And when talking to him, they themselves said a great deal, but never said what their real aim was. Moreover, the peasants (and Levin felt that the irascible landowner was right) put as the first and unalterable condition in any agreement that they should not be obliged to use any new methods of farming or any new kinds of agricultural machinery. They agreed that the new kind of plough ploughed better, that a scarifier did the work more quickly, but they found thousands of reasons why they could not use either the one or the other, and though he was convinced that one had to lower the standard of farming, he was sorry to give up improvements the benefits of which were so obvious. But in spite of all these difficulties he got his way and by autumn his scheme began to work, or at least so it seemed to him.

At first Levin thought of letting the whole of his farm as it stood to the peasants, the laborers, and the bailiff on the new co-partnership lines, but he soon came to the conclusion that it was impossible and decided to divide it up. The cattle yard, the orchard, the kitchen garden, the meadows and the cornfields, divided into several parts, formed separate lots. The simple-minded cowherd Ivan, who Levin thought understood his plan better than the rest, formed a profit-sharing association consisting mostly of his family, and became a partner in the dairy farm. The far field that had lain fallow for eight years was taken over with the aid of the intelligent carpenter Fyodor Rezunov by six peasant families on the new cooperative lines, and the peasant Shurayev took over the kitchen gardens on the same terms. The rest remained as before, but these three sections were the beginning of the new order and fully occupied Levin.

It is true that in the dairy farm things did not as yet go any better than before, and Ivan strenuously opposed the idea that cows should be kept in warm sheds and butter made from fresh cream, asserting that in a cold shed a cow consumed less fodder and that butter made of sour cream was more economical, and he expected his wages to be paid as before and was not at all interested in the fact that the money he received was not wages but an advance on his future share in the profits.

It is true that Fyodor Rezunov's cooperative group did not plough the cornland twice with the new ploughs as had been agreed, their excuse being that time was short. It is true that the peasants belonging to this cooperative group, though they had agreed to farm the land on the new conditions, referred to the land not as cooperatively held but as rented for half the crop, and the peasants of this cooperative group and Rezunov himself kept saying to Levin: "If you would only accept money for the land, sir, it would be less trouble for you and we should feel freer." Moreover, these peasants kept putting off the building of the cattle yard and granary on this land on all sorts of pretexts, and dragged the matter on till winter.

It is true that Shurayev would have liked to sublet the kitchen gardens in small lots to other peasants. He apparently quite misunderstood, in fact, intentionally misunderstood, the conditions on which the land had been let to him.

It is true that often when talking to the peasants and explaining to them all the advantages of the new undertaking, Levin felt that they were only listening to the sound of his voice and were quite determined, whatever he might say, not to let themselves be taken in. He felt it particularly when talking to the most intelligent of them, Rezunov, and noticing the gleam in Rezunov's eyes, which showed very plainly both his ironical amusement at Levin and his absolute conviction that if anyone were going to be taken in, it would not be he, Rezunov.

But in spite of all that, Levin thought that things were moving and that by keeping strict accounts and insisting on his own way he would be able to prove to them the advantages of these new arrangements and that then everything would go of itself.

These affairs together with the management of the rest of his estate still on his hands and the work in his study on his book kept Levin so busy the whole summer that he hardly ever went out shooting. At the end of August he learned from a servant of theirs, who had brought back the sidesaddle, that the Oblonskys had gone back to Moscow. He felt that by his discourtesy in not replying to Dolly's letter (a rudeness which he could not remember without blushing), he had burned his boats and could never go to see them again. He had treated the Sviazhskys just as rudely, having left their house without saying good-by. But he would never go to see them again. He did not care any more now. The business of reorganizing the work on his farm absorbed him more than anything had ever done in his life. He read through the books Sviazhsky had lent him and having copied out everything he did not have, and reading other books on political economy and socialism on the same subject, he found, as he had expected, nothing in them that had any relevance to his undertaking. In the works on political economy, in Mill, for instance, whom he studied first and with great zeal, hoping every minute to find a solution of the problems that interested him, he found the laws deduced from the state of agriculture in Europe; but he absolutely failed to see why these laws, inapplicable as they were to Russia, should be deemed to be universal. It was the same with the books on socialism: these were either beautiful, but useless, utopias, which fascinated him while he was still at the university, or mere attempts at the improving or patching up of the economic situation in Europe, with which the state of agriculture in Russia had nothing in common. Political economy maintained that the laws in accordance with which the wealth of Europe had developed and was developing were universal and absolute. Socialist teaching declared that any development in accordance with those laws led to disaster. But neither the one nor the other had anything to say, or indeed contained the faintest hint, about what he, Levin, and all the Russian peasants and landowners should do with their millions of hands and acres to become as productive as possible for the common good.

Having once taken up the study of this problem, he conscientiously read everything that had any bearing on the subject and he was planning to go abroad in the autumn to study the problem on the spot, so that what had often happened to him with various other questions should not happen to him again. For in the past as soon as he began to grasp what the man he was talking to had in mind, he would suddenly be asked: "And what about Kauffmann, and Jones, and Dubois, and Miccelli? You haven't read them. You should read them: they have made a thorough study of this question."

He now saw clearly that neither Kauffmann nor Miccelli had anything to say to him. He knew what he wanted. He saw that Russia had splendid soil, splendid laborers, and that in some cases, as that of the peasant at whose house he had stopped on his way to Sviazhsky, both soil and laborers produced much; but that in the majority of cases, when capital was used in the European way, they produced little, and that this happened simply because the laborers were only too willing to work and work well in the way natural to them and that their opposition was not accidental but permanent and had its roots in the spirit of the people. In his opinion, the Russian people, whose destiny it was to populate and cultivate enormous unoccupied tracts of land consciously, till all those lands had been occupied, kept to the methods best suited for that purpose, and those methods were not by any means as bad as was generally thought. And he wanted to prove it theoretically in a book and practically on his land.

CHAPTER 30

By the end of September the timber for the construction of the cattle yard on the land let to the cooperative producers' group had been carted and the butter from their cows was sold and the profits divided. In practice the new system was working out beautifully, or so it seemed to Levin. But to explain the whole thing theoretically and finish the book, which, according to his dreams, would not only revolutionize political economy, but totally abolish that science and lay the foundation of a new science—that of the relation of the peasants to the soil—he had only to go abroad and there study on the spot what had been done on that subject and find convincing proofs that what had been done there was not what was needed. Levin was only waiting for the wheat to be sold in order to get the money and leave for abroad. But rain set in, making it impossible to get in what remained of the wheat and rye and potatoes, stopped all the work, and even prevented the dispatch of the wheat. The mud made the roads impassable; two mills had been carried away by floods, and the weather was getting worse and worse.

On the morning of the 30th of September the sun showed itself and, hoping for fine weather, Levin began making serious preparations for his departure abroad. He ordered the wheat to be put into sacks, sent the bailiff to the grain merchant to collect the money, and himself went around the estate to give final instructions before leaving. Having seen to all his business, soaked through with the streams of water that had run in at the neck of his leather coat and the tops of his high boots, but in the most cheerful and animated spirits, Levin returned home in the evening. The weather had grown worse toward the evening, and the sleet lashed his drenched horse so painfully that it walked sideways; but under his hood Levin felt excellent and he looked cheerfully around at the muddy streams running along the ruts, at the drops hanging from every bare twig, at the white patches of unmelted sleet on the planks of the bridge, at the thick layer of the still juicy, fleshy elm leaves lying around the denuded tree. In spite of the gloom of the surroundings, he felt quite extraordinarily elated. His talks with the peasants of a rather remote village showed that they were getting used to the new conditions. An old innkeeper, into whose inn he had gone to dry himself, evidently approved of Levin's plan and had of his own accord offered to join a cooperative group to buy cattle.

"I need only to push on steadily toward my goal and I shall get what I want," thought Levin, "and it's certainly worth working and striving for. It is not a personal matter, but something that concerns the welfare of all. The entire agricultural industry and, above all, the position of the peasants, must be completely changed. Instead of poverty—wealth and contentment; instead of hostility—harmony and a bond of common interests. In short, a bloodless but immense revolution, at first in the small circle of our district, then throughout the province, throughout Russia, and throughout the whole world. For an idea that is just must bear fruit. Yes, it is a goal worth working for. And the fact that the author of it is I, Konstantin Levin, the same fellow who went to a ball in a black tie and who was refused by the Shcherbatsky girl and who seems so pathetic and insignificant to himself—that proves nothing. I am sure Franklin felt just as insignificant and as unsure of himself as I do when he went over his past in his mind. That means nothing. I expect he, too, had his Agafya to whom he confided his plans."

It was while immersed in such thoughts that Levin reached home in the dark.

The bailiff who had been to the merchant's had returned and brought part of the money for the wheat. An arrangement had been made with the innkeeper, and the bailiff had learned on the way that the corn was still standing in the fields, so that his own 160 stacks still in the fields were as nothing to what the others had to worry about.

After dinner Levin, as usual, sat down in an armchair with a book, and, while reading, continued to think of his impending journey in connection with his book. Today the whole significance of his work presented itself to him with special clarity, and whole paragraphs of their own accord shaped themselves in his mind, expressing the essential idea of his plans. "I must write it down," he thought. "This ought to make a brief foreword, which I had considered unnecessary at first." He got up to go to his writing table and Laska, who had been lying at his feet, also got up, stretching herself and looking around at him, as though asking where she was to go. But there was no time to write down his thoughts, for the peasants' foremen came for next day's orders and Levin went out into the hall to them.

Having given his orders for next day's work and seen the peasants who had come to discuss their business with him, Levin went back to his study and sat down to work. Laska lay down under the table, and Agafya with her knitting sat down in her usual place.

After writing for some time, Levin suddenly remembered Kitty with extraordinary vividness and her refusal at their last meeting. He got up and began pacing the room.

"What's the use of fretting?" said Agafya. "Now, why do you always stay at home? You should go to a watering place now you've got everything ready."

"But I am. The day after tomorrow. I have to finish my business first."

"Your business! Haven't you given away enough to the peasants already? They're already saying, 'Your master will be getting some reward from the Tsar for it!' and indeed it's strange: what do you want to bother about the peasants for?"

"I'm not bothering about them: I'm doing it for myself."

Agafya knew every detail of Levin's plans for his estate. Levin often explained his ideas to her in all their minutest details and quite frequently argued with her and did not agree with her comments. But this time she interpreted his words in quite a different sense.

"Of course, a man has to think of his soul before everything else," she said with a sigh. "Parfyon Denisich now, for all that he could neither read nor write, died as good a death as God would grant," she said, referring to a former house serf who had died recently. "Received Holy Communion and extreme unction, he did."

"I did not mean that," he said. "What I mean is that I'm doing it for my own good. It's more profitable for me if the peasants do their work better."

"Do anything you like, if he's bone-lazy, he'll do just anyhow. If he has a conscience, he'll work; if not, you can do nothing with him."

"But you told me yourself that Ivan looks after the cattle much better now."

"All I want to say," replied Agafya, evidently not speaking at random, but in strict sequence of ideas, "is that you ought to get married, that's all."

Agafya's mention of the very thing he had just been thinking about grieved and hurt him. Levin frowned and without replying sat down to his work again, repeating to himself all he had been thinking about the importance of this work. Only occasionally he listened in the stillness to the clicking of Agafya's knitting needles and, remembering what he did not wish to remember, frowned again.

At nine o'clock he heard the sound of harness bells and the heavy lurching of a carriage through the mud.

"Well, now, here's someone come to see you so you won't be bored any more," said Agafya, getting up and going toward the door.

But Levin ran ahead of her. His work was not getting on now, and he was glad of a visitor, whoever it might be.

CHAPTER 31

Halfway down the stairs Levin recognized a familiar sound of coughing in the hall; but he did not hear it clearly because of the noise of his steps and he hoped that he was mistaken. Then he saw the whole, long, bony, familiar figure, and it seemed there could be no further room for doubt now, but he still hoped that he was mistaken and that the tall man taking off his fur coat and coughing was not his brother Nikolai.

Levin was fond of his brother, but to be with him was always a torture. And now, when under the influence of the thought that had come to him and Agafya's reminder, he was in a state of uncertainty and confusion, the forthcoming meeting with his brother seemed particularly painful. Instead of a cheerful, hale and hearty stranger, who would, he hoped, divert him from his mental perplexity, he had to meet his brother, who saw through him, who would call forth his innermost thoughts and force him to make a clean breast of everything. And that was the last thing he wanted to do.

Angry with himself for this bad feeling, Levin ran down into the hall. As soon as he was face to face with his brother, this feeling of selfish disappointment disappeared and gave way to a feeling of pity. Dreadful as his emaciation and illness had made his brother before, he looked still more emaciated and still more wasted now. He was a mere skeleton covered with skin.

He stood in the hall, jerking his long, thin neck, as he pulled his scarf from it, and smiling piteously. When he saw that meek and submissive smile, Levin felt a lump rising to his throat.

"Well, here I am," said Nikolai in a hollow voice, without for a second taking his eyes off his brother's face. "I've wanted to come for a long time, but I'm afraid I did not feel well. But now I'm very much better," he said, wiping his beard with his large, thin hands.

"Yes, yes!" replied Levin. And he felt more dreadful still when, exchanging kisses with his brother, he felt with his lips the dryness of his brother's skin and saw his large, strangely glittering eyes close to him.

A few weeks before, Levin had written to tell his brother that after the sale of a small part of their property which had still remained undivided, Nikolai was now entitled to his share of about two thousand rubles.

Nikolai said that he had now come to get the money and, above all, to spend some time in his old home and touch his native soil in order to gather strength, like the heroes of old, for the work that lay ahead of him.

Though he looked more round-shouldered than ever and though his being so tall emphasized his leanness, his movements were, as usual, quick and abrupt. Levin took him to his study.

Nikolai changed his clothes with particular care, a thing he never used to do, brushed his thin, straight hair, and smiling, went upstairs.

He was in the most affectionate and cheerful mood, just as Levin often remembered him in childhood. He even mentioned their brother Sergey without bitterness. When he saw Agafya, he joked with her and inquired after the old servants. The news of the death of Parfyon Denisich made a painful impression on him. For a moment he looked scared; but he immediately recovered himself.

"He was old, wasn't he?" he said, and changed the subject. "Well, I'll spend a month or two with you and then I'm off to Moscow. Myakhkov, you know, promised me a post and I'm entering the civil service. Now I shall arrange my life quite differently," he went on. "You know, I've got rid of that woman."

"Maria Nikolayevna? Why? Whatever for?"

"Oh, she was a horrible woman. Caused me a lot of trouble." But he did not say what sort of trouble it was. He could not very well tell his brother that he had got rid of Maria Nikolayevna because the tea she made for him was too weak and chiefly because she looked after him like an invalid. "And, generally, I should like to change my life completely now. Like everybody else, I have of course done silly things, but the property is the last consideration, and I don't regret it. Good health is the main thing and, thank God, my health has improved."

Levin listened, trying hard to think what to say, but could not. Nikolai probably felt the same. He began questioning his brother about his affairs, and Levin was glad to talk about himself, because he could talk without dissembling. He told his brother of his plans and activities.

His brother listened, but quite clearly was not interested.

These two men were so akin and intimate with one another that the slightest movement, the tone of voice, told them more than could be said in words.

At this moment both of them were preoccupied with

the same thought—Nikolai's illness and approaching death—which put everything else out of their minds. But neither dared speak of it, and consequently everything they said, since it did not express what they really thought, rang false. Never before had Levin felt so glad when the evening was over and it was time to go to bed. Never with any stranger, never when making a formal call, had he been so unnatural and dishonest as he was that night. And the consciousness of his unnatural attitude and the remorse he felt at it made him more unnatural still. He wanted to weep over his dear, dying brother, and he had to listen and keep up a conversation about how he was going to live.

As the house was damp and only his bedroom heated, Levin put his brother to sleep behind a partition in that room.

His brother went to bed and, whether he slept or not, kept tossing about like a sick man, coughing all the time, and when he could not get over a fit of coughing, muttering something. Sometimes he would sigh deeply and exclaim, "Oh, dear Lord!" Sometimes, when the phlegm choked him, he cried angrily, "Oh, hell!" Levin lay long awake listening to him. He thought of all sorts of things, but his thoughts always led up to one thing: death.

Death, the inevitable end of everything, confronted him for the first time with irresistible force. And death, which was close to his beloved brother, who was moaning in his sleep and by habit calling indiscriminately both on God and the devil, was not so far away as it had hitherto seemed to him. It was in himself too—he felt it. If not today, then tomorrow, if not tomorrow, then thirty years hence—what difference did it make? And what this inevitable death was, he not only did not know, he not only never thought of it, but could not and dared not think of it.

"I'm working, I want to do something, but I had forgotten that it will all come to an end, that it will all end in—death."

He sat on his bed in the dark, crouching and hugging his knees, and, holding his breath with the effort, kept thinking. But the more mental effort he made, the clearer it became to him that it was undoubtedly so, that he had really forgotten, that he had overlooked one little thing in life—that death would come and everything would come to an end and that, in fact, it was not worth beginning anything, and that one could do nothing about it. Yes, it was terrible, but it was so.

"But I am still alive. What am I to do now? What?" he said in despair. He lit a candle and, getting up quietly, walked up to the looking glass and began examining his face and hair. Yes, there were gray hairs at his temples. He opened his mouth. His back teeth were beginning to decay. He bared his muscular arms. Yes, he was still very strong. But dear old Nikolai, who was breathing there with the remains of his lungs, had a healthy body too. And suddenly he remembered how when they were children they used to go to bed together and wait till Fyodor Bogdanych had left the room to start throwing pillows at one another and roar with laughter, laugh so irrepressibly that even fear of Fyodor Bogdanych could not stop that brimming, bubbling over consciousness of the happiness of life. "And now that misshapen, hollow chest and—I who do not know what will happen to me and why. . . ."

"Hell!" Nikolai exclaimed after a violent fit of coughing. "What are you doing there?" he called to Levin. "Why don't you go to bed?"

"Oh, I don't know. Insomnia, I suppose."

"And I've slept well. I don't perspire any more, either. Look for yourself. Here, feel my shirt. Not wet, is it?"

Levin felt it, went back behind the partition, put out the candle, but could not get to sleep for a long time. Just when the question of how to live had become a little clearer to him, he was confronted by a new insoluble problem—death.

"I know he's dying, I know he'll be dead before spring—well, how can I help him? What can I say to him? What do I know about it? I had even forgotten there was such a thing!"

CHAPTER 32

Levin had long ago observed that when people made you feel uncomfortable by their excessive tractability and submissiveness, they would soon make your life unbearable by being excessively demanding and carping.

He felt that the same thing would happen with his brother. And, to be sure, Nikolai's meekness did not last long. The very next morning he became irritable and began studiously finding fault with his brother, touching his most sensitive spots.

Levin felt guilty and he could do nothing to mend things. He felt that if they both did not dissemble and spoke without, as they say, beating about the bush, that is, said what they really thought and felt, they would just have looked into one another's eyes and he, Konstantin, would only have said, "You're going to die, you're going to die, you're going to die!" and Nikolai would only say in reply, "I know I'm going to die, and I'm afraid, I'm afraid, I'm afraid!" And they would not have said anything else, had they really spoken of nothing else but of what was in their minds. But it would be impossible to live like that, and that was why Levin tried to do what he had been trying unsuccessfully to do all his life and what others, as far as he could observe, could do so well and without which it was impossible to live: he tried to say something that was different from what he thought, and he could not help feeling that it sounded false, that his brother detected it and grew irritable.

On the third day of his stay Nikolai again challenged his brother to explain his plans to him and began not only criticizing them but deliberately confusing them with communism.

"All you did was to appropriate somebody else's idea and distort it, and now you want to apply it where it is inapplicable."

"But I'm telling you that the two have nothing in common. They deny the justice of property, capital, and inheritance, while I do not deny the efficacy of this chief stimulus" (Levin felt disgusted with himself for using such words, but ever since he had been engrossed in his work, he found himself using these foreign words more and more), "I merely want to regulate labor."

"That's the trouble! You've taken somebody else's idea, stripped it of all that gave it force, and now you want to convince me that it is something new," said Nikolai, angrily jerking his neck.

"But my idea has nothing in common—"

"There," Nikolai went on, smiling ironically and with

a malicious glint in his eyes, "there, at least, you've got, as it were, the geometrical charm—the charm of clarity and certainty. It may be utopian. But granting the possibility of making a *tabula rasa* of all the past: no private property, no family, then labor comes into its own. But you have nothing. . . ."

"Why do you get it all mixed up? I have never been a communist."

"But I have been and I find that while this is premature, it's rational and has a future as Christianity had in the first centuries."

"All I am driving at is that the labor force must be examined from the point of view of natural science, or in other words it must be scientifically studied, its properties ascertained and—"

"But that's quite unnecessary. That force finds a certain form of activity itself in accordance with the degree of its development. First there used to be slaves everywhere, then villeins, and we have the share-cropping system, leaseholders, and agricultural laborers—so what are you looking for?"

At these words Levin suddenly flared up, for deep inside him he was afraid that it was true, true that he wished to balance between communism and the existing forms and that this was hardly possible.

"I am looking for some means of making labor profitable for myself and for the laborer," he said heatedly. "I want to establish—"

"You don't want to establish anything. You simply want to be original, as you always have done, to show that you are not just exploiting the peasants, but doing so with some idea at the back of your mind."

"Well, if that's what you think, you'd better leave it alone!" replied Levin, feeling that a muscle was twitching uncontrollably in his left cheek.

"You have no convictions and you never had any. All you want is to salve your conscience."

"Oh, all right, then, leave me alone!"

"I will, and high time too! You can go to blazes. And I'm very sorry I came!"

However much Levin tried afterward to pacify his brother, Nikolai would not listen and kept saying that it would be much better for them to part, and Konstantin saw that life had become simply unbearable to his brother.

Nikolai had definitely made up his mind to leave when Levin came to him again and asked him in a rather forced tone of voice to forgive him if he had in any way hurt his feelings.

"Oh, what magnanimity!" said Nikolai and smiled. "If you wish to be in the right, I can let you have that pleasure. You're in the right, but I'm going all the same."

A moment before he left, Nikolai kissed Levin and said, looking at his brother suddenly with a strange and serious expression:

"All the same, don't think too badly of me, Kostya!" And his voice trembled.

Those were the only sincere words that had passed between them. Levin understood that what his brother had meant to say was, "You see and you know that I am in a bad way and perhaps we shall never see each other again." Levin understood it and tears started to his eyes. He kissed his brother again, but did not know what to say, and indeed could not say anything more to him.

Three days after his brother's departure, Levin too went abroad. Meeting young Shcherbatsky, Kitty's cousin, at the railway station, Levin greatly surprised him by his grim look.

"What's the matter with you?" asked Shcherbatsky.

"Oh, nothing. There's little to be cheerful about in this world."

"What do you mean, little? You'd better come to Paris with me instead of going to some wretched Mulhausen. You'll see how cheerful it can be!"

"No, thanks, I've done with it all. It's time for me to die."

"Good Lord," said Shcherbatsky with a laugh, "and I'm only just getting ready to live."

"Yes, I thought so too not so long ago, but now I know that I shall soon be dead."

Levin was only saying what he had really been thinking of late. He saw death and the approach of death in everything. But the work he had started interested him all the more. He had to carry on somehow or other till death came. A pall of darkness covered everything for him; but it was just because of this darkness that he felt that his only thread to guide him through this darkness was his scheme, and he seized on it and held onto it with all his might.

Part Four

CHAPTER 1

The Karenins, husband and wife, continued to live in the same house and to meet every day, but they were wholly estranged. Karenin made it a rule to see his wife every day so as not to give the servants any grounds for surmises, but avoided dining at home. Vronsky never came to Karenin's house, but Anna met him elsewhere and her husband knew it.

The situation was painful to all three of them, and not one of them would have been able to live through a single day in a situation like that, had it not been for the expectation that it would change and that it was merely a temporary distressing ordeal that would pass. Karenin expected that this passion would pass as did everything in the world and that it would all be forgotten and his name would remain undisgraced. Anna, who was responsible for the situation and for whom it was most painful, bore it because she not only expected but was firmly convinced that soon everything would be settled and cleared up. She had not the least idea what would settle it, but was quite certain that something would turn up very soon now. Vronsky, involuntarily taking his cue from her, also expected something to happen independently of him that would clear up all these difficulties.

In the middle of winter Vronsky spent a very dull week. He was attached to a foreign prince who was paying a visit to Petersburg and he had to show him the sights of the city. Vronsky himself had a distinguished appearance and, in addition, he possessed the art of carrying himself with respectful dignity and was used to the company of such exalted personages. And so he was appointed to attend on the prince. But his duties seemed a little too strenuous to him. The prince did not wish to miss anything about which he might be asked at home whether he had seen it in Russia and, besides, he wanted to enjoy as many Russian amusements as possible. Vronsky had to act as his guide in both. In the mornings they went sight-seeing and in the evenings they took part in the national amusements. The prince enjoyed unusually good health even among princes; both by gymnastic exercises and by taking good care of his body he had brought himself to such a state of physical fitness that in spite of the excesses he indulged in when enjoying himself, he looked as fresh as a big shiny green Dutch cucumber. The prince had traveled a great deal, and he found that one of the chief advantages of the facilities of modern communications was that they made national amusements so easily accessible. He had been in Spain, where he had serenaded and became on intimate terms with a Spanish woman who played the mandolin. In Switzerland he had shot a chamois. In England he had taken fences in a pink coat and shot two hundred pheasants for a bet. In Turkey he had been in a harem, in India he had ridden an elephant, and now in Russia he wished to sample all the typically Russian amusements.

Vronsky, who was, as it were, his chief master of ceremonies, found it rather hard to apportion all the Russian amusements offered to the prince by different people, such as trotting races, pancakes, bear hunts, troikas, gypsies, and orgies with smashing of crockery in the Russian fashion. And the prince assimilated the Russian national spirit with quite extraordinary facility, smashed trays of crockery, sat with a gypsy girl on his lap, and seemed to be always asking, "What next? Surely that's not all the Russian national spirit consists of?"

As a matter of fact, of all the Russian amusements the prince preferred French actresses, a ballet dancer, and white-seal champagne. Vronsky was used to princes, but whether it was that he had himself lately changed or whether he had been in too close a proximity to this particular prince, that week seemed to him terribly wearisome. All the week he felt like a man who had been put in charge of a dangerous lunatic, was afraid of that

414

lunatic, and at the same time, being in such close proximity to him, afraid for his own reason too. Vronsky
always felt that he must never for a moment relax his
tone of strict official respectfulness so as not to be insulted. The prince's manner of behaving toward those
very persons who, to Vronsky's astonishment, were
ready to spare no efforts to provide him with Russian
amusements, was contemptuous. His views of Russian
women, whom he wanted to study, more than once made
Vronsky flush with indignation. The main reason, however, why Vronsky found him so hard to stomach was
that he could not help seeing himself in him. And what
he saw in that mirror was not flattering to his self-
respect. The prince was a very stupid, very self-assured,
very healthy, very immaculate man, and that was all. He
was a gentleman—that was true, and Vronsky could not
deny it. He was equable and dignified with those above
him, free and simple with his equals, and contemptuously indulgent with his inferiors. Vronsky was the same
himself and held it something to be proud of; but in his
relations with the prince he was an inferior and that
indulgently contemptuous attitude towards him made
him feel indignant.

"What a stupid piece of beef! Am I really like that?"
he thought.

However that may have been, when he said good-by
to him at the end of the week, before his departure for
Moscow, and received his thanks, Vronsky was happy to
be rid of an embarrassing situation and the unpleasant
mirror. He said good-by to him at the railway station
after their return from a bear hunt, where they had spent
a whole night taking part in a display of Russian
daredevilry.

CHAPTER 2

On his return home, Vronsky found a note from
Anna. She wrote: "I am ill and unhappy. I cannot go
out, but I cannot go on any longer without seeing you.
Come this evening. Alexey goes to the council at seven
and will be there till ten." Wondering for a moment at
the strangeness of her asking him to come to her house,

in spite of her husband's request not to receive him there, he decided to go.

Vronsky had been promoted to the rank of colonel that winter and, no longer quartered with the regiment, he was living alone. Immediately after lunch he lay down on the sofa and five minutes later the memories of the disreputable scenes he had witnessed during the last few days became all mixed up with his mental image of Anna and a peasant who had played an important part as a beater at the bear hunt; and Vronsky fell asleep. He woke up in the dark, trembling with horror, and quickly lighted a candle. "What was it? What? What was the terrible thing I dreamed? Yes, yes. The peasant, the beater, a dirty little man with a tousled beard, was bending down and doing something and all of a sudden began muttering strange words in French. No, there was nothing more in the dream," he said to himself. "But why then was it so terrible?" He vividly recalled the peasant again and those incomprehensible French words he had been muttering, and a chill of horror ran down his spine.

"What nonsense!" thought Vronsky and looked at his watch.

It was half past eight already. He rang for his valet, dressed hurriedly, and went out of the house, completely forgetting his dream and only worried at being late. On driving up to the entrance of the Karenins' house, he again glanced at his watch and saw that it was ten to nine. A high, narrow carriage, with a pair of grays, stood before the front door. He recognized Anna's carriage. "She is coming to me," thought Vronsky. "That would be much better. I hate going into his house. But I'm afraid it can't be helped now. I can't hide myself," he said to himself with the manner, which had become second nature to him since childhood, of one who had nothing to be ashamed of. Vronsky got out of his sledge and went to the door. The door opened and the hall porter with a rug over his arm called the carriage. Vronsky, who did not usually notice details, could not help noticing now the look of surprise with which the hall porter glanced at him. In the doorway Vronsky ran up against Karenin. The gaslight fell straight across his bloodless, pinched face under the black hat and his white tie showing bright from under the beaver collar of his overcoat. Karenin's dull eyes stared fixedly at Vronsky's face.

416

Vronsky bowed, and Karenin, munching his lips, raised his hand to his hat and went out. Vronsky saw him get into the carriage without looking round, take the rug and a pair of opera glasses, and disappear. Vronsky went into the hall. His brows were knit and his eyes glittered with a proud, angry light.

"What a situation!" he thought. "If he'd fight, stand up for his honor, I could have done something, could have expressed my feelings; but this weakness or meanness. He puts me in the position of a deceiver, which I never was and do not want to be."

Since his meeting with Anna in the Wrede garden Vronsky's ideas had changed a great deal. Submitting involuntarily to Anna's weakness—she had given herself up to him entirely, expecting him alone to decide her fate, and was ready in advance to accept anything—he had long ceased to think that their union might end as he had then imagined. His ambitious plans had again receded into the background and, feeling that he had come out of the circle of activity in which everything was clearly defined, he gave himself up completely to his feeling, and this feeling bound him more and more closely to her.

While still in the hall he heard the sound of her retreating footsteps. He realized that she had been waiting for him, listening for him, and was now going back to the drawing room.

"No!" she exclaimed when she saw him, and at the first sound of her voice tears started to her eyes. "No, if things go on like this much longer, it will happen much, much sooner!"

"What will happen, my dear?"

"What? Here I've been waiting, worrying, an hour, two hours. . . . No, I won't! . . . I can't quarrel with you. I suppose you couldn't come. No, I won't!"

She put both her hands on his shoulders and looked long and intently at him with searching, rapturous eyes. She was scrutinizing his face to make up for the time she had not seen him. As at every meeting with him, she tried to blend the picture she had of him in her imagination (incomparably better than, and indeed quite impossible in, reality) with him as he really was.

CHAPTER 3

"You met him?" she asked when they sat down at a table under the lamp. "That's your punishment for being late."

"Yes, but how did it happen? Shouldn't he have been at the council?"

"He had been and had come back and again went out somewhere else. Don't let us talk about it. Where have you been? With the prince all the time?"

She knew all the details of his life. He was about to say that he had been up all night and had fallen asleep, but looking at her excited and happy face he felt ashamed. And he said that he had to go and report the prince's departure.

"But it's over now, isn't it? He's gone?"

"It's over, thank heaven. You have no idea how unbearable it was."

"But why? Isn't it the kind of life all young men lead?" she said, knitting her brows and, picking up her crocheting from the table, she began disentangling the hook without looking at Vronsky.

"I've long since given up that kind of life," he said, surprised at the change in her face and trying to divine its meaning. "And I don't mind confessing," he went on, smiling and showing his tightly packed row of white teeth, "that all this week I seem to have been looking at myself in a glass while watching that kind of life, and I didn't feel pleased, I can tell you."

She held her work in her hand, but did not crochet, looking at him with strange, glittering, unfriendly eyes.

"This morning Lisa called on me—they're not afraid to call on me in spite of the Countess Lydia Ivanovna," she added, "and told me about your Athenian evening. How disgusting!"

"I was only going to say—"

She interrupted him.

"Was it the Thérèse you used to know before?"

"I was going to say—"

"How disgusting you men are! How is it that it never

418

occurs to you that a woman can never forget these things?" she said, getting more and more excited and in this way betraying the cause of her irritation. "Especially a woman who cannot know your life. What do I know? What did I know?" she went on. "Only what you tell me. And how do I know whether you tell me the truth? . . ."

"Anna, I resent that. Don't you trust me? Have I not told you that I have not a thought I would not reveal to you?"

"Yes, yes," she said, evidently trying to banish all jealous thoughts. "But if you knew how miserable I was! I believe you, I do believe you. So what were you going to say?"

But he could not immediately remember what he wished to say. These fits of jealousy, which had been becoming more and more frequent recently, horrified him and, however much he tried to conceal it, made him feel colder toward her, although he knew that the cause of her jealousy was her love for him. How many times had he told himself that her love was happiness; and now that she loved him as only a woman can love for whom love outweighs all that is good in life, he was much farther from happiness than when he had gone after her from Moscow. Then he thought himself unhappy, but that happiness was in the future; but now he felt that his best happiness was already behind. She was not at all like the woman she had been when he saw her first. Both morally and physically she had changed for the worse. She had broadened out, and when she spoke of the actress a spiteful expression had distorted her face. He looked at her as a man might look at a faded flower he had picked, in which he found it difficult to discover the beauty which made him pick and destroy it. And yet he felt that though when his love was stronger, he could, had he wanted it badly, have torn that love out of his heart, now when, as at this moment, it seemed to her that he felt no love for her, he knew that the bond between them could not be broken.

"Well, what were you going to tell me about the prince? I have driven away the demon," she added. The demon was what they called jealousy. "Now, what did you begin to say about the prince? Why did you find it so hard to bear?"

419

"Oh, it was intolerable!" he said, trying to pick up the lost thread of his thought. "He doesn't improve on closer acquaintance. If I had to describe him I would say he was one of those well-fed beasts who take first prizes at cattle shows, and nothing more," he said in a tone of vexation which interested her.

"Oh, but why?" she objected. "After all, he must have seen much and he is well educated, isn't he?"

"It's quite a different kind of education—their education. One can see that he has been educated only to have the right to despise education, as they despise everything except animal pleasures."

"But then you all love these animal pleasures, don't you?" she said, and again he noticed on her face that gloomy look which evaded him.

"Why are you so anxious to take his part?" he said, smiling.

"I don't take his part—it's all the same to me. But I can't help thinking that if you did not like those pleasures yourself, you might have refused to take part in them. But you enjoy seeing Thérèse in the nude like Eve . . ."

"Again, again the demon!" said Vronsky, taking the hand she had laid on the table and kissing it.

"I'm sorry, but I can't help it! You don't know what I've been through while waiting for you! I don't think I'm jealous. No, I'm not. I trust you when you are here with me, but when you are somewhere by yourself leading that life of yours which I cannot understand . . ."

She moved away from him, disentangled at last the hook from her crocheting, and, with the aid of her forefinger, began quickly to draw the loops of white wool, shining in the lamplight, through each other, her slender wrist moving rapidly and nervously in its embroidered cuff.

"Well, what happened? Where did you meet Alexey?" she suddenly asked, her voice ringing unnaturally.

"We ran into each other at the entrance door."

"And did he bow to you like that?"

She pulled a long face and, half shutting her eyes, quickly changed her expression and folded her hands; and on her beautiful face Vronsky suddenly saw the same look with which Karenin had bowed to him. He smiled and she laughed gaily with that delightful, deep laughter which was one of her chief charms.

"I simply can't understand him," said Vronsky. "If after your talk in the country he had broken with you or challenged me . . . but this sort of thing I cannot understand. How can he put up with such a situation? He suffers, that's obvious."

"He?" she said, with a sarcastic laugh. "He's perfectly satisfied."

"Why do we all go on tormenting ourselves when everything might be arranged so well?"

"Oh no, he doesn't torment himself. Do you think I don't know him, that I don't know the falsehood with which he is soaked through and through? Could anyone who is capable of any feeling live as he lives with me? He understands nothing, feels nothing. Could a man with any feelings go on living in the same house with his guilty wife? Could he talk to her? Call her by her Christian name?"

And she could not stop herself mimicking him again: " 'Anna, *ma chère*, Anna, my dear!'

"He's not a man, he's not a human being, he's a—puppet! No one else knows it, but I do. Oh, if I'd been in his place, I'd long ago have killed, torn to pieces, a wife like me, and not have called her 'Anna, *ma chère*.' He's not a man. He's a ministerial machine. He doesn't understand that I am your wife, that he is a stranger, that I don't want him. . . . But don't, don't let's talk about it!"

"You're unfair, darling, you're unfair," said Vronsky, trying to calm her. "But never mind, we won't talk about him. Tell me what you have been doing. What is the matter with you? What is this illness of yours and what did the doctor say?"

She looked at him, gloating. She had apparently remembered other ridiculous and grotesque sides of her husband's character and was waiting for an opportunity to reveal them.

But he went on:

"I realize that it is not illness but your condition. When is it going to be?"

The mocking light was extinguished in her eyes, but another smile—the knowledge of something unknown to him and quiet sadness—replaced her former expression.

"Soon, soon. You were saying that our position is impossible, that we must put an end to it. If only you knew how awful it was for me, what I would give to be able to love you freely and openly! I should not torture myself or torture you with my jealousy. . . . But it's going to be soon, and not in the way we think."

And at the thought of how it would be, she felt so sorry for herself that tears started to her eyes and she could not continue. She laid her hand, gleaming white and sparkling with rings in the lamplight, on his sleeve.

"It won't be as we think. I did not want to tell you, but you made me. Soon, very soon everything will be settled and we shall all, all be at peace and shall no longer torment each other."

"I don't understand," he said, understanding her.

"You asked me when? Soon. And I shall not live through it. Please, don't interrupt me," and she went on hurriedly. "I know it. I know it for certain. I shall die, and I'm glad I shall die and set you as well as myself free."

Tears gushed out of her eyes; he bent over her hand and began kissing it, trying to hide his agitation, which he knew had no foundation, but which he could not control.

"Yes, so, it's better so," she said, squeezing his hand tightly. "That's the one thing, the one thing left to us."

He recovered and raised his head.

"What nonsense! What ridiculous nonsense you are talking!"

"No, it's the truth."

"What, what is the truth?"

"That I'm going to die. I've had a dream."

"A dream?" echoed Vronsky, and instantly remembered the peasant in his dream.

"Yes, a dream," she said. "It's a dream I had a long time ago. I dreamed that I ran into my bedroom to fetch something or find out something, you know how it is in a dream," she said, her eyes wide with horror. "And in the bedroom, in the corner, something was standing."

"Oh, what nonsense! How can you believe—"

But she would not let him interrupt. What she was saying was too important to her.

422

"And that something turned round and I saw that it was a peasant with a tousled beard, small and—terrible. I wanted to run, but he bent over a sack and began fumbling about in it with his hands. . . ."

She showed how he fumbled in the sack. There was an expression of horror in her face. And, remembering his own dream, Vronsky felt the same kind of horror filling his heart.

"He keeps fumbling about and muttering in French, quickly, quickly, and, you know, pronouncing the *r*'s in the French way: '*Il faut le battre le fer, le broyer, le pétrir. . . .*' And I was so terrified I tried to wake up and I did wake up, but it was still in my dream. And I began asking myself what it could mean. And Korney, my husband's valet, said to me: 'You will die in childbirth, ma'am, in childbirth. . . .' And I woke up. . . ."

"Oh, what nonsense! What nonsense!" said Vronsky, but he himself felt that there was no conviction in his voice.

"But don't let us talk about it. Ring the bell, please. I will order tea. But wait, it won't be long now, I—"

But suddenly she stopped. The expression of her face changed instantly. The horror and agitation were suddenly replaced by an expression of quiet, serious, and blissful attention. He could not understand the meaning of this change. She was listening to the stirring of a new life within her.

CHAPTER 4

After meeting Vronsky at the front door of his house, Karenin drove, as he had intended, to the Italian opera. He sat through two acts and saw everybody it was necessary for him to see. On his return home he carefully examined the coat stand and, noticing that no military greatcoat hung there, went as usual straight to his room. But, contrary to his custom, he did not go to bed, but paced up and down his study till three o'clock in the morning. The feeling of anger with his wife, who would not observe the rules of propriety and carry out the only condition he had insisted on—not to see her lover in his house—gave him no rest. She had not complied with his demand, and he had to punish her and carry out his threat to divorce her and take the boy away. He knew all the difficulties connected with such a course, but he had said that he would do it and he must now carry out his threat. The Countess Lydia Ivanovna had hinted to him that this was the best way out of the situation, and lately the procedure of divorce had been brought to such a state of perfection that Karenin saw a possibility of overcoming the formal difficulties. Moreover, misfortunes never come singly, and the affair of the organization of the natives and the irrigation of the Zaraisky province had caused Karenin so much unpleasantness in the ministry that he had for some weeks been in a state of extreme irritability.

He did not sleep all night and his anger, increasing in a sort of enormous progression, reached its extreme limits. He dressed hurriedly and, as though carrying his cup of wrath full to the brim and afraid of spilling it, afraid of losing with his wrath the energy he needed for his talk with his wife, went into her room as soon as he heard that she was up.

Anna, who thought that she knew her husband so well, was amazed at his appearance when he came in. His forehead was furrowed and his eyes stared gloomily before him, avoiding her look; his mouth was firmly and contemptuously closed. In his walk, in his gestures, and in the sound of his voice there was such determination and firmness as his wife had never seen in him. He entered the room and without greeting her, walked straight to her writing table and, taking her keys, opened the drawer.

"What do you want?" she exclaimed.

"Your lover's letters," he said.

"They are not there," she said, closing the drawer.

But her action told him that he had guessed rightly and, roughly pushing away her hand, he quickly snatched a portfolio in which he knew she kept her most important papers. She tried to snatch it from him, but he pushed her away.

"Sit down, I want to talk to you," he said, putting the portfolio under his arm and pressing it so tightly with his elbow that his shoulder rose up.

She looked at him in silence, too startled and abashed.

"I told you that I would not allow you to receive your lover here."

"I had to see him to . . ."

She stopped, unable to think of an excuse.

"I do not want to discuss the reasons why a woman finds it necessary to see her lover."

"I wanted, I only . . ." she began, flushing. His rudeness irritated her and gave her courage. "Don't you feel how easy it is for you to insult me?" she said.

"You can insult an honest man and an honest woman, but to tell a thief that he is a thief is only *la constatation d'un fait*."

"This streak of cruelty in you is something I did not know before."

"You call it cruelty when a husband gives his wife freedom, gives her the protection of his honorable name on the one condition that she should observe the proprieties. Is that cruelty?"

"It's worse than cruelty, it's—baseness, if you want to know!" Anna exclaimed in a burst of anger, and she got up to go.

"No!" he shouted in his squeaky voice, which had risen a note higher than usual, and seizing her by the wrist so powerfully with his long fingers that her bracelet left red marks, he forced her back into her chair.

"Baseness?" he cried. "If you must use that word, it is baseness to abandon a husband and a son for a lover and go on eating the husband's bread!"

She bowed her head. She did not say what she had said the day before to her lover, that *he* was her husband and that her husband was a stranger; she did not even think of it. She felt all the justice of his words and only said quietly:

"Nothing you say can give a worse description of my position than I could have given myself, but why are you saying all this?"

"Why am I saying it? Why?" he went on, as angrily as before. "Because I want you to know that since you have not carried out my wishes that the rules of propriety should be observed, I shall be taking steps to put an end to this situation."

"Soon, very soon it will come to an end of itself," she said, and again tears started to her eyes at the thought of the nearness of death which she longed for now.

"It will come to an end sooner than you and your lover have planned. All you want is the gratification of your animal passions. . . ."

"To hit one who is down is not only ungenerous; it is not even decent."

"I can see that you think only of yourself. You're not interested in the suffering of a man who was your husband. You don't care a damn if his whole life is ruined and how much he has shuff-shuff-shuffered!"

Karenin was speaking so rapidly that his tongue got in the way of his speech and he could not enunciate the word. In the end he pronounced it "shuffered." She felt like laughing and immediately felt ashamed that anything should have made her feel like laughing at such a moment. And for the first time she felt for him for an instant, she put herself in his place and was sorry for him. But what could she say or do? She hung her head and was silent. He, too, was silent for a few moments and then began again in a less squeaky voice, coldly, emphasizing the words that he used without thinking, though they had no special significance.

"I came to tell you . . ." he began.

She looked at him. "No, I did not imagine it," she thought, recalling the expression of his face when he had stumbled over the word "shuffered." "No, a man with those dull eyes and that self-satisfied composure could not possibly feel anything."

"I cannot change anything," she whispered.

"I came to tell you that I am going to Moscow tomorrow and shall not return to this house again, and that you will be notified of my decision by my lawyer, to whom I shall entrust the divorce. My son," Karenin concluded, recalling with an effort what he wanted to say about his son, "will stay with my sister."

"You want Seryozha in order to hurt me," she said, looking sullenly at him. "You don't love him. Please, leave me Seryozha!"

"Yes, I've even lost my love for my son because he is a constant reminder to me of how much I loathe you. But I shall take him all the same. Good-by!"

And he was about to go, but this time she detained him.

426

"Please, Alexey, leave me Seryozha!" she whispered again. "I have nothing more to say to you. Leave Seryozha till my . . . I shall give birth to a child soon, leave him! . . ."

Karenin flushed and, pulling away his hand, left the room without a word.

CHAPTER 5

The famous Petersburg lawyer's waiting room was full when Karenin entered it. Three women—an old lady, a young woman, and a tradesman's wife—and three men—a German banker with a solitaire on his finger, a Russian merchant with a beard, and an angry-looking civil servant in uniform, with an order hanging from his neck—had been waiting for some time. Two clerks sat at their tables writing, their pens scratching. The writing materials, for which Karenin had a weakness, were extraordinarily good. Karenin could not help noticing it. One of the clerks turned to Karenin splenetically, screwing up his eyes.

"What do you want?" he asked.

"I want to see the lawyer on business."

"I'm afraid he is busy," the clerk said sternly, pointing with his pen to the people who were waiting, and he went on writing.

"Can he not find time to see me?" asked Karenin.

"He has no spare time. He is always busy. Be so good as to wait."

"In that case I shall have to trouble you to give him my card," Karenin said with dignity, realizing that it was impossible to preserve his incognito.

The clerk took his card, and though quite evidently not approving what he read on it, went into the other room.

Karenin was in favor of public trials on principle, but for certain high official reasons he did not approve of certain aspects of their application in Russia and condemned them as much as he could condemn anything that had received the highest sanction in the land. All his life had been spent in administrative activities, and therefore when he did not approve of anything, his dis-

427

approval was mitigated by a recognition of the inevitability of mistakes and the possibility of correcting them. In the new legal institutions he did not approve of the position in which the legal profession had been placed. But till now he had had no dealings with the legal profession and he therefore disapproved of it only in theory; now his disapproval was strengthened by the disagreeable impression he received in the lawyer's office.

"He will be here in a moment," said the clerk and, to be sure, two minutes later the tall figure of an elderly jurist who had been consulting the lawyer appeared in the doorway, followed by the lawyer himself.

The lawyer was a small, thickset, bald-headed man, with a dark, reddish beard, long, light-colored eyebrows, and beetling brow. He was as spruce as a bridegroom, from his necktie and double watch chain to his patent-leather boots. His face was intelligent, peasantlike, while his clothes were dandified and in bad taste.

"Come in, please," said the lawyer, addressing Karenin. And gloomily ushering Karenin before him, he closed the door.

"Won't you sit down?" He pointed to a chair at the writing table covered with papers, and himself sat down behind the desk, rubbing his little hands with their short fingers covered with white hair and bending his head to one side. But the moment he had settled down comfortably a moth flew over the table. The lawyer, with a rapidity one could not have expected from him, opened his hands, caught the moth, and resumed his former attitude.

"Before I begin speaking of my case," said Karenin, who had followed the lawyer's movements with astonishment, "I should like to point out that the matter I have to speak to you about must remain secret and confidential."

A hardly perceptible smile distended the lawyer's drooping, reddish mustache.

"I should not be a lawyer if I could not keep the secrets entrusted to me. But if you would like confirmation . . ."

Karenin glanced at his face and saw that his intelligent gray eyes were laughing and seemed to know everything already.

"You know my name?" Karenin continued.

"I know you and, like every Russian, I know," here he again caught a moth, "your valuable services to our country," said the lawyer with a slight bow.

Karenin sighed, trying to pluck up courage. But, having once made up his mind, he went on in his squeaky voice, without quailing or faltering and emphasizing certain words.

"I am in the unfortunate position of a deceived husband," he began, "and I wish to break the matrimonial bonds with my wife legally, that is, to obtain a divorce, but in such a way that my wife is not given the custody of my son."

The lawyer's gray eyes tried not to laugh, but they danced with irrepressible glee, and Karenin saw that it was not only the glee of a man who is getting a profitable order—there was triumph there and delight, there was a gleam resembling the malevolent gleam he had seen in his wife's eyes.

"You want my assistance in obtaining a divorce?"

"Yes, certainly, but I must warn you that I may be wasting your time. I have come only for a preliminary consultation. I want a divorce, but it is the form in which it can be obtained that is important to me. It is quite possible that if the forms do not agree with my demands I may not take any legal action."

"Oh, that is always so," said the lawyer, "and whether you take or do not take any action in the courts depends entirely on you."

The lawyer lowered his eyes and fixed them on Karenin's feet, feeling that the sight of his irrepressible glee might offend his client. He glanced at the moth that flew past his very nose and put out his hand to catch it, but did not catch it out of respect for Karenin's position.

"Although the general outline of our laws relating to this matter is known to me," went on Karenin, "I should like to know the forms in which such cases are conducted in practice."

"You would like me to explain to you the ways in which your desire can be carried out," said the lawyer, without raising his eyes and adopting his client's manner of speech not without a certain pleasure.

And on Karenin's affirmative nod of the head he continued, only from time to time stealing a glance at Karenin's face, which had grown red in patches.

429

"Under our laws," he said with a light shade of disapproval of the laws, "divorce, as you know, can be obtained in the following cases. . . . Wait, please!" he exclaimed to the clerk who had poked his head through the door, but he got up all the same, said a few words to the clerk, and sat down again. "In the following cases: Physical defects in husband or wife, desertion without communication for five years," he said, bending one of his short hairy fingers, "then adultery" (this word he pronounced with evident pleasure) "with the following subdivisions" (he went on bending his thick fingers, though the cases and their subdivisions could hardly be classified together): "physical defects in husband or wife, adultery of husband or wife." As all his fingers had been used, he straightened them and went on: "That is the theoretical view, but I presume you have done me the honor of consulting me to find out the practical application of the law. And, therefore, guided by precedents, I have to inform you that cases of divorce are as follows: there are, I suppose, no physical defects, or desertion? . . ."

Karenin shook his head!

"—are as follows: adultery of one of the parties and the detection of the guilty party by mutual agreement and, failing such an agreement, involuntary detection. I must add that the latter case is seldom met with in practice," said the lawyer and, casting a quick glance at Karenin, paused, like a vendor of pistols who, after describing the advantages of one kind of pistol over another, waits for his customer to make his choice. But Karenin was silent, so the lawyer began again: "The most usual, simple and sensible course, in my opinion, is adultery by mutual consent. I should not have put it like that when talking to an uneducated person," said the lawyer, "but I think that to people like us the thing is quite clear."

Karenin, however, was so much upset that he did not at once realize the reasonableness of adultery by mutual consent, and his perplexity was expressed in his eyes; but the lawyer immediately came to his assistance.

"Two people can no longer live together—here is the fact. And if both agree about that, the details and formalities become unimportant. And at the same time it is the simplest and surest method."

Karenin fully understood now. But he had religious

430

scruples which made it impossible for him to accept this method.

"This is quite out of the question in the present case," he said. "Here only one course is possible: involuntary detection, confirmed by letters which are in my possession."

At the mention of letters the lawyer pressed his lips together and emitted a thin, pitying, and contemptuous sound.

"I'm afraid," he began, "that cases of this kind, as you are aware, fall under the jurisdiction of the ecclesiastical courts, and the reverend Fathers are very keen on the minutest details in all such cases," he said with a smile that showed he sympathized with the reverend Fathers' taste. "Letters can, no doubt, serve as a partial confirmation, but the evidence produced must be direct evidence, that is, of eyewitnesses. In fact, if you are good enough to let me deal with the case, I should advise you to leave me the choice of the measures to be taken. He who wants a result must accept the means of obtaining it."

"If that is so . . ." Karenin began, turning pale suddenly, but at that moment the lawyer got up again and went to the door to speak to his clerk, who had again interrupted him.

"Tell her we're not dealing in secondhand goods," he said and returned to Karenin.

On his way to his seat he furtively caught another moth. "What a mess my furniture will be in by the summer," he thought, with a frown.

"So you were saying . . ." he said.

"I shall let you have my decision in writing," said Karenin, getting up and holding on to the table. After standing like that in silence for a short while, he said: "I may, then, conclude from your words that a divorce is possible. Will you please also let me know your terms?"

"Yes, quite possible, if you let me have full freedom of action," said the lawyer, without replying to the question. "When may I expect to hear from you?" he asked, moving toward the door, his eyes and patent-leather boots shining.

"In a week's time. And please let me know whether you are willing to undertake the case and on what terms."

431

"Very well."

The lawyer bowed respectfully, let his client pass through the door, and, left alone, gave himself up to his joyful feelings. He felt so cheerful that, contrary to his custom, he let the haggling lady have a reduction and stopped catching moths, having finally decided to have his furniture reupholstered next winter in plush, like Sigonin's.

CHAPTER 6

Karenin had gained a brilliant victory at the meeting of the Commission of the Seventeenth of August, but the consequences of that victory brought about his downfall. The new commission for the investigation of every aspect of the life of the natives had been formed and sent off with extraordinary speed and energy inspired by Karenin. Three months later the commission presented its report. The life of the natives had been investigated in its political, administrative, economic, ethnographic, material, and religious aspects. All the questions had received excellently drafted answers, and the answers were not open to doubt because they were not the work of human thought, always liable to error, but were all the work of bureaucratic officialdom. The answers were all based on official data, reports from governors and bishops, founded on reports from district authorities and ecclesiastical superintendents, founded, in turn, on the reports from rural district offices and parish priests; the answers, therefore, left no possible room for doubt. All the questions, for instance, as to why there were failures of crops or why the natives adhered to their own creeds, etc., questions which without the convenience of an administrative machinery do not and cannot be solved for centuries, received clear and unqualified solutions. And they were in favor of Karenin's opinions. But Stremov, who had been stung to the quick at the last meeting, had on the reception of the commission's report made use of tactics Karenin had not expected. Stremov suddenly went over to Karenin's side, bringing with him several other members, and not only declared himself to be warmly in favor of putting Karenin's measures into effect, but proposed other extreme measures of the same nature. These measures, going much beyond Karenin's original idea, were accepted, and only then Stremov's tactics became apparent. These measures, carried to extremes, proved so stupid that statesmen, public opinion, intellectual ladies, and the press unanimously attacked them, expressing their indignation both against the measures and their rightful begetter, Karenin. Stremov, on the other hand, stood aside, pretending to have blindly followed Karenin's plan and to be himself astounded and indignant at what had been done. That finally brought about Karenin's downfall. But notwithstanding his failing health and his domestic troubles Karenin did not give in. There was a split in the commission. Some of the members, with Stremov at their head, tried to justify their mistake by claiming that they had put their faith in the inspection commission directed by Karenin, which had submitted the report, and declared that the commission's report was nonsense and just a waste of paper. Karenin and a number of other members who saw the danger of such a revolutionary attitude to official papers continued to uphold the findings of the commission of inspection. This led to complete confusion in the higher spheres and even in society, and although everybody was greatly interested in the affair, no one could make out whether the natives were facing ruin and starvation or were on the road to prosperity. Karenin's position, in consequence partly of this and partly of the contempt to which he became exposed because of his wife's infidelity, became very precarious. And in these circumstances he took an important decision. To the surprise of the commission, he announced that he would apply for leave to go and investigate the matter personally on the spot. And having obtained permission, he left for the outlying provinces.

Karenin's departure caused a great sensation, particularly as before starting he formally returned the money for traveling expenses to cover the cost of twelve horses all the way to his destination.

"I consider it very noble of him," said Betsy, speaking about it to the Princess Myakhky. "Why spend government money on post horses when everybody knows that we have railways everywhere?"

But the Princess Myakhky did not agree and was even irritated by the Princess Tverskoy's views.

433

"It's all very well for you to talk," she said, "when you possess I don't know how many millions. But I'm very glad when my husband goes on an inspection tour in the summer. It is very good for his health and he enjoys traveling about, and as for me, I have an understanding with him by which this money goes on the upkeep of a carriage and coachman."

On his way to the outlying provinces Karenin stopped in Moscow for three days.

On the day after his arrival he went to call on the governor-general. At the crossing of Gazetny Lane, where there is always a crowd of private and hired carriages, he suddenly heard someone calling him by his name in such a loud and cheerful voice that he could not help looking round. At the corner of the pavement, in a short, fashionable overcoat and a small fashionable hat tilted on one side, his white teeth gleaming between his smiling red lips, stood Oblonsky, gay, young, and beaming, determinedly and insistently shouting and demanding that Karenin should stop. With one hand he was holding onto the window of a carriage, from which the head of a lady in a velvet bonnet and the heads of two little children were leaning out, and with his other he was smilingly beckoning to his brother-in-law. The lady, too, was waving her hand to Karenin with a kind smile. It was Dolly with her children.

Karenin did not want to see anyone in Moscow, and least of all his wife's brother. He raised his hat and was about to drive on, but Oblonsky told his driver to stop and ran across the snow to him.

"Aren't you ashamed not to have let us know. Been here long? I was at Dusseaux's yesterday and saw 'Karenin' on the board, but it never occurred to me that it was you!" said Oblonsky, thrusting his head in at the carriage window. "I should have dropped in otherwise. I'm so glad to see you!" he went on, tapping one foot against the other to shake off the snow. "What a shame not to let us know!"

"I'm sorry I was very busy, I had no time," Karenin replied dryly.

"Come over and speak to my wife. She is so anxious to see you."

Karenin unwrapped the rug which was around his

chilly legs and, getting out of the carriage, made his way over the snow to Dolly.

"What's the matter, my dear Alexey? Why are you avoiding us?" said Dolly with a smile.

"I'm sorry, I was terribly busy. I'm very pleased to see you," he said in a tone of voice that clearly showed that he was anything but pleased. "How are you?"

"Well, and how is my dear Anna?"

Karenin muttered something and was about to go back to his carriage, but Oblonsky stopped him.

"Tell you what we'll do tomorrow. Dolly, ask him to dinner. We'll invite Koznyshev and Pestsov to let him have a taste of our Moscow intelligentsia."

"Yes, please, do come," said Dolly. "We shall expect you at five or six, just as you like. Well, how is my dear Anna? It's so long since . . ."

"She's all right," Karenin muttered, frowning. "Very glad," and he went to his carriage.

"Will you come?" shouted Dolly.

Karenin muttered something which Dolly could not make out in the noise of the traffic.

"I'll call on you tomorrow!" Oblonsky shouted after him.

Karenin got into his carriage and sat so far back that he could neither see nor be seen.

"Funny fellow!" said Oblonsky to his wife and, glancing at his watch, made a gesture with his hand in front of his face as a parting sign of endearment to his wife and children, and walked jauntily away along the pavement.

"Stiva! Stiva!" cried Dolly, reddening.

He turned round.

"I have to buy coats for Grisha and Tanya. Give me some money!"

"Oh, never mind. Tell them I'll pay!" and gaily nodding to an acquaintance who was driving past, he disappeared.

CHAPTER 7

The next day was Sunday. Oblonsky went to a rehearsal of the ballet at the Bolshoi Theater and gave Masha Chibisov, a pretty dancer who had just been accepted as a member of the ballet through his patronage, the coral necklace he had promised her the day before, and in the wings, in the midday darkness of the theater, contrived to kiss her pretty little face, which brightened up at her present. Besides giving her the coral necklace, he had to fix an appointment with her after the ballet. Explaining that he could not be there at the beginning of the performance, he promised to come for the last act and take her out to supper. From the theater Oblonsky drove to the market and himself selected the fish and asparagus for dinner, and at noon he was already at Dusseaux's, where he had to call on three people who, fortunately for him, were all staying at the same hotel: Levin, who had recently returned from abroad; the new head of his department, who had just been appointed to that high post and who was making a tour of inspection in Moscow; and Karenin, his brother-in-law, whom he was determined to take home with him to dinner.

Oblonsky liked to dine out, but he liked even better to give a dinner party, a small but very select one with regard to food and drink and the guests. He was very pleased with the menu for that day's dinner: there would be perch, brought alive from the market; asparagus; and the *pièce de résistance*, a wonderful but quite plain joint of roast beef and the appropriate wines: so much for the food and drink. As for the guests, there would be Kitty and Levin and, not to make it too obvious, there would also be a girl cousin and young Shcherbatsky; and the *pièce de résistance* here was to be Sergey Koznyshev and Alexey Karenin, Koznyshev a Muscovite and a philosopher, and Karenin a Petersburg man engaged in the practical affairs of state. He was also inviting the well-known eccentric and enthusiast, Pestsov, a liberal, a conversationalist, a musician, a historian, and a most charming fifty-year-old youth, who would act as sauce and garnish to Koznyshev and Karenin. He would egg them on and set them by the ears.

The second installment of the money from the merchant who had bought the timber of his wood had been received and was not yet all spent. Dolly had been very nice and kind lately, and the thought of his dinner party pleased Oblonsky in every respect. He was in excellent spirits. There were two circumstances, though, that were not exactly agreeable; but both of them were submerged in the sea of good-humored gaiety which overflowed his heart. These two circumstances were: first, that he had noticed that Karenin was very cold and stern with him when he had met him in the street the day before; and taking into consideration this and the fact that Karenin had not called on them or let them know of his arrival, with the rumors that had reached him about Anna and Vronsky, Oblonsky guessed that all was not as it should be between the husband and wife.

This was one of the disagreeable things. The other slightly disagreeable circumstance was that his new chief, like all new chiefs, already had the reputation of being a terrible fellow who got up at six o'clock in the morning, worked like a horse, and expected his subordinates to do the same. Besides which, the new chief had the reputation of having the manners of a bear and, according to rumor, held views diametrically opposed to those of his predecessor and to those till now held by Oblonsky himself. On the previous day Oblonsky appeared at his office in civil-service uniform and the new chief had been very affable and chatted with him as with an old acquaintance, and that was why Oblonsky thought it his duty to call on him in a morning coat. The thought that his new chief might not receive him with sufficient warmth was the other disagreeable circumstance. But Oblonsky felt instinctively that everything would *come right* in the most satisfactory manner. "They're all human beings; they've all got weaknesses, like us poor sinners: what is there to get angry or quarrel about?" he thought as he entered the hotel.

"Hullo, Vassily," he said as he passed along the corridor with his hat tilted to one side, addressing a servant he knew. "Growing side whiskers, are you? Levin—

number seven, eh? Show me the way, please. And find out whether Count Anichkin" (his new chief) "will receive me."

"Yes, sir," Vassily replied, smiling. "It's a long time since you were here, sir."

"I was here yesterday, but I came in at the other entrance. Is this number seven?"

Levin stood in the middle of the room with a peasant from Tver, measuring a new bearskin, when Oblonsky entered.

"I say, did you kill him?" cried Oblonsky. "A lovely specimen! A she-bear? How do you do, Arkhip?"

He shook hands with the peasant and sat down on a chair without taking off his coat or hat.

"Take your things off! What's the hurry?" said Levin, taking his hat.

"Sorry, I have no time," replied Oblonsky. "I've only come in for a minute."

He threw open his coat, but later he took it off and stayed for a whole hour, talking to Levin about hunting and all sorts of personal matters.

"Well, tell me please what you did abroad?" said Oblonsky after the peasant had gone. "Where have you been?"

"Why, I've been to Germany, Prussia, France, and England, not in the capital cities but in the manufacturing towns, and saw a lot that's new. And I'm glad I went."

"Yes, I know your idea of settling the working-class problem."

"Not at all. There can be no working-class problem in Russia. In Russia you have the problem of the relation of the worker to the land. It exists there too, but with them it is a case of patching up what has been spoiled, while with us . . ."

Oblonsky listened to Levin attentively.

"Yes, yes," he kept saying. "Quite likely you are right," he said. "But I am glad to see you in good spirits: you go bear hunting, you work and you're full of enthusiasm. You see, young Shcherbatsky told me—he met you, I believe—that you looked depressed and kept talking about death."

"Oh well, I never stop thinking of death," said Levin. "It's quite true that it's time I was dead. And all this is just a lot of nonsense. I will tell you frankly: I care a lot

438

for my idea and my work, but, come to think of it, the whole thing, I mean, this whole world of ours is just a speck of mildew grown up on a tiny planet. And we think we can have something tremendous—ideas, actions! It's all grains of sand!"

"But, my dear fellow, this is as old as the hills."

"Old, yes, but, you know, once you grasp it clearly, everything becomes so insignificant. When you've grasped the fact that today or tomorrow you will die and nothing will be left of you, everything becomes so insignificant. I consider my idea very important, but it, too, turns out to be of no more significance, even if it were possible to carry it out, than walking around this bearskin. And so you spend your life diverting yourself with hunting and work, just not to think of death."

Oblonsky smiled shrewdly and affectionately as he listened to Levin.

"Well, of course! . . . So you've come around to my way of thinking. Do you remember how you used to attack me for seeking enjoyment in life? Be not so severe, O moralist!"

"Well, no, there is some good in life, I mean . . ." Levin got confused. "But I don't really know. All I know is that we shall soon be dead."

"Why soon?"

"And, you know, there is less charm in life when you think of death, but it's more peaceful."

"On the contrary, it's much more fun toward the end. However, I must be off," said Oblonsky, getting up for the tenth time.

"No, please, stay a little longer!" said Levin, detaining him. "When shall we see each other again? I'm leaving tomorrow."

"Good Lord, what a fool I am! I came here specially to . . . I mean, you simply must come and dine with us today. Your brother's coming and my brother-in-law Karenin."

"Is he here?" said Levin, and he wanted to ask about Kitty. He had heard that she had gone to Petersburg at the beginning of the winter to stay with her sister, the wife of a diplomat, and he did not know whether she had returned or not, but he decided not to ask. "Whether she is there or not—what difference does it make?" he thought.

"So you'll come?"

"Yes, of course."

"Well, at five o'clock, then, and you needn't change."

And Oblonsky got up and went down to see his new chief. His instinct had not deceived him. The new, terrible chief turned out to be a very well-mannered and urbane person. Oblonsky had lunch with him and sat talking to him so long that it was nearly four o'clock by the time he got to Karenin.

CHAPTER 8

After returning from morning Mass, Karenin spent all the morning at his hotel. That morning he had two matters to attend to: first, to receive and send on a deputation from the native tribes, which was now in Moscow, to Petersburg; secondly, to write the promised letter to the lawyer. The deputation, though summoned on his initiative, presented many difficulties and even dangers, and Karenin was very glad to have been in time to meet it in Moscow. The members of the deputation had not the slightest idea of their role or their duties. They were naïvely convinced that all they had to do was to explain their needs and the existing state of affairs and to ask for government help. They simply did not realize that some of their statements and demands would play into the hands of the hostile party and would therefore ruin the whole thing. Karenin spent a long time with them, wrote out for them a program, which they should not exceed, and having dismissed them, wrote letters to Petersburg and instructions regarding the deputation. The Countess Lydia Ivanovna was to be his chief assistant in this matter. She was a specialist in the art of handling deputations, and no one knew better than she how to prepare the ground for a deputation and guide it in the right direction. Having finished with the deputation, Karenin wrote his letter to the lawyer. Without the least hesitation he authorized him to act as he deemed fit. In the letter he enclosed three of Vronsky's notes to Anna which he had found in the portfolio he had taken away.

Ever since Karenin left his house with the intention of never returning to his family, ever since he had been to see the lawyer and had spoken, though only to one man, of his intention, and especially since he had converted this matter of life into one of official documents, he was getting more and more used to his intention and clearly visualized the possibility of carrying it into effect.

He was sealing the envelope with his letter to the lawyer when he heard the loud sounds of Oblonsky's voice. Oblonsky was arguing with Karenin's servant and insisting that he should be announced.

"What does it matter?" thought Karenin. "It may be better so: I will tell him about my position with regard to his sister at once and explain why I can't dine with him."

"Ask the gentleman in!" he said in a loud voice, collecting his papers and putting them inside a blotter.

"There, you see, you were lying and he is at home!" Oblonsky could be heard saying in reply to the man who had been trying to stop him, and, taking off his coat as he went, Oblonsky entered the room. "I'm awfully glad to have found you in. So I hope—" Oblonsky began gaily.

"I'm sorry I can't come," said Karenin coldly, standing and not asking his visitor to take a seat.

Karenin had intended at once to enter on the cold relationship which he thought he ought to be in with the brother of a wife against whom he was bringing an action for divorce. But he had not counted on that ocean of good nature which was constantly overflowing the banks of Oblonsky's soul.

Oblonsky opened wide his clear and shining eyes.

"Why can't you? What do you mean to say by that?" he asked, looking bewildered, in French.

"What I mean to say is that I can't come because the family relationship that has existed between us must come to an end."

"What? I mean, how? Why?" Oblonsky said with a smile.

"Because I am about to take divorce proceedings against your sister, my wife. I had to—"

But before Karenin could finish what he was going to say, Oblonsky did something he did not expect. Oblonsky uttered a gasp of surprise and sat down in an easy chair.

"No, my dear fellow, it can't be true!" cried Oblonsky, a look of pain appearing on his face.

"It is true."

"I'm sorry, but I simply can't, I can't believe it."

Karenin sat down, feeling that his words had not had the effect he had anticipated, and that he would have to give an explanation and that whatever that explanation might be, his relations to his brother-in-law would remain the same.

"Yes, I'm afraid I am under the painful necessity of seeking a divorce," he said.

"I will say one thing, my dear fellow. I know you to be a first-rate and fair-minded man, I know Anna—I'm sorry, but I cannot change my opinion of her—to be a fine, splendid woman and that is why, forgive me, I cannot believe it. There must be some misunderstanding," he said.

"Well, of course, if it were only a misunderstanding!"

"Of course, I understand," Oblonsky interrupted. "But, you see, you must bear in mind one thing: you must not be in a hurry. You must not, you really must not be in a hurry!"

"I am not in a hurry," Karenin said coldly, "but one can't very well ask anyone's advice in such a matter. My mind's made up."

"This is terrible!" said Oblonsky, sighing deeply. "I would do one thing, my dear fellow. I implore you to do it!" he said. "The action has not yet begun, as I understand. Before you begin it, see my wife. Talk it over with her. She loves Anna like a sister, she is fond of you, and she is a wonderful woman. For God's sake, talk it over with her. Do me a favor, I implore you!"

Karenin pondered, and Oblonsky looked at him with sympathy without interrupting his silence.

"Will you go and see her?"

"I'm afraid I don't know. That was why I did not call on you. I can't help thinking that our relations will have to change."

"But why? I don't see it. If I may say so, apart from our family relations, you share, to some extent at least, the same friendly feelings that I always had for you. And sincere respect," said Oblonsky, pressing his hand. "Even if your worst assumptions were correct, I don't—and I never would—take upon myself to sit in judgment on either side and I see no reason why our relations should change. But now, please, do this. Come and see my wife."

"Well, we look at it differently," Karenin said coldly. "However, don't let's talk about it."

'But why not come? Well, just for dinner tonight. My wife's expecting you. Do come. And, above all, have a talk with her. She's a wonderful woman. Do that, I implore you on bended knees."

"If you wish it so much, I'll come," Karenin replied with a sigh, and wishing to change the subject, he asked him about something that interested them both: Oblonsky's new chief, a comparatively young man who had suddenly been given so high a post.

Karenin had never liked Count Anichkin and had always differed from him in opinions, but now he could not refrain from showing the hatred, comprehensible to anyone in the civil service, of a man who has suffered a setback in the service to one who has received promotion.

"Well, and have you seen him?" asked Karenin with a venomous smile.

"Of course I have. He came to the office yesterday. He seems to know his business perfectly and is very active."

"Yes, but what exactly is his activity directed to?" said Karenin. "Toward getting things done or undoing what has been done? The misfortune of our country is its red-tape bureaucracy, of which he is a worthy representative."

"I'm afraid I don't know what there is to criticize in him. I don't know what his tendencies are; all I know is that he is a nice fellow," replied Oblonsky. "I've just been to see him and really he is a nice fellow. We had lunch, and I showed him how to make that drink, you know, wine and orange slices. It's a very cooling drink. And it's quite amazing he shouldn't have known it. He liked it very much. Yes, he certainly is a very nice fellow."

Oblonsky glanced at his watch.

"Good Lord, it's after four and I've still to go to Dolgovushin's. So, please, come to dinner. You can't imagine how grieved my wife and I will be if you don't come."

Karenin saw his brother-in-law off in a very different manner from that in which he had greeted him.

"I've promised and I'll come," he said dejectedly.

"Believe me, I appreciate it and I hope you won't regret it," said Oblonsky, smiling.

And putting on his overcoat as he was going out of the room, he brushed against the servant's head with his arm, laughed, and went out.

"At five o'clock and don't change, please," he cried once again, coming back to the door.

CHAPTER 9

It was past five and some of the guests had already arrived, when the master of the house got home. He came in together with Koznyshev and Pestsov, who had run into each other at the entrance. Those two were the chief representatives of the Moscow intelligentsia, as Oblonsky called them. Both were men respected for their character and their intellect. They respected each other, but in almost everything they were in complete and hopeless disagreement, not because they belonged to opposite schools of thought, but just because they belonged to the same camp (their enemies confused them with one another), but in this camp each of them had his own shade of opinion. And since there is nothing less capable of agreement than disagreement on semi-abstract subjects, they not only disagreed in their opinions, but had long been accustomed to make fun, without getting angry, of each other's incorrigible delusions.

They were going through the front door talking of the weather when Oblonsky overtook them. Prince Alexander Shcherbatsky, Oblonsky's father-in-law, young Shcherbatsky, Turovtsyn, Kitty, and Karenin were already sitting in the drawing room.

Oblonsky saw immediately that without him things were going badly in the drawing room. Dolly, in her gray silk gala dress, obviously worried about the children, who had to have their dinner by themselves in the nursery, and about her husband, who was late, had not been able in his absence to get all her guests properly mixed. They all sat like "priests' daughters on a visit" (as the old prince expressed it) evidently wondering why they were all there and just forcing out words so as not to remain silent. The good-natured Turovtsyn must have felt completely out of his depth, for the smile with which his full lips greeted Oblonsky seemed to say, "Well, my dear fellow, you have put me among a brainy lot! A couple of drinks and the Château des Fleurs is more in my line." The old prince sat in silence, his shining eyes casting a sidelong glance now and then at Karenin, and Oblonsky realized that he had already hit upon some witty remark with which to polish off that statesman, whom one was invited to savor like a dish of sturgeon. Kitty kept looking at the door, plucking up courage so as not to blush when Levin should enter. Young Shcherbatsky, who had not been introduced to Karenin, did his best to show that he was not in the least put out by it. Karenin himself, as was his custom in Petersburg, when dining with ladies, was in evening dress with a white tie, and Oblonsky could tell from his face that he had come merely to keep his promise and was fulfilling an unpleasant duty by being in that company. It was he who was mainly responsible for the chilly atmosphere which had frozen all the guests before Oblonsky's arrival.

On entering the drawing room Oblonsky apologized for being late, explaining that he had been detained by a certain prince, who was his usual scapegoat whenever he happened to be late or absent. In a moment he had introduced everybody, and having brought Karenin and Koznyshev together, started them on a discussion of the Russification of Poland, which they immediately took up together with Pestsov. Patting Turovtsyn on the shoulder, he whispered something funny to him and made him sit down near Dolly and the old prince. Then he told Kitty that she was looking very pretty that evening and introduced Shcherbatsky to Karenin. In one minute he had kneaded all that society dough in such a way that the drawing room could have served as a model for all drawing rooms and was filled with animated voices. Konstantin Levin alone was missing. But that was all for the best, for going into the dining room, Oblonsky saw to his horror that the port and sherry were from Depret and not from Levé, and having made the necessary arrangements for the coachman to be sent to Levé as soon as possible, he turned to go back to the drawing room.

In the dining room he met Levin.

"I'm not late, am I?"

"You can't help being late, can you?" said Oblonsky, taking his arm.

"Have you a lot of people? Who's here?" Levin asked, blushing involuntarily and knocking the snow off his cap with his glove.

"All our own people. Kitty's here. Come on, I'll introduce you to Karenin."

Oblonsky, in spite of his liberal views, knew very well that to be acquainted with Karenin could not but be an honor and therefore treated his best friends to that honor. But at that moment Levin was quite incapable of appreciating to the full the pleasure of such an acquaintanceship. He had not seen Kitty since the memorable evening when he had met Vronsky, if, that is, one were not to count the moment he had caught a glimpse of her on the highroad. He had known deep inside him, of course, that he would see her here today. But to maintain his freedom of thought he tried to persuade himself that he did not know it. But now when he heard that she was here, he was suddenly filled with such joy and, at the same time, with such terror that it took his breath away and he could not utter what he wanted to say.

"What is she like? What is she like? Is she the same as before or as she was that morning in the carriage? What if Dolly had spoken the truth? Why shouldn't it be true?" he thought.

"Oh yes, please do introduce me to Karenin," he brought out with difficulty and went into the drawing room with a despairingly determined step and saw her.

She was neither the same as before nor as she had been in the carriage; she was quite different.

She was terrified, shy, shamefaced, and therefore all the more charming. She saw him the moment he entered the room. She had been waiting for him. She was filled with joy and so confused at her joy that there was a moment—the moment when he went up to his hostess and again glanced at her—when she, and he, and Dolly, who saw it all, felt that she would not be able to control herself and would burst into tears. She blushed and turned pale and blushed again, and almost fainted, waiting with quivering lips for him to come up to her. He came up, bowed, and held out his hand in silence. Except for the slight quivering of her lips and the moisture that made her eyes look more brilliant, her smile was almost calm as she said:

"What a long time it is since we last saw one another!" and with desperate determination she pressed his hand with her cold hand.

"You've not seen me, but I saw you," said Levin, with a beaming smile of happiness. "I saw you coming from the station on your way to Yergushovo."

"When?" she asked with surprise.

"You were driving to Yergushovo," said Levin, feeling that the happiness that was flooding his heart was choking him. "And how did I dare," he thought to himself, "to connect something that is not innocent with this touching creature? Yes, it certainly seems that Dolly was speaking the truth."

Oblonsky took his arm and led him up to Karenin.

"Let me introduce you," and he gave their names.

"Very pleased to meet you again," Karenin said coldly, as he shook hands with Levin.

"Are you acquainted?" Oblonsky asked with surprise.

"We spent three hours together in a railway carriage," said Levin with a smile, "but we left it, as after a fancy-dress ball, intrigued; I did, at any rate."

"I see! Please," said Oblonsky, pointing in the direction of the dining room.

The men went into the dining room and walked up to the table with the snacks, on which stood bottles with six different kinds of vodka and as many kinds of cheese with or without little silver scoops, caviar, herrings, different kinds of meat and fish, and plates with slices of French bread.

The men stood round the vodkas, each with its special aroma, and the snacks, and the conversation about the Russification of Poland between Koznyshev, Karenin, and Pestsov gradually flagged in anticipation of dinner.

Koznyshev, who knew better than anyone how at the end of a most serious and abstract argument to add a pinch of Attic salt unexpectedly, and by that action to change the mood of the people he was conducting his discussion with, did so now.

Karenin was arguing that the Russification of Poland could only be brought about as a result of high principles which had to be introduced by the Russian administration.

Pestsov insisted that one nation could assimilate another only when it had a larger population.

Koznyshev agreed with both, but with certain reservations. To bring the conversation to an end, he remarked as they were leaving the drawing room with a smile:

"It follows that there is only one way of Russifying alien nationalities—breed as many children as possible. My brother and I are acting very unpatriotically in that respect. But you married gentlemen, and especially you, Oblonsky, are acting most patriotically. How many have you got?" he asked, turning to his host with a kindly smile and holding out a tiny wineglass to be filled.

Everyone laughed, and Oblonsky most gaily of all.

"Yes, that's certainly the best way!" he said, munching some cheese and pouring some very special vodka into the wineglass held out to him. The conversation really came to an end with that jocular remark.

"This cheese is not bad. May I help you to some?" said the host. "You haven't been doing your physical exercises again?" He turned to Levin, feeling Levin's muscles with his left hand.

Levin smiled, tightened his arm, and under Oblonsky's fingers a lump like a Dutch cheese and as hard as steel rose under the fine cloth of Levin's coat.

"What biceps! A real Samson!"

"I should think one needs great strength for bear hunting," said Karenin, who had the vaguest ideas about hunting, as he spread some cheese and broke his slice of bread, which was as thin as a cobweb.

Levin smiled.

"None at all. On the contrary, a child can kill a bear," he said, making room, with a slight bow, for the ladies, who were coming up to the table with the snacks with their hostess.

"You've killed a bear, I hear," said Kitty, vainly trying to catch a recalcitrant, slippery mushroom with her fork and setting the lace quivering over her white arm. "Have you bears near your estate?" she added, half turning her lovely little head toward him and smiling.

There was, it would seem, nothing extraordinary in what she had said, but what unutterable meaning there was in every sound of her words, in every movement of her lips, eyes, and hands as she said it! There was an appeal for forgiveness; there was trust in him and a caress, a tender and timid caress, and promise and hope and love for him, in which he could not but believe and which suffocated him with happiness.

"No, we went to the Tver province. On my way back I met your brother-in-law in the train, or rather your brother-in-law's brother-in-law. It was an amusing meeting."

And he told them gaily and amusingly how after a sleepless night he had burst into Karenin's compartment in his sheepskin.

"Regardless of the proverb, judging by my clothes and not by my wits, the guard wanted to chuck me out, but I started talking to him in highfalutin language and—er—you, too, sir," he said, turning to Karenin, "judging by my sheepskin were about to turn me out, but afterward you took my part, for which I am very grateful."

"Generally speaking, the rights of passengers in the choice of seats are too indefinite," said Karenin, wiping the tips of his fingers on his handkerchief.

"I could see that you could not make up your mind about me," said Levin, smiling good-naturedly, "so I was quick to start an intellectual conversation to make amends for my sheepskin."

Koznyshev, who was continuing his conversation with his hostess and listening with one ear to his brother, glanced at him sideways and thought: "What's the matter with him today? What does he look like a conquering hero for?" He did not know that Levin felt as if he had grown a pair of wings. Levin knew that she was listening to him and took pleasure in listening to him. And that was the only thing he cared about. Not only in that room, but in the whole world there existed for him only himself, who had grown enormously significant and important in his own eyes, and her. He felt on a height that made his head spin and there, somewhere far below, were all these kind and nice Karenins, Oblonskys, and the rest of the world.

Quite casually, without looking at them and as though there were no other place to put them, Oblonsky made Levin and Kitty sit side by side at the dining table.

"Well, I suppose you might as well sit down here," he said to Levin.

The dinner was as good as the dinner service, of which Oblonsky was a great connoisseur. The *soupe Marie-*

Louise was a great success; the minute pasties, which melted in one's mouth, were perfection itself. Two footmen and Matvey, in white ties, served the food and wine inconspicuously, quietly, and expertly. The dinner was a success on the material side, but it was no less a success on the nonmaterial side. The conversation, sometimes general and sometimes between two or three of the diners, never ceased and became so lively at the end of the dinner that the men got up from the table still talking, and even Karenin cheered up considerably.

CHAPTER 10

Pestsov liked to bring an argument to a conclusion, and he had not been satisfied with Koznyshev's remark, particularly as he was aware of the fallacy of his own opinion.

"I never meant," he began over his soup, addressing Karenin, "density of population alone, but in conjunction with fundamentals and not principles."

"I'm afraid," replied Karenin unhurriedly and languidly, "it's one and the same thing. In my view, only a nation that has reached a high standard of civilization can influence another, that—"

"But you see, the question is," Pestsov interrupted in his deep voice, for he was always in a hurry to speak and always seemed to stake his whole soul on what he was saying, "what exactly one must understand by a higher standard of civilization? The English, the French, the Germans—whose standard of civilization is highest? Which is to nationalize the other? We see that the Rhine has fallen under the influence of France, but the Germans are not in any way inferior to the French in culture, are they?" he shouted. "There must be some other law at work!"

"I think that it is always the truly civilized that exerts its influence," said Karenin, slightly raising his eyebrows.

"But how are we to recognize the signs of true civilization?" asked Pestsov.

"I should have thought," said Karenin, "that those signs were well known."

"Are they?" Koznyshev interposed with a sly smile.

"Now, take education, for instance. It is generally agreed that a purely classical education is the only real education; but we hear violent arguments on both sides and it is impossible to deny that the opposite camp has some strong arguments in its favor."

"You're a classicist, my dear fellow," said Oblonsky. "Red wine?"

"I'm not at the moment expressing any opinion of either the one or the other kind of education," said Koznyshev with an indulgent smile, as though speaking to a child, and holding out his glass. "All I say is that both sides have strong arguments," he went on, addressing Karenin. "I had a classical education, but personally I find no place in this controversy. I see no clear reason why classics should be preferred to a scientific education."

"Natural sciences," Pestsov interposed, "have just as great an educational value and are as likely to develop a boy's faculties. Take astronomy, take botany or zoology with its system of general laws!"

"I'm afraid I can't quite agree with you," replied Karenin. "It seems to me that it can't be denied that the process of studying the forms of a language has a beneficial effect on mental development. Besides, it is impossible to deny too that the influence of the classical writers is in the highest degree a moral one, whereas, unfortunately, with the teaching of the natural sciences are associated those harmful and false doctrines which are the bane of our present times."

Koznyshev was about to say something, but Pestsov interrupted him in his deep bass. He began warmly to prove the unfairness of such a view. Koznyshev quietly waited for an opportunity to put in his word, evidently ready with some incontestable retort.

"But," said Koznyshev with a shrewd smile, addressing Karenin, "you must admit that to weigh exactly the pros and cons of a classical or a scientific education is difficult and that the question which kind of education should be preferred would not have been so easily and conclusively decided, if a classical education did not have the advantage which you have just mentioned, namely, its moral and, *disons le mot*, antinihilistic influence."

"Without a doubt."

"If there had not been the advantage of this antinihilistic influence on the side of classical education we

451

should have given much more thought and consideration to the arguments on both sides," Koznyshev went on with a shrewd smile. "We should have allowed full play to both systems. But now we know that those pills of classical education contain the medicinal property of antinihilism and we offer them boldly to our patients. But what if they did not possess that medicinal property?" he concluded, adding his pinch of Attic salt.

At Koznyshev's pills everybody laughed, and Turovtsyn in particular laughed loudly and gaily, having at last heard something funny, the only thing he was waiting for in listening to the conversation.

Oblonsky had not made a mistake in inviting Pestsov. With Pestsov there, intellectual conversation could not cease for a moment. Hardly had Koznyshev put an end to the discussion of that question with his joke before Pestsov immediately raised another.

"One can't even agree," he said, "that the government had that aim in view. The government is evidently guided by general considerations and remains indifferent to the influence its measures may have. For instance, the education of women ought to have been considered injurious, but the government is opening schools and universities for women."

And the conversation at once veered to the new topic of the education of women.

Karenin expressed the view that the education of women was usually confused with the question of the emancipation of women and for that reason only could be considered harmful.

"I consider, on the contrary, that these two questions are indissolubly connected," said Pestsov. "It's a vicious circle. Women are deprived of rights because of their lack of education, and their lack of education arises from their lack of rights. We mustn't forget that the subjection of women is so great and goes back such a long time that we often fail to realize what a gulf separates them from us."

"You said 'rights,'" said Koznyshev, who had been waiting for Pestsov to finish. "Do you mean rights of serving on a jury, of being members of city councils, presidents of local government boards, civil servants, members of parliament . . ."

"Certainly."

452

"But if women, in some rare exceptional cases, can occupy these posts, it seems to me you've been using the term 'rights' incorrectly. It would have been more correct to say duties. Everybody, I think, will agree that when we fill the office of juryman, town councilor, or telegraph clerk, we feel that we are performing a duty. And that is why it would be more correct to say that women are seeking duties and quite legitimately, too. And one can only sympathize with this desire of theirs to help man in his work for the community."

"That's right," said Karenin. "The only question is whether they are capable of performing these duties."

"I should think they will be very capable indeed," Oblonsky put in, "when education is more generally spread among them. We see this . . ."

"And what about the proverb?" said the old prince, who had been listening very carefully to the conversation for some time, with a humorous twinkle in his small, sarcastic eyes. "I'm sure my daughters won't mind my repeating it: long hair, short wits."

"They thought the same of the Negroes before their emancipation," Pestsov said angrily.

"What seems so strange to me," said Koznyshev, "is that women should be seeking new duties, while men, as we unfortunately see, usually try to avoid them."

"Duties entail rights—power, money, honors: that is what women are after," said Pestsov.

"It's the same as though I sought the right to be a wet nurse and felt hurt that women are paid for the work and I'm not given the job," said the old prince.

Turovtsyn burst into loud laughter and Koznyshev was sorry he had not said that himself. Even Karenin smiled.

"Yes, but a man can't be a wet nurse," said Pestsov, "while a woman . . ."

"Oh yes, an Englishman did once nurse his baby on board ship," said the old prince, allowing himself to speak so freely in the presence of his daughters.

"Well, there will be about as many women officials as there are such Englishmen," put in Koznyshev.

"Yes, but what is a girl to do who has no family?" interposed Oblonsky who had been thinking all the time of Masha Chibisov, in agreeing with Pestsov and supporting him.

"If you were to go thoroughly into such a girl's story,

453

you'd find that she had left her family, her own or a sister's, where she might have done a woman's work," said Dolly, breaking unexpectedly into the conversation, in an exasperated tone of voice, no doubt guessing what girl her husband had in mind.

"But we are standing up for a principle, an ideal," Pestsov objected in his sonorous bass. "Women want the right to be independent and educated. They are hampered and oppressed by the consciousness that this is impossible for them."

"And I am hampered and oppressed that they won't give me a job as a wet nurse in a foundling hospital," again said the old prince to the great delight of Turovtsyn, who burst out laughing again, dropping his asparagus with its thick end into the sauce.

CHAPTER 11

All except Kitty and Levin took part in the general conversation. At first, when the influence that one nation has on another was being discussed, thoughts of what he had to say on this subject involuntarily occurred to Levin; but these thoughts, which at one time had been so important to him, seemed to flash through his mind as in a dream and did not have the slightest interest for him. It even seemed strange to him that they were all trying so hard to talk of something that made no difference to anyone. Similarly, what was being said about the rights and education of women should have interested Kitty. How often had she thought about it when she thought of Varenka, her friend abroad, and her painful position of dependence, how often had she thought what would happen to herself if she did not marry and how many times had she argued about it with her sister. But now she was not in the least interested in it. She and Levin were conducting a conversation of their own, and not even a conversation, but a sort of mysterious communion, which every moment bound them closer and closer to one another and aroused in both of them a feeling of joyful terror before the unknown upon which they were entering.

At first Levin, in reply to Kitty's question how he

could have seen her in the carriage last year, told her how he was returning from the haymaking along the highroad and had met her.

"It was very early in the morning. I suppose you must have only just woken up. Your mother was asleep in the corner. It was a glorious morning. I was walking along and wondering who could be in the four-in-hand. Such a splendid team with bells, and you appeared for a moment, I saw you at the window sitting like this and holding the strings of your bonnet with both hands and thinking awfully deeply about something," he said, smiling. "How I wish I knew what you were thinking about then. Something important?"

"I wasn't untidy, was I?" she thought, but seeing the rapturous smile which the recollection of these details evoked, she felt that the impression she had made must have been a very good one. She blushed and laughed joyously.

"I really don't remember."

"What a jolly laugh Turovtsyn has!" said Levin, admiring his glistening eyes and shaking body.

"Have you known him long?" asked Kitty.

"Who does not know him?"

"And I can see you think he's a bad man."

"No, not bad, but worthless."

"Oh, but you're so wrong!" said Kitty. "And don't think of him like that any more, please! I too had a low opinion of him, but he's—he's an awfully nice man and wonderfully kindhearted. He has a heart of gold."

"How could you possibly find out what sort of heart he has?"

"He and I are great friends. I know him very well. Last winter soon after—soon after you came to see us," she said with a guilty and at the same time confiding smile, "Dolly's children all had scarlet fever and he happened to call. And just imagine it," she went on in a whisper, "he felt so sorry for her that he stopped and helped to nurse them. Yes, he stayed three weeks in the house and looked after the children like a nurse.

"I'm telling Konstantin about Turovtsyn and the scarlet fever," she said, leaning over to her sister.

"Yes, it was wonderful! He is a splendid fellow!" said Dolly, looking toward Turovtsyn, who felt that they were talking about him, and gave them a gentle smile.

Levin looked at Turovtsyn again and could not help wondering how he had failed to realize what a splendid fellow he was.

"I'm sorry, I'm sorry, I shall never think ill of people again!" he said gaily, expressing what he genuinely felt at the moment.

CHAPTER 12

In the conversation that had started on the rights of women there were raised some questions concerning the inequalities of rights in marriage that could not very well be discussed in the presence of ladies. During dinner Pestsov touched several times incautiously on these questions, but Koznyshev and Oblonsky carefully steered him away from them.

But when they rose from the table and the ladies had left the room, Pestsov did not follow them, but turned to Karenin and began to expound the chief cause of inequality. In his opinion, the inequality between husband and wife was due to the fact that infidelity of a wife and infidelity of a husband were not punished in the same way either by law or by public opinion.

Oblonsky hurried over to Karenin and offered him a cigar.

"No, thank you, I don't smoke," Karenin replied calmly, and as though deliberately wishing to show that he was not afraid of this subject, he turned to Pestsov with a cold smile.

"I can only assume that the reason for such a view lies in the very nature of things," he said, and was about to walk into the drawing room, but at that moment Turovtsyn suddenly spoke up, addressing Karenin.

"Have you heard about Pryachnikov?" said Turovtsyn, excited by the champagne he had drunk and for a long time waiting for an opportunity to break the silence that had oppressed him. "Poor old Pryachnikov," he said with his good-natured smile on his moist, red lips, addressing himself chiefly to Karenin, the most important guest of the evening, "I've been told today, fought a duel in Tver with Kvytsky and killed him."

As it always seems that, as though on purpose, one

invariably knocks on a sore place, so now Oblonsky felt that, as ill luck would have it, the conversation that evening kept touching Karenin on his sensitive spot. He made another attempt to draw his brother-in-law away, but Karenin himself asked with interest:

"What did Pryachnikov fight about?"

"His wife. Acted like a man. Challenged and killed!"

"Oh!" said Karenin indifferently and, raising his eyebrows, went into the drawing room.

"I'm so glad you came," said Dolly to him with a frightened smile, meeting him in the sitting room through which he had to pass. "I must have a talk with you. Let us sit down here."

Karenin sat down beside Dolly with the same expression of indifference, which his raised eyebrows gave him, and feigned a smile.

"By all means," he said, "particularly as I was about to ask you to excuse me and let me take my leave at once. I'm leaving Moscow tomorrow."

Dolly was firmly convinced of Anna's innocence, and she felt herself going pale and her lips trembling with anger at this cold, unfeeling man who was so calmly determined to ruin her innocent friend.

"I asked you about Anna," she said, looking into his eyes with desperate determination, "and you did not answer me. How is she?"

"I believe she is quite well," replied Karenin without looking at her.

"I'm sorry, I have no right to . . . But I love Anna like a sister and I respect her. I beg, I beseech you to tell me what has happened between you. What do you accuse her of?"

Karenin wrinkled his face, and, almost closing his eyes, bowed his head.

"I suppose your husband has told you the reasons why I consider it necessary to change my former relations with my wife," he said, without looking her in the eyes and glancing with annoyance at Shcherbatsky who was passing through the sitting room.

"I don't, I don't believe it, I can't believe it!" cried Dolly, clasping her bony hands before her with an energetic movement. She got up quickly and put her hand on Karenin's sleeve. "We shall be disturbed here. Let's go in there, please."

Dolly's agitation affected Karenin. He got up and obediently followed her to the schoolroom. They sat down at the table covered with American cloth cut all over by penknives.

"I don't believe it! I don't believe it!" said Dolly, trying to catch his eyes, which avoided her.

"You cannot disbelieve facts, my dear lady," said Karenin, emphasizing the word "facts."

"But what has she done?" asked Dolly. "What is it she has done?"

"She has treated her duties with contempt and been unfaithful to her husband—that's what she has done," he said.

"No, no, it can't be," Dolly said, putting her hands to her temples and closing her eyes. "No, for God's sake, you must be mistaken."

Karenin smiled coldly with his lips only, wishing to prove to her and to himself the firmness of his conviction; but this passionate defense, though it did not shake him, rubbed salt in his wounds. He began to speak with greater animation.

"It is very difficult to make a mistake when a wife herself tells her husband about it. Tells him that eight years of married life and a son have all been a mistake and that she wants to start life afresh," he said angrily, sniffing.

"Anna and vice—I cannot connect the two, I cannot believe it."

"Madam," he said, now looking straight at Dolly's kind, excited face and feeling his tongue involuntarily loosened, "I'd give a great deal still to be able to have any doubts. While I was in doubt, I was unhappy, but I felt better than I do now. While I was in doubt, there was still hope; but now there is no hope left and all the same I doubt everything. I doubt everything so much that I hate my son and sometimes do not believe he is my son. I am very unhappy."

There was no need for him to say that. Dolly had realized it as soon as he looked her in the face; and she felt sorry for him, and her faith in her friend's innocence was shaken.

"Oh, it's dreadful, dreadful! But can it be true that you have decided on a divorce?"

458

"I have decided to take the final step. There is nothing else for me to do."

"Nothing else to do, nothing else to do. . . ." she said with tears in her eyes. "Yes, there is something else to do!" she cried.

"The awful thing about this kind of trouble is that it is impossible to bear one's cross as in any other kind of trouble, such as loss or death, but one just has to act," he said, as though guessing her thought. "One has to get out of the humiliating position in which one is placed. A *ménage à trois* is out of the question."

"I understand, I quite understand," said Dolly, and her head dropped. She paused, thinking of herself, of her own domestic troubles, and suddenly raising her head with an energetic movement, she clasped her hands imploringly. "But wait!" she cried. "You are a Christian. Think of her. What will become of her if you throw her off?"

"I have thought, ma'am, I have thought a lot," said Karenin. His face was covered in red spots and his dull eyes glared at her. Dolly was now sorry for him with all her heart. "I did that very thing when she herself informed me of my disgrace. I left everything as before. I gave her a chance of turning over a new leaf. I did my best to save her. And with what result? She did not comply with the easiest of my demands, the keeping up of appearances," he went on, getting heated. "You can save a person who does not wish to perish. But if a person's whole nature is so corrupt and depraved that ruin itself seems salvation to her, what is one to do?"

"Anything but divorce!" replied Dolly.

"But what is anything?"

"No, this is awful. She will be nobody's wife. She will be ruined."

"But what can I do?" Karenin said, raising his eyebrows and shoulders. The recollection of his wife's last indiscretion so exasperated him that he became as cold as he had been at the beginning of the conversation. "I am very grateful to you for your sympathy, but I'm afraid I must go," he said, getting up.

"No, wait! You must not ruin her. Listen, I will tell you about myself. I was married and my husband deceived me. I was furious and jealous and I was going to give everything up, I wanted to . . . But I came to my senses and who brought me? Anna saved me. And I am carrying on. The children are growing up, my husband is coming back to his family and feels the error and injustice of his ways and is growing purer and better, and I'm carrying on. . . . I have forgiven and you ought to forgive!"

Karenin listened, but her words had no longer any effect on him. All the bitterness of the day when he had decided on a divorce rose up again in his heart. He shook himself and began speaking in a loud, shrill voice.

"Forgive I cannot and do not want to and I don't think it would be just," he said. "I have done everything for that woman and she has trampled everything in the mud, which is natural to her. I am not a spiteful man and I have never hated anyone, but I hate her with all the strength of my soul and I cannot even forgive her because I hate her too much for all the wrong she has done me!" he declared with tears of anger in his voice.

"Love them that hate you . . ." Dolly whispered shamefacedly.

Karenin smiled contemptuously. He had long known all that, but it could not be applied to his case.

"Love them that hate you, but you can't love those you hate. I'm sorry I've upset you. Everyone has troubles enough of his own!" And having recovered his self-control, Karenin calmly bade her good-by and went away.

CHAPTER 13

When they got up from the table Levin wanted to follow Kitty into the drawing room, but he was afraid she would not like it because his attentions to her would be too obvious. He stayed behind with the men, taking part in the general conversation and, without looking at Kitty, was conscious of her movements, her looks, and the place in the drawing room where she happened to be.

He began now, and without the slightest effort, to keep the promise he had made her—always to think well of people and always to love all men. The conversation

460

had turned to the question of village communes, in which Pestsov saw some special principle which he called "the choral principle." Levin did not agree with Pestsov nor with his brother, who in his own curious way seemed to acknowledge and not to acknowledge the significance of the Russian village commune. But he talked to them simply with the idea of getting them to agree and smoothing out their differences. He was not in the least interested in what he was saying himself and still less in what they were saying, and he only wanted one thing: that they and everyone else should be happy and contented. He knew now what was the one important thing. And that was first there in the drawing room, and then it began moving and stopped at the door. Without turning round, he felt a pair of eyes and a smile directed toward him and he could not help turning round. She was standing in the doorway with Shcherbatsky and was looking at him.

"I thought you were going to the piano," he said, walking up to her. "That's the thing I miss in the country, music."

"No, we only came to fetch you and," she added, rewarding him with a smile as with a present, "thank you for coming. What's the use of arguing? They'll never convince one another, anyway."

"Yes, that's true," said Levin. "Mostly you argue heatedly only because you can't make out what your opponent wants to prove."

Levin had often noticed in discussions between the most intelligent people that after tremendous efforts and an immense number of logical subtleties and words, the disputants at last become conscious of the fact that what they had been at such pains to prove to one another had long ago, from the very beginning of the argument, been known to them, but that they liked different things and were therefore loath to mention what they liked best for fear of getting the worst of the argument. He had often experienced the fact that sometimes in the middle of a discussion one grasps what it is that your opponent likes and one suddenly likes it oneself and immediately agrees with him, and then all arguments peter out and become superfluous; sometimes the reverse happened: one says what one likes oneself and for the sake of which one has been devising arguments and if one happens to put one's case sincerely and well, one's opponent will suddenly agree with one and stop arguing. This was what he wanted to express.

She wrinkled her forehead, trying to understand. But the moment he began to explain, she understood at once.

"I see, you have to find out the reason why your opponent is arguing, what he likes, and then you can . . ."

She had completely grasped and put into words his badly expressed idea. Levin smiled with pleasure; he was so struck by the transition from the confused, verbose discussion with his brother and Pestsov to this laconic and clear, almost wordless, in fact, communication of a most complex idea.

Shcherbatsky left them, and Kitty went to a card table, sat down, and picking up a piece of chalk, began to draw spiral circles on the new green cloth.

They resumed the conversation at the dinner table about women's right to freedom and occupations. Levin agreed with Dolly that an unmarried girl could find work in the family. He tried to prove his point by saying that no family can dispense with a help and that in every family, rich or poor, there are and must be nurses, either hired or belonging to the family.

"No," said Kitty, blushing, but looking all the more boldly at him with her truthful eyes, "a girl may find herself in such a position that she cannot enter a family without humiliation, while she herself . . ."

He understood the allusion.

"Oh yes!" he said. "Yes, yes, you are right!"

And he understood everything Pestsov had been trying to prove at dinner about the freedom of women, simply because he glimpsed the terror in Kitty's heart of the humiliation of remaining an old maid and, loving her, he too felt that terror and humiliation and at once gave up his contention.

There was a pause. She went on drawing on the table with the chalk. Her eyes shone with a soft light. Submitting to her mood, he felt in his whole being a continually growing tension of happiness.

"Oh dear, I've scribbled all over the table!" she said and, putting down the chalk, she made a movement as though wishing to get up.

"How can I remain here alone without her?" he

thought with dismay and picked up the chalk. "Wait," he said, sitting down at the table, "I've wanted to ask you something for a long time."

He looked straight into her sweet though frightened eyes.

"Please do."

"Here," he said and he wrote the initial letters: *w, y, t, m: i, c, b, d, y, m, n, o, t?* These letters stood for: "When you told me: it cannot be, did you mean never or then?" There seemed no likelihood that she would be able to make out this complicated sentence: but he looked at her as though his life depended on her understanding what those letters meant.

She glanced seriously at him, then leaned her furrowed forehead on her hand and began to read. Occasionally she looked up at him, asking him with her eyes, "Is it what I think it is?"

"I have understood it," she said, blushing.

"What word is this?" he said, pointing to the *n* which stood for "never."

"This word means 'never,' " she said, "but that's not true."

He quickly rubbed out what he had written, gave her the chalk, and got up. She wrote: *t, I, c, n, a, o.*

Dolly felt completely consoled for the grief caused by her conversation with Karenin when she caught sight of those two figures: Kitty with the chalk in her hand and with a timid and happy smile looking up at Levin, and his handsome figure, bending over the table, his burning eyes fixed now on the table, now on her. He was suddenly radiant: he had understood. It meant: "Then I could not answer otherwise."

He looked at her questioningly, timidly.

"Only then?"

"Yes," her smile replied.

"And *n* . . . And now?" he asked.

"Well, you'd better read. I'm going to say what I wish, what I very much wish!" And she wrote the initial letters: *t, y, c, f, a, f, w, h.* This meant: "That you could forget and forgive what happened."

He seized the chalk with tense, trembling fingers and wrote the first letters of the following sentence: "I have nothing to forget and forgive; I have never ceased to love you."

She looked at him with a smile that did not waver.

"I understand," she said in a whisper.

He sat down and wrote a long sentence. She understood everything and without asking if she was right, took the chalk and at once wrote the answer.

For a long time he could not make out what she had written and kept looking into her eyes. He was dazed with happiness. He could not fill in the words she meant at all; but he understood all he needed to know in her lovely eyes, which shone with happiness. And he wrote down three letters. But before he had finished writing, she read it over his arm and she herself finished it and wrote her reply: "Yes."

"Playing secrétaire?" said the old prince, coming up to them. "But we'd better be going if you want to be in time for the theater."

Levin got up and saw Kitty off to the door.

In their conversation everything had been said: it had been said that she loved him and that she would tell her father and mother that he would call on them in the morning.

CHAPTER 14

When Kitty had gone and Levin was left alone, he felt so restless without her and so impatient a desire for the time to pass quickly, quickly till next morning when he would see her again and have her as his own forever, that he dreaded like death the fourteen hours which he would have to spend without her. He simply had to be and talk with someone in order not to be alone and to kill time. Oblonsky would have been his most agreeable companion, but he was going to an evening party, as he said, though really to the ballet. Levin had just time to tell him that he was happy and that he was fond of him and would never, never forget what he had done for him. Oblonsky's look and smile showed Levin that he interpreted that feeling rightly.

"Well, so it isn't time yet to die, is it?" said Oblonsky, pressing Levin's hand with feeling.

"N-n-n-no!" said Levin.

Dolly, too, when saying good-by to him seemed to congratulate him.

"I'm so glad," she said, "you and Kitty have met again. We must value old friendships."

But Levin resented Dolly's remark. She could not understand how sublime and beyond her it all was, and she should not have dared to mention it. Levin said good-by to them, but, not to remain alone, he attached himself to his brother.

"Where are you going?"

"To a meeting."

"Well, I'll come with you. You don't mind?"

"Why should I? Let's go," said Koznyshev with a smile. "What's the matter with you today?"

"With me? I'm happy!" said Levin, letting down the window of the carriage in which they were driving. "You don't mind, do you? It's so stuffy here. Yes, I'm happy! Why have you never got married?"

Koznyshev smiled.

"I'm very glad," Koznyshev began. "She seems to be a very nice gi—"

"Don't, don't, don't speak!" cried Levin, taking hold of the collar of his brother's fur coat and drawing it over his face. "She is a nice girl" were such ordinary, such common words, so out of tune with his feeling.

Koznyshev laughed gaily, which was a rare occurrence with him.

"But I may say that I'm very glad, mayn't I?"

"You may say it tomorrow, tomorrow, but nothing more now. Nothing, nothing, silence!" said Levin, again wrapping the collar round his brother's face. "I'm very fond of you," he added. "Can I come with you to the meeting?"

"Of course you can."

"What are you debating tonight?" asked Levin, without ceasing to smile.

They arrived at the meeting. Levin listened to the secretary haltingly reading the minutes of the previous meeting, which he did not seem quite to understand himself. But Levin saw from the secretary's face what a nice, kind, splendid fellow he was. That was plain from the nervous and confused way in which he read the minutes. Then the debate followed. They were discussing the assignation of certain sums of money and the laying of some pipes, and Koznyshev offended two members and went on speaking about something for a long time in a triumphant tone of voice, and another member, writing something down on a scrap of paper, stammered at first but went on to answer him very venomously and charmingly. Then Sviazhsky (he, too, was there) also said something very beautifully and nobly. Levin listened to them and saw clearly that neither the assigned sums nor the pipes had any real existence and that they were not at all angry with each other, but were all very kind and splendid fellows and that they conducted their business in a very nice and charming manner. They were not in anyone's way and everybody was pleased. What seemed so remarkable to Levin was that he could see through them all today, and from little signs he had never noticed before he got to know the true character of every one of them and saw distinctly that they were all kindhearted people. They all seemed particularly to be very fond of him, Levin, today. That was obvious from the way they spoke to him and how even those of them he did not know looked at him so affectionately and kindly.

"Well, are you satisfied?" asked Koznyshev.

"Very. I never thought it would be so interesting. Splendid! Excellent!"

Sviazhsky came up and asked Levin to go home with him and have tea. Levin could not for the life of him understand or remember what it was that had made him dissatisfied with Sviazhsky or what he had tried to find in him. He was a clever and a marvelously kindhearted fellow.

"Thank you very much. I shall be glad to," he said, and he asked after his wife and sister-in-law. And by a strange association of ideas, since Sviazhsky's sister-in-law was connected in his mind with the idea of marriage, he imagined that there was no one he could tell of his happiness more appropriately than Sviazhsky's wife and sister-in-law, and he was very glad to go and see them.

Sviazhsky questioned him about how he was getting on in the country and, as always, assuming that there was no possibility of doing anything that had not already been done in Europe, but Levin did not mind that in the least. On the contrary, he felt that Sviazhsky was right, that the whole business was of no consequence, and he was conscious of the wonderful gentleness and delicacy with which Sviazhsky avoided gloating over the fact that he had been right all along. The Sviazhsky ladies were particularly charming. It seemed to Levin that they already knew all about it and were glad of his happiness, but said nothing out of delicacy. He stayed with them an hour, two hours, three hours, talking of all sorts of things but thinking only of the one thing that filled his heart and never noticed that they were sick and tired of him and that it was long past their bedtime. Sviazhsky saw him off to the front door, yawning and wondering at the strange state his friend was in. It was past one o'clock. Levin went back to his hotel and was terrified at the thought that he was alone now with his impatience and did not know how to spend the remaining ten hours. The servant on duty lighted his candles and was about to leave the room, but Levin detained him. The servant, Yegor, whom Levin had never noticed before, appeared to be a very intelligent, good, and above all, kindhearted fellow.

"I say, Yegor, do you find it difficult to keep awake?"

"It can't be helped, sir. That's my job. Private service is easier, but you earn more here."

It appeared that Yegor had a family, three boys and a daughter, a seamstress, whom he wished to marry to an assistant in a harness-maker's establishment.

Levin took this opportunity of informing Yegor that in his opinion love was the main thing in marriage, and that where there is love there is always happiness, because happiness lies only within oneself.

Yegor listened to him very attentively and apparently fully grasped Levin's idea, but in confirmation of this remarked rather surprisingly for Levin that when he was in the service of nice people, he was always satisfied with his masters and that even now he was perfectly satisfied with his master, though he was a Frenchman.

"What a remarkably good fellow he is," thought Levin.

"Well, and you, Yegor, when you got married did you love your wife?"

"Why, of course, sir! Why shouldn't I love her?" replied Yegor.

467

And Levin could see that Yegor, too, was in an exalted state and was about to tell him his most intimate feelings.

"My life, too, sir, was very remarkable. From a child I . . ." he began, with shining eyes, evidently infected by Levin's exalted mood as people get infected with yawning.

But at that moment a bell rang; Yegor went out and Levin was left alone. He had scarcely eaten anything at dinner, had refused tea and supper at Sviazhsky's, but could not think of eating. He had not slept the night before, but he could not think of sleeping. It was cool in his room, but he felt suffocated with heat. He opened both ventilation windows and sat down at a table opposite them. Beyond a snow-covered roof he could see a gilt fretwork cross adorned with chains and above it the rising triangle of the Charioteer and bright yellow Capella. He looked now at the cross, now at the star, inhaled the fresh frosty currents of air which flowed regularly into the room, and, as in a dream, followed the images and memories that rose up in his mind. Toward four o'clock he heard steps in the corridor, and looked out of the door. It was the gambler Myaskin, whom he knew, returning from the club. He walked gloomily, scowling and coughing. "Poor fellow!" thought Levin, and tears started to his eyes from love and pity for that man. He wanted to speak to him, to comfort him, but remembering that he had nothing on but his shirt, changed his mind and sat down again in front of the open window to bathe in the cold air and gaze at that wonderfully shaped, silent cross, which was so full of meaning for him, and the rising bright yellow star. Soon after six o'clock he heard the floor polishers begin their work, church bells began ringing for service, and Levin felt that he was beginning to shiver. He shut the ventilation window, washed, dressed, and went out into the street.

CHAPTER 15

The streets were still empty. Levin walked toward the house of the Shcherbatskys. The front door was locked and everyone was still asleep. He went back to his hotel, went into his room, and ordered coffee. A day waiter, not Yegor this time, brought it to him. Levin was about to enter into conversation with him, but a bell rang and the waiter had to go. Levin tried to drink his coffee and take a bite of his roll, but his mouth did not seem to know what to do with it. Levin spat out the roll, put on his overcoat, and went out to walk about the streets again. It was past nine when he found himself again outside the Shcherbatskys' front door. In the house they had only just got up and the chef was going out shopping. He had to get through at least two more hours.

All that night and morning Levin had lived unconsciously and felt completely withdrawn from the conditions of material existence. He had not eaten for a whole day, he had not slept for two nights, had spent several hours undressed and exposed to the frost, yet he felt not only fresher and healthier than ever, but quite independent of his body. He moved without any effort of his muscles and felt that he could do anything. He was sure that, if necessary, he could fly upward or lift the corner of a house. He spent the rest of the time walking about the streets, continually looking at his watch and gazing all about him.

And what he then saw, he never saw again. He was moved particularly by the children going to school, the grayish-blue pigeons flying from the roofs to the pavement, and the little loaves of bread, sprinkled with flour, that some invisible hand had put outside a baker's shop. These loaves, the pigeons, and the boys were not of this world. It all happened at the same time: one of the boys ran up to a pigeon and, smiling, looked at Levin; the pigeon fluttered its wings and flew away, glittering in the sunshine among the quivering specks of snow in the air; and from the window of the baker's shop came the smell of hot bread and the loaves were put out. All this together was so extraordinarily nice that Levin laughed and cried with joy. After making a big detour round Gazetny Lane and Kislovka, he went back to the hotel again and, putting his watch in front of him, sat down to wait till it should be twelve. In the next room he could hear people talking about some machines and fraud and coughing as people do in the morning. They did not seem to realize that the watch hand was drawing near to twelve. The hand reached twelve. Levin went out of the hotel. The cabbies evidently knew all about it. They surrounded Levin with happy faces, disputing among themselves and offering Levin their services. Trying not to offend the others, he chose one, promising the rest to hire them another time. He told his cabby to drive to the Shcherbatskys'. The cabby looked marvelous with the white band of his shirt showing from under his coat and fitting tightly around his thick, red, sturdy neck. His sledge was high and comfortable, and never after did Levin drive in one like it, and the horse was wonderful, too, and tried its best to go fast but did not move from its place. The cabby knew the Shcherbatskys' house and, rounding his elbows in a way that was meant to be especially respectful to his fare and crying "Whoa!," he drove up to the front door. The Shcherbatskys' hall porter quite certainly knew all about it. Levin could see it from the smile in his eyes and from the way he said:

"It's a long time since you were here last, sir."

But he not only knew all about it, he quite evidently rejoiced at it and had to make an effort to conceal his joy. Glancing into his sweet, aged eyes, Levin became conscious of something new even in his own happiness.

"Are they up?"

"Yes, sir. This way, sir. Leave it here, please," he said, smiling, when Levin came back for his cap. That did mean something.

"Whom shall I announce you to, sir?" asked a footman.

The footman, though a young man and of the new school of footmen, a bit of a fop, was really a very good-hearted and excellent fellow and he, too, knew all about it.

"The prince . . . the princess . . . the young princess . . ." said Levin.

The first person he met was Mademoiselle Linon. She was passing through the ballroom, and her ringlets and her face shone with happiness. He had scarcely had time to say a few words to her when he heard the rustle of a skirt behind the door and Mademoiselle Linon vanished from his sight and he was overcome by the thrilling dismay of the nearness of his happiness. Mademoiselle Linon hurriedly left him and went to the other door. As soon as she had gone out, he heard the sound of very, very rapid light footsteps over the parquet floor, and his happiness, his life, his own self—his better self, which he had sought and yearned for so long—came rapidly toward him. She did not walk but was borne along by some invisible force.

He saw only her clear, truthful eyes, terrified by the same happiness of love which filled his own heart too. Those shining eyes drew nearer and nearer to him, dazzling him with their light of love. She stopped so close to him that she touched him. Her arms rose and her hands dropped on his shoulders.

She had done everything she could—she had run up to him and surrendered to him entirely, shyly and joyfully. He embraced her, pressed his lips to her mouth that sought his kiss.

She too had not slept all night and had been waiting for him all the morning. Her mother and father had given their unqualified consent and were happy with her happiness. She had been looking out for him. She wanted to be the first to tell him of her happiness and his. She had been preparing herself to meet him alone and had rejoiced at the idea, and had felt timid and abashed, and had not known herself what she would do. She had heard his footsteps and his voice, and had waited at the door for Mademoiselle Linon to go. Mademoiselle Linon had gone away. Without thinking or asking herself why and wherefore, she had gone up to him and acted as she had.

"Let us go to Mother," she said, taking him by the hand.

For a long time he could not say anything, not so much because he was afraid of spoiling the loftiness of his emotion by his words as because every time he wanted to say something he felt that instead of words, tears of happiness would gush out of his eyes. He took her hand and kissed it.

"Is it really true?" he said at last in a flat voice. "I can't believe you love me, darling!"

She smiled at the word "darling" and at the timid look he gave her.

"Yes!" she said significantly and slowly. "I am so happy!"

Without letting go of his hand, she went into the drawing room. The princess began breathing rapidly on seeing them and immediately began to cry, then immediately began to laugh and ran up to them with a vigorous step Levin had not expected, and putting her arms around Levin's head, kissed him and wetted his cheeks with her tears.

"So it's all settled! I am glad. Love her. I am glad. . . . Kitty!"

"Settled it quickly, haven't you?" said the old prince, trying to look indifferent; but Levin noticed that his eyes were moist when he turned to him.

"I have long, I've always wished it!" the old prince went on, taking Levin's hand and drawing him nearer. "Even at the time when this scatterbrain thought of—"

"Father!" cried Kitty, closing his mouth with her hands.

"All right, I won't!" he said. "I'm very, very gl— Oh, how silly I am!"

He embraced Kitty, kissed her face, her hand, then her face again and made the sign of the cross over her.

And Levin was seized with a new feeling of affection for this man, the old prince, who had been a stranger to him before, when he watched Kitty kissing his big hand long and tenderly.

CHAPTER 16

The princess sat in her armchair, silent and smiling; the old prince sat down beside her. Kitty stood by her father's chair, still holding his hand. They were all silent.

The princess was the first to put everything into words and bring all their thoughts and feelings back to the practical side of life. And at first this seemed rather strange and painful to them all.

"When is it to be? We shall have to have an engagement and announce it. And when's the wedding to be? What do you think, Alexander?"

"Here he is," said the prince, pointing to Levin. "He is the principal person concerned."

"When?" said Levin, blushing. "Tomorrow. If you ask me, the official engagement today and the wedding tomorrow."

"Well, really, my dear! What nonsense!"

"All right then. In a week's time."

"He seems quite mad."

"But why not?"

"But, good heavens," said the mother, with a pleased smile at this haste, "and what about the trousseau?"

"There's not going to be a trousseau and all that?" thought Levin with horror. "However, a trousseau, an engagement, and all that cannot spoil my happiness, can it? Nothing can spoil it!" And he glanced at Kitty and noticed that she did not in the least resent the idea of a trousseau. "Then it must be necessary," he thought.

"You see, I don't know anything," he said by way of an apology. "I merely expressed my wish."

"We'll talk it over then. We can have the engagement and make the announcement now. That will be all right."

The princess went up to her husband, kissed him, and was about to go out of the room, but he detained her and, embracing her tenderly, like a young lover, kissed her smilingly several times. The two old people were evidently a little confused for a moment and did not know very well whether it was they who were again in love or their daughter. When the prince and the princess had gone, Levin went up to his fiancée and took her hand. He had now regained control of himself and was able to speak, and he had a great deal to say to her. But what he said was not at all what he had intended.

"How well I knew that it would happen!" he said. "I never really hoped, but at heart I was always sure. I believe it was predestined."

"And I," she said "Even when . . ." She paused and then went on, looking resolutely at him with her truthful eyes. "Even when I pushed my happiness away from me. I never loved anyone but you, but I—I was infatuated. I must say that. Can you forget it?"

"Perhaps it was all for the best. You have much to forgive me. I must tell you . . ."

It was one of the things he had decided to tell her. He had made up his mind from the very first to tell her two things, that he was not as pure as she and, secondly, that he was not a believer. It was painful, but he considered he ought to tell her both these things.

"No, not now, later," he said.

"All right, later. But you must certainly tell me. I'm not afraid of anything. I have to know everything. Now it is settled."

He finished what she wanted to say:

"It is settled that you will have me, whatever I may be. You won't give me up, will you?"

"No, I won't."

Their conversation was interrupted by Mademoiselle Linon, who with an artificial but affectionate smile came in to congratulate her favorite pupil. Before she had gone out, the servants came in to offer their congratulations. Then relatives arrived and that blissful confusion began which went on till the day after the wedding. Levin continually felt uncomfortable and bored, but his happiness went on increasing in intensity all the time. All that time he felt that many things he did not know were expected of him, and he did everything he was told, and it all made him feel happy. He had thought that his courtship would be unlike any other courtship, that the ordinary conditions of an engagement would spoil his peculiar happiness; but in the end he did what others do and this only increased his happiness, becoming more and more peculiar to himself and less and less like anyone else's.

"Now we shall have some sweets," Mademoiselle Linon would say, and Levin went off to buy sweets.

"Well, congratulations," said Sviazhsky. "I'd advise you to get your flowers from Fomin's."

"Oh, are they necessary?" And he went to Fomin's.

His brother told him he ought to borrow some money because there would be a great many expenses, presents . . .

"Are presents necessary?" And he galloped off to buy jewelry from Fulde's.

And at the confectioner's, at Fomin's, at Fulde's, he saw that they were expecting him, that they were pleased to see him, rejoiced in his happiness, just like anyone else with whom he had to do during those days. The extraordinary thing was that everyone not only liked him, but that people who had before been unfriendly, cold, and indifferent, admired him, tried to do whatever he wished, treated his feelings with delicate consideration and shared his conviction that he was the happiest man in the world because his fiancée was the height of perfection. Kitty felt the same. When the Countess Nordston ventured to hint that she had hoped for something better, Kitty grew so excited and proved so convincingly that nothing in the world could be better than Levin that the countess had to admit it and never again failed to greet Levin in Kitty's presence without a rapturous smile.

The explanation he had promised her was the one painful episode of that time. He consulted the old prince and, receiving his permission, gave Kitty the diary in which he had put down the things that were tormenting him. He had, in fact, written that diary with the intention of showing it to his future fiancée. He was worried by two things: his lack of chastity and his lack of faith. The confession of his unbelief passed unnoticed. She was religious and had never doubted the truths of her religion, but his outward unbelief did not affect her in the least. She knew through her love his whole soul and in it she saw what she wanted and it did not matter to her that such a condition of the soul was known as agnosticism. But his other confession made her weep bitterly.

Levin had handed her his diary not without an inner struggle. He knew that there could and must not be any secrets between him and her, and therefore he had decided that it was his duty; but he did not realize the effect it would have on her, he had not put himself in her place. It was only when he called that evening before going to the theater, went into her room, and saw in her tear-stained, sweet, pathetic face the unhappiness caused by the irremediable sorrow he had brought about that he realized what a gulf separated his shameful past from her dovelike purity and was horrified by what he had done.

"Take away, take away these horrible books!" she said, pushing away the notebooks that lay on the table before her. "Why did you give them to me? No," she added, moved to pity by the despair on his face, "it's better, after all. But this is dreadful, dreadful!"

He hung his head and was silent. He could not say anything.

"You won't forgive me, will you?" he whispered.

"Yes, I have forgiven you, but it is dreadful!"

However, his happiness was so great that this confession did not mar it, but merely added another shade to it. She forgave him; but since then he considered himself more than ever unworthy of her, morally bowed still lower before her, and prized still more highly his undeserved happiness.

CHAPTER 17

Involuntarily reviewing the impressions left on his mind by the conversations at dinner and after, Karenin was returning to his solitary hotel room. Dolly's remark about forgiveness had merely annoyed him. Whether or not the Christian principle was applicable to his own case was too difficult a question to be discussed lightly, and Karenin had long since answered it in the negative. Of all that had been said, the words of the silly, good-natured Turovtsyn had stuck most in his mind: *"He acted like a man. Challenged and killed."* They all had apparently agreed with it, though they had not said so out of politeness.

"However, the thing's settled and it's no use thinking about it," Karenin said to himself. And thinking only about his impending journey and his work of inspection, he went into his room and asked the doorkeeper, who followed him, where his valet was. The doorkeeper replied that the valet had just gone out. Karenin ordered tea, sat down at a table, took up a railway timetable, and began planning his itinerary.

"Two telegrams, sir," said the valet, coming into the room. "Excuse me, sir, I had only just gone out."

Karenin took the telegrams and opened them. The first telegram contained the news that Stremov had been appointed to the very post Karenin had hoped to get himself. Karenin threw down the telegram, got up and began pacing the room. *"Quos vult perdere dementat,"* he said, by *quos* meaning those who had had a hand in making this appointment. What annoyed him was not so much the fact that he had not got that post, that he had been quite obviously passed over, as the incomprehensible and remarkable fact that those people did not realize that that windbag and phrasemonger Stremov was less suitable than anyone else for such a post. How was it they did not see that they were ruining themselves, their own prestige, by this appointment?

"Something else of the same kind, I suppose," he said to himself bitterly, opening the second telegram. It was from his wife. The signature "Anna," written in blue pencil, was the first word that caught his eye. "I am dying. I beg, I beseech you to come. I shall die easier with your forgiveness," he read. He smiled contemptuously and threw down the telegram. That it was a trick, an attempt to deceive him, he had no doubt whatever at the first moment.

"There is no deception she would not try out. I suppose she is going to have her baby now. Childbirth pains probably. But what can be their object? Legitimize the child, compromise me, and prevent a divorce," he thought. "But it says something about dying. . . ." He reread the telegram, and then was suddenly struck by the plain meaning of what it said. "And what if it is true?" he said to himself. "If it is true that at the moment of suffering and the nearness of death she is sincerely repentant and I, believing it to be a trick, refuse to go? It would not only be cruel and everyone would condemn me, but it would be sheer stupidity on my part."

"Peter, keep the carriage," he said to his valet. "I'm going to Petersburg."

Karenin decided that he would go to Petersburg and see his wife. If her illness was a trick, he would say nothing and go away again. If she was really ill and dying and wished to see him before her death, he would forgive her if she was still alive, and perform his last duty to her if he arrived too late.

On his way back he thought no more about what he should do.

Feeling tired and dirty after a night spent in the train, Karenin drove through the mist of a Petersburg morning along the empty Nevsky Avenue, staring straight before him and not thinking of what awaited him. He could not bring himself to think of it because when he imagined what would happen, he could not dismiss the thought that her death would at one stroke resolve the difficulty of his position. Bakers, closed shops, night cabmen, house porters sweeping the pavements, flashed by before his eyes, and he watched it all, trying to stifle the thought of what awaited him and what he dared not hope for but was still hoping for. He drove up to the front door. A cab and a private carriage with a coachman asleep on the box stood at the entrance. As he entered the hall, Karenin seemed to drag his decision out of a remote corner of his brain and finally made up his mind to stick to it. It was: "If it is a trick, then calm contempt and depart. If it is true, observe the rules of propriety."

The door was opened by the hall porter before Karenin had time to ring. The porter, Petrov, otherwise Kapitonich, looked strange in an old coat without a tie and in slippers.

"How is your mistress?"

"Safely delivered yesterday."

Karenin stopped dead and turned pale. He clearly realized now how intensely he had desired her death.

"And how is she?"

Korney, in his morning apron, came running down the stairs.

"Very bad," he answered. "There was a consultation yesterday and the doctor is here now."

"Take my things," said Karenin, and feeling slightly relieved at the news that there was still some hope of her dying, he entered the hall.

A military coat was hanging on the hall stand. Karrenin noticed it and asked:

"Who is here?"

"The doctor, the midwife, and Count Vronsky."

Karenin walked into the inner rooms.

There was no one in the drawing room; at the sound of his footsteps the midwife came out of Anna's sitting room in a cap with lilac ribbons.

She went up to Karenin and with the familiarity of the nearness of death took him by the hand and led him to the bedroom.

"Thank God you've come!" she said. "She only talks about you, all about you."

"Quick, some more ice!" came the doctor's peremptory voice from the bedroom.

Karenin went into her sitting room. By her writing table, sitting sideways on a low chair, was Vronsky, his face buried in his hands, crying. He jumped up at the doctor's voice, took his hands from his face, and saw Karenin. At the sight of her husband he was filled with such confusion that he sat down again, drawing his head between his shoulders, as if wishing to disappear somewhere; but he made an effort over himself, got up, and said:

"She's dying. The doctors say there is no hope. I'm entirely in your hands, but please let me be here. . . . However, I am in your hands, I . . ."

At the sight of Vronsky's tears, Karenin felt the onrush of that emotional upset that the sufferings of others always produced in him and, turning away his face, he went quickly to the door without waiting to hear the end of what Vronsky was saying. From the bedroom came the voice of Anna, who was talking rapidly. Her voice was gay, animated with extremely distinct intonations. Karenin walked into the bedroom and went up to the bed. She lay with her face turned towards him. Her cheeks were flushed, her eyes glittered, and her little white hands, thrust out from the cuffs of her dressing jacket, toyed with the corner of the blanket and kept twisting it about. She seemed to be not only in excellent health, but in the best of spirits. She was talking rapidly, in a ringing voice, with extraordinarily correct intonations and full of feeling.

"For, you see, Alexey, I am speaking of my husband— how funny and how terrible that they should both be called Alexey, isn't it?—Alexey would not refuse me. . . . But why doesn't he come? He is kind, he himself does not know how kind he is. Oh dear, what agony! Give me some water, quick! Oh, but it would be bad for her, for my little girl! Oh, all right, get a wet nurse for her. Yes, I agree. It's much better so. He will come and it will hurt him to see her. Give her away."

"He has come, ma'am! Here he is!" the midwife said, trying to draw her attention to Karenin.

"Oh, what nonsense!" Anna went on, not seeing her husband. "But give her to me. Give my little girl to me! He has not come yet. You say he won't forgive me because you don't know him. No one knew him. I alone did, and even for me it was painful. His eyes. One must know his eyes. Seryozha's are just the same, and that's why I can't bear to see them. Has Seryozha had his dinner? You see, I know they'll all forget. He would not forget. Seryozha must be moved into the corner room and Mariette must be asked to sleep with him."

All of a sudden she shrank back, lay silent, and in terror, as though expecting a blow and, as though in self-defense, raised her hands before her face. She had seen her husband.

"No, no," she began, speaking rapidly. "I'm not afraid of him. I'm afraid of death. Alexey, come here. I'm in a hurry because I have no time. I haven't much longer to live. I shall get feverish again in a minute and I shan't understand anything any more. Now I understand. I understand everything. I see everything."

A look of suffering came over Karenin's drawn face. He took her hand and was about to say something, but he could not utter a word. His lower lip quivered, but he was still struggling with his agitation and only now and then glanced at her. And every time he glanced at her he saw her eyes looking at him with such tender and ecstatic emotion as he had never seen in them before.

"Wait, you don't know. . . . Wait a minute, wait a minute. . . ." She paused, as though trying to collect her thoughts. "Yes," she began. "Yes, yes, yes. This is what I wanted to say. Don't be surprised at me. I am still the same. . . . But there is another person in me and I am afraid of her. It was she who fell in love with that man, and I wanted to hate you, and I could not forget her—the woman I was before. That one is not me. I am the real one now, all of me. I'm dying now. I know I'm going to die. You ask him. I feel it already now. My hands, and feet, and fingers—it's as if there were enormous weights on them. Look at my fingers—see how huge they are! But it will soon be over. . . . I only want one thing—I want you to forgive me, forgive me completely! I'm terribly wicked, but my nurse used to tell me: a holy martyr—what was her name?—she was much worse. And I'll go to Rome, too—there's a wilderness there, and I shan't be in anybody's way. Only I shall take Seryozha and the little girl with me. . . . No, you can't forgive me! I know this can't be forgiven! No, no! Go away! You're too good." With one burning hand she held his and with the other she kept pushing him away.

Karenin's distress was growing stronger and stronger

till it had reached a point when he gave up struggling against it; he suddenly felt that what he had thought was an emotional upset was, on the contrary, a blissful state of his soul that suddenly gave him a new happiness he had never known before. It never occurred to him that the Christian law which he had been wishing to follow all his life ordered him to forgive and love his enemies; but a joyous feeling of love and forgiveness of his enemies filled his soul. He knelt down and laying his hand in the bend of her arm, which burned through the sleeve of her jacket like fire, he sobbed like a child. She put her arm round his bald head, moved closer to him, and raised her head with a look of proud defiance.

"There, I knew! Now good-by, good-by all! They've come again. Why don't they go away? Oh, take these furs off me!"

The doctor put her arms back on the bed, carefully laid her back on the pillows, and covered her shoulders. She lay down obediently on her back, gazing with shining eyes straight before her.

"Remember one thing: I only wanted your forgiveness. I want nothing more. Why doesn't *he* come?" she cried, turning to Vronsky at the door. "Come here, come here. Give him your hand!"

Vronsky went up to the side of the bed and, seeing Anna, buried his face in his hands again.

"Uncover your face and look at him. He's a saint!" she said. "Yes, yes, uncover your face!" she cried crossly. "Alexey, uncover his face. I want to see him."

Karenin took Vronsky's hands and drew them away from his face, which looked terribly distorted with suffering and shame.

"Give him your hand. Forgive him."

Karenin held out his hand, without restraining the tears that streamed down his face.

"Thank God, thank God," she cried, "now everything is ready. Just stretch out my legs a little. So—now it's lovely. How badly those flowers are drawn," she went on, pointing to the wallpaper. "Not a bit like violets. Dear, oh dear, when will it all end? Doctor, give me some morphia. Give me some morphia. Oh God, oh God!"

And she began tossing about in the bed.

*　　*　　*

481

The doctor and his colleagues said it was puerperal fever, which in ninety-nine cases out of a hundred was fatal. All day she ran a high temperature and she was delirious and unconscious. At midnight she was in a coma and with hardly any pulse.

The end was expected every moment.

Vronsky went home, but he returned in the morning to find out how she was.

"Won't you stay?" said Karenin, who had met him in the hall. "She may ask for you," and himself led him into his wife's room.

Toward morning again agitation, excitement, rapidity of thought and speech, and once more a lapse into unconsciousness. On the third day it was the same and the doctors said there was hope. That day Karenin came into Anna's room where Vronsky was sitting, closed the door, and sat down opposite him.

"Please," said Vronsky, who felt that Karenin was intending to have it out with him. "I'm unable to speak, I'm unable to understand. Spare me. However painful it is for you, believe me, it is much more terrible for me."

He was about to get up, but Karenin took him by the hand and said:

"I beg you to listen to what I have to say. It is necessary that you should. I must explain to you my feelings, the feelings that have guided me and will guide me in the future, so that you may not misunderstand me. You know I had decided on a divorce and had even begun proceedings. I will not conceal from you that at first I was in two minds about it and was greatly distressed. I tell you frankly that I was motivated by a desire to revenge myself on you and on her. When I got the telegram, I came here with the same feelings, and indeed more than that: I wished for her death. But," he paused, wondering whether or not to reveal his feelings to him, "I saw her and I forgave. And the happiness of forgiving showed me where my duty lay. I have forgiven her completely. I want to turn the other cheek, I want to give my shirt if my cloak is taken, and I only pray to God not to take from me the joy of forgiving!" There were tears in his eyes and Vronsky was struck by their bright and calm expression. "That is my position," he went on. "You may trample me in the mire, you may make me the laughingstock of the world, I will not forsake her

482

and I shall never utter a word of reproach to you. My duty is clear to me: I must and I will remain with her. If she wishes to see you, I shall let you know, but now, I think, it will be best for you to leave."

He got up, and sobs choked his voice. Vronsky, too, got up, and stooping and without unbending his back, gazed sullenly at him. He did not understand Karenin's outlook on life; that was quite beyond him and, in fact, utterly inaccessible to him.

CHAPTER 18

After his talk with Karenin, Vronsky went out on the front steps and stopped, trying with difficulty to remember where he was and where he had to go. He felt ashamed, humiliated, guilty, and deprived of the chance of washing away his humiliation. He felt kicked out of the normal way of life he had hitherto trodden so proudly and lightly. Everything that seemed so firmly established, all the rules and habits of his life, suddenly turned out to be false and inapplicable. The deceived husband, whom he had in the past regarded as a pitiful creature, an incidental and rather ridiculous obstacle to his happiness, had suddenly been summoned by herself, raised to an awe-inspiring pinnacle, and that husband of hers had shown himself on that pinnacle to be not vindictive, false, or ludicrous, but kind, simple, and dignified. Vronsky could not help being aware of it. They had suddenly exchanged roles. Vronsky felt Karenin's greatness and his own humiliation; he felt that Karenin was right and he was wrong; he felt that the husband was magnanimous in his grief, while he was despicable and mean in his deceptions. But this consciousness of his own mean treatment of the man he had unjustly despised was only a small part of his distress. He was terribly unhappy now because his passion for Anna, which he believed had of late begun to cool, had become stronger now that he knew he had lost her forever. During her illness he had learned to know her thoroughly, to see into her very soul, and it seemed to him that he had never loved her before. And it was now when he had got to know her so well and to love her as she should be loved, that he had been humiliated before her and lost her forever, leaving her nothing but a shameful memory of himself. Most horrible of all was the ridiculous and shameful figure he had cut when Karenin pulled his hands away from his face, which was burning with shame. He stood on the steps of the Karenins' house, looking lost and not knowing what to do.

"Shall I call a cab for you, sir?"

"Yes, do."

On returning home after three sleepless nights, Vronsky flung himself full-length on the sofa, his head on his folded hands. His head was heavy. The strangest images, memories, and thoughts followed each other with extraordinary rapidity and distinctness: one moment he saw himself pouring out medicine for the patient and spilling some of it, then he saw the midwife's white hands, then Karenin's queer position on the floor beside the bed.

"To sleep! To forget!" he said to himself, with the calm assurance of a healthy man that if he is tired and sleepy he will fall asleep at once. And, to be sure, the instant his thoughts became confused, he began to sink into the abyss of oblivion. The waves of the sea of unconscious life began to close over his head when suddenly, just as though he had received a violent electric shock, he gave a start so that his whole body leaped upward on the springs of the sofa and, leaning on his hands, he jumped to his knees in terror. His eyes were wide open as though he had not slept at all. The heaviness of his head and the limpness of his limbs, of which he had been conscious a minute before, had suddenly vanished.

"You may trample me into the mire," he heard Karenin's words; and he saw him before him, saw Anna's face, with its flushed cheeks and glittering eyes, looking with tenderness and love not at him, but at Karenin; he saw his own, as he imagined, stupid and ridiculous figure when Karenin took his hands away from his face. He stretched out his legs again, flung himself on the sofa in the same position as before, and closed his eyes.

"To sleep! To sleep!" he repeated to himself. But with his eyes closed he could see more distinctly than ever Anna's face as it had been on that memorable evening before the races.

"All that is at an end and it will never be again, and she wants to erase it from her memory. But I can't live without it. But how can we be reconciled? How can we be reconciled?" he said aloud and began unconsciously repeating these words. This repetition of the words prevented other images and memories, which he felt thronging his head, from arising. But the repetition of those words did not long keep his imagination in check. Again, following each other with extraordinary rapidity, his happiest moments rose in his mind and with them his recent humiliation. "Take away his hands," Anna's voice says. He takes away his hands and becomes aware of the look of shame and stupidity on his face.

He still lay, trying to fall asleep, though he felt that there was not the slightest hope of it, and kept repeating in a whisper random words of some thought, hoping that by doing so he might prevent other images from arising in his head. He listened intently and he heard repeated again and again in a strange and insane whisper the words: "Didn't know how to appreciate, didn't know how to make use of your opportunity. . . . Didn't know how to appreciate, didn't know how to make use of your opportunity. . . ."

"What is this? Am I going off my head?" he said to himself. "Perhaps I am. What else makes people go mad? What else makes them shoot themselves?" he replied to his own questions and, opening his eyes, he was surprised to see near his head a cushion, embroidered by Varya, his brother's wife. He touched the tassel of the cushion and tried to think of Varya and when he had last seen her. But it was agonizing to think of anything that had nothing to do with his present feelings. "No, I must sleep!" He moved the cushion towards him and pressed his head against it, but he had to make an effort to keep his eyes closed. He jumped up and sat down. "This is finished for me," he said to himself. "I must think what to do. What is there left?" He rapidly surveyed in his mind what there was in his life apart from his love of Anna.

"Ambition? Serpukhovskoy? Society? The Court?" There was nothing that interested him there. They had all had a meaning for him once, but now he no longer cared for any of it. He got up from the sofa, took off his coat, loosened his belt, and, baring his shaggy chest to breathe more freely, began pacing the room. "That's the way to go mad," he repeated. "That's how one shoots oneself so as not—not to be ashamed," he added slowly.

He went up to the door and locked it; then with staring eyes and tightly clenched teeth he approached the table, picked up his revolver, examined it, turned it to a loaded chamber, and sank into thought. For two minutes he stood motionless with bowed head, an expression of a strained effort of thought on his face, holding the revolver in his hand and thinking. "Of course," he said to himself, as though a logical, prolonged, and clear-cut trend of thought brought him to an obvious conclusion. In reality, however, that irrefutable "Of course" was merely the outcome of the repetition of exactly the same round of images and memories he had already gone over dozens of times in the last hour. They were the same memories of happiness that were now lost forever, the same sense of the meaninglessness of everything that he might still hope from life, the same consciousness of his own humiliation, and all of them followed in the same sequence of images and feelings.

"Of course," he repeated when for the third time his thought began running round in the same vicious circle of memories and ideas and, putting the revolver to the left side of his chest and with a strong wrench of his whole hand as if to clench his fist, he pulled the trigger. He did not hear the sound of a shot, but a violent blow on his chest knocked him off his feet. He tried to hold onto the edge of the table, dropped the revolver, swayed and sat down on the floor, looking about him in astonishment. He did not recognize his room as he looked up at the curved legs of the table, the wastepaper basket and the tiger-skin rug. The quick, squeaking steps of his servant, coming through the drawing room, brought him to his senses. He made an effort to think and realized that he was on the floor and, seeing the blood on the tiger skin and on his hand, realized that he had tried to shoot himself.

"Stupid! . . . Missed!" he said, feeling with his hand for the revolver. The revolver was close to him, but he looked for it further away. Still looking for it, he stretched over to the other side and, unable to keep his balance, fell, bleeding profusely.

The elegant servant with side whiskers, who more than once complained to his friends of the weakness of his nerves, was so terrified at the sight of his master lying on the floor that he left him to bleed to death and ran for help. An hour later Varya, his brother's wife, arrived and with the aid of three doctors, whom she had summoned from every quarter, and who all arrived at the same time, got the wounded man to bed and remained to nurse him.

CHAPTER 19

The miscalculation Karenin had made when, preparing to meet his wife, he had not thought of the possibility that her repentance might be sincere and that he might forgive her, and she might not die—this miscalculation presented itself to him in all its force two months after his return from Moscow. But the miscalculation he had made had arisen not only because he had failed to consider this contingency, but also because up to the very day when he saw his dying wife he had not known his own heart. . . . By his sick wife's bedside he had for the first time in his life given way to that feeling of deep-felt compassion which the suffering of other people aroused in him and which he had hitherto been ashamed of as a harmful weakness; and pity for her, and remorse at having wished her death, and above all, the very joy of forgiving made him suddenly feel not only relief from his own sufferings, but peace of mind such as he had never experienced before. He suddenly felt that what had been the source of his sufferings had become the source of his spiritual joy and that what had seemed insoluble when he condemned, reproached, and hated had become clear and simple when he forgave and loved.

He forgave his wife and pitied her for her sufferings and remorse. He forgave Vronsky and pitied him, especially when reports of Vronsky's desperate action reached him. He pitied his son, too, more than he had in the past, and reproached himself for having paid so little attention to him. But for the newborn little baby girl he had a sort of special feeling not only of pity but also of tenderness. At first it was only his feeling of pity that made him turn his attention to the delicate little girl, who was not his child and had been so badly neglected during her mother's illness that she would certainly have died had he not taken care of her, and he did not notice himself how he grew to love her. Several times a day he went to the nursery, and he used to sit there so long that the wet nurse and the nurse, who were at first abashed by his presence, became quite used to him. Sometimes he would sit gazing for half an hour at the saffron-red, downy, wrinkled little face of the sleeping baby, watching the movements of the frowning forehead and the chubby little hands with their curled-up fingers, rubbing the tiny eyes and nose with the backs of its fists. At such moments especially Karenin felt absolutely calm and at peace with himself, and saw nothing unusual in his position, nothing that ought to be changed.

But the longer it went on, the more and more clearly did he realize that, however natural his position might appear to him now, he would not be allowed to remain in it. He felt that in addition to the beneficent spiritual force that governed his heart, there was another force, harsh and powerful, if not indeed more powerful, which governed his life, and that this force would not let him have the humble peace he longed for. He felt that everybody looked at him with questioning astonishment, that they did not understand him, that they expected something from him. And he was especially aware of the precariousness and unnaturalness of his relations with his wife.

When the softened mood caused by the nearness of death had passed, Karenin began to notice that Anna was afraid of him, found his presence irksome, and could not look him straight in the eyes. She seemed to be wanting something but could not make up her mind to tell him about it and, foreseeing that their relations could not go on as at present, expected something from him too.

At the end of February it happened that Anna's baby daughter, also named Anna, fell ill. Karenin had been in the nursery in the morning and, after giving orders to send for the doctor, had left for the Ministry. Having finished his business, he returned home at about four o'clock. Entering the hall, he saw a handsome footman in braided livery and a bearskin cape, holding a silver mink coat.

"Who is here?" Karenin asked.

"Princess Tverskoy," the footman replied with a smile, as it seemed to Karenin.

All through that difficult time Karenin noticed that all his high-society acquaintances, especially the women, took a special interest in him and his wife. He noticed in all these acquaintances a sort of joy, which they had difficulty in concealing, the same sort of joy he had noticed in the lawyer's eyes and now in the eyes of this footman. They all seemed elated, just as though they had come from a wedding. When they met him, they asked after his wife's health with badly concealed glee.

The presence of the Princess Tverskoy, because of the memories associated with her and because he had never really liked her, was disagreeable to Karenin, and he went straight to the nursery. In the front nursery Seryozha, lying with his chest on the table and his legs on a chair, was drawing something and chattering away merrily. An English governess, who since Anna's illness had replaced the French one, who was sitting near the boy and doing some *mignardise* crocheting, got up hurriedly, curtseyed, and nudged Seryozha.

Karenin stroked his son's hair, answered the governess' inquiries about his wife's health, and asked what the doctor had said about the baby.

"The doctor said it was nothing serious and ordered baths, sir."

"But she's still in pain," said Karenin, listening to the crying child in the next room.

"I think the wet nurse is unsuitable, sir," said the Englishwoman firmly.

"Why do you think so?" he asked, stopping short.

"It was the same thing at Countess Paul's, sir. The child was given all sorts of treatment, but it turned out that it was simply hungry. The wet nurse had no milk, sir."

Karenin reflected for a moment and then went into the other room. The little girl was lying with her head thrown back, wriggling in the wet nurse's arms, and would neither take the plump breast offered it nor stop screaming, in spite of the hushing of the wet nurse and the other nurse who was bending over her.

"Still no better?" asked Karenin.

"Very restless she is, sir," the nurse answered in a whisper.

"Miss Edwards says that perhaps the nurse has not enough milk," he said.

"I think so too, sir."

"Then why didn't you say so?"

"Who to, sir? The mistress is still ill," said the old nurse in a disgruntled tone.

The nurse was an old family servant. And in those simple words Karenin thought that he noticed a hint at his position.

The baby screamed louder than ever, choking and growing hoarse. The nurse, with a gesture of annoyance, went up to the wet nurse, took it from her arms, and began rocking it as she walked up and down the room.

"The doctor must be asked to examine the wet nurse," said Karenin.

The healthy-looking, smartly dressed wet nurse, afraid of losing her job, muttered something under her breath and, covering her large breast, smiled contemptuously at the idea of her not having sufficient milk. In this smile, too, Karenin thought he saw a sneer at his position.

"Poor little mite," said the nurse, hushing the baby and continuing to walk up and down with it.

Karenin sat down on a chair and with a dejected, suffering look gazed at the nurse as she paced the room.

When the child at last grew quiet and had been laid in her cot and the nurse, smoothing the pillow, went away, Karenin got up and walking with difficulty on tiptoe went over to the baby. For a minute he stood still, gazing with the same dejected expression at the child: but suddenly a smile, wrinkling the skin over his forehead and moving his hair, spread over his face and he went as quietly out of the room.

In the dining room he rang and told the servant who came in to send for the doctor once more. He was annoyed with his wife for not taking proper care of the sweet baby, and he did not want to go in and see her while he felt like that, nor had he any wish to see the Princess Betsy; but his wife might wonder why he did not come in to see her as usual, and that was why, making an effort over himself, he went to her bedroom. As he approached the door over the soft carpet, he could not help overhearing a conversation he did not want to hear.

"If he hadn't been going away," said Betsy, "I could have understood your refusal and his too. But your husband must be above that."

"It isn't for my husband's sake but for my own that I do not wish it," Anna replied in an agitated voice. "Don't say that!"

"But surely you can't possibly refuse to say good-by to a man who has tried to shoot himself on your account."

"That's exactly why I do."

Karenin stopped short with a frightened and guilty face and was about to go away unobserved. But on second thought he decided that it would be undignified and, turning again, he cleared his throat, and went toward the bedroom. The voices fell silent and he went in.

Anna, in a gray dressing gown, with her black hair cut short and standing out like a brush over her round head, was sitting on a settee. As usual at the sight of her husband, all her animation suddenly vanished from her face; she dropped her head and glanced uneasily at Betsy. Betsy, dressed in the very latest fashion, with a hat soaring somewhere high above her head like a shade over a lamp and in a dove-colored gown with very pronounced diagonal stripes going one way on the bodice and the other way on her skirt, was sitting beside Anna, her flat, tall figure very erect, and bending her head, met Karenin with an ironical smile.

"Oh," she said, as though in surprise, "I'm so glad you are at home. You never show yourself anywhere and I haven't seen you since Anna's illness. I've heard everything—all about your solicitude. Yes, you're a wonderful husband!" she said with a significant and gracious air, as though conferring an order of magnanimity on him for his conduct to his wife.

Karenin bowed coldly and, kissing his wife's hand, asked how she was.

"Better, I think," she said, avoiding his eyes.

"But you look feverish," he said, emphasizing the word "feverish."

"I'm afraid we've been talking too much," said Betsy. "I feel it was selfish of me and I'm going."

She got up, but Anna, suddenly blushing, quickly seized her hand.

"No, please stay a moment. I have something to say to you—no," she addressed Karenin, the color spreading over her neck and forehead, "to you. I can't and I don't want to hide anything from you."

Karenin cracked his fingers and bowed his head.

"Betsy says that Count Vronsky wants to come and say good-by before leaving for Tashkent," she went on, not looking at her husband and evidently in a hurry to tell him everything, however difficult it was for her. "I said I could not receive him."

"You said, my dear, that it would depend on your husband," Betsy corrected her.

"No, I'm sorry, I can't see him and it wouldn't lead to . . ." She stopped suddenly and looked questioningly at her husband (he did not look at her). "In short, I don't want to."

Karenin came nearer and was about to take her hand.

Her first impulse was to pull away her hand from his damp hand with the thick swollen veins that sought hers, but with an evident effort she pressed his hand.

"I'm grateful to you for your confidence, but . . ." he said, looking embarrassed and annoyed and feeling that what he could easily and clearly decide by himself he could not discuss in the presence of the Princess Tverskoy, whom he regarded as the personification of that harsh force which must govern his life in the eyes of the world and which prevented him from giving way to his feeling of love and forgiveness. He stopped short, looking at the Princess Tverskoy.

"Well, good-by, my sweet," said Betsy, getting up. She kissed Anna and went out. Karenin saw her off.

"I know you to be a truly magnanimous man," Betsy said to Karenin, stopping in the small drawing room and pressing his hand again with special warmth. "I'm only an outsider, but I am so fond of her and I respect you so much that I take the liberty of offering advice to you. Let him come. Alexey Vronsky is the embodiment of honor and he is leaving for Tashkent."

"I thank you for your sympathy and advice, Princess.

492

But the question whether or not my wife will receive anyone she must decide for herself."

He said it, as was his custom, with dignity, raising his eyebrows, but immediately reflected that whatever he might say there could be no dignity in his position. And he saw that clearly in the discreet, malicious, and ironical smile with which Betsy glanced at him when he had spoken.

CHAPTER 20

Karenin took leave of Betsy in the ballroom and went back to his wife. She was lying down, but hearing his footsteps, quickly sat up in her former place and looked apprehensively at him. He saw that she had been crying.

"I'm very grateful to you for your confidence," he gently repeated in Russian the phrase he had said in French in Betsy's presence and sat down beside her. When he spoke in Russian to her he used the familiar turns of speech and that invariably irritated her. "And I'm very grateful for your decision. I too am of the opinion that as he is going away there is no need whatever for Count Vronsky to come here. Besides—"

"But I've said so already, so why repeat it?" Anna suddenly interrupted him, unable to control the irritation in her voice. "No need whatever," she thought, "for a man to come and say good-by to a woman whom he loves and for whose sake he wanted to die and has ruined himself and who cannot live without him. No need whatever!" She tightened her lips and dropped her glittering eyes, looking at his hands with the swollen veins, which he was slowly rubbing together.

"Don't let us ever talk about it any more," she added more calmly.

"I have left this question to you to decide and I'm very glad to see—" Karenin began.

"—that my wish coincides with yours," she quickly finished the sentence for him, exasperated by the slowness with which he spoke, while she knew perfectly well what he was going to say.

"Yes," he assented, "and Princess Tverskoy's intrusion into our difficult family affairs is entirely uncalled for. Especially as she—"

"I don't believe a word that people say about her," Anna interjected quickly. "I know she is genuinely fond of me."

Karenin sighed and was silent. She was playing nervously with the tassels of her dressing gown, glancing at him with that agonizing feeling of physical loathing for which she reproached herself, but which she could not overcome. All she wanted now was to get rid of his hateful presence.

"I've just sent for the doctor," said Karenin.

"I'm quite well—what do you want the doctor for?"

"Yes, but the baby keeps screaming and they say the nurse hasn't enough milk."

"Then why didn't you let me feed her when I begged you to? Oh, never mind" (Karenin understood what the "never mind" meant), "she's a baby and they'll starve her to death." She rang and ordered the baby to be brought. "I begged to nurse her, I wasn't allowed to, and now I'm blamed for it."

"I'm not blaming you. . . ."

"Yes, you are! Oh God, why didn't I die?" And she burst out sobbing. "I'm sorry, I'm upset, I'm unfair," she said, recollecting herself. "But please, go now. . . ."

"No, it can't go on like this," Karenin said to himself firmly as he went out of his wife's room.

Never before had the impossibility of his situation in the eyes of the world and his wife's hatred of him and altogether that harsh, mysterious force which, contrary to his inner mood, governed his life and demanded fulfillment of its decrees and a change in his attitude to his wife appeared as evident as it did now. He saw clearly that the world as a whole and his wife demanded something from him, but what precisely it was he could not understand. He felt that it was this that aroused a feeling of malice and anger in his soul which destroyed his peace of mind and the whole merit of his magnanimous behavior. He thought that it would be better for Anna to break off her relations with Vronsky, but they were all of the opinion that it was impossible; he was even ready to allow these relations to be resumed, provided the children had not to suffer any disgrace because of it and he was not deprived of them or forced to change his position. Bad as this would be, it was a hundred times better than a complete rupture, which would leave her in a hopeless and shameful position and would deprive him of everything he loved. But he felt that he could do nothing; he knew in advance that everybody would be against him and that they would not let him do what now seemed so natural and good to him, but would force him to do what was wrong, though they considered it the proper thing to do.

CHAPTER 21

Before Betsy had time to walk out of the ballroom, Oblonsky, who had just come from Yeliseyev's, where a consignment of fresh oysters had arrived, met her in the doorway.

"Ah, Princess, what a delightful meeting!" he cried. "I've just been at your house."

"I'm afraid we meet only for a moment as I'm just going," said Betsy, smiling and putting on her glove.

"Wait a moment, Princess, before putting on your glove, let me first kiss your hand. There's nothing I'm so thankful for than for the revival of the old custom of hand kissing." He kissed Betsy's hand. "When shall I see you again?"

"You don't deserve it," said Betsy, smiling.

"Yes I do, because I've become a most serious person. I not only settle my own domestic affairs but other people's as well," he said with a significant expression.

"Oh, I'm so glad," replied Betsy, immediately realizing that he referred to Anna. And they went back to the ballroom and stood in a corner. "He'll kill her," said Betsy in a meaningful whisper. "It's impossible, impossible. . . ."

"I'm awfully glad you think so," said Oblonsky, shaking his head with a grave expression of woebegone commiseration. "That's why I've come to Petersburg."

"The whole town is talking of it," said Betsy. "It's an impossible position. She's pining away. Pining away. He does not realize that she is one of those women who can't trifle with their feelings. He should do one of two things: either take her away and act with energy, or give her a divorce. But this is stifling her."

495

"Yes, yes . . . exactly," said Oblonsky. "That's what I've come for. Well, actually, not entirely because of it. . . . I mean, I've been made a Court Chamberlain and, well, I have to show my appreciation in the proper quarters. But the chief thing is to get this affair settled."

"Well, may God help you," said Betsy.

Having seen the princess down to the hall and once again kissed her hand above her glove, where the pulse beats, and telling her some more indecent nonsense so that she did not know whether to be angry or to laugh, Oblonsky went to see his sister. He found her in tears.

Though he was brimming over with high spirits, Oblonsky tried to accommodate himself to her mood by quite naturally assuming a sympathetic and poetically inflated tone of voice. He asked her how she was and how she had spent the morning.

"Oh, very, very wretchedly. Today and this morning and all the other days, past and future," she said.

"I think you give way to melancholy. You must snap out of it. You must look life straight in the face. I know it's hard, but . . ."

"I've heard it said that women love men even for their vices," Anna began suddenly, "but I hate him for his virtues. I can't live with him. Please, understand, I am physically repelled by him. I fly into a rage. I can't, I can't live with him. But what am I to do? I was unhappy and I thought one couldn't be more unhappy, but I could never have imagined the dreadful position I am in now. Can you believe it that knowing what a good, excellent man he is and that I'm not worth his little finger, I still hate him? I hate him for his generosity. And there is nothing left for me but—"

She was going to say "death," but Oblonsky did not let her finish.

"You're ill and agitated," he said. "Believe me, you are exaggerating. There's nothing terrible about it."

And Oblonsky smiled. Having to deal with such despair, no one else in Oblonsky's place would have permitted himself to smile (a smile would have appeared too callous), but in his smile there was so much kindness and almost feminine tenderness that it did not hurt, but soothed and calmed. His soft, comforting words had a soothing, calming effect like that of almond oil. And Anna soon felt this.

"No, Stiva," she said. "I'm done for, done for. Worse than done for. I am not done for yet; I cannot say that all is at an end. On the contrary, I feel that it is not. I am like a tightly wound-up string which must snap. But it's not ended yet and—the end will be terrible."

"No, no, the string can be loosened gently. There is no situation from which there is no escape."

"I've thought and thought. There's only one. . . ."

Again he understood from her terrified look that the only way of escape she had in mind was death, and he did not let her finish.

"Not at all," he said, "just listen to me. You can't see your position as I can. Let me tell you what I think frankly." Again he smiled guardedly his almond-oil smile. "I'll begin from the beginning: you married a man twenty years older than yourself. You married him without love and without knowing what love was. Let us just say it was a mistake."

"A terrible mistake!" said Anna.

"But I repeat: it is an accomplished fact. Then, let us say, you had the misfortune to fall in love with a man who was not your husband. That was a misfortune, but that, too, is an accomplished fact. And your husband has accepted it and forgiven it." He stopped after each sentence, waiting for her to object, but she said nothing. "It is so, isn't it? Now the question is, can you go on living with your husband? Do you wish it? Does he wish it?"

"I don't know, I don't know at all."

"But you said yourself that you can't stand him."

"No, I didn't. I take it back. I know nothing. I understand nothing."

"Yes, but . . ."

"You can't understand. I feel I'm flying headlong over some precipice, but that I have no right to save myself. And I can't."

"Oh, well, we'll hold something out and catch you. I understand you. I understand that you have not the courage to express your wishes, your feelings."

"I want nothing, nothing except that it should be all over and done with."

"But he sees that and knows it. And do you really think that he doesn't find it as hard to bear as you? You're unhappy, he's unhappy, and what do you think

497

can come of it? But," Oblonsky, not without some effort, expressed his main idea and looked at her significantly, "a divorce would solve everything."

She made no answer and merely shook her cropped head. But from the expression of her face, which suddenly became radiant with her former beauty, he realized that she did not want it only because it seemed to her a happiness she could not hope for.

"I'm terribly sorry for you both, and I can't tell you how happy I'd be if I could arrange it," said Oblonsky, smiling more boldly now. "Don't, don't say a word! I only pray I can tell him exactly what I feel. I'm going to speak to him."

Anna looked at him with dreamy, shining eyes and said nothing.

CHAPTER 22

Oblonsky entered Karenin's study with the same solemn expression with which he was in the habit of taking the chair at council meetings. Karenin, with his arms crossed behind his back, was pacing the room, thinking about the very same thing which his wife and Oblonsky had been discussing.

"I'm not disturbing you, am I?" said Oblonsky, experiencing an unwonted feeling of embarrassment at the sight of his brother-in-law. To conceal his embarrassment he took out a cigarette case with a new kind of clasp which he had only just bought and, sniffing the leather, took out a cigarette.

"No," Karenin replied reluctantly. "Do you want anything?"

"Yes, I'd like to—er—I have to—er—yes, I must have a talk with you," said Oblonsky, becoming aware with surprise of his unaccustomed timidity.

That feeling was so unexpected and strange that Oblonsky could not believe it was the voice of conscience telling him that what he was about to do was wrong. But making an effort, Oblonsky conquered the timidity that had come over him.

"I hope," he said, blushing, "you believe in my love

for my sister and my sincere affection and respect for yourself."

Karenin stopped and made no reply, but Oblonsky was struck by his expression of resignation to his fate.

"I intended—er—I wanted to have a talk to you about my sister and the position both of you find yourselves in at the moment," said Oblonsky, still struggling with his unwonted timidity.

Karenin smiled sadly, looked at his brother-in-law, and without replying, went up to his writing table, took from it an unfinished letter and gave it to Oblonsky.

"I keep thinking about it all the time, and that's what I've begun to write in the hope that I could put it better in writing and seeing that my presence irritates her," he said, handing Oblonsky the letter.

Oblonsky took the letter, looked with perplexed surprise at the dull eyes fixed on him, and began to read.

"I can see that my presence is painful to you. Hard as it was for me to convince myself of this, I can see that it is so and cannot be otherwise. I don't blame you, and God is my witness that when I saw you at the time of your illness I decided with all my heart to forget what had happened between us and to begin a new life. I do not regret and will never regret what I did; my only desire was for your welfare, for the welfare of your soul, and now I see that I have not achieved it. Tell me yourself what would give you true happiness and peace of mind. I am entirely in your hands and I shall do whatever you consider to be just."

Oblonsky handed back the letter and continued looking at his brother-in-law with the same perplexed expression, not knowing what to say. The silence was so oppressive that Oblonsky's lips twitched painfully as he kept staring at Karenin without uttering a word.

"That's what I wanted to tell her," said Karenin, turning away.

"Yes, yes . . ." said Oblonsky, who felt unable to reply as tears were choking him. "Yes, yes, I understand you," he brought out at last.

"I'd like to know what she wants," said Karenin.

"I'm afraid she does not understand her position herself. I mean," Oblonsky corrected himself, "she is no judge of it. She feels crushed, yes, crushed by your generosity. If she reads this letter, she will not be able to say anything—she will only hang her head lower than ever."

"Yes, but in that case what's to be done? How explain—how find out her wishes?"

"If you will permit me to express an opinion, I think it is for you to say plainly what steps you consider necessary to put an end to this situation."

"Then you think an end must be put to it?" Karenin interrupted him. "But how?" he added, moving his hands before his eyes in a gesture that was unusual with him. "I don't see any possible way out."

"There's a way out of every situation," said Oblonsky, getting up and becoming more animated. "There was a time when you wanted to break off . . . If you are quite sure now that you can't be happy together . . ."

"Happiness can mean all sorts of things to all sorts of people. Suppose I agree to everything. I want nothing. What way out is there in our situation?"

"If you want to know my opinion," said Oblonsky with the same soothing, almond-oily, tender smile with which he had spoken to Anna—his kindly smile was so convincing that, feeling his own weakness and yielding to it, Karenin was ready to believe anything Oblonsky should say—"she would never tell you in so many words, but there is only one possible solution, one thing she might desire. This is," Oblonsky went on, "the termination of your relations and of everything that reminds her of them. In my view, what is necessary in your case is the clarification of your new relationship. And this new relationship can only be established by both sides regaining their freedom."

"Divorce," Karenin interrupted with repugnance.

"Yes, it is divorce I have in mind. Yes, divorce," Oblonsky repeated, reddening. "That is from every point of view the most sensible solution for a married couple who find themselves placed as you are. What is to be done if they find that life together has become impossible for them? It's the sort of thing that can always happen."

Karenin sighed deeply and closed his eyes.

"In such a situation the only thing that ought to be considered," Oblonsky went on, overcoming his embarrassment more and more, "is whether one of them desires to marry again. If not, it is very simple."

Karenin, his face drawn with agitation, muttered something under his breath and made no reply. What seemed so simple to Oblonsky, Karenin had thought over thousands of times, and far from being simple, it all seemed utterly impossible to him. Divorce, now that he knew all the details of such an action, seemed impossible to him because his feelings of self-respect and his regard for religion would not allow him to plead guilty to a fictitious act of adultery, and still less to permit his wife, whom he had forgiven and whom he loved, to be exposed and disgraced. And there were other and still more important reasons that made divorce appear impossible to him.

What would become of his son in the event of a divorce? To leave him with his mother was out of the question. The divorced mother would have her own illegitimate family, in which the position and education of a stepson would in all probability be a bad one. Should he keep the boy himself? He knew that it would be an act of revenge on his part, and he did not want that. But apart from this, what made divorce seem to Karenin utterly impossible was that by agreeing to it he would ruin Anna. He could not forget what Dolly had said to him in Moscow. By deciding on a divorce, she had told him, he was only thinking of himself and not considering that he would be irretrievably ruining Anna by it. And having forgiven her and having become attached to the children, he interpreted those words of Dolly's in his own way. To agree to a divorce, to give her her freedom, would mean, as he understood it, to deprive himself of the only thing that bound him to the life of the children, whom he loved, and to deprive her of the last support on the path of virtue and cast her to perdition. If she became a divorced wife, she would form a union with Vronsky, and this union would be both illegal and sinful, for, according to ecclesiastical law, a wife may not remarry as long as her husband is living. "She will form a union with him and within a year or two he will abandon her or she will enter into a new liaison," thought Karenin. "And by consenting to an illegal divorce, I shall be the cause of her undoing." He had thought it all over hundreds of times and he was convinced that a divorce was not at all as simple as his brother-in-law was saying, that, in fact, it was quite out of the question. He did not believe a word of what Oblonsky was saying and had a thousand objections to every argument he used, but he listened to him, feeling that his words were the expression of that powerful, brutal force which governed his life and to which he would have to submit.

"The only question that remains to be decided is on what conditions you will agree to a divorce. She wants nothing and she dare not ask you for anything. She leaves it all to your generosity."

"Oh God, oh God! What for?" thought Karenin, recalling the particulars of a divorce suit in which the husband took all the blame on himself, and with the same gesture with which Vronsky had covered his face, he hid his own face in shame with his hands.

"You're upset, I can understand that. But if you think it over carefully . . ."

"Whosoever shall smite thee on thy right cheek, turn to him the other also, and if any man will take away thy coat, let him have thy cloak also," thought Karenin.

"Yes, yes," he cried in a shrill voice, "I will take the disgrace upon myself and I will even give up my son, but—don't you think we'd better leave it as it is? However, do as you like. . . ."

And turning away so that his brother-in-law could not see him, he sat down on a chair by the window. He felt bitter, he felt ashamed, but with the bitterness and shame he experienced a sense of joy and deep emotion at the greatness of his own humility.

Oblonsky was touched. He said nothing for a minute or two.

"Believe me," he resumed, "she will appreciate your generosity. But," he added, "it was evidently God's will," and having said it, felt that it was a stupid thing to say and could not refrain from smiling at his stupidity.

Karenin wanted to say something, but tears stopped him.

"I'm afraid this sort of misfortune is inevitable and one has to accept it. I regard it as an accomplished fact and I'm doing my best both for you and her," said Oblonsky.

When Oblonsky left his brother-in-law's room, he was touched, but that did not prevent him from feeling satisfied with having successfully accomplished what he had set out to do, for he was certain that Karenin would not go back on his word. To his feeling of satisfaction was added the thought that when the affair was settled he would be able to put the following conundrum to his wife and intimate friends: "What is the difference between me and the emperor? The emperor orders a dissolution and no one's the better for it, but I have made a dissolution and three people are happy. . . . Or: Why am I like an emperor? When . . . However, I'll think of something better," he said to himself with a smile.

CHAPTER 23

Vronsky's wound was a dangerous one even though it missed the heart, and for several days he lay between life and death. The first time he was able to talk again, his brother's wife Varya was alone with him.

"Varya," he said, looking sternly at her, "I shot myself by accident. And, please, never speak of it, and tell everybody else that. Otherwise it would be too stupid for words!"

Without answering, Varya bent over him and looked into his face with a happy smile. His eyes were bright, not feverish, but their expression was stern.

"Well, thank God!" she said. "You're not in pain, are you?"

"A little here," he said, pointing to his chest.

"Then let me change the dressing."

He looked at her in silence, his broad jaws set, while she bandaged him. When she had finished, he said:

"I'm not delirious. Please do all you can to prevent people from saying that I shot myself deliberately."

"But no one does say so. I only hope that you will never again shoot yourself by accident," she said with a questioning smile.

"I don't suppose I shall, but it would have been better . . ."

And he smiled gloomily.

In spite of these words and the smile, which greatly frightened Varya, when the inflammation passed and he began to get better, he felt that he was completely free from one part of his grief. By his action he seemed to have washed away the shame and humiliation he had previously felt. He could now think calmly about Karenin. He admitted his magnanimity and no longer felt humiliated by it. Besides that, he got into his old rut again. He found he could look people in the face once more and was able to live in accordance with his former habits. The one thing he could not tear out of his heart, though he continually struggled against it, was a regret, bordering on despair, that he had lost her forever. That now, having atoned for his guilt toward her husband, he had to give her up and never again stand between her repentance and her and between her and her husband, was a firm decision he had taken and intended to keep. But he could not tear out of his heart a regret for the loss of her love and could not erase from his mind the moments of happiness he had known with her and had valued so lightly at the time and which haunted him now with all their seductive charm.

Serpukhovskoy had offered him a post in Tashkent, and Vronsky accepted the offer without the slightest hesitation. But the nearer the time of his departure approached, the heavier seemed to him the sacrifice he was making to what he thought to be his duty.

His wound had healed, and he was driving out making preparations for his journey to Tashkent.

"To see her just once more and then to bury myself, to die," he thought, and while making a round of farewell visits, expressed this thought to Betsy. With this message Betsy went to Anna and brought back a refusal.

"So much the better," thought Vronsky, when he received the news. "It was a weakness which would have shattered what strength I have left."

Next day Betsy herself came to see him in the morning and informed him that she had received the definite news through Oblonsky that Karenin had agreed to a divorce and that consequently he could see Anna.

Without even taking the trouble to see Betsy off, forgetting all his resolutions, and without asking when he could see Anna or where her husband was, Vronsky at once went to the Karenins'. He ran up the stairs without seeing anyone or anything and with rapid steps, almost at a run, burst into her room. Without thinking or noticing whether there was anyone else in the room or not, he flung his arms round her and began showering kisses on her face, arms, and neck.

Anna had been preparing herself for the meeting, had considered what she would say to him, but she had no time to say any of it: his passion overwhelmed her. She wished to calm him, to calm herself, but it was too late. His feeling communicated itself to her. Her lips trembled so that for a long time she could not utter a word.

"Yes, you've taken possession of me and I am yours," she brought out at last, pressing his hand to her bosom.

"It had to be," he said. "As long as we live, it will have to be. I know that now."

"That is true," she said, growing paler and paler and putting her arm round his head. "Still, there's something terrible in this after all that's happened."

"It will pass, it will all pass, and we shall be happy! Our love, if it could grow stronger, would grow stronger just because there is something terrible in it," he said, raising his head and with a smile that showed his strong teeth.

And she could not help replying with a smile—not to his words, but to his lovelorn eyes. She took his hand and stroked her cold cheeks and cropped hair with it.

"I can hardly recognize you with this short hair. You look prettier than ever. A sweet little boy. But how pale you are!"

"Yes, I am very weak," she said, smiling. And her lips trembled again.

"We'll go to Italy and you'll soon get well," he said.

"Is it really possible that we should be like husband and wife, by ourselves, with our own family?" she said, peering closely at him.

"The thing that surprises me is that it could ever have been otherwise."

"Stiva says that *he* agrees to everything, but I can't accept *his* generosity," she said, looking thoughtfully past Vronsky's face. "I don't want a divorce. I don't care now. Only I don't know what he will decide about Seryozha."

He was quite unable to understand how she could, at the moment of their reunion, remember and think of her son, of divorce. What difference did it make?

"Don't talk and don't think about it," he said, turning her hand over in his and trying to draw attention to himself; but she still did not look at him.

"Oh, why didn't I die? It would have been much better!" she said, and tears streamed silently down her cheeks; but she tried to smile so as not to hurt him.

To refuse the flattering and dangerous mission to Tashkent would, according to Vronsky's former ideas, have seemed impossible and disgraceful. But now he did refuse it without a moment's hesitation and, noticing the disapproval of his superiors at this step, at once resigned his commission.

A month later Karenin was left alone in the house with his son, and Anna went abroad with Vronsky, not only without obtaining a divorce, but having firmly refused one.

Part Five

CHAPTER 1

Princess Shcherbatsky considered it quite out of the question to have the wedding before Lent, to which only five weeks remained, since half of the trousseau could not be ready by that time; but she could not help agreeing with Levin that after Lent it would be too late, for Prince Shcherbatsky's old aunt was very ill and likely to die soon, and then mourning would delay the wedding still further. Therefore, having decided to divide the trousseau into two parts, a larger and a smaller, the princess agreed to have the wedding before Lent. She decided to get the smaller part of the trousseau ready at once and to send on the larger part later, and she was very cross with Levin because he seemed quite incapable of giving her a serious answer as to whether he agreed with this compromise or not.

Levin continued in the same state of lunacy in which it seemed to him that he and his happiness were the chief and only purpose of all existence and that he had no longer to think or bother about anything, that everything was being done and would be done for him by others. He had not even any plans or aims for the future: those too he left to others to decide in the belief that everything would be splendid. His brother Sergey Koznyshev, Oblonsky, and the princess advised him what to do. He merely agreed to everything they suggested. His brother borrowed money for him, the princess advised him to leave Moscow for the country after the wedding, and Oblonsky advised them to go abroad. He agreed to everything. "Do what you like, if it amuses you. I am happy and my happiness cannot be greater nor less because of anything you do," he thought. When he told Kitty of Oblonsky's suggestion that they should go abroad, he was very surprised that she did not agree and seemed to have such definite ideas of her own about their future. She knew that Levin had work he loved in the country. So far as he could see she neither understood nor wished to understand what it was. That, however, did not prevent her from considering it very important. She consequently knew that their home would be in the country and she wanted to go not abroad where they were not going to live, but where their home would be. This intention, expressed in no unmistakable terms, surprised Levin. But since it made no difference to him, he at once asked Oblonsky, as though it were Oblonsky's duty to do so, to go to the country and make all the necessary arrangements there, according to his own good taste, which he possessed in such abundance.

"But, look here," Oblonsky said to Levin on his return from the country, where he had made all the preparations for the arrival of the newlyweds, "have you got a certificate to show that you have received Communion?"

"No. Why?"

"You can't have a church wedding without it."

"Good Lord!" exclaimed Levin. "I don't think I've been to Communion for the past nine years. I never thought of it."

"Dear me, you're a fine one!" Oblonsky said, laughing. "And you call *me* a nihilist! But I'm afraid it won't do. You must go to confession and receive the sacrament."

"When? There are only four days left."

Oblonsky arranged that too. And Levin began to fast as a preliminary to receiving the sacrament. To Levin, as to any unbeliever who respects the beliefs of others, to attend and to take part in all church services was a very painful business. And now, in his present softened state of mind, sensitive to everything, the necessity of pretending was not only painful to him, but seemed utterly impossible. Now, at the time of his glory and his florescence, he had either to lie or to commit sacrilege. He felt incapable of doing either. But however much he questioned Oblonsky whether it was possible to obtain a certificate without going to Communion, Oblonsky insisted that it was quite out of the question.

"Besides, what does it matter—only a couple of days! And the priest's such a nice, sensible old man. He'll extract that tooth for you so that you will scarcely feel it."

Standing in church at the first service, Levin tried to refresh his memory about the strong religious feeling he had experienced as a boy between the ages of sixteen and seventeen. But he was immediately convinced that it was quite impossible for him to do so. Then he tried to look on it all as a meaningless, empty custom, like the custom of paying visits; but he felt that he could not do that either. Levin, like the majority of his contemporaries, had most indefinite ideas as to his attitude towards religion. He could not believe, and at the same time he was not firmly convinced that it was all untrue. And therefore, being both unable to believe in the significance of what he was doing and to regard it with indifference as an empty formality, he felt uncomfortable and ashamed all the time he was getting ready for the sacrament, doing something he did not understand and therefore, as an inner voice told him, something that was false and wrong.

During the service he would sometimes listen to the prayers, trying to invest them with a meaning that would not disagree with his own views; or, finding that he could not understand and must disapprove of them, he would try not to listen but to occupy his mind with the observations and memories and thoughts that passed through his head with extraordinary vividness as he stood idly in church.

He stood through the Mass, vespers, and evensong, and the next morning, getting up earlier than usual, he went to church before breakfast for morning prayers and confession.

There was no one in the church except a soldier-beggar, two old women, and the clergy.

A young deacon, the two sides of his long back clearly visible under his thin under-cassock, met him, and going at once to a small lectern by the wall, began reading the prayers. As the reading went on and especially at the frequent and rapid repetitions of the same words: "Lord, have mercy upon us," which sounded like *"Loravmercypons,"* Levin felt that his mind was closed and sealed and that to attempt to stir it now would only result in confusion, and, therefore, standing behind the deacon, he kept thinking his own thoughts without listening or trying to grasp what was being said. "How wonderfully expressive her hand is!" he thought, recalling how he and Kitty had sat at the corner table the day before. As almost always at that particular time, they had nothing to talk about, and she had put her hand on the table and kept opening and closing it until she herself began to laugh at its movements. He remembered how he had kissed that hand and then begun to examine the converging lines on the rosy palm. "Again loravmercypons," thought Levin, crossing himself, bowing and watching the movements of the supple back of the bowing deacon. "Then she took my hand and examined the lines. 'You have a nice hand,' she said." And he looked at his hand and the deacon's stumpy hand. "Yes, it will soon be over now," he thought. "No, I think he's starting it all over again," he thought, listening to the prayers. "Yes, it is coming to an end. Bowing down to the ground now. That's always before the end."

Clandestinely receiving a three-ruble note into his hand under his velveteen cuff, the deacon said that he would put Levin's name down and went briskly into the chancel, his new boots clattering over the flagstones of the empty church. A minute later he put his head out and beckoned to Levin. Levin's thoughts, till then sealed up in his head, began to stir, but he hastened to drive them away. "It will come right, somehow," he thought and walked to the steps of the enclosure in front of the altar screen. He walked up the steps and turning to the right he saw the priest. The priest, a little old man with a sparse, grizzled beard and kind, weary eyes, was standing beside the lectern turning over the leaves of a missal. With a slight bow to Levin, he began at once to chant the prayers in the usual way. Having finished them he bowed down to the ground and turned to Levin.

"Here Christ stands invisibly before you to receive your confession," he said, pointing to the crucifix. "Do you believe in the teachings of the Holy Apostolic Church?" the priest went on, turning his eyes away from Levin's face and folding his hands under his stole.

510

"I have doubted and I still doubt everything," said Levin in a voice that sounded unpleasant to him, and fell silent.

The priest paused a few seconds to see if he would add anything more and then, closing his eyes, said rapidly with a strong provincial accent:

"Doubts are natural to human frailty, but we must pray that our merciful God should strengthen us. What are your particular sins?" he added without the slightest pause, as if anxious not to waste time.

"My chief sin is doubt. I doubt everything and am in doubt most of the time."

"Doubt is natural to human frailty," the priest repeated. "What do you doubt in particular?"

"I doubt everything. Sometimes, I even doubt the existence of God," Levin said involuntarily and was horrified at the impropriety of what he was saying. But Levin's words did not seem to have had any effect on the priest.

"What doubts can there be of the existence of God?" the priest said hurriedly with a barely perceptible smile.

Levin was silent.

"What doubt can you have of the Creator when you contemplate His works?" went on the priest in his rapid, customary voice. "Who adorned the celestial vault with stars? Who invested the earth with her beauty? How could these things be without a Creator?" he said with an inquiring glance at Levin.

Levin felt that it would be unseemly to start a philosophic discussion with a priest and therefore merely said in reply what had a direct bearing on the question.

"I don't know," he said.

"You don't know?" said the priest with amused bewilderment. "Then how can you doubt that God created it all?"

"I don't understand anything," said Levin, blushing and feeling that what he said was stupid and that anything he said could not but be stupid in the present circumstances.

"Pray to God and beseech Him. Even the holy Fathers doubted and besought God to strengthen their faith. The devil is very powerful and we must not give in to him. Pray to God, beseech Him. Pray to God," he repeated.

The priest paused for some time, as though lost in thought.

"I hear you are about to enter into holy matrimony with the daughter of my parishioner and spiritual son, Prince Shcherbatsky," he added with a smile. "A fine girl!"

"Yes," answered Levin, blushing for the priest. "Why has he to ask that at confession?" he thought.

And, as though in answer to his thought, the priest said:

"You are about to enter into matrimony and God may reward your union with children, is that not so? Well then, what sort of education can you give your little ones if you do not conquer in yourself the temptation of the devil who is leading you into unbelief?" he said with gentle reproach. "If you love your children, then you, as a good father, will desire not only riches, luxury, and honors for them, but you will also desire their salvation, their spiritual advancement in the light of truth. Isn't that so? What will you say to your child, when the innocent baby asks you: 'Daddy, who has created everything that pleases me so much in the world—the earth, the water, the sun, the flowers and the grass?' Will you really reply 'I don't know'? You cannot help knowing, since God in his infinite mercy has revealed it to you. Or what if your child asks you, 'What awaits me in the life beyond the grave?' What will you say to him if you yourself know nothing? How will you answer him? Will you abandon him to the temptations of the world and the devil? That would be wrong!" he said and paused and, with his head on one side, regarded Levin with his kind and gentle eyes.

This time Levin said nothing in reply, not because he did not want to enter into a discussion with a priest, but because no one had ever put such questions to him and there would be plenty of time to consider what to reply when his little children started asking these questions.

"You are entering upon a time of life," went on the priest, "when one must choose one's path and keep to it. Pray to God that in His goodness He may help you and have mercy upon you," he concluded. "May our Lord Jesus Christ, in the grace and bounty of His love for mankind, pardon this His child. . . ." And having

512

pronounced the absolution, the priest blessed him and let him go.

When he returned home that day, Levin experienced a great feeling of relief at the conclusion of an awkward situation and that it had come to an end without his having to tell lies. He had, besides, a rather vague recollection that what the nice, kind old man had said to him was not as stupid as it had seemed to him at first and that there was something in it that had to be elucidated.

"Not now, of course," thought Levin, "but at some other time." Levin felt more than ever now that there was something vague and unclean in his soul and that, so far as religion was concerned, he was in the position he saw so distinctly and disliked in others and for which he found fault with his friend Sviazhsky.

He spent that evening with his fiancée at Dolly's and was in particularly high spirits. In explaining to Oblonsky why he felt so elated, he said he was as happy as a dog who was being trained to jump through a hoop and who, realizing at last what was wanted and having done it, barks and wags its tail and jumps for joy on the table and the window sills.

CHAPTER 2

On the day of the wedding, according to custom (the princess and Dolly insisted on all customs being strictly observed), Levin did not see his bride and dined at his hotel with three bachelors who happened to be there by chance. They were his brother Koznyshev; Katavasov, an old fellow student of Levin's who was now a professor of natural sciences, whom Levin had met in the street and dragged to his hotel; and Chirikov, his best man, a Moscow magistrate and a bear-hunting comrade of Levin's. The dinner was a very merry one. Koznyshev was in excellent spirits and was hugely amused by Katavasov's originality. Feeling that his originality was appreciated and understood, Katavasov showed it off. Chirikov gaily and good-naturedly backed up whatever any of them happened to say.

"Now, you see," said Katavasov with a drawl, a habit

he had acquired while lecturing at the university, "what a talented fellow our dear friend Konstantin Levin used to be. I am speaking of absent friends, for, alas, he is no longer with us. He was fond of learning in those days, when he left the university, and the interests he had were human; but now half of his abilities are employed in deceiving himself and the other half in justifying the deception."

"A more determined enemy of matrimony than yourself I have never come across," said Koznyshev.

"No, I'm no enemy of marriage. I am all for the division of labor. People who can't do anything else ought to carry on with the work of propagating the race, and the rest must work for its enlightenment and happiness. That's how I look at it. There are hosts of aspirants who would like to mix the two occupations, but I am not one of them."

"You can't imagine how glad I shall be when I learn that you've fallen in love," said Levin. "You won't forget to invite me to your wedding, will you?"

"I'm in love already!"

"Yes, with a cuttlefish. You know, I suppose," Levin turned to his brother, "that Katavasov is writing a treatise on the digestive organs and—"

"Now, please, don't get it all wrong! It makes no difference what it is about. The fact is that I really do love cuttlefish."

"But it shouldn't prevent you from loving your wife, should it?"

"It wouldn't, but the wife would."

"Why?"

"Oh, you'll soon find out. Now you like farming and sport—well, just wait and see!"

"Arkhip came to see me today," said Chirikov. "He says there are hundreds of elks in Prudino and two bears."

"Oh well, I'm afraid you'll have to get them without me."

"There you are!" said Koznyshev. "You'd better say good-by to bear hunting in future—your wife won't let you."

Levin smiled. The idea that his wife wouldn't let him seemed so delightful that he was ready to forgo the pleasure of ever setting eyes on a bear again.

"But," said Chirikov, "it's all the same a pity that those two bears would be caught without you. Do you remember that time in Khrapilovo? What wonderful sport we had!"

Levin did not wish to disillusion him of the idea that there could be something good without sport anywhere, and so he said nothing.

"There is a good reason for the custom of taking leave of one's bachelor life," said Koznyshev. "However happy you may be, you can't help regretting your freedom."

"Now, confess you do feel a little like the bridegroom in Gogol's play who jumped out of the window, don't you?"

"I'm sure he does, only he won't own up," said Katavasov, and burst out laughing.

"Well," said Chirikov, smiling, "the window is open. . . . Let's go off to Tver at once. One of them is a she-bear. You can go straight to her lair. Come now, let's catch the five-o'clock train. And leave them to their own devices here."

"I swear to you," said Levin with a smile, "I can't find in my heart a trace of the feeling of regret for the loss of my freedom."

"Why," said Katavasov, "your heart is in such a chaos just now that you wouldn't be able to find anything there. Wait till you get used to your new state a little, then you'll find it all right!"

"Oh no, if that were so I should have felt besides my feeling" (he did not want to use the word "love" in Katavasov's presence) "and my happiness just a little sorry to lose my freedom. But quite the contrary. It is this loss of freedom that I am so glad of."

"That's bad! A hopeless case!" said Katavasov. "Well, let's drink to his recovery or let's wish that at least a hundredth part of his dreams come true. Even that would be happiness such as never was on this earth!"

Soon after dinner the guests went away so as to be in time to change for the wedding.

Left alone and thinking over the remarks of those bachelors, Levin asked himself again whether there was in his heart any of that feeling of regret for his freedom they had been talking about. He smiled at the question. "Freedom? Who wants freedom? Happiness consists only in loving and desiring, in wishing her wishes, thinking her thoughts, which means having no freedom whatever—that is happiness!"

"But do you know her thoughts, her wishes, her feelings?" a voice suddenly whispered. The smile faded from his face and he sank into thought. And suddenly a strange feeling came over him. He was overwhelmed by fear and doubt, doubt of everything.

"What if she doesn't love me? What if she is only marrying me because she wants to get married? What if she doesn't know herself what she is doing?" he asked himself. "She might come to her senses and only after she is married realize that she does not love me and never could love me." And strange and most evil thoughts about Kitty began to come into his mind. He became jealous of Vronsky just as he had been a year ago, just as if that evening he had seen her with Vronsky had been only yesterday. He suspected that she had not told him everything.

He leaped to his feet. "No, this won't do!" he said to himself in despair. "I'll go to her and ask her. Say to her for the last time: we are free, and don't you think it's better that we should remain so? Everything is better than everlasting unhappiness, disgrace, infidelity!" With despair in his heart and bitterness toward all men, toward himself, and toward her, he left the hotel and drove to her house.

He found her in one of the back rooms. She was sitting on a trunk and giving orders to one of the maids as she sorted out piles of dresses of different colors hanging over the backs of chairs or lying on the floor.

"Oh!" she cried when she saw him and her face lit up with joy. "Why, darling, I mean, why are you here?" (To the very last day she addressed him at times formally and at other times caressingly.) "This is a surprise! And I've been sorting out my old dresses and deciding which of them to give away and to whom."

"Oh," he said, looking gloomily at the maid, "that's very nice."

"You can go now, Dunyasha, I'll call you presently," said Kitty. "What's the matter, darling?" she asked, addressing him resolutely in this intimate fashion as soon as the maid had gone out. She noticed his agitated and gloomy expression and she was seized with panic.

"Kitty, I'm terribly unhappy and I can't be unhappy alone," he said with despair in his voice, standing before her and looking imploringly into her eyes. He could already see from her loving, truthful face that nothing could possibly come of what he intended to say, but he simply had to hear her undeceive him. "I've come to say that there is still time. We can still put a stop to it all and put it right."

"Put what right? I don't know what you're talking about. What is the matter with you?"

"I've said it a thousand times and I can't help thinking of it—I mean, that I am not worthy of you. You cannot possibly consent to marry me. Think it over. You have made a mistake. Think it over properly. You can't love me. . . . If . . . I mean, you'd better say so," he said, not looking at her. "I shall be unhappy. Let them say what they like: anything is better than misfortune. . . . Better now, while there is still time. . . ."

"I don't understand," she said, looking frightened. "Do you mean you want to retract . . . that you don't want to . . ."

"Yes, if you don't love me."

"You're mad!" she cried, flushing with vexation. But he looked so wretched that she suppressed her vexation and, flinging some clothes from an armchair, sat down closer to him. "What are you thinking? Tell me everything."

"I am thinking you can't love me. What could you love me for?"

"Oh God, what else can I do?" she said and burst out crying.

"Oh, what have I done?" he cried and, going down on his knees before her, he began kissing her hands.

When the princess came into the room five minutes later, she found them quite reconciled. Kitty not only convinced him that she loved him but, in answer to his question, even explained to him why. She told him that she loved him because she completely understood him, because she knew that he had to love and that everything he loved was good. And that seemed quite clear to him. When the princess came in, they were sitting on the trunk side by side, sorting out the dresses and arguing about the brown dress she had been wearing when Levin had proposed to her and which she wanted to give

517

to Dunyasha, while he insisted that she ought not to give that dress to anyone and should give Dunyasha the blue one instead.

"How is it you don't see it? She is a brunette and it won't suit her. . . . I have thought it all out."

When the princess found out why he had come, she lost her temper half humorously and half seriously, and sent him home to dress and not to waste Kitty's time, for she had to have her hair done and Charles, the hairdresser, was due to arrive any moment.

"As it is, she has scarcely been eating anything for days and is losing her looks, and now you come along and upset her with your nonsense," she said. "Away with you, away with you, my dear sir!"

Levin, looking guilty and ashamed, but comforted, went back to his hotel. His brother, Dolly and Oblonsky, all in evening dress, were waiting for him to bless him with the icon. There was no time to lose. Dolly had to go back home to fetch her son who, his hair well oiled and curled, was to drive in the bride's carriage with the icon. Then a carriage had to be sent for the best man and another was to take Koznyshev and return again. There were, in fact, all sorts of highly complicated arrangements to be made. One thing was certain: there was no time to lose, for it was already half past six.

Nothing came of the blessing with the icon. Oblonsky, standing in a comically solemn pose beside his wife, took the icon and, ordering Levin to bow down to the ground, blessed him with a kind and ironical smile and kissed him three times; Dolly did the same and immediately hurried off, and once more they got all muddled up about the arrangements for the carriages.

"Now, this is what we're going to do: you go and fetch him in our carriage, and Koznyshev, if he will be so good, can go and send the carriage back."

"Of course, I shall be glad to."

"And I'll come immediately with him. Have your things been sent off?" asked Oblonsky.

"Yes," replied Levin and told Kuzma to put out his clothes for him to dress.

CHAPTER 3

A crowd of people, mostly women, had gathered round the church lighted up for the wedding. Those who had been too late to get into the middle of the crowd thronged round the windows, pushing, wrangling, and trying to peer through the gratings.

More than twenty carriages had already been parked by the police along the street. A police officer, ignoring the frost, stood at the entrance, resplendent in his uniform. More carriages kept driving up, and the guests got out, the ladies with flowers in their hair, holding up their trains, and the men taking off their képis or black hats as they entered the church. In the church itself the candles in the chandeliers were all lit, as well as all the candles in front of the icons. The golden glitter on the crimson background, the gilt setting of the icons, the silver of the chandeliers and candlesticks, the flagstones of the floor, the mats, the gonfalons above the choir, the steps to the chancel, the ancient books black with age, the cassocks and surplices—all were flooded with light. On the right-hand side of the well-heated church, in the crowd of swallow-tail coats and white ties, the uniforms, brocades, velvets, and satins, hair, flowers, bare shoulders and arms, and long gloves, a restrained and lively conversation was going on and the sound of it re-echoed strangely from the high dome above. Every time the door creaked there was a hush in the crowd and everyone turned around expecting to see the bride and bridegroom. But the door had opened over a dozen times and each time it turned out to be either a guest, man or woman, who was late and joined the circle of invited guests on the right, or a woman spectator who had managed to elude or propitiate the police officer and who joined the crowd of strangers on the left. Both the relatives and the spectators had passed through every phase of suspense.

At first it was supposed that the bride and bridegroom would arrive at any moment and no importance was attached to the delay. Then people began looking more and more often toward the door, asking each other whether anything could have happened. At length the delay became rather awkward, and relatives and friends tried to look as if they were not thinking of the bridegroom, but were absorbed in their own conversation.

The archdeacon, as if to draw attention to the value of his time, kept clearing his throat impatiently, making the windows rattle. In the choir the bored choristers could be heard trying out their voices or blowing their noses. The priest kept sending the beadle and deacon to see whether the bridegroom had arrived, and he himself, in his purple surplice and embroidered sash, went with increasing frequency to the side door in expectation of the bridegroom. At last one of the ladies looked at her watch and said, "This *is* strange!" and all the guests became restless and began loudly to express their surprise and displeasure. One of the groomsmen went to find out what had happened.

All this time Kitty, who had long been ready and waiting in her white dress, long veil, and wreath of orange blossoms, stood in the drawing room of her parents' house with the old lady who was to act as her sponsor at the wedding and her sister, Princess Lvov, looking out of the ballroom window and for the last half hour waiting in vain for the best man to arrive and announce that the bridegroom had reached the church.

Meanwhile, Levin, in his trousers but without coat or waistcoat, was pacing up and down his hotel room, incessantly thrusting his head out of the door and glancing along the corridor. But there was no sign in the corridor of the man he was waiting for and, brandishing his arms, he returned and addressed Oblonsky, who was quietly smoking.

"Was there ever a man in such a terribly idiotic position?" he exclaimed.

"Yes, it is stupid," Oblonsky concurred with a soothing smile. "But calm down, it will be here in a minute."

"The hell it will!" Levin said with suppressed fury. "And these idiotic open waistcoats! It's impossible!" he cried, glancing at the crumpled front of his shirt. "And what if the things have already gone to the station!" he exclaimed in despair.

"Then you'll put on mine."

"I should have done that long ago!"

"One mustn't look ridiculous. . . . Wait. It will all *come right*."

What happened was that when Levin had told his old servant to get his things ready, Kuzma brought his dress coat, waistcoat, and everything else he thought necessary.

"And the shirt?" Levin cried.

"You've got it on, sir," replied Kuzma with a self-complacent smile.

Kuzma had not thought of leaving out a clean shirt and, having been told to pack everything and take it to the Shcherbatskys', from where the newlyweds were to start that evening, he had done so, packing everything except the dress suit. The shirt Levin had put on in the morning was all crumpled and quite impossible to wear with the fashionable low-cut waistcoat. It was too far to send to the Shcherbatskys'. A servant was sent out to buy one, but he came back with the news that the shops were all closed: it was Sunday. They sent to Oblonsky's for one, but it was much too wide and too short. At last they sent to the Shcherbatskys' to have Levin's things unpacked. Everyone was waiting for the bridegroom in the church, while he was pacing the room like a wild beast in a cage, looking out along the corridor and recalling with horror and despair what he had said to Kitty and what she must be thinking now.

At last the culprit Kuzma rushed into the room with the shirt, panting and out of breath.

"Only just in time, sir. They were already putting the trunk into the cart."

Three minutes later Levin, not looking at the clock for fear of upsetting himself still more, tore down the corridor.

"That won't help matters," Oblonsky said with a smile, as he followed him unhurriedly. "It will all *come right*, it will all *come right*, I tell you."

CHAPTER 4

"Here they are!" "That's him! Which one? The younger one, you mean? And look at her, poor dear! More dead than alive!" people in the crowd were saying as Levin met his bride at the door and went into the church with her.

Oblonsky told his wife the reason of the delay, and the guests smiled and whispered among themselves. Levin saw nothing and no one; he looked at his bride without taking his eyes off her.

Everyone said that she had lost her looks during the last few days and, standing at the altar, was nothing like so pretty as usual; but Levin did not think so. He looked at her hair dressed high under the long veil and white flowers, at the high, stand-up, gathered collar, covering her long neck at the sides and showing it in front in so virginal a way, and at her strikingly slender waist, and he thought she was prettier than ever—not because those flowers, that veil, or the dress ordered from Paris added anything to her beauty, but because, in spite of the finished gorgeousness of her dress, the expression on her sweet face, her eyes, her lips had still the same look of innocent truthfulness.

"I was beginning to think you were going to run away," she said and smiled at him.

"What happened to me was so silly that I'm ashamed to speak of it!" he said, reddening, and then he had to turn around to Koznyshev, who came up to him.

"Lovely story that—about your shirt!" said Koznyshev, shaking his head and smiling.

"Yes, yes," Levin replied, unable to understand what was being said to him.

"Well, my dear fellow," said Oblonsky with an air of feigned consternation, "you've got to settle an important point now. And I can see you're in the right frame of mind to appreciate it properly. I have been asked whether you will have new candles or used ones to hold? The difference is ten rubles," he added, pursing his lips into a smile. "I have made up my mind, but I'm afraid you mightn't agree."

Levin realized that it was a joke, but he could not smile.

"So what do you say? New or used ones? That is the question."

"Yes, yes, new ones."

"Well, thank you very much. The question is settled!" said Oblonsky, smiling. "Dear me, how stupid people become in these circumstances," he remarked to Chirikov, when Levin, after an embarrassed glance at him, moved back to his bride.

522

"Mind you step first on the mat, Kitty," said the Countess Nordston, coming up to them. "You're a fine one!" she added, addressing Levin.

"Well, frightened, are you?" said Kitty's old aunt, Maria Dmitriyevna.

"Are you cold? You look pale. Wait, bend your head down," said Kitty's sister, Princess Lvov, and, raising her plump, beautiful arms, she smilingly adjusted Kitty's flowers on her head.

Dolly came up, wanted to say something, but could not speak and started crying and laughing unnaturally.

Kitty gazed at everybody with the same unseeing eyes as Levin. To everything that was said to her she could only reply with a smile of happiness which was so natural to her now.

Meanwhile the clergy put on their vestments and the priest and deacon came forward to the lectern near the entrance of the church. The priest turned to Levin and said something. Levin did not hear what he said.

"Take the bride's hand and lead her," said the best man to Levin.

For a long time Levin could not understand what was required of him. For a long time they were trying to put him right and were about to give it up as a bad job, for he kept taking her by the wrong hand or himself using the wrong hand, when at last he understood that he had to take her right hand in his right hand without changing his position. When at last he had taken his bride's hand properly, the priest walked a few paces ahead of them and stopped at the lectern. The crowds of friends and relations, in a buzz of conversation and a rustle of ladies' trains, moved after them. Someone bent down and arranged the bride's train. It became so still in the church that one could hear the drops of wax falling from the candles.

The little old priest, in his high, sacerdotal headgear, and with his locks of gray hair glistening like silver and combed back behind his ears, freed his old hands from under the heavy silver vestment with the gold cross on the back, and began fumbling with something at the lectern.

Oblonsky went up to him cautiously, whispered something in his ear, and winking at Levin, went back again.

The priest lit two candles decorated with flowers, holding them askew in his left hand, so that the wax dripped slowly from them, and turned, facing the bridal pair. It was the same priest who had heard Levin's confession. He looked with sad and weary eyes at the bride and bridegroom, sighed, and freeing his right hand from under the vestments, blessed the bridegroom with it, and afterward, but with a shade of solicitous tenderness, placed his fingers on Kitty's bowed head. Then he gave them the candles and, taking the censer, walked slowly away from them.

"Is it really true?" thought Levin and glanced around at his bride. He could see her profile slightly from above, and from the barely perceptible movements of her lips and eyelashes he knew that she was aware of his look. She did not look around at him, but her high, gathered collar stirred, rising to her pink little ear. He perceived that a sigh was suppressed in her breast and that her little hand in the long glove, in which she held the candle, shook.

All the bother about his shirt, about being late, his conversation with friends and relations, their displeasure, his ridiculous position—all suddenly vanished and he felt happy and terrified.

The tall, handsome head deacon, in his alb of silver cloth, his curly hair parted on either side of his head, stepped briskly forward, and lifting his stole with the practiced movement of two fingers, stopped in front of the priest.

"Bless us, O Lord!" slowly one after the other the solemn sounds resounded through the church, vibrating through the air.

"Blessed be our Lord, now and hereafter, for ever and ever," meekly intoned the old priest in response, still fumbling with something on the lectern. And filling the entire church from the windows to vaulted roof, a chord sung by the invisible choir rose in full diapason, swelled, hung motionless for a moment, and softly died away.

Prayers were said, as usual, for peace on high and for salvation, for the Holy Synod and the emperor; they also offered up prayers for the servants of the Lord betrothed that day, Konstantin and Katherine.

"Give unto them perfect love, peace and help, O Lord, we beseech Thee." The whole church seemed to be filled with the archdeacon's voice.

524

Levin listened to the words and was struck by them. "How did they know that it is help, yes, help that one needs?" he thought, recalling his recent fears and doubts. "What do I know? What can I do in this awful matter without help? Yes, it is indeed help that I want now."

When the priest finished the litany, he turned to the bride and bridegroom with a book in his hand.

"Eternal God who unitest them that were separated," he read in his gentle, singsong voice, "and who hath ordained for them an indissoluble union in love; Thou who didst bless Isaac and Rebecca and hast kept Thy promise to their descendants, bless these Thy servants Konstantin and Katherine and lead them into the path of righteousness. For Thou art merciful, O Lord, Lover of mankind, and we praise Thee. Glory be to the Father, and to the Son, and to the Holy Ghost, now and for ever and ever."

"A-amen!" Again the church was filled with the strains from the invisible choir.

" 'Who unitest them that were separated and who hast ordained for them an insoluble union in love,' how profound those words are and how they fit in with what one feels at this moment!" thought Levin. "Does she feel the same as I do?"

And, looking around, he met her eyes.

And from the expression of her eyes he concluded that she understood them as he did. But that was not so; she understood scarcely anything of the service and was not even listening to the words of the ceremony. She could not listen to them or understand them: so powerful was the one feeling which filled her soul and which was growing stronger and stronger. It was a feeling of joy at the full fruition of what had been going on in her soul for the last month and a half and what had during those six weeks gladdened and worried her. On the day when, in the ballroom of the house in the Arbat, she had gone up to him in her brown dress and silently given herself to him, on that day there took place in her heart a complete rupture with her former life, and a completely new, different, and quite unknown life began for her, though in reality her old life was still going on. Those six weeks had been the happiest and the most agonizing time for her. All her life, all her desires and

525

hopes were concentrated on this one man, whom she still did not understand, to whom she was bound by a feeling which she understood even less than the man himself, a feeling that attracted her to him and at the same time repelled her, and yet all the time she went on living her former life. Living the old life, she was horrified at herself, at her utter and complete indifference to all her past: to the things, habits, and people who had loved and still loved her; to her mother, who was hurt by her indifference; to her dear affectionate father, whom she had loved before more than anyone else in the world. At one moment she was horrified at this indifference and at the next she rejoiced at what had brought it about. She could not think of anything, nor desire anything that was not part of that man's life; but this new life had not yet begun and she could not even picture it clearly to herself. There was only anticipation—fear and joy of the new and the unknown. And in a few moments now, the anticipation and the unknown, the remorse and the renunciation of her old life—everything would come to an end, a new life would begin. This new life could not but be terrible because no one could tell what it would be like, but terrible or not it was something that had already been accepted by her as a fact six weeks ago and what was happening now was merely the consecration of what had taken place in her soul long ago.

Turning again to the lectern, the priest with some difficulty picked up Kitty's little ring and, asking Levin for his hand, put it on the tip of his finger. "With this ring I wed thee, Konstantin, servant of God, to the servant of God, Katherine." And putting the big ring on Kitty's slender, rosy finger, pathetic in its weakness, the priest repeated the same words.

Several times Levin and Kitty tried to guess what they had to do, and every time they were wrong and the priest corrected them in a whisper. At last, having done what was necessary, he again made the sign of the cross over them with the rings and again gave the large ring to Kitty and the little one to Levin, again they got confused and twice passed the rings backward and forward without getting it right.

Dolly, Chirikov, and Koznyshev came forward to help them. The result was more confusion, whispering, and smiles, but the touchingly solemn expression on the faces of the young couple did not change; on the contrary, while mixed up over their hands, they looked more serious and solemn than before, and the smile with which Oblonsky whispered to them to put on their rings involuntarily died on his lips. He could not help feeling that any kind of smile would hurt them.

"Thou hast from the beginning created them male and female," the priest read after they had exchanged rings, "and it is through Thee that the wife is joined to her husband to be a helpmeet to him and for the procreation of the human race. Do thou, O Lord, who hast sent down Thy truth upon Thy heritage and gavest Thy promise to our fathers from generation to generation of Thy chosen people, look down upon Thy servant Konstantin and Thy servant Katherine and confirm their union in faith, in concord, in truth, and in love. . . ."

Levin felt more and more that all his ideas about marriage and his dreams of how he would arrange his life had been mere childishness, and that this was something he had never understood and was now still further from understanding, although it was happening to him; and in his breast a tremor rose higher and higher and uncontrollable tears started to his eyes.

CHAPTER 5

All Moscow was in the church, relatives and friends. During the ceremony, in the brilliantly lit church, among the crowd of elegantly dressed women and girls, and men in white ties, frock coats, and uniforms, conversation in seemly low tones never flagged. It was usually started by the men, the women being mostly absorbed in watching every detail of the service that always concerned them so intimately.

In the circle nearest the bride were her two sisters: Dolly and the eldest one, Princess Lvov, a placid beauty, who had arrived from abroad.

"Why is Marie in lilac at a wedding?" asked Mrs. Konsunsky. "It's almost like black."

"With her complexion it is the only thing," replied Princess Drubtskoy. "I can't understand why they are having the wedding in the evening. It's the sort of thing tradespeople would do."

"It's prettier. I was married in the evening too," replied Mrs. Konsunsky, and sighed as she remembered how sweet she had looked that day, how absurdly in love her husband had been with her, and how different things were now.

"They say that if one has been best man more than ten times one never marries," said Count Sinyavin to the pretty Princess Charsky, who had designs on him. "I wanted to be one for the tenth time to insure myself against marriage, but the place was already taken."

Princess Charsky only answered with a smile. She was looking at Kitty and thinking of the time when she would be standing where Kitty now stood, beside Count Sinyavin, and how she would then remind him of his present joke.

Young Shcherbatsky was telling Mrs. Nikolayev, an old lady-in-waiting, that he was going to put the crown on Kitty's chignon for luck.

"She shouldn't have worn a chignon," replied Mrs. Nikolayev, who had long ago made up her mind that if the old widower she was trying to catch ever married her, she would have a quiet wedding. "I don't like all this *faste*."

Koznyshev was talking to Dolly, jokingly assuring her that the custom of going away after the wedding was spreading because newly married couples always felt a little conscience-stricken.

"Your brother ought to be proud of himself. She is wonderfully sweet. I expect you must envy him. Don't you?"

"I'm afraid I'm past all that," he replied, and his face unexpectedly assumed a sad and serious expression.

Oblonsky was telling his sister-in-law the pun he had made about divorce.

"I must put her wreath straight," she said, not listening to him.

"What a pity she has lost her good looks," Countess Nordston said to Princess Lvov. "He's not worth her little finger for all that. Don't you think so?"

"No, I like him very much," replied the princess. "Not because he will be my brother-in-law, either. Look how well he carries himself. And it is so difficult to carry oneself well in such a situation and not look ridiculous. And he is not ridiculous or stiff. You can see he is moved."

"You expected it, didn't you?"

"Almost. She always liked him."

"Well, let's see which of them will be the first to step on the mat. I told Kitty to step on it first."

"It won't make any difference," replied Princess Lvov. "We are all obedient wives. It's a family tradition with us."

"And I purposely stepped on the mat before Vassily. And you, Dolly?"

Dolly was standing near them, she heard them, but made no answer. She was deeply moved. There were tears in her eyes, and she could not have uttered a word without bursting out crying. She was glad for Kitty and Levin; going over her own wedding in her thoughts, she kept looking at the beaming Oblonsky, and, forgetting the present, she remembered only her first innocent love. She remembered not herself only, but all the women who were near her or with whom she was acquainted; she thought of them at that most solemn hour of their lives when, like Kitty, they had stood at the altar with love, hope, and fear in their hearts, renouncing their past and entering upon the mysterious future. Among all these brides that came into her mind she recalled her dear Anna, about whose impending divorce she had recently heard. She, too, had once stood there just as innocent in her veil and orange blossoms. And now what?

"How awfully strange!" she murmured.

The two sisters, the friends and relatives were not the only ones to follow every detail of the ceremony; the women spectators, who were complete strangers, watched it with breathless excitement, afraid of missing a single movement or expression of the bride and the bridegroom. They did not bother to reply to the men, who remained indifferent, and often did not hear their jocular or irrelevant remarks.

"Why has she been crying? Is she being married against her will?"

"Against her will for such a handsome man? A prince, isn't he?"

"And is that her sister in white satin? Just listen to the deacon bellowing: 'And obey thy husband.'"

"Is it the Chudovsky choir?"

"No, the Synod's."

"I asked the footman. Says he's taking her straight to his estate. They say he's rolling in money. That's why they made her marry him."

"Not at all, they make a lovely couple."

"You were saying crinolines were not worn fuller at the sides, but look at that one in puce—an ambassador's wife, they say—see how they stand out?—first one side and then the other."

"What a sweet thing the bride is, like a lamb decked for the slaughter! Say what you like, one can't help feeling sorry for the poor girl."

That was what they were saying in the crowd of the women spectators who had succeeded in slipping in at the church door.

CHAPTER 6

When the rite of betrothal was over, a verger spread a piece of pink silk in front of the lectern in the middle of the church, the choir began singing a psalm to some elaborate and complicated setting in which the bass and tenor exchanged the same phrase with one another, and the priest turned round and motioned the couple to the outspread piece of pink silk. Often as they had heard the saying that he who stepped first on the mat would be the head of the house, neither Levin nor Kitty could think of that as they took those few steps. They did not hear the loud remarks and arguments of some who maintained that he was first and others who claimed that they did it both together.

After the usual questions whether they wished to be married and whether they were promised to anyone else and their replies, which sounded strange to themselves, the second part of the marriage service began. Kitty listened to the words of the prayer, trying to understand their meaning but unable to do so. A feeling of triumph and radiant joy filled her heart more and more as the ceremony proceeded and robbed her of her ability to attend to it.

They prayed "that they may live in chastity for the

benefit of the fruit of the womb, and find joy in their sons and daughters." Mention was made of the creation of woman from Adam's rib and "therefore shall a man leave his father and his mother, and shall cleave unto his wife: and they shall be one flesh," and that "this is a great mystery"; they prayed that God should make them fruitful and bless them as He blessed Isaac and Rebecca, Joseph, Moses, and Zipporah, and that they should see their children's children. "It is all very beautiful," thought Kitty as she heard those words, "and it cannot be otherwise." And a smile of happiness, which involuntarily communicated itself to all those who looked at her, shone on her radiant face.

"Put it right on!" were the words of advice heard when the priest brought out the crowns, and Shcherbatsky, his hand shaking in its three-buttoned glove, held the crown high above Kitty's head.

Levin looked around at her and he was struck by the joyous radiance of her face, and her feeling involuntarily communicated itself to him. He felt as bright and happy as she did.

They enjoyed hearing the reading of the Epistle and the reverberation of the head deacon's voice in the last verse, an event that was awaited with impatience by the outside public. They enjoyed drinking the warm red wine and water from the shallow cup, and they liked it even more when the priest, throwing back his chasuble and taking their hands in his, led them round the lectern while a bass voice chanted *Rejoice, O Isaiah!* Shcherbatsky and Chirikov, who were holding up the crowns and getting entangled in the bride's veil, also smiled and were happy without knowing why, lagging behind or stumbling over the bride and bridegroom every time the priest happened to stop. The spark of joy glowing in Kitty's heart seemed to have spread to everyone in the church. Levin could not help feeling that the priest and deacon wanted to smile just as he did.

Lifting the crowns from their heads, the priest read the last prayer and congratulated the married couple. Levin glanced at Kitty and he thought he had never seen her like that before. She was ravishingly beautiful with the new light of happiness shining in her face. Levin wanted to say something to her, but he did not know whether the ceremony was over yet. The priest helped him out of the difficulty. He said softly, with a smile on his kindly mouth: "Kiss your wife, and you, kiss your husband," and took the candles from their hands.

Levin kissed her carefully on her smiling lips, offered her his arm, and with a new strange sense of closeness, led her out of the church. He did not believe, he could not believe that it was true. Only when their surprised and timid glances met did he believe it, for he felt that they were one already.

After supper, the same night, Levin and Kitty left for the country.

CHAPTER 7

Vronsky and Anna had already been traveling together in Europe for three months. They had visited Venice, Rome, Naples, and had only just arrived in a small Italian town where they planned to stay for some time.

A handsome headwaiter, his thick, oiled hair parted from the nape of his neck upward, wearing a swallow-tail coat with a broad, white lawn shirt front and with a string of charms hanging round his paunch, with his hands in his pockets and his eyes screwed up contemptuously, was answering in a severe tone the questions of a gentleman standing beside him. Hearing steps mounting the staircase at the other side of the entrance, the head-waiter turned around and, seeing the Russian count who occupied the best rooms in the hotel, took his hands out of his pockets and, bowing respectfully, said that the courier had been, and that the business of renting the palazzo had been settled. The agent was ready to sign the agreement.

"Oh, that's good," said Vronsky. "And is Madame at home?"

"Yes, sir. She has been out for a walk, but has returned now."

Vronsky took off his soft, wide-brimmed hat and with his handkerchief wiped his perspiring forehead and his hair, grown well over his ears and brushed back so as to hide his bald patch. And glancing absent-mindedly at the man who was still standing there watching him, was about to go in.

"This gentleman, sir, is a Russian and he has been asking about you," said the headwaiter.

With a mixed feeling of annoyance at being unable to get away from acquaintances anywhere and a desire to find some sort of diversion from the monotony of his life, Vronsky cast another glance at the man who had stopped a short distance away, and at one and the same moment the eyes of both lighted up.

"Golenishchev!"

"Vronsky!"

It was indeed Golenishchev, a comrade of Vronsky's at the Corps of Pages. In the Corps, Golenishchev belonged to the liberal party, had left it with a civil-service rank, but had never actually served in any government office. The two friends had drifted apart after leaving the Corps and had only met once since.

On that occasion Vronsky gathered that Golenishchev had chosen some highly intellectual "liberal" activity and as a consequence was prone to look down on Vronsky's profession and activities. At that meeting, therefore, Vronsky had treated Golenishchev with the cold, proud indifference of which he was master and the meaning of which was: "You may like or dislike my way of life—I don't care a damn about that—but if you want to know me, you must respect me." Golenishchev, for his part, was contemptuously indifferent to Vronsky's attitude. It would seem therefore that this meeting ought to have estranged them still more. Yet now they both brightened up and exclaimed with delight at recognizing one another. Vronsky would never have expected to have been so pleased to see Golenishchev, but probably he did not realize himself how bored he was. He forgot the disagreeable impression left by their last meeting and stretched out his hand to his old schoolfellow, looking genuinely pleased. A similar expression of pleasure replaced the former anxious look on Golenishchev's face.

"I'm so glad to see you!" said Vronsky, showing his strong white teeth in a friendly smile.

"I heard the name of Vronsky, but I did not know which Vronsky. I'm very, very glad!"

"Let's go in. Well, and what are you doing?"

"I've been living here for over a year now. I am working."

"Ah!" Vronsky said with interest. "Let's go in."

And as is usually the way with Russians when they do not wish their servants to understand what they are saying, he began speaking in French instead of in Russian, as he should have done.

"You know Mrs. Karenin? We are traveling together. I am going to see her now," he said, scanning Golenishchev's face attentively.

"Oh, I didn't know," Golenishchev replied in a casual tone of voice (though he knew quite well). "Have you been here long?" he added.

"Me? Three days," replied Vronsky, again peering intently at his friend's face.

"Yes," Vronsky said to himself, catching the meaning of Golenishchev's look and of the way he had changed the subject, "he is a decent fellow and looks at the matter in the right way. I can introduce him to Anna: he looks at it in the right way."

During the three months he had spent abroad with Anna, Vronsky asked himself every time he came across new people how they would regard his relations with Anna, and found that for the most part the men looked at it *in the right way*. But had he and those who looked at it *in the right way* been asked what they understood by that, they would have been at a loss what to reply.

As a matter of fact, those who in Vronsky's opinion understood it *in the right way* did not understand it in any way, but simply behaved as well-bred people do behave when faced with the complicated and insoluble problems which encompass life on every side—they behaved decently, avoiding any indelicate allusions or indiscreet questions. They pretended to understand perfectly the significance and meaning of the situation, to countenance and even approve of it, but to consider it inappropriate and unnecessary to say anything about it.

Vronsky at once guessed that Golenishchev was one of that kind and was therefore doubly pleased to have met him. And, indeed, Golenishchev, when he had been introduced to Anna, behaved to her as well as Vronsky could have desired. He was evidently quite able to avoid without the least effort any subject that might lead to embarrassment.

534

He had never met Anna before and was struck by her beauty and still more by the simplicity with which she accepted her position. She blushed when Vronsky brought in Golenishchev, and this childlike blush which spread all over her frank and beautiful face pleased him very much. But what he liked especially was that apparently intentionally, so as to prevent any misunderstanding with a stranger, she at once called Vronsky simply Alexey and said that they were about to move into a house they had taken, known locally as a palazzo. This straightforward and simple attitude toward her own position pleased Golenishchev. Watching Anna's good-natured, gay, and energetic manner and knowing Karenin and Vronsky, Golenishchev could not help thinking that he quite understood her. It seemed to him that he understood what she herself was quite unable to understand, namely, how she could be so energetic, gay, and happy after having caused her husband's unhappiness, having abandoned him and her son and lost her own good name.

"It's mentioned in the guidebook," said Golenishchev, referring to the palazzo Vronsky was taking. "There is a fine Tintoretto there. Of his last period."

"I tell you what," said Vronsky, addressing Anna. "It's a glorious day, let's go and have another look at the place."

"I'd love to. I'll go and put on my hat. You say it's hot?" she said, stopping at the door and looking inquiringly at Vronsky. And again a bright flush covered her face.

Vronsky understood from her look that she did not know yet on what terms he wished to be with Golenishchev and that she was not sure whether she had behaved as he would have liked.

He gave her a long, tender look.

"No, not very," he said.

And she thought that she had understood everything and, above all, that he was satisfied with her. She gave him a smile and walked rapidly out of the room.

The two friends glanced at each other and both of them looked simultaneously embarrassed, as though Golenishchev, who obviously admired Anna, wanted to say something about her but did not know what, while Vronsky, too, wanted and was afraid of the same thing.

"Well, so you too have settled here?" began Vronsky in order to say something. "And you're still working at the same thing?" he went on, recollecting that he had heard that Golenishchev was writing something or other.

"Yes, I'm writing the second part of *Two Principles*," said Golenishchev, flushing with pleasure at the question. "To be quite exact, I'm not writing yet but preparing and collecting material. The book will be much more comprehensive and will deal with almost all problems. We in Russia don't seem to realize that we are the heirs of Byzantium," and he embarked on a long and heated explanation.

At first Vronsky felt uncomfortable because he did not know even the first part of *Two Principles*, of which its author spoke as of something well known. But afterward, when Golenishchev began to expound his ideas and Vronsky was able to follow them, he listened to him not without interest, though ignorant of *Two Principles*, for Golenishchev talked well. However, Vronsky could not help being surprised and sorry to see the irritable excitement with which Golenishchev spoke of the subject with which he was so preoccupied. The longer he talked, the more his eyes blazed, the more impatiently he refuted the arguments of his imaginary opponents, and the more agitated and hurt became the expression of his face. Remembering Golenishchev as a thin, lively, good-natured, and generous boy, always at the top of his class, Vronsky was wholly at a loss to understand the reason for his irritability and did not approve of it. What he did not like most of all was that Golenishchev, a man of good social standing, should put himself on the same footing with some common scribblers who irritated him and made him angry. Was it worthwhile? Vronsky did not like that, but feeling that Golenishchev was unhappy, he was sorry for him. Signs of unhappiness, of mental derangement almost, could be detected on his mobile, rather handsome face as, without even noticing that Anna had come back into the room, he went on hurriedly and heatedly expounding his views.

When Anna came back in her hat and cloak and stood beside him, toying with her parasol with quick movements of her beautiful hand, Vronsky with a feeling of relief tore himself away from Golenishchev's complaining eyes, which were fixed on him with such intensity, and looked at his enchanting companion, so full of life and gladness, with renewed love. Golenishchev recollected himself with an effort and looked dejected and gloomy at first, but Anna, favorably disposed to everyone (as she was at the time), soon revived his spirits by her simple and cheerful manner. After trying various topics of conversation, she at last got him onto the subject of painting, about which he talked very well, and listened attentively to him. They walked to the house they had taken and went over it.

"I am very glad of one thing," said Anna to Golenishchev, when they were going back to the hotel. "Alexey will have a nice studio. You certainly must use that room, darling," she said to Vronsky in Russian, addressing Vronsky so intimately because she realized that since Golenishchev was likely to become a close friend of theirs in their solitude, it was not necessary to be reserved in his presence.

"Do you paint?" asked Golenishchev, turning around quickly to Vronsky.

"Yes," said Vronsky, coloring. "I used to a long time ago and I've taken it up again a little now."

"He has great talent," said Anna with a happy smile. "I'm no judge, of course. But people who do know say the same."

CHAPTER 8

In that first period of her freedom and rapid recovery Anna felt quite unpardonably happy and full of the joy of life. The thought of her husband's unhappiness did not mar her own happiness. On the one hand, the thought of it was too awful to dwell on. On the other hand, her husband's unhappiness had brought her too much happiness to make her feel sorry. The memory of all that had happened to her after her illness: the reconciliation with her husband, the rupture, the news of Vronsky's wound, his reappearance, the preparations for divorce, the departure from the house of her husband, the parting from her son—all this now seemed like some feverish dream from which she had awakened abroad and alone with Vronsky. The thought of the wrong she had done her husband aroused in her a feeling akin to revulsion such as a drowning man might feel who had shaken off another man who clung to him in the water. It was wrong, of course, but it was better not to think about such terrible details.

One comforting reflection about her conduct had occurred to her at the first moment of the rupture, and when she now recalled the past, she also remembered that reflection. "I have inevitably caused that man's unhappiness," she thought, "but I don't want to profit by his unhappiness; I, too, am suffering and I shall go on suffering: I am losing what I most cherished, my good name and my son. I have done wrong and so I don't want to be happy, I don't want a divorce, and I shall go on suffering because of my disgrace and the separation from my son." But however sincere Anna was in her desire to suffer, she was not suffering. Neither was there any disgrace. With the tact they both possessed in such abundance and by avoiding Russian ladies, they never placed themselves in a false position abroad and everywhere met people who pretended to understand their position far better than they did themselves. The separation from her son, whom she loved, did not trouble her at first, either. The little girl, *his* child, was so sweet and Anna had grown so attached to her ever since she was all that was left to her, that she rarely thought of her son.

Her will to live, increased with her recovery, was so strong and the conditions of life were so new and so pleasant that Anna felt unpardonably happy. The more she got to know Vronsky, the more she loved him. She loved him for himself and for his love of her. To possess him completely was a constant joy to her. His closeness to her was always a delight. All the traits of his character with which she became more and more familiar were inexpressibly dear to her. His appearance, altered by civilian clothes, was as attractive to her as though she were a young girl in love for the first time. In everything he said, thought, and did, she saw something exceptionally great and noble. Her admiration of him often frightened her: she sought but could not find in him anything that was not beautiful. She dared not let him see her consciousness of her own inferiority. It seemed to her that if he knew it he might the sooner fall out of love with her; and she was afraid of nothing more now—although she had no grounds for it—than to forfeit his love. But she could not help being grateful to him for his attitude to her and showing how much she appreciated it. He who in her opinion had such a decided vocation for high office of state, in which he would have been conspicuously successful, had sacrificed his ambition for her and never showed the least regret. He was more than ever lovingly respectful to her, and the thought that she must never be made to feel the awkwardness of her position never deserted him for a moment. So brave and intrepid a man as he not only never contradicted her, but had no will of his own where she was concerned, and seemed to be only occupied in anticipating her every wish. And she could not help appreciating this, even though the very intensity of his solicitude for her, the atmosphere of care with which he surrounded her was occasionally a little too much for her.

Vronsky, meanwhile, although what he had so long desired had come to pass, was not altogether happy. He soon felt that the fulfillment of his desires gave him only one grain of the mountain of happiness he had expected. This fulfillment showed him the eternal error men make in imagining that their happiness depends on the realization of their desires. For a time after uniting his life with hers and putting on civilian clothes, he felt the delight of freedom in general, which he had not known before, and the freedom of love, and he was content; but not for long. He soon became aware that there arose in his heart the desire for desires—boredom. Involuntarily he began snatching at every fleeting caprice, mistaking it for a desire and a purpose. Sixteen hours of the day had to be filled somehow, for they were living abroad in complete freedom, cut off from the round of social life which had occupied most of his time in Petersburg. There could be no question of the pleasures of bachelor life which he had enjoyed on his previous journeys abroad, for one attempt of that kind produced an unexpected fit of depression in Anna quite disproportionate with the offense of a late supper with some acquaintances. Social intercourse with local people or Russians was also out of the question on account of the irregularity of their relations. Sight-seeing, apart from the fact that he had already seen everything, did not have for him, a Russian and an intelligent man, any of that inexplicable significance which the English manage to attach to it.

And just as a hungry animal seizes everything he happens to come across in the hope that it may be food, so Vronsky quite unconsciously seized now on politics, then on new books, and then on pictures.

Since as a young man he had shown an aptitude for painting and, not knowing how to spend his money, had begun collecting engravings, he now decided to take up painting, began working at it, and put into it all the store of unfulfilled desires that clamored for satisfaction.

He had a talent for understanding art and for imitating it with accuracy and good taste, and he imagined that he possessed what a true artist needs. After wavering for some time over which kind of painting to take up, religious, historical, genre, or realistic, he settled down to paint. He understood all the different kinds and could find inspiration in any of them; but he could not imagine that one could be totally ignorant of the different kinds of painting and find inspiration directly in what was within one's soul, regardless of whether what one painted belonged to any particular school. As he did not know this and found inspiration not directly in life but indirectly in the life that had already been embodied in art, he found inspiration very quickly and easily and as quickly and easily produced paintings which were very similar to the particular school he was trying to imitate.

The graceful and effective French school he liked best, and it was in that style that he began to paint Anna's portrait in an Italian costume, and he and everyone who saw it considered this portrait a great success.

CHAPTER 9

The old, neglected palazzo with its high, molded ceilings and its wall frescoes, its mosaic floors and heavy yellow damask hangings at the tall windows, vases standing on consoles and mantel shelves, carved doors and large, somber rooms hung with pictures—this palazzo, as soon as they had moved into it, by its very appearance encouraged Vronsky in the agreeable delusion that he was not so much a Russian landowner and equerry without a post as an enlightened connoisseur and patron of the arts and, in his own way, a modest artist who had renounced the world, his social connections and ambitions for the sake of the woman he loved.

The part chosen by Vronsky with their removal to the palazzo was completely successful, and making the acquaintance through Golenishchev of several interesting persons, he felt composed for a time. He painted studies from nature under the guidance of an Italian professor of painting and studied Italian life in the Middle Ages. He became so taken up with medieval Italian life that he even took to wearing his hat and throwing his cloak over his shoulder in medieval fashion, which became him very well.

"Here we live and know nothing of what's going on," Vronsky said one morning to Golenishchev who had come to see him. "Have you seen Mikhailov's picture?" he went on, handing him a Russian paper that had just arrived and pointing to an article on a Russian artist who was living in that very town and who had finished a picture which had long been talked of and bought before it was finished. The article criticized the government and the Academy for leaving such a remarkable artist without encouragement and help.

"I have," replied Golenishchev. "Of course he is not without talent, but his ideas are quite wrong. It's all the same Ivanov-Strauss-Renan attitude to Christ and religious painting."

"What is the subject of the picture?" asked Anna.

"Christ before Pilate. Christ is represented as a Jew with all the realism of the new school."

And led on by the question about the subject of the picture to one of his favorite topics, Golenishchev began to expound his views.

"I don't understand," he said, "how they can make so gross an error. Christ already has his definite embodiment in the works of the old masters. If, therefore, they want to depict not God but a revolutionary or a sage, let them take some character from history—Socrates, Franklin, Charlotte Corday—but certainly not Christ. They choose the one person that cannot be chosen as a subject for art, and then—"

"But is it true that this Mikhailov is in such straitened

circumstances?" asked Vronsky, thinking that, as a Russian Maecenas, he had to come to the help of an artist irrespective of whether his picture was good or not.

"Well, not entirely. He is a wonderful portrait painter. Have you seen his portrait of Mrs. Vassilchikov? But it seems that he doesn't want to paint any more portraits, so perhaps he really is in straitened circumstances. I say that—"

"Couldn't we ask him to paint a portrait of Anna?" said Vronsky.

"Why mine?" said Anna. "After your portrait of me I want no other. I'd rather he did one of Annie" (as she called her little girl). "And there she is," she added, looking out of the window at their handsome Italian nurse, who had taken the baby into the garden, and immediately glancing round unnoticed at Vronsky. The handsome Italian girl, whose head Vronsky was painting for his picture, was the only secret sorrow of Anna's life. While painting her, Vronsky had admired her beauty, which he thought was peculiarly medieval, and Anna dared not acknowledge to herself that she was afraid of being jealous of this nurse and therefore treated the woman with particular kindness and spoiled her and her little son.

Vronsky, too, glanced out of the window and into Anna's eyes, and at once turned to Golenishchev.

"Do you know this Mikhailov?" he asked.

"I have met him. He's an eccentric fellow and quite uneducated. One of the modern wild men one so often meets nowadays, you know. One of those freethinkers who have been brought up from the very beginning on ideas of atheism, negation, and materialism. Before," Golenishchev went on, either not observing or unwilling to observe that Anna and Vronsky wanted to speak, "a freethinker was a man who had been brought up on ideas of religion, law, and morality and came to be a freethinker through inner struggle and hard work; but now you get a new type of born freethinkers who grow up without ever having even heard that there used to be laws of morality or religion, that there used to be authorities. They grow up in ideas of negation of everything, or in other words, savages. He is one of them. He is, I believe, the son of a Moscow valet and has had no education. When he got to the Academy and won a reputation for himself, he, being no fool, tried to educate himself. And he turned to what he considered to be the true source of education, the periodicals. Now, in the old days, you see, a man, a Frenchman, for instance, who wished to get an education, would have begun to study all the classics, the theologians, the tragedians, the historians, and the philosophers, and you can easily imagine all the mental work that would have involved. But in our country today he at once becomes conversant with the literature of negation, rapidly assimilates the whole essence of the science of negation, and he has got all he wants. And that is not all. Twenty years ago he would have found in that kind of literature signs of the conflict with authorities, with the ideas that had been considered valid for centuries, and he would have gathered from that conflict that there was something else. But today he at once comes upon a literature which does not ever deign to dispute the old ideas but declares straight off: 'There is nothing else! Evolution, natural selection, the struggle for existence—that is all.' In my article I—"

"You know what," said Anna, who had for some time been exchanging furtive glances with Vronsky and who knew that Vronsky was not interested in the education of the artist, but was only concerned to help him and give him a commission for a portrait, "you know what," she determinedly interrupted Golenishchev, who was only just getting into his stride, "let's go and see him!"

Golenishchev recollected himself and readily agreed. But as the artist lived in a remote suburb, it was decided to take a cab.

An hour later Anna, sitting beside Golenishchev with Vronsky facing them, drove up to an attractive new house in the remote suburb. Having learned from the house porter's wife, who came out to meet them, that Mikhailov admitted visitors to his studio, but that at that moment he was at his lodgings a few steps away, they sent her with their cards and a request to view his pictures.

CHAPTER 10

The artist Mikhailov was at work as usual when Vronsky's and Golenishchev's cards were brought to him. In the morning he had been working in his studio at his big picture. On returning home he had got angry with his wife because she had not managed to placate their landlady, who had demanded the rent.

"I've told you a hundred times not to start an argument with her. You're a fool as it is, but when you start arguing in Italian you become a treble fool," he said to her at the end of a long dispute.

"Then you shouldn't get behind with the rent. It's not my fault. If I had any money——"

"Leave me alone, for God's sake!" cried Mikhailov with tears in his voice, and, stopping his ears, went off into his workroom behind the partition and locked himself in. "What a stupid woman!" he said to himself, sat down at the table, and opening a folder, feverishly set to work on a sketch he had begun.

He never worked with such fervor or so successfully as when things were going badly with him and especially after a quarrel with his wife. "Oh, if only I could get away somewhere!" he thought, continuing to work. He was making a sketch of a figure of a man in a fit of anger. He had made one sketch before, but he had not been satisfied with it. "No, that one was better. . . . Where is it?" He went back to his wife and, frowning and not looking at her, asked his eldest little girl what she had done with the paper he had given them. The paper with the discarded drawing was found, but it was dirty and spotted with candle grease. He took it nevertheless, put it on his table, and, stepping back and screwing up his eyes, began examining it. Suddenly he smiled and flung up his hands joyfully.

"That's it! That's it!" he said and, picking up his pencil, at once began drawing rapidly. A grease spot had given the figure a new pose.

He was drawing this new pose when he suddenly remembered the energetic face, with a jutting-out chin, of

544

a shopkeeper from whom he bought cigars, and he gave the man he was drawing that shopkeeper's face and chin. He laughed with delight. The figure he was drawing, instead of being dead and artificial, had sprung to life and could not possibly be altered. It was alive and was clearly and unmistakably defined. The drawing could be corrected in accordance with the requirements of the figure; one could, and indeed one should, find a different position for the legs, change completely the position of the left arm, and throw back the hair. But in making these changes he did not alter the figure, but merely removed what concealed it. He merely removed, as it were, the coverings which made it impossible to see it; each new stroke revealed more and more the whole figure in all its force and vigor as it had suddenly appeared to him by the action of the grease spot. He was carefully finishing the drawing when the cards were brought to him.

"One moment!"

He went out to his wife.

"I'm sorry, Sasha, don't be angry!" he said to her with a timid and affectionate smile. "You were wrong. I was wrong. I shall get it all settled."

Having made it up with his wife, he put on an olive-green overcoat with a velvet collar, and went to the studio. The successful drawing was already forgotten. Now he was pleased and excited by the visit to his studio of these important Russian visitors who had come in a carriage.

About his picture, the one at present on the easel, he felt deep inside him that no one had ever painted a picture like it. He did not think that his picture was better than all the Raphaels, but he knew that what he wanted and what he did express in that picture no one had ever expressed before. He was quite sure of that, he had known it a long time, ever since he had begun to paint it; but the opinions of others, whoever they might be, were of great importance to him all the same and they agitated him profoundly. Every remark, even the most trivial, showing that his critics saw even a small part of what he himself saw in the picture, affected him deeply. He always attributed to his critics a more profound understanding than he had himself and always expected them to see in his work something he had himself failed to see. And he often imagined that he found it in their criticisms.

He walked rapidly to the entrance of his studio and, in spite of his excitement, he was struck by the soft light on Anna's figure as she stood in the shadow of the porch listening to something Golenishchev was heatedly expounding and evidently wishing at the same time to look at the approaching artist. He did not himself notice how, as he approached them, he seized and absorbed this impression, just as he had the tobacconist's chin, and hid it away somewhere at the back of his mind from where he would get it when he needed it. The visitors, already disillusioned by Golenishchev's account of the artist, were even more disillusioned by his personal appearance. Of medium height, thickset, and with a nervous kind of walk, Mikhailov, in his brown hat, olive-green coat, and narrow trousers (when wide ones had long been the fashion), and especially his broad, commonplace face, expressing a combination of timidity and a desire to preserve his dignity, created an unpleasant impression.

"Come in, please," he said, trying to look indifferent, and entering the passage, he took a key out of his pocket and unlocked the door.

CHAPTER 11

On entering the studio, Mikhailov again examined his visitors and made a mental note of Vronsky's face, especially his cheekbones. Although his artistic sense was always on the alert, collecting material, and although he felt more and more excited as the time approached when an opinion would be expressed about his work, he quickly and shrewdly formed an opinion of these three persons out of hardly perceptible signs. That fellow (Golenishchev) was one of the local Russian residents. Mikhailov did not remember his name, or where he had met him or what they had talked about. He only remembered his face as he remembered all the faces he had ever seen, but he also remembered that it was one of those faces whom he had mentally laid aside with the enormous category of pseudo-important faces lacking in expression. Long hair and a very open forehead imparted a semblance of distinction to the face, which had only one insignificant, childish, restless expression, concentrated just above the narrow bridge of the nose. Vronsky and Anna, according to Mikhailov's ideas, must be distinguished and wealthy Russians, who understood nothing about art, but who pretended to be connoisseurs and art lovers. "I suppose they have already done the round of the old masters and are now visiting the studios of the modern ones, the German charlatan and the pre-Raphaelite fool of an Englishman, and have come to me just to complete their sight-seeing program," he thought. He knew very well the dilettanti's way (the more intelligent they were, the worse it was) of visiting the studios of modern painters with the aim of being able to say afterward that art had declined and that the more modern art one saw, the more evident it became that the great old masters were inimitable. He expected all this, he saw it all in their faces, in the careless indifference with which they talked among themselves, looked at the lay figures and busts, and walked about unconcernedly waiting for him to uncover his picture. But in spite of all this, as he turned over his studies, pulled up the blinds, and took the sheet down from his picture, he felt intense excitement, the more so because though in his opinion all distinguished and wealthy Russians were swine and fools, he could not help liking Vronsky and especially Anna.

"There!" he said, fidgeting and stepping aside and pointing to the picture. "This is *Pilate's Admonition*, Matthew, chapter twenty-seven," he went on, feeling that his lips were beginning to tremble with agitation. He moved away and stood behind them.

During the few seconds his visitors were silently looking at the picture, Mikhailov, too, looked at it, looked at it with the indifferent eye of a stranger. For those few seconds he believed in advance that the profoundest and fairest judgment would be pronounced by those very visitors whom he had so despised a few moments ago. He forgot all he had thought of his picture during the three years he had worked on it; he forgot all its fine qualities he had been so certain about—he saw it with the fresh, indifferent eyes of the strangers and saw nothing good in it. In the foreground he saw Pilate's vexed face and the serene face of Christ, and in the background the figures of Pilate's servants and the face of John, watching what was taking place. Each of those faces, which had grown up within him with its own character after so much searching, so many faults and corrections, each face that had given him so much pain and pleasure, and all those faces so often placed and replaced to make sure that they formed one whole, all those shades of color and tone obtained with such effort—all of it seen now with the eyes of those strangers seemed to him like so many commonplaces repeated over and over again. Even the face of Christ that was most dear to him, the focal point of the picture that sent him into transports of joy when he first discovered it, no longer moved him when he looked at the picture with their eyes. He saw a well-painted (and not even so well-painted, for he discovered a multitude of faults now) repetition of those innumerable Christs of Titian, Raphael, Rubens, with the same soldiers and the same Pilates. It was all trivial, poor, stale, and indeed, badly painted—pretentious and weak. They would be justified in saying a few hypocritical and polite things in the presence of the artist and in pitying and laughing at him when left to themselves.

The silence (though it only lasted a minute) became too oppressive for him. To break it and show that he was not excited, he made an effort and turned to Golenishchev.

"I believe I have had the pleasure of meeting you," he said, glancing uneasily now at Anna and now at Vronsky, so as not to miss a single detail of the expression of their faces.

"Why, of course, we first met at Rossi's; remember the party that Italian girl—the new Rachel—recited at," Golenishchev began glibly, turning to the painter and removing his gaze from the picture, without the slightest show of regret.

Noticing, however, that Mikhailov was waiting to hear what he thought of his picture, he said:

"Your picture has progressed a great deal since I last saw it. And now, as then, the thing that strikes me particularly is the figure of Pilate. One can understand that man so well, a kind, good-natured fellow, but a bureaucrat to the tips of his fingers, a man who knows not what he is doing. But it seems to me . . ."

The whole of Mikhailov's mobile face suddenly lighted up: his eyes shone. He wanted to say something, but he was too excited to utter a word and pretended to clear his throat. Low as his opinion was of Golenishchev's ability to understand art, trite as his remark was about the expression of Pilate's face betraying the bureaucrat, and offensive as so trivial a remark seemed before anything had been said about what was important, Mikhailov was absolutely delighted with it. He himself thought the same of Pilate's figure. The fact that it was only one of a million of other opinions which, as Mikhailov well knew, might have been made with equal truth, did not detract for him from the significance of Golenishchev's remark. His heart warmed to Golenishchev for that remark and from being depressed he suddenly became elated. In an instant his whole picture came to life before his eyes with the unutterable complexity of all living things. Mikhailov again tried to say that that was how he understood Pilate, but he could not control the violent trembling of his lips and was unable to utter a word. Vronsky and Anna also said something in the low voice in which—partly not to offend an artist and partly not to say something foolish, which is so easy to do when speaking of art—people usually talk at exhibitions. Mikhailov thought that his picture had made an impression on them too. He went up to them.

"How wonderful Christ's expression is!" said Anna. She liked that expression best of all she saw, and she felt that it was the central point of the picture and that therefore to praise it would be agreeable to the artist. "You can see he is sorry for Pilate."

This again was one of the million just observations which might be made about his picture as a whole and about the figure of Christ. She said He was sorry for Pilate. In Christ's expression there was bound to be pity, for there was love in it as well as peace that was not of this world, a readiness for death, and a consciousness of the vanity of words. Of course there was an expression of a state official in Pilate and of pity in Christ, for the one was the personification of carnal and the other of spiritual life. All this and much more flashed through Mikhailov's mind. And again his face shone with rapture.

"Yes, and how well that figure is done—so much air!

549

You can walk around it!" said Golenishchev, evidently implying by this remark that he did not approve of the content and idea of the figure.

"Yes, marvelous craftsmanship!" said Vronsky. "How those figures in the background stand out! There's technique for you!" he added, turning to Golenishchev and alluding to the conversation they had had about Vronsky's despair of acquiring this technique.

"Yes, yes, marvelous!" Golenishchev and Anna agreed.

In spite of his elation, the remark about technique grated painfully on his ear, and glancing angrily at Vronsky, Mikhailov suddenly scowled. He often heard the word "technique" and could never understand what was meant by it. He knew it meant a mechanical ability to paint and draw quite independent of the subject matter. He had often noticed, as now when his picture was being praised, that technique was contrasted with inner quality, as though it were possible to paint well something that was bad. He knew that much attention and care were required if one did not want to injure one's picture while removing the covering that concealed its inner meaning or, indeed, anything that might conceivably conceal it; but as to the art of painting, technique did not come into it at all. If the things he saw had been revealed to a little child or to his cook, they too would have been able to remove the outer covering of what they saw. And the most experienced and skilled artist who relied entirely on technique could not paint anything by mere mechanical facility if the boundaries of the inner content of his work had not been revealed to him first. Besides, he saw plainly that so far as technique was concerned, he could hardly be praised for it. He saw glaring faults in everything that he painted or ever had painted, faults that were the result of carelessness in removing the outer covering, faults he could not correct now without spoiling the work as a whole. And he saw traces of those outer coverings that had not been entirely removed and that spoiled the picture in almost all the figures and faces.

"There's one thing I'd like to say, if you don't mind. . . ." observed Golenishchev.

"Good heavens, I don't mind in the least," said Mikhailov with a feigned smile. "Please, say it."

"It is that in your picture he is a man made God and not God made man. Still, I suppose that was your intention, wasn't it?"

"I couldn't paint a Christ that was not in my soul," said Mikhailov.

"Yes, but in that case, if you don't mind my saying what I think . . . I mean, your picture is so good that my remark cannot do it any harm, and besides it is only my personal opinion. With you it is different. The idea itself is different. Take Ivanov, for example. Now, I think that if Christ had to be reduced to the level of an historical figure, then Ivanov would have done better to choose a different historical theme, something fresh and untouched."

"But what if this is the greatest theme that presents itself to art?"

"Other themes can be found if one looks for them. The point I want to make is that art does not tolerate discussion and argument. And with Ivanov's picture you can't help asking yourself, 'Is this God or not God?' And the unity of impression is destroyed."

"But why?" asked Mikhailov. "It seems to me that for educated people such a question cannot exist."

Golenishchev did not agree with this, and sticking to his first contention about the importance of a unity of impression in art, he defeated Mikhailov's arguments.

Mikhailov was upset, but he could find nothing to say in defense of his idea.

CHAPTER 12

Anna and Vronsky had for some time been exchanging glances, regretting their friend's clever loquacity, and at last, without waiting for his host, Vronsky crossed over to another, smaller picture.

"Oh, how charming! How charming! Wonderful! It's lovely!" they cried with one voice.

"What do they like so much?" thought Mikhailov. He had forgotten all about that picture painted three years before. He had forgotten all the agonies and ecstasies he had gone through with that picture, when for several months without break it occupied his mind day and night, forgotten as he always forgot all his finished pictures. He didn't even like looking at it and put it on show merely because he was expecting an Englishman who wanted to buy it.

"Oh—er—it's just an old study of mine," he said.

"It's excellent!" said Golenishchev, who evidently genuinely fell under the spell of the picture.

Two boys were angling in the shade of a willow tree. The elder had just cast the line and, entirely absorbed in his occupation, was carefully drawing the float from behind a bush; the younger one lay in the grass, leaning on his elbows with his tousled fair head on his hands, and gazed at the water with dreamy blue eyes. What was he thinking about?

Their admiration of his picture stirred up in Mikhailov his former excitement, but he feared and did not like this idle interest in his past work, and for this reason, though their praises gave him pleasure, he tried to draw his visitors away to a third picture.

But Vronsky asked whether the picture was for sale. To Mikhailov in his excitement over their visit, this mention of money matters was at that particular moment extremely distasteful.

"It's put out for sale," he replied, scowling darkly.

When the visitors had left, Mikhailov sat down in front of his picture of Pilate and Christ and went over in his mind all that had been said, and, if not said, implied by his visitors. And the strange thing was that what had weighed so much with him while they were there and while he had been looking at it from their point of view, suddenly lost all importance for him. He began looking at his pictures from his own uninhibited point of view as an artist and came to the firm conclusion that his picture was perfect and therefore significant, and he needed that to sustain the tension to the exclusion of all other interests without which he could not work.

The foreshortening of Christ's foot was not right all the same. He took his palette and set to work. While correcting the foot he kept glancing at the figure of John in the background, which the visitors had not noticed, but which he knew was the height of perfection. Having finished the foot, he wanted to start working on the figure, but felt that he was too agitated. He could work neither when he felt indifferent nor when he was too overwrought and saw everything too distinctly. There was only one stage in the transition from indifference to inspiration when work was possible. At this moment he was too agitated. He was about to cover the picture, but he stopped and, holding up the sheet, stood for a long time with a rapturous smile looking at the figure of John. At last, tearing himself away from it regretfully, he dropped the sheet over the picture and went home, tired but happy.

On their way back, Vronsky and Golenishchev were particularly animated and in high spirits. They talked about Mikhailov and his pictures. The word "talent," by which they understood an inborn, almost physical, capacity, independent of mind and heart, and which was the word by which they described everything an artist experiences in life, occurred especially often in their conversation, since they required it to describe something they had not the slightest conception of, but wanted to talk about. They said that there was no denying his talent, but that his talent could not develop for want of education—the common misfortune of our Russian artists. But the picture of the boys had stuck in their minds and they kept coming back to it.

"What a charming thing!" said Vronsky. "How well he has brought it off and how simply! He doesn't realize how excellent it is. Yes, we must buy it. We mustn't miss such an opportunity!"

CHAPTER 13

Mikhailov sold Vronsky the picture and agreed to paint a portrait of Anna. On the appointed day he came and began working.

After the fifth sitting the portrait struck everyone, but especially Vronsky, not only by its likeness, but also by its special kind of beauty. It was strange how Mikhailov had been able to discover that special beauty. "One had to know and love her as I love her to discover what is most endearing about her character," thought Vronsky, though it was only through the portrait that he had himself learned this most endearing trait of her character. But this trait was so true that it seemed both to him and to others that they had always known it.

"I have been working hard for ages and was unable to do anything," he said about his own portrait of Anna, "and he just looked and painted it. There's technique for you!"

"It will come," Golenishchev consoled him, for in his opinion Vronsky had talent and, above all, the education that gives one a lofty idea of art. Golenishchev's conviction that Vronsky had talent was supported by his need of Vronsky's sympathy and praise for his own articles and ideas, and he felt that praise and encouragement should be mutual.

In a strange house and, especially, in Vronsky's palazzo, Mikhailov was quite a different man from what he was in his studio. He was pointedly respectful, as though afraid of becoming intimate with people he did not respect. He addressed Vronsky as "sir" and never stayed to dinner, in spite of Anna's and Vronsky's invitations, and never came except for a sitting. Anna was more friendly to him than to others, and was grateful for her portrait. Vronsky was more than polite to him and was evidently interested in the artist's opinion of his picture. Golenishchev did not miss an opportunity of instilling sound ideas of art into Mikhailov. But Mikhailov remained equally cold toward them all. Anna felt that he liked looking at her, but he avoided talking to her. When Vronsky talked about his art, he remained stubbornly silent, and he was as stubbornly silent when shown Vronsky's picture; and he was quite obviously bored by Golenishchev's discourses and never argued with him.

Altogether his reserved, disagreeable, and almost inimical attitude, when they came to know him better, made them dislike Mikhailov, and they were glad when the sittings were over, they were left with the beautiful portrait, and his visits ceased.

Golenishchev was the first to express the thought that was in all their minds, namely, that Mikhailov was simply jealous of Vronsky.

"Well, even if he is not jealous, for after all he has *talent*, he feels annoyed that a rich aristocrat, and a count into the bargain (they all, you know, hate all that), should without any particular difficulty do as well, if not better than, he who has devoted all his life to it. Above all, is the education, which he has not got."

Vronsky defended Mikhailov, but in his heart he agreed with Golenishchev, for in his view a man of another, lower class of society was bound to envy him.

Anna's portraits, his own and Mikhailov's, should have shown Vronsky the difference between himself and Mikhailov; but he did not see it. He merely gave up painting his portrait of Anna, deciding that after Mikhailov's it would be superfluous now. But he went on painting his medieval picture. And he himself, Golenishchev, and especially Anna found that it was very good, because it was far more like the famous pictures of the old masters than Mikhailov's picture.

Meanwhile Mikhailov, though he had been carried away by Anna's portrait, was even more glad than they when the sittings came to an end and he had no longer to listen to Golenishchev's disquisitions on art and was able to forget Vronsky's paintings. He knew that it was impossible to forbid Vronsky to amuse himself with art; he knew that the count and every other dilettante had a perfect right to paint what they liked, but he could not help feeling vexed. A man could not be forbidden to make himself a big wax doll and to kiss it. But if the man came and sat down with this doll in front of a man in love and began caressing his doll as the lover caressed his beloved, the lover could not help feeling vexed. Mikhailov had the same unpleasant feeling when he saw Vronsky's paintings: he felt amused, vexed, sorry, and offended.

Vronsky's passion for painting and the Middle Ages did not last long. He had sufficient taste for art not to wish to finish his picture. He stopped painting it because he was dimly conscious that its defects, little noticeable at first, would become striking if he went on. The same thing happened to him as to Golenishchev, who felt that he had nothing to say and went on deceiving himself that his idea had not yet ripened, that it was maturing in his head, and that meantime he was collecting material. But while Golenishchev grew bitter and depressed, Vronsky could not deceive and torment himself, and he certainly could not become embittered. With characteristic determination he gave up painting without any explanations or justifications.

But without that occupation his life and that of Anna, who was surprised at his disillusionment, appeared so boring in the small Italian town, the palazzo looked so obviously old and dirty, the stains on the curtains, the cracks in the floors, the falling stucco from the cornices became so disagreeably familiar, always the same Golenishchev as well as the Italian professor and the German tourists became so wearisome, that a change became absolutely necessary. They decided to return to Russia and live in the country. In Petersburg, Vronsky intended to get his brother to agree to a division of their property and Anna planned to see her son. The summer they hoped to spend on Vronsky's large family estate.

CHAPTER 14

Levin had been married three months. He was happy, but not in the way he had expected. At every step he found that he was disappointed in his former dreams and discovered new and unexpected enchantments. Levin was happy, but having embarked on married life, he saw at every step that it was not at all what he had imagined. At every step he experienced what a man experiences when, after admiring the smooth, happy motion of a boat on a lake, he finds himself sitting in it himself. He found that it was not enough to sit quietly without rocking the boat, that he had constantly to consider what to do next, that not for a moment must he forget what course to steer or that there was water under his feet, that he had to row, much as it hurt his unaccustomed hands, that it was pleasant enough to look at it from the shore, but very hard, though very delightful, to sail it.

As a bachelor it had often happened that he used to smile inwardly with contempt when watching the married life of others, their petty worries, squabbles, and jealousies. In his future married life, he was convinced, there would not only be nothing of the kind, but even the external forms of his married life would have nothing in common with the life of others. But as it turned out, his life with his wife was in no way different from the married life of other people and made up of the same petty trifles, which he had so despised, but which now against his will had assumed quite an extraordinary and incontestable significance. And Levin realized that these trifles could not be arranged as easily as he had imagined. Though he had thought that he had the most precise ideas about married life, he, like all men, had involuntarily pictured married life as merely the enjoyment of love, which nothing must be allowed to interfere with and from which no petty cares should distract. According to his idea, he had to carry on with his work and then rest from it in the happiness of love. His wife should be loved—and that was all. But like all men, he forgot that she too must work. And he was surprised how she, his poetic, lovely Kitty, during the first weeks and, indeed, the first days of their married life could think, remember, and worry about tablecloths, furniture, spare-room mattresses, a tray, the cook, the dinner, etc. While still engaged to her, he had been struck by the definiteness with which she had rejected the idea of a honeymoon abroad and decided to go to the country, as though she knew something that was wanted and could think of something else besides her love. It had hurt him at the time and now he had several times felt hurt by her petty cares and worries. But he saw that this was necessary to her. And, loving her, though he could not understand what it was all about and though he could not help laughing at those worries of hers, he could not help admiring them, either. He smiled at the way she arranged the furniture they had brought from Moscow, at the way she rearranged his and her own rooms, hung up curtains, decided which rooms were to be for visitors and which for Dolly, got a room ready for her new maid, gave orders for dinner to the old cook, had words with Agafya, taking the catering out of her hands. He saw the old cook smile, admiring her as he listened to her inexperienced, impossible orders; he saw Agafya shake her head thoughtfully and affectionately at her young mistress's new arrangements in the storeroom; he saw that Kitty looked extraordinarily sweet when she came to him, half crying and half laughing, to report that her maid Masha still treated her as a young unmarried girl and that therefore no one in the house obeyed her. This struck him as very sweet, but strange, and he thought that it would have been better without it.

He did not realize the feeling of change she was experiencing after her life at home. There if she sometimes wished for cabbage or kvass or for some sweets, she could not have them; but now she could order whatever she wished, buy pounds of sweets, spend as much money as she liked, and order any pudding she pleased.

She was now looking forward joyfully to the arrival of Dolly with the children, especially because she could order for each child its favorite sweet and Dolly would appreciate her new arrangements. She did not know herself why it was so, but housekeeping had an irresistible attraction to her. She instinctively felt the approach of spring, and knowing that there would be foul weather, built her nest as well as she could, and she was in a hurry to build it and at the same time learn how to do so.

These petty preoccupations of Kitty's, so contrary to Levin's original ideas of elevated happiness, were one of Levin's first disappointments; and these charming preoccupations, which he could not help loving though he could not understand their meaning, were one of his new enchantments.

Another disappointment and enchantment was provided by their quarrels. Levin had never imagined that there could be any relations between him and his wife other than those based on tenderness, self-respect, and love, and all of a sudden in their very early days they had such a violent quarrel that she said to him that he did not love her, that he only loved himself, and she burst into tears and waved him away.

Their first quarrel arose because Levin had ridden over to inspect a new farm. He returned half an hour late because he had attempted a short cut and got lost. He rode home thinking only of her, of her love, of his own happiness, and the nearer he came to the house the warmer grew his tenderness for her. He rushed into the room with a feeling that was even stronger than the one with which he had gone to the Shcherbatskys' house to propose to her and was all of a sudden met with a grim expression he had never seen on her face before. He tried to kiss her, but she pushed him away.

"What's the matter?"

"You're having a nice time . . ." she began, trying to appear calm and venomous.

But the moment she opened her mouth she burst into a flood of reproaches, senseless jealousy, and everything else that had been tormenting her during the half hour she had spent sitting motionless at the window. It was then that he clearly understood for the first time what he had failed to understand when he led her out of the church after the wedding. He understood that she was not only close to him, but that he could not now tell where she ended and he began. He realized it from the agonizing feeling of division into two parts which he experienced at that moment. He felt hurt, but he immediately realized that he could not be offended with her because she was himself. For a moment he felt like a man who, receiving a sudden blow from behind, turns round angrily with the desire to return the blow only to find that he had accidentally struck himself and that there was no one to be angry with and he had to endure and do his best to assuage the pain.

Never again did he feel this so strongly, and it took him a long time to recover his senses. His first impulse was quite naturally to justify himself and explain that she was in the wrong; but to show her that she was in the wrong meant to exasperate her still more and to widen the breach which was the cause of all this trouble. One impulse quite naturally drew him to shift the blame from himself and lay it upon her; another much more powerful feeling drew him to smooth over the breach and prevent it from widening. To remain under so unjust an accusation was painful, but to hurt her by justifying himself would be still worse. Like a man half awake and suffering from pain, he wanted to tear off the aching part and cast it away, but on coming to his senses he realized that the aching part was himself. All he had to do was to try to help the aching part to bear it, and this he did.

They made it up. She, realizing that she was at fault but not admitting it, became more tender to him, and they experienced a new, redoubled happiness in their love. But that did not prevent new collisions from recurring, and very frequently too, for most unexpected and trivial reasons. These collisions also occurred because

559

they often did not know what was important to each other and also because during those early days both were often in a bad mood. When one of them was in a good mood and the other was not, peace was not broken; but when both happened to be in a bad mood, then quarrels occurred for reasons so trifling as to be incomprehensible and they could not remember afterward what it was they had quarreled about. It was true, however, that when they were both in a good mood their happiness was doubled. But all the same this first period of their married life was a trying one.

During all that time they were particularly keenly aware of the tautness of the chain that bound them to one another, of a sort of constant pulling now to one side and now to the other. Altogether their honeymoon, that is, the first month after their wedding, from which Levin had been taught to expect so much, remained in the memories of both not as a time of sweetness but as the most painful and humiliating time of their lives. They both tried in later life to erase from their minds all the ugly, shameful circumstances of that unhealthy period when both were rarely in a normal state of mind and rarely quite themselves.

Only in the third month of their married life, after their return from Moscow, where they had spent a month, did their life begin to run more smoothly.

CHAPTER 15

They had just returned from Moscow and were glad to be alone. He was in his study, writing at the table. She, in the dark, lilac dress she had worn during the first days of their married life and had put on again that day and which was so dear and memorable to him, was sitting with her *broderie anglaise* on the same old leather sofa which had always stood in the study in his grandfather's and father's days. He sat thinking and writing and all the time he never ceased for a moment being joyfully conscious of her presence. He had not abandoned his work on the estate and on the book in which the principles of the new farming methods were to be explained; but just as before his work and thoughts seemed trivial and insignificant to him in comparison with the darkness that overshadowed his whole life, so now they seemed as trivial and unimportant in comparison with his future life bathed in the brilliant sunshine of happiness. He went on with his work, but now he felt that the center of gravity of his attention had shifted and that he consequently saw it all quite differently and more clearly. Before, he regarded this work as an escape from life. Before, he felt that without it his life would be too somber. But now he needed this work to make sure that his life was not too monotonously bright. Having taken up his manuscript again and reread what he had written, he was glad to find that the work seemed worth doing. It was new and useful. Many of his former ideas seemed to him superfluous and extreme, but many omissions became clear to him when he went over the whole thing in his mind. He was now engaged in writing a new chapter on the reasons why agriculture was unprofitable in Russia. He tried to prove that Russia's poverty was not only caused by a wrong distribution of land and a false agricultural policy, but that of late years it was fostered by an alien civilization artificially grafted on Russia, particularly the means of communication, that is, the railways, which led to a centralization in the towns, a growth of luxury, and the resulting development of new industries at the expense of agriculture, as well as credit facilities and, as their concomitant, stock-exchange speculations. He argued that with the normal development of the wealth of a nation all these phenomena would make their appearance only after a considerable amount of labor had been devoted to agriculture and only after the agricultural industry had been placed in proper, or at any rate definite, relations to the other industries; that the wealth of a country must grow in a uniform fashion and especially in such a way that other industries should not outstrip the agricultural industry; that the means of communications should be developed in strict conformance with the condition of agriculture, and that with our wrong methods of using the land, the railways, called into existence not by economic but by political needs, had come prematurely and instead of promoting agriculture, as had been expected, had outstripped it and by stimulating the development of industry and credit facilities had arrested its progress; therefore, just as the one-sided and premature development of a single organ in an animal would impede its general development, so credit, means of communications, and the increased growth of industry, though undoubtedly necessary in Europe where they had arisen at the right moment, had been injurious to us because they had pushed aside the main problem of the organization of agriculture.

While he was writing down his ideas, she was thinking about how unnaturally polite her husband had been to the young Prince Charsky, who had so tactlessly paid court to her on the day before their departure from Moscow. "Why, he's jealous," she thought. "Goodness, how sweet and stupid he is! Jealous of me! If only he knew that all of them are no more than Peter the cook to me," she thought, looking with a strange feeling of proprietorship at the nape of his red neck. "Though it's a pity to disturb him (but he'll have plenty of time for his work!), I must see his face. Will he feel that I'm looking at him? I want him to turn around. . . . I'll will it— well!" and she opened her eyes wider, trying to increase the force of her look.

"Yes, they attract all the sap and shed a false luster," he muttered, putting down his pen and, feeling that she was looking at him, he turned around, smiling.

"Well?" he asked with a smile and got up.

"He did turn around!" she thought.

"Nothing, I only wanted you to turn around," she said, looking at him and trying to guess whether he was annoyed at being interrupted.

"Well, we are happy alone together, aren't we?" he said, going up to her with a radiant smile of happiness. "I am, that is."

"Oh, I feel so good! I shan't go anywhere, least of all to Moscow."

"And what were you thinking about?"

"Me? I was thinking. . . . Never mind, you go back to your writing, don't let me distract you," she said, puckering her lips. "I too must cut out these little holes— see?"

She picked up her scissors and began cutting.

"No, tell me what it was," he said, sitting down beside her and following the circular movement of the tiny scissors.

562

"Oh, now, what was I thinking about? I was thinking about Moscow and the back of your neck."

"What have I done to deserve such happiness? It's unnatural. It's much too good!" he said, kissing her hand.

"Well, so far as I'm concerned, the better, the more natural."

"And you've got a curl here," he said, carefully turning her head round. "A darling little curl. See? Just here. But no, no! We must work."

But their work did not get on, and they jumped guiltily when Kuzma came in to announce that tea was served.

"And have they returned from town?" Levin asked Kuzma.

"Yes, sir, they've just arrived and are unpacking the things."

"Be quick and come," she said to him as she went out of his study, "or I shall read the letters without you. And after that let's play duets."

Left alone, Levin put away his manuscript in the new portfolio she had bought, and began washing his hands at the new washstand with its new elegant fittings which had all made an appearance with her. Levin smiled at his thoughts and shook his head disapprovingly at them. A feeling resembling remorse tormented him. There was something shameful, effeminate, something Capuan, as he called it, in his present mode of life. "It is not good to live like that," he thought. "It'll soon be three months and I have done practically nothing. Today I sat down to work seriously for the first time and what happened? I had scarcely begun when I stopped. Even my ordinary occupations—those too I have practically abandoned. The farm work—why, I hardly go and see about it. Either I'm sorry to leave her or I can see she's bored. And I used to think that life before marriage did not count, that it wasn't anything much, and that real life would only begin after marriage. And now it will soon be three months and I have never spent my time more idly or uselessly. No, this can't go on. I must make a beginning. Of course, she is not to blame. There's nothing to reproach her with. I should have been more firm myself and asserted my independence as a man. If things go on like this, I might get used to it myself and get her to accept it too. Of course, she is not to blame. . . ."

But it is difficult for a man who is dissatisfied not to reproach someone else, and someone, too, who is closest to him, with whatever he happens to be dissatisfied. And Levin could not help feeling vaguely that though she herself was not to blame (she could not possibly be blamed for anything), it was the fault of her upbringing, which was too superficial and frivolous. ("That fool Charsky: I know she wanted to stop him, but did not know how!") "Yes, except for the interest she takes in the house (she has that), except for her clothes and except for the *broderie anglaise*, she has no serious interests. No interest in my work, in the running of the estate, in the peasants, in the music (though she is quite good at that), or in books. She does nothing and is quite content." Levin condemned it in his heart, and he did not realize that she was preparing herself for the period of activity which must come to her when at one and the same time she would be wife to her husband, mistress of the house, and bear, nurse, and bring up his children. It never occurred to him that she knew it instinctively and, preparing herself for this great task, did not reproach herself for the moments of lighthearted and happy love she now enjoyed while gaily building her nest for the future.

CHAPTER 16

When Levin went upstairs, his wife was sitting at the new silver samovar behind her new tea service and, having made old Agafya sit down at a small table with a cup of tea she had poured out for her, was reading a letter from Dolly, with whom she kept up a frequent and regular correspondence.

"See how your lady's made me sit with her," said Agafya, with an affectionate smile at Kitty.

In these words of Agafya's, Levin read the dénouement of a drama which had lately been enacted between her and Kitty. He saw that in spite of Agafya's great disappointment with her new mistress, who had deprived

564

her of the reins of government, Kitty had conquered and made her love her.

"Well, I've opened your letter, as you see," said Kitty, handing him an illiterate letter. "I think it's from that woman, your brother's . . ." she said. "I have not read it. And this is from home and from Dolly. Just fancy! Dolly took Grisha and Tanya to a children's party at the Sarmatskys'. Tanya went as a marquise."

But Levin was not listening. He blushed as he took the letter of Maria Nikolayevna, his brother's former mistress, and began to read it. It was Maria Nikolayevna's second letter to him. In her first Maria Nikolayevna had written that his brother had driven her away for no fault of her own, adding with touching naïveté that though she was again in want she did not ask or desire anything, but that the thought that Nikolai would die without her, his health being so bad, was driving her to distraction, and she begged Levin to look after him. This time she wrote something quite different. She had found Nikolai, gone to live with him again in Moscow and then to a provincial town where he had obtained a post in the civil service. But he had quarreled with his chief and on the way back to Moscow had fallen so ill that she doubted if he would ever get up again. "He keeps talking about you," she wrote, "and, besides, there is no more money left."

"Read this that Dolly writes about you," began Kitty with a smile, but she stopped short, noticing the changed expression on her husband's face.

"What's the matter? What's happened?"

"She writes that my brother Nikolai is dying. I must go."

Kitty's face changed at once. Thoughts of Tanya as the marquise and of Dolly all vanished.

"When will you go?" she asked.

"Tomorrow."

"Can I come with you?" she said.

"Kitty, really!" he said reproachfully.

"What do you mean?" she asked, hurt that he should seem to accept her offer so unwillingly and be vexed with it. "Why shouldn't I come? I won't be in your way. I—"

"I'm going because my brother is dying," said Levin. "Why should you . . ."

"Why? For the same reason as you."

"Even at such a grave moment for me," thought Levin, "all she thinks about is that she will be bored without me here." And such an excuse at so grave a juncture made him angry.

"It's impossible," he said severely.

Agafya, seeing that a quarrel was imminent, put down her cup quietly and went out. Kitty did not even notice her. The tone in which her husband uttered his last words offended her, particularly because he did not seem to believe what she had said.

"And I'm telling you that if you go, I shall go with you. I will certainly go!" she said hastily and angrily. "Why is it impossible? Why do you say it's impossible?"

"Because it means going goodness knows where, by what awful roads and stopping at what sort of inns," said Levin, trying to keep cool. "You would be in my way."

"Not at all. I don't want anything. Wherever you can go, I can too."

"You can't, if only because that woman is there. You can't associate with her."

"I don't know and I don't want to know who and what is there. All I know is that my husband's brother is dying and that my husband is going to him and that I'm going with my husband to—"

"Kitty, please don't be angry. But just think. It's such a grave matter and it hurts me to think that you should get it mixed up with your weakness, your dislike of being left alone. If you feel bored alone, well, go to Moscow."

"There, you *always* attribute mean and contemptible motives to me," she cried with tears of anger and resentment. "There's nothing of the kind—no question of any weakness, nothing. . . . I simply feel that it is my duty to be with my husband at a time of sorrow, but you want to hurt me on purpose, you purposely don't want to understand. . . ."

"Lord, that's terrible—to be a sort of slave!" cried Levin, getting up and no longer able to restrain his annoyance. But at that very instant he felt that he was hitting himself.

"Then why did you marry? You could have been free. Why, if you regret it?" she said, and she jumped up and ran away into the drawing room.

When he came in after her, she was sobbing.

He began to speak, trying to find words not so much to dissuade her as to calm her. But she refused to listen to him or to agree to anything he said. He bent over her and took her resisting hand. He kissed her hand, kissed her hair, and kissed her hand again—she was still silent. But when he took her face in both his hands and said "Kitty!" she suddenly recollected herself, cried a little, and then made it up.

It was decided that they would start together the following day. Levin told his wife that he believed she wanted to go to be of use and agreed that Maria Nikolayevna's presence in his brother's room was in no way improper, but in his heart of hearts he remained dissatisfied both with her and with himself. He was dissatisfied with her because she could not bring herself to let him go when it was necessary (and how strange it was to think that he, who such a short time ago dared not believe in the happiness of her loving him, now felt unhappy because she loved him too much!), and dissatisfied with himself for not having stood his ground. Still less could he agree with any conviction that it did not matter if she did have something to do with the woman who lived with his brother, and he thought with horror of all the encounters that they might have. The very fact that his wife, his Kitty, would be in the same room with a prostitute made him shudder with revulsion and horror.

CHAPTER 17

The hotel in the provincial town in which Nikolai Levin was lying ill was one of those provincial hotels that are built with all the latest improvements, with the best intentions of cleanliness, comfort, and even elegance, but which are transformed with extraordinary rapidity by the people who patronize them into filthy pothouses with pretensions to modern improvements, those very pretensions making them worse than the old-fashioned inns which were simply dirty. This hotel had already reached that stage: the old soldier in a dirty uniform smoking a cigarette at the main entrance who was supposed to carry out the duties of a hall porter, the dismal and unpleasant ornamental cast-iron staircase, the impertinent waiter in his dirty frock coat, the lounge with the dusty bouquet of wax flowers adorning the table, the dirt, dust, and slovenliness everywhere together with a sort of modern, self-complacent railway-station bustle—everything produced a most depressing effect on the Levins after their fresh home life, especially as the artificial impression produced by the hotel was so completely out of keeping with what awaited them.

As always, after being asked what price they wanted to pay for their room, it turned out that not a single room was available: one good room was occupied by a railway inspector, another by a Moscow lawyer, and a third by the Princess Astafyev from the country. There was just one dirty room vacant and they were promised that the room adjoining it would be free by the evening. Annoyed with his wife because what he had expected was coming to pass, namely that at the moment of their arrival, when his heart throbbed with anxiety at the thought of his brother's condition, he had to worry about her instead of rushing immediately to his brother, Levin led his wife into their hotel room.

"Go, go!" she said, with a timid, guilty look at him.

He went out without a word and at the very door came across Maria Nikolayevna, who had learned of his arrival and had not dared to go in to see him. She was just the same as when he saw her in Moscow: the same woolen dress without collar or cuffs and the same good-natured, dull, pock-marked face that had grown a little fuller.

"Well? How is he?"

"Very bad. He can't get up. He's been expecting you all the time. He—er . . . Are you—er—with your wife?"

For a moment Levin did not understand the cause of her embarrassment, but she at once explained it to him.

"I'll go . . . I'll go to the kitchen," she said. "He'll be glad. He heard about it and he knows and remembers her abroad."

Levin realized that she was referring to his wife and did not know what to say.

"Come along, let's go," he said.

But he had hardly moved from the door when it opened and Kitty looked out. Levin blushed with shame and vexation at his wife, who had put him in such an awkward situation; but Maria Nikolayevna blushed still

568

more. She shrank within herself and flushed till her eyes filled with tears, and seizing the ends of her kerchief with both hands, began twisting them with her red fingers, not knowing what to say or do.

At first Levin saw an expression of eager curiosity in Kitty's eyes as she looked at this woman who was so incomprehensible and terrible to her; but that lasted only an instant.

"Well, what's happening? How is he?" she said, addressing first her husband and then Maria Nikolayevna.

"But we can't stand talking here in the corridor!" said Levin, looking round angrily at a man who was just passing along with jerky steps, ostensibly on business of his own.

"Well, then, come in," said Kitty to Maria Nikolayevna, who had recovered herself, but noticing her husband's frightened face, she added, "You'd better go, go and send for me," and she went back to her room. Levin went to his brother.

He had never expected what he saw and felt in his brother's room. He had expected to find him in that state of self-deception, which, he had heard, is so common with consumptives and which had struck him so much at the time of his brother's visit in the autumn. He had expected to find the physical signs of the approach of death more marked, greater weakness, greater emaciation, but still the same sort of condition generally. He had expected that he would experience the same feeling of sorrow at the loss of a loved brother and horror of death he had experienced at the time but to a greater degree. And he had been preparing himself for it; but what he found was something quite different.

In the dirty little room, the painted panels around the walls filthy with spittle, separated by a thin partition from the next room from which people's voices could be heard, the air impregnated with the stifling smell of impurities, on a bed drawn away from the wall, lay a body covered with a blanket. One arm of that body lay on top of the blanket, and the huge hand, like a rake, seemed to be attached in some incomprehensible way to a long, thin spindle quite straight from the wrist to the elbow. The head lay sideways on the pillow. Levin could see the thin hair wet with perspiration on the temples and the drawn, almost transparent, forehead.

"It can't be that this terrible body is my brother Niko-lai," thought Levin. He went nearer, saw the face, and doubt became impossible. In spite of the dreadful change in the face, Levin had only to look at those living eyes raised at him, to notice the slight twitching of the mouth beneath the clammy mustache, to realize the dreadful truth that this dead body was his living brother.

The glittering eyes glanced severely and reproachfully at the brother as he entered the room. And instantly this glance established a living relationship between living people. Levin at once felt the reproach in the look fixed on him and remorse at his own happiness.

When Konstantin took his hand, Nikolai smiled. It was a faint, hardly perceptible smile, and it did not change the stern expression of the eyes.

"You didn't expect to find me like this, did you?" Nikolai said, speaking with difficulty.

"Yes—no," said Levin, not knowing what he was say-ing in his confusion. "Why didn't you let me know sooner, I mean at the time of my wedding? I made in-quiries everywhere."

He had to speak so as not to be silent, but he did not know what to say, particularly as his brother made no reply, but just stared at him, obviously trying to grasp the meaning of each word. Levin told his brother that his wife had come with him. Nikolai said he was glad, but that he was afraid of frightening her by his condi-tion. There was a long pause. Suddenly Nikolai stirred and began to speak. Levin expected to hear something particularly significant and important from the expres-sion of Nikolai's face, but his brother merely talked about his health. He found fault with the doctor, re-gretted that he could not have a celebrated Moscow specialist, and Levin realized that he still hoped to recover.

Taking advantage of the first moment of silence, Levin got up, wishing to escape, if only for a minute, from his painful feeling, and said that he would fetch his wife.

"All right, and I'll have the place cleaned up a bit. It's filthy here and stinking, I shouldn't wonder. Masha, tidy up the room," the sick man said with an effort. "And," he added, glancing questioningly at his brother, "when you've tidied it up, you can go."

Levin said nothing. Going out into the corridor, he stopped. He had said he would fetch his wife, but now, analyzing what he was feeling at that moment, he decided that, on the contrary, he would do his best to dissuade her from going to see the sick man. "Why should she be tortured as I am?" he thought.

"Well, how is he?" Kitty asked with a frightened face.

"Oh, it's dreadful, dreadful! Why did you come?" said Levin.

Kitty was silent for a few seconds, looking timidly and sorrowfully at her husband; then she went up to him and took hold of his elbow with both hands.

"Darling, take me to him," she said. "Together it will be easier for us. Only take me to him, please. Take me to him and go away. Please, try to understand that I find it much harder to see you and not to see him. There I can perhaps be of help to you and to him. Please, darling, let me!"

Levin had to give in and, recovering his composure and completely forgetting about Maria Nikolayevna, he went back with Kitty to his brother.

Stepping lightly and glancing repeatedly at her husband, showing him a brave face full of sympathy, she went into the room of the sick man and, turning round unhurriedly, closed the door. With inaudible steps she went up quickly to the sick man's bedside and, going around so that he need not turn his head, at once took his huge skeleton of a hand into her fresh, young one, pressed it, and with that sympathetic, quiet animation, which gives no offense and which is natural only to women, she began talking to him.

"We met in Soden, but we've never been introduced," she said. "You never thought I'd be your sister-in-law, did you?"

"You wouldn't have recognized me, would you?" he said with a smile that lighted up his face at her entrance.

"Yes, I would. I'm so glad you let us know you were here. Not a day passed without Konstantin's mentioning you and being anxious about you."

But the sick man's animation did not last long.

Before she had finished speaking, his face once more assumed the severe, reproachful look of envy a dying man feels for the living.

"I'm afraid you're not very comfortable here," she

said, turning away from his penetrating glance and looking around the room. "We shall have to ask the landlord
for another room," she said to her husband, "one nearer
to us."

CHAPTER 18

Levin could not look calmly at his brother, he could
not be natural and calm in his presence. When he entered the sick man's room, his eyes and his attention
became unconsciously clouded over and he did not see
or distinguish the details of his brother's condition. He
smelled the awful foul air, he saw the filth and disorder,
his brother's painful condition, and he heard his groans,
but he felt that nothing could be done about it. It never
occurred to him to analyze the details of the sick man's
condition, to consider how that body was lying there
under the blanket, how the emaciated legs, loins, and
back were lying there in their doubled-up position, and
whether it might not be possible to get them into a more
comfortable position or do something to make things, if
not easier, then at least not so uncomfortable. A shiver
ran down his spine when he began to think of those
details. He was absolutely convinced that nothing could
be done to prolong his brother's life or to alleviate his
suffering. The sick man felt that his brother considered
every kind of help of no avail and this exasperated him.
And this made Levin's position still more painful. To be
in the sickroom was torture to him, but not to be there
was still worse. And he kept coming in and going out
on all sorts of excuses, incapable of remaining alone.

But Kitty thought, felt, and acted quite differently.
When she saw the sick man, she was filled with pity for
him. And pity in her woman's heart aroused a feeling
not of horror or repulsion, which it had aroused in her
husband, but a need for action, a need to find out all
the details of his condition and to remedy them. As she
had not the slightest doubt that she had to help him, she
had no doubt either that she could help him, and set to
work at once. The very details, the mere thought of
which threw her husband into a panic, at once engaged
her attention. She sent for the doctor, sent to the chem-

ist's, made the maid she had brought with her and Maria Nikolayevna sweep and dust and scrub, washed and rinsed something herself, and spread something under the blanket. She ordered some things to be brought into the room and others taken out. She herself went several times to her room, paying no attention to the people she met in the corridor, and brought back clean sheets, pillowcases, towels, and shirts.

The waiter, who was serving a meal to some engineers in the general dining room, came several times to her summons with a surly face and found it impossible to ignore her orders, for she gave them with such gentle insistence that he could not help carrying them out. Levin did not approve of all this; he did not believe that any good would come of it for the sick man. What he dreaded most, however, was that his brother might fly into a temper. But the sick man, though apparently indifferent to it all, did not lose his temper, but was only ashamed, and on the whole appeared rather interested in what she was doing for him. Returning from the doctor, to whom Kitty had sent him, Levin opened the door at the moment when his brother, at Kitty's orders, was having his shirt changed. The long, white, emaciated back with the huge, protruding shoulder blades and sticking-out ribs and vertebrae was bare, and Maria Nikolayevna and the waiter got the sleeve of the shirt tangled up and could not get the long limp arm into it. Kitty, who quickly closed the door after Levin, was not looking that way, but the sick man groaned and she hurried over to him.

"Hurry up," she said.

"Don't come here," muttered the sick man angrily, "I can do it myself."

"What did you say?" Maria Nikolayevna asked.

But Kitty had heard and understood that he felt embarrassed and uncomfortable at being undressed in her presence.

"I'm not looking, I'm not looking!" she said, helping his arm in. "Maria Nikolayevna," she added, "please go round the other side and put it right."

"Please go and fetch a little bottle from my handbag," she went on, turning to her husband. "It's in the side pocket. Bring it, please, and by the time you come back they'll be quite finished here."

When he returned with the bottle, Levin found the sick man lying in bed and everything around him completely changed. The foul smell was replaced by the smell of scent and vinegar, which Kitty, pouting her lips and puffing out her rosy cheeks, was sprinkling by blowing through a little tube. There was not a speck of dust anywhere; beside the bed a mat had been put. On the table, medicine bottles and a decanter of water were neatly arranged as well as a pile of linen, which would be required later, and Kitty's *broderie anglaise*. On the other table by the patient's bed stood a glass of some drink, a candle, and powders. The sick man himself, washed and combed, lay between clean sheets propped up on high pillows, in a clean shirt, its white collar round an abnormally thin neck, gazing fixedly at Kitty with a new look of hope and without taking his eyes off her.

The doctor whom Levin had brought and whom he had found at the club was not the same who had been attending Nikolai, with whom the patient was dissatisfied. The new doctor took out a stethoscope and sounded the patient, shook his head, prescribed some medicine, and gave minute instructions, first how the medicine was to be administered and, secondly, what diet he should keep to. He ordered raw or very lightly boiled eggs and seltzer water, with milk fresh from the cow at a certain temperature. When the doctor had gone, Nikolai said something to his brother; but Levin made out only the last words, "your Katya," though from the way his brother glanced at her, Levin realized that he was praising her. Nikolai asked Katya, as he called Kitty, to come nearer.

"I feel much better already," he said. "Why, with you I should have got better long ago. . . . It feels so nice!"

He took her hand and drew it toward his lips, but changed his mind, as though afraid that she might find it disagreeable, put it back, and merely stroked it. Kitty took his hands in both hers and pressed them.

"Now turn me over on my left side and go to bed," he said.

No one caught what he said; Kitty alone understood him. She understood because she never stopped thinking of what he might need.

"The other side," she said to her husband. "He always sleeps on that side. Turn him over. I don't like calling

the servants. I can't do it. Could you?" she asked
Maria Nikolayevna.

"I'm afraid to," replied Maria Nikolayevna.

Much as he dreaded to put his arms around that terrible body to grasp those parts under the blanket he did
not wish to remember, Levin submitted to the influence
of his wife and with the determined expression on his
face his wife knew so well, thrust his arms under the
blanket and in spite of his great strength was amazed at
the unusual heaviness of those emaciated limbs. While
he was turning him over, feeling his neck embraced by
his brother's huge, emaciated arm, Kitty quickly and
noiselessly turned and beat the pillow and arranged the
sick man's thin hair that again stuck to his temples.

Nikolai retained his brother's hand in his. Levin felt
that he wanted to do something with his hand and was
pulling at it. He yielded with a sinking heart. Yes, he
raised it to his mouth and kissed it. Levin, shaking with
sobs and unable to utter a word, went out of the room.

CHAPTER 19

"Thou hast hid these things from the wise and prudent, and hast revealed them unto babes," thought Levin
about his wife, as he talked to her that night.

Levin thought of the Gospel text not because he considered himself wise and prudent. He did not, but he
could not help knowing that he was more intelligent than
his wife and Agafya, and he could not help knowing that
when he thought about death he thought with all his
heart and soul. He knew, too, that many men of great
intellect, whose thoughts on death he had read, had pondered deeply about it and did not know a hundredth
part of what his wife and Agafya knew. Different as
those two women were, Agafya and Katya, as his
brother Nikolai called Kitty and as Levin particularly
liked to call her now, were absolutely alike in this. Both
knew without any doubt whatever what was life and
what was death, and though they could not possibly have
answered or even have understood the questions that
presented themselves to Levin, neither of them had any

doubts about the significance of these phenomena and both looked upon them in the same way, sharing this view with millions of other people. The proof that they knew firmly what death was lay in the fact that they never doubted for a moment how to deal with the dying and had no fear of death. Levin, however, and others like him, though they could say a great deal about death, quite obviously did not know, because they were afraid of death and had not the faintest idea what to do when people were dying. Had Levin now been alone with his brother Nikolai, he would have looked at him with terror and would have sat waiting there in still greater terror, and that would have been all he could do.

And that was not all. He did not know what to say, how to look, how to walk. To talk of things that did not matter seemed an outrage, something quite impossible to him; to talk of death, of something else that was grim and depressing, was equally impossible. To keep silent was impossible too. "If I look at him, he'll think I'm watching him, afraid of him; if I don't look at him, he'll imagine that I'm thinking of something else. If I walk on tiptoe, he won't like it; to walk in the ordinary way seems wrong somehow." But Kitty evidently did not think and, indeed, had no time to think of herself; she was thinking of Nikolai all the time because she seemed to know something, and everything turned out well. She was telling him about herself and about her wedding, smiled, sympathized, petted him, mentioned cases of recovery, and everything turned out well; so she evidently knew. The proof that Agafya's and her behavior was not instinctive, animal, irrational, lay in the fact that in addition to nursing the patient and alleviating his suffering, both demanded something more important for the dying man, something that had nothing to do with physical conditions. Agafya, speaking of the old man who had died, said: "Well, the Lord be praised, he took the sacrament and received extreme unction, God grant each of us to die like this!" In the same way Kitty, besides all her cares about linen, bedsores, and cooling drinks, had succeeded on the very first day in persuading the sick man of the necessity of receiving Communion and extreme unction.

When Levin returned to their two rooms for the night, he sat with bowed head, not knowing what to do. Quite apart from the fact that he could not even bring himself to talk to his wife about supper, about getting ready for bed, about planning what they were going to do; he was ashamed to. Kitty, on the other hand, was more active than usual. She was even more animated than usual. She ordered supper to be brought, unpacked their things herself, helped to make the beds, and did not forget to sprinkle them with insect powder. She was in the state of excitement when one's reasoning powers act quickly, the state of a man before battle or a struggle, in dangerous and decisive moments of life—the moments when a man proves once and for all his mettle and that his entire past has not been wasted, but has been a preparation for these moments.

Everything she did was right, and before midnight everything was unpacked, clean and neat, and the hotel room began to look like home, like her rooms: the beds made, combs, brushes, looking glasses laid out, table napkins spread.

Levin thought that it was inexcusable to eat, to sleep, or even to talk, and he felt that every movement he made was unseemly. She, on the other hand, arranged the brushes, but did it all in such a way that there was nothing offensive about it.

However, they could not eat anything; they did not go to sleep for a long time, and did not even go to bed till very late.

"I'm very glad I persuaded him to receive extreme unction tomorrow," she said, sitting in her dressing jacket before her folding looking glass and combing her soft, fragrant hair with a fine comb. "I have never been present, but Mother told me that prayers are said for the restoration of health."

"Do you really think he can recover?" said Levin, watching the narrow parting at the back of her round little head, which closed every time she drew the comb forward.

"I asked the doctor. He said he couldn't live for more than three days. But how can they know? I'm very glad, anyway, that I persuaded him," she said, peering at her husband through her hair. "Everything is possible," she added with that special, rather cunning expression that always appeared on her face when she spoke of religion.

After their talk about religion during their engagement, neither he nor she had ever started a conversation on the subject, but she carried out the rites of her religion, went to church, said her prayers, always with the quiet conviction that it was necessary to do so. In spite of his assurances to the contrary, she was firmly convinced that he was as good a Christian as herself, if not indeed a better one, and that all he said about it was just one of his amusing masculine whims, like the thing he said about her *broderie anglaise*: that good people darned holes, while she cut them out on purpose, etc.

"Well, yes," said Levin, "that woman Maria Nikolayevna did not know how to manage at all. And—er—I must admit I'm very, very glad you came. You are purity itself, and . . ." He took her hand, but did not kiss it (to kiss her hand with death so near seemed highly improper to him), but only pressed it with a guilty look, gazing into her brightening eyes.

"It would have been so painful for you alone," she said, and raising her arms high so that they hid her cheeks, which flushed with pleasure, she coiled her plaits at the nape of her neck and pinned them. "No," she went on, "she did not know how. . . . Luckily I learned a lot at Soden."

"There weren't such sick people there too, surely?"

"Oh, much worse."

"What is so awful is that I cannot help seeing him as he was when he was young. . . . You would not believe what a delightful young fellow he was, but I did not understand him then."

"I can quite believe it. I can't help feeling that we *might* have been friends, he and I," she said and, dismayed at her own words, she looked round at her husband, and tears started to her eyes.

"Yes, you *might*," he said sadly. "He really is one of those people who are said to be not for this world."

"Well, I'm afraid we have many more hard days before us," said Kitty, looking at her tiny watch. "We'd better go to bed."

CHAPTER 20

The next day the sick man received Communion and extreme unction. During the ceremony Nikolai prayed fervently. In his large eyes, fixed on the icon, placed on a card table covered with a colored napkin, there was such passionate entreaty and hope that Levin was afraid to look at them. Levin knew that this passionate entreaty and hope would merely make the parting from life, which he loved so much, much harder for him. Levin knew his brother and the workings of his mind; he knew that his skepticism was not the result of his finding it easier to live without faith, but that it arose because modern scientific explanations of the phenomena of the universe had driven out his faith; and that was why Levin knew that his present recantation was not genuine, that it had not been the result of the same careful reasoning, but was merely temporary and selfish, caused by an irrational hope of recovery. Levin knew, too, that Kitty had strengthened that hope by her stories of the extraordinary recoveries she had heard of. Levin knew all that and he found it unbearably painful to look at those imploring eyes, which were so full of hope, and at the emaciated hand lifted with difficulty to touch the drawn skin of the forehead in making the sign of the cross, at the protruding shoulder blades and the hollow, rattling chest, which could no longer contain the life for which the sick man was praying. During the sacrament Levin prayed, too, and did what he, unbeliever that he was, had done a thousand times before. He said, addressing himself to God: "If you exist, heal this man (for this thing has happened many times before) and you will save him and me."

After the anointing the sick man suddenly felt much better. He did not cough once during a whole hour, smiled, kissed Kitty's hand, thanking her with tears in his eyes, and said he felt well, had no pain anywhere and that he had an appetite and was stronger. He even sat up when his soup was brought and asked for a cutlet too. Hopeless as his condition was, obvious as it was that he could not possibly recover, Levin and Kitty were for that hour in the same state of excitement, happy, and at the same time fearful of being mistaken.

"Better?"

"Yes, much better."

"Wonderful!"

"There's nothing wonderful about it."

"Anyway, he's better," they said in a whisper, smiling at one another.

This illusion did not last long. The patient fell asleep quietly, but half an hour later his coughing awakened him. And all of a sudden every hope disappeared in those around him and in himself. The reality of his suffering shattered it in Levin and Kitty and in the sick man himself, and they no longer had any doubt, nor even a recollection of their former hopes.

Without mentioning what he had believed half an hour before, just as though he were ashamed even to recall it, he asked for iodine to inhale in a bottle covered with perforated paper. Levin handed him the bottle, and the same look of passionate hope with which he received extreme unction, was now fixed on his brother, demanding from him a confirmation of the doctor's statement that inhaling iodine worked wonders.

"Why isn't Katya here?" he asked in a hoarse whisper, looking around after Levin had reluctantly confirmed the doctor's words. "I can tell you now. . . . It was for her sake that I went through that farce. She is so sweet, but you and I can't deceive ourselves, can we? This is what I believe in," he said, clutching the bottle with his bony hand and beginning to inhale from it.

About eight o'clock in the evening Levin and his wife were having tea in their room when Maria Nikolayevna rushed in breathless. She was pale and her lips were trembling.

"He's dying!" she whispered. "I'm afraid he's going to die immediately."

Both ran to his room. He was sitting up, leaning with one hand on the bed, his long back bent and his head hanging low.

"How do you feel?" Levin asked in a whisper, after a pause.

"I feel I'm going," Nikolai said with an effort, but very distinctly, squeezing the words out of himself slowly. He did not raise his head, merely turning up his eyes without, however, reaching his brother's face. "Katya," he added, "go away!"

Levin jumped up and with a peremptory whisper made her leave the room.

"I'm going," he said again.

"What makes you think so?" said Levin, in order to say something.

"Because I'm going," he repeated as though he had taken a liking to that expression. "It's the end."

Maria Nikolayevna went up to him.

"You'd better lie down," she said. "You'd feel better."

"I'll soon be lying quietly," he said. "Dead," he went on derisively, gruffly. "Oh well, lay me down if you like."

Levin laid his brother on his back, sat down beside him, and hardly daring to breathe, gazed at his face. The dying man lay with closed eyes, but from time to time the muscles on his forehead moved, just as though he were thinking deeply and intently. Levin involuntarily tried to think with him of what was taking place within him, but in spite of all the efforts of his mind to go along with his brother, he saw by the expression of that calm, stern face and the play of a muscle above his eyebrow, that something was becoming clear to the dying man, something which for Levin remained as dark as ever.

"Yes, yes, that's it," the dying man muttered slowly, pausing between each word. "Wait, wait!" Again he was silent. "That's it!" he suddenly exclaimed slowly in a tone of relief, as if everything had become clear to him. "O Lord!" he murmured with a heavy sigh.

Maria Nikolayevna felt his feet. "Growing cold," she whispered.

For a long time, it seemed a very long time to Levin, the sick man lay motionless. He was still alive and from time to time he sighed. The mental strain made Levin tired. He felt that notwithstanding all mental efforts he could not grasp what *that's it* meant. He felt that he was already lagging far behind the dying man. He could no longer think of the problem of death, but he could not help thinking of what he would have to do very soon: close the dead man's eyes, dress him, order the coffin. And the strange thing was that he felt completely indifferent, experiencing neither sorrow nor sense of bereavement, and still less of pity for his brother. If he did have any feeling for his brother at that moment, it was rather one of envy for the knowledge the dying man possessed, but which he could not possess.

He sat for a long time like that, expecting the end. But the end did not come. The door opened and Kitty appeared. Levin got up to stop her. But as he got up he heard the dying man make a movement.

"Don't go," said Nikolai, and stretched out his hand. Levin gave him his hand and angrily motioned his wife away with his other hand.

With the dying man's hand in his, he sat for half an hour, an hour, another hour. He was no longer thinking of death. He was wondering what Kitty was doing, who lived in the next room, whether the doctor owned the house he occupied. He felt hungry and sleepy. He carefully disengaged his hand and felt his brother's legs. The legs were cold, but his brother was still breathing. Levin tried again to leave the room on tiptoe, but the sick man stirred again and said:

"Don't go."

Day began to break; the sick man's condition remained the same. Quietly disengaging his hand and without looking at the dying man, Levin went to his room and fell asleep. When he awoke, instead of the news of his brother's death which he expected, he learned that the sick man had returned to his earlier condition. He was again sitting up, coughing, eating, and talking; he ceased talking of death, again began expressing hopes of recovery, and became more irritable and gloomier than ever. No one, neither Kitty nor his brother, could calm him. He was cross with everybody, was rude to everybody, blamed everybody for his sufferings and demanded that they should fetch a specialist from Moscow. Whenever they asked him how he felt, he invariably replied with an expression of malice and reproach:

"I'm suffering terribly, unbearably!"

The sick man suffered more and more, especially from bedsores, which would no longer heal, and was more and more cross with those about him, reproaching them for everything and especially for not bringing the specialist from Moscow. Kitty tried her best to help him and calm him, but all was in vain, and Levin could see that she was worn out physically and mentally, though she would not admit it. The feeling of death evoked in them all by his taking leave of life on the night he had sent for his brother was destroyed. They all knew that he would quite inevitably die soon, that he was half dead already. They all had only one wish that he would die quickly, and they all did their best to conceal it and went on giving him medicines out of bottles, tried to discover new remedies and doctors, and deceived him and themselves and one another. It was all a lie, a disgusting, offensive, blasphemous lie. And because of his character and because he loved the dying man more than the others did, Levin felt this lie most painfully.

Levin, who had long been thinking of reconciling his two brothers, if only before one of them died, wrote to Koznyshev and, receiving his reply, read it to Nikolai. Koznyshev wrote that he was sorry he could not come, but in touching terms begged his brother's forgiveness.

Nikolai said nothing.

"What shall I write to him?" asked Levin. "You're not angry with him, I hope?"

"No, not at all!" Nikolai answered, vexed at this question. "Write and tell him to send me a doctor."

Three more agonizing days passed; the sick man was still in the same condition. A desire for his death was now felt by everybody who saw him: by the hotel servants and the proprietor, by all the people staying at the hotel, by the doctor, Maria Nikolayevna, Levin, and Kitty. The sick man alone did not express that desire, but, on the contrary, was cross because the specialist had not been sent for, and he went on taking medicines and talking of life. Only in rare moments, when opium made him find momentary oblivion from his incessant sufferings, he sometimes when half asleep expressed what he felt more intensely in his heart than all the others: "Oh, if only it was all over!" or "When will this end?"

His sufferings, gradually growing more severe, did their work and prepared him for death. There was no position in which he could lie without pain, there was not a moment in which he could forget his suffering, there was not a spot, not a limb, in his body that did not ache and cause him excruciating pain. Even the memories, the impressions, the thoughts of that body

583

aroused in him the same feeling of repugnance as the body itself. The sight of other people, their remarks, his own reminiscences—all that was sheer agony to him. Those about him felt this and unconsciously did not permit themselves to move or speak freely or to express their own wishes in his presence. His whole life had now become merged into one feeling of suffering and a desire to be released from it.

It seemed that a violent change was taking place within him, a change that would make him look upon death as a fulfillment of his desires, as happiness. Before, every separate desire caused by suffering or privation, such as hunger, fatigue, or thirst, was gratified by some function of the body that brought enjoyment; but now privation and suffering obtained no relief and any attempt to obtain it only occasioned fresh suffering. And that was why all his desires were merged into one—a desire to get rid of all the sufferings and their source, the body. But he had no words to express this desire for deliverance, and therefore he did not talk about it, but from force of habit demanded the satisfaction of those desires that could no longer be satisfied. "Turn me over on the other side," he said, and immediately demanded to be put back again. "Give me some clear soup. Take away the soup. Say something—why are you all silent?" And as soon as they began to speak, he closed his eyes and expressed weariness, indifference, and disgust.

On the tenth day after their arrival in town Kitty fell ill. She had a headache; she was sick and could not leave her bed all the morning.

The doctor explained that her illness was caused by fatigue and overexcitement, and he prescribed rest and quiet.

After dinner, however, Kitty got up and, as always, went to the sick man's room with her embroidery. He gave her a stern look when she came in and smiled contemptuously when she said she had not been feeling well. That day he was continually blowing his nose and moaning piteously.

"How do you feel?" she asked him.

"Worse," he brought out with an effort. "Awful pain!"

"Where does it hurt?"

"All over."

584

"It will end today, you'll see," said Maria Nikolayevna in a whisper, but as the sick man's hearing, as Levin had noticed, was very acute, Nikolai must have heard her. Levin hissed at her to be silent and looked around at the sick man. Nikolai had heard, but the words made no impression on him. His look was still reproachful and strained.

"What makes you think so?" Levin asked, when she followed him out into the corridor.

"He has begun picking himself."

"How do you mean?"

"Like that," she said, pulling at the folds of her woolen dress.

And indeed he had noticed all that day that the sick man was clutching at himself as if trying to pull something off.

Maria Nikolayevna's predictions came true. Toward evening the sick man was no longer able to lift his hands and just kept staring before him without changing his fixed, concentrated gaze. Even when his brother and Kitty bent over him so that he could see them, he kept staring like that. Kitty sent for the priest to read the prayers for the dying.

While the priest was reading the prayers, the dying man showed no sign of life; his eyes were closed. Levin, Kitty, and Maria Nikolayevna stood at the bedside. Before the priest had finished the prayer, the dying man stretched, sighed, and opened his eyes. Having finished the prayer, the priest put the cross to the cold forehead, then slowly wrapped it in his stole and, after standing in silence for another minute or two, touched the huge, bloodless hand that was turning cold.

"He's passed away," said the priest, turning to go; but suddenly the clammy mustache of the dying man stirred and from inside his chest came the sounds, clear and harsh in the stillness:

"Not yet. . . . Soon."

And a minute later his face brightened, a smile appeared under the mustache, and the women, who had gathered round, began carefully to lay out the body.

The sight of his brother and the presence of death revived in Levin's mind the feeling of horror at the enigma, as well as the nearness and inevitability, of death, which had seized him on that autumn evening when his brother had arrived at his country house. This feeling was now much stronger than before; he felt even less able than before to apprehend the meaning of death, and its inevitability appeared more terrible than ever to him: but now, thanks to his wife's presence, this feeling did not drive him to despair: in spite of death he felt the need for living and loving. He felt that love saved him from despair and that under the threat of despair this love became still stronger and purer.

Scarcely had the one inexplicable mystery of death been enacted before his eyes, when another mystery, equally inexplicable, had arisen, calling to love and to life.

The doctor confirmed his suspicion about Kitty. Her indisposition was pregnancy.

CHAPTER 21

From the moment Karenin realized from his talks with Betsy and Oblonsky that all that was demanded of him was that he should leave his wife alone and not trouble her with his presence, and that his wife herself desired it, he felt so lost that he could not decide anything for himself, did not know what he wanted now, and having put himself in the hands of those who took so much pleasure in arranging his affairs, gave his consent to everything. It was only after Anna had left the house and the English governess sent to ask whether she should dine with him or separately by herself that he clearly realized for the first time his position and was horrified by it.

The most painful part of this situation was that, try as he might, he could not find any link between his past and the present, nor could he reconcile the one with the other. It was not the past, when he lived happily with his wife, that troubled him. The transition from that past to the knowledge of his wife's infidelity had been like a nightmare to him, but he had been through it already; his situation had been painful, but it was comprehensible. If his wife had at the time, after confessing her infidelity, left him, he would have been grieved and unhappy, but he would not have found himself in his

586

present hopeless and incomprehensible position. He could not now reconcile in any way his recent act of forgiveness, his deeply felt emotion, his love for his sick wife and for another man's child with what was happening to him now, that is, with the fact that, as if in return for all this, he now found himself alone, disgraced, ridiculed, unwanted, and despised by all.

For the first two days after his wife's departure Karenin received petitioners, saw his private secretary, attended committee meetings, and had dinner in the dining room as usual. Without realizing why he was doing it, he strained every nerve during those two days to appear calm and even indifferent. When answering the servants' questions as to what should be done with Anna's rooms and belongings, he did his utmost to seem like a man who had not been in the least surprised by what had taken place and who did not regard it as something out of the ordinary, and in this he succeeded: no one could have observed any signs of despair in him. But on the third day after her departure, when Korney brought him a bill from a fashionable milliner's which Anna had forgotten to pay and announced that the manager of the shop had come in person, Karenin said he would like to see him.

"I'm sorry to trouble you, sir," said the shop manager, "but if you want us to send the bill to your wife, would you be so kind as to let us have her address."

Karenin—so it seemed to the manager—was wondering what to do when, suddenly, he turned around and sat down at the table. Dropping his head on his hands, he sat like that for a long time; he tried to say something a few times, but stopped short.

Realizing what his master must be feeling, Korney asked the shop manager to call another time. Left alone once more, Karenin became aware of the fact that he would no longer be able to maintain an appearance of firmness and self-composure. He gave orders for the carriage that was waiting to be sent away, said that he would receive no one, and did not appear for dinner.

He felt that he would not be able to endure the general pressure of pitiless contempt which he had clearly seen in the faces of the shop manager and Korney and of everyone without exception whom he had met during the last two days. He felt that he could not avert people's hatred from himself, because that hatred was caused not by his being bad (for in that case he could have tried to be better), but because he was disgracefully and disgustingly unhappy. He knew that for that, for the very reason that his heart was lacerated, they would be merciless to him. He felt that people would destroy him, as dogs tear the throat out of some crippled dog that is whining with pain. He knew that the only way of escape from people was to hide his wounds from them, and he had unconsciously tried to do just that for two days, but he felt that now he was no longer able to continue the unequal struggle.

His despair was intensified by the consciousness that he was quite alone in his misfortune. It was not only in Petersburg that he had no one to whom he might unburden his mind, who would be sorry for him not as a high official and not as a member of high society, but simply as a suffering human being; but nowhere in the world had he such a friend.

Karenin had grown up as an orphan. There were two brothers. They did not remember their father; their mother died when Karenin was ten years old. Their fortune was small. They were brought up by Karenin's uncle, a distinguished government official and at one time a favorite of the emperor.

Having finished school and university with distinction, Karenin, with his uncle's help, had at once obtained an important post in the civil service and from that time devoted himself entirely to the career of an ambitious civil servant. Neither at school nor at the university, nor afterward in the service, did he make any close friends. His brother had been the one closest to his heart, but he had been in the foreign service and had always lived abroad, where he died soon after Karenin's marriage.

At the time when Karenin was governor of a province, Anna's aunt, a wealthy provincial lady, had brought together her niece and him, a young governor though a middle-aged man, and placed him in such a position that he had either to propose or leave the town. Karenin hesitated for a long time. At the time there were as many arguments for the step as against it, and there was no decisive reason to make him change his rule of refraining when in doubt. But Anna's aunt had impressed upon him through a common acquaintance that he had already compromised the girl and that he was in honor bound to propose to her. He proposed bed and lavished on his fiancée and his wife all the feeling of which he was capable.

His attachment to Anna made any close relationship with other people unnecessary. And now he had not a single intimate friend among all his acquaintances. He had many so-called social connections, but he had no one he could call a friend. Karenin had a great number of people he could invite to dinner, whom he could ask to take part in anything he took an interest in or whose influence he could use for someone he would like to help, or with whom he could freely discuss the actions of other people or of members of the government; but his relations with these people were confined to a sphere strictly limited by custom and habit from which it was impossible to depart. There was one man, a former fellow student, with whom he had become friendly later on, and with whom he might have talked over his personal troubles, but this friend was now a school inspector in a remote part of the country. Of the people in Petersburg the closest to him and in whom he could confide were his private secretary and his doctor.

Mikhail Slyudin, his private secretary, was a simple, intelligent, kindly, and moral man, and Karenin felt that he was favorably disposed to him personally; but the five years of their official relationship had put a barrier in the way of any intimate talk between them.

Having finished signing official papers, Karenin had remained silent for a long time, glancing every now and then at Slyudin, and had tried several times to speak, but could not bring himself to start. He had prepared the opening phrase: "You've heard of my misfortune, haven't you?" But he ended by saying as usual: "So you'll see to it for me, won't you?" and let him go.

The other person, the doctor, was also favorably disposed toward him; but they had long ago come to a silent understanding that both were snowed under with work and always in a hurry.

Of his women friends, including the principal among them, the Countess Lydia Ivanovna, Karenin did not think at all. All women, simply as women, filled him with apprehension and were repugnant to him now.

CHAPTER 22

Karenin had forgotten Countess Lydia Ivanovna, but she had not forgotten him. At that most painful moment of lonely despair she came to see him and walked into his study without being announced. She found him in the posture in which he had been sitting for a long time, with his head resting on both hands.

"*J'ai forcé la consigne,*" she said, walking in hurriedly and breathing heavily from excitement and rapid movement. "I've heard everything. My dear, dear friend!" she went on, pressing his hand warmly in both of hers and gazing with her beautiful, dreamy eyes into his.

Karenin got up with a frown and, freeing his hand, moved a chair toward her.

"Won't you sit down, Countess? I'm afraid I can't see anyone today because I don't feel well," he said and his lips trembled.

"My dear, dear friend!" the countess repeated without taking her eyes off him, and suddenly the inner corners of her eyebrows rose, forming a triangle on her forehead; her plain yellow face looked plainer still, but Karenin felt that she was sorry for him and that she was about to burst into tears. He felt deeply moved, seized her podgy hand, and began kissing it.

"My dear friend," she said in a voice breaking with emotion, "you must not give way to sorrow. Your sorrow is great, but you must find consolation."

"I'm shattered, crushed, I'm no longer a man," said Karenin, letting go of her hand, but continuing to look into her eyes, which were brimful of tears. "My position is all the more terrible because I can find no support anywhere, not even in myself."

"You will find support, but don't look for it in me, although I beg you to believe in my friendship," she said with a sigh. "Our support is love, the love which He has bequeathed us. His yoke is light," she declared with the ecstatic look he knew so well. "He will support and help you."

Though from the way she talked he could feel that

590

she was touched by her own lofty sentiments, and though there was also in it something of the new, ecstatic mystical mood which had recently spread in Petersburg and which Karenin considered excessive, it was gratifying to hear her speak like that now.

"I'm weak. I am shattered. I did not foresee it and I don't understand it now."

"My dear friend," the countess kept repeating.

"It isn't the loss of what no longer exists, it isn't that," went on Karenin. "I don't feel sorry for that. But I cannot help being ashamed before people of the position I am in. It's wrong, but I can't help it. I can't."

"It was not you who performed the great act of forgiveness, which I and everyone else cannot help admiring, but He who dwells within your heart," said Countess Lydia Ivanovna, turning up her eyes ecstatically. "And that is why you cannot possibly be ashamed of your action."

Karenin frowned and, bending his hands backward, began cracking his fingers.

"One must know all the facts," he said in a thin voice. "A man's strength has its limits, Countess, and I have reached the limits of mine. All day long I have had to make arrangements, arrangements about household matters, arising" (he stressed the word "arising") "out of my new solitary position. The servants, the governess, the bills. . . . These petty flames have burned me. I was not able to endure it. At dinner . . . yesterday I very nearly left the table. I could not bear to see the way my son looked at me. He did not ask me the meaning of it all, but he wanted to, and I could not bear to see the look in his eyes. He was afraid to look at me, but that is not all. . . ."

Karenin wanted to mention the bill that had been brought to him, but his voice shook and he paused. He could not recall that bill on blue paper, for a bonnet and ribbons, without feeling sorry for himself.

"I understand, my dear friend," said Countess Lydia Ivanovna. "I understand everything. Succor and consolation you will not find in me, but all the same I have come to help you if I can. If only I could take these petty, humiliating cares off your shoulders! . . . I can see that what is needed is a woman's word, a woman's authority. Will you entrust it to me?"

Karenin pressed her hand gratefully and in silence.

"We will take care of Seryozha together. I'm afraid I'm not very good at practical things, but I will undertake it—I will be your housekeeper. Don't thank me. It is not I who am doing it. . . ."

"I can't help thanking you."

"But, my dear friend, don't give way to the feeling you were speaking about—of being ashamed of what is a Christian's glory: *'he that humbleth himself shall be exalted.'* And you cannot thank me. You must thank Him and ask His help. In Him alone we will find peace, comfort, salvation, and love," she said and, raising her eyes to heaven, she began to pray, as Karenin gathered from her silence.

Karenin listened to her now, and those expressions which before seemed to him, if not unpleasant, at least excessive, now seemed natural and comforting. Karenin did not like this new ecstatic spirit. He was a believer who was interested in religion chiefly from a political point of view, and the new teaching, which allowed itself some new interpretations, was distasteful to him on principle just because it paved the way for argument and analysis. Hitherto his attitude to the new teaching had been cold and even hostile, and he never argued with Countess Lydia Ivanovna, who was carried away by it, but carefully passed over in silence her challenging remarks. But now he listened to her words for the first time with pleasure and without any mental reservations.

"I'm very, very grateful to you, both for your deeds and for your words," he said, when she had finished praying.

Countess Lydia Ivanovna once more pressed both the hands of her dear friend.

"Now," she said after a pause, with a smile, wiping away the last traces of her tears, "I must set to work. I'm going to Seryozha. I shall only apply to you in the last resort."

And she got up and went out of the room.

Countess Lydia Ivanovna went to Seryozha's part of the house and there, wetting the frightened boy's cheeks with tears, told him that his father was a saint and that his mother was dead.

Countess Lydia Ivanovna kept her word. She really

did take over all the cares of arranging and managing Karenin's household. But she had not exaggerated when she said that she was not very good at practical things. All her orders had to be changed, for it was impossible to carry them out, and they were changed by Korney, Karenin's valet, who now managed Karenin's household without anybody's being aware of it, quietly and tactfully informing his master of anything that was necessary while helping him to dress. But Lydia Ivanovna's help was nevertheless extremely valuable: she gave Karenin moral support in the consciousness of her affection and respect and especially, as it comforted her to think, in almost converting him to Christianity, that is to say, in turning him from an apathetic and indifferent believer into a fervent and steadfast supporter of the new interpretation of the Christian doctrine, which had recently spread in Petersburg. Karenin did not find the conversion very difficult. Like Lydia Ivanovna and others who shared her views, Karenin was quite devoid of that depth of imaginative power, of that spiritual faculty which makes the concepts of the imagination so real that they demand to be brought into conformity with other concepts and with reality itself. He saw nothing impossible or incongruous in the notion that death, which exists for the unbelievers, did not exist for him, and that being in possession of complete faith, of the measure of which he was himself the judge, his soul was free from sin and he was already experiencing full salvation here on earth.

It is true that Karenin was dimly aware of the shallowness and error of this idea about his faith. He knew that when, without thinking that his forgiveness was the act of a Higher Power, he gave himself up spontaneously to this feeling, he had experienced more happiness than when, as now, he was every moment thinking that Christ dwelt in his soul and that by signing official papers he was carrying out His will. But it was necessary for Karenin to think like that; it was so necessary for him in his humiliation to possess at least this imaginary height from which he, despised of all, could despise others, that he clung to his sham salvation, as though it were true salvation.

CHAPTER 23

Countess Lydia Ivanovna, when a very young and highly romantic girl, had been married to a rich, aristocratic, good-natured, jovial fellow who was one of the notorious libertines of high society. About two months after their wedding her husband left her and met her rapturous protestations of tender affection with ridicule and even hostility, which those who knew the count's good nature and saw no fault in the ecstatic Lydia were quite unable to explain. Since then, though not divorced, they lived apart, and whenever the husband met his wife he always treated her with the never-changing, biting sarcasm which baffled people so much.

Countess Lydia Ivanovna had long ago ceased to be in love with her husband, but she had never ceased being in love with someone. She would be in love with several persons at once, men and women; she had been in love with almost every person of eminence. She was in love with all the new princes and princesses who married into the imperial family; she was in love with a metropolitan, a suffragan bishop, and a priest. She was in love with a journalist, three Slavs, with Komisarov, a cabinet minister, a doctor, an English missionary, and Karenin. All these loves, now waxing, now waning, did not prevent her from keeping up the most widespread and complicated relations with the Court and high society. But from the time she took Karenin under her wing after his misfortune, from the time she took over the supervision of Karenin's household, looking after his welfare, she felt that all her other loves were not real and that she was now genuinely in love only with Karenin. It seemed to her that her feeling for Karenin now was stronger than any she had ever had before. Analyzing that feeling and comparing it with her previous loves, she saw clearly that she would never have been in love with Komisarov if he had not saved the life of the Tsar, that she would never have been in love with Ristich-Kudzhitsky if there had been no Slav question, but that she loved Karenin for himself, for his lofty, misunderstood soul, for the

594

high-pitched sound of his voice, for his character, and for his soft white hands with their swollen veins. She was not only glad when she saw him, but she searched his face for signs of the impression she was making on him. She wanted to please him not merely by what she said, but also by her whole person. For his sake she devoted more time now to her dress than ever before. She caught herself dreaming of what might have been if she had not been married and he had been free. She blushed with excitement when he entered the room, and she could not repress a smile of delight when he said something agreeable to her.

For several days now Countess Lydia Ivanovna had been in a state of the most violent agitation. She had heard that Anna and Vronsky were in Petersburg. She had to save Karenin from meeting her, she had even to save him from the painful knowledge that that dreadful woman was in the same town as he and that he was liable to meet her any minute.

Lydia Ivanovna tried to find out through her friends what *those disgusting people*, as she called Anna and Vronsky, intended to do and tried so to guide the movements of her dear friend that he should not meet them. A young aide-de-camp, a friend of Vronsky's, through whom she obtained her information and who hoped through her influence to obtain a government concession, told her that they had finished their business and were going away next day. Lydia Ivanovna was already beginning to breathe freely again when the next morning she received a note and it was with horror that she recognized the handwriting. It was Anna's handwriting. The envelope was as thick as a cheap popular print; there was a huge monogram on the oblong yellow sheet, and the letter exhaled a delicious scent.

"Who brought it?"

"A commissionaire from the hotel."

It was some time before the countess could sit down to read the letter. Her agitation brought on a fit of asthma, to which she was subject. When she composed herself, she read the following letter, written in French:

MADAME LA COMTESSE,

The Christian sentiments which fill your heart encourage me, I feel, to the unpardonable boldness of writing

595

to you. I am unhappy at being parted from my son. I implore you to let me see him once before my departure. Forgive me for reminding you of myself. I address myself to you instead of to Mr. Karenin only because I do not wish to cause any suffering to that generous man by reminding him of myself. Knowing your friendship for him, I feel you will understand me. Will you send Seryozha to me, or shall I come to the house at an appointed hour? Or will you let me know where and when I could meet him away from home? I do not anticipate a refusal, knowing the magnanimity of the person on whom a decision depends. You cannot imagine how I long to see my son, and so cannot imagine how grateful I shall be to you for your help.

ANNA

Everything in that letter exasperated Countess Lydia Ivanovna—its contents, the allusion to magnanimity, and especially what seemed to her its free and easy tone.

"Say there is no answer," said the countess, and at once, opening her blotting book, wrote to Karenin that she hoped to see him at the birthday reception at the Palace.

"I have to talk to you about a grave and painful matter. We can arrange there where to meet. Best of all at my house, where I shall have *your* tea ready. It is urgent. He sends a cross, but He also sends strength to bear it," she added, so as to prepare him a little.

Countess Lydia Ivanovna generally wrote two or three notes a day to Karenin. She liked that way of communicating with him, a way that combined elegance and mystery, which were absent from their personal relations.

CHAPTER 24

The congratulations were drawing to a close. Those who were leaving, meeting acquaintances, chatted about the latest news, the newly awarded honors, and the changes among the high officials.

"Don't you think it would be a splendid idea to appoint Countess Maria Borisovna Minister of War and Princess Vatkovsky Chief of Staff?" a gray-haired old man in a gold-embroidered uniform said to a tall and beautiful lady-in-waiting who had asked him about the government changes.

"And me aide-de-camp," the lady-in-waiting replied with a smile.

"You have an appointment already—in the ecclesiastical department with Karenin as your assistant."

"How do you do, Prince?" said the old man, shaking hands with a man who had just come up.

"What were you saying about Karenin?" said the prince.

"He and Putyatov have received the Order of Alexander Nevsky."

"I thought he had it already."

"No. Just look at him," said the old man, pointing with his gold-embroidered hat to Karenin, who was standing at the door of the hall in Court uniform with a new red sash over his shoulder, talking to one of the influential members of the State Council. "Pleased as Punch," he added, stopping to shake hands with a handsome, athletic Court chamberlain.

"No," said the chamberlain, "he's aged."

"From too much worry. He's always writing memoranda now. He won't let a poor fellow go until he has expounded everything point by point."

"Aged? *Il fait des passions.* I expect Countess Lydia Ivanovna is jealous of his wife now."

"Oh, come, you mustn't say anything bad about Countess Lydia Ivanovna."

"But is it bad that she is in love with Karenin?"

"Is it true that Mrs. Karenin is here?"

"Not here at the Palace, but she is in Petersburg. I met her yesterday with Alexey Vronsky, *bras dessus, bras dessous*, on the Morskaya."

"C'est un homme qui n'a pas . . ." the Court chamberlain began, but he stopped to make room for a passing member of the imperial family.

So they went on talking about Karenin, censuring him and laughing at him, while he, barring the way to the member of the State Council he had buttonholed, never ceased for a moment expounding his new financial project to him point by point, for fear that he might escape.

Almost at the same time as his wife had left Karenin, he had experienced the bitterest moment in any high

597

official's life—his civil-service career had come to a stop. It had come to a stop and everyone was fully aware of it, but Karenin himself had not yet realized that his career was at an end. Whether it was due to his conflict with Stremov, or to his misfortune with his wife, or simply to the fact that he had reached his predestined limit, it had become obvious to everyone that year that his career in the civil service was over. He still occupied an important post, he was still a member of many commissions and committees, but he was a man who had done all he was ever likely to do and nothing more was expected of him. Whatever he might say, whatever he proposed, he was listened to as if what he proposed was what everyone had long known and what no one wanted.

But Karenin was not aware of this and, on the contrary, having been removed from any direct participation in the work of the government, he now saw more clearly than ever the shortcomings and mistakes of others and deemed it his duty to point out how they could be corrected. Soon after his wife had left him he began writing his memorandum on the new legal procedure, the first of an innumerable series of unwanted memoranda on every branch of the administration that he was fated to write.

Karenin not only failed to notice his hopeless position in the official world, he was not only not troubled by it, but he was more than ever satisfied with his activity.

"He that is married careth for the things that are of the world, how he may please his wife. . . . he that is unmarried careth for the things that belong to the Lord, how he may please the Lord," says the Apostle Paul, and Karenin who was now guided in all his actions by the Scriptures, often remembered this text. It seemed to him that ever since he had been left without a wife, he had been serving the Lord more than ever by those very projects of his.

The obvious impatience of the member of the State Council, who wished to get away from him, did not trouble Karenin; he stopped expounding his project only when the member of the Council, taking advantage of the passing of the royal personage, slipped away from him.

Left alone, Karenin lowered his head, collecting his thoughts, looked around absent-mindedly, and went

598

toward the door, where he hoped to meet Countess Lydia Ivanovna.

"And how strong and healthy they all are physically," he thought, glancing at a powerfully built Court chamberlain with well-brushed and perfumed whiskers and at the red neck of a prince in a tight-fitting uniform, whom he had to pass on his way. "It is truly said that everything in the world is evil," he thought, casting another sidelong glance at the Court chamberlain's calves.

Moving his legs unhurriedly, Karenin with his usual air of weariness and dignity bowed to the gentlemen who had been talking about him and, looking in the direction of the door, began searching for Countess Lydia Ivanovna.

"Ah, Karenin!" cried the old man, with a malicious gleam in his eyes as Karenin passed him with a cold nod of the head. "I haven't congratulated you yet," he said, pointing to the new order.

"Thank you," replied Karenin. "What a *nice* day we are having," he added, as was his wont, with a special emphasis on the word "nice."

He knew that they were laughing at him, but he had never expected anything but hostility from them; he was used to it by now.

Catching sight, as she entered, of Countess Lydia Ivanovna's sallow shoulders rising from her corset and of her beautiful, dreamy eyes calling to him, Karenin smiled, showing his well-preserved white teeth, and went up to her.

Lydia Ivanovna's toilette had cost her a great deal of trouble, as had all her efforts at dressing up of late. The purpose of her dressing up now was the reverse of what she had in mind thirty years ago. At that time she had wished to adorn herself with something, and the more the better. Now, on the contrary, she had to dress in a way so inconsistent with her age and figure that all she was concerned about was that the contrast between her adornments and her own appearance should not be too horrifying. As far as Karenin was concerned she achieved her object, for to him she seemed attractive. Indeed, for him she was the only island not only of kindly feelings, but of affection, in the sea of hostility and sneers that surrounded him.

As he ran the gantlet of those sneering eyes of the

599

people around him, he was drawn to her adoring looks as naturally as a plant to the light.

"I congratulate you," she said, indicating the decoration with her eyes.

Suppressing a smile of pleasure, he shrugged his shoulders and closed his eyes, as if to say that a thing like that could hardly be expected to make him happy. Countess Lydia Ivanovna was well aware that this was one of his chief sources of happiness, though he would never admit it.

"How is our angel?" asked the countess, meaning Seryozha.

"I'm afraid I can't say that I'm quite satisfied with him," said Karenin, raising his eyebrows and opening his eyes. "Sitnikov isn't satisfied with him either." (Sitnikov was the tutor to whom Seryozha's secular education had been entrusted.) "As I think I told you, he shows a certain coldness to those most important questions which ought to touch the heart of every man and every child," said Karenin, beginning to expound his ideas about the only subject that interested him outside the service—his son's education.

When Karenin with Lydia Ivanovna's help had again been restored to life and activity, he felt it to be his duty to occupy himself with the education of the son left on his hands. Having taken an interest in matters of education before, Karenin devoted some time to a theoretical study of the question. After reading several books on anthropology, pedagogics, and teaching practice, Karenin drew up a plan of education and, engaging the best tutor in Petersburg to supervise it, set to work. And this work occupied him continually.

"Yes, but his heart!" said Countess Lydia Ivanovna with enthusiasm. "I see in him his father's heart, and with such a heart a child can't be bad."

"Well, perhaps. . . . As for me, I do my duty. That's all I can do, I'm afraid."

"You must come and see me," said Countess Lydia Ivanovna after a pause, "for we have to talk over that rather sad business of yours. I'd have given anything to spare you certain memories, but I'm afraid other people think differently. I had a letter from *her*. *She* is here in Petersburg."

Karenin gave a start at the mention of his wife, but

his face immediately assumed that look of deathlike immobility, which expressed his utter helplessness in the matter.

"I expected it," he said.

Countess Lydia Ivanovna looked rapturously at him, her eyes filled with tears of admiration at the grandeur of his soul.

CHAPTER 25

When Karenin entered Countess Lydia Ivanovna's cozy little boudoir, which was full of old china and hung with portraits, the countess herself was not there. She was changing her dress.

On a round table covered with a cloth stood a Chinese tea service and a silver spirit lamp and teakettle. Karenin glanced absently at the countless familiar portraits adorning the room and, sitting down at the table, opened a New Testament that was lying on it. The rustle of the countess' silk dress diverted his attention.

"Well, we can sit down quietly now," said Countess Lydia Ivanovna, with an agitated smile, squeezing herself in between the table and the sofa, "and let's talk over our tea."

After a few words of preparation, the countess, breathing hard and blushing, handed him the letter she had received.

After reading the letter, he was silent for a long time.

"I don't think I have a right to refuse her," he said timidly, raising his eyes.

"My dear friend, you don't see evil in anyone."

"On the contrary, I see that everything is evil. But is it fair?"

There was a look of indecision on his face and a desire to seek advice, support, and guidance in a matter he did not understand.

"Yes," the countess cried. "There is a limit to everything. I can understand immorality," she went on, not altogether truthfully, because she never could understand what it was that led women to immorality, "but I don't understand cruelty, and to whom? To you! How can she stay in the town where you are? Yes, indeed, one lives and learns. And I'm learning to understand your high-mindedness and her baseness."

"But who will throw the stone?" said Karenin, who seemed to be enjoying his role. "I've forgiven her everything, and therefore I cannot refuse her what is so essential to her as a mother—love for her son."

"But is it love, my friend? Is it sincere? Suppose you have forgiven her, that you forgive her, but—er—have we the right to subject the soul of that little angel to such an ordeal? He thinks she is dead. He prays for her and asks God to forgive her her sins. . . . And it is better so. But now, what will he think?"

"I have not thought of that," said Karenin, evidently agreeing with her.

Countess Lydia Ivanovna covered her face with her hands. She was praying.

"If you ask my advice," she said, having finished her prayer and uncovering her face, "then I do not advise you to do it. Don't you think I can see how you are suffering and how this has reopened your wounds? But supposing that, as usual, you do not think of yourself—what can it lead to? More suffering for yourself and torture for your child? If she's still got some human feeling, she ought not to desire it herself. No, I have no hesitation in advising you not to allow it, and with your permission I will write to her."

Karenin agreed, and the countess wrote the following letter in French:

Dear Madam,

To remind your son of you might lead to his asking questions which it would be impossible to answer without implanting in the heart of the child a spirit of condemnation of what should be sacred to him, and I therefore beg you to take your husband's refusal in the spirit of Christian love.

Praying to Almighty God to have mercy on you,

I remain,

Yours sincerely,

Countess Lydia

This letter achieved the secret purpose which Countess Lydia Ivanovna concealed even from herself. It hurt Anna's feelings deeply.

On returning home from Lydia Ivanovna's, Karenin could not carry on with his usual work and find the spiritual peace of a believer who has found salvation that he had felt before.

The thought of his wife who was so guilty toward him and toward whom he had been so saintly, as the Countess Lydia Ivanovna so justly told him, should not have upset him; but he was not feeling at ease with himself: he could not understand the book he was reading, he could not drive away poignant memories of his relations with her, of the mistakes which, so it seemed to him now, he had made in regard to her. The memory of the way in which he had received her confession of unfaithfulness when they were returning home from the races (especially that he had demanded that she should only keep up appearances and had not challenged Vronsky) tormented him like remorse. He was also tormented by the memory of the letter he had written to her; and especially his forgiveness, which no one wanted, and his care for another man's child, wrung his heart with shame and remorse.

He felt exactly the same kind of shame and remorse now when, reviewing his whole past with her, he recalled the clumsy way in which, after much hesitation, he had proposed to her.

"But how am I to blame?" he kept asking himself. And this question invariably gave rise to another: did those others—those Vronskys, Oblonskys, those Court chamberlains with their fat calves—did they feel differently, did they love differently, did they marry differently? And there passed before his mind's eye a whole row of those full-blooded, virile, self-confident men, who always and everywhere involuntarily aroused his curiosity and attention. He drove those thoughts from him, he tried to convince himself that he was not living for this transient life but for the life eternal, that his soul was full of peace and love. But the fact that in this transient, trivial life he had made, as it seemed to him, a few trivial mistakes, disturbed his peace of mind as much as if the eternal salvation in which he believed did not exist. But this temptation did not last long and soon the tranquillity and loftiness of spirit, which helped him to forget the things he did not wish to remember, were restored in his soul.

CHAPTER 26

"Well, Kapitonych?" said Seryozha, returning red-cheeked and happy from his walk on the day before his birthday and giving his overcoat to the tall old hall porter, who was smiling down from his height at the little fellow. "Well, has the bandaged civil servant been here today? Did Daddy see him?"

"He did," the hall porter said with a good-humored wink. "The minute the secretary came out, I announced him. Here, let me take it off, young master."

"Seryozha," said his Slav tutor, standing at the door leading to the inner rooms, "take it off yourself, please."

But Seryozha, though he heard the tutor's weak voice, paid no attention to him. He stood holding on to the hall porter's shoulder belt, and looking up into his face.

"Well, and did Daddy do what he wanted?"

The hall porter nodded.

The bandaged civil servant, who had been seven times to ask Karenin to do something for him, interested both Seryozha and the hall porter. Seryozha had happened to meet him one day in the entrance hall and heard him begging the hall porter plaintively to announce him to Karenin and saying that he and his children were dying of starvation.

Since then, having met the civil servant in the entrance hall a second time, Seryozha took a great interest in him.

"Well, was he very glad?"

"Of course he was. Almost jumping for joy as he went away."

"Anything come?" Seryozha asked after a pause.

"Well, sir," replied the hall porter in a whisper, shaking his head, "there is something from the countess."

Seryozha at once understood that the hall porter was speaking of a present from Countess Lydia Ivanovna for his birthday.

"Are you sure? Where?"

"Korney has taken it to your father. Something nice, I expect!"

"How big? Like that?"

"Not quite, but it's all right."

"A book?"

"No, something else. You'd better run along now, young master, Vassily Lukich is calling," said the hall porter, and hearing the tutor's approaching footsteps, he gently disengaged the little hand in the half-drawn-off glove from his shoulder belt and motioned with his head toward the tutor.

"Vassily Lukich, one moment, please," said Seryozha with that cheerful and affectionate smile which always got the better of the conscientious Vassily Lukich.

Seryozha was feeling too pleased, he was too happy not to share with his friend the hall porter a piece of family good news which he had heard during his walk in the Summer Gardens from the niece of Countess Lydia Ivanovna. This piece of good news seemed particularly important to him because it coincided with the good news about the civil servant and the good news of his own birthday present. Seryozha felt that it was a day on which everyone ought to be happy and gay.

"Do you know Daddy has received the Order of Alexander Nevsky?"

"Of course I do. People have already been coming to congratulate him."

"Well, is he pleased?"

"He can't help being pleased at the Tsar's favor, can he? It shows he's deserved it," said the hall porter sternly and gravely.

Seryozha became thoughtful as he peered into the hall porter's face, which he had studied to the minutest detail, especially his chin, which lay suspended between his gray side whiskers and which no one ever saw except Seryozha, who always looked at him from below.

"Well, and has your daughter been to see you lately?" The hall porter's daughter was a ballet dancer.

"She couldn't come on weekdays, could she? They too have to study. And so must you, sir. Run along now."

When he entered his room, Seryozha, instead of sitting down to his lessons, told his tutor that he thought that the present they had bought him must be a railway engine.

"What do you think?" he asked.

But all Vassily Lukich thought was that Seryozha had to prepare his grammar lesson for his master who was coming at two.

"Please, just tell me, Vassily Lukich," said Seryozha suddenly, when already sitting at his desk with a book in his hands, "what is higher than the Alexander Nevsky? You know, Daddy has received the Order of Alexander Nevsky, don't you?"

Vassily Lukich replied that the Order of Vladimir was higher than the Alexander Nevsky.

"And higher than that?"

"The highest is the St. Andrew."

"And higher than the St. Andrew?"

"I don't know."

"Oh, you don't?" And, leaning his elbows on the table, Seryozha sank into thought.

His reflections were most complex and varied. He imagined his father suddenly receiving the orders of Vladimir and St. Andrew and how, because of it, he would be much kinder at lesson time, and how when he himself grew up, he would receive all the orders and even the one they would introduce that would be higher than the St. Andrew. The moment they introduced it, they would confer it on him.

It was in such reflection that the time passed and when his master came, the lesson about the adverbs of time, place, and manner of action had not been prepared, and the teacher looked not only dissatisfied but hurt. This touched Seryozha. He did not feel guilty for not having learned the lesson, for, try as he would, he could not do it. While the teacher was explaining, he believed that he understood, but as soon as he was left alone, he simply could not remember or understand why such a short and familiar word as "suddenly" should be *an adverb of manner of action*. But he felt nevertheless sorry for his teacher and he wanted to say something nice to him.

He chose a moment when the teacher was silently scanning the book.

"When is your name day, sir?" he suddenly asked.

"You'd better think of your work," replied the teacher. "Name days are of no importance to a rational being. It's just a day like any other, one on which one has to work."

Seryozha looked attentively at the teacher, at his thin

little beard, at his spectacles, which had slipped down below the mark left by them on his nose, and fell into such a deep reverie that he heard nothing of what the teacher was explaining to him. He realized that the teacher did not believe what he had said; he felt it from the tone in which it had been spoken. "But why have they all conspired to speak in the same way, and all about the dullest and most useless things? Why does he push me away from him? Why doesn't he love me?" he asked himself sadly, and could find no answer.

CHAPTER 27

After the teacher's lesson came his father's lesson. Seryozha sat down at the table, playing with his penknife and thinking. One of his favorite occupations was keeping a lookout for his mother during his walks. He did not believe in death generally and in her death in particular, in spite of what Lydia Ivanovna had told him and his father had confirmed, and therefore even after he had been told that she was dead, he kept looking out for her during his walks. Every plump, graceful woman with dark hair was his mother. At the sight of such a woman his heart was filled with such tenderness that his breath failed him and tears started to his eyes. And he was waiting for her to approach him any moment and raise her veil. He would then be able to see all her face, she would smile and embrace him, he would smell her familiar scent, feel the tender touch of her hand and he would burst out crying happily as he had done one evening when he had curled up at her feet and she had tickled him and he had shaken with laughter and bitten her white hands with the rings on the fingers. Later on, when he accidentally found out from his old nurse that his mother was not dead and his father and Lydia Ivanovna had explained to him that she was dead to him because she was not a good woman (this he simply refused to believe because he loved her), he went on looking for and waiting for her in the same way. That day there had been a lady in the Summer Gardens with a lilac veil whom he had watched with a sinking heart, wondering if it was her as she came up toward him along

607

the path. That lady never came up to them and disappeared somewhere. Today he felt more strongly than ever a surge of love for his mother and now, sunk in a reverie and in expectation of his father, he notched all the edge of the table with his knife, staring before him with shining eyes and thinking of her.

"Your father's coming," Vassily Lukich said, rousing him.

Seryozha jumped up, went up to his father, and after kissing his hand, looked up at him attentively, trying to discover some traces of his joy at receiving the Alexander Nevsky.

"Did you have a nice walk?" asked Karenin, sitting down in an armchair. Drawing the Old Testament toward him, he opened it. Although Karenin had more than once told Seryozha that every good Christian must have a thorough knowledge of Bible history, he had often to look up the Old Testament during the lesson, and Seryozha noticed it.

"Yes, it was very nice, Father," said Seryozha, sitting down sideways on his chair and rocking it, which he had been forbidden to do. "I saw Nadenka." (Nadenka was Lydia Ivanovna's niece, who was being brought up by her aunt.) "She told me that you've been given a new star. Are you pleased, Father?"

"First of all don't rock your chair, please," said Karenin. "And, secondly, it is the work and not the reward that is precious. I'd like you to understand that. You see, if you're going to work and learn in order to receive a reward, the work will seem hard to you; but when you work" (Karenin said this remembering how he had sustained himself that morning by sense of duty in the dull task of signing 118 official papers), "loving your work, you will find your reward in the work itself."

Seryozha's eyes, which had been shining with affection and joy, lost their brilliance under his father's gaze. It was the same long-familiar tone in which his father always addressed him and to which Seryozha had already learned how to adapt himself. His father always talked to him, so Seryozha felt, as though he were addressing some imaginary boy out of a book who was quite unlike Seryozha. And when he was with his father Seryozha always tried to pretend to be that boy out of a book.

"You understand that, I hope?" said his father.

"Yes, sir," replied Seryozha, pretending to be that imaginary boy.

The lesson consisted in learning by heart some verses from the gospels and repeating the beginning of the Old Testament. The verses from the gospels Seryozha knew fairly well, but just as he was reciting them he became so absorbed in the contemplation of a bone in his father's forehead which turned very abruptly at the temple that he got muddled and put the end of one verse where the same word occurred to the beginning of another verse. It was obvious to Karenin that he did not understand what he was saying, and this irritated him.

He frowned and embarked on an explanation that Seryozha had heard lots of times and never could remember because he understood it too clearly, just as he could not remember that the word "suddenly" was an adverb of manner of action. Seryozha looked at his father with frightened eyes and the only thing he could think of was whether his father, as he sometimes did, would make him repeat what he had just said. This thought frightened Seryozha so much that he could understand nothing any more. But his father did not make him repeat it, but passed on to the lesson out of the Old Testament. Seryozha related the events themselves very well, but when he had to answer questions as to what events served as a prophecy of what was to come, he knew nothing, though he had been punished before for not knowing this lesson. The passage about which he could not say anything at all, but only floundered, cut the table, and rocked his chair, was the one about the patriarchs before the Flood. He did not know any of them except Enoch, who was taken up to heaven alive. Before he had remembered their names, but now he had completely forgotten them, chiefly because Enoch was his favorite character in the whole of the Old Testament and there was a whole train of thought in his head in connection with Enoch's being taken up alive to heaven, to which he gave himself up entirely now, staring fixedly at his father's watch chain and a half-unfastened button on his waistcoat.

In death, of which he had been told so often, Seryozha did not believe at all. He did not believe that people he loved could die and more especially that he himself would die. That seemed to him quite impossible and

609

incomprehensible. But he had been told that everyone died; he had asked people whom he trusted about it and they confirmed it; his nurse, too, said the same thing, though reluctantly. But Enoch had not died, so not everybody died. "But why shouldn't anyone deserve the same in God's sight and be taken alive to heaven?" thought Seryozha. The bad ones, those, that is, whom Seryozha did not love, might die, but the good ones might all be like Enoch.

"Well, who were the patriarchs?"

"Enoch, Enos . . ."

"You've said it already. This is bad, Seryozha. Very bad. If you don't try to know what is most necessary for a Christian," said his father, getting up, "then what can interest you? I am not pleased with you and Peter Ignatych" (this was the chief teacher) "is not pleased with you. . . . I shall have to punish you."

His father and his teacher were both dissatisfied with Seryozha, and, indeed, he did his lessons very badly. But it could not possibly be said that he was a dull boy. On the contrary, he was far more capable than the boys his teacher held up as examples to Seryozha. The boy, his father thought, did not try to learn what he was taught. But, as a matter of fact, he could not learn it. He could not because there were much more urgent claims in his mind than those which his father and the teacher made upon him. Those claims were contradictory and he was in direct conflict with his instructors.

He was nine years old, he was a child, but he knew his own mind, it was dear to him, and he guarded it as the eyelid guards the eye, and without the key of love he let no one into it. His instructors complained that he did not want to learn, but his mind was full to the brim with a thirst for knowledge. And he learned from Kapitonych, from his nurse, from Nadenka, from Vassily Lukich, but not from his teachers. The water which his father and his teacher expected would turn their millwheels had long since leaked away and was doing its work somewhere else.

His father punished Seryozha by not letting him go and see Nadenka, Lydia Ivanovna's niece; but that punishment turned out luckily for Seryozha. Vassily Lukich was in a good mood and showed him how to make windmills. He spent the whole evening making them and dreaming of making a windmill on which you could turn around either by catching hold of the sails or tying yourself on and spinning around and around. He did not think about his mother all the evening, but when in bed he suddenly remembered her and prayed in his own words that for his birthday tomorrow his mother should stop hiding herself and come to him.

"Do you know, sir," he asked his tutor, "what I have been saying an extra prayer for?"

"To learn your lessons better?"

"No."

"For toys?"

"No. You'll never guess. It's something wonderful, but it's a secret. When it comes true I'll tell you. You haven't guessed, have you?"

"No, I'm afraid I haven't. Come, tell me," said Vassily Lukich with a smile, which was rare for him. "Oh, well, lie down now. I'm going to blow out the candle."

"But I can see better without a candle what I've been praying for. There, I nearly told you the secret!" said Seryozha with a merry laugh.

When the candle was taken away, Seryozha heard and felt his mother. She stood over him and caressed him with a loving look. But then windmills appeared and a penknife, and all got mixed up, and he fell asleep.

CHAPTER 28

On arriving in Petersburg, Vronsky and Anna put up at one of the best hotels, Vronsky separately on the lower floor, and Anna with the baby, the wet nurse, and a maid on the floor above in a large suite of four rooms.

On the day they arrived Vronsky went to see his brother. There he found his mother, who had arrived from Moscow on business. His mother and sister-in-law met him as usual, asked him about his trip abroad, spoke of mutual acquaintances, but did not say a single word about his liaison with Anna. But his brother, who came to see him at his hotel the following morning, asked about her himself, and Vronsky told him frankly that he regarded his union with Mrs. Karenin as marriage, that he hoped that a divorce could be arranged and that he would then marry her, and that meanwhile he considered her his wife, just like any other wife, and he asked his brother to tell that to their mother and to his wife.

"I don't care if society does not approve of it," said Vronsky, "but if my relations want me to treat them as such, they will have to treat my wife as their relation, too."

The elder brother, who always deferred to his brother's views, was not quite sure whether he was right or not till society had decided the question; but for his part he had nothing against it and went up with Alexey to see Anna.

In his brother's presence Vronsky spoke to Anna as to a close acquaintance, as he always did in the presence of a third party, but it was understood that his brother knew of their relations and they talked of Anna's going to Vronsky's estate.

In spite of all his experience of high society, Vronsky, as a result of the new position in which he found himself, labored under a strange delusion. It would seem that he of all people should have realized that high society was closed to him and Anna; but some vague notion got into his head that all that was true of the old days, but that today, when there was so much progress everywhere (without realizing it himself, he had become a supporter of every kind of progress), the views of society had changed and that the question whether they would be received in society was not yet determined. "Of course," he thought, "they will not receive her at Court, but intimate friends can and must look at it in the right way."

A man can sit cross-legged for several hours in one and the same position, if he knows that there is nothing to prevent him from changing it whenever he should wish; but if he knows that he has to go on sitting cross-legged like that, he will get cramps and his legs will begin to twitch and strain in the direction in which he would like to stretch them. This was what Vronsky experienced with regard to society. Although in his heart of hearts he knew perfectly well that society was closed to them, he tried to see whether it would not change and whether it would not receive them. But he very soon noticed that, though society was open to him personally, it was closed to Anna. As in the game of cat and mouse, the arms that were raised to allow him to get inside the circle were instantly lowered to prevent Anna from getting into it.

One of the first Petersburg ladies Vronsky met was his cousin Betsy.

"At last!" she cried joyfully. "And Anna? Oh, I'm so glad! Where are you staying? I can imagine how horrible our Petersburg must seem to you after your delightful journey. I can imagine what your honeymoon must have been like in Rome! And what about the divorce? Is it all settled?"

Vronsky observed that Betsy's delight diminished when she learned that no divorce had as yet taken place.

"They will cast stones at me, I know," she said, "but I shall come and see Anna. Yes, I certainly will. You're not staying here long, are you?"

And she did go to see Anna the same day; but her manner was quite different from what it used to be. She was evidently proud of her daring and wanted Anna to appreciate what a true friend she was. She did not stay more than ten minutes, retailing society gossip, and as she was leaving, said:

"You haven't told me when the divorce is to be. Of course, I've flung convention to the wind, but other strait-laced people will give you the cold shoulder until you are married. And this is so simple nowadays. *Ça se fait.* So you're leaving on Friday? What a pity we shan't see each other again."

From Betsy's tone Vronsky might have guessed what he had to expect from society; but he made another attempt in his own family. Of his mother he had no hopes. He knew that his mother, who had been so full of admiration for Anna when they first met, was now implacably hostile toward her for having been the cause of the ruin of her son's career. But he placed great hopes on his sister-in-law Varya. It seemed to him that she would not cast a stone, but with that simple and determined way of hers would call on Anna and receive her at her house.

The day after his arrival Vronsky took a cab to her house and, finding her alone, frankly expressed his wish.

"You know, Alexey," she said, when she had heard him out, "how fond I am of you and how gladly I'd do anything in the world for you. But I've said nothing because I knew that I could be of no help to you and Mrs. Karenin," she said, with particular stress on the "Mrs.

613

Karenin." "Don't, please, think that I am condemning anyone. Never! In her place I should perhaps have done the same. I do not and I cannot go into all the details," she went on, gazing timidly at his gloomy face, "but one must call things by their names. You want me to call on her, to receive her in my house, and rehabilitate her in society, but, please, understand that I simply cannot do it. I have daughters growing up and I have to mix in society for my husband's sake. Suppose I call on Mrs. Karenin—she will have to understand that I cannot ask her to my house or make sure she doesn't meet anybody here who looks at things differently: that would offend her. I can't raise her. . . ."

"But I don't consider that she has fallen more than hundreds of women whom you do receive," Vronsky interrupted her, looking gloomier than ever, and he got up in silence, realizing that his sister-in-law's decision was final.

"Alexey," Varya said, looking at him with a timid smile, "do not be angry with me. Please, understand that it's not my fault."

"I'm not angry with you," he said just as gloomily, "but I'm doubly hurt. I'm hurt, too, because this means breaking up our friendship. Well, if not breaking it up, then weakening it. You see, for me too there can be no other course."

And with that he left her.

Vronsky realized that any further efforts were useless and that they would have to spend these few days in Petersburg as though in a strange town, avoiding any contact with his former world in order not to run the risk of the unpleasantness or humiliation which was so painful to him. One of the most annoying things about his position in Petersburg was that Karenin seemed to be everywhere and his name on everyone's lips. It was impossible to start a conversation without its turning to Karenin; it was impossible to go anywhere without meeting him. So at least it seemed to Vronsky, just as it seems to a man with a sore finger that, as though on purpose, he keeps knocking it against everything.

His stay in Petersburg seemed to Vronsky even more distressing because he discerned all the time a kind of new mood in Anna that he could not understand. One moment she seemed to be in love with him and the next she would become cold, irritable, and inscrutable. Something was worrying her, something she concealed from him, and she did not seem to notice the humiliations which poisoned his life and which should have been even more painful to a person of her sensibility.

CHAPTER 29

One of Anna's reasons for returning to Russia had been to see her son. From the day she left Italy the thought of seeing him had not ceased to agitate her. And the nearer she got to Petersburg, the greater she imagined the joy and significance of that meeting would be. She never asked herself how such a meeting could be arranged. It seemed to her the most natural and simple thing in the world to see her son when she was in the same town as he; but when she arrived in Petersburg she realized clearly her present position in society and she recognized the fact that it would be difficult to arrange the meeting.

She had been two days in Petersburg. The thought of her son did not leave her for a moment, but she had not yet seen him. She felt she had no right to go straight to the house where she might meet Karenin. They might not even admit her and might insult her. It was painful to her to think of writing to and entering into any sort of communication with her husband: she could be calm only when she did not think of her husband. To see her son when he was out for a walk, to find out where and when he went out was not enough for her: she had so looked forward to this meeting, she had so much to tell him, she wanted so much to hug and kiss him. Seryozha's old nurse might have helped and advised her, but she was no longer in Karenin's house. Two days went by in this uncertainty and in efforts to find the nurse.

Having heard of Karenin's close relations with Countess Lydia Ivanovna, Anna decided on the third day to write the letter which cost her so much effort and in which she purposely stated that permission to see her son must depend on her husband's generosity. She knew that if her letter were shown to her husband, he would keep up his part of a generous husband and not refuse her request.

The commissionaire who took the letter brought back the most cruel and unexpected answer—that there would be no answer. She had never felt so humiliated as when, having sent for the commissionaire, she heard from him a detailed account of how he had had to wait a long time and how afterward he had been told: "There will be no answer." Anna felt humiliated and insulted, but she realized that from her own point of view the countess was right. Her grief was all the more powerful because she had to bear it alone. She could not and she would not share it with Vronsky. She knew that to him, though he was the chief cause of her misery, the question of her meeting with her son would seem a matter of very little importance. She knew that he would never be able to understand the whole depth of her suffering; she knew that, if it were mentioned, his cold tone would make her hate him. And she dreaded that more than anything else in the world, and that was why she concealed from him everything concerning her son.

After spending the whole of that day at the hotel, trying to think of a way of arranging a meeting with her son, she at last came to a decision to write to her husband. She was composing the letter when they brought her Lydia Ivanovna's note. The countess' silence humbled and subdued her, but her note and all that she read between the lines so irritated her, this malice seemed so outrageous to her when compared with her passionate and legitimate love for her son, that she was filled with indignation against other people and stopped blaming herself.

"That coldness, that pretense of feeling!" she said to herself. "They only want to insult me and torture the child! Am I going to submit? Not for anything in the world! She's worse than I. At least, I don't lie."

And she made up her mind there and then that next day, Seryozha's birthday, she would go straight to her husband's house, bribe the servants, cheat, if necessary, but see her son, cost what may, and destroy that monstrous atmosphere of deception with which they had surrounded the unfortunate child.

She drove to a toy shop, bought a lot of toys, and

thought over her plan of action. She would go there early in the morning, at eight o'clock, when Karenin would quite certainly not be up. She would have money in her hand which she would give the hall porter and the footman to let her in and, without raising her veil, would say that she had come from Seryozha's godfather to wish him many happy returns and that she had been asked to leave the toys at his bedside. The only thing she did not prepare for was what she was going to say to her son.

However much she thought about it, she could not think of anything.

Next day, at eight o'clock in the morning, Anna got out of a hired cab and rang the bell at the front door of her former home.

"Go and see what she wants. . . . It's some lady," said Kapitonych, who, not yet dressed, in his overcoat and galoshes, had looked out of the window and caught sight of a lady in a veil standing close to the door.

The assistant hall porter, a young fellow Anna did not know, had hardly opened the door when she went in and, taking a three-ruble note out of her muff, thrust it hurriedly into his hand.

"Seryozha . . . Sergey Alexeyich," she said and was about to walk past.

After examining the note, the hall porter's assistant stopped her at the other glass door.

"Who do you want?" he asked.

She did not hear what he said and made no answer.

Noticing the unknown lady's embarrassment, Kapitonych himself came out, opened the second door to her, and inquired what she wanted.

"From Prince Skorodumov to Sergey Alexeyich," she brought out.

"The young master isn't up yet," said the hall porter, looking at her intently.

Anna had never expected the entirely unaltered appearance of the hall of the house where she had lived for nine years to have affected her so strongly. Memories, happy and painful, rose one after another in her heart and for an instant she forgot why she was there.

"Will you wait, please?" said Kapitonych, helping her off with her fur cloak.

Having done so, he glanced at her face, recognized her, and silently bowed low to her.

"Come in, ma'am," he said.

She wanted to say something, but her voice refused to utter a sound. Glancing at the old man with silent entreaty, she went with light, swift steps up the stairs. Bending forward, with his galoshes catching on the stairs, Kapitonych ran after her, trying to overtake her.

"His tutor is there, ma'am. He may not be dressed. I'll announce you."

Anna continued to run up the familiar stairs, not understanding what the old man was saying.

"This way, please, ma'am. To the left. I'm sorry it's not quite clean. He's in the old sitting room now," said the hall porter, panting. "Please, wait a little, ma'am, I'll have a look first," he went on, and having overtaken her, he opened the big door and disappeared behind it. Anna stopped and waited. "He's only just woken up," said the hall porter, coming out of the door.

Just as he spoke Anna heard the sound of a childish yawn. From the very sound of this yawn she recognized her son and seemed to see him before her.

"Let me in, let me in, you can go!" she said and went in through the high door.

To the right of the door stood a bed and sitting up on the bed was the boy, in an unbuttoned nightshirt, his little body bent over backward, stretching himself and finishing his yawn. At the moment when his lips were about to close, they extended into a blissful, sleepy smile, and with that smile he again fell slowly and happily on his pillow.

"Seryozha!" she whispered, walking up to the bed noiselessly.

During the time they had been parted and more recently when she had been feeling an upsurge of love for him, she had imagined him as a little boy of four, when she had loved him most. Now he was not even the same as she had left him; he was still further from a four-year-old boy, he had grown and he was thinner. Goodness, how thin his face was and how short his hair! And how long his arms! How changed he was since she had left him! But still it was he, with the same formation of the head, the same lips, the same soft neck and broad little shoulders.

"Seryozha!" she called again, almost in the child's ear.

He raised himself on the elbow again, turned his tou-

sled head from side to side, as though looking for someone, and opened his eyes. He gazed quietly and
inquiringly for a few seconds at his mother standing
motionless before him, then he suddenly smiled blissfully and, again closing his eyes, which he seemed unable to keep open, fell not backward but forward into
her arms.

"Sezyozha, my darling!" she said breathlessly, putting
her arms round his plump little body.

"Mummy!" he said, wriggling about in her arms in
order to touch them with different parts of his body.

Smiling sleepily, still with closed eyes, he removed his
chubby little hands from the back of the bed and flung
them round her shoulders, clinging close to her, envel-
oping her in that sweet scent of warmth and sleepiness
which only children possess, and began rubbing his face
against her neck and shoulders.

"I knew," he said, opening his eyes. "Today's my
birthday. I knew you'd come. I'll get up now. . . ."

And while saying this, he was falling asleep.

Anna examined him with intense interest. She could
see how he had grown up and changed in her absence.
She recognized and did not recognize his bare legs, so
big now, which were showing from under the blanket;
she recognized the cheeks that had grown thinner, the
short curls on the back of his neck, where she had so
often kissed him. She touched it all and could not utter
a word; tears choked her.

"What are you crying about, Mummy?" he said, fully
awake now. "Mummy, what are you crying about?" he
asked in a tearful voice.

"Me? I won't cry . . . I'm crying for joy. It's such a
long time since I saw you. I won't, my darling, I won't,"
she said, gulping down her tears and turning away.
"Well, it's time you got dressed," she said after a pause
when she had recovered and, without letting go of his
hand, she sat down on the chair beside the bed, on which
his clothes were lying ready.

"How do you dress without me? How . . ." she tried
to speak naturally and cheerfully, but she couldn't and
she turned away again.

"I don't wash with cold water. Daddy says I mustn't.
You haven't seen Vassily Lukich, have you? He'll be
coming in soon. And you are sitting on my clothes!"

And Seryozha burst out laughing loudly. She looked at him and smiled.

"Mummy, darling, darling Mummy!" he cried, flinging himself on her again and throwing his arms round her. It was as though seeing her smile made him realize clearly what had happened. "You don't want that," he said, taking off her hat. And as though he had seen her afresh without a hat, he started kissing her again.

"Well, what did you think about me? You didn't think I was dead, did you?"

"I never believed it."

"You didn't believe it, my darling?"

"I knew, I knew!" he repeated his favorite phrase and, seizing her hand, which was stroking his hair, he began pressing the palm to his mouth and covering it with kisses.

CHAPTER 30

Meanwhile Vassily Lukich, who had not at first understood who the lady was, realized from what he had heard that she was the mother who had left her husband and whom he did not know because he had come to the house only after her departure, but he could not make up his mind whether to go in or whether to inform Karenin. Deciding finally that his duty was to get Seryozha up at a fixed hour and that consequently it was not his business to consider who was sitting there—the boy's mother or anyone else—but that he must do his duty, he dressed, went up to the door, and opened it.

But the caresses of the mother and son, the sound of their voices and what they were saying, made him change his mind. He shook his head and with a sigh closed the door again. "I'll wait another ten minutes," he said, clearing his throat and wiping away tears.

In the meantime a great commotion was going on among the servants. They all knew that the mistress had come and that Kapitonych had let her in and that she was now in the nursery. But the master always went into the nursery at nine, and they all realized that a meeting between husband and wife was inconceivable and that it must be prevented. Korney, the valet, went down to the hall porter's room to ask who had let her in and why, and hearing that it was Kapitonych who had let her in and taken her up, reprimanded the old man. The hall porter kept obstinately silent, but when Korney said that he ought to be turned out of the house for that, Kapitonych rushed up to him and, waving his hands before Korney's face, burst out:

"I suppose you wouldn't have let her in, would you? I've been in service here ten years and have had nothing but kindness from her, and you, of course, would have gone and said: get out of here! You're a clever fellow, aren't you? Yes, indeed! You'd better mind your own business, my lad, and go on fleecing the master and pinching his raccoon coats!"

"*Peasant!*" said Korney contemptuously, and turned to the nurse who was just coming in. "Now what do you think of that, Marfa Yefimovna?" Korney appealed to her. "He's let her in without telling anyone. The master will be up any minute and go to the nursery."

"Trouble, trouble!" said the nurse. "Couldn't you, Korney, keep him, the master, I mean, in his room a little longer while I run and get her out of the way. Trouble, trouble!"

When the nurse entered the nursery, Seryozha was telling his mother how he and Nadenka had rolled down a hill and turned three somersaults. She listened to the sound of his voice, saw his face and the play of his features, felt his hand, but did not understand what he was saying. She had to go, she had to leave him—that was the only thought in her mind. She heard Vassily Lukich's steps as he came to the door, she heard him clear his throat, and now she heard the footsteps of the nurse as she came into the room; but she sat as though turned to stone, unable to speak or get up.

"Madam, dear madam!" began the nurse, going up to Anna and kissing her hands and shoulders. "It's joy indeed the Lord has brought our little one on his birthday! You haven't changed a bit, ma'am."

"Oh, nurse, dear, I didn't know you were in the house," said Anna, recollecting herself for a moment.

"I'm not, ma'am. I'm living with my daughter. I've just come to congratulate our little darling on his birthday, ma'am."

The nurse suddenly burst into tears and again began kissing her hand.

621

Seryozha, smiling and with beaming eyes, holding on to his mother with one hand and to his nurse with the other, was jumping up and down with his plump bare feet on the carpet. The tenderness of his favorite nurse to his mother delighted him.

"Mummy, she often comes to see me and when she comes . . ." he began, but stopped short, noticing that the nurse was whispering something to his mother, and that a look of fear and something like shame appeared on her face, which did not at all become his mother.

She went up to him.

"My darling," she said.

She could not say good-by, but the look on her face said it, and he understood.

"Darling, darling Kootik!" she said, calling him by the pet name she had used when he was a baby. "You won't forget me, will you? You . . ." but she could say no more.

How many things she thought of afterward that she might have said! But now she did not know what to say and she could not speak. But Seryozha understood everything she wanted to say to him. He understood that she was unhappy and that she loved him. He even understood what it was the nurse had whispered. He had caught the words: "Always at nine," and he understood that it referred to his father and that his father and mother must not meet. This he understood, but one thing he could not understand: why did she look frightened and ashamed? She could not have done anything wrong, but she was afraid of his father and was ashamed of something. He wanted to ask a question that would clear up his doubts, but he dared not: he saw that she was suffering and he felt sorry for her.

"Don't go," he said in a whisper, clinging close to her. "He won't come in just yet."

His mother pushed him away from her a little to see whether he really understood what he was saying, and in the frightened look on his face she read that he was not only speaking of his father, but was asking her what he ought to think about his father.

"Seryozha, my darling," she said, "you must love him. He's better and kinder than I am, and I've treated him badly. When you're grown up, you'll be able to judge."

"There's no one better than you!" he cried in despair through his tears and, seizing her by the shoulders, he hugged her with all his might, his arms trembling with the effort.

"Oh, my darling, my little one!" said Anna, bursting into tears and crying in the same weak, childlike way as he.

At that moment the door opened and Vassily Lukich came in. Footsteps were heard approaching the other door, and the nurse said in a frightened voice: "He's coming!" and handed Anna her hat.

Seryozha sank down on his bed and burst into sobs, covering his face with his hands. Anna moved his hands away from his face, kissed him again on his wet cheeks, and went rapidly toward the door. Karenin was coming toward her. Seeing her, he stopped and bowed his head.

Although she had just said that he was better and kinder than she was, after casting a swift glance at him, which took in his whole figure to the minutest detail, she was seized by a feeling of revulsion and hatred for him. She quickly let down her veil and, quickening her step, almost ran out of the room.

She had no time even to take out the toys she had chosen with so much love and sadness the day before, and she took them back with her.

CHAPTER 31

Dearly as Anna had desired to see her son, much as she had thought of it and prepared herself for it, she had never expected it to have had such a powerful effect on her. When she returned to her lonely suite at the hotel, she could not for a long time understand why she was there. "Yes, it's all over and I'm alone again," she said to herself, and without taking her hat off sat down in an armchair by the fireplace. Staring motionless at a bronze clock on the table between the windows, she sank into thought.

The French maid, whom they had brought from abroad, came in and asked whether she would like to change. She looked at her in surprise and said:

"Later."

A waiter offered her coffee.

"Later," she said.

The Italian wet nurse came in with the baby girl, whom she had just dressed, and held her out to Anna. The plump, well-nourished little girl, as she always did when she saw her mother, turned her little hands—so fat that they looked as if a thread had been tied tightly round the wrists—down, and smiling with her toothless little mouth, began waving them, like a fish waving its fins, making the starched folds of her embroidered little frock rustle. It was impossible not to smile, not to kiss the little thing, not to hold out a finger for her to clutch, shrieking with delight and jumping up and down; it was impossible not to hold up one's lips to her, which she would draw into her mouth by way of a kiss. And Anna did all this. She took her into her arms, and made her dance up and down, and kissed her fresh little cheek and bare little elbows; but the sight of this child made it clearer than ever to her that what she felt for it was not even love when compared with what she felt for Seryozha. Everything about the baby was sweet, but for some reason she did not grip the heart. Upon her first child, though by a man she did not love, she had bestowed all the love that had never found satisfaction; the girl had been born under the most trying conditions and had not received a hundredth part of the care lavished on the first child. Besides, everything about the little girl was still to come, while Seryozha was almost a grown-up man, and a beloved one; thoughts and feelings were already struggling in his mind; he understood, he loved, he judged her, she thought, recalling his words and looks. And she was forever separated from him not only physically but spiritually, and there was nothing to be done about it.

She gave the baby girl back to the wet nurse, let her go, and opened the locket with Seryozha's portrait, taken when he was almost the same age as the little girl. She rose, and removing her hat, took from the table an album in which were photographs of her son at different ages. She wanted to compare them and began taking them out of the album. She took them all out but one, the last and the best photograph. He was sitting astride a chair in a white shirt, a frown in his eyes and a smile on his lips. That was his most characteristic and best expression. With her deft little hands, whose slender white fingers moved with a peculiar tenseness that day, she caught hold of the corner of the photograph several times, but each time it slipped out of her grasp and she could not get it out. There was no paper knife on the table, so she took out the photograph next to it (it was a photograph of Vronsky taken in Rome in a round hat and long hair) and pushed her son's photograph out with it. "Yes, there he is!" she said, glancing at Vronsky's photograph and suddenly remembering that he was the cause of her present grief. She had not thought of him once during the whole of that morning. But now, seeing that manly and noble face, a face so familiar and dear to her, she suddenly felt an unexpected upsurge of love for him.

"But where is he? Why does he leave me alone with my suffering?" she thought all of a sudden with a feeling of reproach, forgetting that she herself had concealed from him all that concerned her son. She sent down to ask him to come up to her at once, and she waited for him with a sinking heart, trying to think of the words with which she would tell him everything and of the expressions of his love with which he would comfort her. The servant returned with the answer that he had a visitor, but that he would come immediately and he further wished to know whether he could bring up Prince Yashvin, who had just arrived in Petersburg. "He won't be coming alone and he hasn't seen me since dinner yesterday," she thought. "He'll be coming with Yashvin and not so that I can tell him everything." And suddenly a strange idea crossed her mind: what if he did not love her any more?

And going over in her mind the events of the last few days, she imagined that she could see a confirmation of that dreadful thought in everything: in the fact that he had not dined at home yesterday, in the fact that he had insisted on their taking separate suites in Petersburg, and lastly, in the fact that even now he was not coming up alone, just as though he were trying to avoid a tête-à-tête with her.

"But he must tell me if it is so. I must know. If I know it, then I shall know what to do," she said to herself, quite unable to imagine the position she would be in if she were to convince herself of his indifference. She thought he was no longer in love with her, she felt on the verge of despair, which made her feel particularly excited. She rang for the maid and went into the dressing room. While dressing, she paid more attention to her toilet than she had done all these days, as though, having fallen out of love with her, he could again fall in love with her because she wore the dress and arranged her hair in the style most becoming to her.

She heard the bell before she was ready.

When she went into the drawing room, it was not he but Yashvin whose eyes she met. Vronsky was examining the photographs of her son, which she had forgotten on the table, and he was not in a hurry to look at her.

"We've met before," she said, placing her small hand in the huge hand of the embarrassed Yashvin (which was so strange considering his enormous figure and coarse face). "We met last year at the races. Give them to me," she said, taking from Vronsky her son's photographs, which he was looking at, with a rapid movement and glancing at him significantly with glittering eyes. "Were the races good this year? I saw the races on the Corso in Rome instead. But then I don't think you care for life abroad, do you?" she said with a nice smile. "I know you and I know all the things you like, though we've met so seldom."

"I am very sorry to hear that," said Yashvin, biting the left side of his mustache, "because, you see, the things I like are mostly bad."

After talking to her for a few minutes and noticing that Vronsky had glanced at the clock, Yashvin asked her whether she would be staying long in Petersburg and, unbending his huge figure, picked up his képi.

"Not long, I think," she said, looking embarrassed and glancing at Vronsky.

"In that case I don't suppose I shall see you again," said Yashvin, getting up and addressing Vronsky. "Where are you dining?"

"Come and dine with us," Anna said determinedly, as though angry with herself for her embarrassment, but blushing as she always did whenever she had to make clear her position before a fresh person. "The dinner here is not good, but at least you will see each other. Of all his regimental friends Alexey likes you best."

"I shall be glad to," said Yashvin with a smile, from which Vronsky could see that he liked Anna very much.

Yashvin took his leave and went out. Vronsky remained behind.

"Are you going too?" she said to him.

"I'm afraid I'm late," he said. "You go on," he called after Yashvin. "I'll catch up with you in a minute."

She took his hand, and without taking her eyes off him looked at him as though trying to think what to say to him to make him stay.

"Wait, there's something I want to say to you," she said, and raising his stubby hand, she pressed it to her neck. "You didn't mind my asking him to dinner?"

"Not at all," he said with a calm smile, showing his compact row of teeth and kissing her hand.

"Alexey, you haven't changed toward me, have you?" she said, pressing his hand in both of hers. "Alexey, I'm having an awful time here. When are we going?"

"Soon, soon. You wouldn't believe how painful our life here is to me, too," he said, drawing away his hand.

"All right, go, go!" she said, feeling hurt, and moved away from him quickly.

CHAPTER 32

When Vronsky returned Anna had not yet come back home. Soon after he had gone, he was told, a lady came to see her and she had gone out with her. That she had gone without letting him know where she was going, that she had not come back yet, that she had gone out somewhere that morning without saying anything to him—all this together with her strangely excited look that morning when Yashvin was there and the hostile way with which she had practically snatched her son's photographs out of his hands made him wonder what was the matter with her. He decided that he must talk things over frankly with her. He waited for her in the drawing room. Anna did not return alone, but brought with her her old maiden aunt, Princess Oblonsky. It was she who had called on Anna in the morning and it was with her that Anna had gone out shopping. Anna pretended not to notice the worried and inquiring look on

Vronsky's face and began telling him gaily about the purchases she had made. He saw that something peculiar was going on inside her: there was a look of strained attention when her eyes rested on him and in her speech and movements there was that nervous rapidity and grace which had appealed to him so much during the first period of their intimacy, but which worried and frightened him now.

The table was laid for four. They were all assembled and about to go into the small dining room, when Tushkevich arrived with a message for Anna from Princess Betsy. The Princess asked to be excused for not having come to say good-by; she was not well and she begged Anna to come and see her between half past six and nine. At the mention of this specific time, Vronsky glanced at Anna, for it showed that the necessary steps had been taken that she should not meet anyone; but Anna did not appear to have noticed it.

"I'm terribly sorry, but between half past six and nine is just when I cannot possibly come," she said with a faint smile.

"The princess will be very disappointed."

"Me too."

"I suppose you're going to hear Patti?" said Tushkevich.

"Patti? You've given me an idea. I would go if I could get a box."

"I could get you one," Tushkevich volunteered.

"I should be very, very grateful indeed!" said Anna. "But won't you stay and have dinner with us?"

Vronsky gave a barely perceptible shrug. He simply could not understand what Anna was doing. Why had she brought that old princess, why had she asked Tushkevich to stay to dinner, and most amazing of all, why was she sending him to get a box for the opera? Did she really think it possible in her position to go to the opera when Patti was singing, where she would meet all her society acquaintances? He looked gravely at her, but she responded with the same defiant half-gay and half-desperate look, the significance of which he could not make out. At dinner Anna was aggressively gay: she seemed to flirt with both Tushkevich and Yashvin. When they rose from table, Tushkevich went to get a box at the opera and Yashvin to have a smoke. Vronsky went

628

down with Yashvin to his own rooms. After sitting with Yashvin for a while, he ran upstairs. Anna was already dressed in her light silk dress trimmed with velvet and cut low in front, which she had had made in Paris; on her hair she wore some rich white lace that framed her face and set off her dazzling beauty to great advantage.

"Are you really going to the theater?" he said, trying not to look at her.

"And why do you ask in such a frightened tone of voice?" she said, once again hurt that he did not look at her. "Why shouldn't I go?"

She pretended not to grasp the meaning of his words.

"Well, of course, there's no earthly reason why you shouldn't," he said, frowning.

"That's just what I say," she declared, deliberately pretending not to understand the irony of his tone and calmly pulling up her long, perfumed glove.

"Anna, for heaven's sake, what's the matter with you?" he said, bullying her, just as her husband once used to talk to her.

"I don't know what you mean."

"You know you can't go."

"Why not? I'm not going alone. The Princess Varvara has gone to dress. She is coming with me."

He shrugged with an air of bewilderment and despair.

"But don't you know—" he began.

"I don't want to know!" she almost shouted. "I don't want to. Am I sorry for what I have done? No, no, and no! And if I were to do it again from the beginning, I'd do the same. For us, for you and me, only one thing matters: whether we love each other. There are no other considerations. Why do we live here separately and not seeing each other? Why can't I go to the theater? I love you and nothing else matters," she said in Russian, glancing at him with a peculiar glitter in her eyes which he could not understand, "so long as you have not changed toward me. Why don't you look at me?"

He looked at her. He saw all the beauty of her face and of her dress, always so becoming to her. But now it was just her beauty and her elegance that irritated him.

"My feelings cannot change, you know that, but I beg you not to go, I implore you not to go," he said again in French, with tender entreaty in his voice, but with a cold look in his eyes.

She did not hear his words, but she saw the cold look in his eyes.

"And I'd like to ask you to explain," she answered irritably, "why I mustn't go."

"Because it might cause you . . ." He faltered.

"I don't understand a thing. Yashvin *n'est pas compromettant,* and Princess Varvara is no worse than other people. And here she is."

CHAPTER 33

Vronsky for the first time experienced a feeling of exasperation, almost anger, for her deliberate refusal to understand her position. This feeling deepened because he could not tell her why he felt so exasperated. Had he told her frankly what he thought, he would have said: "To appear in the theater in this dress, accompanied by the princess, whom everyone knows, means not only to acknowledge your position of a fallen woman, but also to throw down a challenge to society, or in other words, to renounce it forever."

But he could not say that to her. "But how is it she does not realize it? What is going on inside her?" he asked himself. He felt his respect for her was diminishing while at the same time his consciousness of her beauty was increasing.

He went back frowning to his rooms and, sitting down beside Yashvin, who was drinking brandy and soda, his long legs stretched out on a chair, he ordered the same for himself.

"You were talking about Lankovsky's Powerful. It's a good horse and I advise you to buy it," said Yashvin, glancing at his friend's gloomy face. "His hindquarters are not quite perfect, but his legs and head leave nothing to be desired."

"I think I'll take him," said Vronsky.

The talk about horses interested him, but not for a moment did he forget Anna, and he involuntarily listened to the sound of footsteps in the corridor and kept glancing at the clock on the mantelpiece.

"Anna Arkadyevna sent me to say that she has gone to the theater," a servant came in to announce.

Yashvin, emptying another glass of brandy into the sparkling water, drank it, got up, and began buttoning his coat.

"Well, let's go," he said, smiling faintly under cover of his mustache and showing by his smile that he understood the cause of Vronsky's gloom, but attached no importance to it.

"I'm not going," Vronsky replied gloomily.

"But I must," said Yashvin. "I promised. Well, goodby. But why not come to the stalls? You can take Krasinsky's seat," added Yashvin as he went out.

"No, I've something to do."

"One has trouble with a wife," thought Yashvin, as he left the hotel, "but it's much worse with one who is not a wife."

Left alone, Vronsky got up and began pacing the room.

"What is it tonight? The fourth subscription performance. Yegor and his wife are there and Mother too, I suppose. That's to say, the whole of Petersburg will be there. Now she's gone in, taken off her cloak, and come forward into the light. Tushkevich, Yashvin, Princess Varvara . . ." He pictured the scene to himself. "And what about me? Am I afraid or have I put her under Tushkevich's protection? Whichever way you look at it, it's stupid, stupid. . . . And why does she put me in such a position?" he said, giving it up with a wave of the hand.

As he did so, he knocked against the table on which the soda water and the decanter of brandy were standing and nearly knocked it over. In trying to steady it, he upset it and in his vexation kicked it over, and rang.

"If you want to keep your job," he said to the valet who entered, "you'd better remember your duties. See that it never happens again. You should have cleared it away."

The valet, conscious that he was not to blame, was about to protest, but, glancing at his master, realized from his face that he'd better keep silent, and so, bending down quickly, he knelt on the carpet and began sorting out the whole and the broken glasses and bottles.

"That's not your business. Send the waiter to clear it away, and get out my dress suit."

*   *   *

631

Vronsky went into the theater at half past eight. The performance was in full swing. The old attendant helped him off with his fur coat and, recognizing him, called him "Your Excellency" and suggested that he need not take a ticket for his coat but simply call "Fyodor!" when he wanted it. There was no one in the brightly illuminated corridor except the attendant and two footmen with fur coats over their arms listening at the door, which was slightly ajar and through which came the sounds of the discreet staccato accompaniment of the orchestra and a woman's voice rendering a musical phrase with precision. The door opened to let an attendant slip through, and the phrase, drawing to a close, struck Vronsky's ear distinctly. But the door was closed immediately and Vronsky did not hear the end of the phrase nor the cadenza after it, but he knew from the thunder of the applause that it was finished. When he entered the auditorium, which was brilliantly lit by chandeliers and bronze gas brackets, the noise was still going on. On the stage the prima donna, in a glitter of bare shoulders and diamonds, was bowing and smiling as she picked up with the help of the tenor, who was holding her hand, the bouquets that had been clumsily flung across the footlights; she then walked over to a gentleman, his hair parted in the middle and shining with pomatum, who was stretching with his long arms across the footlights to hand her something, and the whole audience in the stalls as well as in the boxes was astir, leaning forward, shouting and clapping. From his raised seat the conductor helped in passing the present and straightened his white tie. Vronsky entered in the center of the stalls and stopped, looking around him. That night he paid less attention than ever to the surroundings he knew so well—the stage, the noise, and all that familiar and uninteresting variegated herd of spectators in a packed theater.

As usual, in the boxes sat the same kind of ladies with the same kind of officers behind them; as usual, the same—goodness only knew who they were—gailydressed women and men in uniforms and evening dress; the same dirty crowd in the gallery; and in all that crowd, in the boxes and in the front seats of the stalls, there were only about forty *real* men and women. To these oases Vronsky at once turned his attention and at once exchanged greetings with them.

The act had come to an end when he came in, and he did not therefore go straight into his brother's box, but walked down to the front row of the stalls and, with his back to the stage, stopped beside Serpukhovskoy, who was standing at the footlights with his knees bent and was tapping the wall of the orchestra with his heel. He had noticed Vronsky from a distance and beckoned to him with a smile.

Vronsky had not yet seen Anna; he purposely avoided looking her way. But he knew from the direction in which everybody's eyes were turned where she was. He was looking around furtively, but he was not looking for her; prepared for the worst, he was looking for Karenin. Luckily for him, Karenin did not happen to be in the theater that evening.

"How little of the soldier there is left in you," Serpukhovskoy said to him. "A diplomat, an artist, or something of the kind."

"Yes, as soon as I got home I put on a frock coat," replied Vronsky, smiling and slowly taking out his opera glasses.

"Now in that, I must say, I do envy you. When I come back from abroad and put on these" (he touched his shoulder knots) "I regret my freedom."

Serpukhovskoy had long dropped all idea of Vronsky's career, but he was as fond of him as ever and was particularly nice to him now.

"A pity you were late for the first act."

Vronsky, listening with one ear, moved his glasses from the stalls to the dress circle and was examining the boxes. Next to a lady in a turban and a bald-headed old man, who blinked angrily just as Vronsky's glasses were focused on him, he suddenly caught sight of Anna's proud, strikingly beautiful head, smiling in its frame of lace. She was in the fifth box in the stalls, about twenty paces from him. She sat in the front of the box and, turning around slightly, was saying something to Yashvin. The poise of her head on her beautiful, broad shoulders and the restrained excitement and radiance of her eyes and her whole face reminded him of what she had looked like when he had seen her at the ball in Moscow.

But now he was affected by this beauty in quite a different way. There was nothing mysterious now in his feeling for her, and for this reason her beauty, though it attracted him more powerfully than ever, also offended him. She was not looking in his direction, but Vronsky felt that she had already seen him.

When Vronsky directed his opera glasses that way again, he noticed that the Princess Varvara was very red in the face and was laughing unnaturally and kept glancing around at the next box, while Anna, tapping the red plush edge of the box with her closed fan, was looking fixedly somewhere else without seeing, and obviously without wishing to see, what was taking place in the next box. Yashvin's face wore the expression it usually had when he was losing at cards. He was scowling, shoving the left side of his mustache deeper and deeper into his mouth, and casting sidelong glances at the same box.

In that box, on the left, were the Kartasovs. Vronsky knew them and he knew that Anna was acquainted with them. Mrs. Kartasov, a thin little woman, was standing in her box with her back to Anna and putting on an opera cloak which her husband was holding up for her. Her face was pale and angry and she was saying something excitedly. Kartasov, a fat, bald-headed man, kept glancing round at Anna and tried to calm his wife. When his wife had gone out, the husband stayed behind for some time, trying to catch Anna's eye and apparently wishing to bow to her. But Anna seemed not to be noticing him on purpose. Turning around, she was saying something to Yashvin, who was bending toward her with his cropped head. Kartasov went out without bowing and the box was left empty.

Vronsky could not make out what exactly had happened between the Kartasovs and Anna, but he realized that what had happened was something humiliating for Anna. He gathered that from what he had seen and more particularly from Anna's face, for he knew that she was summoning her last strength to keep up the role she had undertaken. And that role of outward calm was completely successful. Those who did not know her or her circle, who had not heard any of the expressions of pity, indignation, and amazement by the women that she should have allowed herself to appear in society and so conspicuously too in her lace headdress and in all her beauty, admired the calmness and good looks of the woman and did not suspect that she was experiencing the sensation of one who had been put in the pillory.

Knowing that something had happened but not knowing exactly what, Vronsky was painfully perturbed and, hoping to find out, he thought of going to his brother's box. Deliberately choosing an exit from the stalls at the opposite side from where Anna was, he ran across his former regimental commanding officer, who was talking to two acquaintances. Vronsky heard them mention the name of the Karenins and noticed how the colonel hastened to call him loudly by name with a significant glance at his companions.

"Ah, Vronsky," said the colonel, "when are you coming to see us at the regiment? We can't let you go without a dinner. You're one of our old comrades."

"I shan't have time for it now. I'm sorry, some other time," said Vronsky and ran upstairs to his brother's box.

The old countess, Vronsky's mother, with her steel-gray curls, was in his brother's box. Varya with Princess Sorokin bumped into him in the corridor of the dress circle.

Having conducted Princess Sorokin to her mother-in-law, Varya held out her hand to her brother-in-law and at once began talking about what interested him. He had rarely seen her so excited.

"I think it's despicable and disgusting, and Mrs. Kartasov had no right to act as she did. Mrs. Karenin—" she began.

"What happened? I don't know."

"Don't you? Haven't you heard?"

"You know I shall be the last to hear of it."

"I wonder if you could find a creature more spiteful than that Mrs. Kartasov."

"But what has she done?"

"My husband told me. She insulted Mrs. Karenin. Her husband began talking to her across the box, and she made a scene. I understand she said something offensive in a loud voice and went out."

"Count, your mother is asking for you," said Princess Sorokin, looking out of the door of the box.

"I've been expecting you all the time," his mother said to him, smiling sardonically. "You're nowhere to be seen."

Her son saw that she could not help smiling with delight.

"Good evening, Mother," he said coldly. "I was just coming to see you."

"Why don't you go *faire la cour à Madame Karénine?*" she added, when Princess Sorokin had moved away. "*Elle fait sensation. On oublie la Patti pour elle.*"

"Mother, I've asked you not to speak to me about that," he replied, frowning.

"I'm merely saying what everybody is saying."

Vronsky made no reply and after saying a few words to Princess Sorokin, he left the box. In the doorway he met his brother.

"Ah, Alexey!" said his brother. "What a disgusting business! The woman's a fool, that's all. . . . I was just going to her. Let's go together."

Vronsky did not listen to him. He ran downstairs: he felt he had to do something, but he did not know what. His exasperation with Anna for putting herself and him in such a false position and his compassion for her sufferings made him feel agitated. He went down to the stalls and walked straight toward Anna's box. At the side of her box stood Stremov, talking to her.

"There are no more tenors," he said. "*Le moule en est brisé.*"

Vronsky bowed to her and stopped to shake hands with Stremov.

"I believe you came late and missed the best aria," said Anna to Vronsky with—as he thought—a mocking look at him.

"I'm afraid I'm a poor judge," he said, looking severely at her.

"Like Prince Yashvin," she said, smiling, "who finds that Patti sings too loud."

"Thank you," she said, taking the program Vronsky picked up in her small hand with its long glove, and suddenly at that very moment her lovely face quivered. She got up and went to the back of the box.

Noticing that in the next act her box was empty, Vronsky, amid the suppressed hissing of the audience, which had grown quiet at the beginning of a *cavatina*, left the stalls and went home.

636

Anna was already at the hotel. When Vronsky entered she was alone and still in the dress in which she had gone to the theater. She was sitting in the first armchair by the wall and was staring blankly before her. She glanced at him and immediately resumed her former position.

"Anna," he said.

"It's you, it's you who're to blame for everything!" she cried with tears of despair and malice in her voice, and got up.

"I begged you, I implored you not to go. I knew it would be unpleasant for you."

"Unpleasant!" she cried. "It was horrible! I shan't forget it as long as I live! She said it was a disgrace to sit near me."

"Why worry about what a silly woman says?" he replied. "But why run the risk? Why provoke—"

"I hate your calmness! You shouldn't have brought me to this. If you loved me . . ."

"Anna, what has my love got to do with it?"

"If you loved me as I love you, if you were as unhappy as I am . . ." she said, peering at him with a look of terror.

He was sorry for her, but he couldn't help feeling vexed. He assured her of his love because he could see that that was the only thing that would calm her now, and he did not reproach her with words, but in his heart he reproached her.

She drank in eagerly the assurances of love, which he thought so vulgar that he was ashamed to utter them, and gradually grew calm. Next day, completely reconciled, they left for the country.

Part Six

Part Six

∾

CHAPTER 1

Dolly and her children were spending the summer with her sister Kitty Levin at Pokrovskoye. The house on her own estate was completely dilapidated, and Levin and his wife had persuaded her to spend the summer with them. Oblonsky was entirely in favor of this arrangement. He declared that he was terribly sorry his duties prevented his spending the summer with his family in the country, which would have made him very happy indeed, and while remaining in Moscow, he paid an occasional visit to the country for a day or two. Besides the Oblonskys with all their children and the governess, old Princess Shcherbatsky was staying with the Levins this summer, for she considered it to be her duty to keep an eye on her inexperienced daughter in her *present* condition. There was also Varenka, Kitty's friend from abroad, who kept her promise to visit Kitty when she was married and who was now staying with her friend. All these people were friends and relations of Levin's wife. And though he was very fond of them all, he could not help regretting a little his own Levin world and order of things, which was being submerged by this influx of the "Shcherbatsky element," as he described it to himself. Only one of his own relations, Sergey Koznyshev, was visiting him that summer, but even he was a Koznyshev rather than a Levin, so that the Levin spirit was completely obliterated.

There were so many people in Levin's country house, so long deserted, that almost all the rooms were occupied and almost every day the old princess, when sitting down to a meal, had to count them all and tell the thirteenth grandson or granddaughter to sit at a separate table. As for Kitty, who was very conscientious in carrying out her household duties, she had no little trouble in getting the chickens, turkeys, and ducks, a great number of which were consumed to satisfy the summer appetites of the visitors and children.

The whole family was at dinner. Dolly's children, the governess, and Varenka were making plans where they should go to gather mushrooms. Sergey Koznyshev, who was looked upon by the visitors with such awe for his intellect and learning that it almost amounted to veneration, astonished everyone by joining in the conversation about mushrooms.

"Please, take me with you too," he said, looking at Varenka. "I'm very fond of mushrooming. I consider it a very excellent occupation."

"Why, of course, we shall be very pleased," replied Varenka, blushing.

Kitty and Dolly exchanged meaningful glances. That the learned and intellectual Koznyshev should propose to go gathering mushrooms with Varenka confirmed certain theories of Kitty's that had greatly occupied her mind of late. She hastened to say something to her mother so that her glance should not be noticed. After dinner Koznyshev sat down with his cup of coffee at the window in the drawing room, continuing his conversation with his brother and glancing now and again at the door through which the children, who were about to set out on their mushrooming expedition, would come out. Levin sat down on the window sill near his brother.

"You've changed a lot since your marriage and for the better," said Koznyshev, smiling at Kitty and apparently little interested in the subject of their conversation. "But you've remained faithful to your passion for defending the most paradoxical theses."

"Katya, it isn't good for you to be standing," said her husband, moving a chair toward her with a meaning look.

"Oh well," said Koznyshev, seeing the children, who came running out, "I've no time for it now."

In front of everyone, sideways and at a gallop, came Tanya in her tightly pulled-up stockings. She ran straight toward Koznyshev, flourishing a basket and his hat.

Running up boldly to Koznyshev, with her eyes, which were so like her father's beautiful eyes, shining, she handed him his hat, pretending that she would like to put it on him and softening the undue familiarity of her action by a shy and gentle smile.

"Varenka's waiting," she said, carefully putting the hat on his head, having seen from his smile that she might do it.

Varenka was standing in the doorway. She had changed into a yellow print dress and had tied a white kerchief round her head.

"I'm coming, I'm coming, Mademoiselle Varenka," said Koznyshev, drinking up his coffee and putting his handkerchief and cigar case into their respective pockets.

"What a charming girl my Varenka is, don't you think so?" said Kitty to her husband as soon as Koznyshev got up from his chair. She said it so that Koznyshev could hear, which apparently was what she meant him to do. "And how beautiful, how nobly beautiful! Varenka," cried Kitty, "will you be in the wood by the mill? We'll drive out to you there."

"You forget your condition, Kitty!" said the old princess, hurrying in through the door. "You mustn't shout like that."

Hearing Kitty's voice and her mother's reprimand, Varenka ran up to Kitty with a light step. The rapidity of her movements, the color covering her excited face, everything showed that something unusual was going on inside her. Kitty knew what it was and watched her attentively. She had called Varenka only because she wanted to give her a silent blessing on the important event which, Kitty thought, was bound to take place in the woods that afternoon.

"Varenka," Kitty whispered, kissing her, "I should be very happy if a certain thing were to happen."

"And are you coming with us?" Varenka asked Levin, looking embarrassed and pretending not to have heard what Kitty had said.

"I will, but only as far as the threshing floor. I shall stay there."

"What do you want to do that for?" asked Kitty.

"I must have a look at the new wagons and check up how much they hold," said Levin. "And where will you be?"

"On the terrace."

CHAPTER 2

The women of the house were all gathered on the terrace. They always liked to sit there after dinner, but now there was a special reason for it. Besides the sewing of baby vests and the knitting of swaddling bands, on which they were all engaged now, jam was being made there that afternoon without the addition of water, which was quite a new way of jam making for Agafya. Kitty was introducing this new method, which had always been used in her mother's house. According to Agafya, to whom this work had formerly been entrusted, nothing that was done in the Levin household could be wrong, and she therefore put water with the garden and wild strawberries, insisting that it was quite impossible to make jam otherwise; but her crime had been detected, and now the raspberry jam was being made in the presence of all, to convince Agafya that even without water the jam could turn out well.

Agafya, with a face flushed from the fire and an aggrieved air, her hair ruffled and her thin arms bared to the elbow, was moving the preserving pan over the brazier with a circular motion, looking gloomily at the raspberries and praying that the jam should set before the fruit was ready. The old princess, feeling that Agafya's wrath ought to be directed against her as the chief adviser in the matter of raspberry jam making, tried to look as though she were busy with other things and was not interested in the raspberry jam, but while talking of other matters, she kept watching the brazier out of the corner of her eye.

"I always buy cheap material for dresses for my maids' presents myself," said the old princess, continuing the conversation. "Isn't it time to take the scum off, my dear?" she added, addressing Agafya. "There's no need at all for you to do it, it's much too hot," she said, stopping Kitty.

"I'll do it," said Dolly and, getting up, she began carefully passing the spoon over the foaming sugar, removing what had stuck to it from time to time by tapping the spoon on a plate already covered with yellowish-pink scum and blood-red streaks of syrup. "How they will lick it up with their tea," she thought about her children, recalling how she herself as a child had wondered why grownups did not eat the best part of the jam, the scum.

"Stiva says it's much better to give them money," Dolly meantime continued the interesting topic of the best kind of presents to give to servants, "but—"

"How can one give them money?" the old princess and Kitty cried with one voice. "They appreciate presents."

"Well, last year, for instance, I bought our Matryona Semyovna not poplin exactly, but something like it," said the old princess.

"I remember she was wearing it on your name day."

"A most charming pattern, so simple and refined. I should have made myself a dress of it if she hadn't had it. It's something like Varenka's. Cheap and charming."

"Well, I think it's ready now," said Dolly, letting the syrup drip from the spoon.

"When it begins to set, it's ready. Let it boil a little longer, Agafya."

"Drat the flies!" cried Agafya angrily. "It'll be just the same," she added.

"Oh, he's so sweet! Don't frighten him!" exclaimed Kitty unexpectedly, looking at a sparrow that had alighted on the railing and, turning a raspberry stalk over, began pecking at it.

"Yes, but keep away from the brazier," said her mother.

"*A propos de Varenka,*" said Kitty in French, which they had been talking all the time so that Agafya should not understand them, "you know, Mother, I rather think it will be settled today. You know what I mean. Oh, it would be so wonderful!"

"What an excellent matchmaker you are, though,"

said Dolly. "How carefully and cleverly she throws them together!"

"Please, Mother, tell us what you think of it."

"What am I to think? He" (*he* meant Koznyshev) "could have made the best match in Russia at any time. Now, of course, he isn't so young, but all the same I know many a girl who'd be glad to marry him. She's a very good girl, but he might—"

"But, please, try to understand, Mother, why there could be nothing better for him and for her. To begin with, she's charming!" said Kitty, bending one finger.

"He likes her very much, that's true enough," confirmed Dolly.

"Then, he occupies such a position in the world that he can afford to overlook his wife's fortune and social position. All he wants is a good, sweet girl, a quiet one. . . ."

"Yes, he'll certainly have a quiet life with her," confirmed Dolly.

"Thirdly, she ought to love him. Well, he's got that too. You see, it would be so wonderful! I'm just waiting for them to come out of the wood and—everything settled! I shall see it at once by their eyes. Oh, I'd be so glad! What do you think, Dolly?"

"Don't get so excited," said her mother. "You mustn't get excited—it's bad for you."

"I'm not excited, Mother. I think he'll propose to her today."

"Oh, it's so strange, I mean, the way a man proposes and the time he chooses for it. There seems to be a sort of barrier and then all of a sudden it collapses," said Dolly, smiling dreamily as she recalled her past with Oblonsky.

"Mother, how did Daddy propose to you?" asked Kitty suddenly.

"There was nothing unusual about it—it was all very simple," replied the old princess, but her face lit up at the memory.

"Oh, but how? You were already in love with him, weren't you, before you were allowed to speak?"

Kitty felt a particular pleasure in being able to speak to her mother as an equal about those very important questions in a woman's life.

"Of course, I loved him. He used to visit us in the country."

"But how was it settled, Mother?"

"I suppose you think you've discovered something new, don't you? It's always been the same: it was settled by the eyes, by smiles . . ."

"How well you put it, Mother! Yes, by the eyes and— by smiles," Dolly confirmed.

"But what did he say?"

"What did Kostya say to you?"

"He wrote it down with a piece of chalk. That was wonderful. . . . How long ago it seems!" she said.

And the three women thought about one and the same thing. Kitty was the first to break the silence. She recalled the whole of the winter before her marriage and her infatuation with Vronsky.

"There's one thing, though. . . . I mean Varenka's old love affair," she said, remembering by natural association of ideas. "I meant to say something to Sergey about it, prepare him. They are all, I mean, all men are terribly jealous of our pasts," she added.

"Not all," said Dolly. "You're judging by your own husband. He's still upset by what happened between you and Vronsky. Isn't he? It's true, isn't it?"

"Yes, it's true," replied Kitty, with a pensive smile in her eyes.

"Still," the princess-mother interposed in defense of her maternal care of her daughter, "I don't quite see why your past should trouble him. That Vronsky paid his addresses to you? That happens to every girl."

"Well, actually we're not talking about that," said Kitty, blushing.

"No, I'm sorry," her mother continued, "but it was you who wouldn't let me have a talk with Vronsky. Remember?"

"Oh, Mother!" cried Kitty, with a pained expression on her face.

"There's no holding you back nowadays. But your relations with him could not possibly have gone farther than what was proper. I should have spoken to him myself. However, you must not get excited, darling. Please, remember that and calm yourself."

"I'm quite calm, thank you, Mother."

"How happily it turned out for Kitty that Anna arrived just then," said Dolly, "and how unhappily it turned out for her. Yes," she added, struck by the thought, "it's exactly the reverse now. At that time Anna was happy and Kitty thought that she was unhappy. It's exactly the reverse now. I often think of her."

"Found someone to think of! A horrid, disgusting woman, a woman without a heart," said the mother, who was unable to forget that Kitty had not married Vronsky but Levin.

"What's the use of talking about it?" said Kitty with vexation. "I don't think about it, and I don't want to. . . . And I don't want to think about it," she repeated, listening to the sound of her husband's familiar steps as he was coming up onto the terrace.

"What is it you don't want to think about?" asked Levin as he came up.

But no one answered him, and he did not repeat the question.

"I'm sorry to have barged into your female kingdom," he said, looking disgruntledly upon them and realizing that they were talking about something they would not have mentioned in his presence.

For a moment he felt that he shared Agafya's feeling, her discontent at having to make jam without water and, generally, with the alien Shcherbatsky element. However, he smiled and went up to Kitty.

"Well, how do you feel?" he asked, looking at her with the expression everyone looked at her with now.

"Oh, I'm quite all right," said Kitty with a smile. "And what did you find out about those wagons of yours?"

"They hold more than three cartloads. Well, shall we go for the children? I've ordered the horses to be harnessed."

"You're not going to take Kitty in the trap, are you?" said her mother reproachfully.

"Only at a walking pace, Princess."

Levin never called the princess "Mother," as sons-in-law do, and the princess did not like it. But though Levin liked and respected the old princess very much, he felt that he could not call her that without profaning his feeling for his dead mother.

"Won't you come with us, Mother?" said Kitty.

"I'll be no party to such folly!"

"Well, I'll walk then. It's good for me."

Kitty rose, went up to her husband, and took his arm.

"It may be good for you, but everything in moderation," said the old princess.

"Well, Agafya, is the jam ready?" said Levin, smiling at Agafya and wishing to cheer her up. "Has it turned out well the new way?"

"I suppose so. According to our way, it's overcooked."

"It's better like that, Agafya," said Kitty, immediately realizing her husband's intention and addressing the old woman in the same spirit. "It won't ferment. Our ice in the cellar has melted and there's nowhere we could keep it cool. On the other hand, your pickling is so good that Mother says she hasn't tasted anything like it," she added, smiling and putting Agafya's kerchief straight.

Agafya gave Kitty a peevish look.

"You needn't comfort me, ma'am. Every time I look at you with him, I feel happy," she said, and this disrespectful *him* touched Kitty.

"Come with us to gather mushrooms, you'll show us the best places!"

Agafya smiled and shook her head, as if wishing to say: "I'd be glad to be angry with you, but I just can't."

"Please follow my advice," said the old princess. "Put a piece of paper soaked in rum on top of the jam and then there won't be any mildew even without ice."

CHAPTER 3

Kitty was particularly glad of the opportunity of being alone with her husband, for she had noticed a shadow of chagrin pass over his face, which reflected everything so vividly, when he came up on the terrace and asked what they were talking about and got no reply.

When they had walked on ahead of the others and had passed out of sight of the house on to the hard, dusty road, strewn with rye ears and grain, she leaned more heavily on his arm and pressed it closer to her. He had already forgotten the momentary disagreeable impression and alone with her, now that the thought of her pregnancy never left him, he experienced a joyful

646

feeling, still new to him, a feeling entirely free from sensuality, a feeling of pleasure at being near the woman he loved. They had nothing to say to each other, but he wanted to hear the sound of her voice, which like her eyes had changed since her pregnancy. In her voice as well as in her eyes there was a softness and a seriousness that can be found in people who are constantly concentrated upon one favorite task.

"You're not tired? Lean more on me," he said.

"No. I'm so glad of a chance to be alone with you. I must say, however much I like to be with them all, I miss our winter evenings together."

"That was nice, but this is nicer. Both are nicer," he said, pressing her arm.

"Do you know what we were talking about when you came in?"

"The jam?"

"Yes, about the jam too. But afterward about how men propose."

"Oh!" said Levin, listening more to the sound of her voice than to the words she was uttering, thinking all the time of the road, which now passed through the woods, and going around the places where she might stumble.

"And about Sergey and Varenka. Have you noticed? Oh, I'd like it to happen so much," she went on. "What do you think about it?" and she peered into his face.

"I don't know what to think," replied Levin with a smile. "I could never make Sergey out so far as this is concerned. I told you about—"

"Yes, that he was in love with a girl who died."

"It happened when I was still a child. I only know it from what I've been told. I can remember what he was like then. He was wonderfully charming. But I've observed him since with women: he's polite, some of them he likes, but you can't help feeling that they are just people to him, not women."

"Yes, but now with Varenka. . . . I think there's something there. . . ."

"Perhaps there is. But one has to know him. He's a peculiar, an extraordinary man. He leads only a spiritual existence. He's too pure and high-minded a man."

"But that won't degrade him, will it?"

"No, of course not. But, you see, he's so used to living

647

a spiritual life that he can't come to terms with reality, and Varenka is, after all, reality."

Levin had grown accustomed by now to expressing his thoughts boldly without going to the trouble of putting them into precise language; he knew that at such loving moments as the present his wife would understand what he meant to say even from a hint, and she did understand him.

"Yes, but there isn't so much of this reality in her as there is in me. I can see that he would never have fallen in love with me. She is all spirit."

"Oh no, he is very fond of you, and it's always such a pleasure to me that my people are fond of you."

"Yes, he's kind to me, but . . ."

"But it's not the same as with poor Nikolai—you did love each other," Levin finished her sentence for her. "Why not speak of him?" he added. "I sometimes reproach myself: it will end by our forgetting him. Oh, what a terrible and what a charming man he was. . . . Yes, well, what were we talking about?" said Levin after a pause.

"You don't think he can fall in love?" said Kitty, putting his thoughts into her own words.

"It isn't that he can't fall in love," said Levin with a smile, "but that he does not possess the kind of weakness that is necessary. . . . I always envied him that, and I do even now when I am so happy."

"You envy him for not being able to fall in love?"

"I envy him for being better than I am," said Levin with a smile. "He does not live for himself. His whole life is subordinated to duty. And that is perhaps why he is so calm and contented."

"And you?" asked Kitty with a mocking, affectionate smile.

She would never have been able to put into words the train of thought that made her smile; but the conclusion she drew was that her husband, who so admired his brother and thought so little of himself compared with him, was not sincere. Kitty knew that that insincerity of his arose from his love for his brother, from his sense of shame at being so inordinately happy himself, and especially from his ever-present desire to perfect himself—she loved this in him and that was why she smiled.

648

"And you?" she asked with the same smile. "What are you so discontented about?"

Her disbelief in his dissatisfaction with himself pleased him and he unconsciously tried to get her to express the reason for her disbelief.

"I'm happy," he said, "but I am dissatisfied with myself."

"But how can you be dissatisfied if you are happy?"

"Well, how can I explain it to you? You see, at heart I desire nothing else except that you shouldn't stumble. Good heavens, you mustn't jump like that!" he interrupted his speech to scold her for making too quick a movement in stepping over a twig in their path. "But when I analyze myself and compare myself with others, especially with my brother, I feel that I'm bad."

"In what way?" Kitty went on with the same smile. "Don't you do anything for others? What about your smallholdings, your farming, your book?"

"No, I'm afraid I feel it more than ever now—and it's your fault, you know," he said, pressing her arm, "that I'm not doing what I should be doing. I'm doing it anyhow, a bit here and a bit there. If I could love all that work as I love you. . . . But recently I've been just doing it as though it were a task set me. . . ."

"Well, what then would you say about Father?" asked Kitty. "Isn't he bad, too, because he has done nothing for the common good?"

"He? Oh, no! But one has to have the simplicity, clarity of mind, and goodness of your father. And I haven't got it. Have I now? I do nothing and it worries me. And it's you who have been the cause of it. Before you were here and before *that*," he said, glancing at her figure, which she understood, "I put all my energies into my work. But now I can't, and I feel ashamed. I do it all just like a task that has been set me. I am just pretending. . . ."

"Then would you now like to change places with Sergey?" said Kitty. "Would you like to work for the common good and love the task set you as he does, and nothing more?"

"Of course not," said Levin. "However, I'm so happy that I don't understand anything. And do you really think that he will propose today?" he added after a pause.

"Yes and no. But I do want him to terribly. Wait a moment," she said and, bending down, she picked a wild camomile at the edge of the path. "Come, count. He will propose, he won't . . ." she said and she handed him the flower.

"He will, he won't," said Levin, pulling off the little white petals one by one.

"No, no!" cried Kitty, seizing his hand and stopping him, having watched his fingers with excitement. "You pulled off two at once."

"We won't count this little one then," said Levin, tearing off a short, half-grown petal. "And here's the trap overtaking us."

"Are you tired, Kitty?" the old princess called out.

"Not a bit."

"If you are, you'd better get in, provided the horses are quiet and go at a walking pace."

But it was not worth while getting in. They were quite near the place, and they went the rest of the way on foot.

CHAPTER 4

Varenka, with her white kerchief over her black hair, surrounded by children and good-humoredly and gaily busy with them, and apparently excited at the possibility of a proposal from a man she liked, looked very attractive. Koznyshev walked beside her and did not stop admiring her. Looking at her, he remembered all the charming things he had heard her say, all the good he knew about her, and he was getting more and more conscious of the fact that what he felt for her was something uncommon, something he had experienced a long, long time ago and only once in his life in his early youth. His feeling of happiness at being near her was getting stronger and stronger and at last reached such a point that, as he placed an enormous birch mushroom with a slender stalk and a curled-up rim into her basket, he looked into her eyes and, observing the flush of joyful and frightened agitation that suffused her face, he became embarrassed himself and, without uttering a word, gave her a smile that said too much.

"If that is so," he said to himself, "then I must think

650

it over and come to a decision and not be carried away like a boy by the impulse of the moment."

"I think I'd better go and gather mushrooms by myself," he said, "otherwise my contributions won't be noticed." And he went away from the edge of the wood where they were walking in the short, silky grass amid the sparsely growing old birch trees, to the middle of the wood, where among the white birch trunks the aspens stood out clearly with their gray trunks and the hazel bushes with their dark foliage. After having gone about forty yards, he walked behind a spindle bush in full flower with pinkish-red catkins, from where he could not be seen, and stopped there. Everything around him was dead still. Only from the tops of the birches under which he was standing came the continuous buzzing of flies, like a swarm of bees, and from time to time he could hear the voices of the children coming from a long distance away. Suddenly, not far from the skirts of the wood, he heard Varenka's contralto voice calling Grisha, and a joyous smile lit up his face. Conscious of the smile, Koznyshev shook his head in disapproval of his condition and taking out a cigar began to light it. For a long time he could not strike a match against the trunk of a birch. The delicate pellicle of the white bark stuck to the phosphorus and the light went out. At last one of the matches did burn, and the fragrant smoke of the cigar, like a broad, clearly defined, swaying sheet, moved forward and upward over the bush and beneath the drooping branches of the birch tree. Watching the puff of smoke, he strolled on slowly, thinking over his position.

"And why not?" he thought. "If it were just a flash in the pan or a sudden infatuation, if I only felt this attraction—this *mutual* attraction (I think I can say that)—but felt that it was contrary to the whole tenor of my life, if I felt that in giving way to this attraction I should be false to my vocation and my duty. . . . But there is no question of that. The only thing I can find against it is that when I lost Marie, I told myself that I would remain faithful to her memory. That is the only thing I can say against my feeling. . . . That is important," Koznyshev said to himself, feeling at the same time that this consideration could not be of any importance to him personally, but only perhaps compromised

651

his romantic role in the eyes of others, "but apart from that, I should find nothing whatever to say against my feeling, however much I searched. If my choice depended on reason alone, I could not have chosen anything better."

However many women and girls he recalled whom he had known, he could not remember a single girl who combined to such a degree all, absolutely all, the qualities which, considering it coolly, he would like to see in his wife. She had all the freshness and charm of youth, but she was no longer a child, and if she loved him, she loved him consciously, as a woman ought to love. That was one thing in her favor. Another thing was that she was not only far from showing any desire to mix in high society, she loathed it and at the same time knew it and had all the manners of a woman of the best society without which a life partner would be unthinkable for him. Thirdly, she was religious, but not unintelligently religious and good like a child, like Kitty, for example; but her life was based on religious principles. Even in small things Koznyshev found that she possessed everything he desired in a wife of his: she was poor and had no family, so that she would not bring with her a crowd of relatives with their influence into her husband's house, as he saw Kitty doing. She would be indebted to her husband for everything, which was something he had always desired for his future married life. And this girl, who combined all these qualities, loved him. He was a modest man, but he could not help seeing it. And he loved her. The only reason against it was his age. But he came of a long-lived stock, he had not a single gray hair, no one thought he was forty, and he remembered Varenka saying that it was only in Russia that men of fifty considered themselves old, and that in France a man of fifty considered himself *dans la force de l'age* and a man of forty *un jeune homme*. But what did his age matter when he felt as young at heart as he had been twenty years ago? Was it not youth to feel as he felt now when, coming out again from the other side to the edge of the wood, he caught sight, in the bright slanting sunbeams, of the graceful figure of Varenka in her yellow dress with a basket on her arm, walking with a light step past the trunk of an old birch tree, and when the impression of Varenka merged so harmoniously with the

652

view that had so struck him with its beauty—the view of the field of yellowing oats flooded with the slanting rays of the sun, and the old forest beyond, flecked with gold and fading away into the bluish distance. His heart contracted with joy. He was overcome with a feeling of tender emotion. He felt that his mind was made up. Varenka, who had just bent down to pick a mushroom, rose with a supple movement and looked around. Throwing away his cigar, Koznyshev went toward her with a determined step.

CHAPTER 5

"When I was very young, Varenka, I formed my ideal of the woman I should love and whom I should be happy to call my wife. I have lived a long time and now for the first time I have met in you what I was looking for. I love you and I offer you my hand."

Koznyshev was saying this to himself when he was within ten steps of Varenka. She was on her knees, trying to defend a mushroom with her hands from Grisha, while she was calling to little Masha.

"Come here, here, little ones! There are lots here!" she cried in her lovely deep voice.

When she saw Koznyshev approaching, she did not move or change her position; but everything told him that she felt his approach and was glad of it.

"Well, have you found anything?" she asked, turning to him her beautiful, gently smiling face from under her white kerchief.

"Not one," said Koznyshev. "And you?"

She did not reply, busy with the children who surrounded her.

"There's another one there, near that branch," she said to little Masha, pointing to a small russula, cut across its firm pinkish crown by a dry blade of grass from under which it was trying to escape. She got up when Masha, breaking the mushroom into two white halves, picked it up. "It reminds me of my own childhood," she added, moving away from the children with Koznyshev.

They walked a few steps in silence. Varenka saw that

653

he wanted to speak; she guessed what it was about and grew faint with joy and fear. They had gone so far that they could not be overheard by anyone, but still he did not speak. Varenka would have done better not to break the silence, for after a silence it would have been easier for them to say what they wanted to say than after talking about mushrooms; but almost against her will, almost by accident, Varenka said:

"So you haven't found anything? But then of course there are always fewer in the middle of the wood."

Koznyshev heaved a sigh and made no answer. He was vexed that she should have spoken about the mushrooms. He wanted to bring her back to her first remark about her childhood; but as though against his own will, after a longish pause, he made a remark in reply to her last words.

"I've only heard that white mushrooms grow mostly at the edge of the woods, though I can't tell which are the white ones."

A few more minutes passed; they had gone still farther from the children and were quite alone. Varenka's heart was thumping so hard that she could hear it and she felt herself turning red, then pale, then red again.

To be the wife of a man like Koznyshev, after her position with Madame Stahl, seemed to her the height of happiness. Besides, she was almost sure she was in love with him. And now in another moment it had to be decided. She was terrified. Terrified of what he might and what he might not say.

Now or never was the moment when he had to make their position clear; Koznyshev, too, felt this. Everything about Varenka—her look, her blush, her lowered eyes—showed that she was in a state of painful suspense. Koznyshev saw it and was sorry for her. He even felt that to say nothing now would be to offend her. He quickly went over in his mind all the arguments in favor of his decision. He repeated to himself the words in which he had intended to propose to her. But instead of those words, by some sort of unaccountable idea that came into his mind, he suddenly asked:

"What is the difference between a white and a birch mushroom?"

Varenka's lips trembled with agitation when she replied:

"There is hardly any difference in the cap. It's the stalks that are different."

And the moment those words were uttered, both he and she understood that it was all over, that what should have been said would never be said, and their agitation, having reached its climax, began to subside.

"The stalk of a birch mushroom," said Koznyshev, who had completely regained his composure, "reminds me of the stubble on the chin of a dark man who has not shaved for two days."

"Yes, that's true," Varenka replied with a smile, and involuntarily the direction of their walk changed. They began walking toward the children. Varenka felt hurt and ashamed, but at the same time she experienced a sense of relief.

When he got home and went over all his reasons again, Koznyshev came to the conclusion that his first decision had been wrong. He could not be unfaithful to the memory of Marie.

"Quiet, children, quiet!" Levin shouted quite angrily as he stepped in front of his wife to protect her when the crowd of children came rushing at them with shrieks of delight.

After the children came Koznyshev and Varenka out of the wood. Kitty had no need to question Varenka: she saw from the calm and somewhat shamefaced expressions of both that her plans had not materialized.

"Well?" inquired her husband on their way back home.

"Not biting," said Kitty. Her smile and manner of speaking were like her father's, which Levin often observed in her with pleasure.

"Not biting? What do you mean?"

"This is what I mean," she said, taking her husband's hand, raising it to her mouth, and just touching it with closed lips. "The way one kisses a bishop's hand."

"Who isn't biting?" he said, laughing.

"Neither. This is how it should have been. . . ."

"Some peasants are coming. . . ."

"They didn't see. . . ."

CHAPTER 6

During the children's tea the grownups sat on the balcony and talked as if nothing had happened, though all of them, and particularly Koznyshev and Varenka, knew perfectly well that something had happened, something very important, though of a negative nature. They both felt like children who have failed their examinations and have to stay behind in the same class or who have been expelled from school for good. All the others, feeling that something had happened, talked animatedly about extraneous subjects. Levin and Kitty felt particularly happy and in love with one another that evening. And the fact that they were happy in their love appeared like an unpleasant reflection on those who had desired but failed to achieve the same sort of happiness—and they could not help feeling a little ashamed.

"Mark my words, Alexander will not come," said the old princess.

They were expecting Oblonsky by the evening train, and the old prince, too, had written to say that he might come.

"And I know why," the princess went on. "He says a young couple should be left alone at first."

"But Father has left us alone. We haven't seen him for ages," said Kitty. "And we're not a young couple, anyway. We're a very old couple now."

"Only if he doesn't come, I shall have to say good-by to you, my dears," said the old princess with a mournful sigh.

"What an idea, Mother!" both her daughters objected violently.

"Just think what he must be feeling! Why, now . . ."

And suddenly the old princess' voice trembled unexpectedly. The daughters were silent and looked at one another. "Mother will always find something to be sad about," their look seemed to say. They did not know that however much the old princess enjoyed staying at her daughter's house and however much she felt that she was needed there, she was terribly sad for her husband and for herself ever since they had married their last favorite daughter and their home was left empty.

"What is it, Agafya?" asked Kitty suddenly, turning to Agafya, who had stopped in front of her with a mysterious, significant look on her face.

"About supper."

"Oh, well, that's all right," said Dolly. "You go and see about supper and Grisha and I will go and do his lesson. He hasn't done anything today."

"It's my turn to do his lesson with him," said Levin, jumping up. "I'll go, Dolly."

Grisha, who was already going to school, had to do some homework during the summer holidays. Dolly, who had begun learning Latin with him when they were still in Moscow, had made it a rule on coming to the Levins' to go over with him, even if only once a day, the most difficult lessons—arithmetic and Latin. Levin volunteered to take her place, but the mother, having once heard Levin give the lesson and noticing that he did it differently from the master who had coached the boy in Moscow, though embarrassed and trying not to offend Levin, told him resolutely that they must keep to the textbook as the teacher had done and that she had better give the lessons herself. Levin felt vexed both at Oblonsky for being so unmindful of his son's education that he let his mother, who knew nothing about it, supervise it, and at the teachers for teaching so badly; but he promised his sister-in-law to conduct the lessons exactly as she wished. And he went on teaching Grisha not according to his own method, but according to the book, and going about it in a half-hearted way, he often forgot the hour of the lesson. So it had happened that day.

"No, Dolly, I'll go," he said. "You stay here. We shall do it all properly by the book. Only when Stiva comes and we go shooting, I shall have to miss the lessons."

And Levin went to Grisha.

Varenka told Kitty the same thing, for even in the happy and well-run Levin establishment Varenka found ways to be useful.

"I'll see to the supper, and you stay here," she said and got up to go to Agafya.

"Thank you," said Kitty. "I suppose they could not get any chickens. We'll have to have ours then. . . ."

657

"Agafya and I will see what's to be done," said Varenka, and she went out with Agafya.

"What a nice girl," said the old princess.

"Not *nice*, Mother. She's so charming you won't find anyone like her anywhere."

"So you're expecting Oblonsky today?" said Koznyshev, who was apparently unwilling to pursue the conversation about Varenka. "It would be difficult to find brothers-in-law more unlike each other," he went on with a subtle smile. "One terribly active, living always in society, like a fish in water; the other, our Kostya, lively, quick, sensitive, but as soon as he finds himself in society, he either shuts up or flounders about like a fish on dry land."

"Yes," said the old princess, "he is rather thoughtless. I wanted to ask you," she went on, turning to Koznyshev, "to tell him that she" (she pointed to Kitty) "can't possibly stay here, but must come to Moscow. He says he's going to get a doctor to come down. . . ."

"Mother," Kitty said, annoyed that her mother should be appealing to Koznyshev on such a matter, "he'll do everything, he's agreed to everything."

In the middle of their conversation they heard the snorting of horses and the scraping of wheels on the gravel of the drive.

Before Dolly had had time to get up and go and meet her husband, Levin had jumped out of the window of the room where he was teaching Grisha and lifted the boy out too.

"It's Stiva," Levin shouted from under the balcony. "We've finished, Dolly, don't worry!" he added and began running like a boy to meet the carriage.

"*Is, ea, id, eius, eius, eius,*" cried Grisha, skipping along the drive.

"And there's someone else, probably Father," cried Levin, stopping at the end of the avenue. "Kitty, don't come down those steep steps—go around!"

But Levin was wrong in thinking that the second man in the carriage was the old prince. When he got nearer he saw sitting beside Oblonsky not the prince, but a stoutish man in a Scotch cap with long ribbons behind. It was Vasenka Veslovsky, a second cousin of the Shcherbatskys, one of the flashy men-about-town of

Moscow and Petersburg, "an excellent fellow and a keen sportsman," as Oblonsky introduced him.

Not in the least embarrassed by the disappointment he caused by appearing instead of the old prince, Veslovsky greeted Levin gaily, reminded him that they had met before, and picking up Grisha, lifted him into the carriage over the pointer Oblonsky had brought with him.

Levin did not get into the carriage, but followed it on foot. He was a little annoyed that the old prince, whom he liked more and more the better he knew him, had not come, while Veslovsky, a complete stranger whom he did not care for a bit, had come. Veslovsky appeared even more alien and out of place to him when they got to the steps—at which the whole animated crowd of grownups and children had gathered—and he saw Vasenka Veslovsky kissing Kitty's hand with a particularly affectionate and gallant air.

"Your wife and I are cousins and very old friends," said Veslovsky, again pressing Levin's hand very warmly.

"Well, is there any game?" Oblonsky, who seemed to be in a hurry to say a word of greeting to everybody, asked Levin. "This young gentleman and I have the most ruthless intentions. Why, of course, Mother, they haven't been in Moscow since. Well, Tanya, I've got something for you. Get it, please, it's in the carriage, at the back," he kept talking in all directions. "How much refreshed you're looking, Dolly, dear," he said to his wife, kissing her hand again and holding it in his own and patting it with his other hand.

Levin, who a minute before had been in the most cheerful frame of mind, now looked gloomily at everyone, feeling displeased with everything.

"Whom did he kiss yesterday with those lips?" he thought, as he looked at Oblonsky's affectionate greeting of his wife. He looked at Dolly and did not like her, either.

"Why, she doesn't believe in his love! So why is she so pleased? Disgusting!" thought Levin.

He looked at the old princess, who had been so dear to him a minute ago, and he did not like the manner with which she welcomed Veslovsky with his ribbons, just as though it were in her own house.

Even Koznyshev, who had also come out on the steps,

displeased him by the simulated friendliness with which he greeted Oblonsky, whom, Levin knew very well, he neither liked nor respected.

And he even found Varenka disgusting as, with her air of a *sainte nitouche,* she exchanged greetings with the young fellow, while all she now thought about was getting married.

But most of all he disliked Kitty for having allowed herself to succumb to the gay tone of that young bounder, who seemed to regard his arrival in the country as an event of general rejoicing, and he was particularly displeased with the special smile with which she returned his smiles.

Talking noisily, they all went into the house; but as soon as they were all seated Levin turned and left the room.

Kitty saw that there was something wrong with her husband. She tried to have a talk with him alone, but he hurried away from her, saying that he must go to the office. Not for a long time had the farm work seemed so important to him as at that moment. "For them every day is a holiday," he thought, "but this work is no holiday matter. It can't wait, and you can't go on living without it."

Chapter 7

Levin returned home only when they sent to call him to supper. On the stairs stood Kitty and Agafya, conferring what wines to serve.

"What are you making such a fuss for? Serve the same as usual."

"No, Stiva doesn't drink. . . . Kostya, wait—what's the matter?" cried Kitty, hurrying after him, but he did not wait for her and strode off pitilessly into the dining room, where he at once joined in the animated general conversation carried on by Veslovsky and Oblonsky.

"Well, what about it? Are we going shooting tomorrow?" said Oblonsky.

"Yes, please, let's go," said Veslovsky, sitting down sideways on another chair and tucking a fat leg under him.

"Yes, let's go by all means. And have you had any shooting this year?" Levin asked Veslovsky, gazing intently at his leg, but with that simulated air of agreeableness which Kitty knew so well and which did not become him at all. "I don't know if we shall find any double snipe, but there are plenty of snipe. Only we shall have to go early. You won't be tired, will you? You're not tired, Stiva, are you?"

"Me tired? I've never been tired. Don't let's go to bed all night. Let's go for a walk."

"An excellent idea!" Veslovsky put in. "Don't let's go to bed!"

"Oh, we all know you can do without sleep and don't let anyone else sleep, either," said Dolly to her husband with that barely perceptible irony in her voice with which she now almost always addressed him. "But, if you ask me, it's high time to go to bed now. . . . I'm going. I don't want any supper."

"No, please, darling, stay a little longer," said Oblonsky, going around to her side at the long dining table. "I've so many things to tell you."

"Nothing much, I shouldn't wonder."

"Do you know, Veslovsky has been to see Anna. And he's going to see her again. It's only about fifty miles from here. I, too, am seriously thinking of going over. Veslovsky, come here a minute!"

Veslovsky came over to the ladies and sat down beside Kitty.

"Oh, do tell us!" Dolly exclaimed, turning to him. "You've been to see her? How is she?"

Levin remained sitting at the other end of the table, and while he kept talking to the old princess and Varenka, he could see that an animated and mysterious conversation was going on between Oblonsky, Dolly, Kitty, and Veslovsky. And it was not only the mysterious conversation that interested him. He saw on his wife's face an expression of more than interest as she gazed steadily at the handsome face of Veslovsky, who was telling something with great animation.

"It's very nice at their place," Veslovsky was saying, speaking of Vronsky and Anna. "I do not, of course, take it upon myself to judge, but at their place you feel yourself to be in a family."

"What do they mean to do?"

"I believe they mean to go to Moscow for the winter."

"It would be nice for us to meet there. When are you going?" Oblonsky asked Veslovsky.

"I'm spending July with them."

"Will you go?" Oblonsky asked his wife.

"I've been wanting to for a long time, and I'll certainly go," said Dolly. "I feel sorry for her and I know her. She is a splendid person. I shall go alone after you've gone and I shan't be in anyone's way. As a matter of fact, it will be much better without you."

"That's excellent," said Oblonsky. "And what about you, Kitty?"

"Me? Why should I go?" Kitty said, flushing and glancing around at her husband.

"Why, do you know Anna?" asked Veslovsky. "She's a very attractive woman."

"Yes," she answered Veslovsky, with a still deeper flush, and she got up and went over to her husband.

"Will you be going shooting tomorrow?" she said.

Levin's jealousy during those few minutes, especially after he had seen the flush that covered Kitty's cheeks when she was talking to Veslovsky, had gone far. Now, listening to her, he interpreted her words in his own way. Strange as the whole thing appeared to him when he recalled it later, at that moment it seemed quite clear to him that by asking whether he was going shooting she was only interested to find out whether he would give that pleasure to Vasenka Veslovsky, with whom, as he imagined, she was already in love.

"Yes, I will," he replied in an unnatural voice, which he hated himself.

"Don't you think you'd better stay at home tomorrow, for Dolly hasn't seen anything of her husband, and go the day after tomorrow?" said Kitty.

Levin now interpreted the meaning of her words in this way: "Don't part me from *him*. You can go if you like, but let me enjoy the society of this charming young man."

"Oh, well, if you wish, we can stay at home tomorrow," Levin replied with particular amiability.

Meanwhile Veslovsky, without in the least suspecting the suffering his presence was causing, got up from the table and followed Kitty, looking at her with an affectionate smile.

Levin saw that look. He turned pale and for a moment he could hardly breathe. "How dare he look like that at my wife?" he thought, seething with rage.

"Tomorrow then? Do let's go!" said Veslovsky, sitting down again, and again, as was his habit, tucking his leg under him.

Levin's jealousy increased still more. He already saw himself as the deceived husband, whom his wife and her lover needed only in order to provide them with the comforts and pleasures of life. . . . But in spite of this he inquired in a very polite and hospitable way of Vasenka about his shooting, his gun, his boots, and agreed to go shooting next day.

Happily for Levin, the old princess put an end to his suffering by getting up and advising Kitty to go to bed. But even here Levin had another pang in store for him. When saying good night to his hostess, Veslovsky was about to kiss her hand again, but Kitty, blushing and with naïve rudeness, for which her mother reprimanded her later, said, pushing his hand away:

"I'm sorry, but that's not customary in our house."

In Levin's eyes, Kitty was to blame for having laid herself open to such behavior and even more for having shown so awkwardly that she did not like it.

"Oh, why go to bed?" said Oblonsky, who after the several glasses of wine he had drunk at supper was in his most charming and romantic mood. "Look, Kitty," he said, pointing to the moon rising from behind the lime trees. "How lovely! Veslovsky, that's the time for a serenade! You know, he has a fine voice. We were singing together on the way here. He's brought some beautiful love songs with him, two new ones. He ought to sing them with Varenka."

When they had all gone to their rooms, Oblonsky and Veslovsky kept walking up and down the avenue for a long time and their voices could be heard rehearsing one of the new songs.

Listening to them, Levin sat scowling in an armchair in his wife's bedroom, obstinately refusing to answer her questions as to what was the matter with him; but when at last she asked him herself with a timid smile: "Is there something you didn't like about Veslovsky?" he could not contain himself any longer and told her everything;

what he was telling her hurt his pride, and that exasperated him still more.

He stood before Kitty, his eyes flashing terribly under his knit brows, pressing his strong hands against his breast, as though straining every nerve to keep himself under control.

The expression of his face would have been harsh and even cruel were it not for a look of suffering which touched her. His jaws quivered and his voice faltered.

"Please, understand, I'm not jealous—that's a horrible word. I can't be jealous and believe that. . . . I'm sorry I can't say what I feel, but it is dreadful. . . . I'm not jealous, but I'm offended and humiliated that anyone should dare to think—should dare to look at you with such eyes. . . ."

"What eyes?" asked Kitty, trying conscientiously to recall every word and gesture of that evening and every shade of meaning they could possibly have had.

In her heart of hearts she thought that there had been something just at the moment when Veslovsky followed her to the other end of the table, but she dared not acknowledge it to herself, much less tell him about it and so increase his suffering.

"And what could there be so attractive about me, as I am now?"

"Oh!" he cried, clutching his head. "You shouldn't have said that. . . . So that if you had been attractive . . ."

"No, no, Kostya, wait—listen!" she said, looking at him with an expression of compassionate pain. "What can you be thinking of? Why, men just don't exist for me. They don't, I tell you. Well, would you like me not to see anyone at all?"

At the first moment she had been hurt by his jealousy; she resented the fact that she should be forbidden any kind of diversion, even the most innocent; but now she would have gladly sacrificed not merely trifles like that, but anything for his peace of mind, to save him from the agony he was suffering.

"Please, understand the horror and the comic absurdity of my situation," he went on in a desperate whisper. "I mean that he is in my house, that after all he has done nothing improper, except by that free and easy manner of his and that tucking in of his leg. He thinks it's the best possible form and and I have to be polite to him."

"But, darling, you're exaggerating," said Kitty, but in her heart she was glad of the force of love for her which found expression in his jealousy.

"What is so awful about it is that you're just as you always are, and now, when you are my holy of holies and we are so happy, so particularly happy, this rotter . . . I'm sorry, he isn't really a rotter. I shouldn't call him names. He's no concern of mine. But our happiness, yours and mine, why . . ."

"You know I think I understand now how it all started," began Kitty.

"How? How?"

"I saw the way you looked at us when we were talking at supper."

"Yes, yes," Levin said in dismay.

She told him what they had been talking about. And as she told him that, she was breathless with agitation. Levin was silent for some minutes, then, looking intently at her pale, frightened face, he suddenly clutched at his head.

"Darling, I've worn you out! My darling, forgive me! It was madness. I'm sorry, it's all my fault. And, really, how could I torture myself over such nonsense?"

"Oh, no, I am sorry for you!"

"For me? Me? Why, I'm a madman! And why did I torture you? It's terrible to think that any stranger can destroy our happiness."

"Why, yes, that's what hurts so much."

"Well, in that case I'll make him stay the whole summer and vie with him in expressions of politeness," said Levin, kissing her hands. "You'll see. . . . Tomorrow . . . though, of course, we're going shooting tomorrow, aren't we? . . ."

CHAPTER 8

Next day, before the ladies were up, the shooting conveyances—a shooting brake and a cart—stood at the door, waiting for them, and Laska, having realized since early morning that they were going shooting, after a great deal of yelping and jumping about, was sitting in the cart beside the coachman, looking excitedly and disapprovingly at the door, through which the sportsmen had not yet come and fretting at the delay. The first to come out was Vasenka Veslovsky, in new high boots that reached halfway up his thighs, a green shirt girdled with a new cartridge belt smelling of leather, and a Scotch cap with streamers, and with a new English hammerless shotgun without a sling. Laska jumped down to him, greeting him by leaping about, asked him in her own language how soon the others would come out, and receiving no reply, returned to her post of expectation and grew motionless again, her head turned to one side and one ear pricked up. At length the door opened with a bang and Oblonsky's yellow spotted pointer, Krak, flew out of it followed by Oblonsky himself with a gun in his hand and a cigar in his mouth. "Down, down, Krak!" he said affectionately to the dog, who was pawing his stomach and chest and getting entangled in his game bag. Oblonsky was wearing rawhide boots, linen bands wound around his feet, a pair of torn trousers, and a short coat. On his head he wore a wreck of a hat, but his gun of the latest model was a beauty and his game bag and cartridge belt, though much worn, were of the very best quality.

Vasenka Veslovsky had not realized before that a truly smart sportsman's turnout consisted of being dressed in rags but having shooting implements of the best possible quality. He realized it now as he gazed at Oblonsky dressed in his tattered clothes but looking radiant with his elegant, well-nourished, and cheerful figure, a real gentleman if ever there was one. Veslovsky decided that on his next shooting expedition he would most certainly follow Oblonsky's example.

"Well," he said, "and what about our host?"

"He's got a young wife," Oblonsky said, smiling.

"Yes, she's so lovely too!"

"He was already dressed. I expect he must have run back to her."

Oblonsky had guessed right. Levin had run back to his wife to ask her again if she had forgiven him his foolishness of the night before, and also to ask her for goodness' sake to be more careful and not to forget to keep away from the children who might push against her. Then he had to get another assurance from her that she was not angry with him for going away for two days and to beg her to be sure to send him a note next morning by a servant on horseback, just a few words to let him know that she was well.

As always, Kitty found it difficult to part from her husband for two days, but seeing his animated figure, which seemed particularly large and powerful in his shooting boots and white shirt and beaming with the excitement, so incomprehensible to her, of the sportsman setting out on a shoot, she forgot her own chagrin in his gladness and took leave of him cheerfully.

"Sorry, gentlemen," he said, rushing out on the front steps. "Have they put the lunch in? Why the chestnut on the right? Oh, never mind. Laska, stop it, go and sit down!"

"Let them out with the heifers," he said to the herdsman, waiting for him at the front steps for orders about some bullocks. "Sorry, here comes another rascal."

Levin jumped off the shooting brake, in which he had already taken his seat, to have a talk with the carpenter, who was coming up with a footrule in his hand.

"You didn't come to the office yesterday, and now you're detaining me," said Levin. "Well, what is it?"

"Let me make another turning, sir. A mere matter of three more steps. We'll get it just right, sir. It will be much more convenient."

"I wish you'd have listened to me," Levin replied, looking vexed. "I told you to fix the string boards first and then fit the treads. Now it's too late to do anything about it. Do as I tell you and make a new staircase."

What happened was that in the new wing that was being built the carpenter had spoiled the staircase, having made it without calculating the elevation, so that when it was put in position the steps all sloped. Now the carpenter wanted to keep the same staircase, adding another three steps.

"It would be much better, sir."

"But where will it reach to with three extra steps?"

"Good Lord, sir," said the carpenter with a disdainful smile, "it will fit perfectly. You see, sir," he went on with a persuasive gesture, "it starts from the bottom, and it will go up and up till it gets there."

"But the three extra steps will add to the length. . . . Where will it get to?"

"Why, sir, provided it starts from the bottom, that is, it's sure to get there," the carpenter repeated obstinately and persuasively.

"It will get to the ceiling and go up the wall."

"Lord, no, sir, it'll start from the bottom. It will go up and up and get there."

Levin pulled out his ramrod and began sketching the plan of a staircase in the dust.

"There, you see now?"

"As you say, sir," said the carpenter, his eyes suddenly brightening, having evidently at last understood. "Yes, sir, it seems I'll have to make a new one."

"Well, then, do as you're told," Levin shouted as he climbed into the shooting brake. "Drive on! Hold the dogs, Philip!"

Having left behind him all his family and estate worries, Levin was overcome by such a strong sense of the joy of life and anticipation that he did not feel like talking. Besides, he experienced that feeling of mounting excitement which every sportsman experiences as he approaches the scene of action. If anything worried him now it was whether they would find anything in Kolpensky marsh, how Laska would compare with Krak, and what sort of shot he himself would prove that day. He only hoped he would not disgrace himself before the stranger. He hoped Oblonsky would not outshine him.

Oblonsky experienced the same feelings, and he did not feel like talking, either. Veslovsky alone went on chattering gaily without stopping. Listening to him now, Levin felt ashamed as he recalled how unfair he had been to him the night before. Veslovsky really was a nice fellow, simple, good-natured, and very jolly. If Levin had met him before his marriage, he would have made a friend of him. Levin did not quite like his attitude to life as a never-ending holiday and the sort of free and easy air of elegance about him. He seemed to think that his long nails, his Scotch cap, and all the rest showed that he was unquestionably a person of superior tastes; but this could be forgiven for the sake of his good nature and general decency. Levin was attracted by his good upbringing, his excellent French and English, and by the fact that he was a man of his own class.

Veslovsky greatly admired the Don steppe horse attached on the left. He kept expressing his delight with it.

"It must be glorious to gallop across the steppes on a Cossack horse! Don't you think so?" he kept saying.

He seemed to imagine something wild and romantic about a ride on a steppe horse, but there did not appear to be any substance in his fancies; however, his naïveté, especially combined with his handsome looks, his charming smile, and graceful movements, was extremely attractive. Whether it was that Veslovsky's nature was congenial to Levin or that, to expiate his sins of the previous evening, he tried to see nothing but good in him, Levin found his company agreeable.

After they had gone about two miles, Veslovsky suddenly discovered that he missed his cigars and pocketbook. He did not know whether he had lost them or left them behind on the table. As there were 370 rubles in his pocketbook, it was impossible to ignore the matter.

"Do you know what, Levin? Let me gallop home on that left trace horse. That would be glorious, eh?" he said, already getting ready to mount.

"No, why bother?" replied Levin, who calculated that Vasenka could hardly weigh less than two hundred pounds. "I'll send the coachman."

The coachman rode back on the trace horse, and Levin drove the remaining pair himself.

CHAPTER 9

"Well, what's our itinerary? Tell us all about it," said Oblonsky.

"The plan is as follows: now we're going as far as Gvozdevo. On this side of Gvozdevo there is a double-snipe marsh, and behind Gvozdevo there are marvelous snipe marshes and you can bag double snipe there too. It's hot now, but we shall get there toward evening (it's about fifteen miles), and we shall have some shooting there in the evening. We shall then spend the night there and tomorrow we shall tackle the big marshes."

"And is there nothing on the way?"

"Yes, there is, but it would delay us, and, besides, it's

hot. There are two lovely spots, but I'm not sure we shall find anything there."

Levin would have liked to stop at those two spots himself, but they were both near home and he could always do some shooting there, and they were rather small, not big enough for three persons to shoot in. And that was why he was prevaricating and saying that they would hardly find any game there. When they came to one of the small marshes, Levin wanted to drive past, but Oblonsky's experienced sportsman's eye already descried the marsh grass from the road.

"Shall we try this?" he said, pointing to the marsh.

"Please, Levin, let's! It looks splendid!" Veslovsky begged, and Levin could not but agree.

They had scarcely stopped before the dogs, racing one another, made a beeline for the marsh.

"Krak! Laska!"

The dogs returned.

"There's no room for the three of us. I'll wait here," said Levin, hoping that they would find nothing but the peewits which the dogs had flushed and which were wheeling over the marsh with their plaintive cries.

"No, let's all go, Levin. Please, come along!" pleaded Veslovsky.

"There's no room, I tell you. Back, Laska! Laska! You won't need another dog, will you?"

Levin stayed behind at the shooting brake, watching the two sportsmen enviously. They went all over the little marsh, but except for a moorhen and peewits, one of which Veslovsky shot, there was no game there.

"Well, you see, I was not grudging you the marsh," said Levin. "It was just a waste of time."

"It was jolly all the same. Did you see?" said Veslovsky, clambering awkwardly into the brake with his gun in one hand and the peewit in the other. "I got this one cleverly, didn't I? Well, how soon shall we get to the real place?"

Suddenly the horses dashed forward. Levin knocked his head against the barrel of someone's gun and a shot rang out. Actually, the shot came first, but to Levin it seemed the other way round. What happened was that Veslovsky, while uncocking the triggers, had pulled one trigger while uncocking the other. The charge went into the ground without hurting anybody. Oblonsky shook his head and laughed reproachfully at Veslovsky. But Levin had not the heart to reprove him. To begin with, any reproach would have seemed to have been provoked by the danger he had just escaped and by the bump which had come up on his forehead; secondly, Veslovsky was so naïvely heartbroken at first and then laughed so good-naturedly and infectiously at their general alarm that it was impossible not to laugh oneself.

When they came up to the second marsh, which was fairly large and would take some time to go over, Levin again tried to persuade them not to get out. But Veslovsky again prevailed over him. Once more, the marsh being narrow, Levin, like a hospitable host, stayed behind with the vehicles.

As soon as he got to the marsh, Krak made for the hummocks. Veslovsky was the first to run after the dog. Before Oblonsky had time to approach, a double snipe rose in the air. Veslovsky missed it and it flew over to an unmown meadow. The bird was left to Veslovsky. Krak found it again and pointed, and Veslovsky killed it and went back to the vehicles.

"Now you go and I'll stay with the horses," he said.

Levin was beginning to be filled with the envy sportsmen know so well. He handed the reins to Veslovsky and walked into the marsh.

Laska, who had been whining and complaining for some time of the injustice of being kept back, made straight for a reliable spot covered with hummocks which Levin knew very well and which Krak had not yet come upon.

"Why don't you stop her?" shouted Oblonsky.

"She won't flush them," replied Levin, pleased with his dog and hurrying after her.

The nearer Laska got to the familiar hummocks, the more and more intent did she become in her pursuit. A small marsh bird distracted her only for an instant. She described one circle in front of the hummocks, and had begun describing another when suddenly she stopped dead.

"Come along, Stiva, here!" shouted Levin, feeling his heart beat more rapidly and suddenly as though some bolt had been withdrawn from his strained sense of hearing, all the sounds, having lost the limits imposed on them by distance, came tumbling over his ears with quite unnatural distinctness. He heard Oblonsky's footsteps and took them for the distant tramp of horses, he heard the brittle sound of a broken-off corner of a hummock on which he had stepped and which crumbled, pulling out the grass by the roots, and he took it for the noise of a double snipe on the wing. He also heard behind him a sound of splashing which he could not account for.

Picking his way, he approached the dog.

"Sick it!"

It was not a double snipe but a snipe that the dog had flushed. Levin raised his gun, but as he was taking aim the same sound of splashing grew louder, came nearer and was mingled with Veslovsky's voice shouting something strangely and loudly. Levin saw that he was aiming behind the snipe, but fired nevertheless.

Making sure that he had missed, Levin turned round and saw that the shooting brake and the horses were no longer on the road but in the marsh.

Wishing to watch the shooting, Veslovsky had driven into the marsh and the horses got stuck in the mud.

"Where the devil does he think he's going?" Levin muttered to himself, returning to the carriage that had sunk in the mud. "Why did you leave the road?" he remarked dryly to Veslovsky and, calling the coachman, he began getting the horses out.

Levin was vexed both at having been put off his shot and at his horses having been led into the bog, and above all at having to unharness the horses in order to get them out, for neither Oblonsky nor Veslovsky helped him or the coachman because they had no idea how to harness or unharness horses. Without a word in reply to Veslovsky, who was assuring him that it was quite dry there, Levin worked in silence with the coachman to extricate the horses. But later on, when he finished with the work and saw how painstakingly Veslovsky was pulling at the splashboard so that in the end he wrenched it off, Levin reproached himself for having been too curt to Veslovsky under the influence of his sentiments the day before, and did his best to make amends for his brusqueness by being particularly nice to the young man. When everything was in order again and the vehicles had been brought back on the road, Levin gave orders for lunch to be served.

"Bon appétit—bonne conscience! Ce poulet va tomber

jusqu'au fond de mes bottes," Veslovsky, who had cheered up again, repeated a French saying as he finished his second chicken. "Well, now our calamities are at an end and now everything will go right. Only to expiate my sin I must sit on the box. Don't you think so? Yes, I must! I'm Automedon. You wait and see how I will drive you!" he answered Levin's plea to let the coachman drive, refusing to let go of the reins. "No, I must atone for my sin and I'm very comfortable on the box." And he drove off.

Levin was a little afraid that he would tire out the horses, especially the roan on the left, whom he did not know how to control; but he could not help falling under the spell of Veslovsky's high spirits, and listened to the songs he sang all the way while sitting on the box, or the stories he told and his demonstration of the way one ought to drive four-in-hand in the English fashion. And after lunch they drove in the best of spirits to the Gvozdevo marsh.

CHAPTER 10

Veslovsky had driven so fast that they arrived at the marsh too soon, while it was still too hot.

When they got to the real marsh, the chief object of their journey, Levin involuntarily tried to think how to get rid of Veslovsky and go about without his being in the way. Oblonsky evidently wanted the same thing, and Levin discerned on his face the anxiety every true sportsman felt before the beginning of a shoot, and also a little good-natured cunning that was characteristic of him.

"Well, how shall we go? It's an excellent marsh and I can see some hawks," said Oblonsky, pointing to two large birds hovering over the reeds. "Where there are hawks, there's sure to be game."

"Well, gentlemen," said Levin, pulling up his boots and examining the percussion caps of his gun with a somewhat gloomy expression, "do you see that sedge?" He pointed to a little island of dark green vegetation in an enormous half-mown meadow stretching along the right bank of the river. "The marsh begins here, straight in front of us, do you see, where it is greener? From here it runs to the right, where those horses are grazing. There are hummocks there and double snipe, and all around that sedge right up to the alder grove and down to the mill. There, you see, by that creek. That's the best place. I once shot seventeen snipe there. We'll separate and go in different directions with the two dogs and meet again at the mill."

"Well, who goes to the right and who to the left?" asked Oblonsky. "There's more room on the right, so you two go that way and I'll keep to the left," he added, as though in a casual tone of voice.

"Splendid! We'll get the best bag. Come along, come!" Veslovsky cried.

Levin had to agree, and they separated.

As soon as they entered the marsh the two dogs began searching together and made toward the brown pool. Levin knew what that cautious and indeterminate search of Laska's meant; he also knew the place and expected a whole covey of snipe.

"Veslovsky, walk beside me, beside me!" he said in a faltering voice to his companion, who was splashing in the water behind him and the direction of whose gun after the accidental shot by the Kolpensky marsh willy-nilly interested Levin.

"No, I won't be in your way. Don't worry about me."

But Levin could not help worrying as he remembered Kitty's parting words: "Mind you don't shoot one another!" The dogs drew nearer and nearer, keeping out of each other's way, each following its own scent; the expectation of snipe was so strong that the squelching of his own foot as he drew it out of the yellow mud sounded like the call of a snipe to Levin, and he grasped the butt end of his gun firmly.

"Bang! Bang!" he heard just above his ear. That was Veslovsky firing at a flight of ducks which wheeled over the marsh and which were at that moment flying far out of range toward the sportsmen. Before Levin had time to look around, he heard the cry of one snipe; then another and a third, followed by about eight more, rose one after the other.

Oblonsky got one just as it was beginning its zigzag flight, and the snipe fell like a lump into the bog. Oblonsky unhurriedly aimed at another, still flying low over the sedge, and that snipe too fell just as the shot rang out; and they could see it fluttering over the cut reeds, flapping its uninjured white-edged wing.

Levin was not so lucky. He aimed at his first bird too low and missed it; he turned his gun at it again as it was rising, but at that very moment another one flew from under his feet and distracted his attention, and he missed again.

While they were loading their guns, another snipe rose in the air and Veslovsky, who had managed to finish reloading before the others, fired two charges of small shot over the water. Oblonsky picked up his brace of snipe and glanced at Levin with sparkling eyes.

"Well, now we separate again," said Oblonsky and, limping with his left leg and holding his gun ready, he whistled to his dog and went off in one direction. Levin and Veslovsky went in the other.

It was always like that with Levin: if he missed his first shots, he got excited, lost his temper, and shot badly for the rest of the day. So it was this time. There were a great many snipe. They kept rising from under the dogs, from under the sportsmen's feet, and Levin might have recovered himself, but the more he fired, the more he disgraced himself in front of Veslovsky, who was firing away merrily, in and out of range, never hitting anything and not in the least put out by it. Levin was in a hurry, could not restrain himself, got more and more excited, and reached the point where he fired almost without hoping to hit anything. It seemed Laska too understood it. She searched less eagerly and kept glancing back at the sportsmen as though in perplexity and with reproach. Shot followed shot. Powder smoke hung about the sportsmen, but in the large, roomy net of the game bag there were only three light, small birds. And even of these one had been shot by Veslovsky and another belonged to them both. Meanwhile from the other side of the marsh came not frequent, but, as it seemed to Levin, significant reports from Oblonsky's gun, followed almost every time by a shout of "Krak, Krak, fetch it!"

This excited Levin still more. The snipe kept wheeling in the air over the reeds. From every side could be heard the squelching sounds of birds rising from the marshy ground and their cries in the air; the snipe that had been previously flushed and had been flying in the air descended in front of the sportsmen. Instead of two hawks,

675

there were dozens of them circling and screeching over the marsh.

Having walked over more than half of the marsh, Levin and Veslovsky came to the place where the peasants' meadow land was divided into long strips, reaching to the reeds and marked off either where the grass had been trodden down or by a mown strip of grass. Half of those strips were already mown.

Though there was little hope of finding as many birds on the unmown part of the meadow as on the mown one, Levin, having promised to meet Oblonsky, walked with his companion farther along the mown and unmown strips.

"Hey there, sportsmen!" shouted one of the peasants, who were sitting beside a cart without a horse. "Come and have a bite with us! A drink of vodka!"

Levin looked round.

"Come on, sir! It's all right!" shouted a merry, bearded, red-faced peasant, showing a row of white teeth and raising a greenish pint bottle that glittered in the sunshine.

"*Qu'est-ce qu'ils disent?*" asked Veslovsky.

"They're inviting us to have a drink of vodka with them. I expect they must have been dividing the meadow. I should go and have a drink," said Levin, not without cunning, hoping that Veslovsky would be tempted by the vodka and go and join them.

"Why do they treat us?"

"Oh, they're just making merry. Do go along. You'd find it interesting."

"*Allons, c'est curieux.*"

"Go, go! You'll find the way to the mill!" shouted Levin and, looking around, was pleased to see Veslovsky, bending down and stumbling with his weary feet and holding his gun at arm's length, making his way out of the marsh toward the peasants.

"You come too, sir!" the peasant shouted to Levin. "What are you afraid of? Have a bite of our pie!"

Levin would have very much liked a drink of vodka and a piece of bread. He was exhausted and could hardly drag his stumbling feet out of the swampy ground, and for a moment he was in doubt. But his dog pointed. And at once all his weariness vanished and he stepped lightly through the marsh toward his dog. A snipe rose from

676

under his feet; he fired and killed it. The dog continued to point. "Sick it!" Another bird rose from under the dog. Levin fired. But it was his unlucky day and he missed, and when he went in search of the one he had killed, he could not find it. He trudged all over the sedge, but Laska would not believe that he had shot anything and when he sent her to look for it, she pretended to search, but did not really do so.

Even without Veslovsky, whom Levin blamed for his bad luck, things did not improve. There were lots of snipe there too, but Levin missed one after another.

The slanting rays of the sun were still hot; his clothes, wet through with perspiration, stuck to his body; his left boot, full of water, was heavy and squelched; beads of perspiration rolled down his face grimy with powder; there was a bitter taste in his mouth, a smell of powder and stagnant water in his nose, and his ears were full of the incessant sound of snipe rising from the boggy marsh; the barrels of his gun were so hot that he could not touch them; his heart thumped with quick, short beats; his hands shook with agitation, and his tired feet stumbled as he dragged them over the hummocks and through the bog; but still he went and still he fired. At last, after a disgraceful miss, he threw his hat and gun on the ground.

"No, I must pull myself together," he said to himself. He picked up his gun and hat, called Laska to heel, and got out of the marsh. When he reached a dry place he sat down on a hummock, took off his boots, emptied the water from one of them, then went up to the marsh, drank some of the rust-tasting water, wetted the heated barrels, and washed his face and hands. Feeling refreshed, he returned to the same spot where a snipe had settled with the firm intention of not getting flurried.

He tried to keep calm, but the same thing happened again. His finger pulled the trigger before he had taken aim. Things went from bad to worse.

There were only five birds in his game bag when he left the marsh and walked toward the alder grove where he was to meet Oblonsky.

Before he saw Oblonsky, he caught sight of his dog. Krak, black all over with the stinking marsh slime, sprang out from under an upturned root of an alder and started sniffing Laska with the air of a conquering hero.

677

Behind Krak, in the shade of the alders, appeared Oblonsky's stately figure. He walked toward Levin, red and perspiring, with an unbuttoned collar, still limping a little as before.

"Well?" he said, smiling merrily. "You've been firing a lot, haven't you?"

"And what about you?" asked Levin.

But there was no need to ask because he could see the full game bag.

"Oh, not bad!"

He had fourteen birds.

"A fine marsh! I suppose Veslovsky must have interfered with you. It's a bit awkward with two men and one dog," said Oblonsky, to soften his triumph.

CHAPTER 11

When Levin and Oblonsky arrived at the peasant's cottage where Levin always put up, Veslovsky was already there. He was sitting in the middle of the room, holding on with two hands to the bench, while a soldier, the brother of the peasant's wife, was trying to pull off his slime-covered boots, and he was laughing his infectious, gay laugh.

"I've only just come. *Ils ont été charmants.* Just imagine, they gave me food and drink. Marvelous bread! *Délicieux*! And the vodka! I never tasted better. And they just wouldn't accept any money. They just kept on saying 'No offense meant' for some reason."

"Why take money? They were just treating you, you see, sir. Their vodka isn't for sale, is it, sir?" said the soldier, at last succeeding in pulling off one wet boot together with a blackened sock.

In spite of the dirt brought into the cottage by the soiled boots of the sportsmen and the filthy dogs that were licking themselves clean, and the smell of bog and gunpowder which filled the room, and the absence of knives and forks, they drank their tea and ate their supper with a relish which only people who go out shooting know. Washed and clean, they retired to a hay barn where the coachman had made up beds for the gentlemen.

Though dusk had fallen, none of the sportsmen wanted to sleep.

After exchanging a few reminiscences and stories about shooting, dogs, and old-fashioned shooting parties, their conversation turned to a subject that interested them all. Following Veslovsky's repeated ecstatic remarks about how delightful the arrangements made for them for the night were, the exquisiteness of the scent of hay, the charm of a broken cart (it seemed to be broken to him because its shafts had been removed), about the good nature of the peasants who had treated him to their vodka, about the dogs, each lying at its master's feet, Oblonsky told them about the delights of a shooting party he had been invited to last summer on the estate of a certain Malthus. Malthus was a well-known railway magnate. Oblonsky told them of the marshes in the province of Tver which Malthus had leased and preserved and about the carriages and dogcarts which had driven the sportsmen to the shoot and the wonderful marquee that had been set up for lunch beside the marsh.

"I can't understand you," said Levin, sitting up on his heap of hay. "How is it that those people don't disgust you? I realize, of course, that lunch with Lafitte is very nice, but don't you find that very luxury disgusting? All those people, just like our spirit monopolists in the old days, make their money in a way that earns the contempt of all decent men, but they don't care a rap for this contempt and then afterward use the money they have dishonestly earned to buy off that contempt."

"Perfectly true!" cried Veslovsky. "Absolutely. Oblonsky, of course, does it out of *bonhomie*, but the others say, 'Well, if Oblonsky stays with them . . .' "

"Not a bit of it," Oblonsky said, and Levin could hear that he was smiling as he spoke. "I simply don't consider him more dishonest than any other wealthy merchant or nobleman. All of them have made their money by work and intelligence."

"But what kind of work? Do you call it work to get hold of a concession and then sell it at a profit?"

"Of course it is. It's work in the sense that if he and others like him did not exist we should have no railways."

"But it's not work in the sense that we understand it as the work of a peasant or a scholar."

"You may be right, but it is still work in the sense that his activity produces a result—the railways. But then, of course, according to you, railways are useless."

"That is quite another question. I'm ready to admit that they are useful. But every acquisition that is disproportionate to the labor spent on it is dishonest."

"But who is to say what is disproportionate?"

"The acquisition by dishonest means and cunning," said Levin, feeling that he was incapable of clearly defining the borderline between honesty and dishonesty. "Like the profits made by banks," he went on. "This is evil, I mean, the acquisition of enormous fortunes without work, as it used to be with the spirit monopolists. Only the form has changed. *Le roi est mort, vive le roi!* Hardly were the monopolies abolished before railways and banks appeared: just another way of making money without work."

"Yes, well, what you say may all be true and clever. . . . Down, Krak!" Oblonsky shouted at the dog that was scratching itself and turning over the hay, evidently convinced of the justness of his case and, therefore, speaking calmly and unhurriedly. "But you haven't defined the borderline between honest and dishonest work. The fact that I draw a bigger salary than my head clerk, though he knows the work better than I do—is it dishonest?"

"I don't know."

"Well, then let me tell you. That you receive for your work on the estate a profit of let's say five thousand rubles, while our peasant host, however hard he may work, can never get more than fifty, is just as dishonest as my earning more than my head clerk and Malthus more than an engine driver. It seems to me that the hostile attitude of the public toward men like Malthus is absolutely unjustified and is, in my opinion, due to envy. . . ."

"I don't think that's fair," remarked Veslovsky. "There can be no question of envy. There is something dirty about that kind of business."

"Please, let me finish," said Levin. "You say it is unjust for me to get five thousand while a peasant gets only fifty. That's true. It is unjust, and I feel it, but . . ."

"Yes, indeed. Why should we eat, drink, go shooting,

and do no work, while he is always, always working?" said Vasenka Veslovsky, the thought evidently having occurred to him for the first time in his life and therefore speaking quite sincerely.

"Yes, you feel it, but you don't give him your property," said Oblonsky, who seemed purposely trying to provoke Levin.

A covert sort of hostility had recently sprung up between the two brothers-in-law: ever since they had married sisters a rivalry seemed to have arisen between them as to which of them had ordered his life best, and now this hostility found expression in the discussion which was beginning to assume a personal note.

"I don't give it away because no one demands it of me, and even if I wanted to, I couldn't have given it away," replied Levin. "And, besides, there's no one to give it to."

"Give it to this peasant here. He won't refuse."

"Yes, but how am I to give it to him? Take him to town and make out a deed of conveyance?"

"I don't know how, but if you are convinced that you have no right . . ."

"I am not at all convinced. On the contrary, I feel I have no right to give it, that I have duties to the land and to my family. . . ."

"I'm sorry, but if you consider this inequality unjust, why don't you act accordingly?"

"I do, only in a negative way, in the sense that I don't try to increase the difference in our positions."

"Now that, if you don't mind my saying so, is a paradox."

"Yes," Veslovsky agreed, "that is something like sophistry. Ah, mine host," he said to the peasant, who had opened the creaking doors and was coming in, "aren't you asleep yet?"

"No, sir, it's too soon to think of sleep. I thought the gentlemen were asleep, but I could hear you talking. I've come for a hook. She won't bite?" he added, stepping cautiously with bare feet.

"And where will you sleep?"

"We're going to take the horses out to graze tonight."

"Oh, what a night!" said Veslovsky, looking through the large frame of the open barn doors at a corner of the cottage and the unharnessed brake, visible in the faint afterglow. "Listen! It's women's voices singing and not at all badly. Who is it singing?" he asked the peasant.

"The maidservants, sir. From close by."

"Come along, let's go and see! We shan't sleep anyway. Come along, Oblonsky!"

"Oh, I don't know whether to go or lie here," Oblonsky said, stretching himself. "It's so lovely to lie here."

"Oh well, I'll go by myself then," said Veslovsky, getting up quickly and putting on his boots. "Good-by, gentlemen. If it's jolly, I'll tell you. You've let me have some shooting, and I won't forget you."

"He is a nice fellow, isn't he?" said Oblonsky, when Veslovsky had gone and the peasant had shut the door after him.

"Yes, he's nice," replied Levin, still thinking of what they had just been discussing.

It seemed to him that he had expressed his thoughts and feelings as clearly as he could, and yet both of them—sincere and far from stupid men—had declared with one voice that he was comforting himself with sophistries. That troubled him.

"Yes, my dear fellow, that's how it is. One of two things: either you admit that the existing social order is just, in which case you ought to uphold your rights, or else you admit that you are enjoying unfair privileges, as I do, and get all the pleasure you can out of them."

"No, if it were unjust you couldn't possibly enjoy these good things of life with pleasure. At least, I couldn't. The main thing, so far as I'm concerned, is not to feel guilty."

"Don't you think we'd better go, after all?" said Oblonsky, evidently feeling tired with the mental strain. "We shan't sleep, you know. Come on, let's go!"

Levin did not reply. The remark he had made during the conversation about his acting justly in a passive sense made him wonder. "Could one be unjust only in a passive sense?" he asked himself.

"What a strong scent the fresh hay has!" said Oblonsky, sitting up. "I know I shan't go to sleep. Vasenka seems to be up to something there. Can you hear the laughter and his voice? Hadn't we better go too? Come on!"

"No," said Levin, "I won't go."

"Surely, not on principle too?" said Oblonsky, smiling and looking in the dark for his cap.

"No, not on principle. Why on earth should I go?"

"You're going to have a lot of trouble, you know," said Oblonsky, getting up and putting on his cap.

"Why?"

"Don't think I can't see the position you've put yourself in with your wife. I heard how you two consider it to be a question of prime importance whether or not you should go away shooting for two days. That's all very well for an idyll, but it can't go on like this all your life. A man must be independent. He has his own masculine interests. A man must be manly," said Oblonsky, opening the doors.

"What exactly do you mean? Go and make love to housemaids?" asked Levin.

"Why not, if it amuses you? *Ça ne tire pas à conséquence.* My wife won't be the worse for it, and I shall get a bit of fun. The main thing is to keep the sanctity of your home inviolate. Nothing of that kind at home. But you needn't tie your hands."

"Perhaps so," said Levin dryly and turned on his side. "We'll have to start early tomorrow and I'm not going to wake anyone. I'll be off at daybreak."

"Messieurs, venez vite!" cried Veslovsky, coming back. *"Charmante!* It's my discovery. *Charmante!* A perfect Gretchen. I've already made her acquaintance. A real peach, I tell you!" he went on in so approving a voice as though she had been made pretty specially for him and he was expressing his satisfaction with the maker.

Levin pretended to be asleep, but Oblonsky put on his slippers and, lighting a cigar, left the barn, and their voices soon died away.

Levin could not fall asleep for a long time. He heard his horses munching hay, then how their host and his eldest son got ready and set out for the night watch; then he heard the soldier settling down to sleep on the other side of the barn with his little nephew, their host's son; he heard the boy telling his uncle in his treble voice what he thought of the dogs, which seemed enormous and terrible to him; then he heard the boy asking what those dogs were going to hunt and the soldier replying in a hoarse, sleepy voice that the sportsmen would go off to the marshes in the morning and would fire their guns and then, to stop the boy's questions, adding: "Go to sleep, Vaska, go to sleep, or else . . ." Soon after that the soldier began snoring himself and everything grew still, and all he could hear was the neighing of the horses and the harsh cries of the snipe. "Could it only be in a passive sense?" he asked himself again. "Well, what if it is? It's not my fault." And he began thinking of the next day.

"I'll go early tomorrow and I'll make a point of not getting excited. There are thousands of snipe. And double snipe too. And when I come back there will be the note from Kitty. Yes, perhaps Stiva is right: I'm not manly enough with her. I've become weak-willed. . . . But what's to be done about it? In a passive sense again!"

As he was falling asleep he could hear the laughter and the merry voices of Veslovsky and Oblonsky. He opened his eyes for a moment: the moon had risen and they were standing chatting in the open doorway, in the bright moonlight. Oblonsky was saying something about the freshness of a girl, comparing her to a fresh kernel just taken out of its shell, and Veslovsky, laughing his infectious laugh, kept repeating something a peasant must have told him: "Go and get your own girl!"

Levin muttered drowsily: "Tomorrow at dawn, gentlemen!" and fell asleep.

CHAPTER 12

Waking just as day was breaking, Levin tried to rouse his companions. Veslovsky, lying on his stomach with one stockinged leg outstretched, slept so soundly that it was impossible to get a response from him. Oblonsky sleepily refused to go so early. Even Laska, curled up and asleep on a corner of the hay, got up reluctantly and straightened and stretched her hind legs lazily one after the other. Having put on his boots and taken his gun, Levin cautiously opened the creaking doors of the barn and went out. The coachmen were asleep beside the carriages; the horses were dozing. Only one of them was lazily munching some oats, scattering and blowing them about all over the trough. It was still quite dark outside.

"Why are you up so early, my dear?" the old hostess, who had just come out of the cottage, asked him, as if he were an old friend of the family.

"Why, I'm off shooting, Granny. Is this the way to the marsh?"

"Go straight along the back of the cottages, past our threshing floor, my dear, and then across the hemp field. There's a path there."

Stepping cautiously with her bare, sunburned feet, the old woman took him as far as the threshing floor, and pushed back the fence for him.

"Keep on straight and you'll come to the marsh. Our lads drove the horses that way last night."

Laska ran gaily ahead along the path; Levin followed her with a light, brisk step, continually glancing at the sky. He did not wish the sun to rise before he got to the marsh. But the sun did not wait for him. The moon, which was still shining when he first came out, now only glittered like quicksilver; the morning star, which one could not help seeing before, now had to be looked for; what had been indistinct patches in the distant field could now be clearly seen: they were sheaves of rye. The dew, still invisible till the sun had risen, on the tall fragrant hemp which had already shed its pollen, drenched Levin's legs and shirt above the waist. In the transparent stillness of the morning the faintest sounds could be heard. A bee whistled past Levin's ear like a bullet. He looked more closely and saw another, then a third. They all came from behind the wattle fence of an apiary and disappeared over the hemp field in the direction of the marsh. The path brought him straight to the marsh, which could be recognized by the mist rising from it, dense in some places and thin in others, so that the reeds and the willow bushes looked like little islands swaying in the wind. At the edge of the marsh, beside the road, the peasant boys and men, who had kept watch over the grazing horses, were lying under their coats, having fallen asleep before daybreak. Three hobbled horses were moving about nearby. One of them clattered its shackles. Laska walked beside her master, asking to be allowed to run forward and looking round. Having passed the sleeping peasants and coming to the first bog,

Levin examined his percussion caps and let Laska go. One of the horses, a well-fed, three-year-old chestnut, on seeing the dog shied and, raising its tail, snorted. The other horses were also startled and, splashing through the water with their hobbled feet and making a sucking sound every time they drew their hoofs out of the thick, clayey mud, began floundering their way out of the marsh. Laska stopped dead, threw a quizzical glance at the horses and a questioning one at Levin. Levin stroked the dog and whistled to her in sign that she might start.

Laska ran gaily and anxiously across the bog, which swayed under her feet.

Having run into the marsh, Laska at once discerned from among the familiar smells of roots, marsh grasses, stagnant water, and the unfamiliar smell of horse dung, the scent of the bird, the bird with the peculiar smell that excited her more than anything else. Here and there among the moss and marsh docks the smell was very strong, but it was impossible to say in which direction it grew stronger or weaker. To find out, it was necessary to go further afield to the lee of the wind. Hardly aware of the legs under her, Laska ran on with a strained gallop, so that she could stop at each bound, if the occasion should arise, first to the right, away from the morning breeze which blew from the east, and then turned to face the wind. Inhaling the air with dilated nostrils, she felt at once that it was not their scent only but that they themselves were right in front of her, and not only one but many of them. Laska slackened her speed. They were there all right, but where she could not yet determine exactly. To find the exact spot she was already beginning to circle around when her master's voice distracted her. "Laska, here!" he said, pointing to the other side. She stood still, as though asking him whether it would not be better to carry on as she had begun. But he repeated his order in an angry voice, pointing to some hummocks covered with water, where there could not possibly be anything. She obeyed, pretending to search and to please him, went all over the place, and then returned to the first spot and immediately got on their scent again. Now, when he no longer interfered with her, she knew what to do, and without looking where she was stepping, stumbling over high mounds, and falling into the water, but overcoming every obstacle with her

686

strong, supple legs, she began the circle which was to make everything clear to her. *Their* scent was getting stronger and stronger and more and more distinct, and suddenly it became quite clear to her that one of them was right there behind that hummock within five paces of her, and she stopped dead and froze into immobility. On her short legs she could see nothing in front of her, but she knew from the scent that it was not five paces off. She stood still, more and more conscious of its presence and enjoying the suspense. Her tail was stretched straight and tense, only its tip quivering. Her mouth was slightly open, her ears pricked. One of her ears had turned back while she ran, and she was breathing heavily and cautiously and looked around even more cautiously, with her eyes rather than with her head, at her master. With his familiar face but terrible eyes, he was coming along, stumbling over the hummocks and quite unusually slowly, as it seemed to her. She thought he came slowly, but actually he was running.

Noticing Laska's peculiar manner of searching when she seemed to be dragging her hind legs along with her mouth half open and her whole body clinging to the ground, Levin realized that she was pointing at a snipe, and with an inward prayer for success, especially with his first bird, he ran up to her. Having come up close to her, he began looking in front of him and from his height he saw with his eyes what she had seen with her nose. In a little space between the hummocks he could see a double snipe. It had turned its head and was listening. Then, spreading its wings a little and folding them again, it wagged its tail awkwardly and disappeared behind the corner of a hummock.

"Sick it! Sick it!" Levin cried, pushing Laska from behind.

"But I can't go," thought Laska. "Where am I to go? From here I can scent them, but if I go forward I shan't know where they are." But he gave her a push with his knee and said in an excited whisper: "Sick it, Laska, old girl! Sick it!"

"Oh well, if he wants it I will, but I can't answer for myself now," she thought, and rushed headlong between the hummocks. She could scent nothing any more now, but only saw and heard, without understanding anything.

Ten paces from its former place a double snipe rose

in the air with its deep cry and its peculiarly distinct whirr of wings. And immediately following the report, it dropped heavily on its white breast in the wet bog. Another one did not wait to be flushed, and rose in the air without the dog.

When Levin had turned toward it, it was already some distance away. But his shot caught it. After flying about twenty feet, the second double snipe rose steeply upward and then, turning over and over like a ball, fell with a thud on a dry spot.

"This is more like it!" thought Levin, putting the warm, fat double snipe in his game bag. "Eh, Laska, old girl, it does look more like it, doesn't it?"

When Levin, having reloaded his gun, moved on, the sun, though invisible behind the clouds, had already risen. The moon had lost all its brilliance and looked like a little white cloud in the sky; not a single star was to be seen any longer. The marsh grasses, silvery with dew before, were now golden. The patches of rust-colored water were amber. The bluish grass had turned into a yellowish green. Marsh birds were moving about in the bushes that sparkled with dew and cast long shadows near the brook. A hawk had woken up and was sitting on a stook, turning his head from side to side and gazing discontentedly at the marsh. Jackdaws were flying to the fields, and a barefooted boy was already driving the horses toward an old man who had got up from under his coat and was scratching himself. The smoke from the gun, as white as milk, spread over the green grasses.

One of the boys ran up to Levin.

"There were lots of ducks here yesterday, sir!" he shouted to Levin and followed him at a distance.

And in the sight of the boy, who so obviously approved of what he was doing, Levin felt doubly pleased to kill three snipe one after another.

CHAPTER 13

The huntsman's saying that if the first beast or bird is not missed, the sport will be good, proved to be true.

Tired, hungry, and happy, Levin returned toward ten

o'clock, having tramped some twenty miles, with nineteen first-class game birds and one wild duck, which he tied to his belt, as there was no room left in his game bag. His companions had long been awake and had had time to get hungry and have breakfast.

"Wait, wait, I know I had nineteen," said Levin, counting again the snipe and double snipe, which no longer looked as handsome as when they had been on the wing, but were twisted, dried up, and bloodstained with their heads bent on one side.

The count was correct, and Oblonsky's envy gratified Levin. Another thing that pleased him was that on his return he found the messenger who had already arrived from Kitty with a note.

"I am very well and happy. If you were worried about me, you can be easier in your mind about me now. I have a new bodyguard, Maria Vlasyevna" (this was the midwife, a new and important person in Levin's household). "She came to see how I was and found me in excellent health, and we have got her to stay till your return. Everyone is cheerful and well, and if you are having good sport please don't hurry and stay another day."

These two joyful events, his successful shooting and the note from his wife, were so great that the two mishaps that followed them passed lightly over Levin. One was that the chestnut trace horse, which had evidently been overworked the previous day, was off its feed and seemed also off color. The coachman said that it had been strained.

"They overdrove it yesterday, sir," he said "Why, driven so hard for seven miles!"

The other mishap, which at first upset his good humor, though afterward he laughed heartily at it, was that nothing was left of all the provisions Kitty had provided in such abundance and which it seemed ought to have lasted for a whole week. Returning tired and hungry from the shooting, Levin conjured up in his mind such a vivid picture of the pies that when approaching his lodgings he could already smell and taste them in his mouth, just as Laska scented game, and he immediately told Philip to serve them. But it appeared that there were no pies and not even any chickens left.

"What an appetite that fellow's got!" said Oblonsky,

laughing and pointing to Vasenka Veslovsky. "I don't suffer from loss of appetite, but he's just a seven days' wonder!"

"Well, it can't be helped," said Levin, looking gloomily at Veslovsky. "Let's have some beef then, Philip."

"The beef's been eaten, sir, and the bones were given to the dogs," replied Philip.

Levin was so annoyed that he said crossly:

"You might have left me something!" and he felt like crying.

"Well, then, draw the birds and stuff them with nettles," he said in a trembling voice to Philip. "And see if you can get some milk for me."

It was only afterward, when he had satisfied his hunger, that Levin felt sorry he had shown his annoyance before a stranger, and he began laughing at his hungry animosity.

In the evening they went shooting again, and Veslovsky, too, shot several birds, and at night they set off for home.

The return journey was as cheerful as their journey to the marshes. Veslovsky sang songs and recalled with relish his adventures with the peasants, who had treated him to vodka and said, "No offense meant!" as well as his nocturnal exploits, the games and his attempt to have fun with a servant girl and the peasant who asked him whether he was married and, on finding out that he was not, said to him: "Don't you run after other men's wives, but see if you can't get one of your own." This seemed to have amused Veslovsky very much.

"I am altogether very pleased with our trip. And you, Levin?"

"I'm very pleased too," said Levin sincerely, for he was particularly glad not only to feel no hostility such as he had felt for Vasenka Veslovsky at home, but, on the contrary, to be very friendlily disposed to him.

CHAPTER 14

Next morning at ten o'clock Levin, having made the round of his estate, knocked at the door of Vasenka Veslovsky's room.

"Entrez," called Veslovsky. "You must excuse me, I've only just finished my ablutions," he said, smiling, as he stood before Levin in his underclothes.

"Don't mind me," said Levin, sitting down by the window. "Have you slept well?"

"Like a top. What sort of day is it for shooting?"

"What do you take, tea or coffee?"

"Neither, thank you. I'll wait for lunch. I really feel ashamed of myself. I expect the ladies must be up already. It would be nice to have a little stroll now. Show me your horses."

They had a stroll round the garden, visited the stables, and even did some physical exercises together on the parallel bars. Then Levin returned to the house with his visitor and entered the drawing room with him.

"Oh, we've had such wonderful sport and so many new impressions!" said Veslovsky, going up to Kitty, who was sitting at the samovar. "What a pity ladies are deprived of these pleasures!"

"Well, I suppose he has to say something to the lady of the house," Levin said to himself. Again it seemed to him that there was something in the smile and the conquering air with which the visitor addressed Kitty.

The old princess, who sat at the other side of the table with Maria Vlasyevna and Oblonsky, called Levin to her and began speaking to him about moving to Moscow for Kitty's confinement and getting an apartment there. Just as all the preparations for the wedding had been distasteful to Levin because by their triviality they detracted from the grandeur of the event, so the preparations for the forthcoming birth, the time of which they seemed to be reckoning on their fingers, seemed even more offensive to him. For a long time he tried not to listen to those conversations about the best methods of swaddling the new baby, trying to turn away and not see those mysterious endless strips of knitting, three-cornered pieces of linen, to which Dolly attached special importance, etc. The birth of a son (he was sure it was going to be a son), which they promised him, but which he could still not believe in—so extraordinary did it seem—appeared to him on the one hand such an immense and therefore impossible happiness, and on the other such a mysterious event that the assumed knowledge of what was going to happen and, as a result of it, preparations as for something ordinary, something human beings themselves were responsible for, seemed scandalous and degrading to him.

But the old princess did not understand his feelings and explained his unwillingness to think and talk about it as due to thoughtlessness and indifference, and consequently gave him no peace. She was commissioning Oblonsky to look for an apartment and now called Levin to her.

"I don't know anything about it, Princess. Do as you think best," he said.

"You'll have to decide when to move."

"I'm afraid I don't know. I know that millions of babies are born without their parents going to Moscow and without doctors . . . so why—"

"Well, of course, if that's what you—"

"No, no. Just as Kitty likes."

"One can't talk to Kitty about it. You don't want me to frighten her, do you? Why, only this spring Natalie Golitsyn died because her midwife was incompetent."

"I'll do anything you say," he said gloomily.

The princess began talking to him, but he did not listen to her. Though his conversation with the princess upset him, it was not that but what he saw by the samovar that made him look so ill-humored.

"No, this is impossible," he thought, glancing now and then at Vasenka Veslovsky, who was bending over Kitty and saying something to her with his handsome smile, and at Kitty, blushing and agitated.

There was something indecent in Vasenka's pose, his look, and his smile. And Levin even saw something indecent in Kitty's pose and look. And again the light went out in his eyes. Again, as on the previous occasion, he suddenly, without the slightest intermission, felt himself cast down from the height of happiness, peace, and dignity into an abyss of despair, hatred, and humiliation. Again they all became hateful to him.

"Yes, you do just as you think best, Princess," he said, looking round again.

"Heavy is the head that wears a crown!" Oblonsky said jestingly to him, hinting no doubt not only at the princess' conversation, but also at the cause of Levin's agitation, which he had noticed. "How late you are today, Dolly!"

They all got up to greet Dolly. Vasenka rose for an

instant and with the absence of politeness to women so characteristic of the modern young men he barely bowed and once more continued the conversation with Kitty, laughing at something.

"Masha has worn me out," said Dolly. "She slept badly and is terribly capricious this morning."

The conversation Vasenka had started with Kitty again concerned Anna and the question whether love can rise above social conventions. Kitty did not like this kind of conversation, and it excited her both because of its subject and because of the tone in which it was conducted and, particularly, because she knew very well how her husband would react to it. But she was too innocent and simple-minded to be able to stop it and even to conceal the superficial pleasure which the young man's obvious attention gave her. She wanted to put an end to the conversation, but she did not know how. She knew that whatever she did would be noticed by her husband and would be construed into something wrong. And indeed when she asked Dolly what was the matter with Masha, and Vasenka, waiting for the uninteresting conversation to end, began to gaze indifferently at Dolly, the question struck Levin as an unnatural and disgusting piece of hypocrisy.

"Well, shall we go mushrooming today?" said Dolly.

"Yes, let's please, and I will come too," said Kitty, and blushed. She wanted to ask Vasenka, out of politeness, whether he would go with them, but did not. "Where are you off to, Kostya?" she asked her husband with a guilty look as he walked past her with resolute steps. This guilty look confirmed all his suspicions.

"The mechanic came while I was away," he said without looking at her, "and I haven't seen him yet."

He went downstairs and was just leaving his study when he heard his wife's familiar footsteps hurrying after him at a reckless speed.

"What's the matter?" he said dryly to her. "We're busy."

"I'm sorry," she said to the German mechanic, "I'd like to say a few words to my husband."

The German wanted to go, but Levin said to him:

"Don't trouble."

"The train's at three?" asked the German. "I hope I won't miss it."

Levin did not answer him, but went out with his wife.
"Well, what have you to say to me?" he said in French.

He did not look at her face and he did not want to see how she in her condition stood with her whole face twitching, looking miserable, and crushed.

"I—I wanted to say that it is impossible to live like this—it's torture!"

"The servants are there—in the pantry," he said angrily. "Please, don't make a scene."

"Well, then, let's go in there!"

They were standing in a passage. Kitty wanted to go into the next room. But the English governess was there, giving a lesson to Tanya.

"All right, come into the garden!"

In the garden they came across a gardener weeding the path. But without thinking that the gardener could see her tear-stained and his agitated face, without thinking that they looked like people running away from some calamity, they walked on with rapid steps, feeling that they had to speak out and clear up their misunderstanding, to be alone together and free themselves from the torment they were both suffering.

"One can't live like this! It's torture! You're suffering, I'm suffering. And what for?" she said when they had at last reached a secluded garden seat at the corner of the lime-tree avenue.

"But just tell me one thing: wasn't there something improper, indecent, horribly degrading in his tone?" he asked, standing before her with his fists pressed to his chest, as he had stood on that night before her.

"Yes, there was," she said in a trembling voice. "But, darling, can't you see that I'm not to blame? Ever since this morning I wanted to adopt a tone that . . . but these people . . . Why did he come? How happy we were, you and I!" she said, choking with sobs that shook her full figure.

The gardener saw with surprise that although nothing had been pursuing them and there had been nothing to run away from, and that they could not have found anything particularly wonderful on that seat—he saw that they passed him on the way home with composed and radiant faces.

CHAPTER 15

After seeing his wife upstairs, Levin went to Dolly's part of the house. Dolly, too, was greatly upset that day. She was walking up and down the room, talking angrily to a little girl who stood howling in a corner.

"You'll stand in that corner all day long," she was saying, "and have your dinner by yourself, and you will not see a single doll, and I won't make you a new dress," she went on, unable to think of any further punishment for the child.

"Oh, she's such a wicked girl!" Dolly said, turning to Levin. "I don't know where she gets her nasty habits from!"

"But what has she done?" asked Levin in a rather indifferent tone of voice, for he wanted to ask her advice about his own affairs and was therefore annoyed at having come at an inopportune moment.

"She and Grisha went away behind the raspberry bushes and there—I can't even tell you what she did. I'm sorry Miss Elliot is not with us any more. This one doesn't seem to notice anything—she's just a machine. . . . *Figurez-vous que la petite* . . ."

And Dolly told him Masha's crime.

"This doesn't prove anything," Levin tried to calm her. "It's not bad habits, it's just mischievousness."

"But why do you look so upset?" asked Dolly. "Why have you come? What's going on there?"

And from the tone of her voice Levin realized that it would not be difficult for him to say what he had come to say.

"I've not been there. I've been in the garden with Kitty. We've quarreled for the second time since . . . Stiva's arrival."

Dolly looked at him with intelligent, comprehending eyes.

"Well, tell me honestly, don't you think there was . . . not in Kitty, but in the way that . . . that gentleman behaved . . . something that might be unpleasant, no . . . not unpleasant, but horrible, offensive to a husband?"

"Well, I mean, how shall I put it? . . . Stand, stand in the corner there!" she said, turning to Masha, who, noticing a barely perceptible smile on her mother's face, was about to turn round. "Men of the world would say that he is behaving like all young men behave. *Il fait la cour à une jeune et jolie femme*, and a man of the world should only be flattered by it."

"Yes, yes," Levin said gloomily, "but you did notice it, didn't you?"

"Not only I, but Stiva too. He told me straight after tea: *'Je crois que Veslovsky fait un petit brin de cour à Kitty.'* "

"Well, that's excellent. Now I am content. I'm going to kick him out," said Levin.

"What do you mean? Have you gone off your head?" Dolly exclaimed, horrified. "Really, Kostya, do talk sense!" she said, laughing. "Well, you can go to Fanny now," she said to Masha. "No, if you insist, I'll speak to Stiva. He'll take him away. We could tell him that you were expecting visitors. I don't think he quite fits in with us here, anyway."

"No, no, I'm going to do it myself."

"But you won't quarrel with him, will you?"

"Not at all. I'm going to enjoy it," said Levin, his eyes sparkling with real enjoyment. "Come, forgive her, Dolly. She won't do it again," he said about the little delinquent, who had not gone to Fanny but was standing irresolutely before her mother, waiting and glancing from under her brows to catch her mother's eye.

The mother looked at her. The little girl burst out sobbing bitterly, buried her face in her mother's lap, and Dolly put her thin, tender hand on her head.

"And what has he in common with us?" thought Levin, and went in search of Veslovsky.

Passing through the hall, he gave orders for the carriage to be harnessed to drive to the station.

"One of the springs broke yesterday, sir," said the footman.

"Well, then, the trap, and make haste, please. Where's the visitor?"

"He's gone to his room, sir."

Levin came upon Vasenka at the moment when, after unpacking his trunk and spreading out his new songs,

696

he was trying on a pair of leggings and preparing to go riding.

Whether there was something unusual in Levin's face or whether Vasenka himself felt that *ce petit brin de cour* which he had started was out of place in this family, he was a little (as far as a man of the world can possibly be) disconcerted by Levin's entry.

"You wear leggings for riding?"

"Yes, it's much cleaner," said Vasenka, putting his fat leg on a chair, fastening the bottom hook, and smiling good-naturedly and gaily.

He was without doubt a nice fellow and Levin felt sorry for him and ashamed of himself as his host when he caught the timid look on Vasenka's face.

On the table lay a piece of the stick they had broken when doing their physical exercises that morning and trying to straighten the warped parallel bars. Levin picked it up and began breaking off the splintered bits at the end, at a loss how to begin.

"I—er—wanted . . ." He fell silent, but suddenly remembering Kitty and all that had happened, he said, looking him firmly in the eyes, "I have ordered the carriage for you."

"How do you mean?" Vasenka began in surprise. "Where are we going?"

"You're going to the railway station," Levin said darkly, breaking off the splinters of the stick.

"Are you going away or has anything happened?"

"It happens that I'm expecting visitors," said Levin, breaking off the splintered ends of the stick more and more rapidly with his strong fingers. "No, as a matter of fact, I am not expecting visitors and nothing has happened, but I ask you to leave. You may explain my incivility as you please."

Vasenka drew himself up.

"I ask *you* to explain it to me . . ." he said with dignity, having understood at last.

"I'm sorry I cannot explain it to you," said Levin, quietly and slowly, trying to control the trembling of his jaw. "And I think you'd better not ask."

And as the splintered end had all been broken off, Levin got hold of the thick ends with his fingers, split the stick in two, and carefully caught the end piece as it fell.

Probably the sight of those tensed arms, the muscles of which he had felt that morning during their physical exercises, the glittering eyes, the low voice, and the trembling jaw convinced Vasenka more than any words. Shrugging his shoulders and smiling contemptuously, he bowed.

"I can see Oblonsky, can't I?"

The shrug and the smile did not irritate Levin. "What else could he do?" he thought.

"I will send him to you at once."

"What nonsense is this!" said Oblonsky, having learned from his friend that he was being driven out of the house and finding Levin in the garden, waiting for the departure of the visitor. "*Mais c'est ridicule!* What's bitten you? *Mais c'est du dernier ridicule!* What did you imagine if a young man . . ."

But it seemed that the place where Levin had been bitten was still sore because he turned pale again and quickly cut Oblonsky short when he was about to explain the reason for his indignation.

"Please, don't go into it! I just can't help it. I'm very much ashamed of myself before you and him. But I don't think he will really mind very terribly going away, and my wife and I do not particularly enjoy his presence here."

"But it's insulting to him! *Et puis c'est ridicule.*"

"It's insulting to me also and painful! And it was not my fault and there's no reason why I should suffer!"

"Well, I must say I never expected it from you. *On peut être jaloux, mais à ce point, c'est du dernier ridicule!*"

Levin turned away from him quickly and walked off to the far end of the avenue, where he continued walking up and down alone. Soon he heard the rattle of the trap and through the trees saw Vasenka, wearing his Scotch cap, sitting in it on some straw (unfortunately there was no seat in the trap), jolting over the ruts as he was driven along the avenue.

"What's happening now?" thought Levin, when a footman ran out of the house and stopped the trap. It was the mechanic, whom Levin had quite forgotten. The German bowed and said something to Veslovsky, then climbed into the trap and they drove away together.

Oblonsky and the old princess were shocked by Levin's conduct. And he himself felt not only extremely *ridicule*, but completely to blame for everything and utterly disgraced; but when he remembered what his wife and he had suffered and asked himself how he would have acted another time, he answered that he would do just the same again.

In spite of all this, toward the end of the day everyone with the exception of the old princess, who could not forgive Levin for his behavior, became extraordinarily animated and gay, like children after a punishment or grownups after a very painful official reception, so that by the evening they talked in the absence of the old princess about Vasenka's expulsion as of something that had happened a very long time ago. And Dolly, who had inherited from her father the gift of making people laugh, made Varenka split her sides with laughter when she related for the third or fourth time, always with fresh humorous additions, how she had only just put on some new ribbons in the visitor's honor and was on the point of going out into the drawing room when she heard the clatter of an ancient rustic cart. And who should be in that rustic cart? Why, dear old Veslovsky himself, Scotch cap, love songs, leggings, and all, sitting on the straw!

"At least you might have let him have the carriage! And then I hear: 'Stop!' Well, I thought, he has been reprieved. But not at all! They put a fat German beside him and they took them away together. And my new ribbons were just wasted! . . ."

CHAPTER 16

Dolly carried out her intention and went to see Anna. She was very sorry to hurt her sister or do anything that Kitty's husband might dislike; she understood how right the Levins were in not wishing to have anything to do with the Vronskys; but she thought it was her duty to go and see Anna and show that her feelings toward her were not changed in spite of the changed circumstances.

Not to depend on the Levins for the journey, Dolly sent to the village to hire horses; but learning about that, Levin came to her to protest against it.

"What has given you the idea that I am against your

going? And even if I were against it, I should resent it even more if you did not take my horses," he said. "You never told me definitely that you were going. And that you should hire horses in the village, in the first place, casts a rather unpleasant reflection on me and, besides, they'll undertake to drive you, but they will never get you there. I have horses, and if you don't want to hurt my feelings, you will take them."

Dolly had to agree, and on the appointed day Levin had a team of four horses ready for his sister-in-law and a change of horses waiting for her at the post station. He had made it up of farm and riding horses, and though they were not very smart-looking, they were quite capable of getting Dolly to her destination in one day. Now, when horses were also needed for the old princess, who was leaving, and for the midwife, it was rather difficult for Levin, but by the laws of hospitality he could not allow Dolly to hire horses when staying at his house; besides, he knew that she needed the twenty rubles that the journey would have cost her, and Dolly's financial affairs, which were in a rather distressing state, were taken to heart by Levin as if they were his own.

Acting on Levin's advice, Dolly started before daybreak. The road was good, the carriage comfortable, the horses ran along at a spanking pace, and beside the coachman sat the clerk from the estate office, whom Levin sent with her for greater safety instead of a footman. Dolly dozed off and only woke up when they were approaching the inn where the horses had to be changed.

After drinking tea at the well-to-do peasant's house where Levin had stopped on his way to Sviazhsky's, and chatting with the women about their children and with the old man about Count Vronsky, of whom he spoke highly, Dolly continued her journey at ten o'clock. She had never enough time to think at home, being too busy looking after the children. But now, during her four hours' drive, all the thoughts she had kept back before came crowding into her head, and she reviewed her whole life from every possible angle as she had never done before. Her thoughts seemed strange even to herself. At first she thought of her children, about whom, though the princess and, above all, Kitty had promised to look after, she was worried all the same. "I only hope Masha won't be naughty again, or Grisha get kicked by

700

a horse, or Lily's stomach get more upset." But soon the problems of the present began to be replaced by those of the immediate future. She began thinking that they would have to move to a new apartment in Moscow for the winter, to reupholster the furniture in the drawing room, and to have a new winter coat made for the eldest girl. Then came problems of a more remote future: how she would launch the children into the world. "It's not so difficult with the girls," she thought, "but what about the boys?

"It's all very well my coaching Grisha now, but that is only possible because I am free now and not having a baby. It's no use counting on Stiva, of course. But I may be able to bring them up with the help of kind people, but what if another baby should come. . . ." And it occurred to her how untrue was the saying that a curse had been imposed upon woman to bring forth her children in sorrow. "To give birth to a child is nothing, it's pregnancy that is a torture," she thought, recalling her last pregnancy and the death of her last child. And she recalled the talk she had had with the young peasant woman at the inn. In answer to her question whether she had any children, the good-looking woman replied:

"I had a little girl, but God has set me free. I buried her last Lent."

"And did you grieve very much for her?"

"Why should I? The old man has lots of grandchildren as it is. They're only a lot of trouble. You can't work or do anything. Like a millstone round your neck."

Dolly thought this answer horrible in spite of the young woman's good looks and her obvious good nature; but now she involuntarily remembered her words. There was certainly some truth in those cynical words.

"And, really, when you come to think of it," reflected Dolly as she looked back on the fifteen years of her married life, "pregnancy, sickness, dullness of mind, indifference to everything, and above all, disfigurement. Kitty, young and pretty Kitty, she, too, has lost her looks, and when I am pregnant I look hideous. I know. Childbirth, suffering, horrible suffering, that last minute . . . and then nursing, sleepless nights, and those fearful pains. . . ."

Dolly shuddered at the mere recollection of the pain she had endured from sore nipples, from which she had suffered with almost every baby. "Then the children's illnesses, this everlasting anxiety; then their upbringing, their nasty propensities (she recalled little Masha's misdemeanor in the raspberry bushes), lessons, Latin—and this is so incomprehensible and difficult. And, as if that were not enough, the death of these children." And once more the cruel memory that always weighed so heavily on her mother's heart rose in her mind of the death of her last baby, a boy who had died of croup. She recalled his funeral, the general indifference shown to the little pink coffin, and her own heartrending, lonely grief as she looked at the pale little forehead with the curly hair at the temples, and the open, surprised little mouth she caught sight of at the moment they closed the pink lid with its gold lace cross over him.

"And what is it all for? What will come of it all? So that I, who have not a free moment for myself, either pregnant or nursing a child, always cross and grumbling, worried to death myself and constantly worrying others, repugnant to my husband, shall live out my life and watch my unhappy, badly reared, and penniless children grow up? And even now I don't know how we should have managed if the Levins had not asked us to spend the summer with them. Of course, Konstantin and Kitty are so tactful that we don't feel it; but it can't go on like that. As soon as they have children of their own, they won't be able to help us. Even now they feel cramped. Will Father, who has hardly anything left for himself, be able to help us? No, I can't possibly give the children a start myself; it can be done only with the help of others and by humbling myself. Why, even supposing that, at best, I am lucky enough not to lose any more of them and bring them up somehow, even then, the best I can possibly expect is that they will not be scoundrels. That is all I can hope for. And for this so much suffering, so much hard work! . . . My whole life is ruined!" She recalled the young peasant woman's words again and again and she felt disgusted to remember them; but she could not help admitting that there was a measure of crude truth in those words.

"Is it still far, Mikhailo?" Dolly asked the estate-office clerk, to dismiss from her mind the thoughts that frightened her.

"About five miles from this village, I understand, ma'am."

The carriage drove down the village street to a small bridge. A crowd of cheerful peasant women, with ready-twisted sheaf binders hanging from their shoulders, were crossing the bridge, chattering loudly and merrily. The women stopped on the bridge, staring inquisitively at the carriage. All the faces turned to her seemed to Dolly healthy and gay, mocking her with their joy in life. "Everyone is alive, everyone is enjoying life," Dolly went on thinking when, after passing the peasant women and having reached the top of the hill, the horses went at a trot again and she was swaying comfortably on the springs of the old carriage, "but I, released as from a prison from the world that is killing me with worry, have only now recovered myself for a moment. Everyone is alive—those peasant women, and my sister Natalie, and Varenka, and Anna, to whom I am going now—everyone except me.

"And they are all attacking Anna. What for? Am I better than she? At least I have a husband whom I love. Not as I would have liked to love him, but I do love him, but Anna did not love hers. How is she to blame? She wants to live. God has put that need into our hearts. Quite possibly I should have done the same. And I still don't know whether I did well to listen to her at that terrible time when she came to see me in Moscow. I should have left my husband then and begun life afresh. I might have loved and been loved in the right way. And is it any better now? I don't respect him. I merely need him," she thought about her husband, "and I put up with him. Is that any better? At that time I was still attractive, I still had my good looks," Dolly went on thinking, and she felt like taking a look at herself in a glass. She had a little traveling mirror in her handbag and she wanted to get it out, but glancing at the backs of the coachman and the clerk who sat swaying beside him, she felt that she would be ashamed if one of them happened to look around, and she did not take it out.

But even without looking at herself in the glass she thought that it might not be too late even now, and she remembered Koznyshev, who was particularly nice to her, and Stiva's friend, kind-hearted Turovtsyn, who had helped her nurse her children when they had scarlet fever and who was in love with her. And there was someone else, a very young man who, as her husband told her jokingly, considered that she was the prettiest of the three sisters. And the most passionate and impossible romances came into her mind. "Anna has been absolutely right and I will most certainly not reproach her. She is happy, she is making another person happy, and she is not as depressed as I am, but most likely as fresh, clever, and fully alive as ever," thought Dolly, and a mischievous smile wrinkled her lips, chiefly because while thinking of Anna's love affair, she conjured up parallel with it an almost identical love affair with an imaginary composite man who was in love with her. Like Anna, she confessed everything to her husband. And Oblonsky's astonishment and embarrassment at the news of her unfaithfulness made her smile.

Immersed in such daydreams, she reached the turning leading from the highroad to Vozdvizhenskoye.

CHAPTER 17

The coachman stopped the horses and looked round to a field of rye on the right, where some peasants were sitting beside a cart. The estate-office clerk was about to jump down, but changed his mind and shouted peremptorily to a peasant, beckoning him to come up. The breeze, which they had felt while driving, died down as soon as they had stopped; the horseflies settled on the sweating horses, which angrily tried to whisk them off. The metallic sound of a scythe being sharpened near the cart ceased. One of the peasants got up and came toward the carriage.

"Taking things easy, aren't you?" the estate clerk shouted angrily at the peasant, who was slowly stepping with bare feet over the ruts of the dry, unbeaten part of the road. "Hurry up, will you?"

The curly-headed old man, with a bit of bast tied around his head, his hunched back dark with perspiration, quickened his steps, walked up to the carriage, and put his sunburned arm on the splashboard.

"Vozdvizhenskoye? The manor house? To the count's?" he repeated. "As soon as you get to the top of that hill,

704

turn to the left. That'll bring you straight to the drive. But who do you want? The count himself?"

"Why, are they at home, my good man?" Dolly said rather vaguely, not knowing how to ask even a peasant about Anna.

"I expect so," said the peasant, shifting from one bare foot to the other and leaving a clear imprint of it with its five toes in the dust. "I expect so," he repeated, evidently desirous of entering into a conversation. "More visitors arrived yesterday. They've got lots of them— visitors, I mean. What do you want?" he asked, turning around to a lad who was shouting something to him from the cart. "Yes, of course! They passed here on horseback a while ago, to see the harvester. I expect they must be home again by now. And who may you be?"

"We've come a long way," said the coachman, climbing back onto the box. "So it isn't far, is it?"

"I tell you it's just here. As soon as you get to . . ." he repeated his directions, rubbing his hand along the splashboard of the carriage.

The young, sturdy, thickset lad also came up.

"There wouldn't be some job going harvesting, ma'am?" he asked.

"I'm sorry, I don't know," replied Dolly.

"So you just turn to the left and you'll get straight to it," said the peasant, who seemed to be reluctant to let the visitors go and anxious to continue the conversation.

The coachman started the horses, but before they had time to go around the corner, the peasant shouted again.

"Stop! Stop there! Wait!" shouted two voices.

The coachman stopped.

"They're coming! There they are!" the peasant shouted, pointing to four persons on horseback and two in a charabanc, coming along the road.

It was Vronsky with a jockey, Veslovsky and Anna on horseback, and Princess Varvara and Sviazhsky in the charabanc. They had been for a ride to see some of the newly-arrived reaping machines in operation.

When the carriage stopped, the riders went on at a walking pace. Anna rode in front beside Veslovsky. She rode quietly on a small, sturdy English cob with a cropped mane and short tail. Dolly was struck by Anna's beautiful head with the black curls escaping from under her top hat, her full shoulders, her slender waist in the black riding habit, and the whole ease and grace with which she sat on the horse.

At first she thought it indecorous for Anna to be riding on horseback. Dolly's idea of horse riding for a woman was associated with that of light flirtatiousness, which, to her mind, was all right for a young girl, but not becoming to a woman in Anna's position. When she saw her closer, however, she became at once reconciled to her riding. In spite of her elegance, everything about her was so simple, quiet, and dignified—her bearing, clothes, and movements—that nothing could have been more natural.

At Anna's side, on a steaming gray cavalry horse, his fat legs thrust forward and evidently full of self-admiration, rode Vasenka Veslovsky in his Scotch cap with fluttering ribbons, and Dolly could not restrain an amused smile when she recognized him. Vronsky rode behind them. He was on a thoroughbred dark bay horse, which was obviously overheated with galloping. He was pulling on the reins to hold it in.

Behind him rode a little man in the dress of a jockey. Sviazhsky and the princess in a brand-new charabanc, to which was harnessed a big, black trotter, were trying to overtake the riders.

Anna's face suddenly brightened with a joyful smile as she recognized Dolly in the little figure pressed against a corner of the old carriage. She uttered a little cry, started in her saddle, and touched her horse to a gallop. Riding up to the carriage, she jumped down unaided and, holding up her habit, ran toward Dolly.

"I thought it was you but I dared not believe it! What a wonderful surprise! You can't imagine how glad I am!" she cried, one moment pressing her face to Dolly's and kissing her and another leaning back and gazing smilingly at her.

"What a wonderful surprise, Alexey!" she said, looking round at Vronsky, who had dismounted and was walking toward them.

Taking off his gray top hat, Vronsky went up to Dolly.

"You've no idea how glad we are to see you," he said, with peculiar emphasis to his words and showing his strong white teeth in a smile.

Vasenka Veslovsky took off his cap without dismounting and greeted the visitor, gaily waving the ribbons over his head.

"That is Princess Varvara," Anna said in reply to Dolly's questioning glance as the charabanc drove up.

"Oh!" said Dolly, and her face involuntarily expressed displeasure.

Princess Varvara was her husband's aunt, and she had long known her and did not respect her. She knew that Princess Varvara had spent all her life as a poor relation at the houses of her rich relatives; but that she should now be living in the house of Vronsky, who was a perfect stranger to her, seemed to Dolly to reflect unfavorably on her husband's family. Anna noticed Dolly's expression and looked embarrassed, blushed, let her riding habit slip out of her hands, and stumbled over it.

Dolly walked up to the charabanc and coldly greeted Princess Varvara. She was acquainted with Sviazhsky too. He asked how his eccentric friend was getting on with his young wife and, throwing a cursory glance over the ill-matched horses and the patched splashboards, suggested that the ladies should drive the rest of the way in the charabanc.

"I'll go in that *vehicle*," he said. "The horse is a quiet one and the princess is an excellent driver."

"No, stay as you are, please," said Anna, coming up. "We'll go in the carriage," and taking Dolly's arm, she led her away.

Dolly was dazzled by the elegant open carriage, the like of which she had never seen before, by the beautiful horses, and by the elegant, brilliant people about her. But what struck her most of all was the change that had taken place in Anna, whom she loved and knew so well. Any other woman, who was less observant and who had not known Anna before and, moreover, who had not thought the thoughts Dolly had thought on the way, would not even have noticed anything special in Anna. But now Dolly was struck by that transitory beauty which only comes to women in moments of love and which she now discovered in Anna's face. Everything in that face: the well-defined dimples in her cheeks and chin, the curve of her lips, the smile that seemed to hover over her face, the light in her eyes, the grace and swiftness of her movements, the full timbre of her voice, and even the manner in which she replied—half crossly and half kindly—to Veslovsky, who asked permission to ride her cob, so as to teach it to lead with the right leg

707

when starting to gallop—it was all remarkably attractive; and she apparently knew it and was glad of it.

When the two women got into the carriage, both were suddenly seized with shyness. Anna was embarrassed by the intent, questioning look with which Dolly regarded her; Dolly, because after Sviazhsky's remark about the "vehicle," she felt ashamed of the dirty old carriage in which Anna sat beside her. Philip the coachman and the estate agent's clerk experienced the same feeling. To conceal his embarrassment, the estate agent's clerk bustled about, helping the ladies in, but Philip the coachman became sullen and made up his mind not to be impressed in future by this show of superiority. He smiled ironically as he cast a glance at the black trotter, having already decided in his own mind that all the black trotter was good for was taking people for a *promenade* in a charabanc and that it could never do thirty miles at a stretch on a hot day.

The peasants had all got up from beside the cart and looked on with cheerful inquisitiveness at the way the visitor had been met, making their own comments.

"They're glad all right," said the curly-headed old man with the piece of bast round his head. "Haven't seen each other for a long time, I warrant."

"Now if that raven gelding had been carting our sheaves, Uncle Gerasim, we'd be done in no time!"

"Look, look," said one of them, pointing to Veslovsky, getting into the sidesaddle, "that's a woman in breeches, isn't it?"

"No, it's a man. See how easily he jumped up!"

"Well, lads, it don't look as if we're going to have a nap today!"

"Not a chance!" said the old man, blinking at the sun. "It's getting late! Take your scythes and let's go!"

CHAPTER 18

Anna looked at Dolly's thin, careworn face with its wrinkles filled with dust and was about to tell her what she was thinking, namely, that Dolly looked thinner; but remembering that her own looks had improved and that

Dolly's eyes had told her so, she sighed and began talking about herself.

"You are looking at me," she said, "and wondering whether I can be happy in my position. Well, I'm ashamed to confess it, but I—I am quite inexcusably happy. Something magical has happened to me, like a dream when you feel frightened and scared and suddenly, when you wake up, you feel that all these terrors are gone. I have wakened up. I have lived through something too harrowing and awful, but now for a long time past, especially since we came here, I've been so happy!" she said, looking at Dolly with a timid, questioning smile.

"Oh, I'm so glad!" said Dolly, smiling, but involuntarily in a colder tone than she had intended. "I'm very glad for you. Why did you not write to me?"

"Why? . . . Because I did not dare. . . . You forget my position."

"To me? You dared not? Oh, if you knew how I . . . I consider . . ."

Dolly wanted to tell Anna what she had been thinking that morning, but for some reason it seemed out of place now.

"However, we can talk about that later," she said, wishing to change the subject. "What are all those buildings?" she asked, pointing to the red and green roofs that could be seen through a hedgerow of acacia and lilac. "It looks like a little town."

But Anna did not answer her.

"No, no. Tell me what you really think of my position. What is your opinion of it?" she asked.

"Well, I think," began Dolly, but at that moment Vasenka Veslovsky, having got the cob to lead with the right leg, galloped past in his short jacket, jumping heavily up and down on the chamois leather of the sidesaddle.

"It's all right!" he shouted.

Anna did not even glance at him, but once more Dolly thought that the carriage was hardly the right place to start upon a long conversation and she cut short what she wanted to say.

"I don't think anything," she said. "I've always loved you, and when you love someone, you love the whole person, just as he or she is, and not as you would like them to be."

Turning her eyes away from her friend and screwing them up (this was a habit of hers which was unfamiliar to Dolly), Anna pondered, trying to understand the full significance of that remark. And, having evidently understood it to mean what she wanted it to mean, she glanced at Dolly.

"If you have any sins," she said, "they will all be forgiven you for coming to see me and for what you have just said."

And Dolly saw that tears started to her eyes. She pressed Anna's hand in silence.

"Well, what are those buildings?" she repeated her question after a minute's silence. "What a lot of them there are!"

"Those are the buildings of the people employed on the estate, the stud farm, and the stables," answered Anna. "And here the park begins. It had all been terribly neglected, but Alexey has had it all made good again. He is very fond of this estate and, something I never expected, he has become passionately interested in farming. But then he is such a highly endowed nature! Whatever he sets his mind to, he does beautifully. Not only is he not bored, he throws himself into his work with passionate interest. He—and I have only just learned to appreciate him—he has become a careful, first-rate landlord—why, in farming matters he has become a real miser! But only in farming matters. Where it is a question of thousands he does not mind," she went on with that joyously cunning smile with which women often talk of the secret characteristics of the man they love which are known only to them. "You see that large building? It's the new hospital. I think it will cost more than a hundred thousand rubles. That is his hobby now. And do you know how it all started? The peasants asked him to let them some meadow land, at a lower rent, I think, and he refused. I reproached him with being stingy. But, of course, it was not that alone, but everything taken together led him to build the hospital just to show, you see, that he was not stingy. If you like, *c'est une petitesse*, but I love him all the more for it. In another moment now we shall see the house. It was his grandfather's house and he hasn't altered anything at all on the outside."

710

"How beautiful!" said Dolly, looking with involuntary surprise at the beautiful house with columns appearing from the variously colored foliage of the old trees in the garden.

"It is beautiful, isn't it? And you get a wonderful view from upstairs."

They drove into a graveled courtyard surrounded by flowerbeds, in one of which two gardeners were making a border of rough, porous stones, and stopped under a covered portico.

"Oh, they've already arrived!" said Anna, looking at the horses that were being led away from the front door. "Look at that horse. Don't you think it's lovely? It's my cob. My favorite. Bring it here, please, and get me some sugar. Where's the count?" she asked the two footmen in resplendent liveries who rushed out of the front door. "Ah, here he is!" she said, seeing Vronsky and Veslovsky coming out to meet her.

"Where are you putting the princess?" asked Vronsky in French, addressing Anna and, without waiting for a reply, welcomed Dolly again and this time kissed her hand. "In the large room with the balcony, I expect."

"Oh no, that's much too far away! The corner room will be better, I think. We shall be able to see more of each other there. Well, come along," said Anna, who had been giving her favorite horse the sugar the footman had brought.

"Et vous oubliez votre devoir," she said to Veslovsky, who had also come out into the portico.

"Pardon, j'en ai tout plein les poches," he replied with a smile, putting his fingers into his waistcoat pockets.

"Mais vous venez trop tard," she said, wiping her hand the horse had wetted in taking the sugar with her handkerchief. "How long can you stay?" she addressed Dolly. "One day? That's impossible."

"That's what I've promised and—the children," said Dolly, feeling embarrassed because she had to take her bag out of the carriage and also because she knew that her face must be covered all over with dust.

"No, Dolly, darling. . . . Well, we'll see. Come along!" and Anna took Dolly to her room.

It was not the grand room Vronsky had suggested, but one for which Anna apologized to Dolly. This room that seemed to need an apology was so luxuriously furnished that Dolly had never seen anything like it. It reminded her of the best hotels abroad.

"Well, darling, I can't tell you how happy I am to have you here," said Anna, sitting down in her riding habit for a moment near Dolly. "Tell me about your children. I saw Stiva only for a moment but he doesn't know how to talk to children. How is my favorite Tanya? A big girl now, I suppose?"

"Yes, quite big," Dolly replied shortly, herself surprised that she could talk so coldly about her children. "We are very comfortable at the Levins'," she added.

"You see, had I known that you don't despise me," said Anna, "you could have all come to us. After all, Stiva is an old and great friend of Alexey's," she added, and suddenly blushed.

"Yes, but we are all right as it is," Dolly replied, looking embarrassed.

"I'm afraid I'm talking a lot of nonsense, I'm so pleased to see you. The only thing that matters, darling, is that I'm so pleased to see you," said Anna, kissing her again. "You haven't told me yet how and what you think of me, and I want to know everything. But I'm glad you will see me just as I am. Above all, I shouldn't like people to think that I wish to prove anything. I don't want to prove anything. I simply want to live without hurting anyone but myself. I have a right to do that, haven't I? However, that's something that has to be discussed at length and we shall talk it all over properly later. I will go and dress now and send you a maid."

CHAPTER 19

Left alone, Dolly surveyed the room with the practiced eye of a housewife. Everything she had seen when driving up to the house and walking through it, and everything she saw now in her room, gave her the same impression of abundance and gracious living, and of that new European luxury which she had only read about in English novels but had never seen in Russia and in the country. Everything was new, from the new French wallpaper to the carpet which covered the whole floor. The bed had a spring mattress with a special kind of bolster and small pillows with silk slips. The marble washstand and the dressing table, the settee, the tables, the bronze clock on the mantelpiece, the curtains, and the door hangings were all new and expensive.

The smart lady's maid who came to offer her services was more fashionably dressed and had her hair done more stylishly than Dolly. She was as new and expensive as the room itself. Dolly liked her politeness, tidiness, and obligingness, but she felt uncomfortable with her; she was ashamed to let her see her patched dressing jacket which, as ill luck would have it, had been packed for her by mistake. She felt ashamed of the very patches and darns of which she had been so proud at home. At home it was clear that six jackets required eighteen yards of nainsook at sixty-five kopecks a yard, which, besides the trimmings and the making, comes to over fifteen rubles, and she had to save up all that. But before the maid she was, if not exactly ashamed, at least uncomfortable.

Dolly felt greatly relieved when Annushka, whom she had known a long time, came into the room. The smart French maid had to go to her mistress and Annushka remained with Dolly.

Annushka was apparently very pleased to see Dolly, and she kept talking without stopping. Dolly noticed that she was very anxious to tell her what she thought of her mistress' position, particularly of the count's love and devotion to Anna, but Dolly carefully stopped her whenever she began to speak about it.

"I grew up with my mistress and she is dearer to me than anything. But, I suppose, it's not for us to judge, ma'am. And he does love her very much, ma'am. . . ."

"So, please, get it washed for me if you can," Dolly interrupted her.

"Yes, ma'am. We have two women specially kept for washing small things, but the laundry is done by machine. The count sees to everything himself. He's such a splendid husband, ma'am. . . ."

Dolly was glad when Anna came in and put a stop to Annushka's chatter.

Anna had changed into a very simple lawn dress. Dolly examined this simple dress very carefully. She knew what such simplicity meant and what it cost.

"An old acquaintance," said Anna, referring to Annushka.

Anna was no longer embarrassed. She was entirely at her ease and self-composed. Dolly saw that she had completely recovered from the shock of her arrival and assumed that superficial, indifferent tone which, as it were, closed the door to the compartment where her feelings and innermost thoughts were kept.

"Well, and how is your little girl, Anna?" asked Dolly.

"Annie?" (This was what she called her little daughter Anna.) "She's quite well. She's quite a big girl now. Would you like to see her? Come along, I'll show her to you. Oh, I've had so much trouble with her nannies," she began telling her. "We had an Italian wet nurse. She was very good, but so stupid. We wanted to send her back home, but the little darling is so used to her that we're still keeping her."

"But how did you manage . . ." Dolly began, intending to ask what name the child would bear, but noticing the sudden frown on Anna's face, she changed the purport of her question. "How did you manage to wean her? You have weaned her, haven't you?"

But Anna had understood.

"That wasn't what you were going to ask, was it? You wanted to ask about her name, didn't you? Well, that worries Alexey. You see, she has no name. I mean," she corrected herself, "she is a Karenin," and as she said it, Anna screwed up her eyes till only the meeting lashes could be seen. "However," she went on, her face brightening suddenly, "we shall talk about it all later. Come along, I'll show her to you. *Elle est très gentille.* She's already crawling."

In the nursery the luxury, which had so struck Dolly in the rest of the house, was still more striking. Here were perambulators ordered from England and appliances for teaching babies to walk and a specially constructed low sofa in the shape of a billiard table for the baby to crawl on, and swings, and baths of a new special kind. All this of English make, solid, and of good quality and apparently very expensive. The room was very large, lofty, and light.

When they came in, the baby was sitting in a little armchair at the table, with nothing on but a vest, and having her dinner of broth, which she had spilled all over her little chest. The child was being fed by a Russian nursemaid, who seemed to be having her dinner at the same time. Neither the wet nurse nor the head nurse was to be seen: they were in the next room, where they could be heard talking in a peculiar kind of French, which was their only means of communication.

Hearing Anna's voice, a smartly dressed, tall Englishwoman, with an unpleasant face and coarse expression, came into the room, rapidly shaking her fair curls, and at once began excusing herself, although Anna had not found fault with her. To every word of Anna's the Englishwoman would say hurriedly, "Yes, my lady."

The dark-browed, dark-haired little girl, with her sturdy, ruddy little body covered with gooseflesh, won Dolly's heart in spite of the severe look she gave the new visitor; she even felt a little envious of the child's healthy appearance. The way the little girl crawled also pleased Dolly very much. Not one of her own children had crawled like that. The baby looked wonderfully sweet when she was put on the carpet with her dress tucked up behind. Glancing around at the grown-up people with her bright black eyes, like a little animal, apparently pleased that she was being admired, smiling and holding her feet apart, she supported herself energetically on her hands, rapidly drew her little behind forward, and again advanced on her hands.

But the general atmosphere of the nursery and particularly of the English nurse, Dolly did not like at all. Dolly could only explain the fact that Anna, with her knowledge of people, could have engaged such an unsympathetic and disreputable-looking Englishwoman for her little girl by the assumption that no respectable nurse would have accepted a position in so irregular a household as Anna's. Moreover, Dolly gathered at once from a few words she heard that Anna, the wet nurse, the head nurse, and the child did not get on together and that the mother's visit was an exceptional event. Anna wanted to give the baby one of her toys, but could not find it.

Most astonishing of all was that when Dolly asked how many teeth the child had, Anna made a mistake and knew nothing at all about the latest teeth.

"Sometimes I can't help feeling bad because I don't seem to be needed here," said Anna, as she was leaving the nursery, lifting her train to avoid the toys lying near the door. "It was different with my first."

"I thought," Dolly said timidly, "it was the other way around."

"Oh no! I think you know I have seen him, Seryozha, I mean," said Anna, screwing up her eyes as though trying to descry something in the distance. "But we'll talk about it later. You'll hardly believe me, but I'm just like someone who's starving and has a full dinner before her and does not know what to start on first. The full dinner is you and the talks I'm going to have with you and which I could not have had with anyone else, and I don't know what to begin with first. *Mais je ne vous ferai grâce de rien.* I have to make a clean breast of everything. But, I suppose, I'd better give you a brief account of the people you will meet here," she began. "I will begin with the ladies. The Princess Varvara. I think you know her and I also know your and Stiva's opinion of her. Stiva says that the one aim of her life is to prove her superiority over Aunt Katerina Pavlovna. That's quite true, but she is kind and I am grateful to her. There was a time in Petersburg when I had to have a chaperon. Just then she turned up. But she really is kind. She made my position much easier. I can see that you don't realize all the difficulties of my position—there in Petersburg," she added. "Here I am quite at ease in my mind and happy. But of that later. I must continue the list. There is Sviazhsky—he is a marshal of nobility and a very decent person, but he wants something from Alexey. You see, now that we have settled in the country, Alexey, with his wealth, can exercise a great deal of influence. Then there is Tushkevich—I believe you have met him—he was always at Betsy's. Now he has been turned out and he has come to stay with us. He is, as Alexey says, one of those people who can be very pleasant if you accept them for what they wish to appear, *et puis, il est comme il faut*, as the princess says. Then there is Veslovsky . . . you know him, don't you? A very charming boy," she said, and a roguish smile puckered her lips. "What is this extraordinary story about him and Levin? Veslovsky told Alexey about it, but we just can't believe it. *Il est très gentil et naïf*," she added with the same smile. "Men need some diversion and Alexey needs an audience, and that's why I value all this com-

pany. It must be lively and gay here so that Alexey shall
not wish for anything new. Then you will see our estate
agent. He is a German, an excellent person, and he
knows his business. Alexey thinks the world of him.
Then there's the doctor, a young man, not exactly a nihilist, but eats with his knife, you know—he's a most
excellent doctor, though. Then there is the architect. . . .
Une petite cour."

CHAPTER 20

"Well, here's Dolly, Princess! You wanted so much to
see her," said Anna, as she and Dolly came out on to
the large stone terrace where the Princess Varvara was
sitting in the shade before an embroidery frame, embroi-
dering a cover for Vronsky's easy chair. "She says she
doesn't want anything before dinner, but will you please
order some lunch for her and I'll go and find Alexey
and bring them all here."

The Princess Varvara gave Dolly an affectionate and
somewhat patronizing reception and immediately
began explaining that she was staying with Anna because she had always loved her more than did her sister
Katerina Pavlovna, who had brought Anna up, and
that now when everyone had thrown Anna over, she
considered it her duty to help her in this most trying,
transitional period.

"Her husband will give her a divorce and then I shall
go back to my solitude, but at present I can be of use
and I shall do my duty, however hard it may be, not like
some people I know. And how sweet and kind of you
to have come. They live absolutely like the most perfect
married couple. It is for God to judge them, not for us.
And, after all, what about Biryuzovsky and Mrs. Aven-
yev? And even Nikandrov, and Vasilyev and Mrs. Ma-
monov, and Lisa Neptunov? No one ever said a word
against them, and in the end they were all received
again. And then *c'est un intérieur si joli, si comme il faut.
Tout-à-fait à l'anglaise. On se réunit le matin au breakfast
et puis on se sépare.* Everyone does what he likes till
dinner. Dinner at seven. Stiva did very well to send you.
He must keep in with them. You know he can do any-

thing through his mother and brother. And they do so much good too. Has he told you about his hospital? *Ce sera admirable*—everything from Paris."

Their conversation was interrupted by Anna, who had found the men in the billiard room and brought them back with her to the terrace. There was still plenty of time before dinner, and the weather being excellent, several proposals for passing the time for the next two hours were made. There were a great many ways of spending the time at Vozdvizhenskoye, and they were all different from those at Pokrovskoye.

"*Une partie de lawn tennis,*" Veslovsky proposed with his beautiful smile. "You and I will be partners again, Anna Arkadyevna."

"No, it's too hot. Let's go for a stroll around the garden and for a row in the boat to show Dolly the riverbanks," Vronsky proposed.

"I think Dolly would like a walk best. Wouldn't you? We can go for a sail in the boat afterward," said Anna.

So it was decided. Veslovsky and Tushkevich went to the bathing pavilion, promising to get the boat ready there and wait for the others.

Two pairs, Anna with Sviazhsky and Dolly with Vronsky, walked along a garden path. Dolly was a little troubled and embarrassed by the entirely novel environment in which she found herself. In the abstract, theoretically, she not only justified but even approved of Anna's conduct. As is quite often the case with women of unimpeachable moral conduct who are rather tired of the monotony of a virtuous life, she not only condoned from afar an illicit love affair but even envied it. Besides, she loved Anna with all her heart. But faced with such a situation in real life, and seeing Anna among all those people who were so alien to her, with their observance of good form, Dolly felt ill at ease. She particularly disliked seeing the Princess Varvara, who forgave them everything for the sake of the comforts she enjoyed there.

In general, in the abstract Dolly approved of Anna's conduct, but to see the man for whose sake Anna had behaved in so unconventional a fashion made her feel uncomfortable. Besides, she never really liked Vronsky. She considered him very proud, and she saw nothing in him of which he could be proud except his wealth. But here in his own house he impressed her in spite of herself more than ever, and she could not feel at ease with him. In his presence she felt the same as she had felt when the French maid helped her to unpack. Just as with the maid, she was not so much ashamed as uncomfortable at the patches in her dressing jacket, so now with him she felt not so much ashamed of herself as uncomfortable.

Dolly felt embarrassed and was trying to think of something to talk about. She thought that with his pride he would not be pleased to hear her expressing admiration for his house and garden, but unable to find any other subject of conversation, she told him that she liked his house very much.

"Yes," he said, "it's a very beautiful building and in the good old style."

"I like the courtyard in front of the entrance very much. Was it like that before?"

"Oh, no!" he said and his face lit up with pleasure. "You should have seen that courtyard in the spring!"

And he began, quietly at first and then more and more carried away by his subject, to draw her attention to the various details of the improvements he had carried out in the house and the garden. One could see that, having devoted a great deal of trouble to the improvement and the restoration of the estate, Vronsky felt the need of bragging about them to a fresh person and he was delighted by Dolly's praises.

"If you'd like to have a look at the hospital and are not too tired, it isn't very far from here," he said, peering into her face to make sure that she really was not bored.

"Will you come, Anna?" he asked, turning to her.

"We shall, shan't we?" she said to Sviazhsky. "*Mais il ne faut pas laisser le pauvre Veslovsky et Tushkevich se morfondre là dans le bateau.* We must send to let them know. Yes, it's a monument he'll leave behind him here," said Anna, addressing Dolly with the same sly, knowing smile with which she had spoken about the hospital before.

"Oh, it's a great undertaking!" said Sviazhsky, but not to appear to be making up to Vronsky, he at once added a slightly critical remark. "I am surprised, though,

Count," he said, "that you, who're doing so much for the health of the peasants, should be so indifferent to the schools."

"*C'est devenu tellement commun les écoles,*" said Vronsky. "But that's not the real reason. I have simply been carried away. This way to the hospital," he said, turning to Dolly and pointing to a side path that led out of the avenue.

The ladies opened their parasols and entered the sidewalk. After a few more turnings they passed through a gate and Dolly saw on the high ground before her a large, red, nearly completed building of a rather fanciful design. The iron roof, as yet unpainted, shone dazzlingly in the bright sunshine. Beside the finished building another was being erected. It was surrounded by scaffolding and workmen in aprons stood on it laying bricks, pouring mortar from small wooden tubs, and smoothing it with trowels.

"How quickly the work is progressing," said Sviazhsky. "When I was here last there was no sign of a roof."

"It will all be ready by the autumn," said Anna. "Inside it's practically finished."

"And what's this new building?"

"That will be the doctor's house and the dispensary," replied Vronsky and, seeing the architect in his short coat coming toward him, he excused himself to the ladies and went to meet him.

Avoiding the lime pit from which the workmen were taking the slaked lime, he stopped and began discussing something heatedly with the architect.

"The pediment is still too low," he said to Anna in reply to her question what it was all about.

"I said all along that the foundation ought to be raised," said Anna.

"Well, yes, that would certainly have been better," remarked the architect, "but I'm afraid it's done now."

"Yes, I'm very much interested in it," said Anna to Sviazhsky, who expressed his surprise at her knowledge of architecture. "The new building ought to be in keeping with the hospital. But it was an afterthought and begun without a plan."

Having finished his discussion with the architect, Vronsky rejoined the ladies and led them inside the hospital.

Although they were still working at the cornices outside and painting on the ground floor inside, the upper story was nearly finished. Mounting the broad iron staircase to the landing, they entered the first large room. The walls were plastered to look like marble, the enormous plate-glass windows were already put in, only the parquet floor was not yet finished, and the carpenters, who were planing a square of parquet, stopped their work and, taking off the bands that kept their hair out of the way, exchanged greetings with the gentry.

"This is the reception room," said Vronsky. "There will be a desk, a table, and a cupboard here and nothing else."

"This way, let's go through here, but don't go near the window," said Anna, feeling whether the paint was dry. "Alexey," she added, "the paint's dry already."

From the reception room they passed into the corridor. Here Vronsky pointed out the new ventilation system that had been installed. Then he showed them the marble baths and the curiously sprung beds, the wards, the storeroom, the linen room, the stoves of a new design, the noiseless trolleys to convey all sorts of necessary articles along the corridor, and lots of other things. Sviazhsky expressed his admiration of everything like a man who was well acquainted with all the newest improvements. Dolly simply expressed her surprise at things she had never seen before and, wishing to understand it all, inquired about everything, which seemed to please Vronsky very much.

"Yes," said Sviazhsky, "I think this will be the only correctly planned hospital in Russia."

"And won't you have a maternity ward?" asked Dolly. "It is so necessary in the country. I've often—"

In spite of his courtesy, Vronsky interrupted her.

"This isn't a maternity home, but a hospital for all diseases except infectious ones," he said. "And have a look at this," he went on, rolling up an invalid chair for convalescents that had just arrived from abroad. "Look!" He sat down in the chair and began moving about in it. "The patient can't walk, he is too weak or there's something the matter with his legs, but he needs fresh air, so he just goes out in it and takes a ride. . . ."

Dolly was interested in everything and she liked everything she saw very much, but it was Vronsky himself with his unassuming, naïve enthusiasm that she liked most. "Yes, he's a very nice, good person," she thought again and again, not listening to him, but looking at him and trying to make out the meaning of his expression and mentally putting herself in Anna's place. She liked him so much in his state of great animation that she understood how Anna could have fallen in love with him.

CHAPTER 21

"No, I don't think so. The princess is tired and horses don't interest her," said Vronsky to Anna, who had suggested that they should go to the stud farm, where Sviazhsky wanted to see the new stallion. "You go and I will see the princess back to the house and we'll have a talk together," he said, "if," he added, turning to Dolly, "you don't mind, that is."

"I don't understand a thing about horses and I shall be very glad to," replied Dolly, not without surprise.

She saw by Vronsky's face that there was something he wanted of her. She was not mistaken. As soon as they had passed through the gate and gone back to the garden, he glanced in the direction where Anna had gone and having made sure that she could neither hear nor see them, began:

"I suppose you must have guessed that I wanted to have a private talk with you," he said, looking at her with laughing eyes. "I don't think I'm wrong in thinking that you are Anna's friend."

He took off his hat and, getting out a handkerchief, mopped his head, which was beginning to go bald. Dolly said nothing and only gave him a frightened look. Left alone with him, she suddenly felt terrified: his laughing eyes and stern expression frightened her.

The most diverse suppositions as to what he was about to say flashed through her mind: "He'll start asking me to stay with them and bring the children and I shall have to refuse, or he'll ask me to get together a circle of friends for Anna in Moscow. . . . Or can it be about Vasenka Veslovsky and his relations with Anna? Or possibly about Kitty and that he feels that he treated her shabbily?" She did not really guess what he actually wanted to talk to her about, anticipating only the unpleasant things.

"You have great influence with Anna and she is very fond of you," he said. "I should like you to help me."

Dolly looked timidly and inquiringly at his energetic face, one moment in the shadow of the lime trees and another wholly or partly in the sunlight that fell between them, and waited for him to say more; but he walked by her side in silence, prodding the gravel with his stick as he went.

"If you, the only one of Anna's women friends—I do not count the Princess Varvara—have come to see us, you've done so, I'm sure, not because you consider our position normal, but because you realize all the hardships of that position and still love her and wish to help her. I am right, am I not?" he asked, looking around at her.

"Yes, of course," said Dolly, shutting her parasol, "but—"

"I'm sorry," he interrupted her and, forgetting that he was placing her in an awkward position, stopped involuntarily, so that she too had to stop, "but, you see, no one feels the whole hardship of Anna's position more than I do. And that is understandable, if you do me the honor of believing that I am a man with a heart. I am the cause of that position and that is why I feel it."

"I understand," said Dolly, finding it impossible not to admire him for the sincerity and the firmness with which he had said it. "But I wonder if you don't exaggerate it just because you feel that you're the cause of it. Her position in society is rather difficult, I can see that."

"In society it's hell," he said quickly, with a dark frown. "It's impossible to imagine moral torments worse than those she went through for two weeks in Petersburg . . . and I beg you to believe that."

"Yes, but here, so long as neither Anna nor you—er—feel that you have any need of society . . ."

"Society!" he exclaimed contemptuously. "What need can I have of society?"

"Well, till then—and that may be always—you are happy and need not worry. I can see that Anna is happy, perfectly happy—she has already told me so," said Dolly with a smile and, having said that, she quite involuntarily felt a twinge of doubt as to whether Anna was really happy.

But it seemed that Vronsky had no doubt whatever about it.

"Yes, yes," he said. "I know she has recovered from all her sufferings. She is happy. She is happy in the present. But I'm afraid I can't say as much for myself. I'm afraid of what is in store for us. . . . I'm sorry, you wouldn't like to go on, would you?"

"No."

"Well, in that case let's sit down here."

Dolly sat down on a garden seat in a corner of the avenue. He stood in front of her.

"I see that she is happy," he repeated, and the doubt whether Anna was really happy struck Dolly more forcibly than before. "But can it go on like this? Whether we've acted rightly or wrongly is another question, but the die is cast," he said, passing from Russian to French, "and we are bound together for life, united by what we consider the most sacred ties of love. We have a child, we may have other children. But the law and all the circumstances of our position are such that thousands of complications arise which she, resting now after all her sufferings and trials, neither sees nor wishes to see. And it's understandable. But I can't help seeing them. Legally my daughter is not mine, but Karenin's. I don't want this deception!" he said with an energetic gesture of denial, looking at Dolly with a gloomily inquiring expression.

She made no answer, but just gazed at him. He continued.

"Some day we may have a son, my son, and by law he will be a Karenin. He will not be heir to my name or to my property, and however happy we may be in our family life and however many children we may have, there will be no legal bond between them and me. They will be Karenins. Just think of the hardship and horror of this situation. I've tried to talk to Anna about it. It irritates her. She does not understand and I can't speak openly to *her* about all this. Now look at another side. I am happy in her love, but I must have some occupation. I have found this occupation and I am proud of it. I consider it far more honorable than the occupations of my former comrades at Court and in the army. And I most certainly would not exchange it for theirs. I am working here without leaving my estate, and I am happy and contented, and I do not want anything more for our happiness. I love this work. *Cela n'est pas un pisaller*, on the contrary . . ."

Dolly noticed that at this point of his argument he got confused and she could not quite understand why he had digressed, but she felt that having once begun to speak of his private affairs, of which he could not speak to Anna, he was now telling her everything and that the question of his work in the country belonged to the same category of his innermost thoughts as the question of his relations with Anna.

"Well, to continue," he said, recovering himself. "The main thing is that you must be convinced that the work you do will not die with you, that you will have heirs to carry on with your work—and I have none. Just imagine the position of a man who knows beforehand that his children and the children of the woman he loves will not be his but someone else's, someone who hates them and will have nothing to do with them. Why, it's dreadful!"

He fell silent, looking greatly agitated.

"Yes, of course, I quite understand. But what can Anna do?" asked Dolly.

"Well, that brings me to the chief point of my talk," he said, making an effort to keep calm. "Anna can do it. It depends on her. Even to petition the emperor for permission to adopt the child, a divorce is absolutely necessary. And that depends on Anna. Her husband agreed to a divorce—your husband had almost arranged it. And I know he would not refuse now. It is only necessary to write to him. At the time he said quite definitely that if she expressed the wish he would not refuse. Of course," he said gloomily, "that is one of those pharisaic cruelties of which only heartless men like him are capable. He knows what torture it is for her to think of her life with him and, knowing her, he demands a letter from her. I realize that it must be very painful to her. But what is at stake is so important that one must *passer pardessus toutes ces finesses de sentiment. Il y va du bonheur de l'existence d'Anne et de ses enfants.* I do not speak of myself, though it is very hard on me, very hard," he said in a menacing voice, as if threatening someone for making it so hard on him. "So that's why, Princess, I am shamelessly clutching at you as a sheet anchor. Help me to persuade her to write to him and ask for a divorce."

"Yes, of course," said Dolly, pensively, remembering vividly her last meeting with Karenin. "Yes, of course," she repeated resolutely, remembering Anna.

"Use your influence with her, but get her to write. I don't want to, and it is practically impossible for me to speak to her about it."

"Very well, I'll speak to her. But how is it she does not think of it herself?" Dolly asked, for some reason suddenly remembering Anna's curious new habit of screwing up her eyes. And she recalled that it was just when the most intimate side of her life was touched on that Anna screwed up her eyes. "As if she half shut her eyes to her life so as not to see it all," thought Dolly. "Yes, certainly, I will talk to her for my own sake and for hers," replied Dolly in reply to his expression of gratitude.

They got up and walked back to the house.

CHAPTER 22

Finding that Dolly had already returned, Anna looked intently at her, as though asking about the talk she had had with Vronsky, but she did not put her question into words.

"I think it's almost dinnertime," she said. "We haven't really seen anything of one another. I am counting on this evening. Now I must go and dress. You too, I suppose. We all got dirty on the site."

Dolly went to her room, and she could not help feeling amused. She had nothing to change into, for she had already put on her best dress; but to show in some way that she had changed for dinner she asked the maid to brush her dress, put on new cuffs and a fresh ribbon, and placed some lace in her hair.

"This is all I could do," she said with a smile to Anna, who came out to her in a third dress, also an extremely simple one.

"I'm afraid we are rather formal here," Anna said as though apologizing for her own smartness. "Alexey is seldom so pleased with anything as he is with your visit. He is positively in love with you," she added. "You're not tired, are you?"

There was no time to discuss anything before dinner. When they entered the drawing room, they found the Princess Varvara and the men already there. The men wore frock coats. The architect alone wore a swallowtail. Vronsky introduced the new visitor to the doctor and the estate agent. The architect had already been introduced to her at the hospital.

The fat butler, his round, clean-shaven face and starched white necktie shining, announced that dinner was served and the ladies rose. Vronsky asked Sviazhsky to take Anna in and himself went up to Dolly. Veslovsky offered his arm to the Princess Varvara before Tushkevich, so that Tushkevich, the estate agent, and the doctor went in by themselves.

The dinner, the dining room, the dinner service, the servants, the wine, and the food were not only in keeping with the general atmosphere of the house, but were, if anything, more sumptuous and modern. Dolly observed all this luxury, which was so new to her, and as a housewife herself in charge of a household, involuntarily made a mental note of all the details—though she had no hope of ever being able to introduce anything she saw into her own house, since such luxury was far above her way of life—and asked herself how it was all done and by whom. Vasenka Veslovsky, her own husband, and even Sviazhsky and a great many other people she knew would not have given it a thought, believing firmly that every decent host wishes his guests to feel that everything that is so well ordered in his house has not cost him, the host, any trouble, but has come about by itself. But Dolly knew very well that even porridge for the children's breakfast does not come of itself and that for that reason alone so complicated and magnificent an establishment must have needed someone's concentrated attention. From the glance with which Vronsky surveyed the table and from the nod he gave the butler and from the way he offered Dolly her choice of hot or cold soup, she concluded that it was all done and kept up by the care of the master of the house himself. Anna quite obviously had as little to do with it as had Veslovsky. She,

Sviazhsky, the princess, and Veslovsky were all equally guests, all of them gaily enjoying what had been provided for them.

Anna was the hostess only in so far as the conversation was concerned. And, as Dolly observed, Anna conducted that conversation (most difficult for a hostess of a small dinner party which included the estate agent and the architect, who, belonging to quite a different world, tried not to show their discomfiture at such unfamiliar luxury and could not take any sustained part in the general conversation) with her usual tact, naturalness, and even pleasure.

The conversation turned on the row Veslovsky and Tushkevich had had by themselves in a boat, and Tushkevich began to tell them about the last races at the Petersburg Yacht Club. But taking advantage of a break in the conversation, Anna at once turned to the architect to draw him out of his silence.

"Mr. Sviazhsky," she said, "was amazed by the way the new building has grown since he was here last. But I'm there every day and I cannot help being amazed at the speed with which it grows."

"It is easy to work with Count Vronsky," the architect said with a smile (he was a respectful and quiet man, who was conscious of his own dignity). "It's not like having to do with the local authorities. Instead of writing a whole ream of papers, I merely report to the count, we talk it over, and in a few words the business is settled."

"American methods," said Sviazhsky with a smile.

"Yes, sir. There they put up buildings in a rational manner. . . ."

The conversation passed to the abuse of power by the United States authorities, but Anna at once changed it to another topic, so as to draw the estate agent out of *his* silence.

"Have you ever seen a reaping machine?" she asked Dolly. "We had been to have a look at them when we met you. It's the first time I ever saw them."

"How do they work?" asked Dolly.

"Exactly like a pair of scissors. A plank and a lot of little scissors. Like this. . . ."

Anna took a knife and a fork in her beautiful white hands with beringed fingers and began to demonstrate. She realized apparently that her explanation would not

728

be understood, but she carried on with it because she knew that she spoke pleasantly and that her hands were beautiful.

"More like penknives," Veslovsky remarked flirtatiously, without taking his eyes off her.

Anna smiled faintly, but did not answer him.

"They are like scissors, aren't they?" she asked, turning to the estate agent.

"O ja," replied the German. *"Es ist ein ganz einfaches Ding,"* and he began to explain the construction of the machine.

"A pity it doesn't bind too," said Sviazhsky. "I saw one at the Vienna exhibition that bound the sheaves with wire. Those would have been much more profitable."

"Es kommt drauf an . . . Der Preis vom Draht muss ausgerechnet werden." And, drawn from his silence, he turned to Vronsky. *"Das lässt sich ausrechnen, Durchlaucht."* The German was about to put his hand in his pocket where he kept the pencil and notebook in which he made all his calculations, but remembering that he was at dinner and noticing Vronsky's cold look, he checked himself. *"Zu compliciert, macht zu viel Klopot,"* he concluded.

"Wunst man Dochots, so hat man auch Klopots," said Vasenka Veslovsky, making fun of the German. *"J'adore l'allemand,"* he said, turning to Anna with the same smile.

"Cessez," she said to him with mock severity.

"And we expected to find you in the fields, Doctor," she addressed the doctor, a sickly-looking man.

"I was there, but I disappeared into thin air," replied the doctor with gloomy jocularity.

"Then you had some good exercise at least."

"Magnificent!"

"Well, and how is the old woman? I hope it's not typhus."

"Typhus or not, she's hardly what you might call a hopeful case."

"I'm sorry," said Anna, and having thus, as it were, paid the tribute of courtesy to the members of the household, she turned to her own friends.

"All the same," Sviazhsky said jestingly, "it would be difficult to construct a machine from your description."

"And why not, pray?" said Anna with a smile which showed that she knew that there had been something engaging in the way she explained the construction of the machine and that Sviazhsky, too, was aware of it.

This new trait of youthful coquetry made a disagreeable impression on Dolly.

"Anna Arkadyevna's knowledge of architecture, on the other hand, is quite marvelous," said Tushkevich.

"Why, of course," said Veslovsky. "Yesterday I heard Anna Arkadyevna say 'entablatures' and 'podiums.' I've got it right, haven't I?"

"There's nothing marvelous about it, considering how much I see and hear of it," said Anna. "I don't suppose you know what houses are made of, do you?"

Dolly saw that Anna was displeased with Veslovsky's flirtatious tone, but she could not help falling in with it herself.

Vronsky behaved in this matter quite differently from Levin. He obviously did not attach any importance to Veslovsky's chatter and, indeed, encouraged these playful exchanges.

"Tell us, Veslovsky, what keeps the bricks together?"

"Cement, of course."

"Bravo! And what is cement?"

"Well, it's a sort of paste—no, putty," said Veslovsky, amid general laughter.

The conversation among the diners, except the doctor, the architect, and the estate agent, who sat in gloomy silence, never ceased for a moment, now moving along smoothly, now catching on something and touching one or the other to the quick. Once Dolly was stung to the quick and got so excited that she even got red in the face and only afterward tried to remember whether she had said anything too much or disagreeable. Sviazhsky had begun talking about Levin, mentioning his peculiar views that machines only did harm to Russian agriculture.

"I have not the pleasure of knowing this Mr. Levin," said Vronsky with a smile, "but I don't suppose he has ever seen the machines he condemns. Or if he has seen and tried one, it must have been some Russian machine and not one imported from abroad. So what sort of views can he possibly have?"

"Turkish views no doubt," said Veslovsky, turning to Anna with a smile.

"I can't defend his opinions," Dolly said, flushing, "but I can say that he is a highly educated man, and if he were here he would be able to answer you. I'm afraid I can't."

"I'm very fond of him and we're great friends," said Sviazhsky with a good-natured smile. "*Mais pardon, il est un peu toqué.* For instance, he maintains that rural councils and magistrates are quite unnecessary and he won't have anything to do with any kind of public work."

"That's just our Russian indifference," said Vronsky, pouring water from an iced decanter into a thin glass with a stem. "We don't realize the duties our privileges impose upon us and for that reason deny the existence of these duties."

"I know no man who is more strict in the performance of his duties," said Dolly, irritated by Vronsky's tone of superiority.

"So far as I'm concerned," went on Vronsky, evidently for some reason stung to the quick by this conversation, "I am, on the contrary, very grateful for the honor they have done me, thanks to Mr. Sviazhsky here, in electing me a justice of the peace. I consider the duty of attending the sessions and hearing the case of some peasant's horse as important as anything else I can do. And I shall consider it an honor to be elected to the town council. It is only in this way that I can repay the advantages I enjoy as a landowner. Unfortunately, people do not understand the important position the big landowners should occupy in the state."

Dolly could not help feeling it strange to hear how calmly self-assured he was in being in the right at his own table. She recalled how Levin, who held diametrically opposed views, was equally positive in his opinions at his own table. But she was fond of Levin and therefore on his side.

"So we can depend on you, Count, to be present at the next sessions?" said Sviazhsky. "But you'll have to leave in good time so as to be there on the eighth. I hope you will do me the honor of staying with me."

"And I rather agree with your brother-in-law," said

731

Anna. "Only I wouldn't go as far as he," she added with a smile. "I'm afraid we've got too many of these public duties lately. Just as before we used to have so many officials that we had to have an official for every little thing, so now we have all sorts of public workers. Alexey has been here six months and I believe he is already a member of five or six public institutions—a member of the board of trustees, a justice of the peace, a town councilor, a juryman, a member of some commission on horses. *Du train que cela va*, all his time will be taken up by it. And I fear that with such a multiplicity of official duties, the whole thing will become a mere form. Of how many official bodies are you a member?" she asked, turning to Sviazhsky. "More than twenty, aren't you?"

Anna was saying it in a jocular tone of voice, but one could feel a touch of irritation in it. Dolly, who had been observing Anna and Vronsky closely, at once noticed it. She also perceived that at this conversation Vronsky's face at once assumed a serious and obstinate expression. Noticing it as well as the fact that the Princess Varvara hastened to change the subject by talking of their Petersburg acquaintances, and recalling how irrelevantly Vronsky had started talking about his public activities in the garden, Dolly realized that this question of public activity was connected with some deep private disagreement between Anna and Vronsky.

The dinner, the wines, the service were all excellent, but it was all the sort of thing Dolly had seen before at public dinners and balls she no longer relished, and it had the same impersonal and strained character about it; and that was why on an ordinary day and in a small gathering all this produced a disagreeable impression on her.

After dinner they sat on the terrace for a while. Then they played lawn tennis. The players, having chosen their partners, took up their places on a carefully leveled and rolled croquet lawn on either side of a net stretched between two gilt posts. Dolly tried to play, but could not understand the game for a long time, and when she did, she was so tired that she sat down beside the Princess Varvara and only watched the players. Her partner Tushkevich also gave up; but the rest went on playing for a long time. Sviazhsky and Vronsky both played very well and seriously. They followed carefully the ball served to them, ran up adroitly to it without hurry and without dallying, waited for it to bounce, and hitting it with the racquet neatly and with precision, sent it back across the net. Veslovsky played worse than the others. He got too excited, but made up for it by his gaiety, which inspired the other players. His laughter and shouts never ceased. He as well as the other men had, with the ladies' permission, taken off their coats, and his large handsome figure in white shirt sleeves, his red, perspiring face and impetuous movements imprinted themselves on the memories of the onlookers.

When Dolly had gone to bed that night she had only to close her eyes to see Vasenka Veslovsky rushing about the croquet lawn.

Dolly did not feel particularly cheerful while they were playing. She did not like the flirting Veslovsky carried on with Anna and the general unnaturalness of grown-up people carrying on a children's game in the absence of children. But not to disconcert the others and to while away the time in some way or other, she joined the players and pretended to be enjoying herself. All that day she had the strange feeling that she was taking part in a theatrical performance with better actors than herself and that her own bad performance was spoiling the whole show.

She had come with the intention of staying two days if she found their way of life congenial to her. But in the afternoon, during the game, she decided that she would leave the next day. The painful worries about her children which she had so hated on the way, appeared in quite a different light after a day spent without them and drew her back to them.

Dolly felt greatly relieved when, after evening tea and a sail in the boat at night, she got back to her room alone, took off her dress, and sat down to do up her thin hair for the night. Indeed, she hoped that Anna would not be coming in presently to talk to her. She wished to be alone with her thoughts.

CHAPTER 23

Dolly was about to get into bed when Anna came into the room in her dressing gown.

Several times during the day Anna had begun to speak about the things that affected her closely and every time after a few words she stopped, saying, "We'll talk it all over when we are alone. I have so much to say to you."

Now that they were alone Anna did not know what to talk about. She sat near the window, looking at Dolly and trying to call to mind all the store of intimate topics that seemed so inexhaustible and—could not find anything to say. At that moment it seemed to her that everything had already been said.

"Well, how is Kitty?" she said with a deep sigh and a guilty glance at Dolly. "Tell me the truth, Dolly. She isn't angry with me, is she?"

"Angry? Good heavens no!" said Dolly with a smile.

"But does she hate and despise me?"

"Why, no! But, of course, there are things that cannot be forgiven."

"Yes, yes," said Anna, turning away and looking out of the open window. "But it was not my fault. Whose fault was it? Well, what does being at fault mean? Could things have been otherwise? What do you think? Could it possibly have happened that you did not become Stiva's wife?"

"I'm afraid I don't know. But you'd better tell me. . . ."

"Yes, yes, but we haven't finished about Kitty. Is she happy? I'm told he is a very nice man."

"He's much more than that. I don't know a better man."

"Oh, I'm so glad! I'm very glad. Much better than that," she repeated.

Dolly smiled.

"But tell me about yourself. I have lots of things I should like to talk to you about. And I have had a talk with . . ." Dolly did not know what to call Vronsky. She did not feel like calling him "Count" or "Alexey."

"With Alexey," said Anna. "I know. I'd like to ask you frankly what you think of me and of my life?"

"How can I tell you all of a sudden? I really don't know."

"Oh, but you must tell me. You see what my life is like. But don't forget that you're seeing us in summer, when you've come, and we're not alone. We arrived here in early spring. We lived quite alone and I don't wish for anything better. But just think of me living alone, without him, quite alone, and that is bound to happen. . . . I can see quite clearly that it is going to happen quite often, that he will spend half his time away from home," she said, getting up and sitting down closer to Dolly.

"Naturally," she interrupted Dolly, who was going to object, "naturally, I'm not going to keep him by force. In fact, I am not keeping him. There will be the races soon, his horses are running, he will go. I am very glad. But just think of me, try to imagine my position. . . . Still, it's no use talking about it, is it?" She smiled. "Well, what did he talk to you about?"

"He talked about something I wanted to talk to you about too, so that it is easy for me to be his advocate. I mean, whether it isn't possible . . . whether you ought not to try to . . ." Dolly hesitated for a moment, "to— to put things right—er—to improve your position. . . . You know what I think of it. . . . But all the same, if it is possible, you ought to get married. . . ."

"You mean a divorce?" said Anna. "The only woman who called on me in Petersburg was Betsy Tverskoy. You know her, don't you? *Au fond c'est la femme la plus dépravée qui existe.* She was Tushkevich's mistress, deceiving her husband in the most discreditable way. And she told me that she did not want to know me so long as my position was irregular. Don't think I am making any comparisons. . . . I know you, darling. But I could not help remembering . . . Well, so what did he say to you?" she repeated.

"He said that he suffers on your account and on his own. You may say it is egoism, but what legitimate and noble egoism! He wants first of all to legitimize his daughter and be your husband and have a right to you."

"What wife, what slave could be more of a slave than I am in this position?" Anna interrupted her gloomily.

"But what he wants most of all is that you should not suffer."

"That's impossible. Well?"

735

"And his most legitimate desire is that your children should have a name."

"What children?" said Anna, not looking at Dolly and screwing up her eyes.

"Annie and the others that will come. . . ."

"He needn't worry about that. I shall have no more children."

"How can you say that?"

"I won't have any because I don't wish to."

And in spite of her agitation Anna could not help smiling on observing the naïve expression of curiosity, amazement, and horror on Dolly's face.

"You see, the doctor told me after my illness . . ."

"Impossible!" said Dolly, opening her eyes wide.

To her it was one of those discoveries which lead to consequences and deductions so enormous that at first it is quite impossible to grasp it all, and one that one has to think a great deal about first.

This discovery, which suddenly explained to her all those families, hitherto incomprehensible to her, where there were only one or two children, aroused so many thoughts, reflections, and contradictory feelings in her that she did not know what to say and merely gazed at Anna in amazement with wide-open eyes. It was the very thing she had been dreaming of on the way to Anna's that morning, but now, learning that it was possible, she was horrified. She felt that it was too simple a solution of too complicated a problem.

"N'est-ce pas immoral?" was all she said after a pause.

"Why? You must remember that I have to choose between two alternatives: either to be pregnant, that is, to be ill, or to be the friend and comrade of my husband, well, practically my husband," Anna said in a deliberately casual and light-hearted tone.

"Well, yes, yes," said Dolly, hearing the same arguments she had used herself and not finding them as convincing as before.

"For you as well as for other people," Anna said as though guessing her thoughts, "there may still be some doubt about it, but for me . . . You must realize that I am not his wife: he loves me as long as he is in love with me. And what else have I got to keep his love? Not like this?"

736

And she stretched her white arms in front of her stomach.

With unusual rapidity, as happens in moments of great agitation, thoughts and memories crowded into Dolly's head. "I," she thought, "did nothing to attract Stiva. He left me for others, and the first woman for whom he betrayed me did not keep him by being always pretty and gay. He left her and took up a third. And can Anna really attract and keep Count Vronsky in this way? If it is *that* he looks for, he will find dresses and manners more attractive and gay. And however white and shapely her bare arms may be, however beautiful her full figure and her flushed face under that black hair, he will find other women still lovelier, as that disgusting, pathetic, and dear husband of mine does."

Dolly made no answer and only sighed. Her sigh, expressing disagreement, did not escape Anna, and she went on. She had a store of arguments so powerful that one could find no answer to them.

"You say it is wrong, but consider it carefully," she continued. "You forget my position. How can I want children? It's not the suffering I'm thinking of. I'm not afraid of it. But think who my children would be. Unhappy children bearing another man's name. By the very fact of their birth they would have to be ashamed of their mother, their father, their birth!"

"But that's exactly why you ought to get a divorce."

But Anna did not listen to her. She wanted to finish the arguments with which she had so often convinced herself.

"What has my reason been given to me for, if I am not to make use of it to avoid bringing unhappy human beings into the world?"

She glanced at Dolly and went on without waiting for a reply.

"I should always feel guilty toward those unhappy children," she said. "If they do not exist, they are not unhappy, and if they are unhappy, I alone should be to blame for it."

These were the very arguments Dolly had put to herself; but now she listened to them and could not understand them. "How can one be guilty toward beings that do not exist?" she thought. And suddenly she asked herself whether her darling Grisha would be better off if he had never existed. And this seemed so absurd and strange to her that she shook her head to dispel the jumble of insane thoughts that whirled in her brain.

"No, I don't know," she merely said with an expression of disgust on her face. "But it isn't right."

"It may not be right, but please don't forget what you are and what I am. Besides," added Anna, who in spite of the wealth of her arguments and the poverty of Dolly's could not help admitting that it was not right, "don't forget the chief thing—that I am not in the same position as you. For you the question is whether you want to have any more children, while for me it is a question whether I want to have them at all. And that is a great difference. You see, I can't possibly wish to have them in my position."

Dolly did not argue. She suddenly felt that the distance separating them had become very big and that there were questions on which they could never agree and about which it was better not to talk.

CHAPTER 24

"There is all the more reason, then, why you should regularize your position, if possible," said Dolly.

"Yes, if possible," said Anna in a voice that had become suddenly quite different, quiet, and sad.

"Why, isn't a divorce possible? I was told your husband had agreed."

"Dolly, I don't want to talk about it."

"Very well, we won't," Dolly hastened to say, noticing the expression of pain on Anna's face. "Only I see you take too gloomy a view of things."

"Me? Not a bit. I'm very happy and contented. You saw, *je fais des passions*. Veslovsky . . ."

"Well, to be quite frank, I did not like Veslovsky's manner," said Dolly, wishing to change the subject.

"Heavens, no! It amuses Alexey and nothing more. He's just a boy and he is entirely in my hands. I can do what I like with him. He's just like your Grisha. . . . Dolly," she suddenly changed the subject, "you say I take a gloomy view of things. You cannot understand.

It's too awful. I'm trying my best not to take any view at all."

"But I think one must. One must do all one can."

"But what can I do? Nothing. You say I should marry Alexey and that I'm not thinking about that. Not thinking about that!" she repeated, coloring. She rose, drew herself up, sighed deeply, and began pacing the room with her light step, stopping now and then. "I'm not thinking! Why, not a day, not an hour passes without my thinking about it and without reproaching myself for doing so. For my thoughts about it are enough to drive me mad. Drive me mad," she repeated. "When I think about it I cannot get to sleep without morphia. Very well, let's talk calmly. They say, divorce. Well, to begin with, *he* won't give it to me. *He* is now under the influence of the Countess Lydia Ivanovna."

Dolly, sitting upright in her chair, turned her head following Anna, as she walked up and down the room, with a pained expression of sympathy on her face.

"One must try," she said softly.

"All right, suppose I do. What does it mean?" she said, evidently expressing a thought she had considered a thousand times and knew by heart. "It means that I who hate him, though I consider myself guilty toward him—and I do think him magnanimous, mind—that I should humiliate myself and write to him. . . . Well, suppose I make the effort and do it. I shall either receive an insulting answer or his consent. Very well, I get his consent . . ." Anna had just at that moment reached the far end of the room and she paused there, doing something to the window curtain. "I get his consent, but my— my son? They won't give him to me, will they? He'll grow up despising me, in the house of his father whom I have left. Do understand that there are only two human beings I love—equally, I believe, but both more than myself—Seryozha and Alexey."

She came out to the middle of the room and stopped before Dolly, her hands pressed against her breast. In her white dressing gown her figure appeared particularly tall and broad. She bent her head and, her eyes glistening with tears, looked from under knitted brows at the small, thin, pitiful figure of Dolly in her patched dressing jacket and nightcap, trembling all over with emotion.

739

"I love these two beings only, and the one excludes the other. I cannot get them both together, and that is the only thing I want. And if I can't get it, nothing matters any more. Nothing, nothing. It will end some way or other and that is why I can't, why I don't like to speak of it. So please don't reproach me. Don't condemn me for anything. You in your innocence cannot understand what I suffer."

She came and sat down beside Dolly and peering into her face with a guilty expression, took her by the hand.

"What are you thinking? What are you thinking of me? Don't despise me. I don't deserve contempt. Yes, I am unhappy. If anyone is unhappy, it is I," she declared and, turning away from Dolly, burst into tears.

Left alone, Dolly said her prayers and got into bed. When she was talking to her, she felt deeply sorry for Anna, but now she could not bring herself to think about her. The thought of her own home and children rose in her mind with a new and peculiar charm, surrounded by a sort of new radiance. That world of hers now seemed so precious and sweet to her that she did not wish on any account to spend another day away from it, and she made up her mind to go back next day.

Meanwhile Anna returned to her boudoir, took a glass and poured into it several drops of medicine, the chief ingredient of which was morphine. She drank it and, sitting still for a few minutes, went into the bedroom, feeling calm and cheerful.

When she entered the bedroom, Vronsky looked closely at her. He tried to find some trace of the conversation which he knew she must have had with Dolly, since she had stayed so long in her room. But in her expression—restrained, agitated, and concealing something—he could find nothing except the beauty which, though familiar, still attracted him violently, and her consciousness of it and her desire that it should exert its influence on him. He did not want to ask her what they had been talking about, but he hoped that she would tell him something of her own accord. But all she said was:

"I'm glad you like Dolly. You do like her, don't you?"

"Why, I've known her a long time. I think she's very kind, *mais excessivement terre-à-terre.* All the same I was very glad to see her."

He took Anna's hand and looked questioningly into her eyes.

Misinterpreting that look, she smiled at him.

Next morning, in spite of the entreaties of her hosts, Dolly got ready to go back home. Levin's coachman, in his far-from-new coat and his hat resembling a postboy's, with his ill-matched horses and the old carriage with mended splashboards, drove up sullenly but bravely to the covered, sand-strewn portico.

Dolly did not feel quite at ease when saying good-by to the Princess Varvara and the men. Having spent a day together, both she and her hosts had a distinct feeling that they did not mix and that it was better for them not to associate. Anna alone felt sad. She knew that with Dolly's departure no one would stir up the feelings in her heart her visit had roused. To have those feelings disturbed was painful; but she knew all the same that they were the best part of her inner self and that that part of her was being rapidly smothered by the life she was leading.

When they had driven out into the open country Dolly experienced a delightful feeling of relief, and she was about to ask the two men how they had liked it at Vronsky's, when suddenly the coachman Philip spoke up himself.

"Rolling in money they may be, ma'am, but they only gave our horses three measures of oats. Before cockcrow it was all gone. For what's the good of three measures? A mere snack. And they charges only forty-five kopecks a measure at an inn. When we have visitors, we gives the horses as much as they'll eat."

"A close-fisted gentleman," the estate-office clerk put in.

"But did you like their horses?" asked Dolly.

"The horses are first class. And the food's good. But I can't say I liked it there. I don't know how you found it, ma'am," he concluded, turning his handsome, kindly face to her.

"I felt the same. Well, shall we be back by the evening?"

"We should, ma'am."

On her return home, Dolly found everyone well and particularly nice. She gave them an excited account of her journey, telling them how well she had been received, the luxury and good taste of the Vronskys, and their games, and would not let anyone say a word against them.

"One has to know Anna and Vronsky—and I've got to know him better now—to realize how nice they are and how touching," she said, speaking now with complete sincerity and quite forgetful of the vague feeling of dissatisfaction and awkwardness she had experienced there.

CHAPTER 25

Vronsky and Anna spent the whole of the summer and part of the autumn in the country in the same way and still taking no steps to get a divorce. They had agreed not to go away anywhere, but the longer they lived alone, especially in the autumn when they had no visitors, the more they realized that they would not be able to endure this sort of life and that it would have to be changed.

It would seem that their life was such that one could not wish for anything better: they had ample means, good health, a child, and both had occupations of their own. Anna devoted as much time to her appearance, even when they had no visitors, and she read a great deal, both novels and serious books that happened to be in fashion. She ordered all the books that received good notices in the foreign papers and periodicals they subscribed to and read them with the attention which is only possible in seclusion. In addition, she studied from books and technical journals all the subjects which were of practical interest to Vronsky, so that he often came straight to her with questions relating to agriculture, architecture, and sometimes even horse breeding or sport. He was amazed at her knowledge and her memory and at first used to doubt her and ask for confirmation, and she would then find what he asked for in some book and show him.

The equipment of the hospital also interested her. There she not only assisted, but arranged and planned many things herself. But her main preoccupation was still herself, herself insofar as she was dear to Vronsky, insofar as she could compensate him for all he had given up. Vronsky appreciated this desire not only to please him but also to serve him, which had become the sole aim of her life, but at the same time he fretted at the love meshes in which she tried to entangle him. As time went on, he saw himself more and more entangled in them, and the desire grew in him not to escape from them as much as to try whether they really interfered with his freedom. But for this ever-growing wish to be free and not to have a scene every time he had to go to town to a council meeting or to the races, Vronsky would have been perfectly satisfied with his life. The role he had chosen for himself, the role of a rich landowner, which in his opinion should form the nucleus of the Russian aristocracy, was not only wholly to his taste, but gave him an ever-increasing sense of satisfaction, now that he had lived like one for the last six months. And his affairs, which occupied and absorbed him more and more, were in excellent order. In spite of the enormous sums he had spent on the hospital, the agricultural machines, the cows imported from Switzerland, and many other things, he was convinced that he was not frittering away but increasing his fortune. Where it was a question of profit from the sale of woods, grain, wool, or the leasing of land, Vronsky was as hard as flint and knew how to hold out for his price. In large-scale farming, both on this and on his other estates, he kept to the simplest and safest methods and was extremely economical and calculating in matters of smaller importance. In spite of all the cunning and ingenuity of his German estate agent, who tried to persuade him into buying all sorts of things by drawing up estimates which seemed rather larger than necessary, but which, on closer examination, could be purchased much more cheaply and make an immediate profit, Vronsky did not let himself be persuaded by him. He would listen to what his agent had to say, question him, and agree to take his advice only when the things to be ordered from abroad or built were the latest, as yet unknown in Russia, and so likely to arouse surprise. Besides, he would agree to a big expenditure only when he had money to spare, and in spending the money, he went into the minutest details and insisted on getting the very best for his

743

money. It was therefore clear from the way he managed his business that he was not wasting but adding to his fortune.

In October there were the nobility elections in the Kashin province, where Vronsky, Sviazhsky, Koznyshev, and Oblonsky had their estates. Levin, too, had some land in that province.

Because of all sorts of circumstances and the persons who took part in them, these elections attracted public notice. They were widely discussed and great preparations were made for them. People in Moscow, Petersburg, and abroad, who had never attended any elections, were taking part in these.

Vronsky had long ago promised Sviazhsky to be present.

Before the elections Sviazhsky, who often visited Vozdvizhenskoye, called for Vronsky.

The day before, Vronsky and Anna had almost had a quarrel about the proposed trip. It was the dullest and dreariest time of the year and for that reason Vronsky, anticipating opposition, informed Anna of his proposed journey in a stern and cold tone he had never used to her before. But to his surprise Anna accepted the news quite calmly and only asked when he would be back. He looked at her attentively, not understanding this composure. She answered his look with a smile. He knew this ability of hers to withdraw within herself and he knew that that only happened when she had decided on some plan of action without telling him about it. He was afraid of that; but he was so anxious to avoid a scene that he pretended to believe, and to a certain extent genuinely did believe, in what he wished to believe—in her good sense.

"I hope you won't be bored."

"I hope so," said Anna. "I received a box of books from Gautier yesterday. No, I shan't be bored."

"She wants to adopt that tone, so much the better," he thought. "Otherwise it would be the usual thing again."

And so without forcing her to disclose what was in her mind, he left for the elections. It was the first time since the beginning of their life together that he had parted from her without coming to a full understanding. On the one hand, it worried him, but on the other hand he thought it was much better so. "At first there

744

will be, as now, something vague and repressed, and then she will get used to it. Anyway, I am quite willing to give her everything except my independence," he thought.

CHAPTER 26

In September Levin moved to Moscow for Kitty's confinement. He had already been living there for a whole month without doing anything, when Koznyshev, who had an estate in the Kashin province and who was taking a very active part in the forthcoming elections, was about to leave for the electoral district. He invited his brother to accompany him, for Levin, too, had a vote in the Seleznev district. Levin had besides some very important business to transact in Kashin in connection with a trusteeship and some money due from a mortgage to his sister who lived abroad.

Levin was still unable to make up his mind, but Kitty, who could see that he was bored in Moscow, advised him to go and, without saying anything to him, ordered the nobleman's uniform necessary for the occasion and costing eighty rubles. It was these eighty rubles paid for the uniform that chiefly decided him to go. He left for Kashin.

Levin had been five days in Kashin, going daily to the electoral meetings and seeing to his sister's affairs, which he was still unable to settle. All the marshals of nobility were busy with the elections and he could not get even the simple matter of the trusteeship settled. The other business—the money from the mortgage—also met with similar difficulties. After a great deal of trouble the injunction on the payment of money had been removed and the money was ready to be paid out; but the notary, a most obliging man, could not issue the check because it had to be signed by the president, and the president, who had not appointed a deputy, was engaged at the meetings. All these worries, the going from place to place, the conversations with good, kindly people who fully realized the unpleasantness of the petitioner's position, but who could do nothing about it, all this strain that produced no results aroused a painful feeling in

Levin, the sort of feeling one experiences in a dream when one tries to use physical force. He felt it frequently when talking to his very good-natured legal adviser, who was apparently doing his utmost, straining every nerve, to get Levin out of his difficulties. "Why not try this," he would say more than once, "and go to so-and-so and so-and-so?" And he outlined a whole plan how to circumvent the fatal obstacle which was at the root of all the trouble. But he invariably added: "They'll put you off all the same, but there's no harm in trying." And Levin tried and went and drove from place to place. They were all very kind and amiable, but it still turned out that the obstacle he was anxious to circumvent rose up again in the end and again barred his way. What Levin resented most of all was that he could not make out who he was fighting against and who could possibly derive any profit from the delay in his business. No one, not even his lawyer, seemed to know this. If Levin could have understood it as he understood why people have to stand in a queue at a railway booking office, he would not have felt so hurt and annoyed; but no one could explain to him the reason for the obstacles he encountered in his business transactions.

But Levin had changed a great deal since his marriage; he had become patient and if he did not understand why things had been arranged that way, he told himself that, not knowing all the facts, he could not judge, that possibly things had to be like that, and he tried not to become exasperated.

And now, being present at the elections and taking part in them, he also tried not to condemn, not to argue, but to do his utmost to understand what it was that good and honest people, whom he respected, were so serious and enthusiastic about. Since his marriage so many serious aspects of life had been revealed to him, which because of his thoughtless attitude to them he considered unimportant before, that he looked for and expected to find some serious significance in this election business also.

Koznyshev explained to him the meaning and importance of the social upheaval which the elections were supposed to bring about. The marshal of nobility for the province in whose hands the law placed so many important public functions—the board of trustees (the very

746

same that was giving Levin so much trouble now), the board supervising the disposal of enormous sums of money belonging to the nobility, secondary schools for boys and girls, military schools, elementary education according to the new law, and finally the rural councils— the marshal of nobility for the province, Snetkov, was a man of the old school, who had run through an enormous fortune. He was a kind man, honest after his own fashion, but quite unable to understand the requirements of the present age. He always took the side of the nobility in everything, he did all he could to oppose the spread of popular education, and gave a class character to the rural councils which should have such enormous importance. It was necessary to put in his place a fresh, up-to-date, practical man of affairs who was abreast of the times and could conduct the business of the nobility in such a way as to extract from the rights granted to it not as the nobilities, but as an element of the rural councils, all the advantages of self-government which could be obtained from them. In the wealthy province of Kashin, always ahead of the others in everything, such forces were now gathered that if matters were here managed in the right way, it could serve as a model for other provinces throughout Russia. That was why the present elections were of such great importance. It was proposed to elect in place of Snetkov either Sviazhsky or, better still, Nevedovsky, a former university professor, a remarkably intelligent man and a great friend of Koznyshev's.

The assembly was opened by the governor of the province, who in his speech to the nobles urged them to elect their officials impartially and according to merit and for the welfare of the country and expressed the hope that the Kashin noblemen would, as in previous elections, do their duty without fear or favor and justify their emperor's high confidence in them.

Having finished his speech, the governor left the hall, and the noblemen followed him noisily, animatedly, and some of them even rapturously, thronging around him while he was putting on his fur coat and speaking amicably to the marshal of nobility. Levin, who wished to investigate everything thoroughly and not miss anything, was standing there too in the crowd and heard the governor say: "Please tell Maria Ivanovna my wife is very sorry she

747

has to go to hospital." Then the noblemen gaily got their fur coats and went in a body to the cathedral.

In the cathedral Levin, with the others, raised his hand and repeated after the priest the words of the most solemn oath to perform everything the governor had hoped for. Church services always affected Levin and when he uttered the words "I kiss the cross," and glanced around at the crowd of young men and old men, repeating the same words, he felt deeply touched.

On the second and third day the assembly dealt with the business of the noblemen's finances and the girls' high school, which, Koznyshev explained, was of no importance whatever, and Levin, busy with his own affairs, did not bother about it. On the fourth day the audit of the provincial funds took place. It was here that the first clash between the new party and the old occurred. The committee which had been entrusted with the task of auditing the funds reported to the assembly that the sums were all correct. The marshal of the nobility rose and with tears in his eyes thanked the nobility for their confidence. The noblemen cheered him loudly and pressed his hand. But at that moment one nobleman who belonged to Koznyshev's party got up and said that he had been informed that the committee had not audited the funds because it considered that a verification would be an insult to the marshal. One of the members of the committee was indiscreet enough to confirm this. Then a small, very young-looking, but very venomous gentleman began saying that he thought the marshal of nobility would be pleased to give an account of the money and that the excessive tactfulness of the members of the committee was depriving him of that moral satisfaction. Thereupon the members of the committee withdrew their report and Koznyshev began to prove very logically that they had to decide whether the accounts had been audited or not and went on to explain the dilemma in which they found themselves in great detail. A long-winded speaker from the opposite party replied to him. Then Sviazhsky spoke and he was followed by the venomous gentleman again. The debate went on for a long time without any decision being reached.

Levin was surprised that they should go on arguing about it so long, especially as when he asked Koznyshev whether he thought the money had been misappropriated, his brother replied: "Oh no! The marshal is an honest man. But this old-fashioned way of patriarchal family management of the affairs of the nobility must be shaken."

On the fifth day the elections of the district marshals took place. It was rather a stormy day in some districts. In the Seleznev district Sviazhsky was elected unanimously without a ballot, and he gave a dinner party at his house that evening.

CHAPTER 27

On the sixth day the election of the marshal of the province was to take place. The large and small halls were full of noblemen in all sorts of uniforms. Many had come for the day only. Friends who had not seen each other for years—some from the Crimea, some from Petersburg, and some from abroad—met at the assembly. At the marshal's table, under the portrait of the emperor, the debate was in full swing.

Both in the large and the small halls the noblemen formed groups belonging to different camps, and from their suspicious and hostile glances, from the way they fell silent as soon as a stranger approached, and from the fact that some of them went whispering together into the farthest corridor, it could be gathered that each party had secrets it kept from the other. By their outward appearance the noblemen were sharply divided into two kinds: the old and the new. The old were mostly wearing either the old-fashioned buttoned-up uniforms of the nobility and carried swords and hats, or the naval, cavalry, or infantry uniform of the rank they had held when they left the army or the navy. The uniforms of the old noblemen were of an old-fashioned cut with puffs at the shoulders; they were clearly too small for them, short and tight in the waist, as though their wearer had grown out of them. The younger men wore unbuttoned uniforms, long in the waist and broad across the shoulders, and white waistcoats, or else uniforms with black collars embroidered with laurel leaves, the emblem of the Ministry of Justice. To the younger, too, belonged the court uniforms which here and there embellished the crowd.

But the division into old and young did not correspond to the division into parties. Some of the young, as Levin observed, belonged to the old party and, on the other hand, some of the oldest noblemen were exchanging whispered confidences with Sviazhsky and were quite obviously warm supporters of the new party.

Levin stood with his group in the small hall, where they were smoking and taking refreshments, listening intently to what was being said and vainly straining his mental powers in an effort to understand what was being said. Koznyshev was the center around which the rest were grouped. He was now listening to Sviazhsky and Khlyustov, the marshal of another district, who belonged to their party. Khlyustov was against going to Snetkov with representatives of his district in order to invite him to stand for re-election, while Sviazhsky was trying to persuade him to do so, and Koznyshev approved of this plan. Levin did not understand why the opposition party was anxious to ask the man whom they wanted to defeat to stand for re-election.

Oblonsky, who had just had something to eat and drink, went up to them in his Court chamberlain's uniform, wiping his mouth with his scented and bordered cambric handkerchief.

"We are taking up our position," he said, addressing Koznyshev and smoothing back his whiskers.

And after listening to the conversation, he expressed himself in favor of Sviazhsky's views.

"One district is enough and Sviazhsky obviously already belongs to the opposition," he said, and everyone but Levin seemed to understand him.

"Well, Kostya, you're getting a taste for it too, it seems," he said, addressing Levin and taking his arm.

Levin would have been glad to get a taste for it, but he could not understand what it was all about and, stepping aside, he told Oblonsky that he simply could not make out why they should be asking the marshal of the province to stand again.

"Oh, *sancta simplicitas*!" said Oblonsky and briefly and clearly explained the situation to Levin.

If, as in former elections, all the districts nominated the marshal of the province, he would have been elected without a ballot. They did not want that. Now, however, eight districts were willing to nominate him; if two refused to do so, Snetkov might decline to seek re-election. Then the old party might put up someone else, because that would upset all their calculations. But if only one district, namely, Sviazhsky's, did not nominate him, Snetkov would stand for re-election. Some of them might even vote for him and let him get a good number of votes so as to mislead the opposition party, and when their own candidate offered himself for election, some of the opposition might even vote for him.

Levin understood, but not entirely, and he was about to put some further questions, when suddenly everyone began talking and moving noisily toward the large hall.

"What's the matter? What? Who? A proxy? Who? What? Rejected? Not a proxy. Flerov not admitted. What if he is under trial? In that case they'd exclude anybody. It's disgraceful! The law!" Levin heard people shout on all sides, and with all the others, who were hurrying somewhere for fear of missing something, he moved toward the large hall and, hemmed in by the crowd of noblemen, approached the provincial marshal's table, at which the provincial marshal, Sviazhsky, and other party leaders were heatedly debating something.

CHAPTER 28

Levin was standing rather far off. One nobleman was breathing heavily and wheezing beside him and another was creaking with his thick-soled boots, and they prevented him from hearing distinctly. He could only hear from a distance the marshal's soft voice, then the shrill voice of a venomous gentleman and then Sviazhsky's voice. They were arguing, as far as Levin could make out, about the meaning of a particular clause of the law and the meaning of the words: "against whom proceedings are pending."

The crowd parted to make way for Koznyshev, who was approaching the table. Koznyshev, after waiting for the venomous gentleman to finish speaking, said that he thought that the best thing to do would be to look up the clause of the law and he asked the secretary to find it. The clause stated that in case of a difference of opinion a vote should be taken.

Koznyshev read out the clause and began explaining its meaning, but he was interrupted by a tall, stout, stooping landowner with a dyed mustache, wearing a tight uniform, the collar of which cut into the back of his neck. Going up to the table, he struck it with the ring on his finger and cried in a loud voice:

"A vote! Put it to the vote! No use talking! A vote!"

Several voices began speaking all at once and the tall landowner with the ring on his finger, getting more and more embittered, shouted louder and louder. But it was impossible to make out what he was saying.

He was merely repeating what Koznyshev had proposed, but he quite obviously hated Koznyshev and the whole of his party, and this feeling of hatred communicated itself to the members of his own party and evoked a similar, though more decently expressed, animosity from the opposing party. There was a great deal of shouting and for a minute or two everything was in confusion, so that the marshal had to call for order.

"Vote! Vote! Everyone who is a nobleman will understand. . . . We shed our blood. . . . The sovereign's confidence. . . . No auditing of the marshal's account! He's not a shop assistant! . . . That's not the point . . . to the vote, please! . . . Disgusting! . . ." furious, angry voices shouted on all sides. The looks and expressions on the faces were even more furious and angry. They expressed implacable hatred. Levin had no idea what it was all about and he was surprised at the passion with which the question whether Flerov's case should be put to the vote or not was discussed. He forgot, as Koznyshev explained to him afterward, the syllogism that it was necessary to get rid of the marshal for the public good, that to get rid of the marshal one had to obtain a majority of votes; that to obtain this majority of votes one had to give Flerov the right to vote, and that to secure Flerov's eligibility one had to elucidate the meaning of the clause of the law.

"You see, a single vote may be decisive and you have to be serious and consistent if you want to devote yourself to public service," Koznyshev concluded.

But Levin had forgotten that and it pained him to see these good men, whom he respected, in such a disagreeable, vicious state of excitement. To escape from this

752

painful sensation, he went, without waiting for the end of the debate, to a room where there was no one except the waiters at the buffet. At the sight of the busy waiters, wiping crockery and arranging plates and wineglasses, at the sight of their calm, eager faces, Levin felt an unexpected sense of relief, just as though he had come out of a stuffy room into the fresh air. He began pacing the room and looking at the waiters with pleasure. He particularly liked the way one waiter with gray whiskers, while showing his contempt for the young waiters who were making fun of him, was teaching them how to fold napkins. Levin was just about to start a conversation with the old waiter, when the secretary of the noblemen's board of trustees, an old man whose specialty it was to know all the noblemen of the province by name, distracted him.

"Please, Konstantin Dimitreyvich," he said, "your brother is looking for you. A vote is being taken."

Levin went into the large hall, was given a white ball, and approached the table behind his brother. Sviazhsky was standing at the table with a meaningful and ironical expression on his face, gathering his beard into his fist and smelling it. Koznyshev put his hand into the box, placed his ball somewhere, and making way for Levin, stopped beside him. Levin went up to the table, but having completely forgotten what the voting was about, turned to Koznyshev with the question, "Where am I to put it?" He spoke in a low voice, while the people around him were talking, so he hoped his question would not be heard. But just at that moment the talk stopped and his improper question was heard. Koznyshev frowned.

"That is something you have to decide for yourself," he said severely.

Several persons smiled. Levin blushed, hastily put his hand under the cloth and, as his ball was in his right hand, dropped it in on the right. Having dropped it, he remembered that he had to put his left hand in also, and he put it in, but it was too late, and, feeling still more confused, he beat a hasty retreat to the back of the room.

"One hundred and twenty-six for and ninety-eight against," rang out the voice of the secretary, who could not pronounce his *r*'s. There was laughter: a button and two nuts had been found in the ballot box. Flerov was allowed to vote and the new party scored its first success.

But the old party did not consider itself defeated. Levin heard Snetkov being asked to stand and saw a crowd of noblemen surrounding the marshal, who was saying something. Levin drew near. In reply to his supporters, Snetkov spoke of the confidence and affection the noblemen had shown him, which he did not deserve, for all he had done was to be loyal to the nobility, to whom he had devoted twelve years of service. Several times he repeated the words, "have done as much as I could, served faithfully and truly, appreciate and thank," then he stopped suddenly, his voice choked with tears, and went out of the room. Whether those tears were the result of the consciousness of the injustice done to him, or of his love for the nobility, or of the strained situation in which he was placed, feeling himself surrounded by enemies, his agitation certainly communicated itself: the majority of the noblemen were touched and Levin was overcome by a feeling of tenderness for Snetkov.

In the doorway the marshal of nobility of the province collided with Levin.

"Sorry," said Snetkov, as though speaking to a stranger, but, recognizing Levin, he smiled timidly.

Levin thought that he wanted to say something, but could not speak because he was too agitated. The expression of his face and his whole figure in his uniform with crosses and white trousers trimmed with gold lace, as he walked hurriedly past, reminded Levin of a hunted animal who sees that things are going badly with him. This expression on the marshal's face affected Levin particularly because the day before he had been at the marshal's house in connection with the matter of the trusteeship and had seen him in all the grandeur of a kindly family man. The big house with the old family furniture; the respectful old footmen, neither too clean nor smart, quite evidently old serfs who had remained with their master; his stout, good-natured wife in a lace cap and Turkish shawl, fondling her pretty little grandchild, her daughter's daughter; his fine-looking young son, a sixth-form schoolboy, who had just come home and who kissed his father's large hand in greeting; his host's impressive cordial words and gestures—all this had aroused an involuntary feeling of respect and sympathy in Levin the day before. Now the old man seemed touching and pathetic and he felt he had to say something pleasant to him.

"So you are going to be our marshal again," he said.

"Hardly," replied the marshal, looking round nervously. "I'm tired and I'm afraid old. There are younger and more worthy men than I. Let them have a go."

And the marshal of nobility disappeared through a side door.

The most solemn moment had arrived. The elections were about to begin. The leaders of both parties were counting on their fingers the white and black balls they might get.

The debate about Flerov had given the new party not only an additional vote but also a gain in time so that they could bring up three more noblemen who were prevented by the machinations of the old party from taking part in the elections. Snetkov's minions had made drunk two of them who had a weakness for drink and had carried off the uniform of the third one.

Having heard of this, the new party had managed during the debate about Flerov to send some of their men in a hired carriage to supply one of the noblemen with a uniform and to fetch one of their drunken supporters to the assembly.

"Brought one. Poured water over him. I think he'll do," said the landowner who had gone to fetch him.

"He isn't too drunk, is he? He won't fall down, will he?" said Sviazhsky, shaking his head.

"No, he's fine. I only hope they don't give him anything to drink here. I've told the barman not to let him have anything on any account."

CHAPTER 29

The narrow room in which they were drinking and smoking was full of noblemen. The excitement was growing and anxiety was noticeable on all faces. Especially excited were the leaders, who knew all the details and kept count of all the votes. These were the commanders of the impending battle. The rest, like the rank and file before a battle, though preparing for the fight, were for the time being looking for some distractions. Some of them were eating, either standing or sitting at the table; others walked about the long room, smoking cigarettes and talking to friends they had not seen for a long time.

Levin did not want to eat and he did not smoke; he did not wish to join his own set, that is to say, Koznyshev, Oblonsky, Sviazhsky, and the others, because Vronsky, wearing the uniform of an equerry, stood engaged in an animated conversation with them. Levin had caught sight of him at the elections the day before and had carefully avoided meeting him. He went up to the window and sat down, looking at the various groups and listening to what was being said around him. He felt sad particularly because he saw that everyone was animated, preoccupied, and busy, while he alone and a very ancient, mumbling, toothless old man in naval uniform who had sat down beside him showed no interest in what was going on around them and seemed to have nothing to do with it.

"He's such a rogue! I told him, but he doesn't care. And no wonder! He couldn't collect it in three years!" a short, round-shouldered landowner with pomaded hair hanging over the embroidered collar of his uniform was saying with loud emphasis, vigorously tapping with the heels of the new boots he had obviously put on for the elections. And casting a discontented look at Levin, the landowner turned his back sharply.

"Yes, it's a dirty business, say what you like," remarked a little man in a thin voice.

Next a whole crowd of landowners, surrounding a fat general, hastily approached Levin. The landowners were evidently looking for a place where they could talk without being overheard.

"How dare he say I gave orders to steal his trousers! He must have pawned them and spent the money on drink. I don't care a damn for him and his princely title! He has no right to say it—it's a swinish thing to do!"

"But, look here, they're basing their claim on the statute," someone was saying in another group. "The wife should have been registered as a noblewoman."

"To hell with the statute! I mean it. That's what noblemen are for. You must have confidence in them."

756

"Come along, sir. *Fine champagne.*"

Another crowd was following a nobleman about who was shouting loudly: it was one of the three men who had been made drunk.

"I've always advised Maria Ivanovna to let her estate because she will never make it pay," said a landowner with gray whiskers, who was wearing a colonel's uniform of a former general staff, in a pleasant voice. It was the same landowner Levin had met at Sviazhsky's. He recognized him at once. The landowner, too, recognized Levin and they shook hands.

"Very pleased to meet you. Indeed, sir, I remember you very well. We met last year at Sviazhsky's."

"Well, and how is your farm?"

"I'm afraid it's just the same, showing a loss," the landowner replied, stopping beside Levin, with a resigned smile but with an air of calm conviction that it could not possibly be otherwise. "And how did you come to be in our province?" he asked. "Have you come to take part in our *coup d'état?*" he went on, pronouncing the French words firmly but with a bad accent. "The whole of Russia is here: Court chamberlains and almost Cabinet ministers." He pointed to the stately figure of Oblonsky in white trousers and Court chamberlain's uniform, walking about with a general.

"I must confess I understand very little about these provincial elections," said Levin.

The landowner looked at him.

"What is there to understand? It's of no importance whatever. A decaying institution which continues in motion merely by the force of inertia. Have a good look: even the uniforms tell you that it's a gathering of justices of the peace, permanent officials and so on, but not of noblemen."

"Then why do you come?" asked Levin.

"Habit, I suppose, for one thing. Then one must keep up one's connections. A moral obligation of sorts. And then, to tell the truth, there's a private reason. My son-in-law wants to stand as a permanent member: they are not well off and I have to lend a helping hand. Now, why do such gentlemen come?" he said, pointing to the venomous gentleman, who had made a speech at the provincial marshal's table.

"That's the new generation of nobility."

"It may be new, but it has nothing to do with the nobility. They are just landowners, while we are country squires. As noblemen they are merely committing suicide."

"But you say it's an obsolete institution."

"It may be obsolete, but it must still be treated with a little more respect. Take Snetkov, for instance. Whether we are any good or not, the fact remains that we've been growing for a thousand years. Now, suppose you want to lay out a garden in front of your house and a century-old tree is growing on that spot. . . . It may be old and gnarled, yet you won't cut it down for the sake of a few flower beds. You will lay out your beds so as to make use of the old tree. It can't be grown in a year," he said guardedly and immediately changed the subject. "Well, and how is your farming going?"

"Not too good. Five per cent."

"Yes, but you don't reckon your own work. You too are worth something, aren't you? Now, take me. I used to get three thousand a year in the service before I took up farming. Now I work harder than I did as a civil servant and, like you, only get five per cent, if I'm lucky, that is. But my own labor goes for nothing."

"Then why do you do it? It's a clear loss, isn't it?"

"Well, you just go on. What else is one to do? Habit, and also you somehow know it has to go on like that. I'll tell you something more," he went on, leaning his elbow on the window and warming to his theme. "My son doesn't want to be a farmer. He's going to be a scholar or a scientist. So there won't be anyone to carry on after me. But I still carry on. This year I've planted an orchard, you see."

"Yes, yes," said Levin, "that's true. I always feel that I'm getting no profit from my farming, but I carry on. . . . You feel a sort of duty to the land."

"Now, let me tell you something else," the landowner went on. "A neighbor of mine, a merchant, came to see me. I took him around the farm and garden. 'Well, sir,' he said to me, 'everything seems to be all right, but your garden is neglected.' But, as a matter of fact it's perfectly in order. 'Now, if I were you,' my neighbor went on, 'I'd cut down those lime trees. Only you must do it when the sap is rising. You must have about a thousand lime trees here and each tree will produce two fine printing boards. And today such boards fetch a good price, and, besides, you'd have a lot of timber, too.' "

"Yes, and with the money he'd buy cattle or some land for a mere song and lease it to the peasants," Levin concluded with a smile, having evidently come across such calculations before. "And he'll make a fortune, while you and I may be thankful if we can keep what we have and leave it to our children."

"I understand you are married," said the landowner.

"Yes," replied Levin with proud satisfaction. "It is strange, though," he went on, "how we live without worrying what is going to happen to us, just as though, like the vestals of old, we were appointed to guard some sacred fire."

The landowner grinned under his white mustache.

"There are also some among us, like our friend Sviazhsky or Count Vronsky, who has just settled here, who'd like to treat agriculture like an industry, but so far this has only resulted in loss of capital."

"But why don't we do like the merchants?" asked Levin, returning to the idea that had struck him. "Why don't we cut down our parks and provide boards for the printers?"

"Why, as you've said, to guard the fire! The other thing is not the sort of thing a nobleman would do. Our business is not here at the elections but in our own homes. There's a class instinct, too, which tells us what to do and what not to do. It's the same with the peasants. I've noticed it again and again: a good peasant tries to get hold of as much land as he can. However bad the soil, he keeps on ploughing. He gets no profit, either. It's a dead loss to him."

"Yes, just like us," said Levin. "Very, very glad to have met you," he added, seeing Sviazhsky approaching.

"We two have met for the first time since we were at your house," said the landowner, "and we've had a good chat."

"Abusing the new order, I suppose?" said Sviazhsky with a smile.

"We plead guilty."

"Got it off our chests."

759

CHAPTER 30

Sviazhsky took Levin's arm and went back to his own group with him.

This time it was no longer possible to avoid Vronsky. He was standing with Oblonsky and Koznyshev, looking straight at Levin as he came up.

"Very glad to meet you," he said, holding out his hand to Levin. "I believe I had the pleasure of meeting you at—er—the Princess Shcherbatsky's."

"Yes, I remember our meeting very well," said Levin and, flushing crimson, at once turned away and began talking to his brother.

Smiling faintly, Vronsky went on talking to Sviazhsky, apparently not having the slightest desire to enter into a conversation with Levin; but Levin, while talking to his brother, kept looking round at Vronsky, trying to think of something to say to him to make up for his rudeness.

"What's holding up things now?" asked Levin, glancing at Sviazhsky and Vronsky.

"Snetkov," replied Sviazhsky. "He must either refuse or consent to stand."

"Well, has he consented or not?"

"That's the trouble, neither the one nor the other," said Vronsky.

"And if he refuses, who will stand then?" asked Levin, casting furtive glances at Vronsky.

"Anyone who likes," said Sviazhsky.

"Will you?" asked Levin.

"Certainly not," said Sviazhsky, casting a frightened glance at the venomous gentleman who was standing beside Koznyshev.

"Who will then? Nevedovsky?" said Levin, feeling that things were getting a little too deep for him.

But this was still worse. Nevedovsky and Sviazhsky were the two prospective candidates.

"Me? Most certainly not!" replied the venomous gentleman.

It was Nevedovsky himself. Sviazhsky introduced him to Levin.

"So it's got you too, has it?" said Oblonsky, with a wink at Vronsky. "It's like the races. Might take a bet on the winner."

"Yes, it certainly gets you all right," said Vronsky. "And having started it, one wants to get it finished. A fight!" he said, frowning and clenching his powerful jaws.

"What a businesslike fellow Sviazhsky is! He puts things so clearly."

"Oh yes," said Vronsky, absently.

There was a pause, during which Vronsky, since he had to look at something, looked at Levin, at his feet, his uniform, and then his face, and noticing Levin's gloomy eyes fixed on him, remarked just for the sake of saying something:

"How is it that you, who always live in the country, are not a justice of the peace? You're not in the uniform of a justice."

"It's because I consider that kind of court an idiotic institution," Levin, who had all the time been waiting for an opportunity to speak to Vronsky to make up for his rudeness at their first meeting, replied sullenly.

"I'm afraid I don't think so—on the contrary," said Vronsky with calm surprise.

"It's just an amusing pastime," Levin interrupted him. "We don't need justices of the peace. I haven't had a single case in eight years. And when I did have one, the decision was all wrong. The nearest justice of the peace is thirty miles from my place. To settle a matter worth two rubles, I have to send an attorney who costs me fifteen."

And he related how a peasant stole some flour from a miller and how when the miller told him about it, the peasant sued him for slander. All this was beside the point and foolish, and Levin himself was aware of it even while he spoke.

"Oh, he's such an eccentric fellow!" said Oblonsky with his most almond-oil smile. "But we'd better go. I believe the balloting has started."

And they separated.

"I can't understand," said Koznyshev, who had observed his brother's clumsy performance, "I can't understand how one can be so entirely devoid of political tact. That is what we Russians lack. The marshal of the province is our opponent and you are *ami cochon* with him and ask him to stand. And Count Vronsky . . . I don't suppose I'd choose him for a friend—he invited me to dinner and I shan't go—but he's one of us, so why make an enemy of him? Then you ask Nevedovsky if he's going to stand. It's not the way to do things."

"Oh, I don't understand anything about it," Levin replied gloomily. "And, anyway, it's all nonsense."

"You say it's all nonsense, but as soon as you begin to do something about it, you make a mess of it."

Levin made no answer and they went into the large hall together.

The marshal of the province, though he could feel in the air the plot that was being hatched against him and though he had not been asked to stand, had still decided to offer himself as a candidate. A hush fell over the room and the secretary announced in a loud voice that Mikhail Stepanovich Snetkov, captain of the Horse Guards, was nominated for the post of marshal of the province and that the balloting would now be taken.

The district marshals, carrying little plates on which were ballot balls, went from their tables to the table of the marshal of the province, and the balloting began.

"Put it on the right," Oblonsky whispered to Levin, when he with his brother followed the marshal to the table. But Levin had forgotten the plan which had been explained to him and was afraid that Oblonsky had made a mistake when he said "on the right." For was not Snetkov their enemy? As he walked up to the box, he held the ball in his right hand, but thinking that it was a mistake, he put it in his left hand just as he reached the box and evidently placed it on the left. An expert, who was standing beside the box and who could tell by the mere movement of the elbow where every ball was put, pulled a wry face. There was no need for him to exercise his sagacity this time.

Everything became silent again and the counting of the balls could be heard. Then a single voice announced the number of the votes cast for and against.

The marshal had received a considerable majority of votes. Everyone began talking and they all rushed headlong toward the door. Snetkov came in and the noblemen surrounded him, offering their congratulations.

"Well, is it all over now?" Levin asked Koznyshev.

"It's only beginning," Sviazhsky smilingly replied for

Koznyshev. "The marshal's opponent may get more votes."

Levin had again forgotten about that. He only remembered now that there was some subtle point about this, but he found it too tedious to remember what it was. He felt depressed and he was anxious to get away from the crowd.

As no one was paying any attention to him and as no one seemed to need him, he went quietly to the small refreshment room and felt greatly relieved to see the waiters again. The old waiter asked him if he would like something to eat and Levin said he would. Having eaten a cutlet and haricot beans and talked to the waiter about his former masters, Levin, not wishing to return to the large hall where he did not feel at ease, went up to the gallery.

The gallery was full of fashionably dressed women, leaning over the balustrade and trying not to miss a single word of what was being said below. Elegantly dressed lawyers, bespectacled high-school teachers, and army officers sat or stood beside the women. Everywhere people were talking about the elections, about how harassed the marshal of nobility looked and how wonderful the debates had been; in one group Levin heard them praising his brother.

"I'm so glad to have heard Koznyshev," one woman was saying to a lawyer. "It was worth while going hungry. Wonderful! So clear and audible! No one speaks like that in your court, except perhaps Meidel, and he's far less eloquent!"

Finding a vacant place at the balustrade, Levin leaned over and began to look and listen.

All the noblemen were sitting behind little partitions according to their respective districts. In the middle of the hall stood a man in uniform, announcing in a loud, shrill voice:

"Captain of Cavalry Yevgeny Ivanovich Apukhtin is invited to stand for election as marshal of the province!"

There was dead silence and then a feeble old man's voice was heard:

"Declines!"

"Civil Servant of Seventh Rank Peter Petrovich Bohl is invited to stand for election as marshal of the province!"

"Declines!" shouted a youthful, high-pitched voice.

A similar announcement was made, and again followed by "Declines." This went on for a quarter of an hour. Leaning over the balustrade, Levin looked and listened. At first he was surprised and wanted to know what it was all about. Then, satisfying himself that he could never understand it, he felt bored. Then, when he remembered the agitation and hatred he had seen on all the faces, he felt sad: he decided to leave and went downstairs. Passing through the corridor behind the gallery, he met a dejected-looking schoolboy with bloodshot eyes walking up and down. On the stairs he met a couple: a woman, who was running up swiftly in her high-heeled shoes, and the nimble-footed assistant public prosecutor.

"I told you you'd be in time," said the assistant public prosecutor just as Levin stepped aside to let the woman pass.

Levin was already going down the stairs leading to the front door and was getting his cloakroom ticket out of his waistcoat pocket, when the secretary caught him. "Please, sir, they are voting!"

Nevedovsky, who had so emphatically declined to stand, was being balloted for.

Levin went up to the door of the hall; it was locked. The secretary knocked, the door was opened and two red-faced landowners darted out past Levin.

"Can't stand it any more," one of the red-faced landowners said.

Then the head of the marshal of the province was thrust out of the door. Exhaustion and fear made his face look dreadful.

"I told you not to let anyone out!" he shouted to the doorkeeper.

"I was letting someone in, sir!"

"Oh, Lord!" said the marshal of the province and, sighing deeply and dragging his weary legs in their white trousers with a bowed head, he made his way to the table in the center of the room.

Nevedovsky was elected by a majority, as had been expected, and he was now the marshal of the province. Many people looked cheerful, many looked happy and contented, many were in ecstasy, and many were discontented and unhappy. The old marshal of the province was in despair and could not conceal it. When Nevedov-sky left the hall, he was surrounded by a crowd of people who followed him enthusiastically as they had followed the governor of the province on the first day when he opened the elections and as they had followed Snetkov when he had been elected.

CHAPTER 31

The newly elected marshal of the province and many members of the triumphant new party dined that evening with Vronsky.

Vronsky had come to the elections because he felt bored in the country, because he had to assert his rights to freedom before Anna, and because he wished to repay Sviazhsky by supporting him at these elections for all the trouble he had taken to get Vronsky elected to the rural council, and, most of all, because he had decided to perform strictly all the duties of the position of a landowner and nobleman that he had assumed. He had never expected that the elections would interest him and thrill him so much, or that he could be so good at that kind of thing. He was quite a new man among the local nobility, but he was obviously a great success and he was not mistaken in thinking that he had already gained some influence among them. This influence was furthered by his wealth, his noble descent, his fine house in the town lent him by his old friend Shirkov, a financier who had founded a flourishing bank in Kashin; by the excellent chef Vronsky had brought from the country; by his friendship with the governor, who had been a former comrade and even protégé of Vronsky's; and most of all by the simple manner in which he treated all alike and which soon made the majority of the noblemen change their opinion about his supposed pride. He felt himself that with the exception of the crazy fellow who was married to Kitty Shcherbatsky and who with rabid animosity had talked a lot of quite pointless nonsense without rhyme or reason, every nobleman whose acquaintance he had made had become his stanch supporter. He saw clearly, and other people recognized it too, that he had contributed a great deal to Nevedovsky's success. And now at his own table, celebrating Nevedovsky's election, he experienced a pleasant feeling of triumph over the success of his candidate. The elections themselves had made such an impression on him that he decided to stand himself in three years' time, if he and Anna were married by then, just as when winning a prize at the races he felt like taking his jockey's place himself next time.

Now they were celebrating the jockey's victory. Vronsky sat at the head of the table; on his right was the young governor, a general of the emperor's suite. All of them regarded the governor as the master of the province, who had solemnly opened the elections, who had made a speech, and who, as Vronsky noticed, aroused a feeling of respect and even servility in those present. But for Vronsky he was just "little Miss Maslov"—such was his nickname in the Corps of Pages—who felt abashed before him and whom he tried to *mettre à son aise.* On his left sat Nevedovsky with his youthful, unflinching, venomous face. With him Vronsky was simple and respectful.

Sviazhsky bore his defeat cheerfully. It was not really a defeat for him, as he said himself, turning, champagne glass in hand, to Nevedovsky: they could not have found a better representative of the new course which the nobility ought to follow. That was why, he declared, every honest person was on the side of today's success and was celebrating it.

Oblonsky too was pleased that he had spent his time so agreeably and that everyone was satisfied. At the excellent dinner the different incidents of the elections were discussed. Sviazhsky gave a comic rendering of the marshal's tearful speech and, turning to Nevedovsky, observed that His Excellency would have to choose another, more complex, way of auditing the accounts than tears. Another witty gentleman told them how footmen in knee breeches and stockings had been engaged for the marshal's ball and that now they would have to be sent back unless, of course, the new marshal of the province decided to give a ball with footmen in knee breeches and stockings.

During the dinner they kept addressing Nevedovsky as "our marshal of the province" and as "Your Excellency."

This was uttered with the same pleasure as a newly married woman is addressed by her married name. Nevedovsky pretended to be not only indifferent to this title, but to despise it, but it was quite clear that he felt happy and that he had to restrain himself in order not to betray his delight, for that would have accorded ill with the new liberal environment in which they found themselves.

During the dinner several telegrams were dispatched to persons interested in the outcome of the elections. Oblonsky, who was enjoying himself hugely, sent one to Dolly. "Nevedovsky," he wired, "elected by majority of twelve. Congratulations. Spread the news." He dictated it aloud, saying: "Must make them feel happy too." But on receiving the telegram, Dolly only sighed over the ruble it cost to send and guessed that it must have been sent at the end of a dinner. She knew that Stiva had a weakness at the end of a dinner party to *faire jouer le télégraph.*

Everything, including the excellent dinner and the wines, which did not come from Russian merchants, but were imported ready-bottled from abroad, was extremely distinguished, simple, and gay. The party of twenty was selected by Sviazhsky from among the new public men holding the same liberal views as he, and they were both witty and well bred. Toasts were drunk, also half in jest, to the new marshal of the province, the governor, the bank director and "our kind host."

Vronsky was satisfied. He never expected to find such charming good form in the provinces.

When the dinner was over, things became gayer still. The governor invited Vronsky to a concert in aid of "our Serbian brothers," arranged by his wife, who wished to make his acquaintance.

"There will be a ball afterward and you'll see our local beauty. She's really quite remarkable."

"Not in my line," Vronsky replied, who liked that English expression, but he smiled and promised to come.

Before they rose from the table and had begun smoking, Vronsky's valet came up to him with a letter on a salver.

"From Vozdvizhenskoye by special messenger, sir," he said with a significant look.

"Extraordinary how like the assistant public prosecutor Sventitsky he is!" remarked one of the guests in French, referring to the valet, while Vronsky, frowning, was reading the letter.

The letter was from Anna. Even before he read it he knew its contents. Thinking that the elections would end in five days, he had promised to return on Friday. It was now Saturday and he knew that the letter would be full of reproaches that he had not returned in time. The letter he had sent off the evening before had probably not reached her yet.

The letter was just what he had expected, but its form was unexpected and particularly unpleasant. "Annie is very ill. The doctor says it may be pneumonia. I lose my head when alone. The Princess Varvara is more of a hindrance than a help. I expected you the day before yesterday and yesterday and am now sending to find out where you are and what you are doing. I wanted to come myself, but changed my mind, knowing you would not like it. Send me some reply so that I should know what to do."

The child was ill and she had thought of coming herself. His daughter was ill, and this hostile tone.

Vronsky could not help being struck by the contrast between the innocent merriment of the elections and the somber, grim love to which he had to return. But he had to go and he set off for home by the first train that night.

CHAPTER 32

Before Vronsky's departure for the elections, Anna, realizing that the scenes they had every time he went away could only estrange instead of bind him to her, made up her mind to make every possible effort to bear the separation from him calmly. But she was hurt by the cold, severe look he gave her when he came to tell her he was going, and her peace of mind was destroyed even before he had gone.

Later on, reflecting in solitude about that look, which expressed his right to freedom, she came, as always, to the same conclusion—the consciousness of her own humiliating position. "He has the right to go when and where he likes. Not only to go away, but to leave me.

He has all the rights, I have none. But knowing that, he shouldn't have done it. . . . But what has he done? He looked at me coldly, severely. Of course, this is something vague and intangible, but it never happened before, and that look means a lot," she thought. "That look shows that he is beginning to fall out of love with me."

And though she was quite sure that he was beginning to fall out of love with her, there was nothing she could do about it. She could not change her relations to him in any way. Just as before, she could hold him only by her love and attractiveness. And just as before, she could stifle the terrible thought of what would happen if he ceased to love her by trying to keep herself occupied by day and by taking morphine at night. True, there was something else she could do: not hold him—she wanted nothing else but his love to do that—but be closely bound up to him, be in such a position that he could not abandon her. That meant divorce and marriage. And she began to desire it and made up her mind to agree the first time he or Stiva should broach the subject to her.

Absorbed in such thoughts, she spent the five days he was away, the five days he was to be away, at the elections.

Walks, talks with the Princess Varvara, visits to the hospital, and, above all, reading, reading one book after another, filled her time. But on the sixth day, when the coachman returned without him, she felt that she would no longer be able to keep in check the thought of him and of what he was doing there. It was just then that her little daughter fell ill. Anna decided to nurse the baby, but even that did not divert her thoughts, particularly as the illness was not dangerous. However hard she tried, she could not bring herself to love the little girl, and she just could not pretend to love her. Toward the evening of that day, Anna, left alone, became so terrified on his account that she decided to go to town, but, thinking it over carefully, she wrote that contradictory letter which Vronsky received and, without reading it over, sent it off by special messenger. The next morning she got his letter and regretted her own. She anticipated with horror a repetition of the severe look he had given her when leaving, particularly when he found out that the little girl was not dangerously ill at all. But she was glad

769

she had written. Though Anna admitted to herself that he was tired of her, that he regretted giving up his freedom to return to her, she was glad he was coming. Let him be tired of her, but let him be there with her so that she could see him, so that she could know his every movement.

She was sitting in the drawing room, under a lamp, with a new volume of Taine, reading and listening to the howling of the wind outside, expecting the carriage to arrive every minute. Several times she fancied she heard the sound of wheels, but she was mistaken. At last she heard not only the sound of wheels, but also the coachman's shout and a muffled noise in the covered portico. Even the Princess Varvara, who was playing patience, confirmed it. Anna got up, flushing, but instead of going downstairs, as she had done twice already, she stopped dead. All of a sudden she felt ashamed of her deception, but she was still more afraid of how he would greet her. The feeling of injury had passed; all she feared now was the expression of his displeasure. She remembered that her daughter had been perfectly well since the day before. She was even annoyed with her for having got better as soon as the letter had been sent. Then she remembered that he was downstairs, all of him, his hands, his eyes. And forgetting everything, ran joyfully to meet him.

"Well, how's Annie?" he asked timidly, looking up at Anna as she ran down to him.

He was sitting on a chair and a footman was pulling off his warm boots.

"Oh, she's better."

"And you?" he said, giving himself a shake.

She took his hand in both hers and drew it to her waist, not taking her eyes off him.

"Well, I'm very glad," he said, looking her over coldly, her hair and her dress, which he knew she had put on for him.

He liked it all, but he had liked it so many times before! And the severe, stony expression she dreaded so much settled on his face.

"Well, I'm very glad. And are you well?" he said, wiping his damp beard with a handkerchief and kissing her hand.

"It doesn't matter," she thought, "so long as he is

here, for when he is here, he cannot, he dare not, fail to love me."

The evening passed happily and cheerfully in the company of the Princess Varvara, who complained to him that in his absence Anna had been taking morphia.

"I'm sorry, but I'm afraid I couldn't help it. . . . I couldn't sleep. . . . My thoughts kept me awake. I never take it when he is here. Hardly ever."

He told them about the elections and Anna knew how to lead him on by her questions to what pleased him most—his own success. She told him everything that interested him at home. And her news was all of a most cheerful nature.

But late at night, when they were alone, Anna, seeing that she had regained her possession of him, was anxious to erase the painful impression left by the look he had given her for her letter.

"Confess," she said, "you were annoyed to receive my letter. You didn't believe me, did you?"

The moment she said it she realized that, however lovingly disposed he might be to her, he had not forgiven her that.

"Yes," he said. "It was such a strange letter, wasn't it? Annie ill, then you wished to come yourself."

"That was all true."

"I don't doubt it."

"Yes, you do. I can see you're not pleased."

"Not for one moment. If I am displeased—and I don't deny it—it's because you don't apparently wish to admit that there are duties—"

"Duties to go to a concert. . . ."

"Oh, don't let's talk about it," he said.

"Why not talk about it?" she said.

"All I want to say is that there may be some unavoidable business. Now, for instance, I shall have to go to Moscow about the house. . . . Oh, Anna, why are you so irritable? Don't you know that I can't live without you?"

"If that is so," said Anna in a suddenly changed voice, "it can only mean that you are tired of this sort of life. Yes, you'll come for a day and go away again, as men usually do."

"Anna, that is cruel. I'm ready to give my whole life . . ."

But she was not listening to him.

"If you go to Moscow, I'll come too. I won't stay here. Either we must separate or live together."

"You know very well that that's the one thing I want. But for that . . ."

"I must get a divorce? I'll write to him. I can see I cannot live like this. . . . But I'm coming to Moscow with you."

"You speak as though you were threatening me," said Vronsky with a smile. "Why, I wish for nothing better than to be always with you."

But as he spoke those tender words, the look that flashed in his eyes was not only cold—it was the vicious look of a persecuted and exasperated man.

She saw that look and rightly guessed its meaning.

"If that is so," his look said, "then it's a disaster!"

It was a momentary impression, but she never forgot it.

Anna wrote to her husband asking him for a divorce, and at the end of November, having taken leave of the Princess Varvara, who had to go to Petersburg, she moved with Vronsky to Moscow. Expecting every day a reply from Karenin, to be followed by a divorce, they now set up house together like a married couple.

Part Seven

✒

CHAPTER 1

The Levins had been over two months in Moscow. The date had long passed on which, according to the most reliable calculations of people conversant with such matters, Kitty should have been confined, but she had still not given birth to the child and there was nothing to show that she was now nearer her time than she had been two months before. The doctor, the midwife, Dolly, her mother, and especially Levin, who could not think of the impending event without dread, were beginning to feel impatient and anxious; Kitty alone felt perfectly happy and calm.

She became distinctly conscious now of the birth in her of a new feeling of love for the coming, and for her to some extent already existing, child, and she gave herself up to this feeling with delight. The child was no longer a part of her, but sometimes lived its own independent life. Sometimes this gave her pain, but at the same time this strange new joy made her wish to laugh.

Everyone she loved was with her, and they were all so kind to her, they took such care of her, she saw everything that was going on around her in so pleasant a light that, if she had not known and felt that it must soon come to an end, she could not have wished for a better and pleasanter life. The only thing that marred the charm of this life was that her husband was not as she loved him best and as he used to be in the country.

She loved his quiet, friendly, hospitable manner in the country. In town he always seemed restless and on his guard, as though afraid lest anyone should offend him or, still worse, her. In the country, feeling himself in the right place, he was never in a hurry and was never idle. In town he was constantly in a hurry, as though afraid to miss something, and yet he had nothing to do. She felt sorry for him. Other people, she knew, did not find him pathetic. On the contrary, when Kitty observed him in society, as one sometimes observes a person one loves, trying to see him as if he were a stranger, so as to find out the impression he makes on others, she saw with a twinge of jealousy that far from being pathetic, he was extremely attractive with his rectitude, his somewhat old-fashioned, bashful politeness to women, his powerful figure, and his unusually, as she thought, expressive face. But she saw him from within and not from without; she saw that in town he was not his real self; otherwise she could not explain his condition to herself. Sometimes she reproached him in her heart that he found it difficult to arrange his life here so that he should be satisfied with it.

And, indeed, what could he do? He did not care for cards. He did not go to the club. To go about with men about town like Oblonsky—she knew now what that meant: it meant drinking and then driving somewhere afterward. She could not think without horror of the places men drove to in such cases. Go into society? But she knew that to do that one had to find pleasure in the company of young women, and she could hardly wish that. To stay at home with her mother and sisters? But agreeable and amusing as she found these everlasting conversations between her sisters—about the Alines and the Nadines, as the old prince called them—she knew that he would find them boring. What then was there left for him to do? Go on working at his book? He did try to do so and at first had gone to the library to take notes and do some research for his book; but, as he kept telling her, the more he did nothing, the less time he seemed to have. Besides, he complained to her that he had talked so much about his book here that all his ideas had become confused and he had lost interest in them.

The only advantage of this life was that in town they never quarreled. Whether the conditions in town were different or whether they had both grown more careful and reasonable in that respect, in Moscow they never had any quarrels arising from jealousy, which they had so feared when they moved to town.

In this respect, an event occurred of the utmost importance to both of them, namely Kitty's meeting with Vronsky.

The old Princess Maria Borisovna, Kitty's godmother, who had always been very fond of her, was very anxious to see her. Kitty was not going out anywhere because of her condition, but she went with her father to see the old lady, and there she met Vronsky.

The only thing Kitty could reproach herself with over that meeting was that the moment she recognized Vronsky's once so familiar figure in his civilian clothes her breath failed her, her blood rushed to her heart, and her face—she felt it—colored deeply. But that only lasted a few seconds. Before her father, who purposely began talking to Vronsky in a loud voice, had finished what he was saying, she was quite able to look Vronsky in the face, to talk to him, if need be, as naturally as she talked to Maria Borisovna and, above all, so that her slightest intonation and smile could have been approved by her husband, whose unseen presence she seemed to feel about her at that moment.

She exchanged a few words with him, even smiled calmly at a joke he made about the elections, which he called "our parliament." (She had to smile in order to show that she saw the joke.) But she at once turned to Princess Maria Borisovna and did not look around at him again until he got up to take his leave; she did look at him then, but only because it would be impolite not to look at a man when he is saying good-by.

She was grateful to her father for not saying anything to her about this meeting with Vronsky; but she could see from his special tenderness after the visit, during their usual stroll, that he was pleased with her. She was pleased with herself. She had never expected to find the strength to keep somewhere deep inside her all the memories of her former feeling for Vronsky and not only seem quite calm and indifferent in his presence, but really be so.

Levin flushed much more than she had when she told him of meeting Vronsky at the Princess Maria Borisovna's. It was very hard for her to tell him that, but it was even harder to go on telling him all the details of the

775

meeting, as he did not ask any questions but only looked at her with a frown.

"I'm very sorry you were not there," she said. "I mean not that you were not in the same room, for I—I shouldn't have been so natural with you there. . . . I'm blushing much more now—much, much more," she said, blushing till tears started to her eyes. "But I'm sorry you could not have watched us through the keyhole."

Her truthful eyes told Levin that she was satisfied with herself and, though she was blushing, he felt composed at once and began questioning her, which was just what she wanted. When he heard it all, down to the fact that it was only at the first moment that she could not help blushing but that afterward she felt as natural and at ease with him as with anyone she might happen to meet, Levin cheered up completely and said that he was very glad it had happened and that now he would not act as foolishly as he had done at the elections, but would try to be as friendly as possible with Vronsky when he next met him.

"It's so painful to think that there exists a man who is almost my enemy and whom I hate to meet," said Levin. "I'm very, very glad."

CHAPTER 2

"Please call on the Bohls," said Kitty to her husband, when he came into her room at eleven o'clock before going out. "I know you are dining at the club. Father put your name down. But what are you going to do this morning?"

"Only going to see Katavasov," replied Levin.

"Why so early?"

"He promised to introduce me to Metrov. I'd like to have a talk to him about my work. He's a well-known Petersburg scholar."

"Oh yes, wasn't it an article of his you were praising so? Well, and then?" Kitty asked.

"I may go around to the courts to see about my sister's business."

"And the concert?" she asked.

"Oh, what's the good of going alone?"

"Oh yes, do go. They're doing those new things there. It used to interest you so much. I should certainly have gone."

"Well, anyway, I'll come back home before dinner," he said, glancing at his watch.

"Put on your frock coat so that you can call on Countess Bohl on the way."

"Is it absolutely necessary?"

"Yes, absolutely. He called on us. I mean, it's not much to ask, is it? You'll call, sit down, talk about the weather for five minutes, and then get up and go away."

"I know you won't believe me, but I'm so out of touch with that sort of thing that it makes me feel ashamed. And really think of it! A perfect stranger arrives, sits down, stays there without doing anything, wastes their time and upsets himself, and goes away again."

Kitty laughed.

"But you paid calls before you were married, didn't you?" she said.

"I did and I always felt ashamed, and now I'm so out of touch that I assure you I'd rather go without dinner for two days than pay that call. It's so embarrassing. I feel the whole time that they will be offended, that they will say to me: Why did you come if you have no business here?"

"They won't be offended, I promise you," said Kitty, looking laughingly into his face. She took his hand. "Well, good-by! . . . Please, call on them."

He kissed his wife's hand and was about to go, when she stopped him.

"Darling, you know I've only fifty rubles left, don't you?"

"Oh, all right, I'll call at the bank and get some money. How much?" he said with a look of dissatisfaction so familiar to her.

"No, wait," she said, holding onto his hand. "Let's talk it over. It worries me. I don't think I'm extravagant, and yet the money is simply disappearing. There must be something wrong about the way we manage things."

"Not at all," he said, clearing his throat and looking askance at her.

She knew what that clearing of the throat meant. It was a sign of his intense displeasure, not with her but with himself. He really was displeased, but not because so much money had been spent, but because he was being reminded of something he wanted to forget, knowing as he did that something was wrong.

"I've told Sokolov to sell the wheat and get an advance on the mill. We shall have the money in any case."

"Yes, but I'm afraid that altogether we're spending too much. . . ."

"Not at all, not at all," he kept repeating. "Well, good-by, darling."

"But sometimes I really am sorry I listened to Mother. How lovely it would have been in the country. As it is, I've worn you all out and we're spending such a lot of money. . . ."

"Not at all, not at all. Not once since our marriage have I said to myself that I'd have preferred it to be otherwise than it is."

"True?" she said, looking into his eyes.

He had said it without thinking, just to comfort her. But when, glancing at her, he saw her dear, truthful eyes fixed on him questioningly, he repeated it with all his heart. "I am absolutely forgetting her," he thought. And he remembered what was awaiting them so soon.

"Will it be soon? How do you feel?" he whispered, taking hold of both her hands.

"I have thought so so often that I've given up thinking and I honestly don't know."

"And you're not afraid?"

She smiled scornfully.

"Not a bit," she said.

"Well, should anything happen, I shall be at Katavasov's."

"Nothing will happen, don't worry. I'll go for a drive on the boulevard with Father. We'll call at Dolly's. I'll expect you before dinner. Oh dear, yes! Do you know that Dolly's position is becoming quite impossible? She's in debt all around and she has no money. Mother and I were talking about it yesterday with Arseny" (that was her sister's husband, Lvov), "and we decided to let him and you loose on Stiva. It's really impossible. We can't speak to Father about it. . . . But if you and he . . ."

"But what can we do?" said Levin.

"All the same, when you see Arseny have a talk to him about it. He will tell you what we decided."

"Oh well, I'm quite ready to agree with Arseny about

anything. I'll go and see him, anyway. If I have to go to the concert, I may as well go with Natalie. Well, good-by."

On the front steps Levin was stopped by his old servant Kuzma, who had been with him before his marriage and who now looked after his household in town.

"Beauty" (the left shaft horse brought from the country) "has been reshod, sir, but is still lame," he said. "What do you want me to do about it?"

When he first came to Moscow, Levin had taken an interest in the horses he had brought from the country. He had been anxious to arrange this side of his household expenses as well and as cheaply as possible; but it turned out that his horses cost him much more than hired ones, and that they used cabs in any case.

"Send for the vet. Maybe it's a sore."

"But what will Mrs. Levin do, sir?"

It no longer struck Levin as strange, as it had done when he first came to Moscow, that to go from Vozdvizhenskoye to Sivtsev-Vrazhek, a distance of less than half a mile, one had to harness a pair of strong horses to a heavy carriage and drive it through the snowy slush and keep it waiting there for four hours and pay five rubles for it. Now it all seemed quite natural to him.

"Hire a pair for our carriage," he said.

"Very good, sir."

And having solved, thanks to the conditions of town life, so easily and simply a problem that would have required so much attention and personal exertion in the country, Levin went out of the house and, hailing a cab, drove to Nikitsky Street. On the way he was no longer thinking about money, but about how he would make the acquaintance of the Petersburg professor of sociology and talk to him about his book.

It was only during the first days in Moscow that Levin had shown any astonishment at the unproductive but inevitable expenditure which seems so strange to one who lives in the country and which was demanded of him on every side. Now he was used to it. In this respect the thing that is said to happen to drunkards happened to him too: the first glass sticks in the gizzard, the second flies down like a buzzard, but after the third all go down like little birds. When Levin had changed his first hundred-ruble note in order to buy liveries for his footman and hall porter, it suddenly occurred to him that those liveries, which were completely unnecessary but seemed to be indispensable, to judge by the look of amazement on the faces of the old princess and Kitty when he had hinted that one could do without liveries—that those liveries would cost as much as the hire of two laborers for a whole summer, that is, about three hundred working days between Easter and Advent, and each day a day of hard labor from early morning till late at night, this hundred-ruble note still stuck in his gizzard. But the next, changed to pay for provisions for a family dinner costing twenty-eight rubles, though it brought to his mind the fact that twenty-eight rubles was the price of about thirty bushels of oats, reaped, bound, threshed, winnowed, sifted, and sacked, went much more easily than the first. Now, however, the notes he changed no longer evoked such reflections, and they flew away like little birds. Whether the labor expended in the acquisition of money corresponded to the pleasure afforded by what it was spent on was a consideration long since lost sight of. The purely business consideration that there is a price below which grain must not be sold was forgotten too. The rye, after he had so long held out for a fair price, was sold at fifty kopecks a measure cheaper than he could have got for it a month earlier. Even the consideration that at such a rate of expenditure he would not be able to live for a year without running into debt—even that had no longer any meaning. The essential thing was to have money in the bank without asking where it came from, so as to be sure that he would be able to pay for tomorrow's meat. Till now he had always observed that condition: he had always had money in the bank. But now he had no more money left in the bank and he did not quite know where to get any. And it was this that had upset him for a moment when Kitty had reminded him about money; but he had no time to think about it now. He was driving along thinking of Katavasov and his forthcoming meeting with Metrov.

CHAPTER 3

During his present stay in Moscow, Levin had become very intimate with his former fellow student, now Professor Katavasov, whom he had not seen since his marriage. He liked Katavasov because of the clarity and simplicity of his outlook on life. Levin considered that Katavasov's clarity of outlook stemmed from the poverty of his nature, while Katavasov thought that the lack of consistency of Levin's ideas was the result of his lack of mental discipline; but Katavasov's clarity pleased Levin and the abundance of Levin's undisciplined ideas pleased Katavasov, and so they liked to meet and discuss things together.

Levin had read several passages of his book to Katavasov, who liked them very much. Happening to meet Levin at a public lecture the day before, Katavasov had told him that the celebrated Metrov, whose article Levin liked so much, was in Moscow and was very interested by what Katavasov had told him about Levin's work, that he would be at his house next day at eleven o'clock and would be very glad to make Levin's acquaintance.

"You're positively improving, my dear fellow, I'm glad to say," said Katavasov as he greeted Levin in the little drawing room. "I heard the bell and thought, Impossible, he can't be on time. . . . Well, what do you say about the Montenegrins? Born fighters."

"Why? What's happened?" asked Levin.

Katavasov told him in a few words the latest news of the war and, entering his study, introduced Levin to a short, thickset man of pleasant appearance. This was Metrov. For a short time they discussed politics and how the latest events were regarded in the highest circles in Petersburg. Metrov told them what the emperor and one of the cabinet ministers had said about them, which he had heard from a reliable source. Katavasov, on the other hand, heard from a source no less reliable that the emperor had said something quite different. Levin tried to think of a situation in which both statements might have been made, and the subject was dropped.

"He has written almost a book about the natural conditions of the agricultural laborer in relation to the land," said Katavasov. "I'm not a specialist but, as a natural scientist, I was pleased to see that he does not consider man as something outside biological laws, but, on the contrary, regards him as dependent on his environment and looks for the laws of its development in this dependence."

"That's very interesting," said Metrov.

"I really started writing a book on agriculture," said Levin, coloring, "but in studying the chief instrument in agriculture, the farm laborer, I involuntarily arrived at quite unexpected results."

Levin began to expound his views cautiously, as though feeling his way. He knew that Metrov had written an article attacking the generally accepted theory of political economy, but he did not know how far he could hope for sympathy with his own novel views and he could not gather from the expression on the professor's calm, clever face.

"But what do you think are the special characteristics of the Russian laborer?" said Metrov. "His, as it were, biological qualities or the conditions in which he is placed?"

This question already revealed an idea with which Levin could not agree. However, he went on expounding his theory that the Russian laborer's view of the land was quite different from that of other nations. And to prove his theory he hastened to add that, in his opinion, this view of the Russian peasant was due to the consciousness of his vocation to populate vast, unoccupied tracts in the east.

"One can be easily led astray when drawing conclusions about the general vocation of a people," said Metrov, interrupting Levin. "The condition of the laborer will always depend on his relation to land and capital."

And without letting Levin finish explaining his idea, Metrov began expounding his theories and how they differed from any others.

What this difference consisted in Levin did not understand because he did not take the trouble to understand: he saw that Metrov, like the others, in spite of his article in which he attacked the teachings of the economists, regarded the position of the Russian farm laborer still from the standpoint of capital, wages, and rent. Though he had to admit that in the largest eastern part of Russia rent still did not amount to anything, that for nine-tenths of Russia's eighty million population wages meant nothing more than a bare subsistence, and that capital did not exist except in the form of the most primitive tools, yet he regarded every laborer only from that point of view, though on many points he disagreed with the economists and had his own new theory of wages, which he expounded to Levin.

Levin listened reluctantly and at first made objections. He felt like interrupting Metrov to explain his own idea which, in his opinion, would have rendered any further exposition unnecessary. But, as he soon realized, they looked at the problem so differently that they would never understand each other. He therefore ceased making objections and merely listened. Although he was no longer interested in what Metrov was saying, he could not help experiencing some pleasure in listening to him. It flattered his vanity that so learned a man should expound his ideas to him so willingly, so painstakingly, and with such faith in Levin's knowledge of the subject, sometimes indicating a whole aspect of the matter by a mere hint. He attributed it to his own merits, not realizing that Metrov, having exhausted the subject with his own intimate friends, was only too ready to talk about it to any fresh person and that, as a matter of fact, he was quite ready to talk to anyone about a subject which occupied his mind to the exclusion of everything else and about which he was not clear himself.

"I'm afraid we shall be late," said Katavasov, glancing at his watch as soon as Metrov had finished his exposition.

"Yes, there's a meeting of the Society of Lovers of Art and Science in honor of Svintich's jubilee," Katavasov explained in answer to Levin's question. "Metrov and I have arranged to go. I promised to read a paper on his work in zoology. Won't you come with us? It will be very interesting."

"Yes, it's time we went," said Metrov. "Do come with us and from there, if you like, we might go to my place. I'd very much like to hear more about your book."

"Well, it's still far from finished, you know. But I'd gladly come to the meeting with you."

"Have you heard? I sent in a special report," said

Katavasov, who was putting on a frock coat in the next room.

And they began a conversation about a question that was just then agitating the university circles. The question concerned a very important event in Moscow university life. Three old professors on the council had not accepted the opinion of the younger professors; the young professors presented a resolution of their own. This resolution was, in the opinion of some people, a dreadful one, but in the opinion of others it was very simple and fair. The professors were thus divided into two camps.

The part to which Katavasov belonged accused their opponents of deception and kowtowing to authority; the others accused them of youthful impertinence and disrespect to the authority. Though Levin was not a member of the university, he had heard about it more than once since his arrival in Moscow and had himself discussed it and formed his opinion on it. He took part in the conversation that was continued in the street until the three of them reached the old university building.

The meeting had already begun. At a table, covered with a cloth, at which Katavasov and Metrov took their seats, six persons were sitting and one of them, bending close over a manuscript, was reading something. Levin sat down on one of the vacant chairs round the table and in a whisper asked a student sitting near what the paper was about.

"A biography," the student replied, with a disapproving glance at Levin.

Though Levin was not interested in the biography of the scientist, he could not help listening to it and he learned some new and interesting facts about the life of the famous man.

When the reader had finished, the chairman thanked him and read a poem the poet Ment had written in honor of the jubilee, adding a few words of thanks to the poet. Then Katavasov in his loud, shrill voice read his paper on Svintich's scientific work.

When Katavasov had finished, Levin glanced at his watch, saw that it was past one, thought that there would be no time to read his work to Metrov before the concert, which in fact he no longer felt like doing. During the reading he had been thinking over their conversa-

784

tion. It was now quite clear to him that though Metrov's ideas might be of some significance, his own ideas too were important. These ideas could be clarified and eventually lead to some results only if each of them would go on working separately in his chosen path. A mere interchange of these ideas, however, would not lead to anything. Having, therefore, made up his mind to decline Metrov's invitation, Levin approached him at the end of the meeting. Metrov introduced Levin to the chairman, with whom he was discussing the latest political news. He was telling the chairman what he had already told Levin that morning, and Levin made the same observations, but for the sake of variety expressed a new view which had just occurred to him. After that they started discussing the university question again. As Levin had already heard it all, he hastened to tell Metrov that he was sorry he could not avail himself of his invitation and, taking his leave, drove off to see Lvov.

CHAPTER 4

Lvov, who was married to Kitty's sister Natalie, had spent all his life in the two Russian capitals and abroad, where he had been educated and where he had been in the diplomatic service.

He had left the diplomatic service the year before, not because of any unpleasantness (he never had any unpleasantness with anyone), and obtained a post in the Moscow branch of the Ministry of the Royal Court in order to give his two boys the best possible education.

Though their habits and views were diametrically opposed and though Lvov was much older than Levin, they had become great friends that winter and grown very fond of each other.

Lvov was at home and Levin went into his study without being announced.

Wearing an indoor jacket with a belt and chamois-leather slippers, Lvov was sitting in an armchair, a pince-nez with blue glasses on his nose, carefully holding a half-smoked cigar in his outstretched, shapely hand, and reading a book on a stand before him.

His handsome, refined, and still youthful-looking face,

to which his glossy, wavy, silvery hair gave a still more aristocratic appearance, lit up with a smile when he saw Levin.

"Capital! I was just about to send over to you. Well, how is Kitty? Sit down here, it's more comfortable," he said, getting up and pushing forward a rocking-chair. "Have you read the last circular in the *Journal de St.-Pétersbourg*? I think it's excellent," he said with a slight French accent.

Levin told him what he had heard from Katavasov about what was said in Petersburg and, after some talk about politics, told him how he had made the acquaintance of Metrov and about the meeting he had been to. This interested Lvov very much.

"You know," he said, "I envy you for having the entry into that interesting scientific world. It is true," he went on as usual in French, in which he found it easier to express himself, "I have no time to spare, my official duties and my occupations with the children make this impossible for me. Besides, my education, I'm not ashamed to confess, is terribly deficient."

"I don't think so," said Levin with a smile and, as always, deeply touched by his brother-in-law's low opinion of himself, which was not in the least put on out of modesty, but was quite sincere.

"But it is. I am now beginning to feel how badly educated I am. Even for the children's lessons I often have to refresh my memory and, indeed, to learn things for the first time. For, you see, it's not enough for them to have teachers, they must also have a supervisor, just as on your estate you must have both laborers and an overseer. Here," he said, pointing to Buslayev's *Grammar*, lying on the reading stand, "I've been reading this—Misha is supposed to know it and it's so difficult. . . . Now will you, please, explain to me—he says here . . ."

Levin tried to explain that it was impossible to understand it, but Lvov would not agree.

"You're just laughing at me!"

"On the contrary, I don't think you quite realize how, looking at you, I'm always learning what I myself shall have to be doing soon—the education of my children."

"You've nothing to learn from me, I'm sure," said Lvov.

"All I know is," said Levin, "that I never saw better

brought-up children than yours, and I don't wish for better children than yours."

Lvov was quite plainly trying to restrain his expression of delight, but he could not manage it.

"If only they turn out better than I. That's all I want. You don't yet know all the difficulties one has with boys like mine, whose education has been neglected through our life abroad."

"They'll catch up. They're such talented children. The main thing is moral training. That's what I learn when I look at your children."

"You say, moral training. You can't imagine how difficult that is. As soon as you've managed to overcome one thing, others crop up, and you have to start all over again. Without the support of religion—you remember I discussed it with you before—no father would be able to bring up his children by his own efforts."

This conversation, which always interested Levin, was interrupted by the entrance of the beautiful Natalie, who came in dressed to go out.

"I didn't know you were here," she said, evidently not at all sorry but rather pleased to have interrupted a conversation she had heard many times before and of which she was heartily sick. "Well, how is Kitty? I am dining with you today. Look here, Arseny," she said, turning to her husband, "you will take the carriage . . ."

And husband and wife began discussing what they would do that day. As her husband had to go and meet someone on official business and she had to go to the concert and then to a public meeting of the Near East Committee, there was a great deal to discuss and arrange. Levin, as one of the family, had to take part in these deliberations. It was decided that Levin would accompany Natalie to the concert and the public meeting, and from there they would send the carriage to the office for Arseny, who would then call for his wife and take her to Kitty's, or, if he was still busy, send the carriage back and Levin would go with her.

"He spoils me," said Lvov to his wife. "He assures me that our children are wonderful while I know that there is so much that is bad in them."

"Arseny goes to extremes, I always say," declared his wife. "If you look for perfection, you'll never be satisfied. And what Father says is perfectly true—when we were brought up people went to one extreme: we were kept in the attic while our parents lived on the first floor. Now it's the other way round: the parents in the lumber room and the children on the first floor. The parents, you see, have no right to live now. Everything is for the children."

"What does it matter, if it's more agreeable?" said Lvov, with his attractive smile, touching her hand. "Anyone who didn't know you would think you were a step-mother and not a mother."

"No," said Natalie, putting his paper knife in its proper place on the table, "extremes are no good in anything."

"Well, come in, you perfect children," he said to the two handsome boys, who entered the room and, after bowing to Levin, approached their father, evidently wishing to ask him something.

Levin would have liked to talk to them, to hear what they were going to say to their father, but Natalie began talking to him and then Makhotin, a colleague of Lvov's, in court uniform, came in to fetch Lvov to meet someone, and an endless conversation began about Herzegovina, Princess Korzinsky, the Duma, and Countess Apraxin's sudden death.

Levin forgot all about the commission he had been charged with. He remembered it only on his way into the hall.

"Oh dear, Kitty asked me to have a talk to you about Oblonsky," he said, when Lvov stopped on the stairs to say good-by to him and his wife.

"I know Mother-in-law wishes us, the two brothers-in-law, to tell him off properly," said Lvov, blushing and smiling. "But why should I?"

"Well, I'm going to tell him off, then," said his wife with a smile, as she stood in her white fur-lined cloak, waiting for them to finish their talk. "Come along!"

CHAPTER 5

Two very interesting works were being performed at the matinée concert.

One was *King Lear on the Heath*, a fantasia, and the other a quartet dedicated to the memory of Bach. Both works were new and in the modern style, and Levin was anxious to form an opinion of them. After he had conducted his sister-in-law to her seat, he took his stand at a pillar and made up his mind to listen as attentively and conscientiously as he possibly could. He tried not to let his thoughts wander or the impression of the music be marred by watching the conductor in a white tie waving his arms, which always so unpleasantly distracts one's attention from the music; or by the ladies in their bonnets, who had so carefully tied the ribbons over their ears for the concert; or by all those faces of people who were either not interested in anything or were interested in all sorts of things except the music. He tried to avoid meeting the musical experts or talkers, and stood looking down on the floor and listening.

But the more he listened to the *King Lear* fantasia, the less did he feel able to form any definite opinion of it. As soon as the musical expression of some feeling seemed to be on the point of starting, it immediately broke up into fragmentary expressions of new emotions and sometimes into disconnected, though extremely complex, sounds, depending entirely on the whim of the composer. But even these fragments of musical expressions, good as some of them were, struck one as unpleasant because they were entirely unexpected and unprepared for. Gaiety, sadness, despair, tenderness, triumph burst upon the ear without any justification, just like the emotions of a madman. And, as with a madman, these emotions vanished just as unexpectedly.

Throughout the performance Levin felt like a deaf person watching people dancing. He was completely bewildered when the performance of the work was over, and he felt utterly exhausted from the strain of unrewarded attention. From all sides came loud applause. People got up, walked about, and began to talk. Wishing to discover the reason for his own bewilderment by finding out the impression of others, Levin went in search of the experts and was glad to see a famous music critic talking to Pestsov, an acquaintance of his.

"Wonderful!" Pestsov said in his deep bass. "How do you do, Levin? Especially picturesque, and, as it were, sculpturesque and rich in color, is the passage where you feel Cordelia's approach, where the woman, *das ewig Weibliche*, enters upon a struggle with fate. Don't you think so?"

"But why, I mean, what has Cordelia to do with it?" Levin asked timidly, completely forgetting that the fantasia represented King Lear on the heath.

"Cordelia appears—here, look!" said Pestsov, tapping his fingers on the glossy program he held in his hand and handing it to Levin.

Only then did Levin recollect the title of the fantasia and hastened to read the Russian translation of Shakespeare's lines printed on the back of the program.

"You can't follow without it," said Pestsov, addressing Levin, as the person he had been speaking to had gone and he had no one to talk to.

In the interval Levin and Pestsov began a discussion on the merits and demerits of the Wagnerian tendency in music. Levin argued that the mistake Wagner and his followers were making was in trying to make music pass into the province of another art, just as poetry makes the mistake of describing the features of a face, which should be done by painting, and as an example of such a mistake he mentioned the case of a sculptor who carved in marble the shades of poetic images rising round the figure of a poet on a pedestal. "These shades are so little like shades that they even cling to a ladder," said Levin. He liked this phrase, but he could not remember whether he had used it before, and to Pestsov, too, and he looked embarrassed after having said it.

Pestsov, on the other hand, argued that art was one and indivisible and that it could only reach its highest manifestations by uniting all the various branches of art.

The second part of the concert Levin could not hear, for Pestsov, who was standing beside him, kept talking to him almost all the time, criticizing the music for its quite unwarranted and mawkish affectation of simplicity and comparing it with the simplicities of the pre-Raphaelites in painting. On his way out Levin met many more acquaintances with whom he talked about politics, music, and mutual friends. Among others, he met Count Bohl. He had quite forgotten that he had to pay a call on him.

"Well, why not go now?" Natalie said, when he told her. "Perhaps they are not at home and then you could come for me at the meeting. I shall still be there."

CHAPTER 6

"They aren't at home, are they?" said Levin, entering the hall of Countess Bohl's house.

"They are, sir," said the hall porter, resolutely helping him off with his overcoat.

"What a nuisance!" thought Levin, and he sighed as he pulled off one glove and smoothed his hat. "Why on earth am I here? What am I going to talk to them about?"

As he passed through the first drawing room, he met Countess Bohl in the doorway, giving some order to a servant with a worried and severe expression on her face.

When she saw Levin she smiled and asked him into the next room, a smaller drawing room, from which came the sound of voices. In that room were the countess' two daughters, who were sitting in armchairs, and a Moscow colonel with whom Levin was acquainted. Levin went up to them, exchanged greetings, and sat down beside the sofa with his hat on his knees.

"How is your wife? Have you been to the concert? I'm afraid we could not go. Mother had to go to the funeral."

"Yes, I heard. . . . She died so suddenly. . . ." said Levin.

The countess came in, sat down on the sofa, and also asked him about his wife and the concert.

Levin replied and repeated his question about Countess Apraxin's death.

"She always was delicate, though."

"Were you at the opera last night?"

"Yes, I was."

"Lucca was very good, wasn't she?"

"Yes, she was," he said, and as he did not care what he said, he began repeating what he had heard hundreds of times about the singer's extraordinary talent. Countess Bohl pretended to be listening. Then, when he had said enough, the colonel, who had so far been silent, carried on. He also talked of the opera and the lighting.

Finally, having said something about the proposed *folle journée* at Turin's, he laughed, got up noisily, and went away. Levin, too, got up, but saw by the countess' face that it was not yet time for him to go. He had to stay another two minutes. He sat down.

But as he kept thinking how stupid it all was, he could not find a subject for conversation and remained silent.

"Aren't you going to the public meeting?" began the countess. "I'm told it will be very interesting."

"No, but I promised my sister-in-law to call for her there," said Levin.

There was another pause. The mother exchanged glances with her daughters again.

"Well," thought Levin, "I believe I can go now," and he got up. The ladies shook hands with him and asked him to tell his wife *mille choses* from them.

As he helped Levin on with his overcoat, the porter asked him where he was staying and at once wrote down his address in a large, well-bound book.

"I don't care, of course, but it's awfully stupid and makes one feel ashamed," thought Levin, consoling himself with the reflection that everybody did it, and he drove off to the public meeting, where he was to find his sister-in-law and take her back home with him.

At the public meeting there were a great many people, most of them belonging to high society. Levin was in time to hear the review of the position in the Balkans, which everyone said was very interesting. After that, people began to gather into groups and Levin met Sviazhsky, who asked him to be sure and come that evening to a meeting of the Agricultural Society where an important paper was to be read. He also met Oblonsky, who had only just come from the races, and many more friends and acquaintances. Levin had again to talk and listen to various opinions about the meeting, the new fantasia, and a trial. But as a result of the mental fatigue he was beginning to feel, he made a mistake when talking of the trial, and afterward he remembered that mistake several times with vexation. Discussing the sentence to be passed on a foreigner who was being tried in Russia and declaring how unjust it would be to punish him merely by deporting him from the country, Levin repeated what he had heard said the day before by a man he knew.

"I think that to deport him would be like punishing a pike by throwing it into the water," said Levin.

It was only later that he remembered that this idea, which he had heard from an acquaintance and given out as his own, was taken from one of Krylov's fables and that his acquaintance had repeated it from a newspaper article.

After taking his sister-in-law home and finding Kitty in good spirits and well, Levin went off to the club.

CHAPTER 7

Levin arrived at the club just at the right moment. Members and visitors were driving up as he got there. Levin had not been at the club for a long time, not since the time when, after leaving the university, he had lived in Moscow and began going into society. He remembered what the club was like, the external details of its layout, but he had completely forgotten the impression it made on him before. But as soon as he drove into the wide, semicircular courtyard and, getting out of the cab, entered the porch where a hall porter, wearing a shoulder belt, noiselessly opened the door and bowed to him; as soon as he saw in the hall the coats and galoshes of the members, who found it less trouble to take their galoshes off downstairs than to go up in them; as soon as he heard the mysterious ring of the bell that announced his ascent and saw, as he mounted the shallow, carpeted staircase, the statue on the landing and, in the doorway, a third porter in club livery, who had grown older and whom he recognized, who at once slowly opened the door for him while examining him closely—Levin felt himself enveloped by the old atmosphere of the club, an atmosphere of repose, contentment, and propriety.

"Your hat, sir," the porter said to Levin, who had forgotten the rule that hats must be left in the porter's room. "It's a long time since you were here, sir. The prince put your name down yesterday. Prince Oblonsky has not arrived yet."

The porter knew not only Levin but all his connections and relatives and at once mentioned some of his closest friends.

Passing through the first hall divided up by screens, where there was a fruit buffet, and having overtaken an old man who was walking very slowly, Levin entered the noisy, crowded dining room.

He walked past the tables, which were nearly all occupied, examining the guests. Here and there he saw all sorts of people—young and old, some of whom he hardly knew and others who were old friends of his. There was not a single worried or preoccupied face among them. They had all apparently left their cares and anxieties with their hats in the porter's room and were about to enjoy the material blessings of life at their leisure. There was Sviazhsky there, and Shcherbatsky, and Nevedovsky, and the old prince, and Vronsky, and Koznyshev.

"Ah, why are you so late?" said the old prince with a smile, giving Levin a hand over his shoulder. "How's Kitty?" he added, putting straight the table napkin which he had tucked in behind a button of his waistcoat.

"She's all right. The three of them are dining at home together."

"Ah, the Alines and Nadines. I'm sorry, there's no vacant place here. Be quick and get a place at that table," said the prince and, turning away, cautiously accepted a plate of turbot soup from a waiter.

"Levin, here!" a good-natured voice shouted a little further off. It was Turovtsyn. He was sitting beside a young man in military uniform, and two chairs were tilted up against their table.

Levin joined them with pleasure. He had always been fond of the good-natured rake Turovtsyn—with him was associated his memory of his proposal to Kitty—but today, after the strain of all those intellectual conversations, Turovtsyn's good-natured face was particularly welcome.

"This is for you and Oblonsky. He'll be here presently."

The army officer, who held himself very erect, with merry, always laughing eyes, was Gagin from Petersburg. Turovtsyn introduced them.

"Oblonsky is always late."

"Ah, here he is!"

"Have you only just arrived?" said Oblonsky, hurrying up toward them. "How do you do? Had any vodka? Well, then, come along!"

Levin got up and followed him to a large table spread with every possible brand of vodka and all sorts of hors d'oeuvres. From the score of hors d'oeuvres on the table it ought to have been possible to choose one to any taste, but Oblonsky asked for something special and one of the liveried waiters brought it at once. They drank a glass of vodka each and returned to the table.

While they were still at their fish soup, Gagin ordered a bottle of champagne and told the waiter to fill the four glasses. Levin did not refuse the proffered wine, and ordered another bottle. He was hungry and ate and drank with great pleasure and with even greater pleasure took part in the gay and simple conversation of his companions. Lowering his voice, Gagin was telling them the latest drawing-room story from Petersburg, and though the story was stupid and indecent, it was very funny and Levin burst out laughing so loudly that people turned round to look at him.

"That is like the 'That's just what I can't bear' story! Do you know it?" asked Oblonsky. "Oh, it's delightful! Another bottle!" he called to the waiter, and began telling his story.

"With Mr. Peter Vinovsky's compliments!" interrupted an old waiter, bringing two slender glasses of still-sparkling champagne on a tray and addressing Oblonsky and Levin.

Oblonsky took the glass and, exchanging a look with a bald-headed man with a ginger mustache at the other end of the table, nodded to him, smiling.

"Who is it?" asked Levin.

"You met him once at my place, remember? A nice fellow!"

Levin did the same as Oblonsky and took the glass.

Oblonsky's story was very funny, too. Then Levin told his story, which was also appreciated. Then they talked about horses, about that day's races, and about how dashingly Vronsky's Atlas had won the first prize. Levin did not notice how the dinner passed.

"Ah, here they are!" said Oblonsky, just as they were

finishing dinner, leaning over the back of his chair and holding out his hand to Vronsky, who was coming up with a tall colonel of the Guards.

Vronsky's face was also lit up by the general good humor prevalent at the club. Leaning his arm gaily on Oblonsky's shoulder he whispered something in his ear, and with the same gay smile held out his hand to Levin.

"Very pleased to meet you," he said. "I looked for you again at the elections, but was told you had already gone."

"Yes, I left the same day. We've just been talking about your horses. Congratulations," said Levin. "It was very good going."

"You've got some race horses too, haven't you?"

"No, my father had. But I remember and know something about them."

"Where did you dine?" asked Oblonsky.

"At the second table, behind the pillars."

"He's been congratulated," said the tall colonel. "It's his second imperial prize. I wish I had the luck at cards that he has with horses. But why waste the golden moments? I'm off to the 'infernal regions,' " the colonel concluded and walked away from the table.

"That's Yashvin," Vronsky said in reply to Turovtsyn, sitting down in the vacated chair beside them. He drank the glass of champagne they offered him and ordered a bottle. Whether influenced by the general atmosphere of the club or by the wine he had drunk, Levin had a long talk with Vronsky about the best breeds of cattle and was pleased to find that he did not feel the slightest animosity toward the man. He even told him among other things that he had heard from his wife that she had met him at Princess Maria Borisovna's.

"Oh, Princess Maria Borisovna! Isn't she wonderful?" said Oblonsky and told a story about her which made them all laugh. Vronsky, in particular, burst out into such good-natured laughter that Levin felt completely reconciled to him.

"Well, have you finished?" said Oblonsky, getting up and smiling. "Let's go!"

CHAPTER 8

On leaving the table, Levin, feeling that his arms were swinging with quite unusual ease and regularity, passed with Gagin through the high-ceilinged rooms to the billiard room. Crossing the large hall, he came across his father-in-law.

"Well, and how do you like our temple of idleness?" asked the prince, taking his arm. "Come, let's walk around a little."

"As a matter of fact, that's just what I was going to do. It's interesting."

"Yes, I daresay you do find it interesting. But my interest is different from yours. Now, for instance, you look at those old men there," he said, pointing to a club member with a bent back and pendant lip, shuffling toward them in soft boots, "and you imagine that they were born shufflers."

"Shufflers?"

"Oh, I see, you don't even know the word. It's a club term of ours. You know the game of egg rolling? When an egg is rolled a lot of times and can't be rolled any more it turns into a shuffler. Well, we too are like that, my boy. You keep on coming and coming into the club till you become a shuffler. You laugh? But people like me are already wondering when we, too, will graduate into shufflers. Do you know Prince Chechensky?" asked the prince, and Levin saw by his face that he was going to tell him something amusing.

"No, I don't."

"You don't? Not the famous Prince Chechensky? Well, no matter. He is always playing billiards. Three years ago he wasn't yet among the shufflers and still pretended to be a fine fellow. Called other men shufflers. Well, one morning he arrives at the club and our hall porter Vassily—you know Vassily, don't you? It's the fat one. He's a great wit. So Prince Chechensky asks him, 'Well, Vassily, who's here? Any shufflers?' and Vassily says in reply, 'Yes, sir, you're the third one!' Yes, my boy, that's how it is!"

Talking and exchanging greetings with acquaintances, Levin and the prince went through all the rooms: the large one in which card tables were already arranged and the habitual partners were playing for small stakes; the sofa room where they were playing chess and where Koznyshev was sitting and talking to someone; the billiard room, where in a recess by a sofa a gay party, including Gagin, were drinking champagne, and "the infernal regions," where around a table, at which Yashvin had already taken his seat, a number of backers were crowded. Taking care not to make any noise, they entered the dimly lit reading room, where under shaded lamps an angry-looking young man sat leafing over one journal after another and a bald-headed general was absorbed in a book. They also went into the room which the prince called "the clever room." In that room three men were engaged in a heated argument about the latest political news.

"We're ready, Prince," said one of his partners, finding him there, and the prince went away.

Levin sat down, listened to the discussion, but remembering all the conversations he had heard that morning, he suddenly felt terribly bored. He got up hastily and went back to look for Oblonsky and Turovtsyn, with whom it was so much more cheerful.

Turovtsyn was sitting on the high sofa in the billiard room with a tankard of some drink, and Oblonsky was talking about something with Vronsky by the door at the far end of the room.

"She isn't exactly depressed, but that indefinite, unsettled position," Levin overheard, and he was about to go away quickly, but Oblonsky called him.

"Levin," cried Oblonsky, and Levin noticed that his eyes, though not actually filled with tears, were moist, as they always were when he was either drunk or in a very sentimental mood. At that moment he was both. "Levin, don't go," he said, pressing his elbow tightly, evidently not wishing to let him go on any account.

"This is my true, almost my best friend," he said to Vronsky. "You, too, are very near and dear to me. And I'd like you two to be good friends and I know that you will be because you are both excellent fellows."

"Well," said Vronsky with good-natured jocularity

holding out his hand, "all we have to do now is to kiss and be friends."

He quickly grasped Levin's hand and pressed it warmly.

"I'm very, very glad," said Levin, pressing his hand.

"Waiter, a bottle of champagne," said Oblonsky.

"And I'm very glad too," said Vronsky.

But in spite of Oblonsky's wish and their own mutual desire, they had nothing to talk about, and both felt it.

"You know," Oblonsky said to Vronsky, "he has never met Anna and I'd very much like to take him to see her. Let's go, Levin!"

"Really?" said Vronsky. "She will be very glad. I'd gladly come with you now," he added, "but Yashvin worries me and I'd like to stay till he has finished."

"Why? Is he in trouble?"

"He's losing all the time and I alone can restrain him."

"What about a game of pyramids? Levin, will you play? Ah, excellent!" said Oblonsky. "Place the balls for pyramids, please," he said to the marker.

"It's been a long time," replied the marker, who had already placed the balls in a triangle and was rolling the red ball about to pass the time.

After the game Vronsky and Levin joined Gagin at his table and at Oblonsky's suggestion Levin began betting on aces. Vronsky sat at the table surrounded by friends who kept coming up to him, or went to "the infernal regions" to see what Yashvin was doing. Levin experienced a pleasant sensation of relief from the mental fatigue of the morning. He was glad the hostility between him and Vronsky was at an end, and the sense of calm, decorum, and contentment never left him.

When they had finished their game, Oblonsky took Levin's arm.

"Well, shall we go to see Anna? Now, shall we? She's at home. I promised to bring you long ago. Where were you going this evening?"

"Nowhere in particular. I had promised Sviazhsky to go to the meeting of the Agricultural Society, but I'll come with you, if you like."

"Excellent, let's go then! Find out if my carriage has come," Oblonsky said to one of the footmen.

Levin went up to the table, paid the forty rubles he had lost, paid his club bill to an old footman standing at the door, who in some mysterious way knew the right amount, and, swinging his arms rather peculiarly, passed through all the rooms to the entrance door.

CHAPTER 9

"The Oblonsky carriage!" the hall porter shouted in a loud bass voice.

The carriage drove up and they got in. It was only at first, while the carriage was driving out of the courtyard of the club, that Levin was conscious of that sense of club composure, pleasure, and the manifest decorum of his surroundings; as soon as the carriage drove out into the street and he felt it jolting on the cobbled roadway, heard the angry shout of the cabman who was coming toward them, saw in the dim light the red signboard of a pothouse and a small shop, that sense was destroyed. He began to think over his actions and ask himself whether he was doing right in going to see Anna. What would Kitty say? But Oblonsky did not give him time to think and, as though divining his doubts, dispelled them.

"I'm so glad you're going to make her acquaintance. You know, Dolly has long wished it. Lvov too called on her and still goes to see her. Though she is my sister," Oblonsky went on, "I can say without fear of contradiction that she is a remarkable woman. You will see. Her position is a very difficult one, especially now."

"Why especially now?"

"We are negotiating with her husband about a divorce. And he is willing to give her one, but there are difficulties about her son. That's why this business that could have been settled long ago has been dragging on for three months. As soon as she gets a divorce, she will marry Vronsky. How stupid it is, I mean, the old custom of walking round and round, singing 'Rejoice, Isaiah!' in which no one believes any more and which stands in the way of people's happiness," Oblonsky put in. "Well, then their position will be as regular as yours or mine."

"What is the difficulty then?" said Levin.

"Oh, it's a long and boring story! Everything is so

800

vague and indefinite in this country. But the point is that she has been living for three months here in Moscow, where everybody knows her and him, waiting for the divorce. She does not go out anywhere, she does not see any woman except Dolly, because, you understand, she does not want people to come and see her just as a favor. Even that stupid fool Princess Varvara has left because she does not think it proper. Well, anyway, in a position like that any other woman would not have found sufficient resources in herself to fall back on. But you will see how she has arranged her life, how calm and dignified she is. To the left, in the lane opposite the church!" shouted Oblonsky, leaning out of the carriage window. "Oh dear, it's so hot!" he said, throwing open his already unfastened overcoat still wider in spite of the twelve degrees of frost.

"But she has a daughter, hasn't she? She is probably occupied with her," said Levin.

"You seem to imagine every woman is just a female, *une couveuse*," said Oblonsky, "occupied, if she is occupied at all, only with children. I believe she is bringing up her daughter splendidly, but one doesn't hear about her. She's busy, first of all, with her writing. I can see you smiling ironically, but you're wrong. She is writing a children's book. She doesn't talk about it to anyone, but she read it to me and I showed the manuscript to Vorkuyev, the publisher, you know, and a writer himself, I believe. He knows a lot about such things and he says it is a remarkable piece of work. But don't run away with the idea that she is a woman writer and nothing else. Not at all. She is first of all a woman with a heart. You will see. Just now she has a little English girl with her and a whole family she is interested in."

"You mean, she does it for charity?"

"Dear me, you always look at things from the worst possible point of view. It is not at all a question of charity. It's something that comes straight from the heart. They had—I mean, Vronsky had—an English trainer, a first-rate man in his own line, but a drunkard. He drank like a fish, got delirium tremens, and deserted the family. She saw them, helped them, got interested, and now the entire family is on her hands. And she doesn't treat them in a patronizing way, just helping them with money. She herself coaches the boys in Russian for the secondary school and she has taken the girl into the house. But you'll see for yourself."

The carriage drove into the courtyard and Oblonsky rang loudly at the front door, before which a sledge was standing.

Without asking the porter who opened the door whether Anna was in, he went into the hall. Levin followed him, wondering more and more whether he should or shouldn't have come.

Glancing at himself in the looking glass, Levin noticed that he was red in the face; but he was certain he was not drunk and he followed Oblonsky up the carpeted stairs. Upstairs Oblonsky asked a footman, who bowed to him as to a member of the family, who was with Anna and was informed that Vorkuyev was with her.

"Where are they?"

"In the study, sir."

Passing through a small dining room with dark-paneled walls, Oblonsky and Levin entered, walking over a thick carpet, into a semi-dark study, lit by one lamp with a large dark shade. Another reflector lamp on the wall threw a light on a large, full-length portrait of a woman, which involuntarily attracted Levin's attention. It was Anna's portrait painted in Italy by Mikhailov. While Oblonsky passed behind a trellis-work screen with climbing plants, and a man's voice that had been speaking fell silent, Levin stood looking at the portrait, which seemed to come out of the frame in the brilliant illumination, and could not tear his eyes away from it. He even forgot where he was and, not listening to what was being said, did not take his eyes off the wonderful portrait. It was not a picture, but a living, lovely woman with black, curly hair, bare shoulders and arms, and a wistful half smile on lips covered with soft down, looking tenderly and peremptorily at him with eyes that disturbed him. The only reason why she could not be a living woman was that she was more beautiful than a living woman could be.

"I'm very glad," he suddenly heard a voice near him say, apparently addressing him, the voice of the selfsame woman he had been admiring in the portrait.

Anna had come out from behind the screen to meet him and Levin saw in the half-darkness of the study the woman of the portrait, in a dark dress of different shades of blue, not in the same attitude nor with the same expression, but of the same remarkable beauty which the artist had caught in the picture. She was less dazzling in reality, but, to make up for it, there was something new about her, something irresistibly captivating, which was not in the portrait.

CHAPTER 10

She had got up to meet him, without concealing her pleasure at seeing him. In the calm, self-composed way in which she held out her energetic little hand to him, introduced him to Vorkuyev, and indicated a pretty, red-haired little girl sitting at her work, whom she called her ward, Levin recognized the familiar pleasant manners of a woman of the world, always self-composed and natural.

"I'm very, very glad," she repeated, and on her lips those simple words for some reason assumed a special meaning. "I have known of you and liked you for a long time both for your friendship for Stiva and for your wife's sake. . . . I'm afraid I only knew her for a very short time, but she left on me the impression of a lovely flower—yes, a flower. And she will soon be a mother!"

She spoke freely and without haste, from time to time glancing from Levin to her brother. Levin sensed that the impression he had made on her was a good one, and he immediately felt at ease and as natural and comfortable with her as though he had known her from childhood.

"Mr. Vorkuyev and I have come to Alexey's room just because we wanted to smoke," she said in reply to Oblonsky's question whether he might smoke. And glancing at Levin, instead of asking him whether he smoked, she drew toward her a tortoise-shell cigarette case and took out a cigarette.

"How are you today?" asked her brother.

"Oh, not so bad. Nerves as usual."

"Don't you think it's remarkably good?" said Oblonsky, noticing that Levin kept looking at the portrait.

"I've never seen a better portrait."

"And it's quite an extraordinary likeness, isn't it?" said Vorkuyev.

Levin glanced from the portrait to the original. Anna's face lighted up with a special brilliance when she felt his eyes on her. Levin blushed and, to conceal his embarrassment, was about to ask her how long it was since she had seen Dolly, but at that moment Anna herself began to speak.

"Mr. Vorkuyev and I have just been talking about Vashchenkov's latest paintings. Have you seen them?"

"Yes, I have," replied Levin.

"But I'm sorry, I interrupted you. You were about to say . . ."

Levin asked whether she had seen Dolly lately.

"She was here yesterday. She is very angry with the school for the way they treat Grisha. It seems the Latin master has been unfair to him."

"Yes, I saw the pictures." Levin went back to the subject she had started. "I'm afraid I didn't like them very much."

Levin's attitude toward art was different from what it had been that morning: he no longer used well-worn clichés in talking about it. Every word he uttered in his talk to her had a special meaning. It was pleasant to talk to her and still more pleasant to listen.

Anna talked not only naturally and intelligently, but also intelligently and carelessly, not attributing any value to her ideas, but attaching much greater value to the ideas of the person she was speaking to.

The conversation turned to the new movement in art and the new Biblical illustrations by a French artist. Vorkuyev criticized the artist for a realism carried to the point of coarseness. Levin said that the French had carried symbolism in art further than anyone else, and that was why they regarded a return to realism as a special kind of merit. They saw poetry in the very fact that they did not lie.

Never had any clever remark uttered by Levin given him more pleasure than this. Anna's face lighted up the moment she appreciated the idea he had expressed. She laughed.

"I laugh," she said, "as one laughs when one sees a very striking likeness. What you just said is a perfect description of present-day French art, painting, and even literature—Zola, Daudet. But perhaps it is always like that—artists form their conceptions from imaginary, symbolic figures, and then when all the possible combinations have been made, they get tired of the imaginary figures and begin inventing more natural and true ones."

"That's perfectly true," said Vorkuyev.

"So you've been at the club?" she said, addressing her brother.

"Yes, yes, she's certainly a wonderful woman!" thought Levin, lost in admiration and gazing fixedly at her beautiful, mobile face, which had now quite changed. Levin did not hear what she was saying to her brother as she leaned over him, but he was struck by the change of her expression. So lovely in its tranquillity before, her face all of a sudden expressed a strange curiosity, anger, and pride. But that lasted only a minute. She screwed up her eyes, as if she were remembering something.

"Still, it's of no interest to anyone," she said and turned to the little English girl.

"Please order tea in the drawing room," she said in English.

The little girl got up and went out.

"Well, did she pass her examination?" asked Oblonsky.

"Yes, with flying colors. She's a very clever girl and has a sweet nature."

"You'll end up by being more fond of her than of your own daughter."

"You talk like a man. There's no such thing as more or less in love. I love my daughter with one kind of love and her with another."

"I'm always telling Anna Arkadyevna," said Vorkuyev, "that if she were to devote a hundredth part of the energy she bestows on this English girl to promoting the general education of Russian children, she would be doing a great and useful work."

"I'm very sorry, but I just could not do it. Count Alexey Vronsky" (as she uttered Vronsky's name she cast a timid and appealing glance at Levin and he involuntarily replied with a respectful and reassuring look) "did his best to induce me to take an active interest in our village school. I went there several times. The children were very nice, but I just couldn't get attached to the work. You say, energy. Energy is based on love. And you can't get love just like that—you can't get it to order. Take this little girl. I've grown fond of her and I don't know myself why."

And again she glanced at Levin. And her look and her smile, everything told him that she was addressing her words to him alone, thinking highly of his opinion and at the same time knowing in advance that they understood one another.

"I can understand it perfectly," said Levin. "One can't put one's heart into a school or any similar institution and that's why, I think, these philanthropic institutions always give such poor results."

For a moment she was silent, then she smiled.

"Yes," she said. "I never could do it. *Je n'ai pas le coeur assez large* to love a whole orphanage full of horrid little girls. *Cela ne m'a jamais réussi.* Think of the women who have created a social position for themselves in that way. And now all the more so," she added with a sad, confiding expression, turning ostensibly to her brother, but quite obviously addressing her words only to Levin. "Even now when I need some occupation so badly I can't do it." And suddenly frowning (Levin realized that she was frowning at herself for talking about herself) she changed the subject. "I've heard it said about you," she said to Levin, "that you are a bad citizen and I've defended you as best I could."

"How did you defend me?"

"It depends on the nature of the attack. But won't you come and have some tea?"

She rose and picked up a book bound in morocco.

"Let me have it, please," said Vorkuyev, pointing to the book. "It's well worth it."

"Oh no, it's so unfinished."

"I've told him about it," said Oblonsky to his sister, indicating Levin.

"You shouldn't have. My writing is like those fretwork baskets made by prisoners Lisa Merkalov used to sell me. She was in charge of the prisons in some society," she added, turning to Levin. "And these unfortunates achieved miracles of patience."

Levin saw a new feature in the character of the woman whom he found so extraordinarily attractive. In addition to intelligence, grace, beauty, she also possessed

806

sincerity. She had no wish to conceal from him the terrible hardship of her position. Having said it, she sighed and her face suddenly assumed a stern expression and seemed to harden. That expression made her look more beautiful than ever; but it was quite a new kind of expression, it was quite out of the range of the expressions radiating and creating happiness, which had been caught by the artist in the portrait. Levin glanced once more at her portrait and at her figure when, taking her brother's arm, she walked through the lofty doors with him, and he felt a tenderness and pity for her which surprised him.

She asked Levin and Vorkuyev to go into the drawing room, while she stayed behind to discuss something with her brother. "About the divorce, about Vronsky, about what he is doing at the club, about me?" wondered Levin. And the question what she might be saying to Oblonsky agitated him so much that he hardly listened to what Vorkuyev was telling him about the merits of the children's story Anna had written.

Over their tea they continued the same kind of pleasant, serious, and discerning conversation. Not only was there not a single moment when they had to look for a topic of conversation, but, on the contrary, one felt that one had not time enough to say what one wanted to and gladly refrained in order to hear the other talk. And everything that was said not only by her, but also by Vorkuyev and Oblonsky, seemed to Levin to assume a special significance thanks to her attention and the observations she made.

While following their interesting conversation, Levin kept admiring her all the time—her beauty, her intelligence, her good education as well as her simplicity and sincerity. He listened, talked, and all the time thought of her, of her inner life, trying to divine her feelings. And just as before he had thought so ill of her, so now, by some strange process of reasoning, he justified her and at the same time was sorry for her and could not help fearing that Vronsky did not fully understand her. At about eleven o'clock when Oblonsky got up to go (Vorkuyev had left earlier), it seemed to Levin that he had only just arrived. Levin, regretfully, also got up.

"Good-by," she said, holding his hand and gazing into his face with a look that seemed to draw him to her. "I am so glad *que la glace est rompue.*"

She let go of his hand and screwed up her eyes.

"Please tell your wife that I'm just as fond of her now as ever and that if she cannot forgive me my position, I don't want her ever to forgive me. To forgive she would have to live through what I have lived through, and may God preserve her from that."

"Yes, I will certainly tell her," Levin said, blushing.

CHAPTER 11

"What a remarkable, charming, pathetic woman!" thought Levin as he went out into the frosty air with Oblonsky.

"Well, I told you, didn't I?" said Oblonsky, seeing that Levin was completely won over.

"Yes," Levin said thoughtfully, "an extraordinary woman! Not only intelligent, but wonderfully warm-hearted. I'm terribly sorry for her!"

"Everything will soon be settled now, thank God. So there, don't be so quick to pass judgment in future," said Oblonsky, opening the door of his carriage. "Goodby. We're not going the same way."

Without ceasing to think of Anna and of the unaffected talk they had had together, recalling every detail of the expression of her face, entering more and more into her position and feeling very sorry for her, Levin returned home.

At home Kuzma informed Levin that Kitty was all right, that her sisters had not long been gone, and handed him two letters. Levin read them in the hall there and then, so as not to let them distract his attention later on. One was from his estate agent, Sokolov, who wrote that the wheat could not be sold because they were only offering five and a half rubles a bushel and that there was no other way of raising money. The other letter was from his sister. She reproached him for not having settled her business yet.

"Well, we'll have to sell it for five and a half rubles if we can't get more," Levin at once settled the first problem with the greatest of ease, though it had appeared to him so difficult before. "It's quite remarkable how one wastes one's time here," he thought in connection with the second letter. He felt guilty for not having done what his sister had asked him. "Today I haven't been to the courts, either, but then I really had no time today." And, resolving that he would attend to it next morning without fail, he went to his wife. On the way to her room, Levin ran over in his mind all he had done that day. All that had happened was that he had listened and taken part in conversations. All these conversations were about matters which, had he been alone in the country, he would never have bothered about, but here he found them very interesting. And they were all extremely good, except for two things which were not so good. One was what he had said about the pike and the other—there was something that was not right about the tender pity he felt for Anna.

Levin found his wife looking sad and depressed. The dinner of the three sisters would have been a great success but for the fact that they had waited and waited for him till they had all become bored, her sisters had left and she remained alone.

"And what have you been doing?" she asked, looking into his eyes, which were somehow suspiciously bright. But, not to prevent him from telling her everything, she concealed the fact that she had noticed anything and listened with an approving smile to his account of how he had spent the evening.

"Well, I was very glad to have met Vronsky. I felt quite at ease and natural with him. You see, I don't mind if I never meet him again, but I'm glad there won't be that constraint again," he said, and remembering that while not thinking of *ever meeting him again*, he had gone at once to call on Anna, he blushed. "We say the peasants drink, but I'm not sure who drinks more, the peasants or our own class of people. At least the peasants only drink on holidays, but . . ."

But Kitty was not interested to hear how the peasants drank. She had seen him blush and she wanted to know the reason.

"Well, and where did you go then?"

"Stiva kept pestering me to go and see Anna."

And having said this, Levin blushed still more and his

doubts as to whether he had done right or wrong in going to see Anna were now finally resolved. He knew now that he should not have gone.

At the mention of Anna's name, Kitty's eyes flashed and opened unusually wide, but making an effort she concealed her agitation and deceived him.

"Oh!" she only said.

"I'm sure you won't be angry with me for going. Stiva asked me to and Dolly wished it," Levin went on.

"Oh no," she said, but in her eyes he saw what an effort she had had to make to take a hold on herself, and it boded him no good.

"She's a very charming, very, very pathetic, and very good woman," he said, and he told her about Anna, her occupations, and what she had asked him to say to her.

"Why, of course, she is very pathetic," said Kitty when he had finished. "Who did you get the letters from?"

He told her and, taken in by her calm tone of voice, went to undress.

On his return he found Kitty still sitting in the same chair. When he went up to her, she looked at him and burst out sobbing.

"What is it? What?" he kept asking, knowing very well *what* it was.

"You've fallen in love with that horrible woman! She has bewitched you. I could see it in your eyes. Yes, yes! What will become of it? In the club you drank and drank, then gambled, and then went to call on—whom? No, we must go away. I shall go away tomorrow!"

It took Levin a long time to calm his wife. At last he was successful, but only after he had admitted that his feeling of pity in combination with the wine he had drunk had led him astray and that in consequence he fell under the artful spell of Anna. He promised to avoid seeing her in future. One thing he was most sincere about in his confession was that living so long in Moscow with nothing to do but eat, drink, and talk, he was losing his senses. They talked till three o'clock in the morning. Only by three o'clock were they sufficiently reconciled to fall asleep.

CHAPTER 12

Having seen off her guests, Anna did not sit down, but began pacing up and down the room. Though she had unconsciously (as she always did to all young men at that time) done all she could during the evening to arouse in Levin a feeling of love, and though she knew that she had succeeded as far as it was possible in one evening with an honorable married man, and though she had liked him very much (in spite of the glaring difference, from a man's point of view, between Vronsky and Levin, for being a woman she saw what they had in common, which had made Kitty fall in love with both Vronsky and Levin), no sooner had he left the room than she ceased to think about him.

One and the same thought kept recurring to her in different forms. "If that's the way I affect men, including this married man who loves his wife, then why is *he* so cold toward me? And it isn't that he is cold—I know he loves me—but something has come between us now, something new. Why has he been away the whole evening? He sent word by Stiva that he could not leave Yashvin, but must keep an eye on his play. Is Yashvin a child? But let's assume it's true. He never tells lies. There is something else hidden in that truth. He is glad of the chance of showing me that he has other obligations. I know that. I don't mind that. But why does he have to prove it to me? He wants to prove to me that his love for me must not interfere with his freedom. But I don't want proofs. All I want is love. He should realize how awful my life is here in Moscow. Is this life? I don't live, I'm merely waiting for something to come to an end, and it's being delayed and delayed. Again there is no reply. And Stiva says he cannot go and see Alexey. And I can't possibly write again. I can't do anything. I can't begin anything or change anything. I am just trying to restrain myself, waiting, waiting, inventing all sorts of distractions—the Englishman's family, writing, reading—but it's all nothing but self-deception, a kind of morphia

811

all over again. He ought to have some pity on me," she said, feeling tears of self-pity starting to her eyes.

She heard Vronsky's impetuous ring at the front door and hastily wiped away her tears. She not only dried her tears, she sat down near the lamp and opened a book, pretending to be calm. She had to show him that she was displeased that he had not come home as he had promised, but she must not show him how unhappy she was and, above all, there must be no hint of self-pity. She might pity herself, but he must not pity her. She did not want any quarrel; she blamed him for wanting one, but she could not help assuming a truculent attitude.

"I hope you haven't been bored," he said, coming up to her cheerfully and gaily. "Oh, what a terrible passion gambling is!"

"No, I was not bored. I've long ago taught myself how not to be bored. Stiva and Levin were here."

"Yes, I knew they were coming to see you. Well, how did you like Levin?" he asked, sitting down beside her.

"I liked him very much. They only left a short while ago. How was Yashvin getting on?"

"He'd won at first—seventeen thousand. I told him to come away and nearly made him do so. But he went back, and now he's lost it all and more."

"Then why did you stay?" she asked, suddenly raising her eyes to him. The expression of her face was cold and hostile. "You told Stiva you were staying on to bring Yashvin away. And now you have left him there."

The same expression of a cold readiness for a fight appeared on his face.

"In the first place, I never asked him to give you a message from me and, secondly, I never tell lies. But the chief reason why I stayed is that I wanted to stay," he said, frowning. "Anna, why? Why?" he added after a moment's pause, bending over toward her and opening his hand in the hope that she would put hers in it.

She was glad of this appeal to tenderness. But some kind of strange evil power prevented her from giving in to her impulse, as if the rules of the fight did not permit her to give in.

"Of course you wanted to stay and you stayed. You always do what you want to. But why tell me this? Why?" she repeated, getting more and more excited.

"Does anyone question your rights? But it seems you want to be in the right, so be in the right!"

His hand closed, he drew back, and his face assumed a still more stubborn expression.

"For you it's a matter of obstinacy," she said, looking intently at him and suddenly finding the right word for the expression of his face which exasperated her so much. "Yes, obstinacy! All you're concerned about is whether you will get the better of me, while I . . ." Again she felt sorry for herself and she nearly burst into tears. "If you only knew what it means to me when I feel as I do now, that you are hostile—yes, hostile—to me. Oh, if you only knew what that means to me! If you knew how near I am to doing something desperate at such a moment—how afraid I am, how afraid I am of myself!" And she turned away to hide her sobs.

"But what are we quarreling about?" he said, horrified by the expression of her despair and, bending over toward her again, he took her hand and kissed it. "What is it all about? Am I looking for any amusement outside our home? Don't I avoid the society of women?"

"I should hope so!" she said.

"Well, then, tell me what I have to do to make sure you don't feel worried? I'm ready to do anything to make you happy," he said, touched by her despair. "I'd do anything in the world to spare you the anguish you're suffering from now, Anna," he said.

"Oh, it's nothing, nothing!" she said. "I don't know myself what it is—my lonely life, my nerves, or what. . . . Well, don't let's talk about it. What about the races? You haven't told me," she asked, trying to conceal her triumph at the victory, for it was hers after all.

He asked for supper and began telling her about the races; but she could see from the tone of his voice, from his eyes, which were growing colder and colder, that he had not forgiven her her victory, that the obstinacy against which she had fought was taking possession of him again. He was colder to her than before, as though he was sorry he had given in. And she, remembering the words which had given her the victory—"I am near to doing something desperate and I am afraid of myself," realized that this weapon was a dangerous one and that she would not be able to use it a second time. But she felt that side by side with the love that bound them together, there had grown up some evil spirit of strife, which she could not cast out of his heart and still less out of her own.

Chapter 13

There are no conditions to which a man cannot get accustomed, especially if he sees that everyone around him lives in the same way. Levin would not have believed it possible three months earlier that he could go quietly to sleep in the circumstances in which he now found himself; that while living an aimless, senseless life, a life, moreover, that was above his means; and after his hard drinking (he could find no other words for what he had been doing at the club), after his clumsy attempt to be friendly with a man with whom his wife had once been in love and the even more inappropriate call on a woman who could only be called a fallen woman; and after having almost fallen in love with that woman and grieved his wife—that after all this he could fall asleep so peacefully. But under the influence of his weariness, of a late night, and the wine he had drunk, he slept soundly and peacefully.

At five o'clock he was wakened by the creaking of an opening door. He sat up and looked round. Kitty was not in bed beside him. But behind the partition a light was moving about and he heard her steps.

"What is it? What?" he asked, half awake. "Kitty, what is it?"

"Nothing," she said, coming from behind the partition with a lighted candle in her hand. "I didn't feel well," she added, with a particularly sweet and meaning smile.

"What? Has it begun? Has it?" he asked in a frightened voice. "We must send . . ." He began dressing hurriedly.

"No, no," she said, smiling and holding him back with her hand. "It's probably nothing. I only felt a little unwell. But it's over now."

She went up to the bed, put out the candle, lay down, and was quiet. Though her quietness, just as though she were holding her breath, seemed suspicious to him, and

814

especially the peculiar tenderness and excitement with which, coming out from behind the partition, she had said, "Nothing," he was so drowsy that he fell asleep at once. It was only afterward that he remembered that bated breath and realized what was going on in her dear, sweet soul when, while lying motionless at his side, she was awaiting the greatest event in a woman's life. At seven o'clock he was awakened by the touch of her hand on his shoulder and a faint whisper. She seemed to be torn between regret at waking him and a desire to speak to him.

"Darling, don't be frightened. . . . It's all right. . . . Only I think . . . I think we'd better send for Lizaveta Petrovna."

She had lit the candle again. She was sitting on the bed, holding in her hand some knitting she had been doing during the last few days.

"Please, don't be frightened. It's all right. I'm not a bit afraid," she said, seeing his alarmed face, and she pressed his hand to her bosom and then to her lips.

He jumped out of bed, hardly conscious of himself, and without taking his eyes off her for a moment, put on his dressing gown, and stood still, gazing at her. He had to go, but he was unable to move, so struck was he by the look on her face. He, who loved her face and knew every expression and look on it, had never seen it like this. The thought of the grief he had caused her the night before made him feel how vilely and horribly he had treated her when he saw her as she was now. Her flushed face, with the soft hair escaping from under her nightcap, was radiant with joy and resolution.

Little as there was of artificiality and conventionality in Kitty's character, Levin was still astonished at what was laid bare to him now when every veil had been removed and the very kernel of her soul shone through her eyes. And in this simplicity and in this baring of her soul he could see her, the woman he loved, more clearly than ever. She looked and smiled at him; but suddenly her brow contracted, she raised her head, and going up quickly to him took his hand and clung close to him, her hot breath engulfing him. She was in pain and seemed to be complaining to him of her suffering. For a moment he felt, from force of habit, that he really was to blame for it. But the tenderness in her eyes told him that far from blaming him, she loved him for her suffering. "If I am not to blame for it, then who is?" he could not help thinking, looking for someone responsible for those sufferings so as to punish him. She suffered, complained, triumphed, and rejoiced in the suffering and loved it. He saw that something beautiful was taking place in her soul—but what? That he could not understand. That was beyond his comprehension.

"I've sent for Mother, and you go quickly for Lizaveta Petrovna. . . . Oh, darling! . . . It's nothing, it's passed."

She moved away from him and rang the bell.

"Well, go along now. Pasha's coming. I'm all right."

And Levin was amazed to see her taking up the knitting she had fetched in the night and starting work on it again.

As Levin was going out of one door he heard the maid coming in at the other. He stopped at the door and heard Kitty give detailed instructions to the maid to help her move the bed.

He dressed and, while his carriage was being made ready (it was too early for a cab), he ran back to the bedroom not on tiptoe but, as it seemed to him, on wings. Two maids were busy moving something in the bedroom. Kitty was walking up and down and knitting, quickly throwing the wool over the needle, and giving orders.

"I'm going to fetch the doctor now. They've already gone for Lizaveta Petrovna, but I'll go around there too. Anything else? Oh yes, shall I go and fetch Dolly too?"

She looked up at him, apparently not hearing what he was saying.

"Yes, yes. Go, go!" she said quickly, frowning and motioning him away with her hand.

He was entering the drawing room when he suddenly heard a pitiful moan coming from the bedroom and lasting only a moment. He stopped and for a long time could not understand.

"Of course, it was Kitty," he said to himself and, clutching his head, ran downstairs.

"Lord, have mercy on us! Pardon and help us!" He kept repeating the words that suddenly and unexpectedly sprang to his lips. And, unbeliever that he was, he kept repeating those words not with his lips only. Now, at this moment, he knew that not only all his doubts, but, as he realized so well, the very impossibility of believing with his reason, did not prevent him in the least from appealing to God. All that fell away, like dust, from his soul. To whom else was he to appeal, if not to Him in whose hands he felt himself, his soul, and his love to be?

The carriage was not ready yet, but in feeling a tremendous access of physical strength and alertness and anxious not to lose a single moment, he did not wait, but started off on foot, telling Kuzma to catch her up.

At the corner of the street he saw a night cabman hurrying along. In the little sledge sat Lizaveta Petrovna in a velvet cloak with a shawl over her head. "Thank God, thank God!" he murmured, overjoyed to recognize the fair-haired woman with her little face, which now wore a particularly serious, even stern expression. Without telling the driver to stop, he ran along beside her.

"Two hours ago, not longer?" she asked. "You'll find the doctor, only don't hurry him. And get some opium at the chemist's."

"So you think it will be all right? Lord, have mercy on us and help us!" said Levin, seeing his horse coming out of the gate. Jumping into the sledge beside Kuzma, he told him to drive to the doctor's.

CHAPTER 14

The doctor was not up yet, and his servant said that he had gone late to bed and given orders that he was not to be called, but that he would be up soon. The servant was cleaning the lamp glasses and seemed very absorbed in his work. His attention to the glasses and complete indifference to what was taking place at Levin's astonished Levin at first, but on thinking it over he at once realized that no one knew or was obliged to know his feelings and that it was therefore all the more necessary to act calmly, deliberately, and firmly to break through this wall of indifference and attain his end. "Do not hurry and do not let anything go by default," Levin said to himself, feeling an ever-increasing access of physical strength and alertness.

Having learned that the doctor was not up yet, Levin

decided, out of the many plans that occurred to him, on the following: Kuzma was to go with a note to another doctor, while he himself would go to the chemist's for opium, and if, on his return, the doctor had not got up yet, he would either bribe the footman or, if need be, force his way into the bedroom and wake him.

At the chemist's a lean dispenser was sealing up a packet of powders for a coachman, who was waiting for it, with the same indifference with which the doctor's servant was cleaning the lamp glasses, and refused to let him have any opium. Levin, trying not to hurry and not to get flustered, gave the names of the doctor and the midwife and explained why the opium was needed. The dispenser asked in German whether he should let him have it and, receiving an affirmative reply from behind the partition, took down a bottle and a funnel, slowly poured some of the drug into a smaller bottle, stuck on a label, though Levin begged him not to do it, and was about to wrap it up. But this was more than Levin could stand: he determinedly snatched the bottle from the dispenser's hands and rushed out of the big glass doors. The doctor had not got up yet and his valet, who was now busy putting down a carpet, refused to wake him. Levin quietly took out a ten-ruble note and, speaking slowly but without losing time, handed him the note and explained that the doctor (how great and important this doctor, so insignificant before, seemed to him now!) had promised to come at any time and that he would most certainly not be angry and must therefore be wakened at once.

The servant consented, went upstairs, and asked Levin to wait in the waiting room.

Levin could hear the doctor behind the door coughing, walking about, washing, and saying something. Three minutes passed; to Levin it seemed more than an hour. He could not wait any longer.

"Doctor, Doctor!" he called in a beseeching voice through the open door. "I'm terribly sorry, Doctor, but, please, for God's sake see me as you are. It's over two hours. . . ."

"Coming, coming. . . ."

"Just for one minute! . . ."

"Coming. . . ."

818

Two more minutes passed while the doctor was putting on his boots and another two minutes while he was putting on his coat and combing his hair.

"Doctor!" Levin began again in a piteous voice, but at that moment the doctor came out, dressed and his hair brushed. "These people have no conscience," thought Levin. "Brushing his hair while we are about to die!"

"Good morning!" said the doctor to him, holding out his hand and almost teasing him by his composure. "There's no need for you to be in a hurry. Well, sir?"

Trying to be as circumstantial as possible, Levin began to tell the doctor all the unnecessary details about his wife's condition, continually interrupting his account with requests that the doctor should come with him at once.

"Don't be in such a hurry. You don't know whether I shall be needed at all. However, I promised and I suppose I'd better come. But there is no hurry. Sit down, please. Would you like some coffee?"

Levin looked at him as though he did not know whether the doctor was laughing at him or not. But the doctor never thought of laughing.

"I know, my dear sir, I know," he said with a smile. "I'm a married man myself. We husbands are the most pathetic creatures at a time like this. I have a patient whose husband always runs away to the stables on such occasions."

"But what do you think, Doctor? Do you think it will be all right?"

"Everything seems to point to a favorable result."

"Then you will come at once?" said Levin, staring furiously at the servant bringing in coffee.

"In about an hour."

"An hour? For heaven's sake, Doctor. . . ."

"Very well, let me have a cup of coffee first."

The doctor began drinking his coffee. Both were silent.

"The Turks seem to be getting a real good beating," said the doctor, munching a roll. "Did you read yesterday's telegram?"

"I'm sorry, I can't stand it!" said Levin, jumping up. "So you'll come in a quarter of an hour, won't you?"

"Half an hour."

"On your word of honor?"

Levin returned home as the old princess arrived, and they went up to the bedroom together. The princess had tears in her eyes and her hands shook. When she saw Levin, she embraced him and burst out crying.

"Well, Lizaveta Petrovna, my dear?" she said, seizing the midwife's hand as she came out of the bedroom with a beaming, but preoccupied face.

"It's going on all right," she said. "Please, persuade her to lie down. It will be easier for her."

From the very moment Levin woke up that morning and realized what the situation was, he had been bracing himself to endure what was before him without reflection and without any unnecessary anticipation, firmly suppressing all his thoughts and feelings, resolved not to upset his wife, but on the contrary to calm her and keep up her spirits. Not allowing himself even to think of what was going to happen or how it would all end and finding out how long a confinement usually lasted, he mentally prepared himself to endure and steel his heart for five hours, which seemed not impossible to him. But when he came back from the doctor's and again saw Kitty's sufferings, he began repeating more and more often: "Lord have mercy on us and help us," sighing and raising his head toward heaven; and he was overcome by a feeling of fear that he might not be able to bear the strain and would either run away or burst into tears. So terrible did he feel. And only one hour had passed.

But after that hour, another passed, a second, a third, and all the five hours that he had imposed on himself as the limit of his endurance, and the situation was still unchanged. He went on enduring because there was nothing else he could do, imagining every moment that he had reached the limit of his endurance and that any moment his heart would burst with pity.

But minutes passed and hours, and more hours, and his suffering and horror and strain grew more and more intense.

All the ordinary conditions of life, without which one can have no idea of anything, no longer existed for Levin. He had lost the sense of time. The minutes—those minutes when she called him to her and he held

820

her perspiring hand, now squeezing his with extraordinary strength and now pushing him away—seemed like hours to him, and hours seemed like minutes. He was surprised when Lizaveta Petrovna asked him to light a candle behind the partition and he learned that it was five o'clock in the afternoon. Had he been told that it was only ten o'clock, he would have been no less surprised. He was as little aware of where he had been all the time as he had of when and where it had been happening. He saw her burning face, sometimes bewildered and suffering and sometimes smiling and trying to calm him. He saw the old princess, red-faced and tense, the curls of her gray hair undone, in tears, which she did her best to keep back, and biting her lips; he saw Dolly, and the doctor smoking fat cigars, and Lizaveta Petrovna with a firm, determined, and reassuring expression on her face, and the old prince pacing up and down the ballroom and frowning. But how they came and went, and where they were, he did not know. The old princess was one moment in the bedroom with the doctor and the next in the study, where a table laid for a meal made its appearance; and then it was not the princess but Dolly. Then Levin remembered that he had been sent somewhere. Once he was sent to move a table and a sofa to another room. He did it with a will, thinking that it was necessary for Kitty, and only afterward did he find out that he had been preparing a bed for himself. Then he was sent to the study to ask the doctor something. The doctor had answered and then began talking about the disorderly scenes in the town council. After that he had been sent to fetch an icon in a silver-gilt case from the old princess' bedroom, and he and the princess' old maid had climbed onto a small cupboard to get it down and had broken the little lamp, and the princess' maid had tried to comfort him about his wife and the lamp, and he had brought the icon back with him and put it at Kitty's head, carefully pushing it behind the pillows. But where, when, and why all this was done he did not know. Nor did he understand why the old princess took his hand and, looking mournfully at him, begged him to calm himself, and Dolly tried to persuade him to eat something and led him out of the room, and even the doctor looked at him gravely and with sympathy, offering him some drops.

He only knew and felt that what was happening was similar to what had happened in the hotel of the provincial town a year ago on the deathbed of his brother Nikolai. Only that had been sorrow and this was joy. But both that sorrow and this joy were equally beyond the ordinary conditions of life. In this ordinary life they were like openings through which something higher became visible. And what was happening now was equally hard and agonizing to bear and equally incomprehensible, and one's soul, when contemplating it, soared to a height such as one did not think possible before and where reason could not keep up with it.

"Lord have mercy on us and help us," he kept repeating incessantly to himself, in spite of his long and seemingly complete alienation from religion, feeling that he was turning to God as trustingly and as simply as in the days of his childhood and early youth.

All this time he was in two distinctly separate moods. One when he was away from her, with the doctor, who smoked one fat cigarette after another and stubbed them out on the rim of the overflowing ashtray, with Dolly and the old prince, where they talked about dinner and politics or Mary Petrovna's illness and where Levin suddenly forgot what was going on in the house and felt as though he were waking up; and the other mood, at her bedside, by her pillow, where his heart was about to burst with pity, and yet did not burst, and where he prayed without stopping to God. And every time that a scream, reaching him from the bedroom, roused him from his momentary forgetfulness, he succumbed to the same strange delusion that possessed him at the very first—every time he heard the scream he jumped up, ran to justify himself, remembered on the way that he was not to blame, and was overcome by a desire to protect and help her. But when he looked at her he again realized that he could not help and was horrified and murmured, "Lord have mercy on us and help us!" And the longer it lasted, the more intense those two moods grew: the calmer he became when away from her, almost indeed forgetting her, the more and more poignantly did he react to her suffering and his own helplessness. He would jump up, wishing to run away somewhere, but ran to her room instead.

Sometimes, when she called him again and again, he

reproached her. But seeing her meek, smiling face and hearing the words, "I've worn you out," he reproached God, but the thought of God made him at once pray for forgiveness and mercy.

CHAPTER 15

He did not know whether it was late or early. The candles had all burned low. Dolly had just been in the study and suggested that the doctor should lie down. Levin sat listening to the doctor's story about a quack magnetizer and looking at the ash of his cigarette. It was a period of rest and he was only half awake. He had completely forgotten what was going on. He listened to the doctor's story and took it in. Suddenly there was a terrible scream. It was so terrible that Levin did not even jump up, but looked questioningly at the doctor with bated breath, too terrified to speak. The doctor bent his head on one side as he listened and smiled approvingly. Everything was so extraordinary that nothing surprised Levin any more. "I suppose that's all right," he thought and went on sitting where he was. But who was screaming? He jumped up, ran on tiptoe into the bedroom, walked round the midwife and the old princess and took up his old position at the head of the bed. The screaming had stopped, but something was different now. What it was he neither saw nor understood and did not want to see or understand. But he read it in the midwife's face, which was stern and pale, but still as resolute, though her jaw trembled a little and her eyes were fixed intently on Kitty. Kitty's flushed, worn-out face, a strand of hair clinging to her perspiring forehead, was turned to him, seeking his eyes. Her raised hands were asking for his hands. Seizing his cold hands with her perspiring ones, she began pressing them to her face.

"Don't go, don't go! I'm not afraid, I'm not afraid!" she said rapidly. "Mother, take off my earrings. They are in the way. You're not frightened, are you? Soon, soon, Lizaveta Petrovna. . . ."

She was speaking very rapidly and she tried to smile. But suddenly her face became distorted and she pushed him away.

"Oh, this is terrible! I'm dying, dying! Go, go!" And again he heard that terrible scream.

Levin clasped his head in his hands and ran out of the room.

"It's nothing, nothing, everything's all right," Dolly called after him.

But whatever they said, he knew that now it was all over. Leaning his head against the jamb of the door, he stood in the next room and heard someone shrieking and howling in a way he had never heard before and he knew that these screams came from what had once been Kitty. He had long ceased wishing for a child. He hated this child now. He did not even wish her to live now. All he wished was that these terrible sufferings should end.

"Doctor, what is it? What is it? Oh, my God!" he said, seizing the doctor's hand as he entered.

"It's the end," said the doctor.

The doctor's face was so grave as he said it that Levin understood him to mean that Kitty was dying.

Beside himself, he rushed into her room. The first thing he saw was the midwife's face. It looked more frowning and more severe than ever. Kitty's face was not there. In its place was something horrible both because of the strained expression and the frightful sounds that issued from it. He pressed his head to the wood of the bedstead, feeling that his heart was breaking. The terrible screaming did not cease; it grew more terrible and, as though reaching the utmost limit of horror, it suddenly ceased. Levin could not believe his ears, but there was no doubt about it: the screaming stopped and all he heard was a soft bustling, a rustling, and the sound of hurried breathing, and her voice, her live, tender, happy voice, saying: "It's over!"

He raised his head. Her arms drooping helplessly on the blanket and looking extraordinarily gentle and beautiful, she gazed silently at him, trying to smile but unable to do so.

And suddenly Levin felt himself transported in a flash from the mysterious, terrible, and strange world in which he had been living for the last twenty-two hours into his old everyday world, now radiant with the light of such new happiness that he could hardly bear it. The taut cords snapped. The sobs and tears of joy he had not foreseen rose with such force within him that his whole body shook and for a long time prevented him from speaking.

Falling on his knees by her bed, he held his wife's hand to his lips and kissed it, and her hand responded to his kisses with a weak movement of fingers. Meanwhile, at the foot of the bed, in the midwife's expert hands, like the flame of a lamp, flickered the life of a human being who had never existed before and who, with the same rights and importance to itself, would live and beget others like himself.

"Alive! Alive! And it's a boy! Nothing to worry about!" Levin heard the midwife's voice saying as she slapped the baby's back with a trembling hand.

"Is it true, Mother?"

The old princess' quiet sobbing was the only reply she got.

And amid the silence, as an unmistakable answer to his mother's question, there came a voice quite unlike the other subdued voices in the room. It was a bold, insolent cry of a human being that had no consideration for anything and that seemed to have appeared out of nowhere.

Had Levin been told before that Kitty was dead, that he had died with her, and that their children were angels, and that God was present before them—he would not have been surprised at anything. But now, having returned to the world of reality, he had to make a great effort to realize that she was alive and well and that the desperately howling creature was his son. Kitty was alive and her sufferings were at an end. And he was ineffably happy. That he understood and it filled him with joy. But the child? Whence and why had he come? And who was he? He just could not understand, he could not accustom himself to the idea. It seemed something superfluous, something too much, something which it would take him a long time to get used to.

CHAPTER 16

About ten o'clock the old prince, Koznyshev, and Oblonsky were sitting at Levin's and, after talking about the young mother, they began discussing other matters.

Levin listened to them, and as they talked, involuntarily thought of what had been happening before that morning and remembered himself as he had been the previous day before the birth of his child. A hundred years seemed to have elapsed since then. He felt as if he were on some inaccessible height from which he was carefully descending so as not to hurt the feelings of those he was talking to. He talked and never for a moment ceased thinking of his wife, of her present condition, and of his son, to the idea of whose existence he was trying to accustom himself. The whole world of woman, which after his marriage had assumed a new, hitherto unsuspected significance for him, now rose so high in his estimation that his imagination could not grasp it. He listened to the conversation about yesterday's dinner at the club and thought, "What is happening to her now? How is she? What is she thinking of? Is our son Dmitry crying?" And in the middle of the conversation, in the middle of a sentence, he jumped up and left the room.

"Send someone to let me know if I can see her," said the old prince.

"All right," replied Levin and, without stopping, went to her room.

She was not asleep, but was talking quietly with her mother, making arrangements for the christening.

Tidied and her hair brushed, a smart cap trimmed with something blue on her head, her hands on the counterpane, she lay on her back and, meeting his glance, drew him to her with a look. Her look, already bright, grew still brighter, the nearer he approached her. Her face showed the same change from the earthly to the unearthly as is seen on the faces of the dead; but there it was a farewell, while here it was a welcome. His heart was again gripped by agitation as at the moment of the child's birth. She took his hand and asked whether he had slept. He could not bring himself to answer and turned away, conscious of his own weakness.

"I've had a good sleep, darling," she said, "and I feel so good now."

She gazed at him and suddenly her expression changed.

"Let me have him," she said, hearing the baby's weak cry. "Let me have him, Lizaveta Petrovna, and let his father see him too."

"Why, yes, let his father have a look at him," said the

826

midwife, lifting something strange, red, and wriggling. "But wait, let's first make him tidy," and she put the wriggling red object on the bed, began unwrapping and wrapping it up again, raising and turning him over with one finger and powdering him with something.

Looking at this tiny, pathetic little creature, Levin tried in vain to discover in his heart anything in the least resembling paternal feeling. He felt nothing for the baby but aversion. But when it was stripped and he caught sight of such thin little hands and feet, saffron-colored, with little fingers and toes, and the big toe even looking quite different from the others, and when he saw the midwife bending the little, sticking-out arms as though they were springs and encasing them in little garments, he was filled with such pity for the little creature and such fear that she might hurt them that he tried to restrain her hand.

Lizaveta Petrovna laughed.

"Don't be afraid, don't be afraid!"

When the baby had been swaddled and transformed into a hard cocoon, the midwife lifted it in her arms, as though proud of her work, and drew back so that Levin could see his son in all his beauty.

Without taking her eyes off the baby, Kitty, glancing around, looked in the same direction.

"Let me have him! Let me have him!" Kitty said and was even going to sit up.

"What are you doing?" the midwife said to her. "You mustn't move like that! Wait, I'll give him to you. Let's first show Daddy what a fine lad we are!"

And Lizaveta Petrovna held out to Levin on one hand (with the other she merely supported the nape of the wobbly head) this strange, wriggly red creature that tried to hide its head in the swaddling clothes. But there was also a nose, a pair of squinting eyes, and smacking lips.

"A beautiful baby!" said Lizaveta Petrovna.

Levin sighed with disappointment. This beautiful baby only inspired him with a feeling of disgust and pity. It was not at all the sort of feeling he had expected.

He turned away while the midwife got the baby to take the unaccustomed breast.

A sudden laugh made him raise his head. It was Kitty who laughed. The baby had taken the breast.

"Well, that's enough, that's enough!" said Lizaveta

Petrovna, but Kitty would not give up the baby. He fell asleep in her arms.

"Have a look at him now," said Kitty, turning the baby so that Levin could see him. The old man's face wrinkled up still more and the baby sneezed.

Smiling and scarcely able to keep back tears of tenderness, Levin kissed his wife and left the darkened room.

What he felt about the little creature was not at all what he had expected. There was nothing happy or cheerful about it; on the contrary, there was a new distressful feeling of fear. It was the consciousness of another sphere of vulnerability. And this consciousness was so painful at first, his fear that that helpless creature might suffer was so strong, that it completely submerged the strange feeling of unreasoning joy and even pride he had felt when the baby sneezed.

CHAPTER 17

Oblonsky's financial affairs were in a parlous state.

Two-thirds of the money he had received for the sale of the wood had already been spent and by allowing a discount of ten per cent he had obtained from the merchant almost the whole of the last third. The merchant would not advance any more money, particularly as Dolly had for the first time that winter asserted her rights to her own property and had refused to sign the contract for the receipt of the money for the final payment. Oblonsky's entire salary went on household expenses and the payment of small pressing bills. There was no money at all.

This was unpleasant and awkward and, in Oblonsky's opinion, ought not to be allowed to go on. The reason for his financial troubles, as he understood it, was that his salary was too small. His job had certainly been a very good one five years ago, but it was different now. Petrov, the bank director, got twelve thousand rubles; Sventitsky, a company director, got seventeen thousand; Mitin, who had founded a bank, got away with fifty thousand. "It looks as though I had been asleep and been forgotten!" thought Oblonsky to himself. And he began pricking up his ears and keeping his eyes open, and toward the end of the winter he had discovered a very good post and launched an attack on it, at first from Moscow, through uncles, aunts, and friends; and then in the spring, when things had gone far enough, he himself went to Petersburg. It was one of those cushy, lucrative jobs with salaries varying from one to fifty thousand rubles which are far more numerous now than they used to be; it was the post of a member of the board of the Joint Agency of the Mutual Credit Balance of the Southern Railways and Banking Houses. This post, like many other similar posts, required such immense knowledge and activity as could hardly be expected from one man, and as no man possessing all these qualities could be found, it was better that the post should be given to an honest rather than a dishonest man. And Oblonsky was not merely an honest man (in the ordinary sense), but an honest man (in quotation marks), with that particular meaning which this word has in Moscow, where an honest public servant, an honest writer, an honest periodical, an honest institution, an honest political tendency or party means not only that the man or the institution is not dishonest, but that, given the right opportunity, they are quite capable of turning "agin the government." Oblonsky moved in those circles in Moscow where that particular meaning was attached to the word "honest," and he was considered there to be an honest man, and for that reason he had a better claim than others to that post.

The job carried a salary of from seven to ten thousand a year and Oblonsky could hold it without giving up his government post. The appointment to it depended on two ministries, one lady, and two Jews; and all these people, though they had already been prepared, Oblonsky had to see in Petersburg. Moreover, he had promised his sister Anna to obtain from Karenin a definite answer about the divorce. So, getting fifty rubles from Dolly, he left for Petersburg.

Sitting in Karenin's study and listening to his draft report on the bad state of Russian finances, Oblonsky only waited for the moment when he finished speaking to broach the subject of his own business and to put in a word about Anna.

"Yes, that's very true," he said, when Karenin took off his pince-nez, without which he could not read now, and looked up inquiringly at his former brother-in-law, "that's very true so far as details are concerned, but still the principle of our age is freedom."

"Yes, but I am formulating another principle which embraces the principle of freedom," said Karenin, stressing the word "embraces" and putting on his pince-nez again to reread the part where he had said it.

Turning over the beautifully written, wide-margined manuscript, Karenin once more read through his cogent argument.

"I do not want protection for the benefit of private individuals, but for the common good—for the lower and the upper classes alike," he said, looking at Oblonsky over his pince-nez. "But *they* cannot grasp that, *they* are only concerned with their own personal interests and are carried away by phrases."

Oblonsky knew that when Karenin began talking about what *they* were doing and thinking—*they* being the people who did not want to accept his projects and who were the cause of all the evil in Russia—the end was in sight. He therefore gladly renounced the principle of freedom and agreed entirely. Karenin fell silent, thoughtfully turning over the pages of his manuscript.

"By the way," said Oblonsky, "I want to ask you something—should you happen to run across Pomorsky, will you just mention to him that I'd very much like to get the vacant post of member of the board of the Joint Agency of the Mutual Credit Balance of the Southern Railways and Banking Houses."

Oblonsky was already very familiar with the name of the post that was so near his heart and he could pronounce it rapidly without mistake.

Karenin put a few searching questions about the activities of the new board and sank into thought. He was wondering whether there was anything in the activities of the new board that would be contrary to his own projects. But as the activities of the new institution were very complicated and his own projects covered a very wide field, he could not decide this all at once.

"No doubt," he said, taking off his pince-nez, "I could mention it to him. But what do you really want this post for?"

"There's a good salary attached to it, about nine thousand, and my means—"

830

"Nine thousand," repeated Karenin and frowned. The large figure of the salary recalled to him the fact that the activities in which Oblonsky proposed to engage were contrary to the main idea of his projects, which always leaned toward economy.

"I consider—and I have written a memorandum on this subject—that the enormous salaries paid nowadays are a symptom of the unsound economic policy of our administration."

"But what would you have?" said Oblonsky. "Let's say a bank director gets ten thousand—why, he's worth it. Or an engineer gets twenty thousand. Say what you like, the work they do is of vital importance."

"In my considered opinion, salary is payment for goods delivered and it must conform to the law of supply and demand. If, therefore, the fixed salary is a violation of this law—as, for instance, when I see two engineers leaving college together and both equally well trained and efficient, and one getting forty thousand while the other only earns two thousand, or when lawyers and hussars, possessing no special qualifications, are appointed directors of banks, with huge salaries—I can only conclude that their salaries are not fixed according to the law of supply and demand but simply by personal influence. And this is an abuse important in itself and having a deleterious effect on government service. I believe—"

Oblonsky hastened to interrupt his brother-in-law.

"Yes, but you must agree that a new and undoubtedly useful organization is being founded. Say what you like, it's a matter of vital importance. They are particularly anxious that it should be conducted in an *honest* way," said Oblonsky, emphasizing the word "honest."

But the Moscow significance of the word "honest" was unintelligible to Karenin.

"Honesty is merely a negative quality," he said.

"But you would greatly oblige me all the same," said Oblonsky, "if you just put in a word to Pomorsky. Just casually, I mean."

"But I should have thought it depended more on Bolgarinov," said Karenin.

"Bolgarinov has nothing against it," said Oblonsky, reddening.

Oblonsky reddened at the mention of Bolgarinov because he had called on the Jewish financier that morning and that visit had left a bad impression on him. Oblonsky was firmly convinced that the business enterprise to which he was offering his services was new, vital, and honest; but that morning when Bolgarinov had, with undisguised intention, made him wait two hours in his waiting room with other petitioners, he had suddenly felt uncomfortable.

Whether it was that he, Prince Oblonsky, a descendant of the princely house of Rurik, was kept cooling his heels for two hours in a Jew's waiting room or that for the first time in his life he did not follow the example of his ancestors of serving the state only and was entering a new field of activity, the fact remained that he had felt very uncomfortable. During those two hours in Bolgarinov's waiting room, walking jauntily about, smoothing his side whiskers, entering into conversation with the other job seekers, and inventing the pun he would tell his friends afterward about adjuring a Jew, Oblonsky carefully concealed his feelings from others and even from himself.

But all the time he felt uncomfortable and vexed without himself realizing why: whether it was because nothing would come of his pun of adjuring the Jew or because of some other reason. When at last Bolgarinov received him and was very polite to him, quite obviously triumphing in his humiliation, and practically refusing his request, Oblonsky tried to forget it as quickly as possible. And it was only now that he remembered and blushed.

CHAPTER 18

"There's another matter I'd like to discuss with you," said Oblonsky after a short pause, shaking off that unpleasant recollection. "I daresay you know what it is. It's about Anna."

At the mention of Anna's name, Karenin's face underwent a complete change: instead of its former animation, it assumed a weary and lifeless look.

"What exactly do you want of me?" Karenin said, fidgeting in his chair and closing his pince-nez with a snap.

"A decision, my dear fellow, some sort of decision. I am addressing you now" ("not as an injured husband," Oblonsky was about to say, but afraid of damaging his case, substituted the words) "not as a statesman" (which sounded quite incongruous), "but simply as a man, a good man and a Christian. You must take pity on her," he added.

"What exactly do you mean?" Karenin said quietly.

"Yes, you must take pity on her. If you had seen her as I have—and I spent the whole winter with her—you would have taken pity on her. Her position is awful—yes, awful!"

"I was under the impression," replied Karenin in a more high-pitched, almost shrill voice, "that she had everything she wished for."

"Oh, my dear fellow, for God's sake don't let's have any recriminations! What's past is past, and you know what she wants and what she is waiting for—a divorce."

"But I thought that she did not want a divorce if I insisted on keeping my son. I replied to her in that sense and I was under the impression that the matter was closed. Anyway," Karenin squeaked, "I consider it closed."

"For heaven's sake don't get excited," said Oblonsky, touching his brother-in-law's knee. "The matter is not closed. If you don't mind my recapitulating, this is how things stood: when you and Anna separated, you were great, you were as magnanimous as a man could be, you were willing to give her everything—freedom, even a divorce. She appreciated that. No, please, don't think I'm exaggerating. She did appreciate it. So much so, in fact, that at the first moment, feeling that she had wronged you, she did not and could not consider everything. She gave up everything. But life and time have shown that her position is agonizing and impossible."

"Anna's life cannot interest me," Karenin interrupted, raising his eyebrows.

"I hope you don't mind if I refuse to believe it," Oblonsky rejoined gently. "Her position is painful for her and of no benefit to anyone. She deserved it, you will say. She knows that and does not ask you for anything. She says quite frankly that she dare not ask you. But I and all her relations, all of us who love her, beg of you and implore you. Why should she suffer so much? Who gains by it?"

"You seem to put me in the position of defendant," said Karenin.

"Why no, no, not at all, try to understand me," said Oblonsky, touching Karenin's hand now, as if he were sure that the contact would mollify his brother-in-law. "All I say is that her position is agonizing, that you can put it right and that you will lose nothing by doing so. I'll arrange it all in such a way that you won't notice anything. You did promise, you know."

"The promise was given before. I thought the question about my son had settled the matter. Besides, I had hoped that Anna had enough magnanimity. . . ." Karenin, who had gone pale, brought out with trembling lips.

"She leaves everything to your magnanimity. She asks you, she implores you only for one thing—get her out of the impossible position she is in. She is no longer asking for her son. Alexey, you're a kindhearted man. Put yourself in her place for a moment. The question of a divorce is now a matter of life and death for her. If you had not promised before, she would have become reconciled to her position and have gone on living in the country. But you did promise; she wrote to you and moved to Moscow. And now she's been living for six months in Moscow, where every meeting is like a knife thrust into her heart, and she is waiting every day for your decision. Why, it's like keeping a condemned man for months with a noose round his head, promising him perhaps death or perhaps a reprieve. Have pity on her and I shall undertake to arrange everything. *Vos scrupules—*"

"I'm not talking about that," Karenin interrupted him in disgust. "But it's quite possible that I promised something I had no right to promise."

"So you're going back on your promise?"

"I'll never refuse to do what is possible, but I must have time to consider how far what I promised is possible."

"No, my dear fellow," said Oblonsky, jumping to his feet, "I don't want to believe it! She is as unhappy as a woman can be, and you can't refuse such a—"

"Inasmuch as my promise is possible. *Vous professez d'être un libre penseur.* But as a believer I cannot act contrary to the Christian law in so important a matter."

"But in Christian societies and in ours too, divorce,

as far as I know, is permitted," said Oblonsky. "Divorce is also permitted by our Church. And we see—"

"Permitted, but not in that sense."

"My dear fellow, I don't recognize you," Oblonsky said after a pause. "Was it not you (and didn't we appreciate it?) who forgave everything and, moved by true Christian feeling, were ready to sacrifice everything? You said yourself, 'Give your cloak, if they take your coat,' and now—"

"Please, I beg you," said Karenin in a squeaky voice, getting up suddenly, pale and with trembling jaw, "I beg you to stop—to—to stop this—er—conversation."

"Oh, no! Please, forgive me, forgive me if I have pained you," Oblonsky declared, smiling with embarrassment and holding out his hand, "but I've only delivered my message as an envoy."

Karenin gave him his hand and thought for a moment.

"I must think it over and seek guidance," he said. "I shall give you a definite answer the day after tomorrow," he added after a moment's consideration.

CHAPTER 19

Oblonsky was about to leave when Korney came into the room.

"Sergey Alexeyich," he announced.

"Who is Sergey Alexeyich?" Oblonsky began, but immediately recollected. "Oh, Seryozha," he said. "I thought Sergey Alexeyich was the director of a department. Anna," he thought, "asked me to see him."

And he remembered the timid, pathetic look with which Anna had said to him at parting: "Do all you can to see him. Find out where he is, who looks after him, everything about him. And, Stiva, if possible . . . It is possible, isn't it?" Oblonsky knew what that "if possible" meant, "If possible arrange a divorce so that I can have my son. . . ." Now Oblonsky realized that there could be no question of that, but he was glad all the same to see his nephew.

Karenin reminded his brother-in-law that they never spoke of his mother to the boy, and he asked him not to say a word to him about her.

"He was very ill after that meeting with his mother, which we had not foreseen," Karenin said. "We even feared for his life. But sensible treatment and sea bathing in the summer restored his health and now, on the doctor's advice, I send him to school. And, indeed, the influence of his schoolmates has had a good effect on him, and he is quite well and is making excellent progress."

"What a fine lad he's grown into! No longer little Seryozha, but big Sergey Alexeyich!" Oblonsky said with a smile, as he looked at the handsome, broad-shouldered boy in a dark blue tunic and long trousers, who came boldly and confidently into the room. The boy looked healthy and cheerful. He bowed to his uncle as to a stranger, but recognizing him he blushed and turned away quickly, as though offended and angry about something. He went up to his father and handed him his school report.

"Well, that's not so bad," said his father. "You can go now."

"He's grown thin and tall and is no longer a child but a real boy—I like it," said Oblonsky. "Do you remember me?"

The boy cast a quick glance at his father.

"Yes, *mon oncle*," he replied, glancing at his uncle and dropping his eyes again.

His uncle called him nearer and took his hand.

"Well, how are things?" he asked, wishing to have a talk with the boy but not knowing what to say.

The boy, blushing and not answering, gently withdrew his hand from his uncle's clasp. As soon as Oblonsky let his hand go, he threw a questioning glance at his father and, like a bird let out of its cage, went quickly out of the room.

A year had passed since Seryozha last saw his mother. Since then he had heard nothing more of her. During that year he had been sent to school and got to know and like his schoolmates. The dreams and memories of his mother, which, after their last meeting, had made him ill, no longer filled his mind. When they came back he took pains to drive them away, regarding them as shameful and fit only for girls and not for a boy and a classmate. He knew that there had been a quarrel between his father and his mother which separated them;

he knew that he would have to remain with his father, and did his best to get used to the idea.

When he saw his uncle, who looked like his mother, he felt uncomfortable because it brought back the memories which he considered shameful. It was the more disagreeable from some words he had overheard while waiting at the door of the study; and especially from the expression on his father's and uncle's faces, he guessed that they had probably been talking about his mother. And in order not to blame his father, with whom he lived and on whom he depended, and, above all, not to give way to sentiment which he considered so degrading, Seryozha tried not to look at his uncle, who had come to upset his peace of mind, and not to think of what he reminded him.

But when Oblonsky, who had come out after him, saw him on the stairs, called to him, and asked him how he spent his playtime at school, Seryozha, his father not being there, got into conversation with him.

"We play at railways now," he said in reply to his uncle's question. "It's like this, you see: two sit down on a form—they are the passengers, and one stands on the same form. The rest all harness themselves to it. They may do it with their hands or with their belts, and then they go rushing off through all the rooms. The doors are opened beforehand. Well, you see, it's jolly difficult to be the guard!"

"You mean the one standing up?" asked Oblonsky with a smile.

"Yes, you must be brave and quick, especially when the train stops all of a sudden or when someone falls down."

"Yes, that's no joke," said Oblonsky, gazing sadly into the boy's animated eyes, so like his mother's, no longer a child's eyes and no longer quite innocent. And though he had promised Karenin not to speak of Anna, he could not restrain himself.

"Do you remember your mother?" he asked suddenly.

"No, I don't," Seryozha said quickly and, blushing scarlet, dropped his eyes. His uncle could get nothing more out of him.

Half an hour later the Slav tutor found his pupil on the stairs, and for a long time he could not make out whether he was in a temper or was crying.

"I expect you must have hurt yourself when you fell down," said the tutor. "I told you it was a dangerous game. I shall have to tell your headmaster about it."

"If I'd hurt myself, no one would have known it. You can depend on that."

"What is it, then?"

"Oh, leave me alone! Remember or not—what business is it of his? Why should I remember? Leave me alone!" he cried, addressing himself not to his tutor, but to the whole world.

CHAPTER 20

Oblonsky, as always, did not waste his time in Petersburg. In Petersburg, in addition to the business he had to attend to—the arrangements for his sister's divorce and the post he wanted for himself—it was as usual necessary for him to refresh himself after, as he expressed it, the mustiness of Moscow.

Moscow, in spite of its *cafés chantants* and omnibuses, was still a stagnant swamp. Oblonsky always felt it. After living in Moscow for some time, especially in the proximity of his family, his spirits flagged. A long time in Moscow without a break reduced him to a state where he began to be upset by his wife's ill-humor and her constant reproaches, by the health and education of his children, and the petty details of his work at the office; even the fact that he had debts troubled him. But he had only to arrive in Petersburg and spend some time there among the set in which he moved, where people lived, really lived, instead of vegetating as in Moscow, and in a twinkling his cares vanished and melted away like wax in front of a fire.

His wife? . . . Only that day he had been talking to Prince Chechensky. He had a wife and a family, grown-up sons who were pages at Court, and he had another, illegitimate family with other children. Though the first family was far from bad, Prince Chechensky felt much happier in his second family. He took his eldest son to visit his second family and told Oblonsky that he considered it useful for his son because it broadened his mind. What would they say to it in Moscow?

Children? In Petersburg children did not interfere with the life of their fathers. Children were sent to boarding schools and there were none of those wild notions that were so prevalent in Moscow—Lvov was a case in point—that the children should have all the luxuries of life and the parents nothing but work and worry. Here they understood that a man ought to live for himself, as every civilized person should.

The Service? Government service too was not that constant, hopeless drudgery here that it was in Moscow. Here there was some personal interest in being a high civil servant. You met all sorts of people who could be of service to you, made witty remarks, performed all sorts of amusing tricks, took off persons and—before he knew it, a man's career was made, as was the case with Bryantsev, whom Oblonsky had met the day before and who was now a most influential state dignitary. This sort of government service was worth while.

But it was the idea of money matters they had in Petersburg that had a particularly soothing effect on Oblonsky. Bartnyansky, who spent at least fifty thousand a year to judge by his style of living, had said something quite remarkable to him on that score the night before.

Oblonsky had a long chat with Bartnyansky before dinner.

"I believe," he said to him, "you know Mordvinsky very well. Now, you could do me a good turn if you would put in a word for me with him. There's a post I should like to get. A member of a board of directors of—"

"I'm sorry, I don't think I could remember the name anyway. Only what the hell do you want to get yourself mixed up with those railway concerns and with Jews for? Whichever way you look at it, it's a disgusting business."

Oblonsky did not tell him that it was something of vital importance; Bartnyansky would not have understood that.

"I want the money. Have nothing to live on."

"But you do live, don't you?"

"Yes, but I'm in debt."

"Oh? How much?"

"Very much. Twenty thousand."

Bartnyansky laughed uproariously.

"Oh, you lucky fellow!" he exclaimed. "I owe a million and a half and I have absolutely nothing! But, as you see, one can still live!"

And Oblonsky saw the justice of this remark not only from hearsay but from actual fact. Zhivakhov's debts amounted to well over three hundred thousand and he had not a penny to bless himself with, yet he lived, and how he lived! Count Krivtsov, whose case had long been given up as hopeless, still kept two mistresses. Petrovsky had run through five million, continued to live in just the same style, and even was in charge of the Finance Department at a salary of twenty thousand. But quite apart from this, Petersburg had a pleasant physical effect on Oblonsky. He felt younger there. In Moscow he sometimes noticed his gray hairs, dozed off after dinner, stretched himself, walked slowly upstairs, breathing heavily, was bored in the company of young women, did not dance at balls. In Petersburg, on the other hand, he always felt ten years younger.

In Petersburg he appreciated fully the wisdom of what the sixty-year-old Prince Peter Oblonsky, who had just returned from abroad, had told him.

"We don't know how to live here," Peter Oblonsky said. "You see, I spent the summer in Baden. Felt quite a young man again. Yes, sir. Every time I saw a young girl, my fancy . . . Dinner, a couple of glasses of wine, and I'd feel strong and full of beans. I arrived in Russia—had to see my wife, and in the country, too, worse luck!—and after only two weeks I started walking about in a dressing gown at home and stopped dressing for dinner. As for thinking of young girls! . . . I've become quite an old man. The only thing left for me is to think of saving my soul. Then I went to Paris and I got better again."

Oblonsky felt just the same in Petersburg. In Moscow he let himself go to such an extent that if he went on living there a little longer, he might for all he knew have really got to the soul-saving stage; but in Petersburg he began to feel alive again.

Between the Princess Betsy Tverskoy and Oblonsky there existed long-established and rather peculiar relations. Oblonsky always jestingly paid court to her and made, also in jest, the most improper remarks to her, knowing that she liked it more than anything. The day after his talk to Karenin he called on her and, feeling a young man again, went so far in his bantering flirtation and silly love talk that he did not know how to extricate himself, for, unfortunately, far from being attracted to her, she positively disgusted him. This sort of relationship had established itself between them simply because she found him very attractive. He was therefore very pleased when Princess Myakhky arrived and put an end to their tête-à-tête.

"Ah, so you are here," she exclaimed on seeing him. "Well, how is your poor sister? Don't look at me like that," she added. "Ever since everyone has been attacking her, and they are all a hundred thousand times worse than she, I've come to the conclusion that she has acted splendidly. I can't forgive Vronsky for not letting me know when she was in Petersburg. I'd have called on her and gone out with her everywhere. Please, give her my love. Well, tell me about her."

"Well, her position is very difficult, she—" Oblonsky began, in the simplicity of his heart putting a literal interpretation on Princess Myakhky's words.

But Princess Myakhky, as was her wont, interrupted him immediately and began to talk herself.

"She did what everyone else, except myself, does, but they hide it. She did not want to deceive anyone and that's splendid. And the best thing she did was to leave that half-witted husband of hers, that brother-in-law of yours. I'm sorry, I always maintained that he was a fool, though everyone kept saying that he was clever, oh, so clever! Now that he has got himself mixed up with Lydia Ivanovna and Landau everyone says that he is crazy and I'd be glad not to agree with them, but this time I can't."

"But tell me, what does it mean?" said Oblonsky. "I went to see him yesterday about my sister's affair and I asked him for a definite answer. He did not give me an answer. He said he had to think it over and this morning, instead of an answer, I receive an invitation to call this evening on the Countess Lydia Ivanovna."

"Why, of course, of course," cried Princess Myakhky gleefully. "They'll ask Landau and see what he says."

"Landau? Why? Who is Landau?"

"Why, don't you know Jules Landau, *le fameux* Jules Landau, *le clairvoyant*? He, too, is crazy, but your sister's fate depends on him. That's what comes of living in the provinces. You know nothing. Landau, you see, was a shop assistant in Paris. One day he went to see his doctor. He fell asleep in the doctor's waiting room and while asleep began giving advice to all the other patients. Most remarkable advice it was, too. Then the wife of Yuly Meledinsky—the invalid, you remember?—got to hear about this Landau and took him to see her husband. He is treating her husband now. I don't think he's done him any good, for he is still as feeble as ever, but they believe in him and take him around with them. They brought him to Russia. Here everyone pounced on him and he began treating them all. He cured Countess Bezzubov and she took such a fancy to him that she adopted him."

"Adopted him?"

"Yes, adopted him. He's no longer Landau now but Count Bezzubov. But that's not the point. The point is that Lydia—I am very fond of her, though I don't think she's in her right mind—naturally pounced upon this Landau, and neither she nor Karenin do anything now without first consulting him, so that your sister's fate is now in the hands of this Landau, alias Count Bezzubov."

CHAPTER 21

After an excellent dinner and a large quantity of brandy at Bartnyansky's, Oblonsky arrived at the Countess Lydia Ivanovna's only a little after the appointed time.

"Who else is with the Countess—a Frenchman?" Oblonsky asked the hall porter, looking at Karenin's familiar overcoat and a strange, rather artless overcoat with clasps.

"Mr. Karenin and Count Bezzubov," replied the hall porter severely.

"The Princess Myakhky was right," thought Oblonsky, mounting the stairs. "Strange! However, it wouldn't be a bad idea to get friendly with her. She has enormous influence. If she were to put in a word with Pomorsky, the job's as good as mine."

It was still quite light outside, but in Countess Lydia Ivanovna's small drawing room the blinds were drawn and the lamps lit.

At a round table under a lamp sat the countess and Karenin, discussing something in low tones. A short, lean man, with hips like a woman's, knock-kneed, very pale, handsome, with beautiful shining eyes and long hair that fell over the collar of his frock coat, stood at the other end of the room, looking at the portraits on the wall. After greeting his hostess and Karenin, Oblonsky could not help glancing once more at the stranger.

"Monsieur Landau," the countess called, addressing him with a gentleness and shyness that astonished Oblonsky. And she introduced them.

Landau turned round hastily, walked up, and, smiling, put his flabby, sweaty hand into Oblonsky's outstretched hand, and immediately went back and continued to gaze at the portraits. The countess and Karenin exchanged meaningful glances.

"I'm very glad to see you, especially today," said the Countess Lydia Ivanovna, motioning Oblonsky to a seat near Karenin. "I introduced him to you as Landau," she went on in a low voice, glancing at the Frenchman and then at once at Karenin, "but he is really Count Bezzubov, as you no doubt know. Only he does not like the title."

"Yes, I have heard," replied Oblonsky. "I am told he completely cured Countess Bezzubov."

"She was here today," the countess said, addressing Karenin. "She was so pathetic. This separation is a terrible blow to her. A terrible blow!"

"Is he really going?" asked Karenin.

"Yes, he's going back to Paris. He heard a voice yesterday," said Countess Lydia Ivanovna, glancing at Oblonsky.

"Ah, a voice!" repeated Oblonsky, feeling that he must be very careful in this company, where something peculiar was about to occur or had already occurred, something to which he so far had no clue.

There was a moment's silence after which Countess Lydia Ivanovna said to Oblonsky with a subtle smile, as though coming to the main subject of their conversation:

"I've known you a long time and I am very pleased to know you better. *Les amis de nos amis sont nos amis.* But to be a friend, one has to enter into the state of one's friend's mind, and I'm afraid you are not doing this in the case of Mr. Karenin. You understand what I am talking about, don't you?" she said, raising her beautiful, dreamy eyes.

"To a certain extent, Countess, I do understand that the position of Mr. Karenin . . ." began Oblonsky, not quite grasping what it was all about and therefore wishing to confine himself to generalities.

"The change has nothing to do with his external position," the countess said sternly while at the same time following with enamored eyes Karenin, who had got up and joined Landau. "His heart is changed. He has been given a new heart and I'm afraid you haven't quite grasped the change that has taken place in him."

"Generally speaking, of course, I can imagine this change. We—er—have always been friendly and now . . ." said Oblonsky, responding with a warm glance to her look and at the same time wondering with which of the two ministers she was more closely connected, so that he should know which of them to ask her to influence on his behalf.

"The change which has taken place in him cannot weaken his feeling of love for his fellow men. On the contrary, that change can only strengthen his love. But I'm afraid you don't understand me. Won't you have some tea?" she said, indicating with her eyes the footman who was handing tea around on a tray.

"Not altogether, Countess. Of course, his misfortune . . ."

"Yes, his misfortune, which has become his greatest good fortune when his heart became new and was filled with Him," she said, looking with lovelorn eyes at Karenin.

"I think I could ask her to put in a word to both," thought Oblonsky.

"Why, of course, Countess," he said, "but I think that these changes are of such an intimate nature that no one, not even the closest friend, cares to speak of them."

"On the contrary, we must speak and so help one another."

"No doubt, but sometimes there are such differences of convictions, and besides . . ." said Oblonsky with a gentle smile.

"There cannot be any differences in a matter that concerns Holy Truth."

"Of course not, but . . ." And, looking embarrassed, Oblonsky stopped short. He realized that she was talking of religion.

"I think he's going to fall asleep," Karenin whispered in a significant tone of voice, approaching Lydia Ivanovna.

Oblonsky looked round. Landau was sitting by the window, leaning against the arm and back of an armchair, with his head drooping. Noticing that they were all looking at him, he raised his head and smiled a naïve, childlike smile.

"Don't take any notice of him," said Lydia Ivanovna, with a light movement pushing a chair up for Karenin. "I have observed . . ." she began, when a footman entered with a note. She ran over the note quickly and, excusing herself, with extreme rapidity wrote an answer, handed it to the footman, and returned to the table. "I have observed," she continued her interrupted sentence, "that Muscovites, especially the men, are most indifferent to religion."

"Oh, no, Countess, I think that Muscovites enjoy the reputation of being the most stanch believers," said Oblonaky.

"Yes, but so far as I know you are unfortunately one of the indifferent," said Karenin, addressing Oblonsky with a weary smile.

"How can one be indifferent!" exclaimed Lydia Ivanovna.

"In this respect I'm not so much indifferent as in a state of suspended judgment," said Oblonsky with his most mollifying smile. "I don't think that the time for those questions has yet come for me."

Karenin and Lydia Ivanovna exchanged glances.

"We can never know whether the time has come for us or not," said Karenin severely. "We ought not to think whether we are ready or not: grace is not influenced by human considerations—sometimes it descends not on those who seek it but on those who, like Saul, are unprepared."

"No, not yet, I think," said Lydia Ivanovna, who had been watching the Frenchman's movements.

Landau got up and came up to them.

"You don't mind my listening?" he asked.

"Why, no," said Lydia Ivanovna, looking tenderly at him. "I did not want to disturb you. Sit down beside us."

"The important thing is not to shut one's eyes to the light," Karenin continued.

"Oh, if you knew the happiness we experience feeling His continual presence in our souls!" said Countess Lydia Ivanovna, smiling beatifically.

"But surely a man may sometimes feel himself incapable of rising to such heights," said Oblonsky, feeling that it was not quite honest of him to recognize the existence of such religious heights and at the same time be unable to bring himself to admit that he was a freethinker to a person who by a single word to Pomorsky might secure him the desired post.

"You mean to say that he is prevented by sin, don't you?" said Lydia Ivanovna. "But that is a false view. There is no sin for a true believer—the sin has already been expiated. *Pardon*," she added, glancing at the footman, who came in with another note. She read it and answered verbally: "Tell him tomorrow at the Grand Duchess's. For a true believer," she went on, "there is no sin."

"Yes, but faith without works is dead," said Oblonsky, remembering the sentence from the catechism, and only by a smile maintaining his independence.

"There it is—from the Epistle of St. James," said Karenin, turning to Lydia Ivanovna with a somewhat reproachful note in his voice, as though referring to something they had discussed more than once. "How much harm has been done by a false interpretation of that passage! Nothing turns people away from religious beliefs as much as such an interpretation. 'I have no works and therefore I have no faith,' and yet that is not said anywhere. It's just the opposite."

"To labor for God, to save one's soul by works and fasting," said Countess Lydia Ivanovna with an expression of disgust and contempt, "those are the barbarous notions of our monks. . . . Yet we do not find it said anywhere. It is much simpler and easier," she added, looking at Oblonsky with the same encouraging smile with which at Court she used to encourage young Maids of Honor who felt embarrassed in their new surroundings.

"We are saved by Christ who suffered for us, we are saved by faith," Karenin put in, showing his approval of her remark by a look.

"Vous comprenez l'anglais?" asked Lydia Ivanovna and, receiving an affirmative answer, got up and began

looking among the books on the shelf. "I'd like to read you *Safe and Happy, or Under the Wing*," she said, with an inquiring look at Karenin. And having found the book and sat down again, she opened it. "It is quite short. Here is described the way in which faith can be acquired and the joy, higher than any bliss on earth, with which faith fills the soul of man. A man who has faith cannot be unhappy, because he is never alone. But you will see. . . ." She was about to begin reading when the footman came in again. "Mrs. Borozdin? Tell her tomorrow at two. Yes," she said, putting her finger in the book to mark the place and sighed, gazing with her beautiful dreamy eyes straight before her, "that is how true faith acts. Do you know Marie Sanin? You have heard about her misfortune? She lost her only child. She was in despair. And what do you think? She found this Friend and now she thanks God for the death of her child. That is the happiness faith gives!"

"Ah, yes, this is very . . ." said Oblonsky, glad that she was going to read and give him time to collect his thoughts. "No," he decided, "I'd better not ask for anything today. I only hope I can get out of here without making a mess of things."

"I'm afraid you'll be bored as you don't understand English," said Countess Lydia Ivanovna, addressing Landau. "But it won't take long."

"Oh, I'll understand," Landau said with the same smile and closed his eyes.

Karenin and Lydia Ivanovna exchanged significant glances and the reading began.

CHAPTER 22

Oblonsky was completely taken aback by the novel, strange language he was listening to. The complexity of Petersburg life had a stimulating effect on him, lifting him out of the stagnation of Moscow. But he liked and understood these complexities in spheres congenial and familiar to him. But in this strange environment he was puzzled, stunned, and did not know what to make of it all. Listening to Countess Lydia Ivanovna and feeling Landau's fine, naïve or knavish—he did not know himself which—eyes fixed on him, Oblonsky began to be conscious of a peculiar heaviness in his head.

The most diverse thoughts went whirling through his head. "Marie Sanin is glad her child's dead. . . . I wish I could have a smoke now. . . . To be saved one must only have faith. . . . The monks themselves do not know how to do it; Countess Lydia Ivanovna alone knows. . . . And why does my head feel so heavy? Is it the brandy or because all this is so very odd? I don't think I have done anything shocking so far. All the same I can't possibly ask her now. I have heard that they make one pray. I hope they won't make me. That would be too absurd. And what nonsense she is reading, but her pronunciation is good. Landau—Bezzubov. Why Bezzubov?" Suddenly Oblonsky felt his lower jaw dropping irresistibly into a yawn. He smoothed his whiskers, concealing his yawn, and shook himself. But the next moment he felt himself falling asleep and was on the point of snoring. He roused himself just as Countess Lydia Ivanovna said: "He's asleep."

Oblonsky looked round in alarm, feeling guilty and caught in the act. But he was immediately relieved to notice that the words "He's asleep" did not refer to him, but to Landau. The Frenchman had fallen asleep just as Oblonsky had done. But Oblonsky's sleep (so he thought) might have offended them (though he did not really believe it, so strange did everything appear to him), whereas Landau's sleep delighted them, the countess especially.

"Mon ami," said Lydia Ivanovna, carefully holding the folds of her silk dress to prevent it from rustling and in her excitement calling Karenin *mon ami, "donnez lui la main. Vous voyez?* Sh-sh . . ." She hissed at the footman who came in again. "I'm not at home."

The Frenchman was asleep or pretended to be asleep, leaning his head against the back of the chair, and making weak movements with his clammy hand, lying on his knees, as if trying to catch something. Karenin got up, knocking against the table in spite of his caution, and put his hand into the Frenchman's. Oblonsky, too, got up, and opening his eyes wide, as though wishing to wake himself in case he was asleep, looked first at one and then at the other. It was all real. Oblonsky felt that his head was getting worse and worse.

848

"Que la personne qui est arrivée la dernière, celle qui demande, qu'elle sorte! Qu'elle sorte!" said the Frenchman without opening his eyes.

"Vous m'excuserez, mais vous voyez . . . Revenez vers dix heures, encore mieux demain."

"Qu'elle sorte," the Frenchman repeated impatiently.

"C'est moi, n'est-ce pas?"

And, receiving an answer in the affirmative, Oblonsky forgetting the request he had wanted to make to Lydia Ivanovna and forgetting his sister's affairs, conscious only of the one desire to get out of there as quickly as possible, tiptoed out of the room and rushed out into the street, as if fleeing from an infected house. He talked and joked a long time with the cabby, trying to regain his senses as soon as possible.

In the French theater, where he arrived in time for the last act, and then at the Tartar restaurant where he had some champagne, Oblonsky was able to breathe freely again to some extent in an atmosphere congenial to him. But all the same he did not feel quite himself that evening.

When he returned to Peter Oblonsky's house, where he was staying, he found a note from Betsy. She wrote that she was very anxious to finish their interrupted conversation and asked him to call next day. He had scarcely finished reading the note, making a wry face over it, when he heard downstairs the ponderous tread of men carrying something heavy.

Oblonsky went out to see what it was. It was the rejuvenated Peter Oblonsky. He was so drunk that he could not walk upstairs, but he told the servants to set him on his feet when he saw Oblonsky. Clinging to Oblonsky, he went back to his room with him and there he began telling him how he had spent the evening, and fell asleep.

Oblonsky was in low spirits, which happened rarely with him, and could not fall asleep for a long time. Everything he recalled was disgusting, but most disgusting of all, like something shameful, was the memory of the evening at Lydia Ivanovna's.

Next morning he received from Karenin a definite refusal to divorce Anna and he realized that the decision was based on what the Frenchman had said in his real or pretended sleep the evening before.

CHAPTER 23

To do anything in married life, husband and wife must be either in complete agreement or at loggerheads with one another. But when the relations between husband and wife are uncertain, neither one thing nor the other, nothing can be undertaken.

Many families continue for years in their old rut, detested both by husband and wife, simply because there is neither complete dissension nor agreement.

Both for Vronsky and for Anna life in Moscow in the heat and dust, when the gentle warmth of the sun in the spring was succeeded by the heat of the summer and all the trees on the boulevards had long been in leaf and the leaves were already covered in dust, was unbearable. But they did not move to Vozdvizhenskoye, as they had long ago decided to do, but stayed on in Moscow, which both of them had begun to loathe, because there had been no agreement between them of late.

The irritation that divided them had no tangible cause, and all their attempts at finding an explanation for it not only failed to remove it, but exacerbated it. It was an inner irritation, based on her suspicion that his love for her had diminished and on his feeling of regret that he had placed himself in a difficult position for her sake, which she, instead of making it easier for him, made more difficult still. Neither of them would speak of the cause of their irritation, but each thought the other in the wrong and at every opportunity tried to prove it to one another.

For her he, with all his habits, thoughts, desires, with all his mental and physical qualities, meant one thing only: love for women, and this love, which she felt should be concentrated on her entirely, was diminishing; consequently, according to her reasoning, he must have transferred part of this love to other women or to one other woman—and she was jealous. She was jealous not of any particular woman, but of the diminution of his love. Not having as yet an object for her jealousy, she

850

was looking for one. At the slightest hint she transferred her jealousy from one object to another. Now she was jealous of the coarse women with whom he might so easily have an affair thanks to his bachelor connections; now she was jealous of the society women he might meet; now she was jealous of some imaginary girl whom he might want to marry after breaking with her. This last idea tormented her most of all, particularly as he himself had carelessly told her in an unguarded moment that his mother understood him so little that she actually tried to persuade him to marry the young Princess Sorokin.

And being jealous, Anna was indignant with him and was constantly seeking reasons to justify her indignation. She blamed him for everything that was painful in her position. The agonizing state of suspense, one moment full of hope and another of despair, in which she lived in Moscow, Karenin's dilatoriness and indecision, her own seclusion—she put it all down to him. If he loved her, he would realize how unbearable her situation was and do something to get her out of it. It was his fault, too, that they were living in Moscow and not in the country. He could not live buried in the country as she would have liked to. He had to have society, and it was he who put her in this awful position, the wretchedness of which he simply refused to understand. And it was he again whose fault it was that she was forever parted from her son.

Even the rare moments of tenderness which occurred between them did not soothe her: in his tenderness she now detected a shade of calm self-confidence, which had not been there before and which exasperated her.

It was already dusk. Anna, all alone, awaiting his return from a men's dinner party, paced up and down his study (the room in which the traffic noises were least audible), going over in her mind every detail of their quarrel the day before. Going back from the abusive words they had exchanged during the quarrel to what had been their cause, she at last got to the beginning of their conversation. For a long time she could not believe that the dispute had arisen from such an innocuous conversation about a matter that was of no consequence whatever to either of them. But so, in fact, it was. It had

851

all begun with his laughing at the girls' high schools, which he considered unnecessary, while she defended them. He spoke disrespectfully of women's education in general and said that Hannah, Anna's little protégée, had no need of any knowledge of physics.

This irritated Anna. She interpreted it as a contemptuous allusion to her own occupations. And she thought of something that should make him pay for the pain he had caused her.

"I don't expect you to understand me or my feelings, as a man who loved me would, but I did expect ordinary delicacy from you," she said.

And, to be sure, he flushed with vexation and said something disagreeable. She could not remember what her reply was, but it was at this point that he had said with the obvious intent to hurt her too:

"It is quite true that I'm not interested in your partiality for this girl because I can see that it is unnatural."

The cruelty with which he shattered the world which she had constructed for herself with such difficulty in order to be able to endure her hard life, the unfairness with which he accused her of hypocrisy and unnaturalness, made her blood boil.

"I am very sorry that only what is coarse and material is comprehensible and natural to you," she said and walked out of the room.

When he came to her in the evening, they did not refer to their quarrel, but both of them felt that it had been smoothed over, not settled.

Now he had been away from home all day and she had felt so lonely and miserable at being on bad terms with him that she was quite willing to forget and forgive everything and make it up with him, and even wished to take the blame on herself and exonerate him.

"I'm alone to blame. I'm irritable. I'm unreasonably jealous. I'll make it up with him and we will go back to the country, where I shall be calmer," she said to herself.

"Unnatural," she suddenly remembered the word that had hurt her most because of his intention to wound her feelings.

"I know what he wanted to say. He wanted to say: it is unnatural not to love your own daughter but someone else's child. But what does he understand of the love for

852

children, of my love for Seryozha, whom I have given up for his sake? But that desire to hurt me! Yes, he loves another woman. It can't be anything else."

And realizing that in wishing to calm herself she had again completed the circle she had been around before and had returned to her former state of irritation, she was horrified at herself. "Is it possible that I can't? Is it possible that I can't take the blame on myself? He is truthful, he is honest, he loves me. I love him. In a few days I shall get my divorce. What more do I want? What I want is calmness and confidence, and I will take it on myself. Yes, now, as soon as he comes, I'll tell him that it was my fault, though it really wasn't, and we will go away."

And so as not to think any more about it and not to give in to irritation, she rang the bell and ordered her trunks to be brought, to pack their things for the country.

At ten o'clock Vronsky arrived.

CHAPTER 24

"Well, did you have a good time?" she asked with a guilty and meek look as she came out to meet him.

"Same as usual," he replied, realizing at once from one look at her that she was in one of her good moods. He was already accustomed to these transitions and was particularly glad of it today because he himself was in the best of spirits.

"What do I see? Ah, that's right!" he said, pointing to the trunks in the passage.

"Yes, we must go away. I went out for a drive and it was so lovely that I longed to be in the country. There is nothing to keep you here, is there?"

"It's the only thing I want. I'll be back in a moment. I just want to change. Let's have some tea."

And he went to his study.

There was something offensive in the way he said, "Ah, that's right!" just as one speaks to a child when it stops being naughty, and even more offensive was the contrast between her penitent tone and his self-confident one; and for an instant she felt a desire for a fight rising in her; but with an effort she suppressed it and met Vronsky with the same cheerful expression as before.

When he came in she told him, partly repeating words she had prepared, how she had spent the day and her plans for their departure.

"You know it came to me almost like an inspiration," she said. "Why wait for the divorce here? Won't it do just as well in the country? I can't wait any longer. I don't want to go on hoping, I don't want to hear anything more about the divorce. I've made up my mind that it shall not influence my life any longer. Don't you agree?"

"Yes, of course," he said, throwing an uneasy glance at her excited face.

"Well, what have you been doing at your dinner party? Who was there?" she asked after a pause.

Vronsky told her the names of the guests. "The dinner was excellent," he said, "the boat race and everything was quite nice, but I'm afraid in Moscow they can't manage things without doing something ridiculous. Some woman turned up, the queen of Sweden's swimming instructress, and gave a display of her art."

"You mean, she swam?" Anna asked, frowning.

"Yes, in some sort of red bathing costume. An old, hideous woman. Well, so when are we off?"

"What a silly idea! Is there anything particular in the way she swims?" asked Anna, without answering his question.

"Absolutely nothing. I quite agree—it was awfully silly. So when do you think of going?"

Anna shook her head as though wishing to drive away an unpleasant thought.

"When are we going? Why, the sooner the better. We can't get ready by tomorrow. The day after tomorrow."

"Wait a moment. The day after tomorrow is Sunday and I must go and see Mother," said Vronsky, looking embarrassed because as soon as he mentioned his mother he felt Anna's intent and suspicious glance fixed on him. His embarrassment confirmed her suspicions. She flushed and turned away from him. Now it was no longer the Swedish queen's swimming instructress she was thinking of but young Princess Sorokin who lived with Countess Vronsky in the country near Moscow.

854

"Couldn't you go there tomorrow?" she said.

"No, I couldn't. The power of attorney and money for the business I'm going there for will not have arrived by tomorrow," he replied.

"In that case we won't go at all."

"Why not?"

"I won't go any later. Monday or not at all!"

"But why?" Vronsky asked as though in astonishment. "There's no sense in that!"

"You can see no sense in that because you don't care a rap about me. You don't want to understand what my life is like. The only thing I was interested in here was Hannah. You say it's all pretense. You said yesterday that I don't love my own daughter, that I pretend to love this English girl and that it is unnatural. Well, I'd like to know what kind of life can be natural for me here."

For an instant she recovered her senses and was horrified at having broken her resolution. Yet though she knew that she was encompassing her own ruin, she could not restrain herself, she could not resist pointing out to him how wrong he was, she could not give in to him.

"I never said that. All I said was that I did not sympathize with that sudden affection."

"Why don't you speak the truth, you who are always boasting of your straightforwardness?"

"I never boast and I never tell a lie," he said quietly, restraining his rising anger. "I'm very sorry you don't respect—"

"Respect is an invention of people who want to cover up the empty place where love should be. And if you don't love me any more, it would be better and more honest to say so!"

"Lord, this is becoming unbearable!" cried Vronsky, getting up from his chair. And stopping in front of her, he said slowly: "Why do you try my patience?" He said it with an air as if he could have said much more, but restrained himself. "It has its limits!"

"What do you want to say by that?" she exclaimed, looking with terror at the undisguised expression of hatred on his whole face and particularly in his cruel, menacing eyes.

"What I want to say is . . ." he began, but stopped short. "I must ask you what it is you want of me?"

"What can I want? I can only want that you should not desert me as you're thinking of doing," she said, having realized what he had left unsaid. "But I don't want that—it's of secondary importance. I want your love, and that does not exist any more. Which means that it is all over."

She walked toward the door.

"Wait! Wait, will you?" said Vronsky, still frowning darkly but holding her back by the hand. "What is the matter? I said we must put off our departure for three days, to which you replied that I was lying, that I was not an honest man."

"Yes, and I repeat that a man who reproaches me because he has given up everything for my sake," she said, recalling the words of an earlier quarrel, "is worse than dishonest—he is heartless!"

"There are limits to one's patience!" he exclaimed and quickly let go of her hand.

"He hates me, that's clear," she thought and went out of the room in silence and without looking back.

"He is in love with another woman—that is clearer still," she said to herself, as she went into her own room. "I want love, and it no longer exists. So it is all over," she repeated the words she had said, "and it must be finished.

"But how?" she asked herself and sat down in an easy chair before the looking glass.

Thoughts of where she should go now—to the aunt who had brought her up, to Dolly, or simply abroad by herself—of what he was doing now alone in his study, of whether this quarrel was final or whether a reconciliation was still possible, of what all her former Petersburg acquaintances would be saying about her now, of how Karenin would regard it, and many other thoughts about what would happen now after the rupture came into her head, but it was not with all her mind that she gave herself up to these speculations. There was one vague idea in her mind which alone interested her, but she could not formulate it clearly. Thinking of Karenin again, she recollected her illness after her confinement and the feeling that never left her at that time. "Why did I not die?" She recalled the words she had uttered then and her feelings at the time. And she suddenly realized what was at the back of her mind. Yes, that would solve everything. "To die! Karenin's shame and disgrace, and Seryozha's, and my own terrible shame—death will wipe out everything! If I die, he too will be sorry. He will pity me, love me, and will suffer on my account." She sat in her chair with a smile of self-pity frozen on her lips, pulling off and on the rings on her left hand, vividly imagining to herself his feelings after her death.

The sound of approaching footsteps, his footsteps, distracted her. She pretended to be busy putting away her rings, and paid no attention to him.

He came up to her and, taking her hand, said softly:

"Anna, let's go the day after tomorrow if you like. I agree to anything."

She made no answer.

"Well?" he asked.

"You know yourself," she said and, unable to restrain herself any longer, burst into sobs.

"Have done with me, have done with me!" she murmured between her sobs. "I'll go away tomorrow. . . . I'll do more. Who am I? An immoral woman. A millstone round your neck. I don't want to torment you any longer. I don't want to. I'll set you free. You don't love me. You love another!"

Vronsky besought her to calm herself, he assured her that there was not the slightest foundation for her jealousy, that he had never ceased loving her and never would, that he loved her more than ever.

"Anna, why torture yourself and me like that?" he said, kissing her hands. There was a look of tenderness in his face, and she thought she detected tears in the sound of his voice and felt their moisture on her hand. And in an instant Anna's despairing jealousy changed into desperate, passionate tenderness; she flung her arms round his neck and covered his neck, head, and hands with kisses.

CHAPTER 25

Feeling that their reconciliation was complete, Anna eagerly began making preparations for the departure to the country. Though it was not settled yet whether they

857

would go on Monday or Tuesday, as the night before each kept giving way to the other, Anna was busily getting ready for their departure, feeling quite indifferent now whether they left a day earlier or later. She was standing in her room before an open trunk, sorting clothes, when he came in earlier than usual, dressed to go out.

"I'll go to Mother now. She can send me the money through Yegorov. I shall be ready to leave tomorrow," he said.

Good as her mood was, the mention of his visit to his mother's made her wince inwardly.

"I don't think I shall be ready myself," she said, and immediately thought: "So it was possible to arrange things as I wanted to!"

"No," she went on, "do as you wished. Go to the dining room, I'll come as soon as I've sorted out these things that are not wanted," she said, piling some more clothes into Annushka's arms.

Vronsky was eating his beefsteak when she entered the dining room.

"You can't imagine how hateful these rooms have become to me," she said, sitting down beside him to her coffee. "There's nothing more horrible than these furnished rooms. There's no personality about them, no soul. This clock, these curtains, and, above all, the wallpaper—what a nightmare! I think of Vozdvizhenskoye as of a promised land. You're not sending off the horses yet?"

"No, they'll come on after us. Are you driving out anywhere?"

"I wanted to go to Mrs. Wilson's to take her some dresses. So it's definitely tomorrow?" she said in a cheerful voice, but suddenly her face changed.

Vronsky's valet came in to get a receipt for a telegram from Petersburg. There was nothing extraordinary in Vronsky's getting a telegram, but as though wishing to hide something from her, he told his valet that the receipt was in his study and then hastily turned to her.

"I shall most certainly have everything settled by tomorrow," he said.

"Who is the telegram from?" she asked, not listening to him.

"From Stiva," he replied reluctantly.

"Why didn't you show it to me? What secrets can there be between Stiva and me?"

Vronsky called the valet back and told him to bring the telegram.

"I didn't want to show it to you because Stiva has a passion for sending telegrams. What's the use of telegraphing when nothing has been settled?"

"About the divorce?"

"Yes. He wires he could get no definite decision. He was promised a final answer soon. Here, read it yourself."

Anna took the telegram with shaking hands and read what Vronsky had said. At the end were added the words: "Little hope, but will do everything possible and impossible."

"I told you yesterday that I don't mind when I get a divorce or whether I get one at all," she said, coloring. "There was not the slightest necessity to hide it from me."

"In the same way," she thought, "he can hide his correspondence with women from me, and for all I know he does hide it."

"Yashvin wanted to call this morning with Voytov," said Vronsky. "It seems he has won from Pestsov all and even more than Pestsov can pay—about sixty thousand."

"But why do you imagine," she said, irritated because by his change of subject he showed so obviously that she was losing her temper, "that this news interests me so much that it must be concealed from me? I said I don't want to think about it and I only wish you were as little interested in it as I am."

"I am interested because I like things to be clear and aboveboard."

"It's not the outward form but love that has to be clear and aboveboard," she said, getting more and more irritated not by what he said, but by the cold, calm tone in which he spoke. "Why do you want it?"

"Good Lord, again about love!" he thought, making a wry face. "You know perfectly well why," he said. "For your sake and for the sake of the children we may have."

"We shan't have any."

"That would be a great pity," he said.

"You want it for the sake of the children, but you

don't think about me, do you?" she said, quite forgetting and indeed not having heard that he had said: "*For your sake* and for the sake of the children."

The question of having children had long been a subject of dispute between them and had always irritated her. His desire to have children she explained as showing his indifference to her beauty.

"Oh, but I said *for your sake*. Most of all for your sake," he added, wincing as though with pain, "because I'm quite certain that a great deal of your irritability is due to the uncertainty of your position."

"Well, now that he has stopped pretending I can see all his cold hatred for me," she thought, not listening to his words, but gazing with horror at the cold, cruel judge that looked provokingly at her out of his eyes.

"That is not the reason," she said, "and I really fail to understand how the reason for what you're pleased to call my irritability can be due to anything but the fact that I am entirely in your power. What uncertainty of position can there be about that? Quite the contrary!"

"I'm very sorry you don't seem to wish to understand," he interrupted her, stubbornly intent on expressing his thought. "The uncertainty arises from your imagining that I am free."

"So far as that is concerned, you needn't worry about it at all," she declared and, turning away from him, began drinking her coffee.

She lifted her cup, sticking out her little finger, and put it to her lips. After a few sips she glanced at him and the expression on his face told her clearly that her hand, her gesture, and the sound she made with her lips were repulsive to him.

"I don't care a damn what your mother thinks and whom she wants to marry you to," she said, putting down the cup with a trembling hand.

"But that's not what we were talking about."

"Yes, it is. And, believe me, I am not interested in a heartless woman, whether she is old or not, whether she is your mother or not, and I don't want to know her."

"Anna, I beg you not to speak disrespectfully of my mother."

"A woman whose heart does not tell her where her son's happiness and honor lie has no heart."

"I must ask you again not to speak disrespectfully of

860

my mother, whom I respect," he said, raising his voice and looking sternly at her.

She made no answer. Looking intently at his face and hands, she recalled every detail of their reconciliation the night before and his passionate love-making. "He will be making love in the same way to other women— he wants to, I'm sure of that," she thought.

"You don't love your mother," she said, looking at him with hatred. "It's all words, words, words!"

"If that is so, we must . . ."

"Make up our minds? Well, I've made up mine," she said and was about to go out, but at that moment Yashvin came into the room. Anna greeted him and stopped.

Why, when a storm was raging in her heart and when she felt she was at a turning point of her life, which might have dire consequences for her, why she should at that moment have to pretend before a stranger who sooner or later would find out everything, she could not tell; but immediately suppressing the storm within her, she sat down and began talking to their visitor.

"Well, how are your affairs? Has the money been paid?" she asked Yashvin.

"Oh, not so bad. I don't think I'll get it all and I have to leave on Wednesday. And when are you leaving?" said Yashvin, screwing up his eyes and looking at Vronsky, evidently guessing that they had been quarreling.

"The day after tomorrow, I believe," said Vronsky.

"You've been meaning to go for a long time, haven't you?"

"But now it's definite," said Anna, looking straight into Vronsky's eyes with an expression which told him that he need no longer think of any possibility of a reconciliation.

"Aren't you sorry for that unfortunate Pestsov?" she continued her conversation with Yashvin.

"I never asked myself whether I was sorry or not. You see," he pointed to his side pocket, "my entire fortune is there. I'm a rich man now, but I shall be going to the club tonight and perhaps leave it a beggar. You see, whoever sits down to play with me also wants to leave me without a shirt to my back, and the same is true of me. So we fight, and that's what is so exciting."

"But suppose you were married," said Anna, "what do you think your wife would feel about it?"

Yashvin laughed.

"Well, you see, that's why I never married and never intend to."

"What about Helsingfors?" said Vronsky, joining in the conversation and glancing at Anna, who had smiled.

Meeting his look, Anna's face instantly assumed a cold and stern expression, as if she wished to say to him: "It's not forgotten. Everything is just the same."

"Have you never been in love?" she said to Yashvin.

"Good Lord, hundreds of times! But, you see, some men can sit down to cards and at the same time be able always to leave for a rendezvous, at the appointed time. But I can have a love affair and at the same time never be late for cards in the evening. That's how I manage it."

"I was not asking you about that, but about the real thing." She was going to say "Helsingfors," but did not want to repeat the word Vronsky had used.

Voytov, who was buying a horse from Vronsky, arrived. Anna got up and went out of the room.

Before leaving the house, Vronsky came to her room. She tried to pretend to be looking for something on the table but, ashamed of the pretense, stared coldly at him.

"What do you want?" she asked him in French.

"Gambetta's pedigree, I've sold him," he said. His tone of voice conveyed more clearly than any words: "I have no time for explanations and it wouldn't lead to anything, anyway."

"I'm not to blame for anything," he thought. "If she wants to punish herself, *tant pis pour elle.*"

But as he was going out, he thought she said something and his heart suddenly turned over with pity for her.

"What, Anna?" he asked.

"Nothing," she replied, coldly and calmly as before.

"Well, if it's nothing, *tant pis pour elle*," he thought, again chilled.

As he was going out, he caught sight of her face in the looking glass: it was pale and her lips were trembling. He wanted to stop and say something nice to her, but his legs carried him out of the room before he could think what to say. He was out all that day and when he came home late at night, the maid told him that Anna had a headache and asked him not to go into her room.

CHAPTER 26

Never before had their quarrel lasted a whole day. Today was the first time. And it was not a quarrel. It was quite a clear admission of a complete estrangement. Could he otherwise have looked at her as he had done when he came into the room for Gambetta's pedigree? Look at her, see that her heart was bursting with despair, and go out in silence with that calm and indifferent expression on his face? He was not only out of love with her, he hated her because he was in love with another woman—that was obvious.

And recalling all the cruel words he had said to her, Anna was thinking of the other words which he had apparently wished to say and indeed could have said to her, and she was becoming more and more irritated.

"I'm not holding you," he could have said. "You can go where you like. I suppose the reason why you did not want to obtain a divorce from your husband is that you would like to go back to him. Well, go back! If you want money, I'll give you some. How many rubles do you want?"

All the cruelest things a coarse man could say she imagined him to have said to her, and she did not forgive him for them just as if he had really said them.

"And wasn't it only yesterday that he swore that he loved me, he—a truthful and honest man? Haven't I many times before been in despair for nothing?" she said to herself a moment later.

The whole of that day, with the exception of her visit to Mrs. Wilson, which took her about two hours, Anna spent wondering whether all was over between them or whether there was still hope of a reconciliation. Ought she to leave at once or see him once more? She waited for him all day and in the evening, having left word for him that she had a headache, went to her room, thinking: "If he comes in spite of the maid's message, it means that he still loves me. If he doesn't come, it means that all is over and then I shall decide what I am to do!"

In the evening she heard his carriage stop, heard his ring at the door, his footsteps, his conversation with the maid: he believed what he was told, he did not want to find out more and went to his room. So all was over.

And death as the only way of restoring his love for her in his heart, of punishing him, and of gaining the victory in the fight which an evil spirit was waging against him in her heart, presented itself clearly and vividly to her.

Now nothing mattered any more: whether they went to Vozdvizhenskoye or not, whether she obtained a divorce from her husband or not—it was all useless. She wanted one thing only—to punish him.

When she poured out her usual dose of opium, it occurred to her that she had only to drink the whole bottle in order to die, and it seemed to her so simple and easy that she again began thinking with relish how he would suffer, be sorry, and cherish her memory when it was too late. She lay in bed with open eyes, staring at the stucco cornice of the ceiling by the light of a single guttering candle and at the shadow the screen cast on it, and she vividly pictured to herself what he would feel when she was no more, when she would be nothing but a memory for him. "How could I have said those cruel things to her?" he would say to himself. "How could I have left the room without saying anything to her? But now she is no more. Now she is gone from us forever. She is there. . . ." Suddenly the shadow of the screen wavered, covered the entire cornice, the entire ceiling, and other shadows rushed toward it from the other side; for an instant the shadows rushed back, but a moment later moved forward with renewed swiftness, wavered, coalesced, and the room was plunged into darkness. "Death!" she thought. And she was seized with such terror that for a long time she could not make out where she was, and for a long time she could not find a match with her trembling hands and light another candle in the place of the one that had burned down and gone out. "No, anything—only to live! Why, I love him and he loves me! All this has been before and it will pass," she said, feeling tears of joy rolling down her cheeks at her return to life. To escape from her fears, she hastily went to him in his study.

He was sound asleep. She went up to him, and holding the lighted candle over his face stood a long time looking at him. Now, when he was asleep, she loved him so much that she could not restrain tears of tenderness at the sight of him; but she knew that were he to wake up, he would look at her coldly, conscious of his own rightness, and that before telling him how much she loved him she would have to prove to him in what way he had wronged her. She returned to her room without waking him and after a second dose of opium fell toward morning into a heavy, troubled sleep during which she never ceased to be conscious of herself.

In the early morning a terrible nightmare she had had even before she became Vronsky's mistress woke her. An old peasant with a tousled beard, muttering some meaningless French words, was doing something as he bent over a piece of iron, while she, as always in this nightmare (which made it so horrible), felt that the little peasant was paying no attention to her but was doing something dreadful over her with the iron. And she woke in a cold sweat.

When she got up, she recalled, as though through a thick mist, the events of the previous day.

"There had been a quarrel. Just as had happened several times before. I said that I had a headache and he did not come to see me. Tomorrow we shall be leaving and I have to see him and get things ready for our departure," she said to herself. And learning that he was in the study, she went to him. As she passed through the drawing room, she heard a carriage stop at the front door and, looking out of the window, she saw a young girl in a lilac hat leaning out of the carriage window and saying something to a footman who was ringing the bell. After some talk in the entrance hall, someone went upstairs and she heard Vronsky's footsteps outside the drawing room. He was coming swiftly downstairs. Anna went up to the window again. There he was on the front steps, without a hat, going down to the carriage. The young girl in the lilac hat handed him a packet. Vronsky smiled and said something to her. The carriage drove off and he ran quickly upstairs again.

The mist, which shrouded everything in her mind, suddenly lifted. The feelings of yesterday wrung her aching heart with fresh pain. Now she simply could not understand how she could have humiliated herself so much as to stay in the same house with him for a whole day. She went into the study to tell him of her decision.

"That was Princess Sorokin and her daughter. They brought me the money and the papers from Mother. I could not get them yesterday. How is your head, better?" he said calmly, not wishing to see or understand the grim, solemn expression of her face.

She gazed intently and in silence at him, standing in the middle of the room. He glanced at her, frowned for a moment, and continued to read his letter. She turned and slowly walked toward the door. He could still have called her back, but she went up to the door and he remained silent and the only sound in the room was the rustle of the paper as he turned over a page.

"By the way," he said when she was already in the doorway, "we are going tomorrow, aren't we?"

"You are, not I," she said, turning round to him.

"Anna, it's impossible to live like this. . . ."

"You are, not I," she repeated.

"This is becoming intolerable!"

"You—you will be sorry for this," she said and went out.

Frightened by the despairing look with which she had uttered those words, he jumped to his feet and was about to run after her, but, recollecting himself, sat down again, clenching his teeth and frowning. This (as he thought) indecent threat of something or other exasperated him. "I've tried everything," he thought, "and there is only one thing left—to take no notice." And he began getting ready to drive into town and then to his mother's again, for he had to get her signature to the power of attorney.

She heard the sounds of his footsteps in his study and the dining room. But he did not come in to see her, but merely gave orders to let Voytov have the horse if he were not back by that time. Then she heard the carriage driving up and the door open, and he went out again. But a moment later he went back into the hall and someone ran upstairs. It was his valet running back for the gloves he had forgotten. She went up to the window and saw him take the gloves without looking up and, touching the driver on the back, say something to him. Then, without looking up at the windows, he sat down in the carriage in his usual posture, crossing one leg over the other, and, putting on a glove, disappeared round the corner.

CHAPTER 27

"He's gone! It's all over!" said Anna to herself, as she stood at the window, and in response to her thought, the impressions of the great darkness when the candle had gone out and of the terrible nightmare merged into one and gripped her heart with icy horror.

"No," she exclaimed, "it can't be!" and, crossing the room, rang loudly. She felt so terrified at being alone that she did not wait for the servant, but went to meet him.

"Find out where the count has gone," she said.

The man replied that the count had gone to the stables.

"The count asked me to tell you, in case you should wish to go out, ma'am, that the carriage would be coming back directly."

"Very well. Wait, please. I'm going to write a note now. Tell Mikhailo to take it to the stables. Make haste."

She sat down and wrote:

"It is all my fault. Come back home. We must talk things over. For God's sake, come. I'm frightened."

She sealed it and gave it to the footman.

She was afraid of being left alone now, and she followed the servant out of the room and went into the nursery.

"Good Lord, that's not him! Where are his blue eyes and his sweet, shy smile?" was her first thought on seeing her plump, rosy-cheeked little girl with her black, curly hair instead of Seryozha who, in the confusion of her mind, she had expected to see in the nursery. The baby, sitting at the table, kept persistently banging it with the stopper of a decanter, looking blankly at her mother with her two black currants—her black eyes. Telling the Englishwoman that she was quite well and that they were leaving for the country next day, Anna sat down beside the little girl and began twirling the decanter stopper round in front of her. But the child's loud, ringing laughter and a movement of her eyebrows reminded her so vividly of Vronsky that, holding back her sobs, she got up hastily and went out of the room. "Is it really over? No, it cannot be," she thought. "He will come back. But how will he explain to me that smile of his, that animation of his after he had spoken to her? But even if he does not explain it, I shall still believe him. If I don't believe him, there's only one thing left for me—and I don't want that."

She looked at the clock. Twelve minutes had passed. "Now he has received my note and is on his way back. It won't be long now—another ten minutes. . . . But what if he does not come? No, that's impossible. He must not see that I've been crying. I'll go and wash my eyes. Heavens, haven't I done my hair this morning?" she asked herself. And she could not remember. She felt her head with her hand. "Yes, I have, but I simply can't remember when." She did not even trust her hand and went up to the cheval glass to see whether she really had done her hair. She had, but she could not remember doing it. "Who's that?" she thought, gazing in the looking glass at the feverish face with strangely glittering eyes looking at her with a frightened expression. "Why, it's me," she realized all at once and, examining herself from top to toe, she suddenly felt his kisses and, shuddering, moved her shoulders. Then she raised her hand to her lips and kissed it.

"What's the matter with me? I'm going mad!" And she went to her bedroom where Annushka was tidying up.

"Annushka," she said, stopping in front of her and looking at her, not knowing herself what she would say to her.

"You were thinking of going to see the Princess Oblonsky," said the maid, as though guessing what was at the back of her mind.

"To Princess Oblonsky? Yes, I'll go."

"Fifteen minutes there and fifteen back. He is already on the way. He'll be here presently." She took out her watch and looked at it. "But how could he go away and leave me in such a state? How can he live without having made it up with me?" She went up to the window and began looking out into the street. By this time he should have been back. But her calculations might have been wrong and she began again trying to remember when he had left and to count the minutes.

Just as she was walking over to the clock to see whether her watch was keeping time, someone drove up to the house. Looking out of the window she saw her carriage. But no one was coming upstairs and she could hear voices below. It was her messenger who had returned in the carriage. She went down to him.

"I was too late to catch the count, ma'am. He had driven off to the Nizhny station."

"What do you want? What?" she said to the cheerful, red-cheeked Mikhailo, as he handed her back her note.

"But he did not get it, of course," she remembered.

"Take this note to the Countess Vronsky's country house. You know it, don't you? And bring back an answer at once," she said to the messenger.

"But what am I going to do myself?" she thought. "Why, I'll drive over to Dolly's. Of course. Or I shall really go mad. And, of course, I can send a telegram as well." And she wrote out a telegram:

"I must talk to you, come at once."

Having sent off the telegram, she went to dress. Already dressed and with her bonnet on, she again glanced into the eyes of the plump, placid Annushka. There was a look of real compassion in those kindly little gray eyes.

"Annushka, my dear, what am I to do?" murmured Anna, sobbing and sinking helplessly into a chair.

"But why be so upset, ma'am?" said the maid. "These things do happen. You go out and shake it off."

"Yes, I think I will go out," said Anna, recollecting herself and getting up. "And if a telegram comes while I'm away, send it on to Princess Oblonsky's. . . . No, I'll come back myself."

"I must not think, I must do something, go out, above all, get out of this house," she said to herself, listening with horror to the terrible thumping of her heart, and she hurriedly went out and got into the carriage.

"Where to, ma'am?" asked Peter before getting onto the box.

"To the Oblonskys', on the Znamenka."

CHAPTER 28

The weather was bright. All the morning a fine drizzling rain had fallen, but it had now cleared up. The iron roofs, the flagstones of the pavements, the cobbles of the roadway, the wheels, the leather, brass, and metalwork of the carriages—all shone brightly in the May sunshine. It was three o'clock and the busiest time in the streets.

Sitting in the corner of the comfortable carriage, swaying lightly on its elastic springs with the swift trot of the pair of grays, Anna, once again reviewing in her mind the events of the last few days amid the unceasing rattle of wheels and the rapidly changing impressions in the open air, saw her position in quite a different light from what it appeared to her at home. Now even the thought of death no longer seemed so terrible and clear, and death itself no longer seemed inevitable. Now she reproached herself for the humiliating position into which she had sunk. "I am begging him to forgive me. I have given in to him. I have admitted that I am in the wrong. Why? Can't I really live without him?" And without answering the question how she proposed to live without him, she began to read the signboards. "Office and warehouse. Dental surgeon . . . Yes, I will tell Dolly everything. She does not like Vronsky. I will feel ashamed and hurt, but I will tell her everything. She is fond of me and I will do as she says. I won't give in to him. I won't allow him to tell me what to do. . . . Philippov, pastry cook. I've heard he sends his pastry to Petersburg. The Moscow water is so good. Oh, those wells in Mytischchen and the pancakes!" And she remembered how long, long ago, when she was only seventeen, she paid a visit to the Troitsa Monastery with her aunt. "In a stagecoach. There were no railways then. Was that really me, that girl with the red hands? How many things that seemed at the time beautiful and inaccessible to me have since become insignificant, and the things I had then are forever unattainable now. Could I have believed then that I would humiliate myself to such an extent? How

870

proud and satisfied he will be when he gets my note! But I'll show him. . . . How nasty that paint smells. Why do they go on painting and building? Dressmaking and millinery," she read. A man bowed to her. It was Annushka's husband. "Our parasites," she remembered Vronsky saying. "Our? Why our? The awful thing is that it is impossible to tear up the past by its roots. It is impossible to tear it up, but it is possible to hide the memory of it. And I will hide it." At this point she remembered her past with Karenin and how she had erased it from her memory. "Dolly will think I am leaving a second husband and that I must therefore be in the wrong. But do I want to be in the right? I can't!" she said, and she was on the verge of tears. But she began at once to wonder what those two girls could be smiling at. "Love, I suppose. They don't know how dismal it is, how humiliating. . . . The boulevard and children. Three little boys running about playing at horses. Seryozha! I shall lose everything and shall never get him back. Yes, I shall lose everything if he does not return. He may have missed the train and be back by now. So you're after more humiliation, are you?" she said to herself. "No, I'll go to Dolly and tell her frankly: I am unhappy, I deserve it, it is all my fault, but I am unhappy all the same, please, help me. These horses, this carriage—oh, how disgusted I am with myself for being in this carriage—they are all his—but I shall not see them again any more."

Trying to think what she was going to say to Dolly and deliberately lacerating her heart, Anna walked up the steps.

"Is anyone with the princess?" she asked in the hall.

"Mrs. Levin, ma'am," the footman replied.

"Kitty! That same Kitty with whom Vronsky had once been in love," thought Anna. "The same girl he keeps thinking of with affection. He is sorry he did not marry her. And of me he thinks with hate and is sorry he ever took up with me."

When Anna arrived, the two sisters were discussing the question of feeding the baby. Dolly went alone to meet the visitor who, having come at that moment, interrupted their talk.

"Oh, you haven't gone yet?" Dolly said. "I was coming to see you myself. I've just got a letter from Stiva."

"We've had a wire from him too," said Anna, looking around for Kitty.

"He writes that he can't make out what it is Alexey really wants, but that he won't leave without getting an answer."

"I thought you had someone with you. May I see the letter?"

"Yes, Kitty," Dolly said, looking embarrassed. "She is in the nursery. She has been very ill."

"I heard about it. May I see the letter?"

"I'll fetch it at once. But he has not refused. On the contrary, Stiva is hopeful," said Dolly, pausing in the doorway.

"I have no hope and I don't even desire it," said Anna.

"Does Kitty really think it beneath her dignity to meet me?" thought Anna when she was left alone. "Perhaps she is right. But it is not for her, the girl who was in love with Vronsky, it is not for her to let me see it, even if it is true. I know that in my position I cannot be received by any decent woman. I knew that from the very first moment I sacrificed everything for him. And this is my reward! Oh, how I hate him! And why did I come here? I feel worse here. It's much harder here." She could hear the voices of the two sisters discussing something in the next room. "And what can I say to Dolly now? Console Kitty by showing her how unhappy I am? Put up with her patronizing airs? No! Besides, Dolly herself would not understand. And I have nothing to tell her. It would be interesting, though, to see Kitty and show her how I despise everybody and everything, how I don't care what happens now."

Dolly came in with the letter. Anna read it and handed it back in silence.

"I knew all that," she said, "and it doesn't interest me in the least."

"But why not? On the contrary, I am hopeful," said Dolly, looking at Anna with curiosity. She had never seen her in such a strange, irritable state. "When are you going to the country?" she asked.

Anna, screwing up her eyes, looked straight before her and did not answer.

"Why does Kitty hide herself away from me?" she said, looking at the door and coloring.

"Heavens, what nonsense! She's nursing the baby and can't get things right somehow. I was giving her some advice. She will be very pleased to see you. She will be here presently," Dolly said awkwardly, not knowing how to tell a lie. "Oh, here she is!"

When she heard that Anna had come, Kitty did not want to come out and meet her, but Dolly had persuaded her. Summoning up courage, Kitty came in and, blushing, went up to Anna and held out her hand.

"I'm very glad," she said in a trembling voice.

Kitty looked embarrassed because she was torn between her hostility to this bad woman and her desire to be forbearing to her. But as soon as she saw Anna's lovely and attractive face, all the hostility disappeared at once.

"I shouldn't have been surprised if you had not wished to meet me," said Anna. "I've got used to everything. You've been ill? Yes, you have changed."

Kitty felt that Anna was looking at her with animosity. She attributed it to the awkward position that Anna, who had once patronized her, felt herself to be in, and she was sorry for her.

They talked about Kitty's illness, about the baby, about Stiva, but it was evident that Anna was not interested in any of it.

"I came to say good-by to you," she said, getting up.

"When are you going then?"

But, again not answering, Anna turned to Kitty.

"Yes, I'm very glad to have seen you," she said with a smile. "I've heard so much about you from all sides and even from your husband. He came to see me and I liked him very much," she added, evidently with a bad intention. "Where is he?"

"He has gone to the country," said Kitty, blushing.

"Remember me to him—please do!"

"Oh, I will!" Kitty exclaimed naïvely, looking compassionately into her eyes.

"Well, good-by, Dolly!" And kissing Dolly and pressing Kitty's hand, Anna hurried away.

"She's just the same and as attractive as ever. She is

very beautiful!" said Kitty when left alone with her sister. "But there is something pitiful about her! Something terribly pitiful!"

"Yes, there is something peculiar about her today," said Dolly. "When I was seeing her out, I thought that she was going to cry."

CHAPTER 29

Anna got into the carriage in an even worse state of mind than when she left home. To her former torments there was now added a feeling of being affronted and rejected, of which she had been clearly conscious during the meeting with Kitty.

"Where to, ma'am? Home?" asked Peter.

"Yes, home," she said, not even thinking now where she was going.

"How they looked at me—as if I were something horrible, incomprehensible, and strange! What can he be telling that other man so warmly?" she thought, looking at two passers-by. "Is it really possible to tell anyone what you are feeling? I wanted to tell Dolly and it's a good thing I didn't. How glad she would have been at my unhappiness. She would have concealed it, but she would have been glad that I've been punished for the pleasures she envied me. As for Kitty, she would have been even more delighted. Oh, I can see her through and through! She knows that I was more than usually nice to her husband, and she is jealous of me. She hates me. And despises me. In her eyes I am an immoral woman. If I were an immoral woman I could make her husband fall in love with me—if I wanted to. And I did want to. How that man there is satisfied with himself," she thought about a fat, red-cheeked man who was driving past in the opposite direction and who, taking her for an acquaintance, raised his shiny hat above his bald, shiny head and then discovered that he was mistaken. "He thought he knew me. And he knows me as little as anyone else in the world. I don't know myself. I know my appetites, as the French say. Now those two want some of that filthy ice cream—they know that for a certainty," she thought, looking at two boys who stopped

874

an ice-cream man, who took down a tub from his head
and wiped his perspiring face with the end of a towel.
"We all want something sweet and tasty. If not sweets,
then dirty ice cream. Kitty is just the same: if not Vronsky, then Levin. She envies me. And hates me. We all
hate each other. I Kitty, Kitty me. Yes that is true. Tyutkin, *coiffeur. Je me fais coiffer par* Tyutkin. I'll tell him
that when he comes home," she thought and smiled. But
at that instant she remembered that she had no one now
to tell anything amusing to. "There isn't anything amusing anyway. Nothing really gay. Everything is disgusting.
They are ringing the churchbells for vespers, and how
devoutly that merchant is crossing himself, just as though
he were afraid to drop something. Why those churches,
the churchbells, and all these lies? Merely to conceal the
fact that we hate one another, like those cabmen who
are so angrily swearing at each other. Yashvin said: 'He
wants to leave me without a shirt and I him.' Now, that's
quite true!"

These thoughts engrossed her so much that she even
forgot to think of her troubles until the carriage drew
up at the front steps of her house. Only when she saw
the hall porter coming out to meet her did she remember
that she had sent the note and the telegram.

"Is there any reply?" she asked.

"I'll go and see, ma'am," replied the hall porter and,
glancing at the desk in the hall, he took up and handed
her the thin square envelope of a telegram. "I cannot
return before ten—Vronsky," she read.

"And isn't the messenger back yet?"

"No, ma'am," replied the hall porter.

"Well, if that's how it is, then I know what to do,"
she said to herself, and conscious of a vague feeling of
anger and a desire for vengeance rising within her, she
ran upstairs. "I'll go to him myself. Before leaving him
for good, I'm going to tell him everything. I have never
hated anyone as much as I hate that man!" she thought.
Catching sight of his hat on the hatstand, she shuddered
with aversion. She never realized that his telegram was
a reply to her telegram and that he had not yet received
her note. She imagined him now calmly talking to his
mother and Princess Sorokin and glad of her sufferings.
"Yes, I must go at once," she said to herself, without
really knowing where to go to. She was anxious to get

away as quickly as possible from the feeling she experienced in that awful house. The servants, the walls, the things in the house—everything aroused a feeling of disgust and anger in her and weighed her down like some heavy load.

"Yes, I must go to the railway station, and if he isn't there, I must go to his mother's house and catch him red-handed." Anna looked at the timetable in the daily newspapers. There was an evening train at two minutes past eight. "Yes, I shall be in time." She gave orders for other horses to be harnessed and began packing a traveling bag with the things she might need for a few days. She knew that she would not return. Among the different things that occurred to her, she vaguely decided that after what would happen at the railway station or in the countess' country house, she would go on by the Nizhny railway to the first town and stay there.

Dinner was on the table. She went up to it, sniffed at the bread and the cheese, and making sure that everything eatable disgusted her, ordered the carriage and went out. The house was already casting a shadow right across the street. It was a bright evening and still warm in the sun. Annushka, who came out with her things, Peter, who put them in the carriage, and the coachman, who was obviously disgruntled—she felt disgusted with them all and they irritated her by their words and movements.

"I shan't want you, Peter."

"But how about your ticket, ma'am?"

"Oh well, just as you like, I don't care," she said with vexation.

Peter jumped up on the box and, arms akimbo, told the coachman to drive to the station.

CHAPTER 30

"There's that girl again! Again I understand it all!" Anna said to herself as soon as the carriage started and, rocking slightly, rumbled over the little cobbles, and again impressions succeeded one another in her mind.

876

"Now, what was the last thing I thought of that was so good?" she tried to remember. "Tyutkin, *coiffeur*? No, it wasn't that. Oh yes—what Yashvin said: the struggle for existence and hatred are the only things that hold people together. No, it's no use, wherever you are going," she mentally addressed a party of people in a coach-and-four who were evidently going for a picnic into the country. "And the dog you're taking with you won't help you. For you can't run away from yourselves." Glancing in the direction in which Peter was looking, she saw a workman, almost dead drunk, his head swaying, who was being led off somewhere by a policeman. "Now, this one," she thought, "is much more likely to. Count Vronsky and I were also not able to find that pleasure, though we expected much from it." And now for the first time Anna turned the searchlight, in which she saw everything, on her relations with him, which she had so far avoided thinking about. "What did he look for in me? Not so much love as the gratification of his vanity." She remembered his words, the expression of his face, suggestive of a faithful setter, in the early days of their love affair. And everything now confirmed it. "Yes, it was vanity that counted most with him. The vanity of success. It was that he was so triumphant about. Of course, there was love too, but mostly pride in his success. He boasted of me. Now that is past. There is nothing more to boast of. Nothing to be proud of, only ashamed. He has taken all he could from me and now he no longer needs me. He is tired of me and is trying not to treat me like a cad. He let the cat out of the bag yesterday—he wants divorce and marriage so as to burn his boats. He loves me, but how? The zest is gone," she said to herself in English. "That one," she thought, looking at a red-cheeked shop assistant riding on a hired horse, "wants to astonish everyone and is very pleased with himself. No, there's not the same flavor about me for him now. If I leave him now, he will be really and truly glad."

That was not a supposition. She saw it clearly in the piercing light which revealed to her now the meaning of life and of human relations.

"My love grows more and more passionate and demanding and his dwindles and dwindles, and that is why we are drifting apart," she went on thinking. "And there's nothing one can do about it. He is everything in the world to me, and I demand that he should give himself up to me more and more completely. And he wants more and more to get away from me. Before we became lovers we were drawn together, but now we are irresistibly drifting apart. And nothing can be done to alter it. He tells me that I am insanely jealous, and I too have kept telling myself that I was insanely jealous. But that is not true. I am not jealous; I am discontented. But . . ." Her mouth dropped open and she changed her place in the carriage, so agitated was she by a sudden thought that occurred to her. "If only I could be anything but his mistress, while caring passionately for nothing except his caresses! But I can't and I don't want to be anything else. And by this desire I arouse his disgust, which in turn arouses resentment and anger in me, and it cannot be otherwise. Don't I really know that he would not deceive me, that he never as much as thinks of marrying the Princess Sorokin, that he is not in love with Kitty, that he will not be unfaithful to me? I know all that, but it does not make it any easier for me. If, no longer loving me, he is kind and affectionate to me out of a sense of *duty* and what I desire is not there—why, that is a thousand times worse than hatred. It is hell! And that's just what it is. He has long stopped loving me. And where love ends, hate begins. I don't know these streets at all. Hills and houses and houses . . . and in the houses people, and more people. . . . Thousands and thousands of them and they all hate each other. Well, suppose I think of something I would like to make me happy. Well? I get a divorce. Alexey lets me have Seryozha, and I marry Vronsky." The thought of Karenin brought him back to her mind with extraordinary vividness—his mild, lackluster, lifeless eyes, the blue veins on his white hands, his intonations and cracking fingers, and remembering the feeling which had once existed between them and which had also been called love, she shuddered with revulsion. "Well, I get a divorce and become Vronsky's wife. What then? Will Kitty no longer look at me as she looked at me today? She will not. And will Seryozha stop asking and wondering about my two husbands? And what kind of new feeling can I invent between Vronsky and myself? Is any kind, if not of happiness, then at least of something that is not torment, possible at all? No and no again!" she answered herself now without the slightest hesitation. "It is impossible! Life is pulling us apart, and I am the cause of his unhappiness and he of mine, and it is impossible to change either him or me. Every attempt has been made, the thread of the screw is worn. . . . Yes, a beggar woman with a baby. She thinks people pity her. Aren't we all flung into the world only to hate each other and therefore to torment ourselves and others? Schoolboys laughing. Seryozha?" she remembered. "I, too, thought that I loved him and was deeply moved with tenderness for him. Yet I lived without him, exchanged him for another love, and did not complain about this change so long as I found satisfaction in that love." And she thought with disgust of what she called "the other love." The clearness with which she now saw her own life and the life of everyone else gave her pleasure. "It's the same with me, and Peter, and the coachman Fyodor, and with that merchant, and with all the people who live there by the Volga where those advertisements invite us to go on holiday, and everywhere and always," she thought as she drove up to the low building of the Nizhny station, and the porters ran out to meet her.

"Shall I take a ticket to Obiralovka, ma'am?" said Peter.

She had completely forgotten where she was going and why, and had to make a great effort to understand the question.

"Yes," she said, handing him her purse with the money and, hanging her little red handbag on her arm, she got out of the carriage.

As she made her way through the crowd to the first-class waiting room, she gradually recalled all the circumstances of her position and the different decisions she was not sure about. And again hope and despair, chafing the old sores, began in turn to lacerate the wounds of her tormented and terribly fluttering heart. Sitting on the star-shaped sofa waiting for the train, she looked with disgust at the people coming in and out (they were all objectionable to her) and thought of how she would arrive at the station, write him a note, of what she would write, of how he was at that very moment complaining to his mother (not understanding her suffering) of his position, how she would enter the room, and what she would say to him. Then she thought how happy life might still be, how agonizingly she loved and hated him, and how dreadfully her heart was beating.

CHAPTER 31

The station bell rang, some young men passed by, ugly and insolent, in a hurry and yet mindful of the impression they were creating; then Peter, in his livery and gaiters, with his dull, animal face, also passed through the waiting room and came up to her to see her into the train. The noisy men fell silent as she passed them on the platform, and one of them whispered something about her to another—something disgusting, of course. She mounted the high step of the railway carriage and sat down in an empty compartment on the dirty seat that was once white. Her bag bounced on the sprung seat and then lay still. With a foolish smile Peter raised his gold-braided hat at the window to take leave of her; an insolent guard slammed the door and turned the handle. A woman, ugly and wearing a bustle (Anna mentally stripped that woman and was appalled at her deformity), and a little girl, laughing affectedly, ran past the carriage window.

"Katerina Andreyevna has it, she has everything, *ma tante*," cried the little girl.

"A little girl—and she too is already crippled in mind and full of affection," thought Anna. Anxious not to see anyone, she got up quickly and sat down at the opposite end of the empty compartment. A grimy, deformed peasant in a cap from under which his tousled hair stuck out, passed by the window, bending down to the carriage wheels. "There's something familiar about that hideous peasant," thought Anna. And remembering her dream, she went to the opposite door. A guard was opening the door to let in a husband and wife.

"Are you going out, ma'am?" he asked.

Anna made no answer. Neither the guard nor the passengers noticed the horror on her face under the veil. She went back to her corner and sat down. The couple sat down opposite her, attentively but stealthily examining her dress. Anna thought both the husband and the wife detestable. The husband asked her permission to smoke, not because he wanted to smoke, but quite obviously in order to enter into conversation with her. Having received her permission, he began to speak to his wife in French about things he wanted to talk about even less than he wanted to smoke. They were saying all sorts of silly things, not because they wanted to say them, but in order that she should hear them. Anna saw clearly that they were sick and tired of each other and hated each other terribly. And how indeed could one help hating such pitiable monstrosities.

The second bell rang, followed by the loading of the luggage, noise, shouting and laughter. Anna saw so clearly that there was nothing to be joyful about, that this laughter exasperated her to the point of physical pain and she felt like stopping her ears not to hear it. At last the third bell rang, the guard whistled, the engine screeched, the coupling chains gave a jerk, and the husband crossed himself. "It would be interesting to ask him what he meant by that," thought Anna, regarding him spitefully. She looked past the woman out of the window at the people on the platform who had been seeing the train off and who seemed to be gliding backward. With rhythmic jerks over the points of the rails, the carriage in which Anna sat rolled past the platform, past a brick wall, past the signals, and past other carriages; the well-greased wheels rolled more smoothly over the rails, making a slight ringing sound; the window was lit by the bright evening sun and a little breeze played against the blind. Anna forgot all about her fellow passengers and, gently rocked by the motion of the carriage and inhaling the fresh air, she resumed the trend of her thoughts.

"Where did I leave off? I was thinking that I could not imagine a situation in which life would not be a torment, that we have all been created in order to be tortured, that we all know that, and that we are always trying to think of something to deceive ourselves. But when you see the truth, what are you going to do?"

"What has reason been given to man for if not to help him to escape from his troubles," said the woman in French, evidently pleased with her phrase, screwing up her face into a grimace.

881

Those words seemed to supply an answer to her thoughts.

"To escape from his troubles," Anna repeated. And glancing at the red-cheeked husband and his thin wife, she realized that the sickly woman considered herself misunderstood and that her husband was unfaithful to her and encouraged her in her opinion of herself. It was as if by directing her searchlight upon them Anna could see the story of their lives and all the secret places of their hearts. But there was nothing of interest there and she continued with her reflections.

"Yes, I am very troubled and reason was given us to escape from our troubles, which means that I too must get rid of them. Why not put out the candle when there is nothing more to look at, when it is disgusting to look at it all? But how? Why did that guard run along the footboard? Why are those young men in the next carriage shouting? Why are they talking and laughing? It is all untrue, all lies, all deception, all evil!"

When the train stopped at the station, Anna got out with a crowd of other passengers and, keeping away from them as if they were lepers, stopped on the platform, trying to remember why she had come there and what it was she had intended to do. Everything that had seemed possible before, she found so difficult to grasp now, especially in this noisy crowd of hideous people who would not leave her in peace. Porters rushed up offering their services. Young men, stamping their feet on the planks of the platform and talking in loud voices, looked her up and down, and the people who came toward her always tried to get out of her way on the wrong side. Recollecting that she had meant to go on if there was no reply, she stopped a porter and asked if there was not a coachman with a note from Count Vronsky.

"Count Vronsky? Someone from there was here just now to meet Princess Sorokin and her daughter. What does the coachman look like?"

While she was talking to the porter, Mikhailo the coachman, rosy-cheeked and cheerful, came up in his smart dark-blue coat with a watch chain and handed her a note, evidently very proud of himself to have carried out his errand so well. She opened it and her heart sank even before she had read it.

"Very sorry your note did not catch me. Shall be back at ten," Vronsky had written in a careless hand.

"Yes, I expected it!" she said to herself with a malicious grin.

"All right, you may go home," she said quietly, addressing Mikhailo. She spoke softly because the rapid beating of her heart interfered with her breathing. "No, I won't let you torment me," she thought, addressing her threat not to him and not to herself, but to that which made her suffer, and she walked along the platform past the station buildings.

Two servant girls, strolling about the platform, turned their heads to look at her, making some remarks about her dress. "Real," they said about the lace she was wearing. The young men did not leave her in peace. As they passed by, they again peered into her face and shouted something in unnatural voices. The stationmaster, as he walked by, asked her if she was going on the train. A boy selling kvass never took his eyes off her. "Oh dear, where am I to go?" she thought as she walked farther and farther along the platform. At the end of it she stopped. Some women and children, who had come to meet a man in spectacles and who were laughing and talking loudly, fell silent and looked her up and down as she came alongside them. She quickened her step and walked away from them to the edge of the platform. A goods train was approaching. The platform began to shake, and she imagined that she was traveling in the train again.

And suddenly, remembering the man who had been run over on the day she first met Vronsky, she realized what she had to do. Quickly and lightly descending the steps that led from the water tank to the rails, she stopped close to the passing train. She looked at the bottom of the trucks, at the bolts and chains and the tall iron wheels of the slowly moving first truck, and tried to estimate by sight the point midway between the front and back wheels and the moment when it would be opposite her.

"There!" she said to herself, looking at the shadow cast by the truck on the sand mixed with coal dust which covered the ties. "There, right into the middle, and I shall punish him and get rid of all of them and of myself."

She wanted to fall midway between the wheels of the first truck, which was drawing level with her. But her red handbag, which she began to take off her arm, delayed her, and it was too late: the middle of the truck had passed her. She had to wait for the next. A feeling similar to the one she always experienced when about to enter the water to bathe seized her now and she crossed herself. The familiar gesture of making the sign of the cross aroused in her mind a whole series of memories of her childhood and girlhood, and suddenly the darkness that enveloped everything for her was torn apart, and for an instant life presented itself to her with all its bright past joys. But she did not take her eyes off the wheels of the approaching second truck. Exactly at the moment when the middle distance between the wheels drew level with her, she threw away her red handbag and, drawing her head down between her shoulders, fell under the truck on her hands, and with a light movement, as though she were getting ready to get up immediately, dropped on her knees. And at that very instant she was horror-struck at what she was doing. "Where am I? What am I doing? Why?" She tried to get up, to throw herself back, but something huge and implacable struck her on the head and dragged her down on her back. "Lord, forgive me everything!" she cried, feeling the impossibility of struggling. The little peasant, muttering something, was working over the iron. And the candle, by the light of which she had been reading the book filled with anxieties, deceits, grief, and evil, flared up with a brighter light than before, lit up for her all that had hitherto been shrouded in darkness, flickered, began to grow dim, and went out forever.

Part Eight

∾

CHAPTER 1

Nearly two months had passed. It was the middle of the hot summer and Koznyshev was only now getting ready to leave Moscow.

Events of some importance had taken place in Koznyshev's life during this time. His book, the fruit of six years' labor—*A Survey of the Foundations and Forms of Government in Europe and Russia*—had been finished about a year ago. Some sections of this book and the introduction had been published in periodicals, and other parts had been read by Koznyshev to people of his own circle, so that the ideas of the work could not be very new to the public. But still Koznyshev expected that the publication of his book ought to make a serious impression on society and create, if not exactly a revolution, then at least great excitement, in learned circles.

After the most painstaking revision the book had been published last year and sent out to the booksellers.

Not asking anyone about it, replying reluctantly and with feigned indifference to his friends' inquiries as to how his book was going, and not even inquiring of the booksellers how it was selling, Koznyshev watched keenly and with strained attention for the first impression his book would make on society and on literature.

But a week passed, and another, and a third and no impression whatever could be noticed in society; his friends, the specialists and the scholars, occasionally, and quite evidently out of politeness, spoke to him about it. The rest of his acquaintances, not interested in a book of a scientific nature, did not bother to speak to him about it at all. Society, too, now particularly occupied with something else, showed itself completely indifferent to it. Neither was there any mention of the book in the periodicals for a whole month.

Koznyshev had calculated to a nicety the time it would take for a review to be written, but one month passed, then another, and still there was silence.

Only in the *Northern Beetle*, in a humorous article about the singer Brabanti who had lost his voice, were a few contemptuous references made apropos of Koznyshev's book, with the implication that the book had long been condemned by everybody and consigned to general ridicule.

At last, in the third month, a critical article appeared in a serious periodical. Koznyshev knew the author of the article. He had met him once at Golubtsov's.

The author was a very young and ailing journalist, extremely clever as a writer, but very badly educated and shy in his personal relations with people.

In spite of his absolute contempt for the writer, Koznyshev set about reading the article with the greatest respect. The article was dreadful.

It was clear that the critic had completely misunderstood the whole book, but he had so cleverly selected his quotations that to those who had not read it (and hardly anyone had read it) it was quite clear that the book was nothing but a collection of high-sounding words and these not always well chosen (which was indicated by marks of interrogation), and that the author of the book was a totally ignorant man. And all this was so witty that Koznyshev himself would have been only too glad to possess such wit; but that was just what made it so dreadful.

Though Koznyshev checked up on the accuracy of the critic's arguments in a most thoroughly conscientious manner, he did not stop to consider the deficiencies and mistakes which were ridiculed—it was all too obvious that it had all been chosen deliberately—but he could not help recalling the minutest details of his meeting and conversation with the author of the review.

"I didn't offend him in some way, did I?" Koznyshev asked himself.

He remembered that when they had met, he had corrected the young man in the use of a word which betrayed his ignorance. This, Koznyshev thought, explained how the article came to be written.

This review was followed by dead silence about the book both in print and in conversation, and Koznyshev realized that the book, which had taken him six years to write and into which he had put so much love and labor, had made no impression on public opinion.

Koznyshev's position was all the more painful because, having finished his book, he had no more research work to do, such as had before occupied the greater part of his time.

Koznyshev was intelligent, well educated, healthy, and active, and he did not know what to do with his superfluous energy. Discussions in drawing rooms, at conferences, meetings, committees, and everywhere where one could talk, occupied part of his time; but having been a town dweller most of his life, he did not allow himself to spend all his energy in talk, as his inexperienced brother did when he was in Moscow; so he had a great deal of time on his hands and a great deal of mental energy to spare.

Fortunately for him, at this most trying time after the failure of his book, the Slav question, which had previously only smoldered in society, came to the fore, displacing such questions as dissenters, our American friends, the Samara famine, exhibitions, and spiritualism, and Koznyshev, who had been one of the first to raise this question, devoted himself entirely to it.

In the circle to which he belonged nothing was written or talked about at that time except the Slav question and the Serbo-Turkish war. Everything the idle crowd usually does to kill time was now done for the benefit of the Slavs. Balls, concerts, dinners, speeches, fashions, beer, restaurants—everything bore witness to sympathy with the Slavs.

With much that was said and written on the subject, Koznyshev did not entirely agree. He saw that the Slav question had become one of those fashionable diversions which one after another serve as a pastime for society; he saw, too, that many people were taking up this question in order to promote their own selfish and vainglorious interests. He was quite aware of the fact that the newspapers published much that was unnecessary and exaggerated for the sole purpose of attracting attention and outdoing their rivals. He saw that amid this general enthusiasm those who were unsuccessful or those who had a grudge against society leaped forward and shouted louder than anyone else: commanders-in-chief without armies, journalists without journals, ministers without ministries, party leaders without followers. He saw that there was a great deal in this thing that was frivolous and ridiculous; but he also saw and recognized the unmistakable and ever-growing enthusiasm, uniting all classes of the population, with which it was impossible not to sympathize. The massacre of Slavs who were coreligionists and brothers evoked sympathy for the sufferers and indignation against their oppressors. And the heroism of the Serbs and Montenegrins, fighting for a great cause, aroused in the whole nation a desire to help their brothers not only with words, but also with deeds.

There was, besides, something else that pleased Koznyshev very much: the manifestation of public opinion. The public had definitely voiced its wishes. The soul of the nation, as Koznyshev put it, had become articulate. And the more active he was in this movement, the clearer it became to him that it was something that was certain to assume vast dimensions and become an event of historic importance.

He devoted himself completely to the service of this great cause and forgot to think about his book.

His whole time now was so taken up that he was unable to answer all the letters and requests addressed to him.

Having worked all through the spring and part of the summer, it was not till July that he got ready to pay a visit to his brother in the country.

He was going for a short two weeks' holiday into the holy of holies of the nation—the heart of the country—to enjoy seeing the uprising of the national spirit of which he and all the inhabitants of the two Russian capitals and the large towns were fully convinced. Katavasov, who had long been meaning to carry out his promise to visit Levin in the country, traveled with him.

CHAPTER 2

Koznyshev and Katavasov had scarcely reached the Kursk station, which was particularly crowded that day, and, getting out of their carriage, looked around for the footman who was following with their luggage, before a party of volunteers drove up in four cabs. They were met by ladies with nosegays, and with the crowd rushing after them, Koznyshev and Katavasov entered the station.

One of the ladies who had met the volunteers spoke to Koznyshev as she came out of the waiting room.

"Have you come to see them off too?" she asked in French.

"No, Princess, I'm traveling myself. Going to my brother's country house for a rest. Do you always come to see them off?" asked Koznyshev with a faint smile.

"Why, of course!" replied the princess. "Is it true we've already sent eight hundred? Malvinsky would not believe me."

"More than eight hundred. Counting those who did not go from Moscow direct there must be more than a thousand," said Koznyshev.

"There now! I said so!" the lady exclaimed joyfully. "And it is true, isn't it, that about a million rubles have already been subscribed?"

"More, Princess."

"And what do you say about today's telegram? The Turks have been beaten again,"

"Yes, I read it," Koznyshev replied.

They were referring to the latest dispatch from the Serbo-Turkish front, which confirmed the report that the Turks had been beaten and put to flight on all fronts for three days in succession and that a decisive battle was expected next day.

"Oh, by the way, there's such a fine young man who wants to go too. I don't know why they are making difficulties. I know him personally and I do wish you could write a note for him. He was sent by Countess Lydia Ivanovna."

Having obtained such particulars as the princess could give about the young man who wanted to go as a volunteer, Koznyshev went into the first-class waiting room and wrote a note to the right people and gave it to the princess.

"You know, Count Vronsky, the—er—notorious—er—is going by this train," said the princess with a rather superior and meaningful smile when Koznyshev had found her again and given her the note.

"I heard he was going, but did not know when. Is he on this train?"

"I've seen him. He's here. Only his mother is seeing him off. I think it's the best thing he could do, don't you?"

"Why, yes, of course."

While they were talking, the crowd rushed past them to the dining table. They too moved nearer to it and they heard the loud voice of some gentleman who, glass in hand, was making a speech to the volunteers. "In the service of faith, humanity, and our brothers," the man was saying, raising his voice more and more. "Mother Moscow gives you her blessing in this great cause. *Zhivio!*" he concluded in a loud and tearful voice.

Everyone shouted *Zhivio!* and another large crowd rushed into the waiting room and nearly knocked the princess off her feet.

"Ah, Princess, how did you like that?" said Oblonsky, suddenly appearing in the middle of the crowd and beaming joyfully. "Spoke well, didn't he? And with such warmth! Bravo! And Koznyshev here, too! Now you ought to say a few words—er—of encouragement, you know. You do it so well," he added, with an affectionate, respectful, and hesitant smile, gently pushing Koznyshev forward by the arm.

"No, thank you, I'm catching my train now."

"Where to?"

"To my brother's in the country," replied Koznyshev.

"Then you'll see my wife. I have written to her, but you'll see her first. Please tell her that you've seen me and it's *all right*," he said in English. "She will understand. And, incidentally, you may as well tell her that I've been appointed a member of the Board of the Joint . . . Oh, well, she'll understand. You know *les petites misères de la vie humaine*," he said, as if apologizing, to the princess. "And Princess Myakhky, not Lisa, but Bibish, really is sending a thousand rifles and twelve nurses. Did I tell you?"

"Yes, I've heard," Koznyshev replied reluctantly.

"A pity you're going away," said Oblonsky. "Tomorrow we are giving a dinner to two who are off to the front, Dimer-Bartyansky from Petersburg and Grisha Veselovsky. They're both going. Veselovsky has only just got married. A brave fellow! Don't you think so, Princess?" he addressed the lady.

The princess, without replying, looked at Koznyshev. But the fact that Koznyshev and the princess seemed anxious to get rid of him did not abash Oblonsky. He looked smilingly now at the feather on the princess' hat and now around the waiting room, as if trying to remember something. Seeing a woman with a collecting box, he beckoned to her and put in a five-ruble note.

"Can't see those collecting boxes without feeling moved while I've money in my pocket," he said. "And what do you say to today's dispatch from the front? Brave fellows, those Montenegrins!"

"You don't say!" he exclaimed when the princess told him that Vronsky was going by that train. For a moment Oblonsky's face looked sad, but a minute later, when with a light spring in his step and smoothing his whiskers, he entered the room where Vronsky was, he had completely forgotten his sobs over the dead body of his sister and saw in Vronsky only a hero and an old friend.

"With all his faults one must do him justice," said the princess to Koznyshev as soon as Oblonsky had left them. "A truly Russian, Slav nature! Only I'm afraid Vronsky won't quite relish meeting him. Say what you like, I can't help being moved by the fate of that man. Do have a talk with him on the journey," said the princess.

"Yes, perhaps, if I get the chance."

"I never liked him. But this atones for a lot. He's not only going himself, he's taking a whole squadron with him at his own expense."

"So I heard."

The station bell rang. Everybody crowded toward the door.

"There he is!" said the princess, pointing to Vronsky, in a long overcoat and a wide-brimmed black hat, walking with his mother on his arm. Oblonsky was walking beside him, talking animatedly.

Vronsky was frowning and looking straight before him, as though not hearing what Oblonsky was saying.

Probably in response to what Oblonsky had told him, he looked round to where the princess and Koznyshev were standing and silently raised his hat. His face, aged and full of suffering, looked as though it had been turned to stone.

Having gone out on the platform, Vronsky let his mother precede him and silently disappeared into one of the compartments.

On the platform "God Save the Tsar" was struck up, followed by cries of Hurrah! and *Zhivio!* One of the volunteers, a tall, flat-chested, and very young man, was bowing in a way that was specially noticeable, waving his felt hat and a bouquet over his head. Thrusting their heads out from behind him, two army officers and an elderly man with a large beard and a greasy cap also bowed.

CHAPTER 3

Having taken leave of the princess, Koznyshev and Katavasov, who had joined him, went into the crowded carriage and the train started.

At Tsaritsyno the train was met by a well-matched choir singing "Glory, Glory to Our Russian Tsar." The volunteers again thrust their heads out of the windows and bowed, but Koznyshev paid no attention to them. He had had so much to do with the volunteers that he was already familiar with the general type and it did not interest him. Katavasov, on the other hand, being busy with his scientific work, had had no opportunity of studying them and he was very much interested and kept asking Koznyshev about them.

Koznyshev advised him to go along to the second-class

carriage and have a talk with some of them. At the next station Katavasov took his advice.

As soon as the train stopped he went into a second-class carriage and made the acquaintance of the volunteers. They were sitting in a corner of the compartment and talking volubly, evidently aware that the attention of their fellow passengers and of Katavasov, who had just entered, was directed toward them. The young man with the hollow chest talked louder than any of them. He was obviously drunk and was telling them about something that had happened at his institute. Opposite him sat a middle-aged officer, wearing the military jacket of the Austrian Guards. He listened to the young man with a smile and tried to stop him. A third volunteer, in an artillery uniform, sat beside them on a trunk. A fourth one was asleep.

Getting into conversation with the young man, Katavasov learned that he was a wealthy Moscow merchant who had run through a large fortune before he was twenty-two. Katavasov did not like him because he was effeminate, pampered, and delicate; he was evidently quite convinced, especially now that he was drunk, that he was doing something heroic and he bragged in a most unpleasant manner.

The second volunteer, the retired army officer, also made a disagreeable impression on Katavasov. He was a man who seemed to have tried everything. He had had a job on the railways, been an estate agent and a factory owner, and he talked about it all without the slightest necessity, using the wrong technical terms.

The third one, the artilleryman, on the other hand, Katavasov liked very much. He was a modest, quiet man, who was evidently very impressed by the knowledge of the retired Guards officer and the heroic self-sacrifice of the young merchant, and he said nothing about himself. When Katavasov asked him what made him go to Serbia, he replied modestly:

"Why, everyone's going. We must go to the assistance of the Serbs. I feel sorry for them."

"Yes, they are particularly short of artillerymen like you," said Katavasov.

"I haven't served long in the artillery. Perhaps they'll put me in the infantry or cavalry."

"Why into the cavalry when they need artillerymen

most of all?" asked Katavasov, concluding from the artilleryman's age that he must have reached a fairly high rank.

"I'm afraid I wasn't long in the artillery. I'm a retired cadet," he said, and began explaining why he did not pass his examination.

All this put together made a very disagreeable impression on Katavasov and when the volunteers got out at a station to have a drink, Katavasov wanted to check his unfavorable impression with someone. One of the passengers, an old man in a military greatcoat, had been listening very carefully to Katavasov's talk with the volunteers. When left alone with him in the compartment, Katavasov addressed him.

"What a difference there is in the social position of all these men who are going to the front," Katavasov said rather vaguely, wishing to express his own opinion and at the same time to learn what the old man thought about it.

The old man was an old soldier who had been through two campaigns. He knew what a soldier should be like, and by the appearance and talk of those gentlemen and by the dashing way in which they applied themselves to the bottle on the way, he regarded them as bad soldiers. Besides, he lived in a provincial town and he was only too ready to tell Katavasov about a discharged soldier from his town, a drunkard and a thief, who could not get a job anywhere and had joined the volunteers. But, knowing by experience that in the present mood of the public it was dangerous to express an opinion contrary to the prevailing one and, in particular, to criticize the volunteers, he too was carefully watching Katavasov.

"Well," he said, laughing with his eyes, "I suppose they need men badly there."

They began talking about the latest news from the front, and both of them concealed from each other their perplexity as to whom tomorrow's battle was to be fought with, seeing that, according to the latest news, the Turks had been defeated on all fronts. And they parted without either of them expressing an opinion.

Katavasov, on returning to his compartment, involuntarily prevaricated and, in telling Koznyshev his impressions of the volunteers, let it appear that they were all excellent fellows.

At the next big station of the chief town of a province the volunteers were again greeted with songs and cheers, men and women again appeared with collecting boxes, and the provincial ladies presented the volunteers with bunches of flowers and accompanied them to the refreshment room; but all this was on a much smaller scale than in Moscow.

CHAPTER 4

During the stop in the chief town of the province Koznyshev did not go to the refreshment room, but walked up and down the platform instead.

Passing Vronsky's compartment the first time, he noticed that the blind was down. But when he passed it the next time he saw the old countess standing at the window. She beckoned to him.

"You see, I'm going with him. Seeing him off as far as Kursk," she said.

"Yes, so I heard," said Koznyshev, stopping at the window and glancing inside. "What a fine thing for him to do," he added, observing that Vronsky was not in the compartment.

"Why, what else could he do after his misfortune?"

"What a terrible thing to happen!" said Koznyshev.

"Oh, you can't imagine the things I've been through! But do come in, please. . . . Oh, what I've been through!" she repeated when Koznyshev had got in and taken a seat beside her. "You can't imagine it! For six weeks he never spoke a word to anyone and I had to beg him on my bended knees to take some food. We dared not leave him alone for a single minute. We took away everything with which he could kill himself. We lived on the ground floor, but one could not foresee what he might do. You know, don't you, that he once tried to shoot himself on her account?" she said, and the old woman's brows knit at this recollection. "Yes, her end was just what you would expect of a woman like her. Even the death she chose was mean and disgusting."

"It is not for us to judge, Countess," Koznyshev said with a sigh, "but I quite understand how distressing it must have been for you."

"It was, indeed. I was living on my estate and he was with me at the time. A note was brought. We had no idea that she was there at the station. In the evening, I had only just retired to my room, my maid Mary told me that a woman had thrown herself under a train. Something seemed to hit me. I realized that it was she. The first thing I said was: 'Don't tell him!' But they had already told him. His coachman was there and saw it all. When I ran to his room he was beside himself—it was terrible to see him. He did not say a word, but at once galloped off to the station. I don't know what happened there, but they brought him back like one dead. I shouldn't have recognized him. *Prostration complète*, the doctor said. Then he went nearly raving mad. Oh, what's the use of talking?" said the countess, with a despairing wave of the hand. "It was a dreadful time. Dreadful. No, whatever you say, she was a bad woman. I mean, why these desperate passions? All because she wanted to prove something special. And she proved it all right. Ruined herself and two splendid men—her husband and my unhappy son."

"And what about her husband?" asked Koznyshev.

"He took her daughter. Alexey at first agreed to anything. But now he is terribly upset at having given up his daughter to a stranger. But he can't take back his word. Karenin came to the funeral. But we did all we could to prevent his meeting Alexey. For him, for her husband, it is easier. She had set him free. But my poor son had given himself up to her entirely. He had flung everything away—his career, myself, and even then she had shown no pity for him, but deliberately dealt him a mortal blow. No, whatever you say, her very death is the death of a wicked woman, a woman without religion. God forgive me, but I can't help hating her memory when I see my son's ruin."

"But how is he now?"

"It is a godsend, this Serbian war. I'm an old woman and I don't understand anything about it, but for him it is a godsend. Of course, as his mother, I am terrified for him, and, what's worse, I hear *cela n'est pas très bien vu à Pétersbourg*. But it can't be helped. It was the only thing that could rouse him. Yashvin, one of his best friends, had lost everything at cards and decided to go to Serbia. He came to see him and persuaded him to join him. Now he's got something to occupy his mind. Please, go and have a talk with him. I'm so anxious for him to have something to distract him. He is so melancholy. And to make things worse, he has toothache. He will be very glad to see you. Please, have a talk with him. He is walking about on the other side."

Koznyshev said that he would be very glad to and crossed over to the other side of the train.

CHAPTER 5

In the slanting evening shadow of some sacks heaped up on the platform, Vronsky, in a long overcoat, his hat pulled down low and his hands in his pockets, was walking up and down like a lion in a cage, turning about sharply after every twenty paces. It seemed to Koznyshev, as he approached, that Vronsky pretended not to see him. Koznyshev did not care. He had no personal scores to settle with Vronsky.

In Koznyshev's eyes Vronsky was at that moment an important public figure working for a great cause and he considered it his duty to encourage and hearten him. He went up to him.

Vronsky stopped short, peered at Koznyshev, recognized him, and advancing a few steps to meet him, clasped his hand warmly.

"I hope you don't mind this intrusion," said Koznyshev, "but is there anything I can do for you?"

"There's no one on earth I'd rather see than you," said Vronsky. "You must excuse me. I'm afraid there's nothing left in life for me that would give me any pleasure."

"I quite understand and I wanted to offer you my services," said Koznyshev, looking intently at Vronsky's face, which bore obvious signs of suffering. "Would you like a letter to Richtich or to Milan?"

"Good Lord, no!" said Vronsky, as though making an effort to understand him. "If you don't mind, let's walk. It's so stuffy in the carriage. A letter? No, thank you. To die one needs no letters of introduction. Unless it be to the Turks. . . ." he said, smiling with his lips only. His eyes retained their look of great suffering.

"Yes, but surely you'd find it easier to establish connections, which you will have to do, anyway, with someone who has been prepared. However, just as you please. I was very glad to hear of your decision. There have already been so many attacks on the volunteers that a man like you raises them in public estimation."

"As a man," said Vronsky, "I am only good insofar as life means nothing to me. I have enough physical energy left to hack my way into a solid square of enemy troops and either overrun them or fall in battle—I know that. I'm glad there's something for which I can lay down my life, which I do not want and am heartily sick of. Let it be of some use to someone," and he made an impatient movement with his jaw because of the incessant, gnawing ache in his tooth, which prevented him from even speaking with the expression he desired.

"You'll become a new man, I predict it," said Koznyshev, feeling touched. "To deliver one's brothers from the yoke of the oppressor is an aim worth dying and living for. God grant you outward success and inward peace," he added, holding out his hand.

Vronsky clasped his hand warmly.

"Yes, as a means to an end I may be of some use, but as a man I am a wreck," he said slowly.

The throbbing pain in his strong teeth, which filled his mouth with saliva, made it difficult for him to speak. He fell silent, gazing at the wheels of the approaching tender, which glided slowly and smoothly along the rails.

And suddenly quite a different feeling, not of pain but of some tormenting inward disquiet, made him forget his aching tooth for a moment. At the sight of the tender and the rails and under the impression of his talk with someone he had not met since his misfortune, he suddenly remembered *her* or rather what was left of her when he had rushed like one demented into the railway shed where on a table, stretched out shamelessly before strangers, lay the bloodstained body still warm with recent life; the head, with its heavy plaits and the curls round the temples, had remained uninjured, and was thrown back, and on the lovely face with its half-open red lips was frozen an expression that was strange and pathetic on the lips and horrible in the fixed open eyes, an expression which repeated, as though in words, the terrible phrase that he would be sorry for it, which she had uttered during their last quarrel.

He tried to remember her as she was when he met her for the first time, also at a railway station, mysterious, charming, loving, seeking and bestowing happiness, and not cruel and vindictive as he remembered her at the last. He tried to recall his best moments with her; but those moments were poisoned forever. He remembered her only in her triumph, after having carried out her threat of inflicting on him a totally useless but ineradicable remorse.

Having twice walked past the sacks in silence and regaining possession of himself, he turned calmly to Koznyshev.

"You don't know of any dispatch from the front since yesterday's? Yes, they've been routed a third time, but a decisive battle is expected tomorrow."

And having exchanged a few words about the proclamation of Milan as king and the vast consequences it might have, they went back to their respective carriages after the second bell.

CHAPTER 6

Not knowing when he would be able to leave Moscow, Koznyshev had not wired to his brother to ask to be met at the station. Levin was not at home when Katavasov and Koznyshev, dark as Arabs with the dust, drove up at about twelve o'clock to the front steps of the Pokrovskoye house in a small, open four-wheeler they had hired at the station. Kitty, sitting on the balcony with her father and sister, recognized her brother-in-law and ran down to meet him.

"Aren't you ashamed not to have let us know?" she said, holding out her hand to Koznyshev and putting her forehead up for him to kiss.

"We've got here without any trouble," replied Koznyshev, "and without inconveniencing you. I'm covered with dust and I dare not touch you. I was so busy, I did not know when I could tear myself away. And you," he went on with a smile, "are as usual enjoying serene happiness outside the current of events in your quiet backwater. This is our friend Katavasov, who has come at last."

"But I'm not a Negro. I shall have a wash and look myself again," said Katavasov, in his usual bantering fashion, holding out his hand and smiling, his teeth looking unusually white in his black face.

"My husband will be so pleased! He has gone to the farm. He should have been back by now."

"Still busy with his farming," said Katavasov. "In his backwater. Yes, indeed. And we in town can see nothing but the Serbian war. Well, and what does my friend think of it? I bet not the same as other people."

"Oh, I don't know. I suppose just what everyone else does," Kitty replied, a little embarrassed, looking around at Koznyshev. "I think I'd better send for him. Father's staying with us. He's only just arrived from abroad."

And having seen to it that Levin should be sent for and that the dusty visitors were shown where to wash— one in Levin's study and the other in Dolly's big room— and having arranged about lunch for them, Kitty, taking advantage of the right to move about freely that she had been denied during the months of her pregnancy, ran out onto the balcony.

"It's Koznyshev and Professor Katavasov," she said.

"Oh dear, it's a bit too much in this heat!" said the prince.

"No, Daddy, he's very nice and Kostya is very fond of him," Kitty said, as if beseeching him about something, with a smile, having noticed the mocking look on her father's face.

"Oh, I didn't mean anything."

"You go and look after them, darling," Kitty said to her sister. "They saw Stiva at the station. He's quite well. And I'll run to Mitya. I'm afraid I haven't fed him since breakfast. He is probably awake and crying now." And feeling the flow of milk, she went quickly to the nursery.

And, to be sure, she did not so much guess (the bond between her and the baby had not yet been sundered) as knew for certain by the flow of her milk that the baby must be hungry.

She knew he was screaming before she got to the nursery. And so he was. She heard him and quickened her

900

step. But the faster she went, the louder he screamed. It was a fine, healthy voice, only hungry and impatient.

"Has he been screaming long, Nurse?" Kitty said hurriedly, sitting down and preparing to feed the baby. "Quick, give him to me! Oh, Nanny, don't be so tiresome. You can tie up his cap afterward."

The baby was convulsed with greedy yells.

"But you can't leave him like that, my dear," said Agafya, who spent almost all her time in the nursery. "He has to be tidied properly. Now, now . . ." she cooed to the baby, without paying any attention to his mother.

The nurse carried the baby to his mother. Agafya followed behind, her face dissolving with tenderness.

"He knows, he knows! As true as I stand here, he recognized me!" Agafya cried, raising her voice above the baby's.

But Kitty was not listening. Her impatience was keeping pace with the baby's growing impatience.

Because of their impatience things took some time to get settled. The baby was not getting hold of what he should and was angry.

At last, after a desperate, breathless scream and swallowing of air, matters were settled and both mother and child calmed down simultaneously and were silent.

"The poor thing is all in a sweat," Kitty said in a whisper, feeling the child with her hand. "Why do you think he recognizes you?" she added, squinting at the baby who, it seemed to her, was looking roguishly at her from under his cap, which had slipped forward, and watching the rhythmic puffing in and out of his cheeks and his tiny hand with its rosy palm, with which he described circular movements.

"Impossible!" said Kitty, in reply to Agafya's repeated assertion, and she smiled. "If he recognized anyone, it would be me."

She smiled because, though she said that he could not recognize her, she knew in her heart that he not only recognized Agafya, but knew and understood everything and, indeed, that he knew lots of things no one else knew and that she, his mother, had found out and begun to understand many things only thanks to him. To Agafya, to the nurse, to his grandfather, and even to his father, Mitya was just a human being requiring only material care; but to his mother he had long been a moral

901

being with whom she already had a whole series of spiritual relations.

"Well, just wait till he wakes and you'll see for yourself," said Agafya. "When I do like this, he immediately beams at me, the little darling. Brightens up like a sunny morning."

"All right, all right, we'll see," whispered Kitty. "You'd better go now. He's going to sleep."

CHAPTER 7

Agafya went out on tiptoe; the nurse pulled down the blind, chased away the flies from under the muslin curtain of the cot and the hornet beating against the windowpane, and sat down, fanning mother and child with a withered birch branch.

"This heat, this terrible heat! Oh, for a drop of rain!" she said.

"Yes, yes, sh-sh-sh . . ." was all Kitty answered, softly rocking herself and tenderly pressing the plump little hand, which looked as if it had been tied tightly round the wrist with a piece of thread, and which the baby still kept waving feebly as he closed and opened his eyes. This little hand disturbed Kitty: she wanted to kiss it, but she was afraid to waken the baby. The hand at last ceased waving and the eyes closed. Only now and again, as he went on sucking, did the baby raise his long curly lashes and glance at his mother with eyes that looked moist and black in the half-darkness. The nurse stopped her fanning and dozed off. From upstairs came the reverberation of the prince's voice and Katavasov's loud laughter.

"I suppose they got into conversation without me," thought Kitty. "But it's all the same a nuisance Kostya isn't back. He must have gone to the apiary again. It may be a pity he goes there so often, but I'm glad of it all the same. It helps to distract him. He's much more cheerful and better now than he was in the spring. He used to be so gloomy and so unhappy that I was beginning to be alarmed about him. And he is so funny!" she whispered, smiling.

She knew what made her husband so unhappy. It was

his want of faith. Although she would have had to agree, had it been put to her, that there would be no salvation for him in the future life if he had no faith, his lack of faith did not make her unhappy; and, though she agreed that there could be no salvation for a man who did not believe in God and though she loved her husband's soul more than anything in the world, she could still think with a smile about his unbelief and say to herself that he was funny.

"Why does he go on reading those works on philosophy all the year around?" she thought. "If it's all written in those books, he can understand them. If, on the other hand, what is written there is not true, then why bother to read them? He says himself that he would like to believe. Then why doesn't he? Is it because he thinks too much? He thinks too much because he's always alone, always alone. He can't talk to us about everything. I think he will be glad of these visitors, especially Katavasov. He likes arguing with them," she reflected, and then at once turned her mind to the problem where to put Katavasov for the night—in a room of his own or together with Koznyshev? Then something occurred to her which made her start with excitement and even disturb Mitya, who gave her a severe look in consequence. "I don't think the laundry woman has brought the washing and there are no sheets for the visitors. If I don't see to it, Agafya will give Koznyshev used sheets," and the very thought of it sent the blood rushing to Kitty's face.

"Yes, I must see to it," she decided, and going back in her mind to what she had been thinking before, she remembered that she had not yet thought out properly something important, something that concerned her deeply, and she was beginning to wonder what it could be. "Oh, yes, Kostya is an unbeliever," she thought again with a smile.

"All right, so he is an unbeliever! I'd rather he was always like that than like Madame Stahl or like what I wanted to be when I was abroad. No, he will never pretend."

And then a recent characteristic example of his kindness came vividly to her mind. Two weeks before, Dolly had received a penitent letter from her husband. Oblonsky implored her to save his honor and to sell her estate to pay his debts. Dolly was in despair. She hated her husband, despised him, was sorry for him, was thinking of asking for a divorce, and her impulse was to refuse, but she ended by consenting to sell part of her estate. After that Kitty remembered with an involuntary smile of tenderness how embarrassed he had been, how he had made many clumsy attempts to broach the subject he had obviously been considering for a long time, and how he at last thought of the only way of saving the situation without offending Dolly and suggested to Kitty that she should give her sister her own part of the estate, something that had never occurred to Kitty herself.

"What kind of unbeliever is he? With his heart, his fear of hurting anyone's feelings, even a child's! Everything for others, nothing for himself. Koznyshev seems to think that it is Kostya's duty to be his manager. And so does his sister. Now Dolly and her children are on his hands as well. All those peasants who come running to him every day, as though it were his business to serve them. Yes, you'll be just like your father, just like him," she said, giving Mitya to the nurse and touching his cheeks with her lips.

CHAPTER 8

Ever since Levin, at the sight of his beloved dying brother, looked for the first time at the questions of life and death in the light of what he called the new convictions which between the ages of twenty and thirty-four imperceptibly replaced the beliefs of his childhood and youth, he had been horrified not so much by death as by life without the slightest knowledge of its origin, its purpose, its reason, and its nature. Organisms, their destruction, the indestructibility of matter, evolution, the law of the conservation of energy, were the terms that had superseded those beliefs. These terms and the conceptions associated with them were very useful for intellectual purposes, but they gave no guidance for life. Levin suddenly felt like a person who had exchanged his warm fur coat for a muslin garment and who, out in the frost for the first time, becomes convinced, not by arguments but with the whole of his being, that he is as good as naked and that he must inevitably die a painful death from exposure.

From that moment, though he was not conscious of it and continued to live as before, Levin never stopped being afraid of his agnosticism. Besides, he was vaguely aware that what he called his convictions were not just agnosticism, but a state of mind which made any knowledge of what he needed impossible.

After his marriage his new joys and responsibilities had at first completely stifled these thoughts; but latterly, after his wife's confinement, when he was staying in Moscow without any occupation, a question that demanded a solution had more and more often and more and more insistently presented itself to him.

The question was: "If I do not accept the replies Christianity offers to the problems of my life, then what replies do I accept?" And in the entire arsenal of his convictions he not only failed to find any answer, but anything resembling an answer.

He was in the position of a man looking for food in a toyshop or at a gunsmith's.

Involuntarily and without being conscious of it himself, he was now looking in every book, in every conversation, and in every man he met for some sort of definite attitude toward these questions and a solution of them.

What amazed and upset him most of all in this connection was that the majority of people belonging to his circle and of the same age as he who had, like himself, replaced their former beliefs by the new convictions, saw nothing to be distressed about and were perfectly calm and contented. So that, besides the principal question, Levin was worried by other questions: Were these people sincere? Were they not dissembling? Or did they understand the answers science gives to the questions he was interested in more clearly than he and in quite a different way? And he made a most thorough study both of the views of these people and of the books which contained their answers.

One thing he had discovered since those questions began to worry him was that he had been mistaken in assuming, as a result of the recollections of his university days, that religion had outlived its purpose and no longer existed. All the people who were near to him and who lived good lives were believers. The old prince, Lvov, whom he admired so much, Koznyshev, and all the women. His wife believed as firmly as he used to do in his early childhood, and ninety-nine out of a hundred of the Russian people, all the common people whose lives inspired him with the greatest respect, were believers.

Another thing he had discovered after reading many books was that the men who shared his views did not understand anything by them and, without explaining anything, merely ignored the questions he considered to be of the utmost importance to him, but tried to solve quite different problems which could not possibly interest him, such as, for instance, the evolution of organisms, a mechanistic explanation of the soul, etc.

Moreover, during his wife's confinement a most extraordinary thing had happened to him. He, an unbeliever, began to pray, and while praying, he believed. But that moment had passed and the state of mind he had been in then meant nothing to him any more.

He could not admit that he had known the truth then, and was mistaken, because as soon as he began thinking calmly about it, it all fell to pieces. Nor could he admit that he had been mistaken then, because he valued his state of mind at the time and to regard it as a weakness would have defiled those moments. He was painfully at odds with himself and he strained all his mental faculties to escape from his predicament.

CHAPTER 9

These thoughts worried and preyed on his mind, now more and now less strongly, but they never left him. He read and thought, and the more he read and thought, the further he felt himself to be from the goal he was pursuing.

During recent months in Moscow and in the country he had become convinced that he could get no answer from the materialists. He read through and reread Plato, Spinoza, Kant, Schelling, Hegel, and Schopenhauer, the philosophers who explain life other than materialistically.

Their ideas seemed fruitful to him when he was either reading or himself thinking of arguments refuting other doctrines, especially those of the materialistic thinkers; but as soon as he began reading or himself devising a solution of the problems, the same thing repeated itself every time. Following the accepted definitions of such vague words as "spirit," "will," "freedom," "substance," and deliberately entering the verbal trap set for him by the philosophers or by himself, he seemed to begin to understand something. But he had only to forget the artificial train of reasoning and to turn from real life to what appeared satisfactory to him so long as he kept to the given train of thought—and suddenly the whole of this artificial edifice collapsed like a house of cards, and it became clear that it had been constructed out of a pattern of words, and regardless of something more important in life than reason.

At one time, when reading Schopenhauer, he substituted the word "love" for "will," and this new philosophy comforted him for a day or two so long as he did not keep away from it; but it, too, collapsed when later on he viewed it from the standpoint of real life, and it turned out to be a muslin garment with no warmth in it.

His brother Koznyshev advised him to read Khomyakov's theological writings. Levin read the second volume of Khomyakov's works, and in spite of its polemical, elegant, and witty style, which at first repelled him, he was struck by its teaching about the church. To begin with, he was struck by the idea that the comprehension of divine truths is not given to man as an individual but to the totality of men united by love—the church. He was particularly pleased by the thought that it was much easier to believe in an existing, living church embracing all the beliefs of men and having God as its head and, therefore, holy and infallible, and from it to accept belief in God, the creation, the fall, and redemption, than to begin with some distant, mysterious God, the creation, etc. But on reading afterward the history of the church by a Catholic writer and another by a Greek Orthodox writer and seeing that the two churches, both in their essence infallible, each repudiated the other, he became disappointed also in Khomyakov's doctrine of the church, and that edifice, too, crumbled into dust as the philosophers' edifices had done.

All that spring he was not himself and lived through terrible moments.

"Without knowledge of what I am and why I am here, it is impossible to live," said Levin to himself, "and since I cannot know that, I cannot live either. In an infinity of time, in an infinity of matter, and an infinity of space a bubble-organism emerges which will exist for a little time and then burst, and that bubble am I."

This was a tormenting fallacy, but it was the sole and last result of centuries-long labor of human thought in that direction.

It was the ultimate belief on which all the systems of human thought in almost all its ramifications were based. It was the ruling conviction, and of all the other explanations Levin, without knowing when and how, adopted it as being at any rate the clearest.

But this was not only a fallacy, it was a cruel mockery of some evil and inimical power, to which one could not submit.

It was necessary to get rid of that power. And the way to get rid of it was in the hands of every man. One had to put an end to this dependence on evil. And there was a way of doing it—death.

And Levin, a happy family man and in perfect health, was several times so near to suicide that he hid away a cord so that he should not be tempted to hang himself and did not go out with a gun for fear of shooting himself.

But he did not shoot or hang himself and went on living.

CHAPTER 10

When Levin thought about what he was and what he was living for, he could find no answer and was driven to despair; but when he stopped asking himself about it, he seemed to know both what he was and what he was living for, because he acted and lived in a positive and determined way; even recently he lived in a more positive and determined way than before.

When he returned to the country at the beginning of June, he resumed his ordinary occupations. Farming, his relations with the peasants and his neighbors, management of his household, his sister's and his brother's affairs, which he had to manage, his relations with his wife and relatives, his care for his baby, his beekeeping—a new hobby of his which he had taken up with enthusiasm that spring—occupied all his time.

These things occupied him now not because he justified them to himself by any kind of general principles, as he had done before; on the contrary, being on the one hand disappointed by the failure of his earlier undertaking for the common good, and on the other hand too much occupied with his own thoughts and the large amount of business heaped on him on all sides, he had completely given up every consideration of the common good and busied himself with his affairs only, for it seemed to him that he had to do what he was doing, that he could not do otherwise.

Before (and this began almost since his childhood and went on increasingly till he reached full maturity), when he tried to do something for the general good, for humanity at large, for Russia, for his own village, he had noticed that the thoughts about it appealed to him while the activity itself had always been unsatisfactory, without conviction that it was really necessary, and the work itself, which at first seemed so great, grew less and less so till it practically disappeared; but now, when since his marriage he had begun to confine himself more and more to his own private life, though he no longer found any delight at the thought of his activity, he felt confident that his work was necessary, saw that it succeeded far better than formerly and that it was taking on larger and larger dimensions.

Now, as though against his own will, he cut deeper and deeper into the earth so that, like a ploughshare, he could not get out without turning up the furrow.

It was undoubtedly necessary for his family to live as their fathers and grandfathers had been accustomed to live, that is to say, at the same educational level, and it was necessary, too, to bring up his children the same way. This was just as necessary as eating when one was hungry; and to make it possible he had to make sure that Pokrovskoye brought in a profit. Just as one had to pay one's debts, so it was necessary to keep the patrimony in such a condition that his son, on inheriting it, would thank his father as Levin had thanked his grandfather for all he had built up and planted. To do this he must not lease the land, but farm it himself, must breed cattle, manure the fields, and plant woods.

It was as impossible not to look after the affairs of Koznyshev, his sister, and all the peasants who came to him for advice and who had grown accustomed to do so as it was impossible to throw down a child you are carrying in your arms. He had to see to the comforts of his sister-in-law and her children, whom he had invited to stay, and of his wife and baby, and it was impossible not to spend at least a small part of the day with them.

All this, together with game shooting and his new bee-keeping hobby, filled up the whole of Levin's life, which, as he thought, had no meaning for him.

But besides knowing thoroughly *what* he had to do, Levin knew just as thoroughly *how* to do it all and which of two things he had to do was more important.

He knew that he must hire laborers as cheaply as possible, but that to take them in bond and pay them less by advancing some of their wages was something he ought not to do, though this would be very profitable. He might demand payment from the peasants in a time of shortage for the straw he sold them, though he felt sorry for them, but he must have nothing to do with the inn and the pothouse, though they were a source of income. The peasants must be punished as severely as possible for felling trees, but no fines must be imposed on them for letting their cattle stray into his fields, and, though it annoyed the watchman and destroyed fear, the strayed cattle must not be impounded.

He must lend money to Peter, who was paying ten per cent a month to a moneylender, to get him out of the moneylender's clutches, but he must neither reduce nor postpone the payment of rent by defaulting peasants. His estate agent must not be excused for failing to have the small meadow mown and wasting the grass; but the two hundred acres planted with young trees must not be mown at all. He must not excuse a laborer who went home in the busy season because his father had died, however much he might be sorry for him, and he had to stop part of his pay for the precious months during which he had been away from work; but he must pay their monthly wage to the old house servants who were no longer of any use.

Levin knew, too, that when he got home he must first

of all go to his wife, who was not feeling well, and that the peasants who had been waiting for three hours to see him could wait a little longer; he knew furthermore that in spite of all the pleasure the hiving of a swarm gave him, he must let the old beekeeper do it without him and go and talk to the peasants who had come to see him in the apiary.

Whether he was acting rightly or wrongly he did not know; and not only did he now avoid laying down the law, he even avoided talking or thinking about it.

Thinking about it led to doubts and prevented him from seeing what he ought and ought not to do. But when he did not think but just lived, he never ceased to feel in his soul the presence of an infallible judge who decided which of two possible actions was the better and which the worse; and as soon as he did what he should not have done, he was immediately aware of it.

So he lived, not knowing and not seeing any possibility of knowing what he was and why he lived in the world, and worried so much by this ignorance that he was afraid he might commit suicide and yet at the same time he resolutely carved out his own individual and definite way in life.

CHAPTER 11

The day Koznyshev arrived at Pokrovskoye was one of Levin's most heartbreaking days.

It was the most pressingly busy season of the year, when the peasants show a most extraordinary self-sacrificing zeal in their work in the fields such as they never show under any other conditions of life, and which would be highly esteemed if the people who exhibited this quality thought anything of it themselves, and if it were not repeated every year, and if the consequences of that zeal were not so simple.

To cut the rye and oats with scythe and sickle and cart them off, to finish mowing the meadows, to replough the fallow land, to thresh the seeds and sow the winter crops—all this seems simple and ordinary; but to get it all done in time it is necessary that all the peasants, from the oldest to the youngest, should work unceasingly and three times as hard as usual for those three or four weeks, living on black rye bread, onions, and kvass, threshing and carting the sheaves by night and sleeping only two or three hours out of the twenty-four.

Having spent most of his life in the country and living in close contact with the peasants, Levin always felt in the busy season that this general feeling of excitement among the peasants communicated itself to him.

Early in the morning he rode to where the first rye was being sown, then to watch the oats carted and stacked, and, returning home when his wife and sister-in-law were getting up, he had coffee with them, and then walked to the farm where the new threshing machine was to be started to thresh the seed corn.

All that day, when talking to his estate agent and the peasants or at home with his wife, Dolly, her children, and his father-in-law, Levin kept thinking of only one thing that formed the sole subject that interested him all the time outside his farming, trying in everything to find what kind of attitude to take up toward his questions: "What then am I? Where am I? Why am I here?"

Standing in the cool shade of the newly thatched barn, with its wattled walls of hazel with the still fragrant leaves, pressed against the freshly stripped aspens of the beams under the thatch, Levin gazed through the open doorway filled with the whirling dry and bitter dust of the chaff, now at the grass around the threshing floor, lit up by the hot sunshine, and the fresh straw that had just been brought out of the barn, now at the variegated heads of the white-breasted swallows that flew in whistling under the roof and, fluttering their wings, hovered in the light of the doorway, and now at the peasants bustling about in the dark and dusty threshing barn, and all the time he was thinking strange thoughts.

"Why is all this being done?" he thought. "Why am I standing here and making them work? Why are they all bustling about and trying to show me how zealous they are? Why is Matryona, the old woman who is such a good friend of mine, working so hard? (I remember administering first aid to her when a girder fell on her in the fire)," he thought, looking at a haggard peasant woman who, raking up the grain, stepped with difficulty on the hard, uneven threshing floor with her sunburned bare feet. "She recovered then, but today or tomorrow

912

or in ten years' time she will be dead and buried and nothing will be left of her nor of that pretty girl in the red, homespun skirt who is beating the chaff from the ears with such nimble, delicate movements. She too will be buried, and that piebald gelding too—that one very soon," he thought, looking at the horse that was breathing heavily through dilated nostrils, its belly rising and falling, as it trod the slanting wheel that turned under it. "They will bury it too, and Fyodor, who is feeding the machine, with his curly beard full of chaff and his shirt torn on his white shoulder. But just the same he goes on loosening the sheaves, giving directions, shouting at the women, and with a quick movement adjusting the strap on the flywheel. And what's more, not only they but I too shall be buried and nothing will be left. What is it all for?"

He thought this and at the same time looked at his watch to see how much they would thresh in an hour. He had to know it in order to set them the day's task accordingly.

"They've been nearly an hour at it and have only just started on the third rick," thought Levin and, going up to the man who was feeding the machine, shouted to him above the din to feed it less frequently.

"You put in too much at a time, Fyodor. You see, it gets jammed and that's why it doesn't go so well. Feed it evenly!"

Fyodor, black with the dust that stuck to his perspiring face, shouted something in reply, but still did not do as Levin wanted him to.

Levin went on to the drum, pushed Fyodor aside, and began feeding the machine himself.

Having worked till the peasants' dinner hour, which soon came, Levin left the barn together with Fyodor and, stopping beside a neat yellow stack of rye ready for threshing, began chatting to him.

Fyodor came from a remote village, the one where Levin had once let the land to be worked cooperatively. Now it was let to an innkeeper.

Levin got into conversation with Fyodor about the land and asked him whether Platon, a well-to-do and good peasant from that village, would not like to rent it for the coming year.

"The rent is too high, sir," replied the peasant, picking

out ears of rye from the inside of his damp shirt. "Platon won't get anything out of it."

"But how does Kirilov make it pay?"

"Mityukha" (as he contemptuously called the inn-keeper), "sir, will make anything pay. He'll squeeze a fellow dry and make sure he gets his own. He will have no pity on a Christian. But Uncle Fokanych" (so he called the old peasant Platon) "will never drive anyone hard, sir. He'll lend a man money and sometimes let him off paying, and sometimes go short himself. Aye, that's the sort of man he is, sir."

"But why should he let anyone off?"

"Why, sir, there are all sorts of people, you see. One man lives only for himself—take Mityukha, sir, just thinks of how to fill his own belly, he does. But Foka-nych is an upright old man. Lives for his soul, he does. Remembers God."

"Remembers God and lives for his soul? What do you mean?"

"Why, sir, that's plain enough. He lives righteously, in a godly way. Now take you, sir. You wouldn't wrong a man, either, would you?"

"No, of course not. Good-by!" said Levin, breathless with excitement and, turning away, took his stick and walked home quickly.

CHAPTER 12

Levin walked along the high road with long strides, attending not so much to his own thoughts (he was as yet unable to sort them out) as to his state of mind, which he had never experienced before.

The peasant's words had the effect of an electric spark on him, suddenly transforming and fusing into one a whole swarm of disjointed, impotent, separate ideas which had never ceased to occupy his mind. These ideas unconsciously had occupied his mind while he was talking to Fyodor about letting the land.

He felt something new in his soul and took delight in probing this new thing, not yet knowing what it was.

"To live not for oneself but for God. For what God? What could be more meaningless than what he said? He said that one must not live for oneself, for the satisfaction of one's own wants, or in other words, that one must not live for what we understand, what we are attracted by, what we want, but for something incomprehensible, for God, whom no one can understand or define. And—well? Did I not understand those meaningless words of Fyodor's? And having understood them, did I doubt their justice? Did I find them stupid, obscure, inaccurate?

"No, I understood them just as he understands them: I understood them perfectly and better than I understand anything in life, and I have never in my life doubted it or could doubt it. And I am not the only one. Everyone, the whole world, understands that perfectly and has never doubted it and everyone is always agreed about this one thing.

"Fyodor says that Kirilov the innkeeper lives for his belly. That is intelligible and rational. All of us, as rational beings, cannot live otherwise than for our bellies. And all of a sudden the same Fyodor says that it is wrong to live for one's belly and that we must live for justice, for God, and at the first hint I understand him! And I and millions of men who lived centuries ago and men who are living now, peasants, the poor in spirit and the wise, who have thought and written about it, saying the same thing in their obscure words—all of us agree on this one thing: what we ought to live for and what is good. With all other men in the world I have only one thing in common that I know is firm, incontestable, and clear, and this knowledge cannot be explained by reason—it is outside it and has neither causes nor consequences.

"If goodness has a cause, it is no longer goodness; if it has consequences, a reward, it is not goodness, either.

"It is just this that I know and that we all know.

"And I was looking for miracles; I was sorry I did not see a miracle which would convince me. And it is this that is the miracle, the only possible, everlasting miracle, surrounding me on all sides, and I never noticed it!

"For can there be a greater miracle than this?

"Can I really have found the solution of everything? Are my sufferings really at an end?" thought Levin, striding along the dusty road, aware of neither heat nor fatigue, filled with a sense of relief after a long period of suffering. The sensation was so joyous that it seemed

915

quite incredible. He was breathless with excitement and, incapable of going further, turned from the road into a wood and sat down in the shadow of an aspen on the uncut grass. He took his hat off his perspiring head, lay down, and leaned his elbow on the lush, broad-bladed forest grass.

"Yes, I must collect my thoughts and consider it carefully," he reflected, gazing intently on the untrodden grass before him and following the movements of a little green insect that was crawling up a stalk of couch grass and was hindered in its ascent by a leaf of goutwort. "Everything from the beginning," he said to himself, turning back the leaf so that it should not be in the way of the insect and bending another blade of grass for it to pass on. "What makes me so happy? What have I discovered?

"I used to say that in my body, that in the body of this grass and this insect (well, it did not want to get onto that blade of grass, spread its wings and flew away) there takes place a transformation of matter according to the physical, chemical, and physiological laws. And in all of us, including those aspens and the clouds and the nebulae, a process of evolution is taking place. Evolution from what and into what? An unending evolution and struggle? As though there could be any sort of direction and struggle in the infinite! And I was surprised that, though I strained my brain to the utmost to find some sort of solution along that path, the meaning of life, the meaning of my own impulses and aspirations, was not revealed to me. And yet the meaning of my impulses is so clear that my whole life is an expression of it, and I was surprised and delighted when the peasant put it into words for me: to live for God, for the soul.

"I have discovered nothing. I have merely found out what I knew. I understood the power that not only gave me life in the past, but gives me life now. I have rid myself of deception. I have found my master."

And he briefly reviewed the whole course of his thoughts during the last two years, which began with the clear and obvious thought of death at the sight of his incurably ill favorite brother.

Realizing then for the first time that there was nothing for every man to look forward to except suffering, death, and everlasting oblivion, he had decided that to live like that was impossible, and that he had either to find an explanation of life so that it should not seem to be a wicked mockery of some devil or to shoot himself.

But he had not done either the one or the other, but went on living, thinking, and feeling, and had even at that very time got married, experienced many joys, and been happy when he was not thinking of the meaning of his life.

What did it all mean? It meant that he lived well but thought badly.

He lived (without realizing it) by those spiritual truths that he had imbibed with his mother's milk, but in his thinking he had not only failed to acknowledge those truths, but had carefully gone around them.

Now it was clear to him that he could live only thanks to the beliefs in which he had been brought up.

"What should I have been and how should I have lived my life had I not had those beliefs, had I not known that one had to live for God and not for the satisfaction of one's needs? I should have robbed, lied, and murdered. Nothing of what constitutes the chief joys of my life would have existed for me." And even by straining his imagination to the utmost he was unable to picture to himself the bestial creature he would have been if he had not known what he was living for.

"I looked for an answer to my question. But reason could not give me the answer, for it is incommensurable with the answer. Life itself has given me the answer, in my knowledge of what is good and what is evil. This knowledge, though, I did not acquire in any way; it was given me as it is given to everyone, *given* because I could not have got it from anywhere.

"Where did I get it from? Was it by reason that I attained to the knowledge that I must love my neighbor and not throttle him? I was told that in my childhood, and I joyfully accepted it because they told me what was already in my soul. And who discovered it? Not reason. Reason discovered the struggle for existence and the law that I must throttle all those who stand in the way of the satisfaction of my desires. This is the deduction of reason. But loving one's fellow men reason could never discover because that is unreasonable.

917

"Yes, pride," he said to himself, rolling over on his stomach and beginning to tie into knots the blades of grass without breaking them.

"And not only the pride of intellect, but the stupidity of intellect. And, above all, the dishonesty, yes, the dishonesty of intellect. Yes, indeed, the dishonesty and trickery of intellect," he repeated.

CHAPTER 13

And Levin remembered a recent scene between Dolly and her children. Left by themselves, the children began cooking raspberries over a candle and pouring jets of milk into their mouths. Their mother, catching them red-handed, tried in Levin's presence to make them realize how much the labor that they were wasting had cost grown-up people, that all that trouble had been taken for them, and that if they broke the cups they would have nothing to drink out of and that if they spilled the milk they would have nothing to eat and would die of starvation.

Levin was struck by the calm, cheerless distrust with which the children listened to their mother's words. They were only distressed that their amusing game had been brought to an end, and they did not believe a single word their mother was saying. They could not, in fact, believe her because they could not imagine the vast quantities of the things they enjoyed and therefore could not imagine that what they were destroying was the very thing they lived by.

"That is all very well," they thought, "and there is nothing interesting or important about it, because those things have always been and always will be. It's the same thing all over and over again. There is no need for us to worry about it; it's all ready for us. What we want is to think of something new, something of our own. So we thought of putting raspberries in a cup and cooking them over a candle and of pouring milk straight into each other's mouths like fountains. This is jolly and new and not in any way worse than drinking out of cups."

"Don't we, and don't I, do just the same when we are trying to find the significance of the forces of nature and

918

the meaning of man's life by reason?" he went on thinking.

"And don't all the philosophic theories do the same when by the way of thought, which is strange and unnatural to man, they bring him to a knowledge of what he has known long ago and indeed known so well that he could not have lived without it? Is it not abundantly clear in the development of every philosopher's theory that he knows in advance, as incontestably as the peasant Fyodor and no whit more clearly than he, the chief meaning of life and is merely trying by a doubtful intellectual process to come back to what everyone knows?

"Just try and let the children get things for themselves, make the cups, milk the cows, and so on. Would they have been naughty in that case? They would have starved to death. Just try and let us loose with our passions, our thoughts, and without any idea of the one God and Creator. Or without any idea of what is good and without any explanation of moral evil.

"Just try and build up anything without these conceptions!

"We destroy only because we have had our fill spiritually. Yes, indeed, we are children!

"Where do I get the joyful knowledge I have in common with the peasant and that alone gives me peace of mind? Where did I get it?

"I, who have been brought up in the conception of God as a Christian, whose life has been filled with the spiritual blessings which Christianity gave me, brimful of these blessings and living by them, I, like a child, not understanding them, am destroying, or rather want to destroy that by which I live. But as soon as an important moment in life comes, like children when they are cold and hungry, I go to Him, and even less than the children, whose mother scolds them for their childish pranks, I feel that my childish attempts at being mischievous because I have plenty of everything are not reckoned against me.

"Yes, what I know, I know not by reason, but because it has been given to me, revealed to me, and I know it in my heart and believe in the chief things the church proclaims.

"The church? The church!" repeated Levin and, rolling over on his other side and leaning on his elbow, he began looking at a herd of cattle in the distance going down to the river on the other side.

"But can I believe in everything the church proclaims?" he thought, testing himself and trying to think of anything that might destroy his present peace of mind. He purposely thought of those doctrines of the church which always seemed most strange to him and led him into temptation. "The creation? But how did I explain existence? By existence? By nothing? The devil and sin? But how do I explain evil? The Redeemer? . . .

"But I know nothing, nothing at all, and I can know nothing but what I am told together with the rest."

And it seemed to him now that there was not a single dogma of the church which could destroy the principal thing—belief in God and in goodness as the only goal of man's existence.

For each of the dogmas of the church one could substitute the belief in serving truth and justice rather than one's personal needs. And each of these dogmas not only did not destroy that belief, but was necessary for the fulfillment of the greatest miracle continually recurring on earth, the miracle that made it possible for everyone together with millions of other most diverse human beings, sages and simpletons, children and old men, peasants, Lvov, Kitty, beggars and kings, to understand with complete certainty one and the same thing and live the life of the spirit, the only life that is worth living and the only life that we prize.

Lying on his back, he was now gazing at the high, cloudless sky. "Don't I know that that is infinite space and not a rounded vault? But however much I may screw up my eyes and strain my sight, I cannot see it except as round and finite, and though I know that space is infinite, I am absolutely right when I see a firm blue vault, far more right than when I strain to see beyond it."

Levin ceased thinking and only seemed to listen to mysterious voices talking joyfully and anxiously to each other about something.

"Can this be faith?" he thought, afraid to believe in his good fortune. "Lord, I thank you!" he murmured, gulping down the rising sobs and with both hands wiping away the tears that filled his eyes.

CHAPTER 14

Levin looked before him and saw the herd of cattle, then he caught sight of his trap with his horse Raven harnessed to it and the coachman, who drove up to the herd and was speaking to the herdsman; then he heard, close by, the sound of wheels and the snorting of the well-fed horse; but he was so absorbed in his thoughts that he did not even wonder why his coachman was coming toward him.

That occurred to him only when the coachman, having driven up, called to him:

"The mistress has sent me, sir. Your brother and another gentleman have come."

Levin got into the trap and took the reins.

As though awakened from a deep sleep, Levin could not collect his thoughts for a long time. He looked at the well-fed horse, lathered between its legs and on its neck where the reins chafed it, he looked at Ivan the coachman sitting beside him, and remembered that he had been expecting his brother and that his wife was probably worried at his long absence, and tried to think who the visitor, who had come with his brother, might be. His brother, his wife, and the unknown visitor appeared in a different light to him now. It seemed to him that now his relations with all men would be different.

"There won't be that lack of sympathy there always used to be between me and my brother; there will be no disputes; with Kitty there will be no more quarrels; I shall be nice and kind to the visitor, whoever he may be, and the servants, Ivan—it will all be different."

Reining in with difficulty the good horse, which was snorting impatiently in its eagerness to quicken its pace, Levin kept glancing at Ivan sitting beside him, not knowing what to do with his idle hands and continually holding onto his shirt against the gusts of wind. Levin tried to think of something to say to start a conversation with him. He was about to say that it was a pity Ivan had pulled the saddle girth too high, but that would have sounded like a reproof, and Levin wanted a frank, friendly talk.

"Bear to the right, sir, there's a stump there," said the coachman, correcting Levin by taking hold of the reins.

"Please leave it alone and don't teach me!" said Levin, annoyed at the coachman's interference. As always, interference made him feel vexed, and he at once felt how sadly mistaken had been his conclusion that his new frame of mind could at once change him when in contact with reality.

When they were still some distance from the house, Levin saw Grisha and Tanya running toward him.

"Uncle Kostya! Mummy's coming, and Granddad, and Sergey Ivanovich, and someone else," they cried, clambering into the trap.

"Who is it?"

"Ugh, an awfully terrible man! He does like this with his hands," said Tanya, standing up in the trap and imitating Katavasov.

"Young or old?" Levin asked, laughing, as Tanya's performance reminded him of someone. "I hope to goodness it's not a tiresome man!" thought Levin.

It was only around the bend of the road that Levin caught sight of the people coming toward him and recognized Katavasov in a straw hat walking along and waving his arms about just as Tanya had shown him.

Katavasov was very fond of talking about philosophy, his ideas of which he had got from the naturalists who had never seriously studied it. Levin had had many arguments with him about it in Moscow.

One of those arguments, in which Katavasov evidently thought that he had come out victorious, was the first thing Levin remembered when he recognized him.

"No," he thought, "I certainly shall never again argue or express my opinions lightly."

After getting out of the trap and greeting his brother and Katavasov, Levin asked where his wife was.

"She's taken Mitya to the wood near the house," said Dolly. "She hopes he'll go to sleep there because it's so hot in the house."

Levin had always tried to dissuade his wife from taking the child into the wood, thinking it dangerous, and he was displeased to hear this news.

"Carries him about from place to place," the old

prince said with a smile. "I told her to try taking him to the ice-cellar."

"She meant to come to the apiary," said Dolly. "She thought you were there. We are going there."

"Well, and what are you doing?" said Koznyshev, falling behind and walking beside his brother.

"Oh, nothing in particular," replied Levin. "Busy on the farm as usual. And what about you? Come to stay for some time, I hope. We've been expecting you for such a long while."

"For about two weeks, I think. I've got a lot to do in Moscow."

At these words the brothers' eyes met and Levin, in spite of the desire he always felt, and now more than ever, to be on friendly and, above all, sincere terms with his brother, felt awkward when he looked at him. He dropped his eyes and did not know what to say.

In his attempt to find a topic of conversation that would be agreeable to Koznyshev and keep him off the Serbian war and the Slav question, at which he had hinted by his reminder of his busy time in Moscow, Levin began talking about his brother's book.

"Well, have there been any reviews of your book?" he asked.

Koznyshev smiled at the premeditation of the question.

"No one cares about it and I least of all," he said. "Look there, Dolly," he added, pointing with his umbrella at some white clouds which appeared over the tops of the aspens, "there's going to be rain."

Those words were enough to re-establish the old relationship between the two brothers, not exactly inimical, but rather cool, which Levin so much wanted to avoid.

Levin joined Katavasov.

"I'm so glad you've decided to come," he said.

"I've been meaning to for a long time. Now we'll have some talk. Have you read Spencer?"

"I haven't finished him," said Levin. "You see, I don't think I need him now."

"Oh? That's interesting. Why not?"

"I've finally come to the conclusion that I shall not find the solution of the problems that interest me in him or anyone like him. Now . . ."

But he was suddenly struck by the calm and cheerful

923

expression of Katavasov's face and he was so sorry to destroy his mood by this conversation that, recollecting his resolution, he stopped short. "We can talk about it later," he added. "If we're going to the apiary," he said, addressing the whole party, "then we have to follow this path."

They walked along a narrow footpath to a little uncut clearing covered on one side with thick clusters of wild pansies and with tall, dark-green bushes of hellebore scattered between them. Levin got his guests to sit down in the deep cool shade of the young aspens on a bench and some tree stumps, specially prepared for visitors to the apiary who were afraid of bees, while he himself went to the hut to fetch bread, cucumbers, and fresh honey for the children and grownups.

Trying to make as few sharp movements as possible and listening to the bees that flew past him more and more frequently, he walked along the path to the hut. At the very entrance one bee began buzzing frantically as it got entangled in his beard, but he extricated it carefully. On going into the shady passage of the hut, he took down his veil from a peg on the wall and, putting it on and thrusting his hands in his pockets, went into the fenced-in apiary in which, standing in regular rows and tied with bast to stakes in a space where the grass had been mown, were the old beehives each with a history of its own and every one familiar to him, and along the wattle fence were the new hives with the swarms that had hives that year. In front of the entrances to the hives, bees and drones flickered before his eyes, dancing and jostling over the same spot, while the working bees flew between them always in one direction, to the wood with the flowering lime trees and back to the hives laden with nectar.

In his ears there was an incessant hum of a variety of sounds, now of a busy working bee flying swiftly past, now of a buzzing, idle drone, or of the excited sentinel bees, guarding their treasure from an enemy and ready to sting. On the other side of the fence an old man was planing a hoop for a cask, not noticing Levin, who stood still in the middle of the apiary and did not call to him.

He was glad of the opportunity to be alone and to recover from the reality which had already succeeded in lowering his mood.

924

He remembered that he had already succeeded in getting angry with Ivan, in treating his brother coldly, and talking thoughtlessly to Katavasov.

"Can it have been only a momentary mood that will pass without leaving a trace?" he thought.

But at that moment, returning to his mood, he felt with joy that something new and important had taken place within him. Reality had only veiled for a time the spiritual peace he had found; it was still intact within him.

Just as the bees, now circling round him, threatening and distracting his attention, deprived him of complete physical calm, forcing him to shrink within himself in order to avoid them, so the cares that had beset him the moment he got into the trap deprived him of his spiritual freedom; but that went on only so long as he was among them. Just as, in spite of the bees, his physical powers remained intact, so his newly realized spiritual powers were intact too.

CHAPTER 15

"Do you know, Kostya, with whom your brother traveled in the train?" said Dolly, after she had distributed cucumbers and honey among the children. "With Vronsky! He's going to Serbia."

"Yes, and not alone, either," said Katavasov. "He is taking a squadron with him at his own expense."

"That's just like him," said Levin. "Are volunteers still going there?" he added, glancing at Koznyshev.

Koznyshev did not reply, for with the blunt side of a knife he was carefully trying to extricate from a bowl in which lay a wedge of white honeycomb a live bee that had got stuck in the running honey.

"I should think so!" said Katavasov, loudly biting through a cucumber. "You should have seen what went on at the station yesterday."

"What's one to make of this? Please, explain it to me in heaven's name, Mr. Koznyshev, where are all these volunteers going and whom are they fighting?" asked the old prince, evidently continuing a conversation that had been started in Levin's absence.

"The Turks," Koznyshev replied with a calm smile. Having at last extricated the bee, which was black with honey and helplessly moving its legs, he was trying to get it off the knife and place it on a firm aspen leaf.

"But who has declared war on the Turks? Ivan Ivanych Ragozov and Countess Lydia Ivanovna with Madame Stahl?"

"No one has declared war," said Koznyshev. "People simply sympathize with the sufferings of their fellow men and wish to help them."

"But the prince was not talking of help," said Levin, sticking up for his father-in-law, "but of war. The prince says that private individuals cannot take part in a war without the consent of their government."

"Kostya, look, there's a bee!" said Dolly, waving away a wasp. "Really, we shall get stung here!"

"It's not a bee, it's a wasp," said Levin.

"Well, sir," said Katavasov to Levin with a smile, evidently challenging him to a discussion, "what is your theory? Why have private individuals no right?"

"Yes, well, my theory, you see, is that, on the one hand, war is such a bestial, cruel, and horrible thing that no man—let alone a Christian—can take upon himself personally the responsibility of starting a war. This only a government can do whose prerogative it is and who is led into war inevitably. On the other hand, according to both science and common sense, in matters of state and especially in the matter of war, citizens renounce their personal will."

Koznyshev and Katavasov, ready with their objections, began speaking both at once.

"You see, my dear sir," said Katavasov, "the trouble is that there may be a case where the government does not carry out the will of the citizens, and then public opinion exerts its own will."

But Koznyshev did not apparently approve of this reply. He frowned at Katavasov's statement and said something else.

"You should not have put the question that way," he declared. "There is no question here of a declaration of war, but simply of an expression of human, Christian feelings. Our brothers by blood and religion are being killed. Well, I mean, even supposing they were not brothers or people of the same religion as ours, but sim-

926

ply women and children and old men. One's feelings are outraged and Russians run to help stop those horrors. Just imagine that you were walking along a street and saw some drunkards beating a woman or a child—I think you would not have stopped to ask whether a war had or had not been declared on those men, but would rush at them and defend the victim."

"But I wouldn't have killed them," said Levin.

"Oh yes, you would."

"I don't know. If I saw it, I might have given in to my spontaneous feeling. I can't say beforehand. But there is not and there can be no question of such a spontaneous feeling about the oppression of the Slavs."

"Perhaps for you there isn't, but for others there is," said Koznyshev, frowning with displeasure. "Among the common people the old beliefs about the suffering of Orthodox Christians under the yoke of 'infidel Mussulmans' are still alive. The Russian people have heard of the sufferings of their brethren and have spoken out."

"Perhaps," Levin said evasively, "only I don't see it. I am one of the people myself and I don't feel it."

"Nor do I," said the prince. "I was living abroad and I read the papers and I confess up to the time of the Bulgarian atrocities I simply could not understand what made all Russians suddenly grow so fond of their Slav brethren while I don't feel any love for them at all. It upset me very much. I thought I must be some monster or else that the Carlsbad water had that effect on me. But ever since I came back I was relieved to find that there are others besides me who are only interested in Russia and not in their Slav brethren. Konstantin here is one."

"Personal opinions don't count in this matter," said Koznyshev. "Personal opinions are of no importance when the whole of Russia—the people has expressed its will."

"I'm sorry but I can't see that. The people know nothing about it," said the prince.

"But, Father, how can you say that?" said Dolly, who had been listening to the conversation. "And what about in church last Sunday? Please, give me a towel," she said to the old man, who was looking smilingly at the children. "It's impossible that all—"

"What about in church on Sunday? The priest was

ordered to read it and he read it. The people didn't understand anything, and they just sighed as they do at any sermon," went on the prince. "Then they were told that there was going to be a collection for some charitable cause and they each took out a kopeck and gave it. But what it was for, they have no idea."

"The common people can't help knowing: the consciousness of its fate is always alive in the common people and at a moment like the present the people have a clear idea of it," said Koznyshev emphatically, glancing at the old beekeeper.

The handsome old man, with his graying black beard and thick silvery hair, stood there motionless, holding a jar of honey and looking kindly and calmly down from his height at the gentlefolk, evidently understanding nothing nor wishing to understand.

"That's right, sir," he said in reply to Koznyshev's words, shaking his head impressively.

"Why not ask him about it?" said Levin. "He neither knows nor thinks about it. You've heard about the war, Mikhailych, haven't you?" he addressed the beekeeper. "I mean what they read in the church. Well, what do you think? Ought we to go to war for the Christians?"

"Why should we think, sir? Alexander Nikolayevich the Emperor has thought for us in the past and will think for us in all matters now. He knows best. Any more bread, ma'am?" he addressed Dolly. "Wouldn't the lad like some more?" he asked, pointing to Grisha, who was finishing his crust.

"I don't need to ask," said Koznyshev. "We have seen and still see hundreds and hundreds of men who give up everything in order to serve the righteous cause. They come from every corner of Russia and express their thoughts and their aims openly and clearly. They bring their mites or go themselves and say straight out why they do it. What does that mean?"

"In my opinion," said Levin, who was beginning to get excited, "it means that in a nation of eighty million there will always be not hundreds, as now, but tens of thousands of men who have lost their social positions, happy-go-lucky people who are ready to go anywhere—into Pugachov's robber band or to Khiva, to Serbia—"

"I'm telling you it's not only hundreds and not happy-go-lucky people but the best representatives of the na-

928

tion!" said Koznyshev, as irritably as if he were defending the last of his possessions. "And the donations! Why, there the whole people is openly expressing its will."

"The word 'people' is so vague," said Levin. "District office clerks, schoolteachers, and one peasant out of a thousand perhaps know what it is about. The rest of the eighty millions, like Mikhailych here, not only don't express their will, but haven't the faintest idea what it is they have to express their will about. What right have we then to say that it is the will of the people?"

CHAPTER 16

Koznyshev, experienced in dialectics, made no reply to Levin's question but at once switched over the conversation to another aspect of the subject.

"Well, of course, if you want to find out the spirit of the people arithmetically, it will be very difficult," he said. "Voting has not been introduced into our country and, indeed, cannot be introduced because it does not express the will of the people. But there are other ways for that. You can feel it in the air. You can feel it with your heart. Not to mention those underwater currents that have been set in motion in the stagnant sea of the nation and which are evident to every unprejudiced person. Look at society in the narrower sense. The most divergent parties of the intellectual world, so hostile to one another before, have all merged into one. All differences are at an end, all the social organs say one and the same thing, all have become conscious of the elemental force that has seized them and carries them all in one direction."

"It's the papers that say one and the same thing," said the prince. "That's true enough. So much so that they are like frogs before a storm. You can't hear anything for them."

"Frogs or no frogs," said Koznyshev, addressing his brother, "I don't publish papers and I don't want to defend them. I am speaking of the unanimity of feeling in the intellectual world."

Levin was about to reply, but the prince interrupted him.

"Oh, well, so far as that unanimity is concerned, there's something else one can say about it," declared the prince. "Now there's that son-in-law of mine, Dolly's husband, you know him. He's now got the post on the committee of a commission or something. I'm afraid I can't remember what it is exactly. Only there's nothing to do there—that isn't a secret, is it, Dolly?—and he gets a salary of eight thousand a year. Try and ask him if his job is of any use and he will prove to you that it is most useful. And he is a truthful man. You see, it's impossible not to believe in the usefulness of eight thousand."

"Why, yes, he asked me to tell his wife that he has got the post," said Koznyshev, looking displeased at what he believed to be an irrelevant remark of the prince's.

"It's the same with the unanimity of the papers. It has been explained to me: as soon as war breaks out their income is doubled. How can they help considering that the fate of the people and of the Slavs . . . and the rest of it?"

"I don't like many papers, but I don't think that is fair," said Koznyshev.

"I would make just one stipulation," went on the prince. "Alphonse Karr put it very well before the war with Prussia. 'You consider this war inevitable? Excellent. He who preaches war—away with him to a special front-line legion and to the assault, to the attack before everybody else!'"

"The newspaper editors would certainly acquit themselves well—I don't think," said Katavasov with a loud laugh as he pictured to himself the editors of his acquaintance in the chosen legion.

"They'd run away," Dolly remarked. "They'd only be in the way."

"If they run," said the prince, "give them a taste of grapeshot from behind the lines or put some Cossacks there with whips."

"It may be a joke, but it's a very bad joke, I'm sorry to say, Prince," said Koznyshev.

"I don't see that it is a joke, it's—" Levin began, but Koznyshev interrupted him.

"Every member of society is called upon to perform his proper task," he said. "Intellectuals perform theirs by giving expression to public opinion. Unanimity and the full expression of public opinion is something the press can be proud of. It is also a highly gratifying phenomenon. Twenty years ago we would have been silent, but now the voice of the Russian people can be heard, ready to rise as one man and sacrifice themselves for their oppressed brethren. This is a great step forward and an earnest of our power."

"But it is not only a question of sacrificing oneself," said Levin, "but of killing Turks. The people sacrifice themselves and are ready to go on doing so for the sake of their souls and not for the sake of murder," he added, involuntarily connecting the conversation with the thoughts that absorbed him.

"What do you mean, for the sake of their souls?" Katavasov said with a smile. "This is a rather puzzling expression for a naturalist. What is a soul?"

"Oh, you know that all right!"

"But I swear I haven't the faintest idea what it is," Katavasov said with a loud laugh.

" 'I came not to send peace but a sword,' said Christ," Koznyshev said for his part, quoting the passage from the Gospels that had always perplexed Levin more than any other, just as if it were the most comprehensible thing in the world.

"That's right, sir," the old peasant, who was standing near them, repeated in reply to a chance look in his direction.

"No, sir, you're beaten, beaten to a frazzle," Katavasov cried merrily.

Levin flushed with vexation, not at being beaten, but because he had not restrained himself and had begun arguing with them.

"No," he thought, "I must not argue with them, for they wear impenetrable armor, while I am naked."

He could see that it was impossible to convince his brother and Katavasov, and still less did he see any possibility of his agreeing with them. What they were preaching was the very pride of intellect which had nearly ruined him. He could not admit that a score of people, including his brother, had the right to assert, on the strength of what they were told by a few hundred volunteers with the gift of the gab who came to Moscow, that together with the newspapers they were expressing the will and the thoughts of the people, especially when those thoughts found expression in vengeance and murder. He could not agree with this because he neither saw any expression of those thoughts in the people among whom he lived, nor did he find such thoughts in himself (and he could not think of himself as other than one of those who made up the Russian people). Above all, he could not agree because while he, in common with the people, did not and could not know what the general welfare was, he knew for a fact that the general welfare could only be attained by a strict observance of the law of good and evil, which has been revealed to every man, and for that reason he could not desire or preach war for any kind of general aims. He said with Mikhailych and the common people who had expressed their thoughts in the legend of the invitation to the Varangians: "Rule and reign over us. We gladly promise you full obedience. All the toil, all the humiliations, all the sacrifices we take upon ourselves; but we neither judge nor decide." And now, according to Koznyshev, the people were giving up the right they had purchased at so high a price.

He further wanted to say that if public opinion was an infallible judge, then why was a revolution and a commune not as lawful as a movement in favor of the Slavs? But all these were thoughts that could not decide anything. One thing, however, was beyond all doubt, namely, that at the moment this dispute was irritating his brother and that it was therefore wrong to carry on with it. And Levin said no more, but merely drew his guests' attention to the clouds that were gathering and suggested that they had better go home before it started to rain.

CHAPTER 17

The prince and Koznyshev got into the trap and drove off; the rest of the party, quickening their pace, went home on foot.

But the cloud, now white and now black, approached so rapidly that they had to quicken their pace still more to get home before the rain. Its forerunners, low and black like sooty smoke, ran across the sky with unusual swiftness. They were only two hundred yards from the house, but the wind had already risen and at any moment a downpour might be expected.

The children were running ahead with frightened and joyful screams. Dolly, struggling with difficulty with the skirts that clung round her legs, no longer walked, but ran, without taking her eyes off the children. The men, holding their hats, walked with long strides. They had just reached the steps when a big raindrop splashed against the edge of the iron gutter. The children, followed by the grownups, ran under the shelter of the roof, talking gaily.

"Where's Kitty?" Levin asked Agafya, who met them in the hall with shawls and rugs.

"I thought she was with you," she replied.

"And Mitya?"

"Still in the wood, I expect, and the nurse with them."

Levin seized the rugs and ran to the wood.

In that brief interval of time the center of the cloud had already moved so far across the sun that it grew as dark as during an eclipse. The wind obstinately, as though insisting on having its own way, kept pushing Levin back and, tearing the leaves and blossoms off the lime trees and baring strangely and hideously the white branches of birches, bent everything in one direction: the acacias, the flowers, the burdock, the grass, and the tops of the trees. The peasant girls, who had been working in the garden, ran screaming under the roof of the servants' quarters. A white curtain of driving rain was already descending over the distant forest and half of the nearest field and advancing rapidly toward the woods. One could feel the moisture of the rain, spattered into tiny drops, in the air.

Lowering his head and battling against the wind, which was tearing the rugs out of his hands, Levin had almost reached the wood and already caught sight of something gleaming white behind an oak, when suddenly there was a blinding flash and the whole earth seemed to have caught fire and overhead the vault of heaven seemed to crack. Opening his blinded eyes, he saw with horror through the curtain of rain the strangely altered position of the green crown of a familiar oak in the middle of the wood. "Has it been struck?" The thought had barely time to cross his mind when, gathering speed, the top of the oak disappeared behind the other trees and he heard the crash of the great tree falling on the others.

The flash of lightning, the peal of thunder, and the sudden sensation of cold that spread over his body merged for Levin into one feeling of horror.

"Dear Lord, dear Lord, not on them!" he said.

And though he thought at once how senseless was his prayer that they should not be killed by the oak that had already fallen, he repeated it, for he knew that he could do nothing better than to utter that senseless prayer.

Rushing up to the spot where they generally went, he did not find them.

They were at the other end of the wood, sheltering under an old lime tree, and were calling to him. Two figures in dark dresses (they had been light-colored dresses before) stood bending over something. It was Kitty and the nurse. The rain was already passing, and it was growing lighter when Levin ran up to them. The lower part of the nurse's dress was dry, but Kitty was drenched through and through and her dress clung to her body. Though the rain had stopped, they were still standing in the same postures they had adopted when the storm broke. Both were bending over a pram with a green hood.

"Alive? Safe? Thank God!" Levin said, running up to them, splashing through a puddle with one shoe half off and full of water.

Kitty's wet and rosy face was turned to him, timidly smiling under her bedraggled hat.

"You ought to be ashamed of yourself," he chided his wife in vexation. "I can't understand how one can be so careless!"

"It really isn't my fault! We were just about to go when he had to be changed. We had hardly . . ." Kitty began defending herself.

Mitya was dry and safe and sound and still fast asleep.

"Well, thank God! I'm sorry, I don't know what I am saying!"

They collected the wet napkins; the nurse picked up the baby and carried him in her arms. Levin walked beside his wife, feeling guilty at having been vexed and stealthily, so that the nurse could not see, squeezing her hand.

934

CHAPTER 18

In the course of the whole of that day, in the most diverse conversations in which he took part only with, as it were, the external part of his mind, Levin did not cease to be joyfully aware of the fullness of his heart in spite of his disappointment at the change that should have taken place in him.

It was too wet after the rain to go for a walk; besides, the storm clouds were still lingering on the horizon, passing, black and thundering, here and there over the rim of the sky. The whole company spent the rest of the day at home.

There were no more disputes; on the contrary, after dinner everyone was in the best of spirits.

Katavasov at first amused the ladies with his original jokes, which went down so well on first acquaintance, but later on Koznyshev made him tell of his very interesting observations on the differences in character and even in physiognomy between the male and female houseflies and on their life. Koznyshev, too, was in good spirits and, challenged by his brother, told them at tea his views on the future of the Eastern question, and he put it all so simply and well that everyone listened with delight.

Kitty alone could not hear him to the end—she was called away to give Mitya his bath.

A few minutes after she had gone, Levin too was called to her in the nursery.

Leaving his tea and sorry to have to leave in the middle of such an interesting conversation and at the same time feeling uneasy at having been called away, for this happened only on important occasions, Levin went to the nursery.

Though Koznyshev's plan, which Levin had not heard to the end, of how the liberated world of forty million Slavs linked with Russia would start a new epoch in history, interested Levin very much as something quite new to him, and though he felt uneasy and disturbed as to why he had been sent for, he immediately recollected his thoughts of the morning as soon as he left the drawing room and found himself alone. All those speculations about the Slav element in world history appeared so insignificant to him in view of what was going on in his own mind that he immediately forgot all about it and was carried back into the frame of mind he had been in that morning.

He did not now, as he used to do before, go over the whole course of his thoughts (he had no need to). He was at once carried back to the feeling that directed him, that was connected with those thoughts, and found that feeling in his soul more powerful and more clearly defined than before. Now it was different from what it used to be when he had to find ways of restoring his peace of mind by recapitulating the whole chain of ideas in order to arrive at the feeling. Now, on the contrary, his feeling of joy and tranquillity was much more vivid than before, and thought could not keep pace with feeling.

He walked across the terrace and looked at two stars that had appeared in the already darkening sky and suddenly remembered: "Yes, when I looked at the sky, I thought that the vault I saw was not a deception and there was something I did not quite think out, something I hid from myself," he thought. "But whatever it was, there can be no question of a refutation. I have only to think it over and all will become clear!"

Just as he was going into the nursery he remembered what it was he had hidden from himself. It was that if the principal proof of the existence of God is His revelation of what is goodness, then why does this revelation confine itself to the Christian church only? What is the relationship of that revelation to the Buddhist and Mohammedan faiths, which also teach to do good?

It seemed to him that he had the answer to this question; but he had no time to formulate it to himself before he entered the nursery.

Kitty was standing, with her sleeves rolled up, beside the bath in which the baby was splashing about and, hearing her husband's footsteps, turned her face to him and beckoned to him with a smile. With one hand she was supporting the head of the plump, kicking baby, who floated on his back, and with the other she squeezed water from a sponge over him with a regular exertion of the muscles of her arm.

"There, look, look!" she said when her husband came up. "Agafya is right. He does recognize me."

What had happened was that Mitya quite incontestably had begun recognizing his own people on that very day.

As soon as Levin approached the bath, the experiment was made and it succeeded perfectly. The cook, who had been called specially for that purpose, bent over the child. He frowned and began shaking his head. Then Kitty bent over him and his face lit up with a smile, he pressed his hands against the sponge, burbling with his lips, producing such a contented and curious sound that not only Kitty and the nurse, but Levin too was surprised and delighted.

The baby was lifted out of the bath with one hand, fresh water was poured over him, then he was wrapped in a bath towel and dried and, after a piercing yell, handed to his mother.

"Well, I am glad you're beginning to love him," said Kitty to her husband, after sitting down in her usual place with the baby at her breast. "I am very glad. You see, I was beginning to be worried about it. You said you did not feel anything for him."

"Did I say that? I only said I was disappointed."

"Disappointed in him?"

"No, not in him, but in my feeling. I had expected more. I had expected that, like some surprise present, some new, pleasant feeling would awaken in me. And then, instead of that, just a feeling of disgust and pity. . . ."

She listened to him attentively, replacing on her slender fingers the rings she had taken off in order to bathe the baby.

"You see, it was really more a matter of fear and pity than of pleasure. Today after the fright during the storm I realized that I loved him."

Kitty's face lit up with a smile.

"Were you very frightened?" she said. "I too was frightened, but I am more terrified now that it is past. I must go and look at that oak. But how charming Katavasov is! It was altogether such a pleasant day. And you are so nice with Sergey when you like. . . . Well, you'd better go to them now. It's always hot and steamy here after the bath. . . ."

CHAPTER 19

When he left the nursery and was alone, Levin at once remembered the thought that had not seemed quite clear to him.

Instead of going back to the drawing room, where he could hear the sound of voices, he stopped on the terrace, and leaning on the balustrade, began looking at the sky.

It had grown quite dark and to the south, where he was looking, there were no longer any clouds. The clouds had passed over in the opposite direction. From there came flashes of lightning and the sound of distant thunder. Levin listened to the regular dripping of the raindrops from the lime trees in the garden and looked at the familiar triangle of stars and the Milky Way intersecting it in the middle with its branches. At each flash of lightning not only the Milky Way but also the bright stars vanished, but as soon as the lightning died out the stars reappeared in the same places as though thrown there by some accurate hand.

"Well, what is it that troubles me?" said Levin to himself, feeling in advance that the solution of his problem, though still unknown to him, was ready in his soul.

"Yes, the one evident and incontestable manifestation of the deity is the law of good and evil disclosed to mankind by revelation, which I feel within myself and in the recognition of which I am not so much united myself as willy-nilly united with other men in one community of believers which is called the church. Well, and what about the Jews, the Mohammedans, the Confucians, the Buddhists—what are they?" he put to himself the question that seemed dangerous to him. "Can those hundreds of millions of human beings be deprived of that highest blessing without which life has no meaning?" He pondered, but immediately corrected himself. "But what am I asking about?" he said to himself. "I am asking about the relation to the deity of all the different religions of mankind. I am asking about the universal revelation of God to the whole universe with all those nebulae. What am I

938

doing? Knowledge, unattainable by reasoning, has been revealed to me personally, to my heart, openly and beyond a doubt, and I am obstinately trying to express that knowledge in words and by my reason.

"Do I not know that it is not the stars that are moving?" he asked himself, looking at a bright planet that had already changed its position to the top branch of a birch tree. "But looking at the movement of the stars I am not able to picture to myself the rotation of the earth and I am right in saying that the stars move.

"And could the astronomers understand and calculate anything if they had to take into account all the complicated and varied motions of the earth? All their marvelous conclusions about the distances, the weight, movements, and deviations of the heavenly bodies are based only on the apparent movement of the stars round a stationary earth, on the very movement that is now before me and that has been the same for millions of men during the centuries and that has been and will be always the same and can always be verified. And just as the conclusions of the astronomers would have been idle and precarious had they not been based on observations of the visible sky in relation to one meridian and one horizon, so would my conclusions be idle and precarious were they not based on that understanding of good and evil which was and will always be the same for all men and which has been revealed to me by Christianity and which can always be verified in my soul. The question of other religions and their relationship to the deity I have neither the right nor the power to decide."

"Oh, you haven't gone yet?" he suddenly heard Kitty's voice saying, as she passed that way to the drawing room. "What's the matter? Has anything upset you?" she said, looking intently at his face in the starlight.

But she would not have been able to discern the expression of his face had not a flash of lightning that hid the stars lit it up. By the light of that flash she could see his face clearly and, observing that he was calm and happy, she smiled at him.

"She understands," he thought. "She knows what I am thinking about. Shall I tell her or not? Yes, I will tell her."

But just as he was going to talk, she herself began to speak.

"Oh, darling, do me a favor," she said. "Go to the corner room and see how they have arranged things for your brother. I can't very well do it myself. Have they put in the new washstand?"

"All right, I'll go at once," said Levin, getting up and kissing her.

"No, it is not necessary to say anything," he thought, when she had passed before him. "It is a secret for me alone, an important and necessary one for me and not to be put into words.

"This new feeling has not changed me, has not made me happy and enlightened me all of a sudden as I had dreamed it would—just the same as with my feeling for my son. There was no surprise about it either. But whether it is faith or not—I don't know what it is—but that feeling has entered just as imperceptibly into my soul through suffering and has lodged itself there firmly.

"I shall still get angry with my coachman Ivan, I shall still argue and express my thoughts inopportunely; there will still be a wall between the holy of holies of my soul and other people, even my wife, and I shall still blame her for my own fears and shall regret it; I shall still be unable to understand with my reason why I am praying, and I shall continue to pray—but my life, my whole life, independently of anything that may happen to me, every moment of it, is no longer meaningless as it was before, but has an incontestable meaning of goodness, with which I have the power to invest it."

Selected Bibliography

Works by LEO TOLSTOY

The Raid, 1853 Story
Sevastopol, 1855 Stories
Two Hussars, 1856 Novel
Youth, 1857 Novel
Family Happiness, 1859 Story
The Cossacks, 1863 Novel
War and Peace, 1869 Novel (Signet Classic 0–451–52326–1)
Anna Karenina, 1877 Novel
The Memoirs of a Madman, 1884 Story
A Confession, 1884 Essay
The Death of Ivan Ilych, 1886 Story (Signet Classic 0–451–52880–8)
The Kreutzer Sonata, 1891 Story
Master and Man, 1895 Story
What Is Art? 1896 Essay
Father Sergius, 1896 Story
Resurrection, 1900 Novel
The Devil, 1911 Story

Selected Biography and Criticism

Arnold, Matthew. "Count Leo Tolstoy." In *Essays in Criticism: Second Series.* New York: St. Martin's Press, 1938.

Bayley, John. *Tolstoy and the Novel.* Chicago: University of Chicago Press, 1988.

Berlin, Isaiah. *The Hedgehog and the Fox.* Chicago: Ivan R. Dee Publisher, 1993.

Bloom, Harold, ed. *Anna Karenina (Modern Critical Interpretations)*. Broomall, PA: Chelsea House Publishers, 1987.

Christian, R. F. *Tolstoy: A Critical Introduction*. Cambridge: Cambridge University Press, 1969.

Gorky, Maxim. *Reminiscences of Tolstoy, Chekhov, and Andreyev*. New York: The Viking Press, 1959.

Holbrook, David. *Tolstoy, Woman, and Death: A Study of* War and Peace *and* Anna Karenina. Madison, NJ: Fairleigh Dickinson University, 1997.

Jones, Malcolm, ed. *New Essays on Tolstoy*. Cambridge: Cambridge University Press, 1978.

Knowles, A. V. *Tolstoy: The Critical Heritage*. London: Routledge & Kegan Paul, 1978.

Mandelker, Amy. *Framing* Anna Karenina*: Tolstoy, the Woman Question, and the Victorian Novel*. Columbus: Ohio State University Press, 1993.

Mann, Thomas. "Goethe and Tolstoy." In his *Essays of Three Decades*. New York: Alfred A. Knopf, 1947.

Maude, Alymer. *The Life of Tolstoy*. 2 vols. London: Oxford University Press, 1930.

Orwin, Donna Tussing, ed. *The Cambridge Companion to Tolstoy*. New York: Cambridge University Press, 2002.

Simmons, Ernest J. *Leo Tolstoy*. 2 vols. Boston: Little, Brown, 1946.

Steiner, George. *Tolstoy or Dostoevsky: An Essay in the Old Criticism*. New Haven, CT: Yale University Press, 1996.

Troyat, Henri. *Tolstoy*. Trans. Ed. Nancy Amphoux. New York: Grove/Atlantic Inc., 2001.

Wilson, A. N. *Tolstoy: A Biography*. New York: W.W. Norton & Company, 2001.

Fact, Fiction, and Film

William R. Pace

All happy men are alike; every unhappy man is unhappy in his own unique way, to paraphrase a great author. If we equate happiness with finding the meaning of life, then Lev Nikolayevich, Count Tolstoy, or, as he is better known, Leo Tolstoy, was a man who spent his entire life dedicated to the search. Literary fame with not one but two books that continually battle it out for the title of World's Greatest Novel was not enough; he was also an education reformer, social rebel, religious iconoclast, and the philosophical forefather of such nonviolence activists as Gandhi.

The fourth of five children, Tolstoy was born, according to the pre–Bolshevik revolution Russian calendar, on August 28, 1828, on his family's country estate, Yasnaya Polyana (Clear Meadow), in the Tula province of Russia. Two years later his mother died and seven years after that his father was murdered, leaving him parentless at age nine. (In light of the constant theme of the negative influence of the city in *Anna Karenina*, it's interesting to note that Tolstoy's father was killed shortly after the family had moved from the country to Moscow.) Because of these tragic events, it's not surprising that death was a continual source of anxiety and literary contemplation for Tolstoy.

At age sixteen, he failed his initial university entrance exam. Once accepted, he found he loved learning yet hated academia, and declined to stay through to graduation. He began keeping a diary and, upon dropping out, wrote in it, "Let a man but withdraw from society and retire into himself and his reason will soon strip off the spectacles through which he has hitherto seen everything in a corrupt light." Not yet in his twenties, he was al-

943

ready expressing a theme that would become fully artic-
ulated in *Anna Karenina* nearly three decades later.

Following his own advice, Tolstoy returned to Yasnaya Polyana, which he soon inherited, and became master of several thousand acres and several hundred serfs,
whose lives he tried to improve. However, establishing
a contradictory pattern that would dog him most of his
life—espousing social reform while unable to stop himself from following the practices of his class—he left the
estate and went to Moscow and, later, St. Petersburg. In
both cities he compiled severe gambling debts and pursued a rather scurrilous and promiscuous agenda that
left him suffering from a "social disease." He was living
the debauched life of the Russian aristocracy, the class
he was born into but in which he was never entirely
comfortable, which is obvious in his treatment of it in
Anna Karenina. His unease wasn't helped by the fact
that he was self-conscious about his looks, especially his
large nose and bushy eyebrows, making him feel even
more the outsider.

Finally wearying of this decadent life, he joined his
brother Nicolai in the army in the Caucasus and during
this period began to add fiction to his writing efforts,
starting with short stories and quickly moving on to novels. He fretted that he might be talentless, writing in his
diary, "Have I talent comparable to that of recent Russian writers? Positively no," but his first novel, *Childhood*, published in 1852, was warmly received, with one
reviewer stating, "If this is the first production of [Tol-
stoy], then one ought to congratulate Russian literature
on the appearance of a new and remarkable talent." It's
doubtful the reviewer realized just how much Russian
literature would be indebted to this new young writer.

Tolstoy wrote several more books during this period.
Moving from stories about his youth to his experiences
in the military, he formed the foundation of his pacifism.
In a story called "The Raid," he wrote, "Can it be that
there is not room for all men on this beautiful earth
under these immeasurable starry heavens?" Upon leaving the military at the end of 1856, he traveled exten-
sively through Europe observing "Western" ways. While
most of Europe was modernizing both industrially and
philosophically, Russia was lagging behind. Some Russians were satisfied with their ways, believing that their

culture was better, and disdained adopting Western ones, while others thought Russia desperately needed to conform. Tolstoy was distrustful of most modernization but did believe a reform in the Russian education system was essential. So in 1859 he began a school for peasant children at Yasnaya Polyana, creating his own textbooks and instituting such radical concepts as dressing himself in peasant garb to blur class distinctions. For three years this remained his creative focus, educational articles and textbooks his only literary output. But he returned to fiction in 1862, the year he married Sofya Andreevna Behrs—or Sonya, as he called her.

Sonya was nearly half Tolstoy's age and, like Kitty in *Anna Karenina*, a sheltered society girl. In fact, much of Levin and Kitty's courtship in the novel is taken directly from Leo and Sonya's real life: Sonya's required reading of her future husband's diaries, the use of chalk to declare love, a wedding day shirt crisis, and much more. But some real events that aren't in the book are the fact that Sonya was shocked at Leo's diary's "appalling experience of male depravity" and that Sonya's father was not in favor of Tolstoy marrying his daughter . . . which may have been due to the fact that Tolstoy had had a long affair with a peasant woman and had fathered a son with her. Regardless, Tolstoy and Sonya married and spent the rest of their lives together, albeit not always happily, and Tolstoy returned to writing novels, including a little piece of literature called *War and Peace*, an epic of the Napoleonic wars published serially from 1865 through 1869. Sonya devotedly hand copied every page of it to ensure the legibility of her husband's work.

Already a well-known and respected writer, Tolstoy sealed his reputation as a Russian literary force with *War and Peace*, drawing admirers from all over Europe. He followed up with two other novels, returned for a while to his pedagogical pursuits, and then prepared to start a novel on Peter the Great, but lost his passion for the project. Instead, he switched to an idea he had had in mind since 1870, one about a "fallen woman." The trick would be "to represent this woman as not guilty but merely pathetic."

While portraying someone as "merely pathetic" can be questioned as a worthy aim, it has to be understood that Tolstoy's wish to represent an adulteress as not guilty was a broad-minded concept for its time. Gustav Flaubert had already caused a stir with *Madame Bovary* (published in 1857, while Tolstoy was in France), but Russia was even less progressive than France. While adulteresses weren't forced to wear scarlet letters on their bosoms, they were shunned just as effectively and could be deprived of everything they possessed; even children they bore to a lover were their *husband's* legal property. Tolstoy dared to consider presenting such a woman as one deserving not contempt but, instead, compassion.

Yet several years passed between his initial idea and actually beginning the novel, and in the interim an event further added to the concept: the jilted lover of a man Tolstoy knew committed suicide by throwing herself under the wheels of a train. Tolstoy attended her autopsy and at some point in the following year coalesced her story with that of his adulteress, and *Anna Karenina* was born.

But originally she was not quite the woman we know today.

Early drafts depicted Anna as "unattractive, with a narrow, low forehead, short, turned-up nose—rather large." And her husband, Karenin—so emotionally distant in the finished book—feels "like sobbing" upon learning of her betrayal, while Vronsky is described as "firm, kind-hearted and sincere." Poor Levin doesn't even make an appearance until the third draft! But with Levin's emergence, the book finally evolved into its familiar narrative: the contrasting of Anna and Vronsky's relationship with Levin and Kitty's. In fact, the early title of the book was *Two Marriages*.

Within a year Tolstoy had most of the book written and in late 1874 began serially publishing it in the periodical the *Russian Messenger*. But then, before it was finished, he stopped writing.

Claiming he couldn't tear himself "away from living creatures to bother about imaginary ones," he once again took up his educational mission. More significant, two very young sons and one premature daughter died in the span of two years as he was writing *Anna*, contributing to a growing spiritual crisis in Tolstoy. In his 1882 book, *A Confession*, he wrote that during this period,

"My life came to a standstill. I could breathe, eat, drink, and sleep, and I could not help doing these things; but there was no life." Devastated, he concluded, "The truth was that life is meaningless."

Having turned his back on religion early in his life, Tolstoy returned to it now, reading the Gospels in the original Greek, a language he amazingly claimed to have learned in only three months, and formed his own personal view of Christ's teachings. Much like Thomas Jefferson had, he excluded the miracles and resurrection and instead adopted, among other things, a nonresistance to evil. This didn't mean evil was to be embraced but, instead, arms were not to be raised against it, creating a spiritual foundation for his pacifism. But as for finishing *Anna*, he wrote a friend in 1875, "My God, if only someone would finish *Anna Karenina* for me. Unbearably repulsive."

But eventually he did complete it and, as the final chapter shows, he invested it with his newfound faith by having Levin experience a spiritual breakthrough. After talking to the peasant Fyodor, Levin, like Tolstoy, discovers a meaning for his life: "I understood the power that not only gave me life in the past, but gives me life now. I have rid myself of deception. I have found my master."

Finally completed, the last serial installment was printed in 1877, and very few readers then or since have found *Anna Karenina* to be "unbearably repulsive." Though certain quarters have been morally outraged by Tolstoy's complex and empathetic view of a woman who finds love outside the sanctified boundaries of marriage, the novel has been hailed as a classic of realistic storytelling that delves deep into the inner consciousness of its leading characters, bringing them and their world alive with amazing detail and insight. And its multiple themes imbue it with a resonance that continues to hold value for the lives of contemporary readers: What is happiness? How does one live with society's hypocrisy? What about the inequality of women's lives? And, of course, what is the meaning of life?

Although he claimed to be repulsed by it, even Tolstoy acknowledged that he had reached a pinnacle: "I wrote everything into *Anna Karenina* and nothing was left over," he later proclaimed. And in a sense, he was right. He would live over thirty years more and continue to write, but for the most part he became more of a teacher and guru than novelist. And although his fictional character Levin was able to find the meaning of life, Tolstoy himself kept searching for it as he focused on promoting the newfound beliefs that eventually got him excommunicated from the Russian Orthodox Church in 1901.

Much to Sonya's chagrin, Yasnaya Polyana became a mecca for like-minded individuals. Tolstoy tried to renounce all his worldly possessions in order to better live the life he preached, but was persuaded he shouldn't for the sake of his wife and children. So instead, he attempted to leave his wife and children living comfortably on the estate and to go off alone to survive without the rich trappings his birth and fame had brought him. The first such attempt was unsuccessful but finally in 1910, at the age of eighty-two, he and a disciple covertly left his home. Unfortunately he didn't make it very far before becoming ill with pneumonia, and was forced to stop in a village named Astapovo. Ironically, the man who so used trains as a symbol for death in *Anna Karenina* died in a train station in November 1910.

Late in his life Tolstoy told his friend I. Teneromo and visiting journalists this about the burgeoning medium of film: "It is a direct attack on the old methods of literary art." However, he went on to add, "But I rather like it . . . it is much better than the heavy, long-drawn-out kind of writing to which we are accustomed." Had he lived to see his work adapted to the silver screen, one wonders if he would have maintained this positive opinion.

Despite its breadth, intellectual scope, and sheer size, *Anna Karenina* has inspired many movie adaptations, a testament not only to the enduring power of Tolstoy's epic, but also to the Herculean—if not Quixotic—efforts of filmmakers. One of the most famous is Greta Garbo's 1935 MGM version (which was actually her second, as she had done a silent one earlier). But thirteen years later another actress appeared in the same role, one who may represent—sadly—a much truer blending of character and performer.

Vivien Leigh leapt to immediate superstar status in 1939 when she was cast over more famous actresses in

948

Gone With the Wind. The search for Margaret Mitchell's Civil War heroine, Scarlett O'Hara, had been one of the biggest casting quests ever. Producer David O. Selznick's pathological perfection had led him to test nearly every actress breathing in America, yet when shooting began he still did not have a leading lady. However, as Atlanta burned for the cameras, Selznick was introduced to Leigh, and she was immediately asked to test for the role. Leigh's appearance at the filming was no mere accident; she had been angling to play Scarlett ever since reading the book. Winning the part, she went on to also win an Oscar, not to mention cinematic posterity.

But afterward it was hard for Leigh to find a film role of equal stature. She made only four films from 1940 to 1945, rare for a contract actress in those days. Married to the dashing premier English actor Laurence Olivier, she suffered a miscarriage that seems to have also been a catalyst for the emergence of a manic-depressive disorder. If that wasn't bad enough, tuberculosis was discovered in her left lung as well. She took time off from film to rest and endure recurring rounds of grueling shock treatment, which was commonly prescribed for mental illness in her day. Such ill health might have stopped others from returning to work, but not the diminutive woman who played the steel-willed Scarlett; instead, she prepared to undertake another famous female role: *Anna Karenina.*

Why Anna? It may be that Leigh felt a strong connection to Tolstoy's protagonist. Like Anna, Leigh had left a husband and child to find true love with another man; before they were married to one another, both she and Olivier had been married to others while conducting a famous affair. By following Olivier to America she had to leave her daughter behind and, once in Hollywood, publicists tried to keep their relationship under wraps; they could rarely appear in public together. Certainly she was not as ostracized as Anna, but parallels were strong, and Leigh was determined to provide her own interpretation of a "fallen woman."

To do so, she teamed up with the Hungarian-born producer Alexander Korda, with whom she had made her very first film and four subsequent ones. Korda had been credited with reviving the flagging English film industry in the early 1930s, and his productions were known for their

949

quality and opulence. Korda assembled a first-rate crew led by director Julien Duvivier, a Frenchman who, like Korda and many other European filmmakers, had done time in the Hollywood studios during the war. He helped adapt Tolstoy's book with writer Guy Morgan and noted French playwright Jean Anouilh (who would later go on to international acclaim with his play *Becket*). Ralph Richardson, one of England's most treasured stage actors, was the film's other above-the-title star, cast as Anna's propriety-obsessed husband, Alexei Karenin.

To adapt one of the world's greatest and longest novels as a commercial film of standard two hours' running time is a daunting task. A filmmaker must execute difficult and painful editing decisions. Historically, most film versions of *Anna Karenina* have focused nearly exclusively on its title character; Korda's production is no different, as Levin makes only two appearances in the entire movie! He's seen once in the beginning, wanting to propose to Kitty (but doesn't get to pop the question before he is shot down), and then later, almost two-thirds of the way through the movie, when Kitty lets him know that, on second thought, she is available. And that's it, the sum total of his time on-screen.

Obviously this is a significant departure from Tolstoy's vision.

Levin's dogged pursuit of the meaning of life through family and honest work is the counterbalance to Anna's struggle—and failure—to fulfill herself through her passionate, sacrificial love for Vronsky. Tolstoy's true story and message are not complete without both halves and there is no doubt much is lost in this bifurcation.

What is a filmmaker to do? A film can be criticized for what is left out but it can only be fairly examined for what is put in. The focus of Korda's version is made clear right from the beginning when it replaces the biblical epigraph "Vengeance is mine; I will repay" with the novel's famous first sentence: "All happy families are like one another; each unhappy family is unhappy in its own way." Immediately this announces that the movie's focus is not Tolstoy's grander themes but, instead, more narrow domestic ones. And if we forgive the film for aborting Levin's story line, we see that it is actually quite faithful to Anna's.

Even with half of the novel jettisoned, a tremendous

amount of cutting and condensing is still required; thankfully, the filmmakers do so adroitly. The film starts as the book does, with Dolly and Stiva on the outs because of his infidelity. Although here his indiscretion is reduced to a mere kiss, due to the infamous Hays Code, which restricted "immoral" behavior on-screen. Of course Anna's infidelity is "okay" to depict, albeit discreetly, because she is "punished" in the end by dying—a double standard that echoes Tolstoy's own theme of hypocrisy. Anna is already en route to Dolly and Stiva's house, allowing for the movie's main catalyst to occur only eight minutes in: Anna and Vronsky meeting at the train station.

The movie beautifully introduces Tolstoy's metaphorical obsession with trains by revealing Anna riding a fabulously frozen one hurtling across the tundra, and by having glamorously ominous shots of trains appear throughout. Glamorous is a key word for this production: it oozes it in a way only rich black-and-white films from Hollywood's heyday can. The money spent on Leigh's costumes, sumptuously designed by Cecil Beaton, could probably finance a dozen gritty independent films today. Anna and Vronsky's first look is also classic Hollywood glamour: shot through a frost-covered window, the moment glowingly conveys the stirring initial attraction Tolstoy described.

Despite the dynamism of this initial encounter, however, there is a lack of chemistry between Leigh and Kieron Moore, the actor playing Vronsky, which is a shame, as the story depends on the palpable force of Anna and Vronsky's love, since they sacrifice children and careers for one another. Leigh always commands as Anna, channeling her own willful nature and bruised psyche into the character, but Moore's Vronsky is a one-note straight arrow with none of Tolstoy's ripples under his smooth surface. Duvivier pulls out cinematic tricks to help boost the verisimilitude of ardor, such as when Vronsky follows Anna onto the train and proclaims his devotion: Duvivier's previously smooth camera work abruptly becomes bumpy as it rushes handheld toward the future lovers, a dramatic effect very little used back in studio days, and which powerfully conveys the surge of their feelings. One wishes there was more of this elsewhere.

The movie continues on, faithfully adhering to the main elements of Anna's story, down to her husband's bad habit of cracking his knuckles, except for one large discrepancy: Anna and Vronsky's child is stillborn. While a significant departure from the book, it is actually a step ahead of Garbo's version. In 1935 the Catholic Legion of Decency and the Hays Code expressed such strong outrage that all references in the Garbo film to the illegitimate child were expunged. Restrictions had softened some in thirteen years, but not enough to allow Anna and Vronsky's love child to live. But all blame shouldn't fall solely on the Hays Code; the filmmakers were probably willing to sacrifice the baby for a few dramatic purposes: One, it engenders sympathy for Anna and her loss. Two, it avoids the issue of showing a mother who does not wholly love her child. And, three, it sidesteps the matter of her leaving a child motherless after she commits suicide. Of course, all three reasons are also *exactly* why Tolstoy had the baby live in the first place: to show aspects of Anna that, while perhaps not the most flattering, reveal her true, deep, complex nature.

But excepting that, the movie really does its cinematic best to follow all the important moments of Anna's journey—the fateful horse race, the trip to Venice, sneaking in to see her son, the humiliating night at the opera—and often uses Tolstoy's own words for dialogue. And as the fire of the lovers' romance abates, Moore's weak Vronsky matters less and Leigh's performance as a woman who cannot stop herself from picking the scabs of her love increases, strengthening the film's power and building nicely to its finest moment: Anna's death.

The chapters of the book relaying this event are some of Tolstoy's best, a pure internal stream of consciousness that keeps the reader trapped in Anna's downward-spiraling thoughts. Definitely difficult material for a film to capture. But the filmmakers made a wise choice in not resorting to a voice-over to convey Anna's inner monologue, as often this device can come off as hokey. Instead, they selected specific lines for Leigh to deliver aloud (but to herself) as she notes all the ugliness of life that she feels surrounds her. Leigh's performance is restrained, yet we feel Anna's tensile strength is at the breaking point. And the beautifully dark cinematogra-

952

phy accentuates the mood, with the visuals of the looming train heightening it. The climax is staged differently than Tolstoy described, but the moment of the train's impact is extremely effective; we expect the camera to cut away, but it refuses to and we're forced to watch as Leigh is propelled to the ground and lies there as the train's iron undercarriage inexorably rolls over her. In a final melodramatic—but poignant—flourish, the last line of Anna's passage fades onto the screen: "And the light by which she had read the book filled with troubles, falsehoods, sorrow, and evil, flared up more brightly than ever before, lighted up for her all that had been in darkness, flickered, began to grow dim, and was quenched forever."

Unfortunately, when it was released the film was not the success Leigh hoped it would be. But a few years later she would triumph once again, winning a second Oscar for her portrayal of another world famous female character: Blanche DuBois in *A Streetcar Named Desire*. As with Anna and Vronsky, the flame went out of her relationship with Olivier as her mental and physical health continued to decline, and they divorced in 1960. She made only a few more films but did manage to win a Broadway Tony for Best Musical Actress in 1963. Finally, on July 7, 1967, suffering from a fatal bout of tuberculosis, "the light by which she had read the book filled with troubles . . . was quenched forever."

Discussion Points

1. Tolstoy was born into an aristocratic land- and serf-owning family. In what ways is this reflected in *Anna Karenina*? What view does Tolstoy hold about the land? About the serfs? About the relationship between serfs and landowners? How is this dramatized in the film?

2. All critics believe that Levin is a stand-in for Tolstoy, but what about the other major character, Anna? Tolstoy fathered a child with a peasant but left her to marry Sonya. In what ways could Anna reflect Tolstoy's own experiences? What views is he expressing through her? Does Tolstoy condemn Anna? If not, why does she commit suicide?

3. Before finishing *Anna Karenina*, Tolstoy suffered a spiritual crisis. Is there an element of spirituality throughout the book, or does it appear at a specific point? If the latter, where? What are the spiritual beliefs the book presents? How are they presented?

4. Trains are mentioned constantly throughout the book. Why the emphasis on trains? What do they represent? How are they used in relation to different characters?

5. The 1948 Vivien Leigh film version almost totally excludes Levin. How does this affect Tolstoy's story? His themes? What kind of effect, if any, does it have on Anna's story?

6. Should movies be allowed to so drastically alter the story lines of literary classics? Why or why not?

7. Does the movie visually represent any of the book's many symbols? Which ones and how? Are there any

954

other ones it could have used to help tell Anna's story? Which ones and how?

8. In what ways does Vivien Leigh's performance fit Tolstoy's description (physical, mental, and emotional) of Anna? In what ways does it differ? If you could cast anyone as Anna, who would you cast? Why?

WILLIAM R. PACE attended New York University's graduate film and television program, receiving his master's of fine arts in film production. A screenwriter and film producer, he has worked on several independent feature films, including *Charming Billy*, which he also directed, and episodes of series television. Pace currently teaches screenwriting at the New School University in New York City, and lives in West Harlem.

Film journalist SUSANNAH GORA appears regularly on national television networks such as NBC, VH1, CNN Headline News, MTV, Court TV, E!, the Fox News Channel, and CNBC. She can also be heard covering entertainment news in a weekly segment for the Associated Press's national radio network. As an editor at *Premiere* magazine, Gora interviewed hundreds of stars, including Anthony Hopkins, Denzel Washington, and Meryl Streep. She lives in New York City.